Orname.

2

1872 - 1982

Chris Fogg is a creative producer, writer, director and dramaturg, who has written and directed for the theatre for many years, as well as collaborating artistically with choreographers and contemporary dance companies.

Ornaments of Grace is a chronicle of ten novels. *Enclave* is the second in the sequence.

He has previously written more than thirty works for the stage as well as four collections of poems, stories and essays. These are: *Special Relationships, Northern Songs, Painting by Numbers* and *Dawn Chorus* (with woodcut illustrations by Chris Waters), all published by Mudlark Press.

Several of Chris's poems have appeared in *International Psychoanalysis* (IP), a US online journal, as well as *in Climate of Opinion*, a selection of verse in response to the work of Sigmund Freud edited by Irene Willis, published by IP in 2017.

Ornaments of Grace

(or *Unhistoric Acts*)

2

Tulip

Vol. 1: Enclave

by

Chris Fogg

flax**books**

Although some of the people featured in this book are real, and several of the events depicted actually happened, *Ornaments of Grace* remains a work of fiction.

For Amanda and Tim

dedicated to the memory

of my parents and grandparents

Ornaments of Grace (*or Unhistoric Acts*) is a sequence of ten novels set in Manchester between 1760 and 2020. Collectively they tell the story of a city in four elements.

Enclave is the second book in the sequence.

The full list of titles is:

1. Pomona (Water)

2. Tulip (Earth)
    Vol 1: Enclave
    Vol 2: Nymphs & Shepherds
    Vol 3: The Spindle Tree
    Vol 4: Return

3. Laurel (Air)
    Vol 1: Kettle
    Vol 2: Victor
    Vol 3: Victrix
    Vol 4: Scuttle

4. Moth (Fire)

Each book can be read independently or as part of the sequence.

"It's always too soon to go home. And it's always too soon to calculate effect... Cause-and-effect assumes that history marches forward, but history is not an army. It is a crab scuttling sideways, a drip of soft water wearing away stone, an earthquake breaking centuries of tension."

Rebecca Solnit: *Hope in the Dark*
(*Untold Histories, Wild Possibilities*)

Contents

ONE

The Moons of Jupiter

TWO

Belle Vue

THREE

The Delph

Ornaments of Grace

"Wisdom is the principal thing. Therefore get wisdom and within all thy getting get understanding. Exalt her and she shall promote thee. She shall bring thee to honour when thou dost embrace her. She shall give to thine head an ornament of grace. A crown of glory shall she deliver to thee."

Proverbs: 4, verses 7 – 9

written around the domed ceiling of the Great Hall Reading Room
Central Reference Library, St Peter's Square, Manchester

"Fecisti patriam diversis de gentibus unam..."
"From differing peoples you have made one homeland..."

Rutilius Claudius Namatianus:
De Redito Suo, verse 63

"To be hopeful in bad times is not just foolishly romantic. It is based on the fact that human history is a history not only of cruelty, but also of compassion, sacrifice, courage, kindness. What we choose to emphasise in this complex history will determine our lives. If we see only the worst, it destroys our capacity to do something. If we remember those times and places—and there are so many—where people have behaved magnificently, this gives us the energy to act, and at least the possibility of sending this spinning top of a world in a different direction. And if we do act, in however small a way, we don't have to wait for some grand utopian future. The future is an infinite succession of presents, and to live now as we think human beings should live, in defiance of all that is bad around us, is itself a marvellous victory."

Howard Zinn: A Power Governments Cannot Suppress

Tulip (i)

"As then the Tulip for her morning sup
Of Heav'nly Vintage from the soil looks up,
Do you devoutly do the like, till Heav'n
To Earth invert you – like an empty Cup..."

The Rubaiyat of Omar Khayyam, verse XL,
translated by Edward Fitzgerald

Earth (i)

"The centuries will burn rich loads
With which we groaned,
Whose warmth shall lull their dreaming lids,
While songs are crooned;
But they will not dream of us poor lads,
Left in the ground."

Wilfred Owen: Miners

Manchester's Tram Network

circa 1920

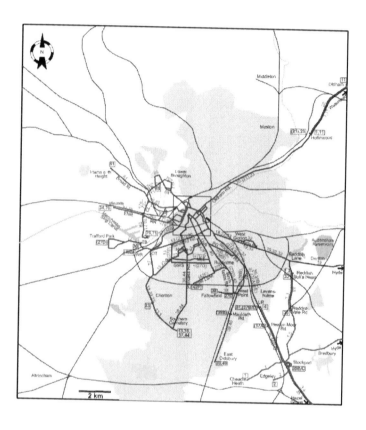

ONE

The Moons of Jupiter

7th May 1922

Sunday 7th May 1922

PHILIPS PARK, BESWICK

TULIP SUNDAY
Returns

After a gap of 9 years
This Popular Annual Event is Revived with a

PROUD PATRIOTIC DISPLAY
FREE ADMISSION

Gates Open at 8.00am

Welcome by the Lord Mayor of Manchester at 11.00am
Official Opening by the Right Hon. John Edward Sutton, MP

Music by
The VICTORIA BRASS BAND
Conductor: Major Gordon Remick, OMM 1st Class

REFRESHMENTS
kindly provided by the Manchester Diocese Mothers' Union

HOOPLA   COCONUT SHY   TOMBOLA
Children's Sports Day
featuring SACK RACES and EGG & SPOON RACES
ELEPHANT RIDES
Courtesy of Jennison's of BELLE VUE ZOOLOGICAL
GARDENS

Gates Close: Sunset
For further information please contact Manchester Corporation
Committee
for Public Walks, Gardens and Playgrounds

Printed by F.G. Wright & Son

Dawn came not a moment too soon for John Jabez Chadwick on Sunday 7th May 1922. He had spent an anxious, sleepless Saturday night, patrolling the thirty acres of Philips Park, to ensure there were no trespassers to trample the displays he had for so many months been labouring to prepare for this especially important Tulip Sunday, the first since the end of The Great War three and a half years before. Shortly after midnight, when the bells of the nearby Church of St Jerome had just finished tolling the hour, Jabez heard a group of lads, probably on their way home from an after hours drinking session at *The Old House and Home*, threatening to climb the railings. Luckily he had Meg, his brother Joe's Welsh collie with him, who gave a low warning growl, which soon sent them on their way, but not before they'd lobbed a few empty bottles into the park. Jabez quickly swept up the broken glass, and after that, all was quiet – until now. The sun began to show through in a clear, cloudless sky just after half-past four, immediately waking up the birds roosting in the trees all across the park, who, as one, launched into a joyous rendition of the avian equivalent of the *Hallelujah Chorus*.

Jabez now had a little over three hours remaining before he must open the gates to let in the public. Crowds were expected to arrive early from all over Manchester. Cheered by the birdsong and the glorious spring morning, he heard himself whistling as he cycled the length of the Carriage Drive, as well as each of the serpentine paths branching from it, which would lead the visitors through the displays of tulips, whose tight buds were just beginning to stir and open as the sun slowly climbed the sky, the early morning drops of dew sparkling on them like finely cut diamonds. He passed by the newly polished Russian cannons captured from the Crimea, gleaming in the sunlight as they overlooked the central lawns from the south-west lodge. He smiled as he caught himself reflected in the recently cleaned and refilled open air swimming pool, with its notice urging "all persons over twelve years and upwards to wear bathing drawers", past the cascade of weirs leading to the six ornamental boating and wild fowl ponds, each fed by a tributary of the River Medlock, whose main channel, following the disastrous flood of 1872, was now culverted beneath the freshly weeded brick path, which Jabez now cycled across. Meg ran alongside him gleefully, as if shepherding him towards his final pen, the gate by the Head Keeper's House, at the park's entrance on Mill Street. Built for Jeremiah Harrison, the park's first Head Keeper and Jabez's grandfather John's mentor, under whom John had learned everything there was to know about soil and drainage, bulbs and seeds, grafts and cuttings, plants and shrubs, a craft he had passed on to Jabez. The house, which was built especially for the purpose of providing the Head Keeper and his family with a home, plus an annual stipend of eighty pounds, should by rights have been where Jabez now lived, with his wife Mary and their children Harriet and Toby, but after Jeremiah died, his widow was allowed to stay on, and then their children too. Jeremiah's grandson, a veteran of the Boer War, lived there now, looked after by his daughter, and Jabez did not begrudge him this, although Mary would remind him from time to time that their two-up, two-down, back-to-back house in Garibaldi Street was already too cramped for their needs, a situation that could only worsen, especially now she was expecting their third child, while the annual stipend barely met the cost of their rent, forcing Jabez to seek additional work in Bradford Pit.

But today was not the day for such a squabble. Today was the first Sunday in May and the long-awaited revival of Tulip Sunday, which had not taken place since the spring of 1914. Today Mary would be bringing Harriet and Toby, each of them scrubbed and polished to within an inch of their lives, like new pins in their Sunday best, in time for the Grand Opening later that morning, and Jabez would be pleased and proud to stand alongside them. Now, leaning against the huge glacial boulder brought down from Ulverston in the Ice Age and deposited in the mud plain of the River Medlock, dug up and erected in this spot when the park was first being laid out to the specifications of designs by William Gay, who had grown up just around the corner from where Jabez now stood, his grandfather's pocket watch in his hand, he waited for St Jerome's Church to strike the hour of eight o'clock, so that he could open the main gates to let in the queues of people already forming outside, good humouredly urging him to, "Come on, Jabez, get a move on."

Jabez said nothing in reply. Savouring the drama of the moment, he waited until the eighth and final stroke of the bell had chimed and then ceremonially took the bunch of keys from his waistcoat pocket, released the padlock, and swung the gates wide open. The people poured in and quickly began to disperse throughout the park. Jabez heard a voice he had been expecting.

"Chadwick?" It was Julian Pettigrew, Chair of the Manchester Corporation Committee for Public Walks, Gardens and Playgrounds formed by the Lord Mayor eighty years before, which still oversaw the running of Philips Park.

"Yes, sir?"

"Splendid day for it, what?"

"Indeed, sir. The tulips will look their best."

"I don't doubt it. Everything in hand?"

"Yes, sir. The Catering Corps arrived by the south-west lodge gate an hour ago and have been setting up their marquees and refreshment tents on the Central Lawn, while the brass band is assembling as we speak, sir, by the Bandstand."

"Capital. Erm..." Here Mr Pettigrew paused, looking about him awkwardly. "Now, concerning the arrangements for our Guest Speaker, the Right Honourable Mr Sutton, MP..." Jabez smiled inwardly, relishing his employer's obvious discomfort. "All in hand, sir. I shall conduct Mr and Mrs Sutton to the Bandstand in time for the official opening as soon as they arrive, sir. There's no need for you to trouble yourself further."

"Splendid. In which case I shall seek out Mrs Pettigrew and ensure that we are ready to take up our positions. She is most anxious to see what the Lady Mayoress is wearing. Oh, and... jolly good show,

Chadwick."

"Thank you, sir. Ah, I believe Mrs Pettigrew is attempting to attract your attention beneath the Avenue of Poplars, sir."

"So she is. Good day."

He raised his cane as he walked over towards the poplars, planted some half a century before in response to Jeremiah Harrison's timely observation that many of the park's trees were suffering from the effects of exposure to the smoke and soot pouring forth from the nearby factories, mills, tanneries and mines. Upon his recommendation the park was replanted with trees that were hardier and, it was hoped, might better withstand the polluted conditions. Jabez's grandfather had planted the black poplars, or, to use their botanical name, *populus nigra*, personally, and they had thrived ever since. Jabez watched Mr and Mrs Pettigrew exchange greetings with their well-to-do acquaintances before commencing to promenade along the avenue towards the Bandstand, where the crowds were all converging, the majority of whom, unlike the Pettigrews, would be delighted to welcome the honourable member for Manchester Clayton, Mr John Edward Sutton, quite unaware that he would unexpectedly lose his seat in the upcoming General Election in November, only to regain it in the by-election a month later, following the unexpected death of the then incumbent Conservative, Mr Edward Hopkinson. Sutton was Labour through and through, a former miner at Bradford Colliery, a trade unionist and, what's more, a local man, having first worked down the pit when he was just fourteen years old. Jabez had met him several times. He understood how important the Park was to the people who lived and worked in and around the streets and canals which bordered it. Jabez was looking forward to the speech he would make in a little over two hours' time.

Meanwhile, if he was quick, he might be able to view the tulips one last time before the ribbons that he had earlier placed along the entrances to the different pathways that led to the display beds were cut and Tulip Sunday was officially declared "open". He looked up. Not a cloud in the sky. It was going to be a perfect day. He ducked under one of the ribbons, Meg following him close at heel, and approached the flower beds. Yes, he felt. These would do nicely. He had planted several stands according to colour – swathes of reds, yellows, purples – before arriving at the central bed, to which all the different pathways ultimately led, in the great dome of the park's Amphitheatre, his *pièce de résistance*, an entire Union Jack, planted meticulously in precise reds, blues and whites. It struck exactly the right patriotic note, he was sure, and his plans had been enthusiastically endorsed by Mr Pettigrew's Committee. For this, the first Tulip Sunday since the end of the war, the overwhelming sense of relief, tinged with national pride that people in Manchester had played their part, struck, the Committee believed, exactly the right note.

All in all Jabez had supervised the planting of more than sixty thousand bulbs to create the day's display. He pushed his hand down into the soil, which was cool, sandy, not too moist, and rich in organic nutrients, helped no doubt by the park's proximity to the cemetery. Jabez paused, watching the soil trickle through his fingers and back into the ground. He had been one of the lucky ones. He'd been posted to Ypres when he'd volunteered and somehow he'd survived. Nothing could have prepared him for what he saw there. Most of his pals had not made it back. But now, he thought, looking at the riot of colour spreading all around him, if he had died and his bones had helped feed bulbs like these, in the earth where his body might have lain, he would have been happy with that.

The Victoria Brass Band struck up the first of their tunes in the Bandstand and Jabez stood up. He dusted the soil from his fingers before heading towards the direction of the music. Mary and the children would be waiting for him there.

The Right Honourable Member for Manchester Clayton stepped up onto the podium especially erected for the purpose in front of the Bandstand to prolonged applause.

"My Lords, Ladies and Gentlemen, boys and girls, thank you for such a warm welcome, warmer even than this beautiful spring morning that we are all of us enjoying so much already. Well, my friends, you all know me. I've lived and worked here all my life, and I am proud to be serving as your Member of Parliament for this wonderful constituency, combining the separate wards of Beswick, Bradford, Miles Platting and Newton Heath, and looking around me, I can see faces I recognise from each of those four districts, and even more from much further afield, and it's not hard to understand why, for today marks a very special day, the revival of that much loved tradition here in Philips Park – Tulip Sunday."

Mr Sutton paused for effect, allowing for another round of prolonged applause.

"And at this point I'd like to invite you all here to join me in giving heart felt thanks to Mr Jabez Chadwick, Head Park Keeper and Gardener, for all the work he and his team have carried out so wonderfully during the cold winter months leading up to today. I am sure you will all agree with me that the displays of tulips throughout the park are quite magnificent. Absence may indeed make the heart grow fonder, and memory may play tricks with us, but I believe that the floral decorations this year surpass all that have preceded them."

Shouts of "Hear, hear!" rang across the park, followed by more generous applause, as the crowds directed their gaze towards Jabez, standing to one side of the podium together with his wife and two children. He sheepishly removed his hat to acknowledge their approval, accompanied by a round of delighted barking from Meg, which produced further laughter and applause.

"Thank you, Jabez. Absence is uppermost in all our hearts and minds this fine May morning, for you don't need me to tell you that today marks the first Tulip Sunday for eight years, the first since the end of that war to end all wars, which has resulted in so very many of our loved ones being absent from us today. But although they cannot be with us here in body, they remain with us in spirit, and we honour each and every one of them for paying the ultimate sacrifice for their country, a sacrifice made all the more real for us with the poignant tribute created for us by Mr Chadwick and his team in that depiction of our Union Flag in tulips of red, white and blue, which lies at the centre of the park just behind where I am standing. And so, before I continue, let us bow our heads in a moment's silent thanks:

"They shall not grow old, as we that are left shall grow old;
Age shall not weary them, nor the years condemn.
At the going down of the sun and in the morning
We will remember them."

He bowed his head, as did nearly all of the assembled throng. A small boy, escaping his mother's outstretched hand, chased after a ball. A tiny girl splashed contentedly in one of the bathing pools, while a legless man, wrapped in an overcoat despite the day's warmth, perched on a low wall by one of the paths, coughed and spat. At a signal from Mr Pettigrew, a bugler from the Victoria Brass Band played *The Last Post*. After this had finished, with a sense of duty done, Mr Sutton continued.

"I'm a plain man and I speak plainly. It is with a great sense of honour nevertheless that I stand here before you today, carrying on that proud tradition begun by my predecessor nearly a century ago, Mr Mark Philips, after whom this beautiful park is named. You don't need me to tell you, I'm sure, that he was also Manchester's first ever Member for Parliament after the great Reform Bill of 1832 or, to give it its proper name, *The Representation of the People Act*, when at last, this great city of ours was finally granted its first seat in Westminster."

More applause.

"I'm not here to make a political speech – that's not what this day is about. No, my friends, whichever side of the political divide we are on, we all stand here today in common purpose, to enjoy fresh air and green pastures. One of Mr Philips's first actions on becoming our first MP was to champion a Bill through the House of Commons to establish public parks in all of England's great cities to provide open spaces for working families to come to and escape the overcrowded yards and cellars, where diseases such as typhoid, cholera and small pox were rife, to offer much needed balm and reparation to damaged lungs. I know only too well, from having worked down the pit from when I was but a lad, just how much we all of us crave the fresher, cleaner air to be found in places such as these. I'm proud to be a miner. I'm proud to be a Mancunian. And I'm especially proud today when, as Mancunians together, we can sample the simple pleasures of a walk in the country, even here in the heart of a city. It is with great pleasure, therefore, that I now officially declare this Tulip Sunday 1922 open."

The brass band immediately began a stirring version

of *"For He's A Jolly Good Fellow"*, which many, though not all, of those standing close by enthusiastically took up, as Mr Sutton was escorted from the podium and led away towards the refreshment tent. Mr Pettigrew, along with several other fellow Committee members, raised a rueful eyebrow. Among his retinue of local VIPs stood Hubert Wright, Managing Director of F.G. Wright & Son, a local firm of printers, and his wife, Annie. Mr Pettigrew made his way towards them, smiling and extending his right hand.

"Hubert, I'm so pleased you have been able to join us. That was a splendid job you did for us with the posters. Look how many people have turned up."

"I think the fine weather might have had more to do with that than any posters of mine."

"As modest as ever, Hubert. But they are so eye-catching. Everyone says so."

"Then you must thank my wife, Mrs Wright, for that. She's the one with the eye for design."

Mr Pettigrew turned towards Annie and acknowledged her contribution. "Mrs Wright," he said, somewhat stiffly and formally, "it's a great pleasure to meet you at last. I trust you will join us for luncheon?"

"I shall be delighted, Mr Pettigrew. Thank you."

At that moment they were joined once again by Mr Sutton.

"A grand day, Pettigrew, a grand day."

"Indeed. Do you know Hubert Wright of Wright & Son, the printers?"

"*Of* him, certainly, but I've never had the pleasure of

actually meeting you till today, sir. You did a first class job with all of my election campaign publicity. I'm delighted to have this opportunity of thanking you in person."

"Thank you, Mr Pettigrew. But I feel bound to point out that we also produced all of the literature for your opponents. We mustn't be seen to be biased in our business."

"Quite so, Hubert. Quite so. Now, Pettigrew, where's this luncheon you promised?"

"If you will just follow me, Mr Sutton."

They all proceeded to join the massed crowds making their way towards the Amphitheatre and the displays of tulips. Hubert turned towards his wife.

"Where's George?" he asked.

"He's with his friends, Hubert, playing by the Boating Lake. Don't worry. I'll keep an eye out for him," and she linked her arm through his as they strolled together in the warm May sunshine.

Less than a dozen yards away Jabez squeezed Mary's hand, picked up his youngest, Toby, and hoisted him onto his shoulders, while Harriet scampered off ahead. "I think ice creams all round, don't you, Mother?"

The children clapped their hands with delight, while Mary rolled her eyes. "You'll spoil them, that's what you'll do, Jabez Chadwick. Come on."

Elsewhere in the park, while listening to Mr Sutton, Miss Esther Blundell had looked around her at the mainly attentive crowds. Gradually people were beginning to wear less sombre colours again, and there was a sense that life was finally beginning, at last, to return to normal after the terrible years of the war. She also noticed, grimly, as her eyes took in the crowds now promenading along the various walkways in the park, how many disabled men there were – on crutches, being wheeled in bath chairs, some, even, propelling themselves on low trolleys – and how, by and large, they were mostly ignored. Was this because, she wondered, we were all accustomed to such sights now, inured perhaps, or was it more because people preferred to avert their gaze? She did not know, but she paused to reach into her purse for a sixpence to drop into a tray that one of the veterans was holding in front of him at a fork in the path. She had been saving this to spend on ice creams for her nephews and nieces, but she felt that this was a better use of the coin.

"Thank you, ma'am," said the soldier, touching his forehead.

"That was kind," said her father, Walter, through whose arm Esther now linked her own as they recommenced their tour of the flower beds. "I never know what to do when I see them," he went on. "They always make me think of Freddie."

"I know," murmured Esther, leaning into her father. "And Arthur."

Her father silently nodded.

Alfred – Freddie – had been the youngest of her five brothers, all but one of them younger than she, who had lied about his age and run away to join The Lancaster

Regiment on his sixteenth birthday, only to be killed within days of his posting at the Battle of Loos. Whereas Arthur, the eldest, two years Esther's senior, had joined the more local Manchester Regiment, the Signal Corps, almost as soon as war had been declared, when the first recruiting posters appeared. He survived Salonika. He survived Gallipoli. But he did not survive the crossing of the Sambre-Oise Canal, exactly one week to the day, almost to the hour, before the signing of the Armistice on 11th November 1918. It was the same action that saw the death of the poet Wilfred Owen, about whom Arthur had written in his letters home, and whose work Esther now knew practically by heart. Had the Right Honourable Mr Sutton uttered "the old lie" *dulce et decorum est pro patria mori* during that blatantly populist speech he had given just a few minutes earlier, she would, she felt certain, have been forced to shout out.

By now she and her father had reached the central display of tulips in the form of the Union Flag, where they had arranged to meet her three other brothers, Frank, Harold and Jim, with their wives and children. They, like their father before them, were all miners and had so been exempted from conscription without stigma on account of their carrying out essential scheduled occupations. At the same time, Esther caught sight of Winifred, alone and anxious, approaching them by a different path. She knew that the sight of Winifred would only upset her father more, and so she indicated that she would join him and her brothers shortly, while she intercepted Winifred before he could see her.

Winifred had been Arthur's fiancée.

She saw Esther approach and waved. Unlike many of the other women walking in the park that morning, Winifred still wore dark clothes, not black, but a deep mauve, as if to acknowledge to the world that she was still in mourning, which in effect she was. She and Esther had been friends for almost ten years. They had met at the Manchester Assizes when they had each independently attended the trial of three suffragettes accused of "the wilful and malicious damage of several illustrious paintings in the City Art Gallery", where they sat next to one another one morning in the public gallery and found themselves in disagreement about the tactics being advocated in pursuit of Votes for Women, a cause they both passionately espoused...

2

23rd April, 1913 – 1st January, 1916

The Manchester Guardian

23rd April 1913

PUBLIC DISTURBANCE AT
SUFFRAGETTES TRIAL

Yesterday the trial began of three suffragettes accused of damaging important paintings in the Manchester Art Gallery three weeks ago. It is alleged that Miss Annie Briggs (48 years), a housekeeper, Mrs Evelyn Manesta (25 years) and Mrs Lillian Forrester (33 years), attacked a number of pictures as part of the militant campaign for Votes for Women, which has now escalated to include the use of violent tactics, such as mass window-smashing, attacks on politicians, damage to property and arson.

Just before nine o' clock on 3rd April 1913, when the Manchester Art Gallery was about to close and few people were about, an attendant in a small chamber leading to the big room of the permanent collection heard what he described as "small crackings of glass following each other rapidly". He immediately rushed into the big room followed by another attendant, who was nearby. They found three women making a rush around the room, breaking the glass of the biggest and most valuable paintings in the collection. They had already completed their work on the right side of the room going in, where pictures by such great artists as Watts, Leighton, Burne-Jones and Rossetti were hung, and were now going around the top of the room. The outrage was quickly carried through, and when the attendants came running in the women were within reach of two more large pictures – one by Millais, another by Watts. The attendants at once rushed to arrest them but the women evaded capture and escaped from the room. The attendants, however, called to the door-keeper and immediately the big doors were closed and their retreat cut off.

The women went quietly and were kept within closed doors while police officers were summoned. The Chief Constable and a superintendent at once went across and took the women to the Town Hall. There they questioned them and, after charging them, allowed them out on bail until the following morning, when they appeared before the stipendiary magistrate.

The full list of paintings damaged were: *The Last Watch of Hero* and *Captive Andromache* by Frederic, Lord Leighton; *The Prayer, Paola and Francesca* and *The Hon J L Motley* by George Frederick Watts; *Astarte Syriaca* by Dante Gabriel Rossetti; *The Flood* and *Birnam Woods* by John Everett Millais; *Sybilla Delphica* by Edward Burne-Jones; *The Last of the Garrison* by Briton Rivière; *The*

Golden Apples of Spring by John Melhuish Strudwick; *The Syrinx* by Arthur Hacker, and *The Shadow of the Cross* by William Holman Hunt.

*

The Manchester Assizes, Great Ducie Street.

The courtroom is packed. The murmur which greets the entrance of the three accused women grows into spontaneous applause and shouts of approval and encouragement from their many supporters gathered in the Public Gallery, among whom sit Esther and Winifred.

CLERK:
　　All rise.

The noise subsides as the Judge enters. The Court is now silent in tense anticipation. The three women stand.

CLERK:
　　Miss Annie Briggs, Mrs Lillian Forrester and Mrs Evelyn Manesta, you are all three members of the

Women's Social and Political Union, are you not?

WOMEN:
We are.

CLERK:
You are hereby charged with unlawfully and maliciously damaging thirteen pictures in the Manchester City Art Gallery on the evening of Thursday 3rd April 1913. How do you plead?

WOMEN: (*tie black pieces of material around their own mouths in the form of a gag*):

Another murmur ripples around the court. The Judge raps his gavel smartly.

JUDGE:
Silence.

CLERK:
Dr Peregrine Gray.

A tall, thin man with white hair and whiskers, and wearing a morning coat, approaches the stand.

CLERK:
Please state your occupation.

GRAY:
Director of the City Art Gallery of Manchester.

CLERK:

Can you confirm for the court the extent of the damages incurred?

GRAY:

The cost of repairing the glass to each of the damaged paintings amounts to £85, and the cost of repairs to two of the canvases has been a further £25. But the consequences of this outrage stretch far beyond the mere monetary. Here in Manchester we are justifiably proud of our art collection, which contains some of the finest examples of Pre-Raphaelite and other acclaimed Victorian paintings unrivalled anywhere in the world, many of them donated by the generous philanthropy of some of our greatest businessmen and benefactors. This collection is available free of charge for the moral and cultural improvement of the general public, and it would be a tragedy indeed if this collection had to be withdrawn from view because of fears for its safety.

JUDGE:

Thank you, Dr Gray. I concur completely.

The Judge now turns his attention to the three women.

JUDGE:

Because you have neither accepted nor denied the charges, you will not be summoned to the Witness Box. You are, however, permitted under law to

make a direct statement to members of the Jury. Do
you have anything you wish to say?

The three women remove their black gags one by one.
ANNIE BRIGGS steps forward first.

ANNIE:

I gave my comrades my fullest possible support but
in no way did I aid them. Our women take their
course on their own deliberate responsibility. This is
not a personal but a world question. We women
must protest against all those things we find
intolerable to us.

She steps aside to allow LILLIAN FORRESTER to make
her statement.

LILLIAN:

I stand before you not as a "malicious" person, but
as a patriot. I appeal to you, gentlemen of the jury,
to bring in a verdict of "not guilty". We have already
been punished by having to appear before the courts
three times and now going through this present
ordeal. I have a degree in history and my knowledge
of it has spurred me to fight for the freedom of
women. I am a loyal and passionate follower of Mrs
Emmeline Pankhurst and all that she represents.
When sentence was passed on her at the Old Bailey
on the morning of our actions later that evening in
the City Art Gallery, committing her to three years
in prison for allegedly inciting persons unknown to

so-called acts of violence, I felt I had to do something to show that here in her home city of Manchester she still had many loyal followers. I considered speaking publicly in Albert Square but chose instead to express my response differently. My husband fully supports and approves of my actions.

JUDGE:

In which case he may consider himself fortunate that he too is not appearing before us this morning.

LILLIAN steps away and EVELYN MANESTA takes her place.

EVELYN:

I regard myself first and foremost as a *political* offender. When I walk about this great metropolis I see poverty and injustice on every street corner, especially for women, whom the law treats differently and unequally when compared to men. I draw the court's attention specifically to the divorce laws, which afford women neither fairness nor dignity. I do not believe that this can ever change unless and until we can secure "Votes for Women".

At this point she turns towards her supporters in the Public Gallery, who take up the cry as if at this given signal. Some of them unfurl a banner declaring the words "Votes for Women", quickly followed by a second containing the slogan "Deeds not Words", and the court is in pandemonium. Esther joins in the chanting enthusiastically, while Winifred watches in silent but diffident admiration. After several minutes, the women who unfurled the banner are evicted from the court, but no further arrests are made. Once order is finally restored, the Judge again raps his gavel and addresses the Jury directly.

JUDGE:

Gentlemen of the Jury, when coming to your verdict, I urge you to remain impartial and not allow yourself to be swayed by any personal opinions you may hold yourselves about the views of the accused as so expressed. Whether you agree or disagree with them is of no consequence. Your duty here today is to administer the Law. No more, no less. You must satisfy yourselves on the basis of the evidence presented by the Prosecution whether the three defendants are guilty or not guilty of the charges with which they have been accused.

The Jury retires but returns after only a very brief period of consideration.

CLERK:

Gentlemen of the Jury, have you reached your verdict?

FOREMAN:
We have.

CLERK:

And are you unanimously agreed upon it?

FOREMAN:

We are.

CLERK:

Do you find Miss Annie Briggs guilty or not guilty?

FOREMAN:

Not guilty.

CLERK:

Do you find Mrs Lillian Forrester guilty or not guilty?

FOREMAN:

Guilty.

CLERK:

And finally do you find Mrs Evelyn Manesta guilty or not guilty?

FOREMAN:

Guilty.

JUDGE:

Thank you. I agree with your findings.

I hereby sentence Mrs Evelyn Manesta to one month's imprisonment, and Mrs Lillian Forrester to three months' imprisonment. This is the maximum sentence permitted to me under the Law. If I had my own way, I would commit them both forthwith to a transport ship to sail around the world until such time that they came to their senses. They claim they were protesting against those things they find intolerable. What I, and I am sure every decent-minded citizen finds intolerable, are the actions of wanton vandalism carried out by women such as these, having indeed been incited so to do by the likes of Mrs Pankhurst and her misguided supporters, such as the attack on eleven post boxes in Manchester with black liquid, thereby damaging more than two hundred and fifty letters, by persons unknown on the same night this uncivilised and illegal act was perpetrated by these women standing before us. We can only hope that the justness of our sentencing may act as a deterrent to anyone else foolish enough to be contemplating similar acts of violence.

He raps his gavel once more, rises and leaves the court. Mrs Lillian Forrester and Mrs Evelyn Manesta are escorted by police officers directly to Strangeways Prison.

*

Afterwards Winifred and Esther travelled by tram together back to Gorton, discussing the details of the trial for the entire journey. Whereas Winifred sympathised with the aims of the suffragists, she had become perturbed by Mrs Pankhurst's increasingly, as she saw it, strident call for "deeds not words", Esther found herself, despite her admiration for, and indeed love of, several of the paintings that had been damaged by the accused, recalling the words of Mrs Ethel Smyth, another leading member of the WSPU, whom she had heard address a rally in Albert Square just a few weeks previously: "There is to me something hateful, sinister and sickening in this heaping up of art treasures, this sentimentalising over the beautiful, while the desecration and ruin of the bodies of women and little children by lust, disease and poverty are looked upon with indifference." Esther could not discuss these matters with anyone at home, except perhaps her older brother, Arthur, and so it was a great source of stimulation for her to have met someone – Winifred – who shared her interest in these, and a whole range of other, topics. They both sensed the world was changing, although in that summer of 1913, when their friendship first blossomed, they could not have anticipated the shocking brutality of the so-called war to end all wars that would make their earlier debates and discussions seem little more than academic tittle-tattle in the face of the numbing statistics of slaughter and loss.

It was shortly after this first meeting that Esther invited Winifred for Sunday tea. She had chosen a Sunday afternoon quite deliberately, believing that this would afford them the best opportunity for time alone, to converse and discuss. Her father would almost certainly be enjoying a nap, or if not, take himself off to his allotment on Melland Road, while her brothers, she felt sure, would be out courting. And so it proved, except for Arthur who, like her, was fond of reading and self-improvement, and who did not currently have a sweetheart he might have been walking out with. He greeted Winifred – Miss Holt – at the door almost as soon as she arrived, and then proceeded to find every possible excuse to remain in her company throughout the afternoon. Esther was both irritated and amused. She had been looking forward to time alone with Winifred herself, but it quickly became clear that Winifred was as attracted to the idea of keeping company with Arthur as he was with her, and it was not long before Winifred became a regular visitor to their home on Sundays, but at her brother's invitation rather than her own.

The following spring, on the occasion of the last Tulip Sunday before the outbreak of hostilities with Germany in fact, Arthur proposed, along the Avenue of the Black Poplars in Philips Park, and Winifred blushingly accepted. The happiness of their engagement was rudely interrupted, however, less than three months later, on 4th August 1914, when Mr Asquith declared that Britain, following Germany's invasion of "poor little Belgium", was now "in a state of war". Arthur enlisted as soon as he could, caught up in the fervour of patriotism that swept the country.

In early October, as the first leaves began to fall, he marched down Deansgate with hundreds of other new recruits of The Manchester Regiment, to the accompaniment of marching bands and cheering crowds towards London Road Station and the trains that would take them to the south coast, where the troop ships were already waiting to carry them across to the fields of Flanders and France.

Watching them disappear, these *Golden Apples of the Sun*, over the brow of the slope that led down from Deansgate, along Hanging Ditch in the lee of Shude Hill, as the bands played *Jolly Good Luck to the Girls Who Love a Soldier*, the crowds gaily sang along, waving their red, white and blue handkerchiefs in the air, Esther and Winifred running alongside, each of them a *Syrinx*, water nymphs carried aloft on a wave by the sound of pipes and drums. Esther felt as though she was watching the early morning shift of men walking in step towards the darkness of the mines at Bradford Pit, like a mockery of *The Pied Piper of Hamlyn*, an army of rats disappearing underground, while Winifred, like *Captive Andromache*, craned her neck, *The Final Watch of Hero*, till the last of them was gone, glimpsing for an instant the child she would never have, its cradle carried away in the rising waters of the flood, before sinking to her knees in silent prayer. Behind her, a dog blithely slept in a shop doorway, *Last of the Garrison*, and Esther, standing tall behind her, a veritable *Astarte Syriaca*, recalled the night before, reading after she had tried to coax the last few embers of the fire in their front room hearth into a prolonged life, her brother, bending low over his kit bag, stretching his arms wide, the crackling flames casting a cruciform shadow on the opposite wall, her light of the world, now a *Scapegoat*.

"And from her neck's inclining flower-stem lean

Love-freighted lips and absolute eyes that wean
The pulse of hearts to the spheres' dominant tune."

*

Exactly nine months earlier the two women had been in attendance at an altogether different march. The Manchester Branch of Suffragists had written to the Chief Constable, Sir Robert Peacock, requesting permission to hold a demonstration in Stevenson Square, behind Piccadilly Gardens in the centre of Manchester, in protest not only against the imprisonment of Lillian Forrester and Evelyn Manesta, but in support of the wider suffragist movement. Esther and Winifred joined the march, along with hundreds of other women from all walks of life, who processed with songs and speeches, from the Square up through Cheetham Hill towards Strangeways, where the two women were still being held.

When they arrived at the prison, they were met by a prison officer, who read the following statement outside the gates on behalf of the governor:

"Since the two women in question are refusing to do any prison work, they will not be allowed to receive any letters or visitors, nor will they receive any remission of sentence."

Esther and Winifred were familiar with the bitter cruelties of the notorious "Cat and Mouse" Act, which attempted to force feed suffragette prisoners, who, if they survived that outrage but continued to refuse food, were released from prison, only to be re-arrested immediately they partook of any substance once free, to begin their sentence all over again. Rumours were already circulating of photographs depicting Mrs Manesta being physically restrained by male prison officers.

After maintaining a candlelit vigil, the women gathered together to sing the Suffragette Anthem, before making their separate ways home.

"March, march, many as one,
Shoulder to shoulder and friend to friend."

Nine months later, after the last of The Manchester Regiment had disappeared from view over the brow of Deansgate, Esther helped Winifred to her feet. The latter wiped her eyes, dusted the front of her dress, and then turned to face her friend.

"We have to stand by them," she said, "our fathers, brothers and sweethearts, and set aside the cause of women's suffrage until there is peace again."

Esther shook her head, but said nothing.

They stood in silence, waiting for the tram to take them home, each in their own thoughts, the few feet of distance between them widening like the division within the Women's Social & Political Union itself. Esther knew that she could not broach the subject with Winifred again. Their lives, like the whole country, were now on temporary hold.

*

They saw less of each other once the war began in earnest. Esther continued to run her household, making sure her four younger brothers got off to work each day at the mine. They frequently worked double shifts as demand for coal increased. Her father insisted on volunteering for everything – it was his duty, he argued – even though his health was deteriorating and his strength diminishing. Inevitably he collapsed one day underground, and the colliery doctor confirmed the early signs of emphysema. But he was not a good patient, and returned as soon as he could. By this time, Esther herself had begun working as a pit brow girl, sorting the coal and moving the heavy wagons on the surface, and she managed to persuade the foreman at the pit to assign lighter duties to her father, such as supervising the new female recruits, ensuring that he now ventured underground as little as possible. Once this pattern had become established, seeing that her father was uncomfortable having his daughter as one of his new charges, she transferred to the nearby rubber factory of Charles Mackintosh & Sons in Chorlton-on-Medlock, where she was originally part of a team of women manufacturing tyres for motor vehicles, before being transferred to meet the growing demand for gas masks. As she fingered one of these strange, trunk-like devices, hanging like the proboscis of some long extinct prehistoric creature which had once walked the earth she now stood upon, she tried to picture her brother fumbling to fit it just in time to ward off the clouds of poisonous gases blowing across the battlefields in France they were beginning to hear more and more about as the months progressed.

She simply could not imagine Arthur as a soldier. Unlike her other brothers, who frequently got into fights as young boys, and who she knew from her brief stint as a pit brow girl still on occasions found fists more eloquent than words, Arthur had been a quiet, studious boy as a child, and at the colliery was already being groomed for white collar work when the war broke out. In his first letter home to her, the single thing that had affected him most up to that point was being issued with a copy of Houseman's *A Shropshire Lad* which, he wrote enthusiastically, he read from last thing each night.

> *"Up, lad, up, 'tis late for lying:*
> *Hear the drums of morning play;*
> *Hark, the empty highways crying*
> *Who'll beyond the hills away...?"*

Winifred, by contrast, left her house at five o'clock each morning to catch the train to Hooley Hill, where she worked in the ordnance factory, swapping the soubriquet of "suffragette" for "munitionette".

*

23 Pearl Street
Denton

5th January 1915

My Dearest Arthur,

It was wonderful to see you, albeit briefly, for your forty-eight hours leave just after Christmas. Thank you for spending so much of it with me, when I know you have other obligations. It was so very good of your family to allow you to come and be with us for the whole of your second day. I have already written and thanked your sister. I do not see as much of Esther as I used to, for as you know, we are each of us so very busy ourselves now with our own war work.

My mother was delighted to be able to cook you a Sunday dinner, for she was certain that they could not be feeding you properly in the Army, but even she had to admit that you were looking well. I don't know what she expected, but my heart was gladdened to see that your face does not yet bear traces of the terrible things you must have witnessed. Perhaps we shall all of us live to see better, brighter days again soon. Everyone said that the war would be over by Christmas. Alas, that prophecy did not come to pass, but now they are saying that it will certainly have ceased by the next. I pray that this is so. We are producing more and bigger shells in the factory with each successive month. Surely, all the destruction that these weapons wreak must be finite?

Sometimes, while I am at work, my thoughts begin to stray. I picture German women, not so very different from ourselves, worrying about loved ones, manufacturing similar armaments, which you and your comrades must face each day while you are out there in the field, and I imagine them having these self-same fears and doubts. We are told we are fighting a just war, and that our efforts are vital to bring it to a swift and victorious conclusion, and I believe this. I do, with all my heart, but I do not like the way our newspapers depict the enemy, "the Hun", as they will insist on describing them, as evil monsters. Their soldiers are young men like you are, my love, with wives and sweethearts, sisters and mothers, back home waiting for them, as I, and Esther, wait for you.

I also think of the German families we knew and were friends with before the war, the various shopkeepers in Denton we would frequent, such as Mr Kaufman, the optician and jeweller, who fashioned the engagement ring you gave me, which I now gaze upon as I write this letter. What will become of them? One hears such troubling rumours. I must try and find out. Already changes have been made. You remember my cousin Janet, who attended our engagement lunch? She works as a waitress at The Midland Hotel in Manchester. Before the war, its main clientele comprised the many German businessmen, who conducted their affairs in the city, and its fare was almost entirely German too. Now, Janet tells me, the décor and menu have all been revised, to reflect the style and taste of our French allies. Not that I shall be dining there any time soon!

I hope you don't mind my writing in such a reflective manner. We have always spoken our minds, you and I, keeping nothing of our thoughts from each other, and these matters do concern me, but for most of the time I am simply too busy to dwell on them for long. Instead, I prefer to spend what few spare moments I have in reading and re-reading your letters to me and in dreaming of when I shall next see you, and when you will be home for good, and we can begin our married life together. Your letters are like the diamonds on my engagement ring, bringing light and lustre to these dark days, and I marvel at your cheerfulness and your ability to write to me in the way that you do from what must be such cramped conditions. You do not describe what it is really like where you are – you are probably not allowed to, for fear of giving away potentially important information, should your letters be intercepted – but I can glean from what you do say that you must all endure such terrible privations, especially in a winter as cold as this one is proving to be. Please know, therefore, that we are all immensely proud of you, Arthur, I especially.

Already you have been promoted to Corporal, about which you said little, for you are naturally so very modest, another of your fine qualities, but one which, I can hear Esther saying with a smile, will soon fade if we heap too much praise upon you! But I cannot help myself, Arthur, for I am certain that these qualities have already been noticed and commented upon by your Commanding Officer, and that the other men will look to you for guidance and strength.

I too have some news. Yesterday I learned that I am to become a film star! But if you are hoping for some glamorous postcard to arrive showing me looking like Theda Bara, I am afraid you must prepare yourself for disappointment! Mr Oxholme, our manager at Hooley Hill, called me to his office just before I was about to leave for home. At first I feared I might be in trouble, although I couldn't imagine why, but he explained to me that he had received a letter from the War Office Cinema Committee, who have been commissioned to make a film to be called 'A Day in the Life of a Munitions Worker', which will be shown in cinemas across the country, so that people can get an idea of what we do, hoping, I suppose, to encourage more young women to come forward to do this type of work, and he has asked me if I will be the munitions worker of the title. I confess that I was very surprised to be asked, but now that I am getting used to the idea, I must say I am intrigued. I shall tell you all about it in my next letter.

Until then, know that the last thing I shall do with this letter is to kiss it, wishing it was you. I keep all of your letters in the drawer by my bed and dream of the day when this terrible war will end and we can be together always.

My darling brave Arthur,

With all my love,

Your fiancée,
Winifred x

*

War Office Cinema Committee Archive

A Day in the Life of a Munitions Worker, 1915

General Description

The film was made at Hooley Hill Munitions Factory, near Ashton-under-Lyne in 1915. The few surviving clips that remain show some of the tasks a female munitions worker would have carried out at the factory. Of all the roles women took on during the 1st World War, that of the "munitionette", as they were sometimes described, was arguably the most vital contribution, for without the bullets and shells they produced, the British Army could not have continued fighting. Seven clips of film remain, each one depicting a different task being carried out by a single female worker during the course of any given day.

Clip 1 shows various women leaving their homes at 5am and then catching a steam train towards the factory site at Hooley Hill.

Clip 2 shows the women changing into boiler suits and rubber boots before clocking in to begin their duties. There is great camaraderie between them.

Clip 3 takes the viewer onto the factory floor itself. The film focuses on the actions of one woman, described as a "Fair Worker", who is using a bradawl to prepare the finished shell to take the detonator.

Clip 4 shows the same woman using an instrument to measure the depth of the internal gauge before inserting the detonator.

Clip 5 depicts a row of women, working along an avenue of completed shells. They each wear protective gloves and a face mask. The individual we have been following stands at the front of this row. She is pouring liquid explosives from a metal measuring jug into the shells. The caption explains that the women are wearing the gloves and masks for protection against poisonous fumes.

Clip 6 shows hundreds of the finished shells, now primed with explosives, which the young woman walks between, making sure the tops are all tightly sealed. A caption reads: "Ready for the Front. One of the Many Avenues of Monster Shells to be presented to the Hun."

Clip 7 then moves to a small side room, where a male doctor, with his female assistant, carries out a series of what are called "regular medical inspections". Two female workers enter one after the other, now wearing their usual day clothes, including a hat and coat, and sit while the doctor briefly examines their eyes and tongues. A third worker enters. It is the woman whose daily routine in the factory has been shown in each of the preceding clips. She has a small sample of blood taken from her, which is placed into a tiny tray. A transparent strip, divided into circular cells of different colours, is run across the tray until a colour match is found, which the male doctor duly makes a note of. After these medical examinations, another caption informs the viewer that "the health of the workers is of paramount importance and is carefully considered at all times." It is compulsory for the women to wash before meals and again before leaving the factory at the end of their shift. The clip now switches to a large wash room. All the women now enter, wearing loose, white shifts, and they vigorously scrub their hands, arms, faces and necks. There is much laughter as they do this.

Finally **Clip 8** is a close up of the individual female worker who has featured

in all sections of the film. She is
facing the camera, looking out towards
the intended audience. She is wearing the
overalls, rubber boots and head scarf
that constitutes her uniform, on the
front of which is her number, 15580. She
is also wearing the protective face mask,
which she removes, and then smiles. A job
well done. The caption now reads:
"Working for Victory". The film then
ends.

*

Walking the short distance home from Denton Station a
few weeks later, Winifred was musing on how the film
makers had chosen to portray her daily routine in a way
that, while not exactly untrue, nevertheless depicted
both her and the work that she and all the other women
did in an almost painterly, heroic fashion, the way she
poured the liquid explosive into the shell seeming to be
almost domestic, reminding her of those Dutch
interiors, like Vermeer's house maid pouring milk,
feminine but quietly strong and reassuringly familiar.
She had been fascinated by the whole process, the
director waiting for the light to fall through the factory
windows at a particular angle in order to emphasise
how the shadow falling across her body from the tower
of shells stacked up behind her heightened their
destructive power, while she moved confidently and
unafraid along those avenues.

"If Leonardo were around today," the director had
proclaimed, "he would not be giving us his *Virgin of the*

Rocks. Instead it would be you, his *Angel of the Shells*."

Winifred had blushed when he said that, and she smiled now, remembering the moment, as he then asked her to repeat the actions she would normally have been doing elsewhere in the factory, at a different time of day, in order to capture a more effective rendition. She had discussed this further with Esther, whom she had visited shortly afterwards one rainy Sunday afternoon, while they had taken a walk during a lull between showers. The way the sun broke through the dark cloud, slanting through the trees in Debdale Park, cast jagged shadows that recalled to her mind the images of barbed wire she had seen in a different newsreel, showing footage of the Western Front at *The Palace* in Ashworth Street, just around the corner from where she lived in Denton.

She had gone with her mother, for it was rumoured that the film with Winifred working in the Hooley Hill Factory was to be shown ahead of the main feature, and her mother was keen to see it. And so it was. Her mother had beamed with pride when she saw Winifred up there on the silver screen "working for victory", until the lights dimmed once more in readiness for Lillian Gish as *Madonna of the Storm*, but not before those heart-stopping minutes of grainy footage showing "Men from The Manchester Regiment" marching along country lanes in northern France, smiling for the camera as they passed by, "on their way to face the Hun", followed by a bleached out foray "over the top", as a few dozen soldiers, pointing their flimsy rifles, with bayonets attached, scaled the barbed wire atop their trenches like jerky marionettes, twitching in the smoke of exploding shells around them, shells not dissimilar to those made by Winifred and all the other munitionettes at Hooley Hill.

The audience in the cinema cheered, but Winifred wondered whether this was something that had really happened, or whether, behind the camera, a director with a megaphone was shouting, "Let's just try that once again, while we still have the light", at the same time shuddering at the thought that her Arthur must be enduring far more terrifying excursions into No Man's Land, even at that very moment they were watching this contrived equivalent. She shut her eyes, for she knew exactly what the shells she helped to manufacture at Hooley Hill were capable of, and the Germans were bound to have their own weapons equally efficient at dealing out similar destruction. The organist in the cinema then began to play the familiar strains of Handel's Largo, *Holy Art Thou, Lord God Almighty*, as on the screen a lone soldier, rifle cradled in his arms, the sun behind him, looked up towards the sky, from where a shining host was smiling down upon him, the Angels of Mons. Winifred's mother's face looked back up towards the screen, wreathed in tears.

Seeing the shadows of trees dancing on the ground in front of her like barbed wire a few weeks later in Debdale Park, she tried to articulate her confusion to Esther.

"A new world is coming. I can feel it, can't you? When this terrible war is over, things will not be allowed to go back to the way they were."

"I wish I shared your confidence," Esther replied. "I look at us now and I see women working in factories, driving ambulances, conducting trams. Do you think that once the men return they're going to want to let us carry on doing those things? They see you up there on the screen and they might cheer, but isn't that because they know, deep down, it isn't real?"

"But it is. I do all of those things they show me doing."

"Though not precisely in that way. You've told me yourself how much of it was contrived, and we both know that the reality is nothing like so glamorous. The cameras don't turn up to Bradford Pit, do they, to film older women, wearing less flattering attire, their faces grimy with coal dust, hauling the surface wagons?"

"No they don't. But this is a powerful new medium, which we might be able to use to our advantage."

"You sound as though you'd like to work in it yourself?"

"I've thought about it. Afterwards maybe."

Esther shook her head. "I've no doubt there might be jobs for women in this new film industry you dream of, but in what capacity? As secretaries, typists, wardrobe assistants? Nothing with any real influence."

"Once we get the vote…"

"But will we? All of that momentum that was building when we marched from Stevenson Square, it's all evaporated now."

"That's what I'm saying. Deeds not words, remember? Our actions, doing the work we are now doing, important work, valuable work that shows us in a completely new light."

"Really? You don't have brothers, Winifred, or a father any more. It's just you and your mother. But with me, with four brothers all working down the mine, plus an ailing father, who do you think cooks and cleans and washes and makes sure the house is running smoothly? And then they have the cheek to complain if their tea's not on the table when they get in, never mind that I've just put in a hard shift at the Rubber Factory myself. No, I'm telling you, vote or no vote, as soon as the soldiers come back, they'll take all those jobs we're currently doing back from us as quick as winking."

"Perhaps that depends on how many come back."

Esther paused. "I'm sorry. Ignore me. I'm just a bit out of sorts today, that's all. Have you heard from Arthur lately?"

Winifred shook her head. "Not for a while. He writes when he can."

Esther nodded. The rain began to fall once more. For a brief moment the sun still angled down through the bare trees. A sudden gust of wind shook the leafless branches, rattling them like bones. Hard drops of rain bounced on the twitching barbed-wire shadows on the pavement until these too disappeared.

Now, a few weeks later, a similar squall began as Winifred made her way home from Denton Station having just completed another hard shift. She relished the prospect of a hot bath in front of the fire in the back kitchen before supper and quickened her pace. Just as she began to lengthen her stride, she thought she heard the sound of glass shattering, followed by a rising, deep-throated roar. Racing around the corner from the next street, an angry, baying mob came charging towards her.

Winifred had to press herself into a doorway as they stormed past. Some were carrying sticks, which they brandished above their heads; some, stones, which they hurled through windows, seemingly at random; while others had tied rags soaked in paraffin onto the ends of broom handles, which they had set alight. Like some many-headed beast they snarled and lashed at all around them. Winifred shrank still further back into the recess of the doorway, trying to make herself invisible. As the final few stragglers at the back bellowed by, she recognised one of them, the son of a neighbour, still only a boy. She managed to catch hold of his sleeve and bring him to a temporary halt.

"Billy! What's going on?"

"This," he replied, his face lit by falling embers of flame from his improvised torch, and thrust a scrunched up piece of newspaper towards her, before barging on down the street to join the others.

Winifred smoothed out the creased news print on her lap as she stood there trembling, and then lifted it towards the gas light to read it.

The Manchester Union

8th May 1915

LUSITANIA SUNK!

NUMBER OF DEAD ESTIMATED AT 1000

NOT MORE THAN 600 KNOWN TO BE SAVED FROM WRECK

The Great Cunarder, *RMS Lusitania*, lies at the bottom of the ocean off the southern coast of Ireland, having been attacked at sea by a German submarine. As the dead and wounded are brought ashore, the death list grows...

*

Two older women, whose faces she knew but whose names she did not, now approached her, each jabbing a finger at the screaming headline.

"Someone's going to pay for this," muttered one of them with dark relish.

"And you don't need to ask twice who that might be," said the other with a grim chuckle.

And indeed Winifred did not. She watched their departing backs cast lengthening shadows along the now deserted, glass-strewn street, knowing exactly where it was they were heading – to the row of German shops along the Hyde Road. But she was too shocked and frightened to follow. She simply remained standing where she was, shaking with guilt and shame.

The following morning, after a night of rioting across the city, Mr Robin Peacock, Chief Constable of Manchester, issued a warrant for the arrest of all German shopkeepers resident in the city.

"In the interests of public safety and for the sake of the Germans themselves," his statement read, "prompt action is now required. Otherwise attacks on property might easily develop, through the natural transition of mob law, into attacks on the person. Accordingly I am ordering the immediate impounding of all German males between the ages of seventeen and fifty-five years in readiness for their deportation in due course, as soon as His Majesty's Government has put the necessary measures in place."

Winifred had not slept at all that night. She had lain awake, shivering, until the sky eventually grew light, thin stripes of grey bleeding from the darker welts above. She crept out into the silent streets. More broken glass crunched beneath her feet. Smoke hung in pockets where buildings had been set ablaze. She saw one or two families scurrying down alleyways, pushing prams piled high with what few possessions remained as they tried to make for places of refuge, which might offer them shelter and a place to hide while the arrests were being made.

She slowly picked her way through the debris and ruin of once familiar streets she now barely recognised. The scene before her resembled something out of

Paradise Lost, when the angels who had sided with Lucifer had been thrown down into hell. Jackdaws, their shaved heads jerking back and forth like hammers, strutted among the burnt out houses, ruthlessly tugging worms from the upturned earth. Children squatted in the open doorways. A rat emerged from an upturned drain and nosed between an untidy heap of fallen bricks before disappearing back among them.

She walked towards Hyde Road, where Mr Kaufman's Optics & Jewellery Shop stood beneath its giant sign of a pair of spectacles now blank and eyeless, between the three brass globes of a Pawnbroker's on one side and a Barber's on the other, its red and white striped pole now spattered with actual blood, all of them owned and run by German families, families known to Winifred personally. By the time she reached the row, the sky was a little lighter. There were more people about, quietly carrying out what they could salvage from their ruined properties into the streets, where they gathered to look back, trying to assess the full scale of the damage and make what sense they could of it.

Winifred paused at the edge of the wreckage. The sight that greeted her appalled her. Less than forty-eight hours ago, these were all thriving shops and businesses, much needed and valued by everyone. Now they were reduced to rubble. What made it even more unbearable for Winifred was the quiet stoicism of the survivors, the women retrieving and re-assembling those things that might still be of use, to be shared amongst everyone, resigned and uncomplaining. A splinter of sun poked and jabbed between the rows of houses, bouncing off the shards of glass littering the streets. Winifred raised a hand to her eyes to shield them from the glare, and as she did so, she began to make out individuals she knew, but no sign at all of the Kaufman family. A servant girl, her hair still tied with rags, carried out a tray, urging the others to rest a few moments and fortify themselves with a sweet, strong cup of tea. They saw Winifred and called her over, insisting that she too have a cup. Despite the sugar, its taste was bitter as she sat beside them on what was still standing of the low brick wall that ran along a narrow ginnel beside the row of still smouldering shops.

"Have you seen the Kaufmans?" she asked.

The servant girl topped up Winifred's tea. "They're not here," she whispered. "It was terrible, what happened here last night. The police just stood by and did nothing. No one wants to talk about it, but I heard they were taken to the new hospital between Oxford Road and Upper Brook Street. I'd try there, Miss."

Winifred nodded and thanked her. She looked up from her tea. The other women were still picking their way through the rubble, carrying out their few saved possessions, which they were vainly trying to sort through. They were clearly still in a state of shock, moving like automata. One older woman, her hair and shoulders thick with white brick and cement dust, suddenly stopped in front of Winifred, not seeing her, her attention distracted by a small child's doll she had spotted, partly buried beneath a pile of stones. She stooped to remove it and then, with a frown of concentration on her face, began to furiously dust it down with a series of compulsively delicate small gestures. She reminded Winifred of a demented but guiltless Lady Macbeth, the object of whose actions would ne'er be clean. As gently as possible, Winifred closed her fingers around the woman's feverish hand until it was stilled. The woman slowly lifted her head and looked directly into Winifred's face, as if searching for somebody she might once have known, and then moved on.

The servant girl, whose name Winifred remembered was Mary, rejoined her. "Poor soul," she said, looking towards the woman still clutching the child's doll. "She's searching for her little one. Only three, she was. They pulled her out from one of the cellars a couple of hours ago, but they were too late. The mother's been out of her mind ever since."

"What happened here, Mary?" said Winifred at last.

"You don't want to know, Miss."

"I do, Mary. I need you to tell me what happened to the Kaufmans."

"They were lovely people, really kind. They took me in when I was only twelve, treated me with such kindness. I lived in a room at t' top of th' house – look, right up there beneath the gable." She pointed to a small window, its glass all smashed, high up near the roof where, Winifred could now see, several slates were missing, which had presumably been torn down during the riots and used as missiles.

The family's sitting room was directly above the shop, with the bedrooms behind at the back. Downstairs was the kitchen, and Mr Kaufman used the cellar for his workshop, where he would make up and polish the jewellery.

"I never went in there," continued Mary, "except for once. It was 'strictly *verboten*', as Mrs Kaufman used to say, even for her. The door was open one time and he asked me to fetch him a glass of water, which I did. He had a magnifying glass fixed to one eye, and he was bent over his desk, grinding lenses. I'd never seen such a thing before, and so he called me over and asked me to look through one of them. It made everything look so much larger than life, so close up, you could see things, little things, that you'd never normally notice, like the whitish crescent at the base of your fingernail..." Mary's voice had trailed almost to a whisper. She was speaking slower and slower, the shock of what had happened increasingly taking hold of her. "The lunula, that's what Mr Kaufman told me it's called... loon-you-lah... a tiny half moon that never stops growing..."

Winifred could see that Mary's hands were shaking. She took them in her own and turned her round, so that she was looking directly at her. "Mary, what happened?"

Mary struggled to return to herself. "I don't like to say, Miss. It was late. After ten, I think. Dark. I was in bed. Suddenly I was woken by a crowd of people running down t' street and shouting. I looked out and someone threw a stone through t' shop window down below, and then others started smashing it with sticks and turning everything upside down. I ran downstairs but Mr Kaufman told me to go back to my room and bolt the door, so I didn't see what happened next, only heard." She shook her head, as if trying to rid herself of the memory. "Such ugly names they called him, and he was the nicest of gentlemen. Then I heard Mrs Kaufman, pleading with them to just leave them alone, but they wouldn't listen. I couldn't stand it, so I unlocked my door and ran down the stairs to see if I could help."

"That was very brave of you, Mary," said Winifred, recalling her own cowardice the night before.

"Stupid, more like. By the time I reached them, Mr Kaufman was lying on t' floor, with a cut to his head, and Mrs Kaufman was kneeling by his side. 'Fetch some water, Mary', she cried, and so that was what I did. By this time, Miss Ruth had come down too, and while Mrs Kaufman and I attended to Mr Kaufman, she really laid into the crowd that were still outside. Some of them were throwing stones and soaking rags with paraffin, which they shoved into bottles that exploded as they hurled them in through all the broken windows. Mrs Kaufman and I managed to get Mr Kaufman down into t' cellar, but Miss Ruth stayed outside. 'Why are you doing this?' she kept asking them. 'We've been your neighbours all our lives. My father's treated many of you for years. And your children'. That's when they started advancing towards her, but still she didn't stop pleading with them. 'I'm even engaged to a soldier who's fighting at the Front,' she shouted. But they wouldn't listen. By the time I got back up out of t' cellar, some men had grabbed her. They... I'm sorry, Miss. I just can't bring myself to say what I saw. Go to

Upper Brook Street, to the hospital, they'll tell you there what happened."

Winifred was silent a long time. It was all too easy to picture what must have happened next. She closed her eyes. Ruth was the same age that she was. Eventually she recovered her composure sufficiently to ask Mary one final question.

"But what about Mr Kaufman? Did he recover?"

"Yes, Miss. It were only a cut, but a deep one. He was very shaken. When the police did finally come, the first thing they did was to arrest him, along with all the other men from German born families, and marched them away. Someone said they're being shipped over to camps on the Isle of Man. I don't know when we'll see him again."

Winifred was reeling with all that she'd seen and heard. She knew she must go to Upper Brook Street to see Mrs Kaufman and Ruth, and put herself at their disposal. She stood up from the low wall, dusted herself down and looked about her. The same, slow, painful clean-up operation was still proceeding, piece by piece, brick by brick.

Almost as if reading her mind, Mary spoke a warning. "You be careful, Miss. It doesn't do just now to say what you're thinking out loud."

"And what about you, Mary? What will you do?"

"Don't you worry about me, Miss. I shall stay here and try and make myself useful till Mrs Kaufman returns from the hospital. I'll make sure she's settled first."

"But she can't come back here. It's not safe,

surely?"

"No, Miss. She has cousins, I believe, in Woodford. Perhaps she'll go there."

"And you?"

"Maybe she'll take me with her."

Winifred nodded, in awe of the girl's plain speaking and the way she looked to live simply from one moment to the next. "Good luck," she said, removing her gloves so that she might hold Mary's grimy fingers firmly with her own, and then she picked her way carefully through the ruins in the direction of Upper Brook Street. A dagger of sun sliced between the skeletal hulks of houses, catching the diamond on her engagement ring, ground for her personally by Mr Kaufman barely twenty yards from where she now walked, just one more broken shard of cut glass. As she skirted the craters and cracks in the pitted surface of pavements and roads, it was as if she were stumbling through No Man's Land.

*

Manchester Royal Infirmary
Upper Brook Street Entrance
Ward C

Date: 10th May 1915
Patient's Notes

Name: Kaufman, Ruth: Miss
Male/<u>Female</u>   <u>Single</u>/Married

Age: 20 years, 5 months
Height: 5ft 2ins

Weight: 8 stones, 4 pounds

Examined by: Nurse Iris McMaster
Doctor in charge: Dr Charles Trevelyan

History:
Miss Kaufman was brought into hospital suffering multiple injuries – see below. She was in severe pain, drifting in and out of consciousness. She was accompanied by her mother, Mrs H. Kaufman, who was able to provide an accurate history. The patient is normally in excellent general health. She has no pre-existing medical conditions. As a child she contracted both measles and chicken pox, neither of which left any lingering complications. When born she had a small infantile haemangioma on her cheek, which mostly faded with the onset of puberty and which is now barely visible. In every other respect the patient is a normal, healthy young female.

Physical Examination:
Upon arrival the patient was examined by Nurse McMaster before being referred to Dr Trevelyan for a more detailed diagnosis. She had sustained serious injuries to her arms, legs, back and ribs, three of which were broken, as was the radius of her left arm. Her face and body were covered with welts and bruises consistent with the patient's mother's account that she had been seized by an angry crowd carrying sticks and other implements and subjected to a vicious beating. Her lips are split, she has a broken nose and fractured right cheek

bone beneath significant swelling. Her right eye has also suffered damage to the point that the patient currently cannot open it. A more detailed optical test will be administered as soon as the swelling around the eye lessens and the patient is more easily able to open it. Her head has been partially shaved and there is evidence that she was tarred and feathered, all physical traces of which have now been removed, an action which caused the patient further pain and distress. In addition there has been severe bruising to the inner thighs and vagina, consistent with repeated aggravated violation. Although over a period of time the patient is expected to make a good recovery from these various physical injuries, Dr Trevelyan remains deeply concerned over the potential longer term psychological effects of the outrage.

*

Eight weeks later, at the start of what threatened to be another cool July day in the wettest summer anyone could remember, Mary stood anxiously at the gates of The Infirmary, waiting for them to open. As soon as they did, she entered and made her way as quickly as she could to Ward C, where she hoped to be allowed to help Miss Ruth get ready. For, if Dr Trevelyan gave the word, and there had been no unforeseen setbacks during the night, today had been earmarked for her to take her first steps back in the world and go home.

Mary knew the circuitous way from the hospital

entrance to the corridor where Ward C was to be found like the back of her hand and could have managed it blindfolded, having walked the route practically every day since the attack had taken place. Nurse McMaster was smiling as she approached.

"Someone's here bright and early, I see," she said.

"Yes, Nurse. Is she ready?"

"Almost. Now Mary, I am relying on you to make sure that your mistress does not try to do too much. She has been a most impatient patient – a good quality, but a dangerous one, especially now, in her condition. She must not – I repeat, not – over-exert herself."

"Yes, Nurse. You can count on me."

"Good. Now, here she is."

The door opened and there stood Ruth. Mary was not shocked by the sight which greeted her, for she had barely left her side, visiting nearly every day, whenever Mrs Kaufman could spare her, but to the middle-aged gentleman in the mackintosh, shaking his umbrella as he stepped in from the insistent drizzle that was now falling outside, Ruth's appearance stopped him in mid-stride. In an instant he took in the pale, gaunt face, the dark circles under the eyes, the left arm in a sling and the less than elegant walking stick to support her, but what shocked him more than any of these was seeing her in the final act of fixing her hat before she turned in his direction. Although her hair had begun to grow back, and the worst of the tufts and patches had been smoothed by Mary on her previous visit, it was nevertheless immediately apparent that the young lady had recently undergone some terrible calamity. The gentleman just managed to recover his composure in time to be able to raise his hat and wish her a good morning before proceeding further along the corridor. Mary looked at her mistress anxiously.

"I'm all right, Mary. Please don't look alarmed. People will just have to get used to me until it all grows back. I've managed to, and so they'll just have to as well. I've done nothing to be ashamed of."

"Quite right, Miss Kaufman," said Nurse McMaster briskly. "That's the spirit. Now – are you quite sure you're ready? I shan't say we're sorry to see you leave us, for that's our job, to make you better, but we shall miss you all the same."

"That we will," said Dr Trevelyan, who at that moment had joined them in the doorway of the ward. "Allow me to escort you. You had us worried for a while, I won't deny it. Didn't she, Mary?"

"Yes, sir."

"But Mary here has been a constant source of strength."

"Thank you, sir."

"And will continue to be, I hope," said Ruth as they reached the exit.

"Well," said Dr Trevelyan, shaking Ruth's free hand, "here we are. I expect Nurse McMaster has already given you the speech about taking things slowly for just as long as you need?"

"Yes, Doctor, she has."

"Good. Now, I don't wish to appear ungracious, but I hope I never have the pleasure of seeing you again. Not inside these four walls, at any rate. Good day to you, and good luck."

"Thank you, Doctor."

As soon as they stepped outside, Ruth paused at the top of the flight of stone steps that led down to the pavement and looked up, letting the rain fall upon her hands and face. "You can't imagine how I've longed for this moment, Mary." She waited a while longer, savouring the fresh air and each separate drop of water. "Now, let us make our way to the tram stop just across the road to take us home."

"But Miss Ruth, I have strict instructions to take you back to Woodford. The train is this way..."

"Mary, listen to me. I have no intention of travelling to Woodford. My home is where it has always been. In Denton. I will not be forced out of it by the actions of the mob. We are going back there, you and I, Mary, and we are going to re-open the shop again, as soon as I am strong enough, and you will be my *Passepartout*."

"Your what, Miss?"

"My trusted right hand and companion."

"Thank you, Miss. But what shall I tell Mrs Kaufman?"

"Leave all that to me, Mary. I shall write to her this afternoon, and you shall post the letter for me, and with luck she should receive it tomorrow."

"Very good, Miss."

"How is she? I have not seen her since the day she took me to the hospital."

Mary paused. "I think you would prefer to hear the truth, Miss, and so I shan't tell a lie. She's not good, Miss, not good at all. It was all just too much for her, you see? What with the attack on the shop, then what happened to you, and…"

"Yes, Mary? What is it?"

"Your father, Miss."

"What about him?"

"It was felt best not to tell you, with you being so weak at first, and then… well, I kept expecting your mother to visit you and tell you herself. It's not my place after all…"

"He's not…?"

"No, Miss. I'm sure we'd have heard. He's… they took him away that night, Miss."

"Who did?"

"The police. He was taken by goods train to Liverpool, and from there put on a ferry to the Isle of Man. To a camp, Miss."

Ruth's shoulders slumped. "Internment," she sighed.

"Yes, Miss. I'm ever so sorry."

"This war will make monsters of us all. Come, Mary. Here's our tram. Will you help me aboard?"

They sat together in an uneasy silence as Mary wondered whether to tell her mistress any more about her mother, the way she now just sat, staring into space, not speaking to anyone, not even her cousin, who had so kindly taken her in and offered to find room for Miss Ruth too. No, thought Mary, best not to say anything just yet. It was going to be difficult enough when they finally got back and Ruth would see for herself the extent of the damage that had been visited upon the place she still insisted on calling home. Mary had done the best that she could to clean up the mess, sweep up all the broken glass, but with no authority of her own, she had merely been able to arrange for boards to be put up where the windows once had been, and a neighbour had replaced the locks on the front and back doors. Mary had managed to clean off the filthy words that had been daubed across them, but you could still make out faint traces of them if the light fell in a certain way.

When they both stood in front of them a few minutes later, Ruth held Mary's hand tightly in her own. The rain had eased, and a pale watery sun was gamely trying to make its presence felt. "Come," she said, "we will not be defeated."

They stepped across the threshold into the room which had formerly been the shop, now quite bare and scrubbed to within an inch of its life by Mary. Ruth looked around. Motes of dust danced in the thin shafts of sunlight that edged their way through the cracks in the wood covering the windows. As her eyes became accustomed to the shuttered light, Ruth's attention was drawn to a vase of yellow tulips on what had once been the shop's counter. Propped against it was a small card. "Wishing you love on your return, Winifred."

Ruth looked around. There on the mantelpiece stood a small wooden plaque, on which was mounted a silver sixpence with the words "presented to Friedrich Kaufman, aged 5 years, upon the occasion of his arrival in Great Britain, 31st August 1865" engraved upon it. She could not equate this sequestered calm with her memories of that night of the riots and her attackers.

"Let us begin at once, Mary," she said with renewed purpose and energy. "Take down these planks of wood from the windows, and then hurry round to Mr Gould, the glazier, and ask him to install new windows at his earliest convenience."

"Yes, Miss."

"We have nothing to be ashamed of. We will not cower in the shadows. What is it our boys shout in the trenches? 'Over the top'?"

"I believe so, Miss."

"Then that is what we shall do."

*

British Army Field Hospital
Salonika

15th August 1915

My Dearest Winifred,

Please do not be alarmed by the address at the top of this letter. While it is true that I am currently convalescing in an army field hospital "somewhere in Salonika" – I am not permitted to say exactly where for obvious reasons – I am not at all badly injured. It is faintly embarrassing in fact, for a piece of shrapnel lodged itself in a part of my anatomy I prefer not to mention. Let me just say that it makes sitting down somewhat painful!

I currently have time on my hands while the excellent nurses keep an eye on all of us here. We have to be careful to do as we're told, otherwise they become most stern with us. I thought I should use some of this time, therefore, to let you know what happened – it's quite a story, and one which I hope will keep you amused when you are at home in the evenings after your long day's work at the Munitions Factory. We saw your film in a tent here a few days ago – very impressive! Some of the boys gave me a bit of a ribbing, as you might imagine, but deep down they are all jealous that I have such a beautiful film star for a fiancée.

Thank you for all your letters. They do reach me eventually and they are such a tonic. Thinking of you, and my sister, keeping the home fires burning, makes everything we are trying to do out here all the more worthwhile. We all of us dream of returning once more to those warm home fires when this is all over and you won't have to work in that factory any more.

But now to my story – it is not a very heroic tale, I'm afraid.

I was laying a length of signal wire between different units and I had to cross a section of No Man's Land. I obviously didn't keep my head down low enough and must have attracted the enemy's attention, for suddenly there was a quick volley of mortar fire, and the next thing I knew I felt a sharp pain in the derrière. I managed to crawl my way back to safety with no further damage, except to my *dignity, when the 2nd Unit's C/O came over, wanting to know what all the commotion was about. A surgeon removed what he could of the offending pieces of metal but then said I'd need to be sent to the nearest Field Hospital, where they could finish patching me up properly. The C/O wasn't best pleased but there was nothing else for it, and a mule was fetched to deliver me post haste.*

While I sat, somewhat painfully it must be said, astride the mule, I asked the C/O which path I should take. "Don't worry," he told me, "the mule knows the way." And indeed he did.

For the rest of the day I rode through cypress groves in a narrow valley flanked by mountains, listening to the sounds of strange birds, insects and running water, the war a world away. Just as the sun was going down I caught sight of the hospital across a river, which the mule refused point blank to cross. Nothing whatever I did could persuade it and the water was too deep for me to cross unaided. So I pulled out my flags from my haversack and signalled my situation to the other side requesting further instructions. Thank goodness for semaphore! Once again I was told not to worry. They signalled me back that the mule would take me the long way round, a few miles downstream to a bridge where I could cross and be with them by the next morning.

It was a long night. I was completely lost and had to trust that the mule would not stumble as we carried on through the dark. When I finally made it to the camp, just as the sun was coming up over the mountains, sleep-deprived and sore from the added insult of a sharp wasp sting to the site of my wound, the field hospital was all but destroyed. A rogue shell must have landed nearby in the night, leaving nothing but a huge crater. Mercifully there were no serious casualties but they were already packing up to find a new, safer base where they could set up, and so there was nothing for it but to continue my weary exodus on foot, the mule being immediately requisitioned to carry supplies and equipment, until we finally reached the spot where I am now sitting up in bed, writing you this letter.

We hear rumours that things got rather sticky further on towards Gallipoli, and so I suppose I have to count myself lucky. Nurse says I should be able to rejoin my unit again in a few days, and so I am just now waiting to receive news of my next posting. It will be good to catch up with the pals once more, but it would be even better to see you again, my love. There's no news yet on when our next leave might be due, but I shall write to you the moment we are informed.

They are saying once again that, with one more determined push, the war may be over by next Christmas, but with the fighting now taking place on so many different fronts, I don't know how they can be certain. We must remain patient and hope the tide will turn for us soon.

I was most distressed to read about what happened to the Kaufmans and even more concerned that you found yourself caught up on the edge of it all. Thank heavens you were not harmed yourself. The sinking of 'The Lusitania' was a most dreadful affair, and passions ran pretty high out here too, I can tell you. I suppose we should not be too surprised that events got out of control for a time. The Lord says to turn the other cheek, but that's a hard thing to master in a war.

Please do all that you can to avoid risking further danger to yourself and know that I think of you every hour of every day.

Yours, with love
Arthur

*

The year turned.

At the end of September Esther's father, Walter, received the telegram stating that Alfred, affectionately known as "young Freddie", had been killed in action during the Battle of Loos. He was just sixteen years old. Walter collapsed in his chair and never returned to work.

The following week, a couple of days after the funeral, Esther took herself to the City Art Gallery on Mosley Street. She always took solace from the paintings that hung there, even after her equivocal feelings about them following the trial of the suffragettes two and a half years before. She had become familiar with so many of them over the years, and now she found herself standing in front of *Autumn Leaves* by Millais. It had always been a favourite. She and Winifred had visited it many times in those distant days before the war, after attending meetings of the Suffragists, or lectures at The Athenaeum next door. The caption beneath it noted that Ruskin considered it "the first perfectly painted twilight", while Millais' wife, Effie, had written that her husband had attempted to create a picture that was "full of beauty but without a subject".

Looking at it now, Esther felt its subject had been found, for it seemed suffused with loss and sorrow. Three beautiful young women and a girl, their auburn hair tumbling loosely round their shoulders, heaped baskets of autumn leaves into a cairn-like pyramid, a funeral pyre, waiting to be burnt, already starting to smoulder, with thin wisps of pale smoke beginning to enfold them like a shroud.

Esther recalled the words of the Psalm sung at Freddie's funeral:

"For my days are consumed like smoke
And my bones are burned as an hearth…"

As the twilight fell behind the figures, the landscape faded into darkness. There were no men, only women inhabiting this scene. Briefly Esther glimpsed a future stretching out ahead of her, and all the women of her generation, alone and barren. Her heart felt smitten and withered, like the piled dead leaves.

She stood before the painting a long time, silent, not moving. Other visitors to the gallery sensed her grieving and kept a respectful distance from her. As they entered this room where the picture was hung, it was almost as if she were an extra figure in the composition, contemplating the view, waiting for the flames to take hold.

Gradually she recovered her composure. This would not do, she thought. She must keep busy. She resolved to seek out Winifred and learn what had become of Ruth Kaufman since she had returned from hospital. She would put others' needs ahead of her own. She quickly turned on her heels and left the gallery. The four figures in the painting continued to pour their baskets of leaves on to the ever growing pyre.

*

There were no trees on Hyde Road from which autumn leaves might fall, and as the days grew shorter, it no longer became possible for Ruth to conceal the true nature of her condition. Mary had known for weeks now, even though Miss Ruth had made no mention of it to her, and so it was with immense relief she opened the front door one Sunday afternoon to see Miss Winifred and Miss Esther standing on the doorstep. They, she was sure, would know what was needed to be done and would counsel her mistress.

MARY:

Miss Esther, Miss Winifred – please: come in.

WINIFRED:

Thank you, Mary.

Esther and Winifred step into the hallway, where Mary helps them with their hats and coats. From the sitting room at the back, Ruth calls out unseen.

RUTH:

Ladies, please come straight through. Mary, will you bring in some tea?

MARY:

Yes, Miss.

Mary hurries into the kitchen, while Esther and Winifred join Ruth in the sitting room, where she is standing, in profile, waiting to greet them. Even allowing for the loose fitting garment she is wearing, it is at once apparent that she is visibly pregnant. She turns to face them, greeting each of them with a kiss to the cheek.

RUTH:

Sit down. Please. No long faces.

WINIFRED:

Oh, Ruth! I don't know what to say.

RUTH:

Then say nothing. The situation is what it is.

ESTHER:

I take it that this is a result of what happened on the
night of the riots?

Ruth inclines her head.

WINIFRED:

The animal. He should be made to pay for what he
has done.

RUTH:

I agree. But I wouldn't know where to begin if asked
to identify them.

WINIFRED:

Them? You mean…?

RUTH:

There were several of them, yes.

Winifred raises her gloved hand to her mouth.

ESTHER:

I am so sorry, Ruth. Who else knows about this?

RUTH:

Mary, obviously. But no one else.

ESTHER:

Have you not seen a doctor?

Ruth shakes her head. Esther looks at her directly.

RUTH:

Yes, you're quite right. I know I should. I will. Soon.

ESTHER:

Urgently.

Ruth nods. Winifred is about to speak when Mary returns with the tray of tea things, which she places on a small occasional table.

RUTH:

Thank you, Mary. Just leave it. We'll pour for ourselves.

MARY:

Yes, Miss.

ESTHER:

Mary?

MARY:

Yes, Miss?

ESTHER:

Ruth, I think Mary should stay. There's much we need to discuss and it makes sense if she hears it. She's the one who's going to have to make sure you're taken care of.

WINIFRED:

But…

Esther throws a sharp look in the direction of Winifred, who thinks better of continuing.

RUTH:

You're quite right. And Mary is already taking care of me. Aren't you? I could not manage without her.

Mary bows her head.

ESTHER:

Good. Then that is settled. Tea, I think now, don't you? Mary, one lump or two?

MARY:

Please, Miss. Let me.

But Esther already has the tea pot in her hand.

In that case, two, Miss. Thank you.

Esther continues to pour and pass everyone their tea.

ESTHER:

Now, Winifred, what was it you were about to say before Mary joined us?

WINIFRED: (*setting down her cup*):

I was going to ask Ruth whether she had told Cecil what had happened and if so, what had been his response?

RUTH:

No. Not yet. As I said before, no one outside this room knows.

WINIFRED:

But you will tell him, surely?

RUTH:

I don't know.

ESTHER:

There are other matters to consider first. Mary?

MARY:

Yes, Miss?

ESTHER:

What do you think Ruth should do?

Winifred's eyes widen in astonishment.

MARY:

Me, Miss?

ESTHER:

Yes, of course you. You know Ruth better than anyone, I imagine?

MARY:

Well, Miss, I think…

She turns to face Ruth directly.

I think there are practical matters that need to be sorted first, before anything gets mentioned to Mr Cecil.

WINIFRED:

Practical matters? What do you mean?

ESTHER:

Don't be naïve, Winifred. Well, Ruth?

RUTH:

Mary's quite right. She's been going on at me for weeks now.

MARY:

It's for your own good, Miss Ruth.

ESTHER:

And what have you decided?

Esther, Winifred and Mary all turn to face Ruth who, for the first time, reveals a slight loss of composure.

RUTH:

I… When I first missed my monthly, I thought it was most probably a reaction to what had happened, the body's way of convalescence, but when I missed a second, and then a third, and I began to experience the most dreadful nausea, I knew there was only one explanation. You suspected before me, I think, didn't you, Mary? (*Mary nods*). I was frightened, and then I was angry, and then I was frightened again. I confess I tried some of the less bizarre old wives' tales – hot baths, a tablespoon of yeast mixed with pennyroyal tea – but as you can see, none of those worked.

WINIFRED:

It's not too late. There are people who… one hears about women, older women, who – well – perform certain procedures…

RUTH:

No. I couldn't do that.

ESTHER:

I'm relieved to hear it.

MARY:

It's too dangerous, Miss. The daughter of a neighbour of ours…

ESTHER:

Thank you, Mary.

RUTH:

I think I must go through with the birth.

ESTHER:

Is there somewhere you could go? The new lying-in hospital on Whitworth Street?

MARY:

Excuse me, Miss. I've been suggesting we might go to Cheshire, to Woodford, where her mother's staying with a cousin. It would be quiet, and no one knows us there.

ESTHER:

Ruth?

Ruth shakes her head.

WINIFRED:

How is your mother?

RUTH:

That's the problem. She's not well at all. Since she learned of my father's internment, she has sunk into an almost unreachable melancholia. She doesn't speak, she hardly eats, she barely registers where she is. When Mary and I went to visit her one Sunday, before I had begun to show, I don't think she even recognised us. Her cousin's doctor has diagnosed delirium. He's advocating electric shock treatment. I can't go there.

ESTHER:

Is there anyone else you might speak to? Your own doctor?

Ruth turns away.

MARY:

Excuse me, Miss. There is someone, I think.

ESTHER:

Yes?

MARY:

Dr Trevelyan. From The Infirmary. He looked after Miss Ruth when she was first attacked. He's ever so kind. He took quite a shine to her.

WINIFRED:

Yes, I remember him. What do you say, Ruth? He might suggest something we've not thought of.

RUTH:

Yes, he might. We'll arrange to see him, won't we, Mary?

MARY:

Yes, Miss. I'll go and make some more tea.

Mary leaves and Winifred goes to sit beside Ruth.

WINIFRED:
But if you do go through with it, what are you going to do afterwards? You're not going to keep the baby, are you?

RUTH:
Why shouldn't I? I've done nothing wrong.

ESTHER:
Indeed you have not, dear. You've been incredibly brave.

WINIFRED:
But what about Cecil?

Ruth looks up at Winifred, biting her lower lip, then shakes her head and turns away.

Ruth: (*barely audible*):
I don't know.

Winifred seems about to press the point further but then changes her mind. Mary returns with the tea.

MARY:
Here we are. Who's for some Angel cake? Miss Ruth baked it this morning.

Esther and Winifred walked the short distance from Ruth's well-furnished apartment above her father's shop to Winifred's much smaller, plainer house, crossing from one side of the railway line to the other. They barely spoke, each deep in their own separate thoughts. When they reached the road where she lived, Winifred grasped Esther's hands tightly in her own.

"I talk too much, I know I do, but I feel so frightened all of the time. What's to become of us, Esther, if none of our men return? It's foolish of me to think this, I know, but I lie awake at nights and my head just feels as if it will explode, and when I do eventually manage some sleep, I dream I am walking down endless avenues of shells in the munitions factory. They seem to stretch on for ever and I am destined to walk between them all, row upon row. And sometimes I think I hear Arthur's voice calling to me, from behind one of the shells, but when I look, he's not there."

Esther placed a gloved finger upon Winifred's trembling mouth. "Hush, darling. Deeds not words, remember?"

They leant into each other and Esther kissed her young friend gently on the brow. From a distance they might have been mistaken for Walter Deverell's *Study of Two Girls Embracing*. A train whistled as it thundered across the stone bridge, issuing a great cloud of steam. When this finally cleared, both women had gone, Winifred into her house to draw her curtains and shut out the world, Esther around the corner to make her way back to her flat on Melland Road, where her father and brothers would be wondering about their tea.

*

Dr Trevelyan alighted from the tram on Hyde Road and looked about him to get his bearings. Yes. He could see the shop at once. Between the red and white striped barber's pole and the three hanging brass globes of a pawnbroker's a pair of outsized spectacles jutted at right angles from the brick wall, where a faded sign announced: G.F. Kaufman & Son, and then in smaller letters underneath: Optics, Lenses, Horology, Jewellers & Engravers.

The doctor crossed the busy road and paused by a stall selling flowers. Should he? Was it proper, he wondered, to buy a young lady flowers, when that young lady was known to him only as a former patient? If he were visiting her in hospital, he would have less hesitation in taking her flowers. Or fruit possibly? He looked around. There was no green grocer he could see. Flowers or nothing then. No. He couldn't possibly arrive empty-handed, even though he had been requested to call in his professional capacity only, to offer advice. Yes. He would take her flowers. Nothing ostentatious. There – a bunch of tulips, still tightly budded. Perfect.

When Mary answered his knock on the shop door, he stepped inside immediately, before being invited, and removed his hat, which he proffered towards Mary, together with his cane and gloves. He kept hold of the flowers himself for the time being.

"You summoned, I came," he said, looking around. "The shop is temporarily closed, I take it?"

"Yes, Doctor. Miss Ruth tried to keep it going at first, but it was too much for her."

"I can well imagine. Now – may I see her?"

"She's resting at the moment. Would you like me to wake her?"

"Presently. Let her sleep a while longer. Perhaps you and I might speak a little first?"

"Me, sir?"

"Yes. Mary, isn't it? You know her better than anyone, so tell me please, in your opinion, how would you describe her current state of mind?"

"Her mind, sir?"

"Yes, Mary, her mind. The body heals, given time. We diagnose, we treat, the patient recovers. But the mind... the scars inflicted there are invisible and much more difficult to treat."

Mary looked down.

"I take it from your expression that you understand something of what I mean?"

"She's like the weather cock on the roof of St Lawrence's Church, Doctor. One minute she's so full of energy she wants to take on the world, the next she can't stop weeping."

"Yes. It's as I thought. Does she remember, do you think, all that befell her?"

"I'd like to think not, sir."

"Does she suffer nightmares?"

"Not that she speaks of, sir. And she doesn't call out in the night. I'd hear her if she did. She was..."

"Yes?"

"She was knocked to the ground, sir."

"She was unconscious?"

"I don't think she knows the full story of what happened to her."

"The brain is a remarkable organ, Mary. A complex network of billions of nerve cells. We know less about it than we do the face of the moon. Yet each year brings new discoveries. It has the capacity to shut down, to repress what may be harmful to us, in a kind of beneficial amnesia."

"You've lost me now, sir."

"Things that are simply too painful to endure, it buries."

"Will she ever remember them, sir?"

"I pray heaven not. There are those – Dr Freud, for example – who urge us to dig deep, to uncover our earliest memories, in a bid to understand better our natures. But I believe that some things are best left where they are. Nature is a great healer, Mary. Nature and time."

"Yes, sir."

Dr Trevelyan nodded, and then once more began to question her. "What other moods have you observed?"

"She hoards things, sir."

"Hoards?"

"She thinks I don't notice. But she's for ever picking up bits of cloth, squirreling them away where she thinks I won't find them. Last week I caught her rooting out the doll's house she'd had as a child. She was holding up all the little toys and looking at them like they might disappear if she didn't hold every one of them close."

"Hmm. What else?"

"In her bedroom…"

"Yes?"

"For months before what happened she'd been saving things in the bottom drawer of her wardrobe for her *trousseau*, ever since her engagement. I know this because from time to time she'd show me certain things she'd bought or been given. But ever since she came home from the hospital, she's not looked at it, not once, and then last week I thought I'd better give it an airing, make sure no moths had got in, and when I opened the drawer…"

"You found…?"

"Things for the baby, sir, all neatly laid out on top."

"And you believe she intends to keep the child once it is born?"

"It's like she's making a nest, sir."

Dr Trevelyan placed the thumb and forefinger of his right hand across the bridge of his nose and closed his eyes. Mary waited, not moving a muscle. After a few moments he addressed her directly once more.

"Perhaps you might enquire whether your mistress is sufficiently rested to be able to see me now?"

"Of course, sir." She bobbed a neat curtsey and hurried out of the room.

The doctor was still clutching the bunch of tulips in his left hand. He'd come across cases of this type of mania in other *pre-partum* women and he'd read some of Dr Freud's more colourful accounts of hysteria among women in his Parisian clinics, but Miss Kaufman had not struck him as hysterical in any way. On the contrary, she seemed extraordinarily resilient in

100

her recovery while she had been his patient in the hospital, heroic even. These sudden vacillations of mood were in complete accord with not only her condition, but the appalling particularity of the circumstances that had caused it. She was to be supported, not argued with, and he tried to prepare himself for what he feared might be a difficult conversation he was about to embark upon. At that moment he was snatched from his reverie by the return of Mary.

"If you please, sir, Miss Ruth will see you now. If you'd care to follow me?"

Mary led the doctor up an elegant staircase with a polished mahogany banister, along a landing with a Turkish rug leading to a window of stained glass, one that had survived the attacks on the shop on the evening following the sinking of *The Lusitania*, where an aspidistra stood in a brass vase on the sill. He paused by a half open door, which Mary indicated he should enter. Inside the curtains were open, as was the window, affording a cool, refreshing breeze. Facing the window Ruth was sitting up in bed, propped up with pillows, a neatly embroidered jacket around her shoulders. Dr Trevelyan noticed immediately the pale face and the dark circles under her eyes.

"Dr Trevelyan, thank you so much for coming to see me at such short notice. You will forgive, I hope, my receiving you like this?"

"Miss Kaufman, I am pleased that you felt you could call on me. I took the liberty of bringing you these." He proffered the tulips towards her. "I hope you do not think me forward?"

"Not at all, Doctor. They are beautiful, a welcome splash of colour in these dark November days. Mary?"

"Yes, Miss?"

"Would you mind putting these in a vase for me please? And then leaving Dr Trevelyan and me alone for a few minutes? Until I call?"

"Of course, Miss."

After Mary had left Dr Trevelyan approached Ruth. "You are most fortunate to have such a capable girl at your side, Miss Kaufman."

"I know it, Doctor, and every day I am grateful for it." She tapped the side of her bed. "Please sit." The doctor hesitated a fraction. "Please," she continued. "I am rather tired today, I fear. I don't believe my voice would carry from here to the chair across the room, and I am long past caring about social improprieties."

Dr Trevelyan smiled and sat beside her. "Miss Kaufman," he began.

"Ruth, please."

"Very well. Ruth. In which case you must call me Charles."

"But you are my doctor."

"Strictly speaking, I am not. Not since you were discharged from my care at the hospital. It's true that I come to you today at your request in my professional capacity, but I also come, I hope, as a friend."

"Thank you. Charles."

"Good. Then we must speak freely and openly. Mary, when she came to see me, said that you needed advice."

"I do. I did."

"I take it then you have already made a decision?"

"I believe I have."

"But you need to go over it with me?"

"Yes, Charles. There are, now, only two choices before me. I never seriously considered a deliberate miscarriage."

"Few would have blamed you if you had, but I am relieved that you didn't. Apart from the legal considerations, the medical risks are extreme."

"I know, and whatever the circumstances of its conception, it is not the fault of the child."

"I agree with you, but that is not the general view of society."

"No. I realise that, and so, as I say, I have two options. I can go away somewhere, deliver the baby in secret, then let it be taken from me, for adoption, or to an orphanage, or worse, to a workhouse…"

"There is no legal framework for adoption, and so unless you know a couple specifically in need of a child, who cannot have one of their own…?"

"I don't."

"I see. And Mary has explained to me the most unfortunate and distressing situation regarding your parents. I am extremely sorry."

"Thank you."

"It would seem, then, that an orphanage would be…"

"What? Easier?"

"I was going to say 'more straightforward'."

"But for whom? For me? What of the child?"

"And the second option?"

"I raise the baby myself."

Dr Trevelyan rose from the side of the bed and walked towards the open window, where he stood, legs astride, hands clasped behind him, looking out, before turning back to address Ruth directly.

"You are one of the most extraordinary women I have ever met, Miss Kaufman – Ruth. What you're suggesting is…"

"Reckless? Foolhardy?"

"Courageous."

"Not so very much. Not really." A tear slid from the corner of her eye and she turned away. "Would you pour me a glass of water please, Charles? There's a jug on the dressing table."

"Of course." He returned with the glass and also passed Ruth his handkerchief.

"Thank you."

Dr Trevelyan waited while she drank some water and composed herself. "Might I ask you a question?"

Ruth nodded and put down the glass.

"It may not be my place, but have you discussed this at all with your fiancé? Or his family perhaps?"

She shook her head, her face screwed up in distress. Without thinking Charles took her hand in his and she did not remove it.

After a further pause, she spoke once more. "While I was in hospital, I managed to write a letter to Cecil's parents, letting them know what had happened – well, not all of it, just what they might have read in the newspapers, about the riots, my being beaten trying to protect my father. They live in a big house, Charles, much grander than ours, in Green Walk, a private road in Whalley Range…"

Charles nodded that he understood.

"I suspect they never really thought me a good match for their son."

"Did they reply?"

"They sent me a *Get Well* card, pre-printed, with their names in italic script at the bottom. They didn't even sign it."

Charles's heart went out to her even more. "And your fiancé?"

"I haven't told him. He has enough to contend with at the Front. I write instead the letters all soldiers hope to receive from their betrothed." She gently took her hand away from his and reached for another sip of water.

After a long silence, Charles spoke again, with extreme gentleness. "I am sure you realise that what you are proposing will cause you immeasurable difficulties."

"Yes."

"At the very least, censure. At worst, ostracism. You will lose customers from your business, your neighbours will shun you, your baby will not be baptised."

"But I've done nothing wrong."

"No. You haven't. Nothing at all. But if you do intend to keep the baby, as I believe you do, you will have to go away, where nobody knows you, where you might pretend that you are a widow, with your husband killed in the fighting – there will be plenty of other women in similar circumstances and so your word will not be doubted…"

"But that would be living a lie. Why should I hide away like that, in secrecy and shame? I have nothing to be ashamed of."

"Forgive me for saying so, Miss Kaufman, but that is not the way the world operates. For centuries this city has been a haven for exiles, for people who have been driven from their places of birth for whatever reasons, Jews, Huguenots, Irish, even Germans like your own family, who have fled persecution, suffering, hardship, to alight here, like migrating birds, with strange customs and different languages, to settle, start again, build new homes, invent new names, make better lives for themselves and their children. It's not running away, Miss Kaufman, it's running towards, and it's not a lie."

Ruth looked at Dr Trevelyan in wide-eyed astonishment. She had not imagined she would hear a speech so passionate from him. Nor, she now realised, had he expected to make one, for even now the colour had risen in his cheeks. He appeared quite flustered and hastily poured himself another glass of water, which he drank in a single draught.

"I do apologise, Miss Kaufman. I did not intend to cause embarrassment." And in truth he did not know quite what had overtaken him. He was not a man to make public pronouncements, but something in this young woman's situation and her demeanour in trying to act with unimpaired moral truthfulness had stirred him beyond measure. "I should be going. You must be tired."

"Yes, Charles, I am tired. But please don't go. Not yet. Sit beside me a little longer."

"I fear I cannot do so, Miss Kaufman."

They held each other's gaze a long time. Outside a train rumbled across the bridge on its approach to the town. A tram clattered past beneath them, its brakes creaking and its bell clanking. A cart spilled its goods. Voices of people calling out angrily to one another across the street rose through the open window. A magpie, swooping among the debris, searched for something shiny, its mocking machine gun cry rattling the air, while a sparrow hopped up on to the sill, a snail shell in its beak, which it tried to crack open, repeatedly banging it against the outside wall.

"I've decided. I shall write to Cecil this evening. I will tell him everything and release him from any obligation. What I do subsequently will depend in part upon his answer."

Charles nodded. He did not yet trust himself to speak.

"And Charles? Will you visit me again?"

"If you wish it."

"I wish it."

"Then let us wait to see how Cecil replies."

Ruth inclined her head, permitting herself the smallest of smiles. Charles was seized with a desire to rush across the room and press his lips against hers, but he merely stood, gently bowed, and moved towards the door.

"Miss Kaufman."

"Dr Trevelyan."

Ruth waited until his footsteps reached the bottom of the stairs and she heard Mary hand him his hat, cane and gloves, followed by their exchange of goodbyes and the front door finally closing behind him as he left, before ringing the bell that was beside her bed. Mary was at her side within moments.

"Well, Miss?"

"Dr Trevelyan has been of great assistance. His advice is invaluable."

The two girls beamed.

"Now, Mary, fetch me pen and paper please. I need to write to Cecil."

*

Announcement in THE TIMES
19th December 1915

Tomorrow at 11.00am a Memorial Service in remembrance of Capt Cecil Young, late of the 9th King's Own Royal Regiment, will take place at the Church of All Saints, Chorlton-on-Medlock, Manchester. Capt Young was killed during a brief skirmish with the 11th Bulgarian Division, who seized the town of Bogdanci on the Macedonian Front. Despite facing overwhelming odds, and with no regard for his own safety, Capt Young attempted the rescue of several comrades who had been ambushed by the roadside and taken prisoner. He single-handedly charged the main body of the enemy troops in a heroic act of self-sacrifice, for which he has been posthumously "Mentioned In Dispatches". We will remember him.

*

A week later, a parcel was delivered to Ruth, containing all of her letters to Cecil. There was no note enclosed. Dry-eyed, Ruth looked across at Mary. She calmly removed her engagement ring and placed it in the back of her dressing table drawer.

"I must write to Dr Trevelyan at once."

*

On the same day that Ruth's letters to Cecil were returned, the following message was printed in *The Manchester Guardian*, a re-issue of the one written the previous Christmas.

To The Women of Germany and Austria: An Open Christmas Letter from the Women of Manchester

Suffragette Sisters,

Some of us wish to send you a word at this sad Christmastide though we can but speak through the press. The Christmas message sounds like mockery to a world at war, but those of us who wished and still wish for peace may surely offer a solemn greeting to such of you who feel as we do. Do not let us forget that our very anguish unites us, that we are passing together through the same experience of pain and grief.

Caught in the grip of terrible circumstance, what can we do? Tossed on this turbulent sea of human conflict, we can but moor ourselves to those calm shores whereon stand, like rocks, the eternal verities of Love, Peace and Sisterhood.

We pray you to believe that, come what may, we hold to our faith in Peace and Goodwill between nations. While technically at enmity in obedience to our rulers, we owe allegiance to that higher law which bids us live at peace with all men.

Though our sons are sent to slay each other, and our hearts are torn by the cruelty of this fate, yet through pain supreme we will be true to our common womanhood. We will let no bitterness enter into this tragedy, made sacred by the life-blood of our best, nor mar with hate the heroism of their sacrifice. Though much has been done on all sides that you will, as deeply as ourselves, deplore, shall we steadily refuse to give credence to those false tales so freely told us, each of the other?

We hope it will lessen your anxiety to learn we are doing our utmost to soften the lot of your civilians and war prisoners within our shores, even as we rely on your goodness of heart to do the same for ours in Germany and Austria.

Do you not feel that the vast slaughter of our opposing armies is a stain on civilisation and Christianity, and that still deeper horror is aroused at the thought of those innocent victims, the countless women, children, babes, old and sick, pursued by famine, disease and death in the devastated areas, both East and West?

Is it not our mission to preserve life? Do not humanity and commonsense alike prompt us to join hands with the women of neutral countries, and urge our rulers to stay further bloodshed? Relief, however colossal, can reach but few. Can we sit still and let the helpless die in their thousands, as die they must – unless we rouse ourselves in the name of Humanity to save them?

There is but one way to do this. We must all urge that peace be made with appeal to Wisdom and Reason. Since in the last resort it is these which must decide the issues, can they begin too soon, if it is to save womanhood and childhood as well as the manhood of Europe?

Even through the clash of arms we treasure our poet's vision, and already we seem to hear:

"A hundred nations swear that there shall be

Pity and Peace and Love among the good and free."

May Christmas hasten that day. Peace on Earth is gone, but by renewal of our faith that it still reigns at the heart of things, Christmas should strengthen both you and us and all womanhood to strive for its return.

We are yours in this sisterhood of sorrow,

(List of more than a hundred signatories attached, including Emily Hobhouse, Millicent Fawcett, Dorothy Smith, Isabella Jones, Hannah Mitchell and, further down, towards the end of the list, Esther Blundell).

*

Wieltje
Belgium

25th December 1915

Dear Winifred,

Merry Christmas to you, my dearest love.

We are camped not far from what was once a small Belgian town. I imagine it used to be quite a pretty place, with a square and a church and a market, but I'm afraid not much of it survives now.

The combined shelling of both armies has seen to that. Where we have dug our trenches used to be fields. Wheat was grown here. Horses pulled ploughs and whole families helped with the harvest. Now it is utterly desolate, a waste land of mud and craters. It makes me think of what the surface of the moon might look like, devoid of any life, except that here there are men, hunkered down for the night, trying to snatch some sleep before daybreak. If you had the power to rise up, like the angel you appear to me as in my dreams, my love, and look down upon this scene, we would resemble two mighty colonies of ants, or rather, moles, each burrowing and tunnelling our way towards the other, and you would not, I am certain, be able to tell us apart.

Please forgive my melancholy mood, Winifred. We are all of us silent tonight. The Christmas season makes us all long to be far, far from here, back at home with our loved ones, sitting before a blazing fire, beside a tree decked with fruit and berries, sparkling with decorations, singing carols. Instead the scene I look out upon is a moonlit monochrome, the grey mud hardened and rutted by a sharp frost that holds us all captive in its icy grip.

When the dawn broke at the start of this Christmas Day, it snowed, and for a time we were children again. There was a lull in the fighting. We threw snowballs at one other. Some of us took to building a snowman.

We tied a belt around his waist and put an army helmet on his head. We nicknamed him Sergeant Jack Frost, and we all saluted him as we passed him. We clubbed together what few provisions we had, and I wrote a Christmas menu in my neatest handwriting, which I passed around to the rest of the unit:

1 tin of best bully beef
1 packet of oat biscuits
Washed down with 1 tin mug of Camp Coffee

We shared what we had, imagining it was roast turkey with all the trimmings.

By now the snow had stopped falling. The sky hung low and heavy. There's always a mist along the front line, and as the pale sun tried to break through on this freezing, grey Christmas morning, we heard a voice calling out to us, not a hundred yards away, across the mud and ice of No Man's Land.

"Hey, Tommy? Merry Christmas..." Then the faint, halting strains of 'Silent Night' floating through the mist.

"Stille nacht
Heilige nacht..."

We tried to join in, but a lump stuck in our throats. Instead, at the end, we offered a quiet round of *applause till, emboldened, Percy down the line started up with 'Good King Wencelas', which was followed by 'God Rest, Ye Merry Gentlemen', which gradually the rest of us took up.*

    "Glad tidings of comfort and joy, comfort and joy
      Glad tidings of comfort and joy..."

Through the mist we noticed a piece of white sheet being waved as a flag.

"Hey – Arthur," Percy called out, "you're the signaller: what does it say?"

"I think we all know what a white flag means," I replied. "We come in peace."

And then, one by one, we climbed stiffly out of the trenches and proceeded to walk gingerly across the space between the two front lines, while, already emerging out of the mist, a small group of the Kaiser's men were walking towards us. There was a brief awkward silence when we finally reached each other, but then one of the Germans put his hand inside his greatcoat – we all tensed – only to smile when he pulled out a small flask of rum which he duly passed around.

As you know, Winifred, I'm a teetotaller. This was the only time I've ever tasted alcohol, but it would have been impolite to have refused.

Then cigarettes were shared, photographs of families and sweethearts admired, yourself included, Winifred, and then I showed them the menu I'd written and asked if they might care to join us for Christmas lunch. But the laughter was cut short by the sound of a shell exploding further down the line and we all beat a hasty retreat back to our respective trenches wishing each other "Good Luck" and "Merry Christmas".

If you'd have asked me then what we were doing fighting men who are just the same as us, I couldn't for the life of me have told you. I still can't. Even though Percy bought it as we were scurrying back. I volunteered to lead a rescue party back out to collect him but the C/O refused. "We don't want to lose anyone else," he said. "Not on Christmas Day."

It's night time now, but there's a full moon, enough light to write by, while out there, in No Man's Land, those that didn't make it back, on either side, lie there on the ground, their bodies bleached and stiff in the moonlight, indistinguishable one from the other. Someone is playing a mouth organ. Its notes seem to fall from the stars. Gradually I recognise the tune. You sang it last Christmas and it comes back to me now.

When the swallows homeward fly
When the roses, scattered, lie
When, from neither hill nor dale,
Chants the silvery nightingale –
In these words my aching heart
Would to thee its grief impart:
Shall we ever meet again?
Parting – ah, parting – is such pain...

I send you all my love this Christmas and pray the next year brings peace, and that I, like the swallows, might fly homeward once again to hold you in my arms.

Yours, with all my love,
Arthur

*

Immediately after Freddie's death, Esther stopped working at the Rubber Factory. She couldn't bear to touch those gas masks, thinking of how her brother must have panicked to try and put his on during the attack at Loos. She recalled the phrase used by Wilfred Owen in the poem she'd recently read in the *Nation* magazine, copies of which could still be found at The Manchester Lit & Phil, where she still attended free lectures on a rare evening off, "*an ecstasy of fumbling*", and it made her shudder. She could no longer bring herself to assist in the manufacture of instruments of war. She knew it was a futile gesture, that others would readily take her place, but she preferred the more honest, if physically more gruelling work of a pit brow girl back at the mine where her brothers still worked. When she'd described the gas masks to them, they'd grimly asked if she might smuggle a few home for them to wear underground.

"Better than carrying those poor canaries down," they'd said, "though probably too hot."

Esther knew full well what conditions were like for them down below, where temperatures rose so high they would frequently be forced to strip naked, except for the helmets on their heads, the belts to carry their tools around their waists and the boots upon their feet.

Now she was working solely at the pit, it meant that she was readily on call to cope with the increasing demands placed on her by her father, who, since Freddie's death, had visibly declined and was more dependant than ever on Esther for his daily needs. She did not show him the poem Arthur enclosed with his most recent letter, nor did she share it with Winifred, who had been to see her just after Christmas, clearly shaken by his last letter to her. She read sections of it to Esther, who found it, unlike Winifred, to be quite comforting. He still retained his humanity and had not, it seemed, become inured to the suffering and brutality he must be witnessing every day. Nor, she was relieved to note, had he succumbed to the blind jingoism, which still infected so much of the nation's press. She was deeply touched by his compassion and sensitivity and felt that, if there were other soldiers with sentiments such as those, which there surely had to be, then there was indeed a genuine hope for future reforms once the war finally came to an end, as end it must, for ultimately there would simply be no more young boys left to send off to the Front.

She picked up Arthur's last letter and read the poem he had included for the hundredth time.

*

Remembrance

'Remember me when I am gone away,
Gone far away into the silent land…'

(from 'Remember' by Christina Rossetti: one of your favourite poems, Esther)

Inching his way forward in mud knee-deep
under a sniper's moon, edging past
the skittering horses, breath freezing in statues
settling on the shoulders of the men, grey ghosts
twitching beneath the humming barbed wire
starred with torn scraps of letters fluttering
in the wind, photographs of sweethearts,
snags of cloth from great coats, puttees,
calico and khaki prayer flags he daily posts,
a silent semaphore of hope he squeezes under,
flicking aside the rats, barely seeing them,
with glove-stiff fingers crawling clear he creeps
into the lunar landscape of no man's land
belaying the signal wire behind him…

Pausing to get his bearings he lets his marksman's
eye accustom to the terrain, the ground hot
despite the winter chill, splintered ice crystals
forming round his upper lip while smoke and ash
from the morning's battle still smoulders
smarting his eyes, he skirts the rims of craters
careful lest the wire catches, stuck fast,
caught in the random ruin of war -
piles of boots like some macabre rummage sale
(sometimes with feet attached, sometimes not)
form scattered cairns that mark his way
to the nearby camp, his second unit's HQ where
he's to join the wire to their transmitter,
a slender long umbilical that can't be cut...

He conjures up his father (miner, reader, vegetable
grower who back home on his allotment plants
prize-winning dahlias twixt rows of runner beans)
looks around him as he crawls thinking
it will be a century at least before this land
bears fruit again despite the fertile bone meal
it's now fed with, the blood red poppies clinging
to the craters' edge silver in the moonlight
leaching the land of all colour,
a mocking monochrome.

Three hours later he reaches the camp
and within minutes he's sending and receiving
Morse code messages he reads like Braille
with his fingers in readiness for the next day's
carnage as clouds cover the moon...

The men on the night watch make room for him
by the fire, they are singing the soldier's anthem –

'and when they ask us,
and they're certainly going to ask us
oh we'll never tell them,
no we'll never tell them...'

He takes out a stub of pencil, scratches
on a scrap of paper a message in Morse
he knows he'll never send, blind dots and dashes
tossed on the dying embers of the flames,
the now cold smoke drifting high into the night sky
to float in a petal shower of ash and dust
down the years, waiting for you, now, at last,
to piece it all together, decipher and decode:
.-- .... .- - / -- . -. / --- .-. / --. --- -.. ... / .- .-. . / - ....
.-- .... .- - / -- .- -.. / .--. ..- .-. ... ..- .- - .. - ...

Trans:
"What men or gods are these...?
What mad pursuits...?"

(from 'Ode to a Grecian Urn' by Keats, another
favourite poem)

*

What disturbed Esther even more than the content, and
what decided her not to share it with Winifred (or
anyone else), was her brother's description of himself in

the third person, as if he had detached himself, necessarily, from what he was experiencing, as if, almost, he saw himself as separate, already beginning to depart from the earth, or perhaps, more accurately, become absorbed into it...

*

Seven months earlier.

Friedrich spent most of the voyage with all of the other internees below deck, where their guards could observe them. It was a rough crossing and several of his fellow travellers were sick, as indeed was he on one occasion, though more through anxiety and agitation than the motion of the sea. His head and body were still sore from when the rioters had attacked him. If it had not been for the bravery of his daughter, who put herself directly between him and the mob, he might have been killed. But what had become of Ruth? No one would tell him, only that Helga, his wife, had had to rush off to the hospital with her, something about concussion, so that he had not had chance to say goodbye to either of them.

His head still raged from the injustice of it. What had the sinking of *The Lusitania* got to do with him, or any of these men standing in the cramped quarters below deck of a ship commissioned from the Isle of Man Steam Packet Company? He may have been born in Germany, but he had lived in England, in

Manchester, ever since he was five years old, when his father brought him with him half a century ago to begin a new life for the whole family. There were thousands of families of original German stock happily settled in the city, so many in fact, that when the Manchester newspapers talked of immigrants, they used the word "Germans" to describe them all. They had been made welcome – as factory owners, mill managers, retailers, bankers, and shopkeepers as he himself was. A cousin of his father's, who had arrived a decade before, had suggested Denton since there were several other German families already established there, Jews and Gentiles alike, and they, as Lutherans, very quickly assimilated. Why, he had even become a sidesman at St Lawrence's Church almost as soon as he turned twenty-one. Helga had attended the inaugural meeting of the Manchester's Women's Institute just a few weeks before and had been invited to serve on its general committee. Theirs was a respectable, integrated community, more English than the English in so many ways, upholders of traditions, loyal to the Crown. What possible threat did they pose to the nation's security? But the newspapers had whipped up such a storm of hatred that people who had formerly been his customers, some of whom he'd even considered friends, he now recognised among the baying mob who'd marched in fury upon his shop, smashing windows, overturning furniture, setting things alight. Such vitriol in their faces.

The ship continued to pitch and roll to a general chorus of groans, and Friedrich took the opportunity to look about him. Since the attack two nights ago, he had been slipping in and out of consciousness. His head had been bandaged and his chest was tightly bound to protect what were suspected to be broken ribs. He put his hand to his right temple and felt the dried blood that had congealed there. His cuts must have opened again while he had been last sleeping. He raised an arm to attract the attention of one of the guards and explained the situation to him. The guard signalled to one of the half dozen nurses who had been brought along to see to any individual needs, and she briskly, but not unkindly, changed his dressing. It was as she was completing this that Friedrich had the chance to take stock of the situation. He estimated there were approximately two hundred of them being interned. Looking more closely now, there were a few faces he recognised. He caught their eye and nodded. These would now be his companions for who knew how many months, or years even.

When land was sighted they were herded up on deck, where they all stood in silence, the off shore wind throwing salt spray into their faces, as the wide Douglas Harbour hove into view. They sailed close to a small, almost submerged reef on the starboard side. Rising from its centre was a bleak, forbidding granite tower. It crossed Friedrich's mind that they might even be abandoned there, marooned in sight of land, but with little hope of reaching it, locked up within those thick eyeless walls. But the nurse who'd changed his dressing, who had taken his arm so that he might steady himself, had evidently done this trip before, and she informed him they were passing what was known as St Mary's Isle, and that the obelisk was the Tower of Refuge, built for shipwrecked sailors, whose ships might founder on the reef.

Friedrich looked beyond the bay, to the hills rising above it. "When you disembark, you will be put on trains to Peel," the nurse whispered, "on the far western side of the island, where the camp has been constructed. Row upon row of white tents."

The reality of what was happening slowly began to dawn upon him. There was a painful lump in his throat and his eyes brimmed with tears. "I want to go home," he said to her.

She nodded and squeezed his hand. "You will be well treated," she said. "Those of you who are fit enough and well enough will work on the land. You will be allowed to write letters, and the Steam Packet brings mail from the mainland three times a week. The time will pass quickly, you will see."

But time did not pass quickly. Not for Friedrich, or for any of the older men or those deemed too weak for agricultural labour. Friedrich was fifty-four years old, just one year within the upper limit of all those being forcibly evicted and removed to Knockaloe, the small village just a couple of miles along the coast from Peel, where the internment camp had been set up. Within just a few weeks, there were almost twenty thousand German men cooped up there, behind high wire fences, patrolled by uniformed, armed guards with fierce dogs.

Over time the white tents began to give way to timber huts, each accommodating sixty men, with a wash house, a cook house and a number of canteens, where they could also purchase tobacco.

The daily routine never altered. At eight o'clock a trumpet sounded and everyone was required to get up, wash and then report for parade, where they were counted to make sure none had tried to escape. A few attempts were made but those who managed to get past the guards were quickly rounded up by the Manx Police and frogmarched back to the Camp. At a quarter past nine there was coffee, after which work duties were assigned. The kind nurse on the ship was correct. This work mostly consisted of agricultural labour, and Friedrich was deemed too weak to undertake it. Lunch was served at midday and was prepared by rotas drawn from the internees themselves, using each individual's daily rations for the ingredients:

1lb of bread
8 oz of fresh meat
4 oz of pressed meat
½ oz of tea or 1 oz of coffee
½ oz of salt
2 oz of sugar
1lb of condensed milk
8 oz of fresh vegetables
2 oz of cheese
2 oz of dried peas, beans, lentils or rice

At two o'clock the mail arrived, followed by a

further shift of work in the afternoons until supper at six, comprising reheated leftovers from lunch, after which the men returned to their tents, and later, once they'd been built, their huts.

The time hung heavily on Friedrich. The arrival of the post was the *alpha* and *omega* of each day, and for weeks he heard nothing. He was beside himself with anxiety. Eventually a letter arrived, from Mary, briefly explaining that Mrs Kaufman was staying with their cousins in Cheshire, for which he was most grateful, but that Ruth was still in the hospital. Her injuries had been severe, Mary wrote, but that she was recovering, and that she would write again as soon as Ruth was allowed back home. It was less than a side in length but Friedrich read it a thousand times, blessing Mary's goodness of heart, for reading and writing did not come easily to her and he knew how she would have laboured over it. He wrote back the same day, enclosing separate letters for Helga and Ruth, which he hoped she would send on. A month later he received a second letter, once again from Mary, this time containing a few additional lines from Ruth, who informed him that she had now returned home, assuring him that she was making good progress, and urging him not to worry. But her weak, spidery handwriting told another story, and he knew at once that she and Mary were each concealing from him the full extent of her injuries. From Helga he heard nothing, only a brief note from their cousin confirming that Mrs Kaufman was still convalescing from the shock of what had happened.

More weeks passed. It was now high summer on the island. The regime at Knockaloe was relaxed a little to allow those older internees, such as Friedrich, to go for supervised walks outside the camp's perimeter. Each day he climbed the path leading out onto the headland, looking down over Peel Harbour. All around him parcels of larks embroidered the sky with their dipping rise and fall. Just out to sea from the bay, connected by a narrow causeway, he could make out St Patrick's Isle, where the ruins of a Viking castle still stood...

The sight of it transported him back to his early childhood, before the family left for England. He'd been born in 1860, in Lübeck, in Schleswig-Holstein in northern Germany, a town which also had its Viking associations, being frequently invaded by the Danes, before becoming a prosperous trading partner in the Hanseatic League. Its many beautiful buildings had their origins from that time. His family had lived within sight of the River Trave, close by the Holstentor, one of the city's four main gates. They could hear the bells from the Marienkirche and Friedrich had been baptised in the Church of St Lawrence. When his family arrived in Manchester, their discovery of a church with the same name in Denton they viewed as a good omen, that they might receive a warm welcome there. Which they did.

When Friedrich had asked his father why they had to leave Lübeck, he was told that the city had changed. It was no longer independent, no longer free. It kept changing hands, like a once precious jewel. From Denmark to Prussia. From Prussia to France. From

France to Austria. From Austria back to Prussia again. It began to lose its lustre, and Friedrich's father wanted a brighter, more secure future for his family. They had relatives in Manchester. It would be an adventure.

And so it had proved.

They followed the old salt route via the Stecknitz Canal, which linked the Trave to the Elbe and took them to Hamburg, from where they caught the ferry across the southern reaches of the North Sea to Tilbury Docks in the county of Essex. Friedrich had strong memories still of the press of people around the docks, of cranes hauling cargo in huge nets like giant catches of fish, of dodging the porters wheeling trolleys, as they made their way to the railway station, which took them to London's Fenchurch Street, where they were met by his Uncle Gustav, who hoisted Friedrich onto his shoulders.

"Here's an English sixpence for you," he had said, before shaking his hand and depositing a whiskery kiss on his forehead.

Friedrich's father held it up to the light. "We shall have this mounted," he said, and display it in pride of place in our new home, as the first native money we received in our new adopted country," before solemnly handing it back to Friedrich.

They climbed aboard a horse-drawn cab that was waiting to take them across the city to Euston Road, where they were to lodge in a hotel overnight, before catching the Milk Train just before dawn the next morning, which would take the whole of one day to transport them all to Manchester's London Road

Station. His father was as good as his word and the mounted sixpence held prime position on the mantelpiece in their sitting room, where he hoped it stood still, having survived the night of the riots...

Day after day Friedrich walked up to the headland outside the camp and deliberately turned his back to the sea, looking east, right across the island as it stretched out before him. On a very clear day he might just make out a different sea on the far coast, some twelve miles distant, and imagine the north-west coast of England beyond the far horizon. He felt, by staring in the direction of what had been his home for half a century, that he might conjure it to materialise right before his eyes, the familiar streets, the rows of houses that were only just being built when his father first guided them from Manchester to Denton...

Back then the sprawl of Cottonopolis had not yet taken hold. The different neighbourhoods were still separate villages, with distinct characters of their own. There were still fields between Ancoats and Ardwick, where there was still a Green, with ducks in a pond and a pump in the square. There were orchards surrounding Droylsden, fish being caught in the Medlock near Gorton, and Denton was a bustling, but small, market town.

His father led them to the front door of their house, where a man in a bowler hat with a thick black moustache handed over a set of keys. Their new house, which no one had lived in before them, and which no one but them had since. The business set up by his father was handed down naturally to him, father to son, after his father had passed away. Now, as Friedrich stretched his eyes towards the thin strip of glittering sea that mocked him like a mirage, he wondered what remained for Ruth, his daughter, to inherit. When she had become engaged to Cecil, the son of the highly respected local Young family, who lived in such a grand house in Green Walk, Whalley Range, the owners of Victoria Mill in Ancoats, he and Helga had hugged each other for joy. They had fulfilled his father's dream for them, the establishment of a small family business and now the joining by marriage to the Manchester merchant gentry. They had arrived, been welcomed, accepted and now they had a legacy, a future. They had reached the promised land. But Cecil was far away, fighting on the fields of Flanders, and he, Friedrich, was here, on this island in the middle of the Irish Sea, unjustly banished, while Ruth was alone and unprotected…

The sun dipped behind a cloud and the air turned colder. A wind was rising, and Friedrich turned to make his way back to the camp. The promised land had indeed become a mirage. A last lark ascended, its song infectious as an infant's laughter. As Friedrich walked, his eyes fell on a young child, a girl of six or seven years old, sitting on a rock, holding a crumpled kite, its tail and string all tangled.

"Excuse me, sir," she said as he approached her.

"Can you mend it please?"

She had a mass of red hair, rather like Ruth, and something about the girl's directness charmed him. He sat down beside her and took the kite from her. "Well," he said, "let me see. I can try. But you'll have to help me."

"Oh yes," she said, "I'm very good at helping."

For a few minutes the two of them sat side by side in concentrated, companionable silence, while the string was unravelled and the tail straightened.

"There," said Friedrich at last. "I think we've done it."

"Yes," she agreed seriously. "I think we have. I was a big help, wasn't I?"

"You were indeed. A very big help. Shall we see if it will fly now?"

"All right. You hold on to the string and I'll run to the top of the hill with the kite and let it go from there."

The wind, which had been gently rising, was now absolutely perfect, and the kite took off at once. The girl clapped her hands with pleasure and ran down the slope to join Friedrich, who was letting out the string a little at a time.

"Higher," cried the girl. "Higher, higher!"

Friedrich duly obeyed, and for several minutes more they delighted in watching the kite dancing in the sky, its ribboned tail riding the wind like a sunburst of larks, until eventually it fell to earth, just as the first few drops of rain began to fall.

"You'd best hurry on home now," said Friedrich, "or you'll get wet."

"Yes," she said. "It's not far, and I expect it's nearly time for my tea. My tummy thinks so anyway. Goodbye." And away she ran. "Thank you for mending my kite," she called back, before she climbed over a gate and skipped off down a grassy lane.

Friedrich waved and watched her till she'd quite disappeared from view. He wondered if she'd been yet another mirage.

He looked down towards St Patrick's Isle and the ruined Viking castle. A sailing dinghy was gracefully plying the inshore waters, tacking into the wind and, from the farthest recesses of his memory, he retrieved an image he thought he'd lost...

1865.

He was standing by the banks of the River Trave, back in Lübeck, not far from the Holstentor, holding a small wooden toy boat, with a sky blue painted hull and a white cloth sail. The water beckoned invitingly. Friedrich bent low and placed it carefully onto the surface where the ripples lapped the shore. He badly wanted to launch it, to watch it glide effortlessly away, like one of the many swans that patrolled this particular stretch of the river, but something held him back. His father had told him to wait. He would follow him down to the water's edge, he said, and together they would cast it with the current and run it with the wind. But where was he? Friedrich looked around but couldn't see him anywhere. He could wait no longer. Taking a deep breath, he blew into the toy boat's sail and gently pushed. The timing was perfect. Almost at once the boat picked up the flow of the river, the evening breeze filled its sail, and away she went.

Friedrich was suddenly aware of a large shadow rising behind him, and there at last was his father.

"I told you to wait," he said. "I warned you."

"I know, Papa, but everything seemed just right and I couldn't wait any longer. Look – she's sailing faster than we ever dreamed."

"And now you have lost her."

Friedrich turned and looked up at his father with a puzzled expression. "What do you mean?"

His father held up a ball of string. "This is what I went back to the house for. This is why I told you to wait. So we could tie this to the small hook at the back of the yacht and then pull her back to the shore. Now there's just no way we can ever reach her."

Friedrich understood at once. How could he have been so stupid? He turned away from his father's stern gaze just in time to see his boat topple over the weir a couple of hundred metres downstream and disappear from view. It was the last sighting he had of her. He wiped his eyes with the flat of his hand. He was determined not to let his father see him cry. "I'm sorry, Papa," he said. "This has taught me a lesson." He turned swiftly on his heel and walked back in the direction of their house. His father watched him, smiling sadly.

Later that evening, after Friedrich had had his bath and was sitting up in bed, looking at a book, his father came in. "What are you reading?" he asked him.

"I'm not," said Friedrich. "I'm looking at an atlas."

"Anything in particular?" his father enquired, sitting beside his son on the bed.

"I'm trying to see where we are."

"Just there," said his father and pointed towards the top of the map. "See? It says 'Lübeck'. Why?"

Friedrich nodded and began to run his finger along a blue line. "Is this the River Trave?"

"Yes, that's right."

"I was trying to find out where my boat might have got to."

Friedrich's father put an arm round his son's shoulders and, with his other, traced the route of the river. "It heads this way, where it joins another river, the Elbe, which is much, much bigger and flows all the way into the sea – just here, do you see?"

Friedrich nodded.

"And across the sea from there is England, where we are all going to live in a few weeks time. It will be quite an adventure, I think, don't you?"

"Will our boat sail right across to England too?"

"I shouldn't think so, Friedrich."

"Why not?"

"It's not big enough."

"Oh."

"Sometimes we have to accept that we have to wait until we are."

"Yes, Papa."

"I'll tell you what we'll do. When we get to England and we have settled into our new home, I'll make you another boat, and we'll find somewhere where we can sail it together. Now – go to sleep."

Friedrich turned over onto his side, shut his eyes and imagined crossing mighty oceans, rocking from side to side until sleep finally took him…

But Friedrich's father never did build another boat. He was always so busy working, and there never seemed to be time. Quite soon Friedrich forgot all about it and, as he explored the disappearing woods and streams around Denton, as more and more houses were being put up, and the fields were all gradually paved with concrete, and new roads were laid and bridges were built, and trains arrived and then trams, he stopped dreaming of crossing oceans to far away places, for he felt as though all roads now led to where he was. To Manchester. The city seemed like the centre of the world and he thought of nowhere else.

His father's business thrived. The giant pair of spectacles he had erected on the side of their house, which now served also as a shop, announced to everyone, even those with sight problems, or to those who could not read, that here was an optician's to be respected and counted on. When he was still small, Friedrich was always rather wary of them. He felt as though, wherever he was, they would see him. There was no escaping their fixed, probing, lidless stare. The eyes behind the pair of spectacles never blinked but seemed to look right into him, even to his innermost, secret thoughts. Whenever the Minister at St

Lawrence's Church would end his sermon, as he frequently did, with the verse from Numbers, "*Be sure your sin will find you out*," Friedrich imagined the eyes of God looking down from on high, piercing clouds and walls, like the sign of the pair of spectacles attached to the side of his house.

But gradually he came to accept them, like any other landmark, and no more frightening than the barber's pole hanging above the shop next door, especially when he learned that its red and white stripes signified blood and bandages. Whenever he went inside to have his hair cut, he was always disappointed never to witness the patching up of wounds on the heads of the older men whose hair was cut and whose chins were shaved, while he sat in a chair and waited his turn.

In his teens he began his apprenticeship to the business, learning all aspects of optics from his father. He acquitted himself well and at the age of twenty-one he was rewarded by having "*& Son*" added by his father to the sign above the shop doorway. He developed a particular interest in, and aptitude for, lenses, and as a result he was able to persuade his father to diversify the business to include, as well as optics, the manufacture and repair of lenses for telescopes, binoculars, magnifying glasses and more specialist jewellers' loupes. It was as a direct consequence of Friedrich's abilities to refine and customise these loupes that they then further expanded their operation to include the cutting and setting of precious gemstones. He would spend hours peering through the various different lenses he had created for their many different instruments, noting the minute gradations in detail that each particular strength accorded. He was fascinated to be able to see right into the heart of things, to penetrate their surfaces to uncover what lay beneath, whether that be the grain of a certain type of wood, the specific qualities of different stones, or the mysteries of the human eye itself, where he would frequently lose himself contemplating the intricacies of the suspensory ligament, probing the depths of the aqueous humour, voyaging through the remoter recesses of the ciliary body, the sclera and the choroid, speculating on the very nature of sight itself, the fovea, the centre of our visual field as little understood as the deepest trenches of the oceans, or the dark side of the moon. When looking through his favourite telescope, a single draw nautical instrument, made by Andrew Ross of Bond Street, a wedding gift to him from Helga, its leather clad body adorned with silver plated brass mounts, which he later adapted with additional lenses of his own, he tried to imagine himself up there in space, looking down from the Milky Way and seeing himself in the window of the attic at the top of their house, where he had constructed a small observatory for himself, and then widening the lens, pulling back to be able to see the intricate spider's web of streets, canals and railway lines, which made up this mighty metropolis, like the veins, arteries and capillaries of a great leviathan, of which he was a tiny, but significant, part, like a delicate cog in one of the more complicated watches, whose mechanisms he lovingly crafted or repaired. If he was no longer there, he himself would not be missed, but the work he did would be, and he turned his head towards the mantelpiece, where the silver sixpence, given to him by his Uncle Gustav on his first day in England, stood mounted before him.

All of this activity afforded little time for leisure, let alone the building and sailing of toy boats, and Friedrich's memory of the loss of his sail boat in Lübeck receded further. The family fell into the predictable and reassuring pattern of six long days of work followed by attendance at St Lawrence's twice each Sunday. It was there that Friedrich first spied Helga, the daughter of a business associate of his father's, so that introductions were straightforward and opportunities for meeting at social engagements not difficult to arrange. They admired each other's seriousness and wanted nothing else from a future together, which promised more of what they had already – growing prosperity and status, not just in Denton, but more widely across Manchester.

Shortly before they were to be married Friedrich's father was seized with a sudden and violent heart attack, and died within the week. It seemed logical for Helga to move in with Friedrich as soon as they were married, and to help look after Friedrich's mother, who was gratefully relieved to cede control of all household matters to her more than capable daughter-in-law.

When Ruth was born, nearly five years later, Friedrich's happiness was complete. This happiness was tempered, however, by the long shadow cast by the collapse of the great banking house of Baring & Brothers. Caught with extensive holdings in Argentine securities, they were forced to suspend trading when the price of these plummeted, and European markets suffered severe contraction in the decade that followed. This gloom and uncertainty was further heightened by the long reign of Victoria finally coming to an end. Only the value of gold remained constant and reliable in those uncertain years and, with shrewd investment and prudent saving, while many businesses faltered, Friedrich's continued to thrive, although he now worked even longer hours than his father had done. Helga never complained, and Ruth quickly learned that she needed to be quiet around her father most of the time. Nevertheless she adored him and would be for ever bringing him little treats and treasures into the cellar, where he cut and set the jewels each night, from things she had found in the places she explored – a hat pin, a thrush's egg, a sycamore leaf, a snail shell. These and others Friedrich would accept with due ceremony, and he put up a special shelf in his work room, where they could be displayed.

A favourite haunt of Ruth's was Denton Wood, which lay little more than a mile from where they lived. Biddy, the first of a number of predecessors to Mary, would look after Ruth, while her mother and father were busy with the shop, and frequently they would walk down Windmill Lane to the wood, where Ruth could run around and explore to her heart's content. Her preferred spot for a picnic was a rough, grassy bank not far from the tiny Dodgeleach Brook, which meandered through the wood as far as the prohibited grounds of Hyde Hall. Carpeting this bank each spring was a secret patch of wild tulips. There was nothing Ruth liked better than to pick a bunch for her father and bring them to him just before she was taken upstairs for bed. Friedrich would receive these from her with a formal bow, inhale their scent, breathe out with satisfied pleasure, and kiss his little princess solemnly on the brow…

Now, walking back to Knockaloe Camp as the moon rose over a grey sea, he knew what he would do to help pass the long, slow hours of each day and the prospect of even longer weeks and months, while he was forced to wait out his internment on this far away island out of time. He would make the replacement for the toy boat he had lost as a child, which his father had never found time to, and which he had forgotten completely until this very afternoon. He would furnish it with all the skill and care he would normally give to the cutting of a rare precious stone, or the grinding of a new ocular lens, and it would take him as long as it needed to, for now he had but world enough and time.

He began by selecting the right wood. Luckily there were still many carpenters on site, constructing more of the timber-framed huts for the hundreds of internees still arriving every week. He managed to get hold of several good-sized off-cuts of ash, birch and cherry. Cherry was the most difficult to work, but he loved its reddish colour, which didn't spoil with carving, and was perfect for the hull. Birch proved ideal for the keel, rudder and mast, while he interlaced thin strips of ash with the cherry for the deck, sanding everything down to a smooth, highly polished finish. He would have preferred linen for the sails, for it was stronger and more water-resistant, but he had to make do with cotton, which he was able to salvage from a surplus bed sheet.

He spent weeks and weeks on it until it was almost perfect. Late summer tipped into autumn, which slid in turn into winter. By then he had become a familiar figure on the headland, where he always sat on the same rock, looking down towards Peel Harbour, and many of the other internees, and even some of the guards, took an interest in the toy yacht's progress, stopping to watch him silently working away with hammer and chisel, sand paper and varnish. Friedrich barely noticed them, or heard their encouragements. More and more he found himself drifting back to when Ruth was a child. Frequently he would speak out loud to her, almost as if she was there, and the passers-by would shake their heads and nod sympathetically, before continuing on their way.

He had not once in all that time seen again the girl with the kite, though he had looked for that flash of red hair and listened for her high, laughing voice, which fell like water running over stones. Then, one afternoon in early December, one of those glorious, unseasonal gifts of a day, with sharp, crystalline air and an unexpected warmth in the sun, he began to feel a little drowsy. The boat was all but complete. The only thing lacking was a name. He laid it in his lap and rested his eyes.

From close by he heard the rise and fall of a lark, its

song running on tiptoe towards him, tripping through the air like a meteor shower, each separate note crackling above him like sparks in the overhead cable of a tram on the Hyde Road. He wondered if he might be dreaming that he was home once again, walking back to the shop, with the giant pair of spectacles, its fixed beam seeking him out from among the crowd. But when he opened his eyes he was still on the headland above the camp. Mingling with the dying fall of the lark's song, he heard a voice singing. He turned his head, and there was the girl with the red hair again, skipping down the hill towards him.

She knelt beside him and picked up the toy boat from his lap. "Have you finished it yet?" she asked him. "You've been making it for such a long time."

"I know," he said, "but I have to make sure it's just right."

"What else is there to do?"

"I have to give it a name," he said, "but I can't think of one."

The girl sat back in the grass, thinking. Then she leant towards him and whispered softly in his ear, spelling it out letter by letter. "T-u-l-i-p…"

Friedrich turned to her and smiled. "That's perfect," he said. "Thank you."

"You'd better paint it on quickly," said the girl, "before the light fades. Here. I've brought you some yellow paint and a brush."

Friedrich looked, and there they were, in the grass by his side. He tried to pick up the brush, but suddenly he felt overcome with tiredness. "I don't think I can manage it," he said. "It seems so heavy. I can barely lift it."

"Don't worry," she said. "I'll help you. I'm good at helping. Remember?"

She placed the brush between the fingers and thumb of his right hand and carefully lifted it towards the tin of paint. She dipped its tip with yellow, bright and delicate like the inside of a flower petal, then steered his hand towards the boat, guiding it, letter by letter, until the name was complete.

Friedrich looked at the boat and the name for a long time. Above him the lark rose higher and higher, until it was nothing more than a distant dot, merging with the early evening stars that had just begun to show in the sky. Where was his telescope, that he might train his eye upon it? The girl had vanished, although he thought he could still feel the gentle pressure of her fingers, guiding his hand. Below he could hear the waves breaking on the shingle, sucking in the pebbles on the beach, then pushing them back, in and out, in and out, like breathing, until at last the tide retreated.

Nobody noticed he was missing in the camp until the final roll call after supper, when a search party was sent out. They found him leaning against a rock on the headland, his body as one with the earth beneath him, clutching a toy boat closely to him. The camp doctor calculated he must have been dead for several hours.

*

Dr Charles Trevelyan was whistling as he did his morning rounds at the new Manchester Infirmary. It was the week before Christmas, 1915.

"Somebody's in a fine mood today," observed Nurse McMaster, smiling.

"Quite," replied the cheerful doctor. "I believe that if we exude happiness and warmth, we may translate such moods to our patients, Nurse, what?"

"Hardly scientific, Doctor, but a good principle by which to live, I've no doubt."

"Precisely so, Nurse."

"Though challenging in a time of war, don't you think?"

"But our duty nevertheless – to smile through adversity is our greatest strength, I believe."

" *'As flies to wanton boys are we to the gods'.*"

Dr Trevelyan paused from his frenetic pace. "Nurse McMaster, I fear you have been the recipient of some recent bad news."

The nurse bowed her head. "My brother."

Dr Trevelyan placed his hand upon her shoulder. "Killed?"

"Wounded. But badly. We are yet to learn the full extent of his injuries."

Such news was now a daily occurrence but still contained the power to stop even such hardened medical professionals as Dr Trevelyan and Nurse McMaster in their tracks, and that was one thing to be grateful for, he supposed, that they were not yet so completely inured as to feel the shock less keenly.

"If there is anything I can do," he offered, somewhat

lamely, but no less sincerely for all that.

The nurse nodded her thanks. "Perhaps you may come to visit him? Once he is home? And give us the benefit of your opinion?"

"Of course, and you must take whatever time you need."

"Thank you, Doctor. But I am needed here."

They reached the end of the corridor and went their separate ways, Nurse McMaster back to the ward and Dr Trevelyan to Radiography, where there was an X-Ray he wished to review.

Ten days had passed since he had received the letter from Ruth, informing him of the death of her fiancé. She was not so explicit as to say directly that she was now free of any obligations, but she inferred without ambiguity that she hoped they may be able to resume and continue their discourse, begun as much with words not spoken, when they had met that first occasion.

She had written: "*As you know, I intend to keep the baby when it is born, if at all possible, and I wonder if you may advise me further, Charles?*"

Charles had taken her at his word and at once formulated a plan. It appeared quite fantastical at first, but, once conceived, it would not leave him, and he had replied at once. He did not have long to wait to hear back from her. Ruth answered by return that she was entirely in favour of his plan: "*I put myself into your hands, Charles. Please make all the necessary arrangements without delay.*"

Charles immediately put his plan into action. What he had suggested was this. He would arrange for

146

somewhere Ruth, accompanied by Mary, could go for the lying-in, and where she could deliver the baby safely, quietly and anonymously. He had connections in Whitefield, a few miles north of Manchester, where she would not be known, but where, he hoped, she would be as comfortable as possible, given the situation. He would ensure that, barring anything unforeseen, he too would be present for the birth, in case the midwife required a doctor's assistance at any point. In the meantime he would make further enquiries about a modest, but comfortably furnished house where she and the baby might live afterwards, where nobody knew of her recent circumstances. Finally, and with a boldness he could scarcely credit, he delicately wondered whether she might possibly consider doing him the honour of listening to a proposal of marriage from him. He was completely willing, he emphasised, to adopt the child as his own, and to the outside world they would appear as a happily married couple with a newly born baby. He realised, he continued, that she may look upon his proposal at worst as abhorrent, or at best as immoderate, and that he would quite understand if she rejected it. If that proved the case, he would proceed to Plan B and let it be known among the more respectable and well-connected of his acquaintances in Whitefield that Ruth was recently widowed, her husband having fallen, like so many, on the field of war. Either of these choices, he believed, would enable Ruth to escape being labelled "a fallen woman", which, he regretted, he felt obliged to point out was the usual fate to be visited on an unwed mother. But of course, the choice was entirely hers, and he finished his letter repeating that he "awaited her instructions".

He did not have long to wait. Ruth once again replied by return, thanking him for his attention to every last detail and for thinking only of her needs. She was not, she added, afraid of scorn or rejection from society. She had, as she consistently maintained, "*done nothing wrong. I have nothing to be ashamed of.*" However, she was, at the same time, "*immensely flattered by your proposal*", and that she would be "*delighted to accept*". He had to look up from the letter at this point and then re-read that last sentence just in case he had imagined it. His heart leapt to discover that his first impressions had not betrayed him. He read again, "*delighted to accept*", and the broadest of smiles spread across his now blushing face. She qualified this by adding that, given the delicacy of public feeling that still pertained, even towards female members of the German community, even though they had been born and raised as English women, it would be advisable that they did not see each other while she was still resident in Denton, except as a doctor might see his patient, but instead communicate only by letter, in order to safeguard her reputation and protect themselves from any unwanted gossip.

Charles replied that her acceptance had thrilled him beyond words, and that he would proceed to set in motion each of the various stages of his plan immediately. He knew, from her time in the hospital after her attack, through the various forms that she had been obliged to fill out, that she was due a birthday soon. On 27th December she would turn twenty-one years old and she would therefore not require written permission from her parents who, he stated gently, were not, he realised, currently in a position either to attend in person or consent by proxy. Therefore he proposed that they should marry early in January, quietly and privately, in Whitefield Town Hall, with just a couple of witnesses, which he would arrange, with Mary as her bridesmaid. He naturally regretted that he could not offer her what he imagined was every bride's wish, to be married in a church, but that Whitefield Town Hall was a magnificent half-timbered building, in the mock Tudor style, within its own grounds, with a lake and an ornate bridge.

Ruth replied that she was delighted with every aspect of the arrangements he was suggesting. She was grateful for his practicality and that circumstances dictated they should act in a way she embraced as one tailored to meet their needs perfectly.

"Manchester is a new city, a modern city, birthplace of Dissent and Radicalism, cradle of Women's Suffrage", adding that, *"even though we do not have it fully yet, it must come one day soon. Let us forge this new path together, with confidence and hope"*.

Friday 7th January 1916 would, she noted, be four weeks away from the date she might expect to give birth, and so perhaps that might be a possible wedding day? *"No later please!"* she added.

In a postscript, she shared with Charles her father's love of telescopes and astronomy, which he had passed down to her. January 7th was the day Galileo first observed the four largest moons of Jupiter – Ganymede, Callisto, Europa and Io – all of which were visible in a clear night sky, if one knew where to look.

"Let these moons be ours, my love," she wrote, and *"let us both look at them each night between now and when we can be together for always."*

Now Charles resumed his whistling, as he walked briskly towards Radiography, to review those X-Rays, believing himself the luckiest man in the world.

The X-Rays were of Ruth.

They had been taken when she had been first admitted to the hospital following the *Lusitania* riots. At the time their concern had been to discover the extent of the damage to her beneath the heavy bruising to her arms, legs and body. The broken ribs and fractured forearm had been immediately apparent, and he had been relieved to see no obvious damage to the skull. He subsequently requested a second set to see how the bones had mended before allowing her to return home.

Now that their future plans had been made, he felt irresistibly drawn towards taking a further, closer look at the skeletal structure of the woman he had grown first to admire and then to love, with whom he was about to spend the rest of his life. He laid the sets of plates inside an Edison fluoroscope so that he could view them in greater detail. Charles still marvelled at the way Röntgen's recent discovery had already transformed his profession. During his training Charles had dissected dozens of cadavers. He was familiar with the human skeleton, in awe at the delicate interplay of tissue and bone, but the facility now afforded him to see inside a *living* body offered unparalleled wonder.

He pored over every detail of Ruth's body as it now appeared before him, when the bones had healed and the bruising subsided. Could this really be the woman he was about to marry? Her beauty took his breath away. The skeleton's symmetry, the way each bone connected to its neighbour, the aesthetic arrangement and display of the vital organs, seemed to him as miraculous as the way Ruth had explained her father's exploration of the night sky. Below him, now, he traced the constellations of her body, the orbit of muscle, ligament and capillaries around the fixed planets of liver, lungs and heart. Here at last was true evidence of what made us who we were, he thought, no longer subject to the prejudices and fancies of ignorance. Even now, in so-called polite society, he had learned to curb his enthusiasm for the intricacies of anatomy, for the public remained squeamish, preferring instead to keep things covered up, hidden and secret.

Once, on a vacation from his studies in Edinburgh, he had been recalling in what he regarded as exquisite detail the *minutiae* of his first surgical procedure, only to be requested to keep such dreadful details to himself, while his aunts and sisters had covered their faces with their handkerchiefs, and his father and uncles had tutted their disapproval. Ruth was different. She wanted to speak out against what she saw as hypocrisy and injustice and, like him, longed for the light of truth to illuminate the darker places of the earth. Charles was reminded of something Thomas Hobbes had written in his *Leviathan*, which was a constant bedside companion.

"And this fear of things invisible is the natural seed of that which everyone in himself calleth 'Religion'; and in them that worship, or fear that power otherwise than they do, 'Superstition'."

He thrilled at the prospect of what he and Ruth might accomplish together, and how the child that was soon to be born would be raised by them equally to go out into the body politic bold and fearless.

He turned his attention back to the X-Ray. He looked again closely at Ruth's heart. For all the new understanding that modern scientific advances were making possible, there was still so much that lay undiscovered. His knowledge of the workings of the human body may be accelerating, but the internal workings of the heart and brain were as unfathomable still as the ocean depths, the further reaches of the universe, the centre of the earth beneath the place where even now he stood. What might X-Rays tell us, he wondered, about how we feel, how we think, how we conceive new ideas, original ways of seeing and interpreting the world around us? Why, for example, did Ruth's heart respond to his irrational proposal of marriage, when the two of them had barely met, had yet to get to know one another, with such an unequivocal *yes*?

Ruth's heart now lay before him on the fluoroscope.

He allowed himself the luxury of looking at it, not for once as a doctor, but as a man. This was the heart of the woman he loved. But then his medical training began to take over once more. He looked closer. Something was not as it should be. The chambers of the heart, particularly the left ventricle, appeared slightly enlarged, dilated. How could he have missed this? He was not at the time, he realised, focused on anything beyond the immediate effects of the injuries she had sustained, but even so, he should have checked this, especially as he had detected signs of possible pulmonary hypertension when checking Ruth's blood pressure during her stay in the hospital.

When the new Infirmary had first opened, Charles had insisted that every modern advancement in medical diagnosis and treatment was, where possible, put at their disposal, and so he had been particularly pleased that one of the Italian physician Scipione Riva-Rocci's sphygmomanometers had been installed, enabling doctors to measure blood pressure easily and accurately. Upon her admission to the hospital, Ruth's reading was unsurprisingly very high, but when this came back down to within what were normal limits as she began to recover, Charles assumed that this was merely following a predictable course of events. Now, however, on examining the enlarged chambers of Ruth's heart so clearly revealed by this second set of X-Rays, when the swelling and bruising had begun to diminish, Charles grew perturbed. Could this dilation be a symptom of a congenital defect, of the type indicated by the research carried out by his German counterpart,

Dr Eberhard Frank, whose paper from 1911 he had read with keen interest in *The Lancet* at the time?

Time would tell. It was something he would need to keep a close eye on, but he was not overly concerned. The last time he saw Ruth she appeared in rude health, while her recent letters gave no cause for immediate concern. Forewarned was forearmed, he told himself, and as he walked away from the Radiography Unit back down the corridors towards the wards where he was next due on his daily rounds, he made a mental note to write that afternoon to Mary, entrusting her to make sure that his bride-to-be remained on a strict, iron-rich diet, together with a list of urgent questions. Was her mistress complaining of headaches? Was she experiencing any pain just below the ribs? Had she detected any recent increase in *oedema*, a sudden swelling in her ankles, feet, face or hands? If the answer to any of these questions was in the affirmative, she must inform him at once and he would hasten to their door immediately. He must remain vigilant for any signs of *toxaemia*, he told himself.

*

On 27th December Ruth turned twenty-one. Together she and Mary had planned a low key celebration. In the last week Mary had been spending every spare moment she had going through all of her mistress's wardrobe, trying to encourage Ruth to make her mind up about which things she would take with her when she made the move to Whitefield. They had also finally settled on which dress she would wear for the wedding, and Mary had been busy taking it out and making all of the necessary adjustments, so that Ruth might wear it in such a way as not to make her condition so immediately obvious.

Let us try at least," she had said to Mary, "to fool the registrar and the witnesses. What a relief it will be finally to go out of doors without immediately setting tongues a-wagging."

Ruth had slept in a little later that morning, and when she did finally emerge, wearing a silk robe that had formerly been wrapped in tissue paper in her bottom drawer, she came downstairs to a breakfast of piping hot beef broth, which Mary was insisting she ate each day, ever since she had received Dr Charles's last letter. Waiting for Ruth on the dining table was a small envelope, on which she recognised Mary's bold, neat, child-like handwriting. Inside was a card she had made herself with pressed tulip petals.

"Oh, Mary – this is beautiful. Thank you."

Mary's cheeks reddened and her smile was broad. "Thank you, Miss."

"Mary, we are friends, are we not?"

"I hope so, Miss."

"Then let us from this day forward put an end to all this mistress/servant business, shall we?"

Mary's eyes widened.

"Please. Call me Ruth."

"Yes, Miss. If you prefer, Miss. Sorry – Ruth, Miss." She took a breath. "Ruth."

"Good. That's better."

"Does it feel any different?"

"What?"

"Being twenty-one? Coming of age?"

"I can't honestly say that it does. I came of age the night of the attack, I think, don't you?"

Mary nodded silently.

"How old are you, Mary? I'm ashamed to say that through all the years you've lived with us, I've never once asked that of you before."

"Twenty."

"Twenty? That must mean you've been here... what? Seven years?"

"Eight. I was just twelve when my mother died. I never knew my father. He died in an accident in the mine when I was just a baby. Your father was so kind taking me in. I've never been so grateful for anything in all my life. When I think what might have happened, I've been so lucky."

"I believe I am the lucky one today, Mary."

"Happy Birthday, Miss." She hastily corrected herself. "Ruth."

The two young women smiled warmly at one another and Ruth stretched out her hand towards Mary, who took it in her own.

"I think this wretched war has been like a coming of age for the whole country, Mary," said Ruth. "Things can't ever go back to how they were before. Too much has happened. Maybe that's one small, good thing to have come out of it all. We're going to have to change. If this really is the war to end all wars, then we're going to have to work extra hard to make the peace that comes after it worth all of this suffering and sacrifice. Let people rise on merit, rather than by accident of birth. Where what we do ourselves matters more than what our fathers did before us. I think Manchester will be a good place to be when that begins, Mary, for haven't we always been at the very start of things here? They say necessity is the mother of invention, do they not? That may be so, but I believe its cradle is here."

Ruth stood up and went to the window, from where she looked out towards the city to the west. She had put on a blue sapphire robe and leaned backwards, placing her hands in the small of her back, like Mariana, in the painting of the same name by Millais.

"I had a dream last night, Mary," she continued. "I dreamed that a great cloud hung above us, filled with a deadly poisonous gas, which killed every living thing, birds, flowers, trees, so that the whole of the earth was like the battlefields of Europe, a grey ocean of mud, devoid of colour, in which we all struggled to keep upright, floundering and drowning. Most of the buildings were flattened too, from the bombardment of the guns and the explosions of the shells, but a few were still standing, and those people who had managed to reach these last few survived, until the gas had cleared and the guns were silent. You and I were among them, Mary, and Charles too, and as we stumbled through the wreckage, where pockets of rats nosed in and out of the shell holes, we came across a patch of ground where a small flower grew, stunted but bravely pushing through from deep underground." She picked up the card Mary had made for her birthday and looked down at the pressed tulip petal inside, when suddenly she stopped.

She placed her hands on her belly and walked back towards Mary. "She's kicking," she said. "Here," and she took one of Mary's hands and placed it there. "Feel."

Mary's eyes lit up. "Yes!" The two women smiled, looking down at the swollen belly and then back up at each other. "*She*, you said?"

Ruth nodded. "Yes. I feel she will be a girl somehow."

They next proceeded to spend a contented couple of hours with Ruth trying on the dress Mary had been altering for her in readiness for the wedding in a little over ten days time, until eventually it was finished, and Ruth stood in front of the mirror on the landing. She tried on a hat, while Mary brushed away the last few snags of cotton thread, before bringing through a Paisley shawl from the bedroom, which she wrapped around Ruth's shoulders. The outfit was complete.

"You look beautiful," said Mary in a whisper.

"Do you really think so?" asked Ruth over her shoulder, as the two women looked at her reflection in the mirror.

"Dr Charles will not be able to keep his hands off you."

"Well, he'll have to till after the baby's been born," giggled Ruth, "and a good while after that too."

Their laughter was interrupted by a sudden, loud knocking on the front door.

"I'll go," said Mary, and she hurried downstairs.

There, waiting on the doorstep, stood the postman.

"Special delivery for Miss Kaufman," he said and thrust forward a large package.

"She can't come to the door just now, but I can take it for her."

"It has to be signed for. Here," and he presented a pencil from behind his ear.

Mary duly signed, took the parcel from the postman, thanking him and wishing him season's greetings, before shutting the door behind her.

"What is it?" called Ruth, coming down the stairs.

"It has an Isle of Man post mark."

It was by now late afternoon. A thick fog hung over the city of Manchester, against which the street lights, the gas flickering and hissing, threw eerie shadows. Inside Mary was going round the house lighting candles. Ruth sat at the foot of the stairs, still unable to move after the shock of reading the letter that was enclosed in the parcel delivered less than an hour before by the postman. She resembled Rossetti's study of his sister, Christina, as the model for the Virgin in *The Annunciation*. Her body shrank from the news, almost as if warding off a physical blow. Her eyes were cast downwards and drawn into herself. Below her on the floor was the wooden toy boat completed by her father on the day of his death, and in her left hand, clenched between two fingers, was the brief note written by the kind nurse who had befriended Friedrich on the voyage from Liverpool.

Dear Miss Kaufman, she had written,

It is with great sadness that I write to inform you of the sudden death of your father while here in the Isle of Man. He was still reeling from the shock of recent events and, although he initially made a good recovery from the physical injuries he incurred on the evening before the internment warrant was issued, he found it increasingly difficult to settle in the camp. In recent weeks he had become confused and distracted, and the Resident Doctor here confirmed that he died as a result of heart failure. When he was found, he had the appearance of somebody sleeping, who has at last found peace, with a blissful smile upon his face. It is our belief that he suffered no pain.

I am enclosing this small wooden boat, which he had spent his last weeks carving. It was something, his fellow internees tell me, that gave him great comfort, and they understood that he had a recipient in mind throughout. It provided him with a much needed purpose in his final days.

Please, on behalf of all of us here at Knockaloe Camp, accept our most sincere condolences for your loss.

Yours truly,
Nurse Jenkins,

Queen Alexandra's Imperial Military Nursing Service, Peel, Isle of Man

After she had lit all of the candles and drawn the curtains, Mary once more tried to rouse Ruth from her state of withdrawal. Eventually she invoked Dr Trevelyan's name, asserting that he would be most concerned to find her in this semi-recumbent position, and finally succeeded in lifting her to her feet, with a promise that, yes, she would eat something, if not for herself, then for baby.

It was as she stood up that she felt the first wave of contractions.

"This can't be happening," she said, her breath coming in sharp, shallow gasps. "It's too soon. We're not ready."

"Remember what Dr Charles told us in his letters – that you may experience these before your waters break. Braxton Hicks, he called them. All perfectly normal and nothing to worry about. It's just your body getting ready for when the real labour starts, which might not be for weeks yet."

"I think these are more than that, Mary. There's something wrong, I know it."

"You must try and relax, you've had a terrible shock, I'm sure that's what's brought this on. Let's get you upstairs and undressed, you'll feel more comfortable in bed."

Mary helped Ruth climb the stairs. As she reached the top, she felt an unusual popping sensation, followed by a sudden rush of fluid coursing between her thighs. There was no denying now what was happening. Ruth's waters had broken and her labour was beginning.

Immediately Mary swung into action. As soon as she had helped Ruth into bed, she set about filling all the kettles, pans and basins she could lay her hands on with water, grateful that the third pumping station constructed by Manchester Corporation between Water Street and the River Irwell was now providing water directly to Denton, although if that failed for any reason, there was still a pump in the yard behind the shop. When she had finished this, she rushed back upstairs to Ruth and began putting on her coat, hat and gloves.

"I'm going to get the midwife, Ruth. I'll be as quick as I can."

"No. Please don't leave me."

Mary could see at once that Ruth was beginning to panic, which was the worst thing possible. Mentally adjusting her plans, she sat beside her on the bed and took her hands in her own.

"Listen. This is what I'm going to do. I'm going to step outside – just for a moment – and find a boy to run and fetch Miss Winifred. She doesn't live far away and, God willing, she can be here in just a few minutes. As soon as she arrives, I'll leave you with her and run to fetch the midwife. Alright?"

Ruth nodded just as another contraction seized her. Mary waited until it had finished. "How often are you having these now?"

"I don't know," whimpered Ruth.

Mary ran downstairs and fetched the carriage clock from the hallway and set it by Ruth's bed. "Start timing them. From now." Ruth agreed that she would. "Now," continued Mary, "I'll go and find a boy."

She dashed into the street. The fog was so thick she could barely see her hand in front of her face, but from close by she heard the unmistakeable sounds of children kicking a ball against a wall.

"Hello?" she called. "Anybody there? Come quickly. I need your help. There's a sixpence for you."

Within seconds two boys appeared beside her. "Yes, Miss?"

"Here," said Ruth, urgently pressing a folded piece of paper on which she had hastily scribbled a message to Winifred. "Do you know where Pearl Street is? Not far from the station?"

"Yes, Miss," said one of the boys, the one with the football tucked under his arm.

"Good. Deliver this to Number 23 and ask her to read it at once, saying that you are to wait for a reply, which you are to bring back directly to me. Do you understand?"

"Yes, Miss."

"Good. Now – here's a sixpence for you, and there'll be another if you bring back a reply."

"Thank you, Miss." And away they ran.

Less than half an hour later, a breathless Winifred was knocking on the front door and hurrying up the stairs to Ruth before even removing her hat.

"Winifred," said Ruth, "I am so grateful."

"What must I do?"

"Listen to Mary. She has everything under control. Please do exactly as she bids you."

Winifred nodded and turned at once to Mary, who led her back downstairs.

"Have you any experience of this, Miss Winifred?"

Winifred shook her head.

"I once helped out at a neighbour's, when I was twelve," said Mary, "but there were always babies being born on our street, so I heard the other women talking. What we need is plenty of hot water. I've filled as many things as I could lay my hands on. If you could begin boiling them and keeping them warm till the midwife comes. I'm going to call on her right now, and then I'm going on to fetch Dr Trevelyan."

Winifred nodded, took off her hat and coat, rolled up her sleeves and immediately began to do as Mary had indicated, while Mary stepped back outside into the night.

She tied her scarf around the lower half of her face, to avoid breathing in too much of the filthy fog that continued to swirl around her, taking on the appearance of some kind of ghostly highwaywoman and, hitching up her skirts, she ran as fast as she could. Within ten minutes she had reached the home of the midwife and knocked loudly upon her door, calling out simultaneously. After what seemed an eternity, the door was finally opened by a much older woman than Mary had been expecting.

"It's my daughter you'll be wanting, not I," she said, coughing and clutching a shawl around her throat.

"Can she come at once please?"

"She's already attending to somebody else. There's no telling when she'll be back."

"What am I to do?"

The old woman coughed again and scratched her head. "You could try Mrs Woakes, I suppose."

"Mrs Woakes?"

"She's a handywoman. She's helped my daughter a few times."

Mary thought for a moment and then nodded. "Very well. Can you direct me to her lodgings please?"

"She's over Reddish way. Broadstone Road. Next to *The Grey Horse*."

"Thank you."

Mary continued to run. Her best chance of reaching Mrs Woakes quickly was to head back to Denton Station and see if there was a convenient train to Reddish, which was only one stop along the line. If not, she hoped, the station would afford her a ready choice of alternatives, being the terminus for both tram and bus services, and if all else failed she would have to take a horse drawn cab. She made some quick calculations as she ran. Mrs Woakes was not a midwife, but as a handywoman she was still permitted to assist at a birth until a doctor arrived. If she put Mrs Woakes on whatever transport she could muster to take her directly back to Hyde Road, while she proceeded to Dr Charles, with a little luck they might be back with Ruth in a couple of hours. Mary hoped that Ruth would not have given birth in that time.

She reached the station just as the train to Reddish was pulling out, to be told that, because of the weather, there would no further trains that evening. Cursing, she rushed back to the forecourt and made enquiries as to the best and quickest way to get to Reddish. She was directed to a bus that was leaving in ten minutes time.

Those ten minutes were among the slowest Mary had ever known.

Eventually they departed and in a further twenty-five minutes she alighted just outside *The Grey Horse*. She knocked on the door of Mrs Woakes's Lodging House, only to be informed that Mrs Woakes was not there, but that she could probably be found in the snug of the adjoining establishment. Mary forsook any qualms she might have held about entering a public house unchaperoned and alone, and boldly went straight up to the bar, ignoring the looks and comments, where the landlord pointed out Mrs Woakes, who was sitting at a table in the next room with two other similarly aged women, nursing a glass of milk stout. She was not best pleased to be thus interrupted but the sight of Mary brandishing a half crown between her gloved fingers was sufficient to overcome her initial reluctance.

Having installed Mrs Woakes on the returning bus, together with directions to Ruth's house, Mary found a cab driver prepared to take her as far as Levenshulme, at the junction of Matthews Lane with Stockport Road, from where, he assured her, she should be able to catch a tram down Plymouth Grove and onto Upper Brook Street, where Dr Trevelyan lived.

The night was bitterly cold and the fog was swirling thicker than ever. The cab driver kindly covered Mary's legs with a rug, climbed aboard beside her, clicked his tongue and gently pulled on his reins, which was all the encouragement his old horse needed to begin the journey. A carriage lamp, hanging on a pole at the front of the cab, cast a sickly orange glow that intermingled with the horse's exhaled breath, making strange, unearthly shapes that seemed to cling and dance around them as they made their slow and painful way towards the city. In Mary's fancy these phantasmagorical shapes took on the form of twisted, anguished babies struggling to be born. It seemed no one else was abroad this dark December night as the final days of 1915 drew to a close. The fog wrapped around them like a shroud, and all she could hear was the slow, rhythmical beat of the horse's hooves on the cobbled streets.

"Here we are, Miss," the cab driver said suddenly, the first words he had uttered since their journey had begun, and he pointed to a tram stop diagonally across the way from the cross roads where he had drawn the horse to a halt.

Calling out her thanks, Mary ran headlong and heedless across the street, leaping aboard the tram just as it was pulling out.

Half an hour later she was standing on Upper Brook Street at the address Dr Trevelyan had given them. Outside the front door were two columns of bells for the various flats within the building. Checking his card she rang the number. No response. She pressed again. Still nothing. A cold fear began to course through her. What if she couldn't find him? That was a possibility she had not allowed herself to consider. She rang again. Just as she did so, the front door opened, from which stepped a middle aged gentleman just on his way out.

He tipped the brim of his top hat with his cane. "May I help you, Miss?"

"Thank you, sir. I am looking for Dr Trevelyan. He is needed most urgently."

"If he is not answering his doorbell, Miss, I imagine he is at the hospital. Come, let me escort you. It is not far, but on such a night as this it would be easy to miss one's way."

"Thank you, sir," said Mary, gratefully accepting the gentleman's offer of his arm. "You are most kind."

In less than ten minutes, the middle-aged gentleman deposited Mary at the front entrance to the Infirmary before continuing on his way. Steadying herself, Mary hastened to the main enquiry desk, where she was coolly informed that Dr Trevelyan was not available.

"It's an emergency," pleaded Mary. "Dr Trevelyan was most insistent that I should alert him should this situation arise. He is needed at once at the home of Mr & Mrs Kaufman, Opticians, Jewellers and Watchmakers of Denton," and she handed across a card.

At that moment Nurse McMaster hurried past.

"Mary?" she called. "Is that you?"

"Yes, Nurse. Thank goodness you're here. I must see Dr Trevelyan."

The woman at the desk attempted to intervene. "I've explained already, Nurse. The doctor is not to be disturbed."

"It's alright, Miss Franks, I'll deal with this."

"As you wish, Nurse," bridled the receptionist.

Nurse McMaster quickly drew Mary to one side. "Is this about Ruth?"

"Yes, Nurse. The doctor said I was to inform him the moment labour has started."

"And it has? When?"

"Almost two hours ago."

"And there's someone with her?"

"Yes. A friend and… a handywoman."

"Not a midwife?"

"None was available."

"I shall inform Dr Trevelyan as soon as he comes out of theatre."

"When will that be?"

"It's impossible to say. There was an accident on Mosley Street. Some kind of collision. I don't know the details, only that the doctor's operating on one of the survivors as we speak."

"I see."

"My advice, Mary, is to go back home. Your good sense will be of great benefit there. I shall inform Dr Trevelyan as I say, and he will come as soon as he can. You need have no fear of that. Now hurry."

"Yes, Nurse. Thank you, Nurse."

Once outside, Mary looked around for where she might catch a tram. The one she had arrived by a few minutes previously was still waiting at the stop. She approached the conductor, alighting from the rear, to seek his advice as to what might be her best course of action from here.

"I'm sorry, Miss. We've instructions to go no further. On account of this fog, Miss, and the accident up ahead. There'll be no more trams running tonight. My advice is to walk, Miss. Take care, mind..."

Mary had begun the walk back to Denton before he had finished speaking. It was four and a half miles at least. In broad daylight that would take her the best part of an hour and a half. Who knows how long in this thick fog at night? From Upper Brook Street she would head down Plymouth Grove once more, till she reached Stockport Road, which she would need to cross into Kirkmanshulme Lane. That would take her to Belle Vue, from where she would join Hyde Road all the way back to Denton. Straightforward enough, she told herself. She'd walked that way many times as a girl with her mother, but she could see so little in front of her, she was worried she might miss a turning, and this slowed her down. She walked past Plymouth Grove, only realising when a man struck a match under a lamp post, and its flare illuminated the sign for Swinton Grove, which she found herself running along as fast as she could, in case the Man with the Match might follow her.

She reached Stockport Road without further mishap, but then once on Kirkmanshulme Lane, which was narrower, less lit and with more twists, she wandered off down Pink Bank Lane, not at first realising her error, until she chanced upon *The Garrat*, a down-at-heel pub, with dirty etched glass windows, and tiles depicting steam locomotives. This was a lonely, abandoned place, with stone steps leading down to damp cellars, where rats loitered, foraging for scraps and leftovers. She passed rouged women standing in doorways and heard coarse shouts from the rooms above. Just as she turned around to retrace her steps, she ran straight into the Man with the Match, who must have been following her after all. He seized her wrist and clamped his other hand roughly across her mouth. His face took on a lurid glow in the light from the pub doorway, the whites of his eyes a sickly yellow. Mary bit his thumb sharply, which caused him to momentarily release his grip on her wrist. She kicked him hard in the shins and ran back up Pink Bank Lane. She heard the Man with the Match curse angrily, but no tell-tale footsteps chasing after her.

She hurried as fast as she could until she found herself back on Kirkmanshulme Lane, turned right and continued running all the way to Belle Vue, whose gates were locked, but whose posters and signs extolling the pleasures of "*All the Fun of the Fair*" mocked her as she passed them. She had longed to go there as a child, and once, as a special treat, her mother had taken her. She'd screamed in delighted terror at the lions and tigers, gasped as the trunk of an elephant swung her onto its back, and was sick after riding the steam-powered Ocean Wave, which simulated a storm at sea.

Her stomach was similarly churning as she continued to make her way back to Ruth. She was sure of her bearings now, despite the fog showing no signs of lifting. Hyde Road was once a Roman way, running directly from the centre of Manchester right into Derbyshire. She knew now she wouldn't get lost, but there were still more than two miles to cover before she reached Denton.

How was Ruth? How was Winifred coping? Had Mrs Woakes arrived and taken control? How long before Dr Charles would be free to join them?

Her mind was racing faster than her feet could carry her. Eventually she could go no further. She had to stop to catch her breath. She had just reached Debdale and was leaning against a wall by Wilton Paddock, alongside the Thirlmere Aqueduct, which conveyed Manchester's drinking water the hundred miles from Cumberland, water which even now, Mary hoped, was being boiled and carried upstairs to where Ruth lay in bed, waiting for her to return.

In the shrouded stillness of this invisible night she became aware of a low, heavy rumbling from deep underground. The earth itself seemed to shift and tilt beneath her. She was aware that the mine workings of Bradford Pit, not far to the north of where she now stood, stretched for many miles in a spider's web of tracks and tunnels under her feet. She fancied she heard a mighty explosion, the crashing fall of thousands of tons of rock, and the cries of the armies of men trapped beneath their weight, struggling to dig and crawl their way out, back to the upper air, in search of the light and warmth and comfort their unseen labours produced, a rough beast, whose hour had come at last. She bent herself double as she waited for the pain from the stitch in her stomach to subside and leave her.

It was in this attitude of supporting herself, breathing in as much air as she could without coughing, that she caught the attention of Police Constable Ernie

Wray, who was wheeling his bicycle along the Hyde Road back in the direction of Manchester.

"Excuse me, Miss, but are you quite alright?"

"Yes, Constable. I must be on my way again at once."

"Are you sure, Miss? It really isn't safe for a young lady to be out unaccompanied on such a night as this?"

Breathlessly Mary explained the crisis.

"In that case, Miss, if you will permit me, sit upon my cross bar, side-saddle so to speak, and I shall escort you there directly."

"Why, thank you, officer. If you're sure you can manage?"

"We'll do our best, shall we?"

Mary eased herself onto the cross bar, Police Constable Wray placed his arms either side of her onto the handle bars, and at once they were off. He rang his bell at regular intervals to let any late night stragglers know they were approaching, and in less than half an hour they had reached the Kaufmans' front door.

"Thank you, Officer. You've been my knight in shining armour."

"All part of the service, Miss," he replied, and then cycled away with a cheery wave and a last ring of his bell. "Good luck," he called, as he disappeared into the fog.

The clock in the hallway was just chiming nine as Mary stepped through the door. She had been away from the house for a little over four hours.

At exactly that moment, Nurse McMaster was waiting to catch Charles as he stepped out of theatre. From the second he saw her, he could tell something was wrong.

"It's Miss Kaufman, isn't it?"

"Her labour has begun. From what I can gather from Mary…"

"Mary was here?"

"Yes, but I had no idea how long you'd be, so I sent her back home. She'd be much more use there, than waiting for you here."

"She's a remarkable young woman."

"She is indeed. But you need to be aware that no midwife is available, only a handywoman, and that Miss Kaufman went into labour approximately four hours ago."

Charles was on his way out before Nurse McMaster had finished speaking.

"Charles – wait. There are no buses or trams running. Because of the fog."

Charles looked thunderstruck. "Is Mr Hart still here?"

"I'm not sure, Doctor."

Mr Hart was the hospital's registrar and he possessed a car. Charles sped back past her along the corridor in the direction of his office and caught him just as he was leaving.

"I have an emergency, sir. Could I possibly impose on you and ask you to drive me to Denton? All public transport has ceased for the night."

Without a moment's hesitation, Mr Hart consented. "Be glad to show her off, Charles. Only had her a fortnight."

They quickly reached it, a Wolseley Stellite, and Charles had to wait patiently while Mr Hart pointed out its various features, its four cylinder engine, its side exhaust valve, its cone clutch, its two speed gearbox, and its armoured wooden chassis. Charles looked up towards the night sky, completely obscured by the thick fog. He badly wished he could have seen the moons of Jupiter, whose position in the heavens he'd been tracing ever since he'd received Ruth's letter. Sensing a pause in Mr Hart's eulogy of the Wolseley Stellite, Charles quickly interjected.

"Will you be able to see your way in this fog, sir?"

"Without a doubt, Trevelyan," he said, pointing to a carriage lamp mounted at the front. "Hop in. Let's put her through her paces, what?"

With a sudden lurch they were on their way. Upper Brook Street was completely deserted.

"An emergency, you say?"

"Yes, sir."

"Best fill me in on the way."

Without revealing his own emotional attachment, Charles summarised the circumstances of the case – the attack on the night of the sinking of *The Lusitania*, Ruth's appalling injuries, a delicate reference to her violation, her subsequent discharge from hospital, followed by the recent discovery of the swelling to the heart.

"You suspect a congenital weakness then?"

"Possibly, sir."

"Then you are quite right to want to monitor the

young lady's progress."

"Indeed. She is strong and resilient but she has commenced labour prematurely, which can be concerning."

"You seem to be taking a particular interest in her welfare, Doctor?"

"You may recall, sir, that she was a patient of ours for several weeks in the summer, when she struck all of us with her stoicism and courage."

"Quite so."

"But her X-Ray does raise concerns about possible *toxaemia.*"

"You are most diligent, Trevelyan."

"If I had my way, sir, all births would take place in hospital, where we might monitor the progress of each particular delivery with the latest medical advancements continuously at hand."

"That may well be desirable, Trevelyan, but what you are advocating is more a social, than a medical, innovation."

"Is Manchester not always the birthplace of innovation?"

"Possibly, but even allowing for such a radical alteration in human behaviour…"

"Sir?"

"… is it not a most primal instinct to wish to bring new life into the world when closest to hearth and home…?"

"Perhaps, sir, but when weighed against the possible risks, surely a hospital birth is preferable?"

"I don't quarrel with you, Trevelyan, although I

might ask you how such universal care is to be paid for."

"With respect, sir, that is a different question."

"True, but not an unrelated one. Moore has some interesting things to say on the matter in his *Principia Ethica*. But theoretically, let us suppose that your Utopian vision came to pass, even that would be of little help on a night such as this."

The fog gripped them in an iron vice. Like some malevolent ghostly army, it pressed on them from all sides.

"Only fools would venture out in this," Mr Hart continued, "fools or doctors! Certainly not women suddenly finding themselves about to give birth before they were expecting to."

Charles recognised a put-down when he heard one and said nothing, aware of his chauffeur's seniority. They continued in companionable silence as Mr Hart ploughed gamely through the empty streets and Charles searched in vain for a familiar landmark, untethered by this other worldly no man's land they travelled through, towards some undiscovered country, from whose bourn he was not sure he would return. Ruth had quoted from elsewhere in *Hamlet* in her most recent letter to him, and her words came back to him now:

"Doubt thou the stars are fire;
Doubt that the sun doth move;
Doubt truth to be a liar;
But never doubt I love..."

Her letters were shot through with snippets of poetry she wanted to share with him, which, as he recollected them now, she seemed to have been saving for the trials of this particular journey on this particular night, "*a dark angel, ever on the wing*."

After three quarters of an hour of snail's pace progress they finally reached their destination.

"I cannot possibly thank you enough, sir," said Charles as he stepped down from the car.

"Nonsense, dear boy. I'm only sorry I couldn't have produced a quicker pair of heels. Another time, what?"

"I hope so, sir."

"Now you go in and deliver that baby, Doctor," and with a cheery wave and a honk from his horn, he turned around and the Wolseley Stellite drove off back into the fog, which swallowed up both sight and sound of them in a matter of seconds.

Charles gathered himself and ran the last few yards to the Kaufmans' front door as though his life depended on it.

The scene that greeted Mary as she stepped back across the threshold, little more than an hour before, was one of devastation.

Winifred was bending over a kettle on the hob. Her hair was unpinned, a single streak of soot across her cheek. "Thank heaven you're back," she whispered.

"Is Mrs Woakes here?"

"Barely. She's upstairs with Ruth."

"Barely? I set her on her way almost three hours

ago. Let me speak with her."

Still not having taken off her hat or coat, she hurried up the stairs.

"Is that you, Charles?" Ruth called out.

"No. Just me. Dr Charles will be here as soon as ever he can."

"No wedding ring, I see?" sneered Mrs Woakes, holding up Ruth's left hand.

"And what's that to you?" demanded Winifred, who'd now joined them.

Mrs Woakes lurched slightly as she stepped away from the bed.

"If you must know," continued Mary, looking towards Ruth, "we had to take it off this afternoon, didn't we, Ma'am, on account of the swelling in our fingers?"

Mrs Woakes sat heavily in an armchair. Ruth mouthed a silent "thank you" in Mary's direction, who lifted Mrs Woakes firmly by the arm, back to a standing position. "And you," she hissed in the older woman's ear, "should have been here hours ago."

"I beg pardon, Miss. I couldn't find it, what with the fog and everything, and I got myself waylaid."

"In the local public house from the smell of you," said Winifred. "Now, Mary, what are we to do until the Doctor arrives? Mrs Woakes?"

Before either could answer, Ruth let out an involuntary gasp of pain. Mary rushed to her side.

"How often are the pains coming?" she asked.

"Often," said Winifred. "She keeps calling out all the time."

"Sure, it's nothing to worry about," remarked Mrs Woakes airily. "These young gentlewomen are all the same. They think they're the first person ever to have a baby. You wait till you start properly, then you'll have something to shout about," and she ensconced herself back into the armchair.

"We need to start timing them," said Mary under her breath to Winifred, who nodded.

"Mary," said Ruth, after the latest wave had passed, "if anything should happen to me tonight…"

"Nothing's going to happen to you…"

"No, listen. I just want you to know, she's to be called Lily. Lily, do you hear me?"

"Yes," said Mary, "Lily, but…"

"I looked it up. It means pure. Pure, innocent, perfect. Lily."

Suddenly she was gripped with another fierce contraction. She squeezed the bed sheets with her hands on either side of her, as her body bucked up and back. Gradually it subsided and she laid her head back on her pillow, closing her eyes. Mary turned to Winifred.

"Something's not right," she whispered.

"Look!" cried Winifred and pointed back down to the bed. The sheets were red. Ruth had started to bleed.

Mrs Woakes sprang up from her chair. "Stand back," she commanded, suddenly sober. "I've seen this before. You," she said, pointing to Winifred, "bring more hot water and towels, and you," to Mary, "look to your mistress."

Ruth appeared to have fainted. Mary picked up her hand and tapped it gently. "Her pulse is so fast," she exclaimed. "Ruth, Ruth, come back to us."

Ruth's eyelids fluttered as she regained consciousness. "The baby," she said, "it seems to have slipped."

"What's happening?" called Winifred, hurrying back up the stairs with hot water and towels.

"I don't know the proper name for it," said Mrs Woakes, as she began to wash between Ruth's legs. "Some kind of rupture or tear. We've got to get the baby out as fast as we can, or it might suffocate."

"I want Charles," cried Ruth. "Where is he?"

"He's on his way," said Winifred, handing more towels to Mrs Woakes. "Isn't that right, Mary?"

Mary nodded, as another contraction struck Ruth.

"Good," said Mrs Woakes. "That's what we need. Now, dear, hold your breath, count to ten, and push, as hard as you can."

This continued for the next half hour, with Ruth regularly pushing, exhorted by the other three women, until Mrs Woakes shouted to make herself heard.

"Stop!" She bent to examine Ruth closely. "It's breech," she said.

Mary and Winifred looked at each other, breathing hard.

"What is it?" gasped Ruth. "What's wrong?"

"Listen to me, dearie. You were right about one thing. Your baby's a lovely wee girl, but she's decided to come out bottom first. So we're going to have to slow ourselves down a little, while I try to turn her round."

"How're you going to do that?" whispered Winifred

Mrs Woakes gave her an old-fashioned look before placing her hands on either side of the baby's hips, which she tried to guide gently back inside Ruth. Then she kneaded Ruth's abdomen firmly with her hands in an effort to get the baby to turn.

"It's no good," she said, shaking her head. "I don't have the skill for this. If your doctor were here, he might manage it, but I can't." She turned back to Ruth. "Very well. Your girl's a stubborn wee miss, and no mistake. I wonder who she takes after? It looks like she's set on coming out hips first, so – when you feel the next pain, start pushing once again. Your two friends here are going to take a leg each and hold them up to give us all a bit more room. Now – push!"

Ruth pushed, and the baby's bottom and then feet slid out.

"Good girl. Let's just have a wee breather now, before we get the head."

She looked back up towards Mary and Winifred anxiously. "We have to be quick," she said, placing her hand further inside Ruth. "I fear the cord might be around the poor thing's neck."

Meanwhile Ruth was slipping away again. Without pausing to think, Mary firmly slapped her face. "Come on, Miss. Now!"

Ruth roared and pushed, Mrs Woakes managed to free the head, the baby was born, followed almost at once by the blood-soaked *placenta*. Quickly she cut the cord, lifted up the baby, who immediately gave vent to a loud and lusty cry.

"That's a fine pair of lungs you have, missy," she

laughed, and she handed her over to Mary, who in turn took her directly to Ruth, while Winifred very gently began to bathe Ruth clean.

Having checked and disposed of the *placenta*, Mrs Woakes returned to start washing the baby, whose shock of red hair was matched by an unmistakeable strawberry mark on her cheek. Her recent kind demeanour was already beginning to desert her. "A sign of sin, I see."

Luckily Ruth did not hear this. She was too weak and had eyes and ears only for the baby. "Lily," she whispered. "My Lily…"

Mary took Mrs Woakes firmly by the shoulder and steered onto the landing. "There'll be no more remarks of that sort, if you please. Not if you want to receive your payment this side of New Year."

"Beg pardon, Miss, I'm sure."

"Now finish what you have to and then leave."

"Mary! Mary, come quickly!" It was Winifred calling from the bedroom.

At the same time there came a loud, rapid knocking on the front door and Charles's voice calling urgently from outside.

"Mrs Woakes," shouted Mary, taking the now crying Lily from the handywoman's cold, rough hands, "the door if you please."

Mrs Woakes bustled from the bedroom down to the front door, which, before she had barely opened it, Charles had burst through and raced immediately upstairs, where time slowed to an agonising standstill for him. He no longer heard the baby's urgent cries, barely registered Mary holding her. His eyes passed over the tangle of blood-soaked sheets, the mess of pans and basins spilling their curdling, dirty liquids. They did not notice Winifred, her hands raised in shock to her lips, her head shaking in disbelief, nor did he hear her cries of anguish.

He saw only Ruth. Her eyes were still open, turned upwards towards a light now hidden from her. Her hands held the tiny space once occupied by Lily, vacated just seconds before, hanging there still, reaching out, as if they anticipated the baby's return at any moment. Charles fell to his knees beside her, enfolding her still warm body in his arms.

Mary, still juggling the baby on one shoulder, took Winifred's hand and led her quietly out of the room, closing the door softly behind them. As they tiptoed down the stairs, they heard Charles's howl of raw pain from behind the closed door, shaking the whole house like a chained beast at bay.

An hour later the house was silent.

Mrs Woakes had been paid and had gone. The baby was sleeping peacefully in a crib by the fire downstairs. Winifred and Mary had restored a sense of peace and tranquillity to Ruth's bedroom, emptying and washing all of the pans and basins, stripping the bed of its mayhem and ruin. Winifred had burned the sheets in the yard at the back, they would never be used again, and Mary had undressed and washed Ruth's broken body. The two young women were lovingly brushing her hair, gently rubbing lotions and ointments into her skin, extracts of chamomile, lavender and myrtle, before covering her with fresh linen sheets, and now they were applying discreet final touches of make-up to her lips, cheeks, eyebrows. A slim volume of poems lay on the bedside table, a particular page marked from when, barely half a day ago, Ruth and Mary had been trying on dresses. It had caught Winifred's eye and she had carefully copied out one of its verses on a piece of scented note paper, which she had laid on the pillow beside Ruth's still glowing flame of red hair.

"Gracile and creamy, white and rose,
Complexioned like the flower of dawn,
Her fleeting colours are as those
That, from an April sky withdrawn,
Fade in a fragrant mist of tears away
When weeping noon leads on the altered day..."

Mary had picked out a simple summer dress of white, fringed with *broderie anglaise*, that Ruth would wear in the coffin once the undertaker had completed his offices the following afternoon.

Mary and Winifred stood side by side at the foot of the bed, handmaidens looking down at their friend, a silent statue, face like marble, skin like alabaster.

All the while Charles sat hunched and mute in the armchair, saying nothing, seeing no one. Finally he stirred himself and took himself away to what had been Mr Kaufman's study at the back of the house. He rooted out pen, ink and paper and set to with all the necessary administrative tasks he knew must be performed. He had written a brief letter to the local undertakers requesting their services, which he had sent round via the same boy Mary had used to fetch Winifred the previous night. He then forced himself to complete, in his professional capacity of attendant doctor, the required legalities of the death certificate.

"The patient died as a result of complications arising during the final stages of delivering her first child. Towards the end of her pregnancy she developed toxaemia and labour began some six weeks ahead of the expected due date. During labour she suffered a uterine rupture, which produced severe haemorrhaging and massive subsequent blood loss. Following a difficult breech birth, the patient experienced a sudden seizure, causing her to lose consciousness, from which, despite the best efforts of all present, she never recovered. Cause of death: heart failure, as a result of peripartum cardiomyopathy."

He read it through twice more and then hastily signed and dated it. He rose from the desk, feeling an acute sense of self-loathing for omitting any mention of the enlarged left ventricle of the heart he had noticed on Ruth's X-Rays, thereby exonerating himself from any threat of professional negligence, while at the same time removing any need for a possible *post mortem*. At least Ruth would be spared that indignity.

He walked towards the window at the far side of the study, where a telescope was trained towards the night sky. He drew back the curtain and noted with grim irony that the fog had now lifted, and that the stars and galaxies shone bright and clear. He put his eye to the telescope, through which he could discern at once the four Galilean moons of Jupiter – Europa, Ganymede, Callisto and Io. Ruth must have observed them nightly from this very spot. They looked back down on him now, hard and glittering, pitiless and mocking, lifeless rocks of ice.

*

For forty-eight hours Charles worked to blunt the edge of grief and guilt, while Mary steered a wide berth around him, all her energies directed towards the looking after of baby Lily. Winifred returned home, for she had shifts at Hooley Hill she must attend.

First there were the funeral arrangements to attend to. While the Reverend Theobald Crowe, the minister at St Lawrence's, the Kaufmans' local church, was sincere in his condolences, he worried nevertheless that anti-German emotions were still running high, and he feared the notoriety of Ruth's circumstances, despite her undoubted blamelessness, might yet stir up that particular hornets' nest once again. Might Dr Trevelyan consider a quieter alternative at St Paul's in Clayton, with the burial to follow at the adjacent Philips Park Cemetery? He had connections with the parish priest there, the Reverend Crowe explained, who would be available, if required, to conduct both services, although the sooner the arrangements could be finalised the better, he urged.

Charles bit his tongue, seething with a silent fury, as he watched Reverend Crowe squirm uncomfortably before him, stammering as he spoke, shifting awkwardly from one foot to the other. Charles felt as though he was looking in the mirror at his own personal reflection, and he was filled with deep self-disgust. An agreement was bitterly struck for the funeral to take place the following morning according to Reverend Crowe's suggestions.

It was a private affair. Apart from Charles, Mary and the baby, only Esther was able to attend, Winifred being unable to take further time away from the Munitions Factory. There was no reading, no eulogy, no hymns of praise, no flowers. Only a verse from Lamentations stutteringly read by a visibly anxious Reverend Archer.

" 'The steadfast love of the Lord never ceases. His mercies never come to an end. They are new every morning. Great is your faithfulness'."

After the briefest of services, they walked behind the coffin the few hundred yards to the cemetery, where a freshly dug open grave was waiting for them. A hard rain began to fall, slanting from the east, drowning the Reverend's final words, snatches of which were carried on the wind, or lost within the urgent hungry cries of Lily, clinging to Mary as if to life itself.

"In sure and certain hope of the resurrection to eternal life through our Lord Jesus Christ, we commend to Almighty God our sister Ruth, and we commit her body to the ground. Earth to earth, ashes to ashes, dust to dust. The Lord bless her and keep her, the Lord make his face to shine upon her and be gracious unto her and give her peace. Amen."

Almost before the Reverend had finished speaking, Charles had turned upon his heels and was walking swiftly away, pausing only to tip the gravediggers. Esther took Lily for a while so that Mary could drop a handful of dirt onto the coffin, before they too began their slow, heart sore journey back home.

That evening, after a cheerless supper of cold meat, which Charles took alone, he summoned Mary to the study.

"I have been poor company these past days," he began.

"We did all we could to save her, sir."

"I know that, Mary. You have been truly heroic, and your continuing presence here since has been an immense comfort to me."

"Thank you, Doctor. And we have sweet Lily here to remind us of her poor, brave mother." She adjusted the baby, who was not quite asleep, from her right to her left shoulder.

"Yes. And it is about Lily, and her future, that I wish to speak."

He looked across the lamp lit room towards where Mary stood, her face fixed on his, the baby nestled into her neck. The scene reminded Charles of William Dyce's *Madonna and Child*, and for an instant his resolve almost waivered. She looked the epitome of the modern Madonna, dressed in contemporary clothes, as clear-eyed as her namesake, determined to protect her charge from the buffetings of the world.

Mary looked back towards him. "If he asks me now," she thought to herself, "if he asks me to take care of the child always, I will say 'yes'."

The fire crackled in the hearth. A sudden spark leapt towards them, forcing Mary to take an involuntary step backwards, while Charles stooped to grab a pair of tongs to remove the offending piece of coal from the rug. The action brought him back to himself.

"I have made a decision, Mary."

"Sir?"

"I know by rights it is not mine to make, but since Miss Ruth's father has now died too, and given her mother's failing mind, I feel that, as the husband to her I was about to become, it is left to me to act." Now that he had begun, the words he had rehearsed in his head sounded hollow and unfeeling as he spoke them out loud, but he felt he had no other choice but to continue. He turned his face away from Mary and the baby, his hands behind his back as he attempted to carry on. "Had Ruth lived, she and I would have married, and I would have raised the baby as my own, to support her through a situation that was not of her making. But..." he paused, turning back to face Mary once more, who remained rooted to the spot, knowing what was to come, "... now that what has happened *has*, the situation is different. Can't you see?"

"I see only a helpless child, with no mother or father, who needs looking after," burst Mary.

"And that is my point. She needs looking after. I cannot do so. I can provide for her, but, without a wife and partner, I cannot look after her. And besides, I have my work…"

"I could look after her, sir," said Mary fervently.

"I know you could, Mary," said Charles gently, at last looking at her directly. "But at what cost to your own reputation and future prospects?"

"I have no mind to them, sir."

"But I do. My mind's made up, Mary. Tomorrow morning, early, we shall take her to St Bridget's at Trafalgar House on the Audenshaw Road."

"The orphanage?"

"I do not wish to sound unfeeling, Mary, but an orphan is what she is, and there she will be safe from harm or exploitation, she will be sheltered, fed and clothed, she will receive a good education, and she will be given every opportunity to be able to make her way in the world when she is old enough to leave their care. She can do this better in Manchester than anywhere, I warrant, for are we not the birthplace of the ragged school here?"

Mary said nothing.

"I know the house," Charles continued, "for the hospital has had dealings with them from time to time before, and I have always been impressed by their kindness. She will be given a fresh start, a new life with a new name."

At this Mary looked up sharply. "It was Ruth's wish that she be called Lily, Doctor. They were almost her last words. As a reminder of her innocence."

"And so she shall be, Mary. I was referring to her surname. And that is all I have to say on the matter. We leave at eight sharp tomorrow morning. Please make sure you have her ready," and he turned away, indicating their conversation was at an end.

Mary, carrying Lily in her arms, left the study without a word. She did not see, after she had gone, Charles close the door behind her, put his head in his hands and silently weep.

At eight the next morning, as instructed, Mary was standing in the hallway with a small suitcase containing all of Lily's few things and a small parcel tucked under her arm, while she carried the baby in a makeshift sling. Charles helped her with her coat, picked up the suitcase and, taking one last look around at the house he would visit no more, put on his hat before opening the door for Mary to step out into another cold, wet morning.

He opened his umbrella and together the three of them took shelter beneath it. It was a Thursday morning, a working day, and already Hyde Road was busy with people. Shops were opening, market stalls were being set up, wagons and carts were bringing in deliveries. The postman was checking a bundle of letters he had taken from his sack, and already there was a queue of people waiting for the tram to Audenshaw. Passers by, if they noticed Charles and Mary at all, might well have assumed them to be just another young married couple with a new baby.

In no time at all the tram arrived and Charles found a space where he and Mary could sit, but it was on the upper deck and was only partly under cover. Charles held the umbrella open above the two of them, and Mary covered Lily as best she could under her coat, concealing her almost completely, except for an occasional glimpse of her face and her tiny starfish hand opening and closing in the outside air. The three of them looked like the figures in Ford Madox Brown's *The Last of England*, leaving one world behind, as they bravely sought a new one, but instead of crossing an ocean, they were merely travelling a few short stops along the route. To Mary, it might just as well have been an ocean, for she knew she was forsaking the only life she had known since she was twelve years old.

Charles and Mary did not speak, not while they were riding on the tram, nor while they walked the short distance from their stop to Trafalgar House, nor again while they waited inside the hallway of what was still a working convent for the final formalities to be agreed and the paper work to be signed. As soon as these were completed, Charles gave a small bow to the sister who had greeted them on their arrival and glanced meaningfully in the direction of Mary. "I shall wait for you outside," he said and then left.

Mary, still holding Lily tightly, looked up at the Sister, who was smiling kindly towards her. She opened out her arms and stretched them towards Mary. "Come," she said gently, "hand her across to me. The sooner you do this, the easier it will be."

Mary had promised herself that she would not permit herself to weep. Even so she felt a pain in her heart more keenly than anything she had known before, but she knew what had to be done, and slowly she carried Lily across the tiny space separating herself from the Sister, so insignificant a distance, yet it was as though the baby was passing from one realm to another.

"There now," said the Sister, "that wasn't so bad, was it?"

"She's called Lily," whispered Mary.

"I know," said the Sister. "I have the certificate. And aren't you the pretty thing," she added, her attention now all with Lily, "with your flaming red hair and that beautiful mark on your cheek? The good Lord must think you're very special to have put that there for you."

Mary continued to watch, smiling bravely through her tears. "Wait," she said suddenly. "I must give her this." She unwrapped the parcel she had carried since they left the house. Inside was the tiny wooden boat carved by Mr Kaufman, which had arrived the day Lily was born. "It's a gift," she explained, "made for her especially by her grandfather before he died."

"Why, isn't that the loveliest thing?" the Sister exclaimed, holding up the boat in front of Lily. "And what does it say on the side? 'Tulip'?"

"Her mother's favourite flower."

"Beautiful," said the Sister. "Now, you'd best be going, I think. The young doctor will be waiting. Time for one last kiss."

Mary walked towards Lily, who was completely easy in the sister's arms, looked for as long as she dared into that face she felt she already knew every molecule of, and kissed her puckered cheek, before walking quickly away, fiercely wiping her eyes with the back of a hand as she did so.

Outside Charles was waiting. "Here," he said, placing a sovereign into her hand.

"I don't want your money, sir," she protested.

"Be sensible, Mary, for you will have expenses until you find yourself another position. Accept it."

She did not want to, but she saw the sense in what he said, and placed it inside her glove.

"What will you do next?"

"I'll go to Woodford, Doctor, to see Ruth's mother." Charles nodded.

"She may not understand what I have to tell her, but she needs to be told."

"You're a fine young woman, Mary. I shall never forget you."

She looked away.

"Goodbye then. Will you not shake my hand?"

Mary turned back to meet his gaze, which was awkward and uncertain. She would not make this any easier for him. "I don't believe I will, sir."

"Very well." Charles raised his hand to his hat and headed off down the drive. Mary watched him turn the corner and disappear. She would never see him again.

*

Births And Deaths Registration Act, 1874

CERTIFICATE OF REGISTRY OF BIRTH
(Fee not to exceed Three-pence)

This Certificate Is Issued For The Purposes of:

The Provision for the Education and Support of Orphan Children Act, 1799 And for NO OTHER USE OR PURPOSE WHATSOEVER

Registration District: Audenshaw
Year: 1915

BIRTH in the Sub-District of:
The township of Ashton
In the County of: Lancashire
Date of birth: 27th Dec 1915
Name: Lily
Sex: Girl
Name & Surname of Father: Unknown
Name & Maiden Name of Mother: Ruth Kaufman
Adopted Surname: Shilling (provided by Sister Clodagh of Trafalgar House)

I, the undersigned, do hereby certify that the above is a true and accurate record

C.M. Trevelyan, Dr

Witness my hand this 30th day of December 1915

*

It took Mary the best part of the following day to make the journey from Denton to Woodford, a distance of only thirteen miles as the crow flies, but the mode of Mary's travel was much more circuitous and nearly twice as far. She was required to take two trains, with the final couple of miles being undertaken by pony and trap, arranged for her by Mr Schneider, the husband of Mrs Kaufman's cousin, who was waiting to greet her when she eventually arrived, just as the last light of the afternoon was fading.

"It is so very good of you to come, Mary," he said, as he helped her down from the trap. He had a full head of thick white hair, a white goatee beard and moustache, and an unmistakeable twinkle in his eye. He was in his sixties and clearly considered himself rather dashing still. Once inside their comfortable cottage, with its gravel drive, wych elm by the gate, neat walled garden at the back, Mr Schneider insisted on pouring Mary, as well as himself, a generous brandy. "To warm you up after your travels," he said, as he trimmed his cigar in front of a luxurious fire. "My wife will be down presently," he continued, "and she will want to know all that has happened. Are you quite comfortable?"

"Yes, sir. Thank you. But..."

"Yes?"

"Might I see Mrs Kaufman please? I feel I should be speaking to her first, if it's all the same, sir?"

"And so you shall, my dear. Quite proper. But warm yourself first. My wife's cousin has a somewhat looser grasp of time these days."

"I'm sorry to hear that, sir, but I am quite recovered

from my journey and would like to see her directly if I may, sir?"

Mr Schneider nodded. "Very well. Follow me."

He led Mary into the hall, from which all the downstairs rooms in the cottage radiated. In a far corner, beneath the staircase, a low wooden door opened into a snug little morning room with a grandmother clock, which ticked pleasingly. Opposite the clock was a small recess where a painting was hung, below which stood a small sewing table and a chair. Sitting on this chair, looking up directly at the painting, was Mrs Kaufman, who did not turn as Mr Schneider and Mary entered. Nor did she register their presence now that they were there.

Mr Schneider gestured towards her with his right hand, almost theatrically, and Mary walked towards this silent, withdrawn woman, whose hands would make occasional, sudden and involuntary movements, as if they were flapping away at some bird on the periphery of her vision.

Mary approached her carefully, knelt by her side, and took both her hands in her own, calming them until at last they fell still. She then began to speak to her, softly in a whisper, so quietly that Mr Schneider could not hear what words she was saying. He could only see her and marvel, as the evening light fell through a small window at the side of the alcove, lighting them in such a way that they appeared to be in a narrow recess in the Lady chapel of an otherwise empty church, and that he had stumbled upon this private scene inadvertently. As Mary continued to speak, still holding her hands and stroking her hair, Mrs Kaufman became less agitated, until she grew almost serene. She picked up once more the embroidery from the sewing table and, head bent in concentration, she continued her needlework, as Mary slowly retreated from her, back to Mr Schneider.

Every now and then Mrs Kaufman would pause to look up at the painting on the wall, where her eyes would rest for a long time, and then they would return to her stitching. Her left hand would sometimes flutter anxiously a moment, and Mary would be by her side in an instant, until the hand became still once more.

Mr Schneider joined them both. "She is much taken with this portrait," he said.

"That doesn't surprise me," replied Mary.

Mr Schneider raised a questioning eyebrow.

"It bears a striking likeness to Ruth," she said.

"I had wondered," he said, half to himself. "The painting is by Rossetti," he said. "A print of course. And the model's name was Fanny Cornforth. Its title is *Bocca Baciata*. The Much Kissed Mouth," he translated. "I hope I do not shock you?"

Mary shook her head.

"It disturbs and attracts equally, I find. The much kissed mouth."

"Not kissed enough to my mind." She looked directly at him. She had the measure of this man. "I speak of Miss Ruth, sir."

"Quite so. A tragic loss."

"And now I think my business is done here, sir. There may still be time for me to catch the last train – if I were to start back right away."

At that point Mrs Schneider burst in on them. "I couldn't possibly hear of such a thing. Henry dear, what can you be thinking of, allowing Mary to leave before she's even taken off her coat?"

"This is a girl who knows her mind, Klara."

"I'm delighted to hear it." She turned back to Mary. "Stay for one night at least. Supper is almost ready. Don't decide until after you've eaten."

Mary smiled and accepted gladly. "I shall be her *Passepartout*," she declared. She decided she liked Mrs Schneider very much.

By midnight it was all arranged. Mary would stay on indefinitely and look after Mrs Kaufman.

"She has such a way with her, Klara," enthused Henry.

Klara narrowed her eyes towards her husband. "I have no doubt of it, Henry. Now come, Mary, let us go upstairs, and tomorrow, bright and early, we will tell my cousin the excellent news."

Mary smiled inwardly. This arrangement would suit her well. It answered the immediate need of where she would live and how she might earn her keep, and as for Mr Schneider, she knew he would trouble her no further. And nor did he.

After breakfast the next morning, the first day of 1916, Mary was walking Mrs Kaufman around the walled garden at the back of the house. As she did so, she became aware of a low, incessant drone emanating from the other side of the far wall.

"What on earth is that noise, I wonder?" she said out loud, and Mrs Kaufman excitedly tugged at Mary's sleeve, pointing to the sky.

Puzzled, but delighted by this sudden burst of energy from her charge, Mary allowed herself to be led by her towards a green wooden gate at the end of the garden. She lifted the latch and pushed it open. It was stiff and difficult to move at first but, with persistence and effort, it opened out into a wide, flat field.

Lined up in rows before her were dozens of bi-planes, their engines all buzzing like giant insects. Men in greatcoats were pulling hard on propellers which, once they caught, whirled around faster and faster until they became a blur, like the colour wheels Mary had made as a child from stiff card which she had spun between her fingers, or the wooden tops she'd chalked rainbow coloured patterns on, which had merged into a single spiral of white as she whipped them along the Stockport Road.

She could just make out the writing on the sides of these mythical flying machines, Avro 504, directly below where the pilots now sat in their open cockpits, giving thumbs up signs to the men who'd cranked the propellers. She watched in wonder as, one by one, they taxied along the central runway in the field and took off high into the sky. Mrs Kaufman clapped her hands as they circled overhead, each of them waiting until they had all made their ascents. They then formed themselves into a tight formation, which resembled a mighty arrowhead, silhouetted black against the clear sky.

Mary watched till they disappeared over the brow of a wooded hill beyond the perimeter of the field. Her whole body was shaking. Like all children, she had sometimes dreamed of flying. Now, after a lifetime of being tethered to the ground, earthbound, always aware of those deep rumblings beneath her feet, she saw that the future was limitless.

Mrs Schneider was now standing by her side.

"You've witnessed our morning aerobatic display, I see. My cousin takes great delight in it."

"As do I."

"This used to be such a quiet spot," Klara recalled. "When my husband retired, we moved here to get away from the city and all of its noise. But now it has followed us. Look."

She pointed to the north. Mary could clearly see a creeping haze of smoke rising from the literally hundreds of factory chimneys, steel mills, cooling towers and smokestacks, which dotted the horizon.

"Manchester," marvelled Mary. "It seems so far away."

Klara smiled. "It grows nearer each month. It shall not be long, I think, until that distant creep reaches all the way down to where we now are standing, and the city will be continuous."

"Would that be such a terrible thing?"

"I don't know, Mary. Since this war began, I'm no longer sure of anything."

"We have to move forward, I think, and we have to

take risks. That's what Miss Ruth did, and even though it ended so badly for her, I will never forget her courage."

"It's a new year after all," agreed Mrs Schneider.

A strange, bird-like cry rose from the back of Mrs Kaufman's throat, as she pointed once more to the skies up above. The phalanx of bi-planes roared overhead, vapour trails streaming behind them, and the three women waved to them as they passed, before walking, arms linked, back towards the house.

3

13th June, 1917 – 29th December, 1918

Eighteen months passed. The world seemed on a treadmill. The wheels of war stuck fast in a churning sea of mud. The mines, mills and factories of Manchester worked round the clock.

*

In the early years of the coal industry it was commonplace for women and children to be found working alongside men underground. This was certainly the case at Bradford Colliery. But following the flash flood at Huskar Pit near Silkstone just across the Pennines in 1838, when twenty-six women and girls were drowned while trying to escape, there was a growing clamour for change. A Royal Commission, chaired by Sir Anthony Ashley Cooper, led to the passing by Parliament of *The Mines and Collieries Act* of 1842, which not only prohibited boys aged under ten years from working underground, but all women and girls. Unsurprisingly, this was not a universally popular move, especially among mine owners, nor among mining families who, in communities which depended solely on coal for their livelihoods, had come to rely on the additional income wives and children might bring in. As a consequence, many pits tended to turn a blind eye to a strict adherence to the new codes of practice set out in the Act, citing the "need for continuity", "respect for tradition" and "supporting the wishes of local families", as ways of circumventing it. So, in Bradford, where, just two years before in 1840, a new shaft for a deep mine was sunk, resentment of the Act was strong and, with the connivance of Mr Thomas Livesey, the new owner, women and girls continued to work eleven and twelve hour shifts underground, the younger ones starting out as "trappers", opening and closing ventilation doors, before going on to become "hurriers" when they were older, pushing tubs of coal to the shaft bottom. There were frequent explosions, usually on account of "firedamp", a highly combustible mix of trapped air and methane, and in 1846 three young women died at the pit, one only eleven years old. As a result, over time, women and girls were only to be found as surface workers.

By the time Esther joined their ranks, there were almost two hundred of them. Her male counterparts still earned nearly twice what she was paid, but the extra income was nevertheless welcome, and it brought her closer to Arthur somehow, as well as her other brothers, who all still worked below.

Lighter work on the surface had been traditionally reserved for older men, or men who had been injured underground and who were no longer deemed strong enough to return to the coal face. As Victorian sensibilities grew, some colliery owners considered pits unsuitable places for women, but this was not the case at Bradford where, over the years, women had proved themselves to be strong and reliable workers, well used to the language and habits of the men. By 1910 yet another new shaft had been sunk, this one almost a mile deep, a massive winding engine had been installed, powered by twin headstocks, and the pit formed but one part of a wider industrial estate, which included a brickworks, using fireclay and shale spoil, a cotton mill, factories producing coal tar, carbolic and sulphuric acids, naphtha and other chemicals, an iron works and an engine shed, all supplied and linked by railway and canal, between them employing tens of thousands of men, women and children.

Esther wore the traditional uniform of these pit brow women, as they had come to be called, which had evolved over time – clogs, trousers covered with an apron, an old flannel jacket, and a headscarf to protect her hair from coal dust. Not a dozen years before, it would have been considered unfeminine, even degenerate, for her to be seen so attired, but the war had changed society's views of what was now deemed acceptable for women to wear. It was quite commonplace to see women in trousers, not only at the work place, but also travelling to and fro, and, on this afternoon of Wednesday 13th June 1917, Esther was to be seen in the garb of a pit brow woman as she made her way back home after completing her day's shift.

She had left the Rubber Factory almost two years before, disgusted by the machinery of war, which was tasking the most ingenious minds of the age with devising ever more intricate ways to kill or maim, and she could no longer stand it. She hated every aspect of the war, the insidious way it wormed into the innermost recesses of every corner of life. Nothing or no one could escape its many-tentacled reach, invading every waking hour, disturbing every conscious thought, haunting every fevered dream. She admired the conscientious objectors, their singular courage in facing down mockery, insults and worse, to uphold their deeply felt moral perspective. She often wondered whether she, had she been born a man, would have had such strength. She hoped that she would, for there was nothing whatsoever she could defend about the decision to prosecute these meaningless hostilities for the sake of so-called national interests. It was not that she was unpatriotic, but surely all men and women shared a common humanity, and the havoc being wreaked upon a whole generation of young men across an entire continent, with millions upon millions of casualties, was, to her, quite literally irredeemable.

She contemplated a future without young men, landscapes reduced to smoke and ash, barren wastelands in which nothing would grow, and felt afraid. Her only hope – and it was a very slim vestige of one – was that possibly all this recent talk, of "a war to end all wars", might perhaps be a single green shoot that she, and everyone else who survived, might cherish and water.

At least here at the pit, she felt as though she was doing work that was useful. Yes, she was not so naïve not to realise that the coal they hauled up was being used by industry to manufacture more and more ways of dealing death, but they were also producing the means of supporting life too, providing light and heat and hope for the thousands of houses and homes, which filled the streets radiating out from the colliery surface, where now she worked, picking out stones from the wagons of coal, fetched from the various seams that were worked below.

They were long days. Esther would rise early, just after five, before even the knocker-up would arrive to rap at their windows with his long pole. She'd rake out the embers of the previous night's fire and lay a new one ready to light when she returned home later from her shift. She'd then make sure her brothers' lunches were all packed (and her father's too if it was a day he also was working, although these were becoming rarer now), after which she'd make breakfast for the boys, waking them in time to be down for when it was on the table. After they'd left the house, she'd then clear away the dishes before changing into her own work clothes to be at the pit yard ready to begin her shift at seven. She worked until four in the afternoon, then, collecting any groceries on the way, walked the mile and a quarter back to their flat in Gorton, where she lit the fire she'd prepared in the morning, before changing out of her pit brow work clothes, having a standing wash, seeing to her father, and afterwards making supper for when her brothers came in from their shifts. At half past six each evening she would then borrow Arthur's bicycle and pedal her way to Brook House, the recently converted auxiliary hospital for wounded soldiers in Levenshulme, where she worked from seven until eleven o'clock each evening as an orderly with the Voluntary Aid Detachment there. This routine she repeated six days each week, except that on Saturdays she would only work at the pit until lunch time. On Saturday afternoons she permitted herself the luxury of visiting the local library. Before the outbreak of the war, Esther had been able to furnish herself with an active and stimulating inner life, attending lectures and public meetings, visiting galleries and museums, the occasional concert, as well as being an avid reader, but since the war began, only the library was left to satisfy this deep longing within her, and she would try each night, upon her return from Brook House, to manage an hour's reading before trimming the lamp, allowing herself four hours sleep, until the next day, when it would all begin again...

When Freddie was a boy, he liked to keep a rat as a pet. It would be in a cage when Freddie wasn't around, but when he was, he'd carry it around with him in his pocket. They all got so used to seeing Freddie sitting there, with his pet rat snuggled on his shoulder, or jumping across from one hand to the other, that they took it for granted. After Freddie was killed, they thought they'd just get rid of it, but their father wouldn't hear of it. "It's Freddie's," he said, "and he would want us to take care of it." Now it spent all of its time in its cage, running on a wheel, round and round, day and night. Sometimes it would keep Esther awake. She'd hear it from the next room and think its tiny squeaks sounded like a lost child...

Sundays were reserved for other household chores, cleaning, laundry, mending, while her brothers slept late and went courting in the afternoons. Sometimes she might see Winifred for tea, but such opportunities for female companionship and conversation proved rarer as the years of the war continued, for other women were similarly pressed as Esther was.

On this particular Wednesday afternoon, therefore, 13th June 1917, Esther had no inkling that it might prove any different from the hundreds of others that had preceded it, as she left the yard of Bradford Colliery shortly after four o'clock.

The first any of the women were aware of anything was the deep rumble they felt beneath their feet, followed by a loud, distant explosion. The air hummed with the sound of it for several seconds, while the wire fence around the perimeter of the colliery rattled with the vibration. They were all of them used to such noises and so, at first, they didn't even comment on it. They momentarily paused, catching their breath, but when the siren in the yard failed to go off, they naturally assumed that it must just have been the usual aftershock from underground when a new seam was being drilled and blasted. But then one of them noticed a large cloud rising up above the line of mills and factories along the Ashton Canal, followed by further, louder explosions, so loud they had to cover their ears, and then everyone began to run.

Two miles to the west of Bradford Colliery, Clayton Mill caught fire and Bridge End Mill collapsed, with hundreds of workers having to be evacuated. Two miles to the east, windows in the shops along the whole of King Street in Dukinfield shattered. Houses over a five mile radius were showered with debris. Even Mary, walking Mrs Kaufman round the Schneiders' garden, more than thirteen miles away in Woodford, was aware of a sudden darkening of the sky.

The Hooley Hill Munitions Factory had exploded.

The Ashton Reporter

15th June 1917

FACTORY EXPLOSION CAUSES HORRIFIC DAMAGE

46 KILLED, INCLUDING 11 CHILDREN, MORE THAN 400 INJURED

At half-past four in the afternoon of Wednesday 13th June 1917, a highly flammable liquid in Nitrator No.9 of the Hooley Hill Munitions Factory leaked during a routine operation being carried out by chemist Nathan Daniels. This leak spontaneously combusted on contact with the wooden staging housing the Nitrator. The fire spread rapidly. Fellow chemist Frank Slater immediately attempted to roll away barrels of TNT out of the building to avert an explosion but he succumbed to the fumes and collapsed. Laboratory Assistant John Morton raised the alarm and removed the body of Mr Slater as the fire raged around him, eventually detonating more than FIVE TONS of dangerous TNT, igniting two adjacent gasometers, resulting in further massive explosions.

46 people were killed by the blasts, with more than 400 others hurt, mostly as a result of glass windows from neighbouring buildings blowing in, 120 of whom remain in hospital with injuries ranging from serious to life-threatening. Of the 46 killed, 11 were children playing nearby. More than 20 railway workers on the adjacent line were killed outright, where the tracks themselves melted, were bent or twisted up into the air into strange and torturous shapes. Nearby Spring Grove Terrace caught the full force of the explosion and the authorities fear that these houses are damaged beyond repair.

The Hooley Hill Factory, which has produced more than 76 million tons of munitions and explosives already this year, is no more, completely obliterated, with the waste acid tanks blown into the canal, also destroying the local sewage works.

Of the men at the centre of the incident in the Nitrating House, John Morton survived, as did Frank Slater, although both suffered major burns. Nathan Daniels died of injuries sustained two days later, while Chief Chemist and Co-Founder of the factory, Mr Sylvain Dreyfus, who had been overseeing the operation, was cut in two by the force of the explosion, identified only by the initials on his clothing.

*

Winifred had clocked off after finishing her shift less

than half an hour before. She had just reached Guide Bridge Station when the explosion occurred. The blast knocked her, along with everyone else in the vicinity, clear off her feet. She experienced what several people commented on afterwards, a sense of time slowing down, almost to a stop. It was as though she floated, hung suspended in mid-air, while thousands upon thousands of infinitesimally small shards of glass danced around her, each one vivid and unique. All sounds slipped away from her as she, and everyone, wheeled through the air, each separate body caught in a perpetual orbit, a new constellation, glinting in the darkening sky. Then, as she hit the ground, chaos returned. People were screaming and crying out for aid. There were sirens and bells, fire engines clanging, brakes screeching, horses whinnying. Water gushed upwards more than twenty feet into the air from a broken water main, almost as if someone had struck oil, black and muddy. She heard voices and footsteps, as gradually her hearing and vision refocused themselves. She tried to get to her feet, only for her legs to buckle beneath her immediately. "Whoa there," someone called, a burly policeman she thought, who sat her back down on the kerb, placing her head between her knees, until eventually the earth's convulsions ceased, and she could begin to make out shapes, distinguish words.

Miraculously, she seemed unhurt. Her skin, what she could see of it, was a pin cushion of hundreds of tiny pricks, each one of them beaded with crimson, but none of them signifying anything deeper than surface cuts. On closer inspection she realised that her entire body was gridded with glass which, as she sat there on the kerb, while chaos reigned around her, she delicately and fastidiously picked out, one by one. It must have taken her almost an hour until she had removed the final one, by which time the scene was calmer. Several bodies still lay prone on the ground. Some, she realised, were dead and were waiting to be taken away, while others were being treated where they lay, too badly injured to be moved. Someone called out for help, and she saw an arm protruding from a pile of bricks, where part of the station had collapsed. Winifred instinctively pulled the bricks away until she revealed a young man, his legs still trapped beneath part of a wall. The arm which she had seen first was bleeding badly and Winifred, without thinking, tore a long strip from her petticoat and tied it tightly around it, like a tourniquet, while she looked around for a doctor who might be able to render more meaningful assistance, but there were none to be spared. She returned to the young man who, she realised, was slipping away. He was frightened and calling out for his mother. All she could think of to say was that she was there, and that she would stay, and he could talk to her, and she would listen.

She held him in her arms until he died. He was about the age Arthur had been when the two of them had first become engaged, before this war had started. She wondered just how many similar sights Arthur must have seen out on the Front, how many of his young comrades he might have held in their final moments, what confessions he had heard, what souls he had absolved. She knew of course something of what went on in the battlefield, the newspapers were daily filled with reports, but mostly they contained little more than statistics, the sheer scale of which in the end simply became too immense to comprehend, or accounts of individual acts of heroism, to make the readers feel better, she presumed, but until today she had simply never considered the intimacy of war. While she daily poured the TNT into the ever gaping mouths of the shells in the Munitions Factory, like hungry babies, she had tried not to think of the devastation such a tiny gesture might cause. From today, that connection would be for ever indelibly imprinted onto the back of her swollen eyes, in the shape of a young man, not much older than a boy, reaching out his hand and calling her "mother".

*

The Ashton Reporter

Monday 18th June 1917

FUNERALS HELD FOR VICTIMS OF BLAST

Yesterday, at Dukinfield Cemetery, funerals were held for the victims of last week's explosion at the Hooley Hill Munitions Factory. These were private ceremonies, for close relatives only, but outside the cemetery gates thousands of mourners came to pay their respects and lend their support.

This support was never more in evidence than in the overwhelming outpouring of grief, not just here in Ashton and her environs, but across the whole country. The Ashton Relief Fund, set up by Mayor Alderman Heap, has already raised in excess of £10,000, with an initial sum of £500 being deposited by no less a figure than Lord Beaverbrook himself, remembered locally as Max Aitken, under which name he stood as Member of Parliament for the Ashton Unionist Party, until his recent peerage.

The fund's primary concern is to ease the suffering being experienced by the more than 2000 people who have been made homeless as a direct consequence of the explosion, which destroyed so many houses in the vicinity. The fund was swelled further by each of the more than 10,000 mourners outside the cemetery gate being requested to contribute 3d each, to which everyone willingly agreed.

At the mass funerals yesterday the cortege assembled outside the Town Hall, where flags flew at half mast. The carriages, drawn by horses bedecked in black plumes, were accompanied to the cemetery by Council officials, clergymen and members of the brass bands of The Manchester Regiment and The Salvation Army, with crowds of 250,000 following behind with mounted police.

A series of memorial concerts is being planned to raise further moneys for the Fund, including one by George Formby Snr at the Theatre Royal, as well as a Charity Cricket Match featuring players from both the Lancashire and Yorkshire County Cricket

Clubs.

Taking pride of place at Dukinfield Cemetery was a special wreath sent on behalf of His Majesty King George V and his wife, Queen Mary of Teck, Empress of India. A statement from Buckingham Palace expressed the profound grief felt by the monarch for all the victims and their families. "We mourn for your loss and we salute you for your courage."

So say we all.

*

Two weeks later the crowds had long gone. The relief operation continued as repairs were carried out to houses in an effort to return the displaced families to their homes as speedily as possible, although it would be many months before that task would be completed. But on Sunday 1st July 1917, Winifred and Esther stood together on the outside of a wire fence, which had been constructed around the perimeter of where the works had once stood, through which they looked at a scene of total devastation, as if it had suffered an all out shell attack, which is exactly what it had.

Nothing whatever of the buildings remained. The site had been completely cleared and what lay before them was a vast crater, stretching for more than an acre. Here and there a few concrete stanchions lurched precariously, with roots of twisted, burnt metal poking through the hard stone crust of earth. Remnants of brick walls, lying where they had fallen, littered the ground, which was hot and smouldering, with coils of smoke still rising up from cracks in the foundations.

Winifred could not recognise the scene to be the same place she had worked in daily for almost three years. She tried to picture the avenues of shells she would walk between but found that she couldn't. All traces of the factory had been obliterated. Threads of wool had been tied to the fence at regular intervals, woven in and out of the wire mesh, in an attempt to soften and humanise the grim phantasmagoria of what lay before them, and as a memorial to those who had lost their lives, especially the children. Someone had tried to attach a small cloth doll to the fence using a piece of cotton, but it had slipped, so that now it simply hung there, swinging in a macabre and disturbing way. Winifred tried to fasten it more securely, but she only seemed to make it worse. She pressed her face up close to the wire, peeping through the narrow gaps in the mesh. She was reminded of a time when she herself was a child and she'd been taken to the Zoological Gardens at Belle Vue to see the lions and tigers. There'd been a fence just like this one there too, except the difference was that at Belle Vue it had been erected to keep the animals in, whereas here it was to keep the likes of her out, an enclosure for death, not life.

A little way further in, emerging from one of the deeper craters, a small straggle of rats nosed around among the smoke and ruin. Winifred remembered how she'd watched, along with all the many thousands of others, the new recruits for The Manchester Regiment, marching down Deansgate at the start of the war, Arthur among them, whistling and singing to brass bands as they went, how for a brief moment she had thought of *The Pied Piper of Hamelin*, leading them as rats to their doom underground. Now, it seemed, only these few returned, nervous and wary, not wishing to be seen.

As if reading her mind, Esther began to speak.

" '*A few, a few, too few for drums and yells,*
May creep back, silent, to still village wells
Up half-known roads'..."

Winifred nodded, took the hand that Esther offered and squeezed it.

"I take it," said Esther, "that Arthur has mentioned his friend Captain Owen in his letters?"

"He has," said Winifred, "several times. He seems quite taken with him."

"I've been trying to find examples of some of his poems, but apart from *The Nation*, nobody's publishing them."

"It's hardly surprising. It's not what people want to read, is it?"

"Arthur says that Captain Owen writes his poems at all times of day, on whatever he has to hand, not just note paper, but cigarette packets, playing cards, anything at all, in case he dies before he's time to finish all he has to say."

"I've not been able to stop thinking about it," added Winifred, turning her gaze back towards the waste land through the mesh of the wire fence. "If it had happened just half an hour earlier, I'd have still been here. I'd have been blown to bits."

"Hush. It's no use thinking like that. If only this, if only that. We have to make the best of how we find things."

"I should have stopped working here when you left the Rubber Factory, but I just didn't think. I didn't make the connection."

"Even if you had, someone else would have stepped into your shoes."

"I find that so depressing, Esther. It's as though you're saying nothing that any of us does, or doesn't do, can make the slightest difference."

"That's not what I mean."

"Then what *do* you mean? Deeds not words, remember? That's what you always used to say. Don't you believe that any more?"

"More than ever. What Mr Marx said about seizing the means of production would serve us all well now, I believe."

"Oh Esther, don't tell me you've become a Bolshevik too, on top of everything else?"

"Not in the way you mean, no. I'm completely against any form of violence. You know that from our times together in the struggle for votes for women..."

"... which we still haven't got – "

" – but which we will get, soon, I think, and so I am optimistic that some of Mr Marx's progressive ideas will also be adopted one day."

"Like seizing the means of production?"

"Exactly."

"Which I don't understand, by the way."

"There are three factors of production, Winifred: labour – the physical act of working; the *subject* of labour – what that work is actually producing, and the *instruments* of labour – the tools and machines we need to do it."

"So? What's wrong with that?"

"Marx believes that if the government seized the means of production, instead of leaving it as it is now, in the hands of just a few rich individuals, we could use them for the greater good of all, rather than the personal gain of a few."

"But that's never going to happen, is it?"

"It might, when women get the vote, for we look at the world differently from men."

Winifred was quiet for a while. She watched the rats, a barely distinguishable grey against the grey dust of the crater, just the other side of the fence, their noses twitching the air, scenting atmospheric changes before they happened. She opened the small bag she was carrying and produced a letter from it.

"This came from Arthur yesterday," she said. "Here. Read it. It pertains to our conversation, I think, and what has happened here." She handed Esther the letter and took a step back so that her shadow would not fall across it as her friend hungrily started to read it.

Dear Winifred,

I've been thinking a lot lately of the work you do at the Munitions Factory. We saw again the film they made of you last week in a makeshift tent behind the front lines. It was intended as a bit of a morale boost for the boys and it certainly did the trick. There's about to be a big push-on – all very hush-hush, but it's all anyone can talk about, especially since they've cancelled all leave for the foreseeable. Sorry, darling. And so watching you, and all the other girls, hard at work making more and more shells for us to launch at the enemy, cheered us up no end. You were splendid by the way. The other chaps are all rather envious of me and say how lucky I am, but I don't need them to tell me that. I know it to be so.

But it also got me thinking more and more about the very nature of this war, how all these new weapons and machines they keep developing help us to deal death at a distance. In some ways I'm all for it. I've seen too many pals close up who've bought it to last me a lifetime. But there's something honest about looking death directly in the eye, feeling the heat of another's blood. When we kill at a distance, we lose this. I keep remembering those German soldiers we shared a drink with two Christmases ago and wonder if they have the same thoughts. I feel certain that they do.

Captain Owen has become something of a friend to me in recent months. Although he is an officer, we talk as equals. I think you would like him if you ever get to meet him. He writes remarkable poems about what he calls "the pity of war", which paint a much more vivid picture of what it is actually like here than a thousand letters of mine ever could, the whole complexity of it. Last night he read me a new one, one that he says is not yet finished, but it seemed to chime perfectly with these thoughts I have been having since watching that film of you last week. It left a deep impression on me and I have committed to memory the following few lines, which I should like to share with you.

> *'It seemed that out of battle I escaped*
> *Down some profound dull tunnel, long since scooped*
> *Through granites which titanic wars had groined.*
> *Yet also there encumbered sleepers groaned,*
> *Too fast in thought or death to be bestirred.*
> *Then, as I probed them, one sprang up, and stared*
> *With piteous recognition in fixed eyes,*
> *Lifting distressful hands, as if to bless.*
>
> *I am the enemy you killed, my friend.*
> *I knew you in this dark: for so you frowned*
> *Yesterday through me as you jabbed and killed.*
> *I parried; but my hands were loath and cold.*
> *Let us sleep now...'*

Your loving fiancé
Arthur

*

Another twelve months passed. The earth completed one more orbit of the sun. The treadmill turned.

*

For Winifred it felt that, whereas a year ago she was standing right at the treadmill's lowest point, now she had mounted its zenith. She could look about her and see the city spread out below. She had become a conductress on Manchester's trams and buses.

"Move on down the bus! Any more fares now please?"

She was wearing trousers once again, the navy of her new uniform replacing the bottle green of her garb as a munitionette, along with a blazer with brass buttons and a rather jaunty cap. She enjoyed the banter with the drivers and other conductors down at the depot, and she liked helping the passengers, even the surly ones, who evidently disapproved of yet another transgression by the weaker sex into what they considered to be inappropriate and unfeminine activity, but these were few and far between, and even their attitudes seemed to alter with time and familiarity, as more and more the Modern Miss, which is what Winifred supposed she now must be, was eulogised in verse and song, mostly in the Music Halls, and Winifred would find herself singing along, especially on a Saturday night, if she was ever on duty just after closing time, to the latest ditty from Vesta Tilley, songs such as *Tilly the Typist, Kitty the Telephone Girl, Polly from the GPO, Dance of the Fire Brigade Girls* and *The Lady Bus Conductor*.

"Where are the girls of the old brigade?
The girls of the once upon a time?"

Most of all she loved the actual journeys themselves. She looked forward to each week's posting, wondering which particular route she might be assigned to next, and before too long she had ridden the entire network, from Wigan in the west to Glossop in the east, and from Bury in the north to Bramhall in the south. She would intone each route like a litany, a church mass she'd got by heart, radiating out from the city centre –

Piccadilly, Ancoats, Miles Platting, Colleyhurst;
Harpurhey, Blackley, Crumpsall Green and Kersal;
Pendlebury, Swinton, Whittle Brook and Wardley;
Walkden, Linneyshaw, Little Hulton, Farnworth;
Hunger Hill, Knutshaw Bridge, Little Lever, Pocket;
Harper Green, Moses Gate, Nob End and Radcliffe

– just one of twenty routes she could roll out at will.

She quickly fell into the routines of early starts and late finishes, of city gents, lost children, amiable drunks and fare dodgers, those who never had change, those who struggled for breath, those on their way to work, or home, or a date, or the pub, those who wanted to talk, and those who wanted a kiss.

She got to know all the landmarks – the statues, the churches, the squares and the high streets – all the junctions and cross roads, blind spots and pot holes. She learned the secret geography of the city, the way one neighbourhood leached into the next, the ponies and traps and occasional cars in wide tree-lined avenues giving way to the wagons and carts in crowded fish markets, how the commercial travellers, bankers and merchants of The Exchanges in their top hats and frock coats or bowler hats and brollies, rubbed shoulders with the tanners and butchers, porters and draymen of The Shambles in their aprons and mufflers and hob-nailed boots. She saw ladies in fine dresses on their way to the theatre and match girls in doorways begging for pennies. She watched the sun break through the early morning mists as the knockers-up, their faces muzzled with thick scarves, rapped on people's windows, and she smiled as the street lights flickered and glowed through the chill evening fogs, with children swinging on lamp posts, whole streets with washing strung across them, coming together to skip through the lines once the clothes had dried and been carried indoors.

"The big ship sails down the alley, alley – oh
The alley, alley – oh, the alley, alley – oh
The big ship sails down the alley, alley – oh
On the last day of September…"

Everywhere the city was heaving, convulsing with activity. Victorian slums of cellars and yards were being razed to the ground, making way for new streets with straight rows of terraced houses stretching their tentacled fingers out across what once were fields. Whole neighbourhoods were being recreated, each of them connected to the ever widening net of rail and tram and bus. As fast as cobbles were set and paving slabs laid, they were being covered with tracks, while overhead, cables formed gridded canopies of spider webbed steel. The whole city spread out around her like a quilted coverlet, each separate village occupying their own distinct square, now stitched together to make a single, unified blanket, with new squares continuously being hastily tacked to its ever-expanding sides and ends. It knew no limits and nothing, it seemed, could stop its relentless march. Winifred gathered this blanket to her, wrapping herself within it. It was as though she had passed through a great wave, her doubts in the city she loved surging like the sea when driven by the wind, but having been called to account, she had, at last, she hoped, found her courage. As the trains hissed with steam, and the trams and buses rattled through the streets like thunder, the sparks cracked in the cables above her, like electric paddles recharging and restarting her heart.

*

Esther, too, felt renewed hope returning to her. Since the beginning of August and the Battle of Amiens, which had seen the allied forces finally breaking through the German lines, the tide of war had turned unstoppably. It was not that Esther was yearning to celebrate victory. It was more that she craved an end to the limitless loss and waste.

At the Battle of Mont Saint-Quentin, the Somme was finally crossed. At the Battle of Havrincourt, the Hindenberg Line was, for the first time, pierced, leading to the 5th and final Battle of Ypres, spearheaded by a squadron of more than a thousand Avro 504s, many of them built in Manchester and tested on the airfield out at Woodford. The Battle of Sharqat brought the war in Mesopotamia to an end and the surrender of the Ottomans, with the Bulgars following suit shortly afterwards, bringing peace to the Balkans. The Scramble for Africa exhaled its last gasp at the Battle of Lioma in Somaliland. September saw the fall of Palestine and the capture of Damascus. In October Austro-Hungarian forces were routed in Italy, and the decisive Hundred Days Offensive came to a close with The Battle of the Canal de la Sambre à l'Oise on 4th November. Less than a week later Kaiser Wilhelm II abdicated, paving the way for the signing of the Armistice of Compiègne, at the eleventh hour of the eleventh day of the eleventh month of the year, which finally signalled the end to all of the fighting.

The following day the owners of Bradford Colliery declared a half day's holiday. While her father and brothers celebrated with work mates at *The Navigation Inn*, Esther took advantage of a quiet afternoon at home by herself. Now that the war was finally over, she could feel the tension beginning to drain from her body. They'd received a letter only recently from Arthur, informing them that he would soon be home on leave, sent before the armistice was signed, and so she also thought she'd stay behind just in case he arrived that day.

She sat down briefly in an armchair, feeling the fatigue of years overtaking her. When she looked up, Arthur was sitting on the arm of the chair, looking down on her and smiling.

"Oh," she said, "I must have nodded off. I didn't hear you come in."

"I hope you've been taking good care of that bike of mine," he said. "I shall be wanting it back now this show's over." He bent over his kit bag, rummaging inside, trying to find something.

"I'll put the kettle on, shall I?" she asked.

"Well," he went on, "I just want you to know that you're not to worry about it."

"About what?" She carried on into the kitchen to fetch some water for the kettle. She heard a knock at the front door. "I'll get it," she called. "You just make yourself comfortable."

Arthur didn't reply.

Esther walked to the front door, opened it, and there on the step was a postman, with a telegram. She knew immediately what it was.

*

REGRET TO INFORM YOU STOP ARTHUR BLUNDELL CORPORAL MANCHESTER REGIMENT STOP KILLED IN ACTION BATTLE OF SAMBRE STOP FULL DETAILS TO FOLLOW STOP DEEPEST SYMPATHY STOP LIEUT J FOULKES STOP

*

The bells of St Philip's Church across the road all at once began to peal.

*

The Manchester Regiment
Ladysmith Barracks
Mossley Road
Ashton-under-Lyne

15th November 1918

Dear Mr Blundell,

It is with enormous sadness that I write to you this day. In my previously sent telegram I promised to furnish you with further details, for I am sure you are anxious to learn more about the circumstances that led to the untimely death of your son. Such news must always be terrible to bear, but learning of this on the day after the signing of the armistice and the conclusion of this terrible war must be especially difficult.

Your son died bravely during the final battle of the war, at the crossing of the Sambre-Oise Canal on 4th November 1918. During an attempt to bridge the canal he successfully fought alongside Captain Owen, his company commander, and secured a narrow pontoon, enabling his fellow soldiers to safely cross, *but was then himself shot by a German machine-gunner, as was Captain Owen. His unselfish gallantry, in risking his own life to protect those of his comrades, bought his company invaluable time, enabling them to advance towards and subsequently capture many enemy forces as a result. His actions were typical of the brave soldier I had come to recognise and value during our service together.*

As the good book tells us: "Greater love hath no man than this, that a man lay down his life for his friends." (John: 15, verse 13)

I do not believe he suffered.

I know that he greatly appreciated the love and support he received from you in the many letters you wrote to him. I also know that he had a fiancée, whose photograph he carried with him always. If you would be so kind as to supply me with her address, I shall then write to her separately.

Arthur died a hero, a credit to himself, his family, his regiment and his country.

Yours truly,
Lt. James Foulkes, Manchester Regiment

*

Enclosed with the letter from Lieutenant Foulkes was Arthur's kit bag containing a few pitiful items that belonged to him – his cap, his corporal's stripes, his belt, a tin containing letters tied together with a shoe lace, the Christmas menu he'd jokingly written for the amusement of his pals, a photograph of Winifred.

Esther flung these across the sitting room with a sudden ferocity. She was so angry she was trembling. Her brothers watched her in silent trepidation, not one of them daring to speak. This was not an every day kind of crossness, the sort that might have caused her to raise a pointed finger at them for not wiping their feet when they came in from work, or for leaving a milk bottle on the table, or for flicking cigarette ash onto the floor instead of using an ash tray. This was a fury as cold as steel. She turned abruptly on her heels and headed towards the front door, on the back of which hung her coat and hat, which she threw on carelessly, and then slammed out into the front yard towards the ginnel at the side of the building, from where she grabbed Arthur's bicycle and pedalled furiously away, down Melland Road, around the corner and out of sight, just as a biblical rain began to fall.

Esther did not pause to consider the direction she was taking. She simply cycled as though her life depended on it, oblivious to the rain crashing in stair rods all around her. Already the roads were becoming like streams, through which she ploughed regardless, spraying fountains of water on either side of her as she made her way by Crowcroft Hall, Ryder Brow, Darras Road, past the iron foundry at Clayton Vale, until she found herself skirting the edge of the Ashton Canal, whose waters were beginning to lap the tow path, before heading off down Bank Street towards Philips Park. Water was gushing up now out of the grids, man hole covers had been thrust aside, between which she had to weave her way over the increasingly broken and uneven ground. Eventually, the inevitable happened. Her front wheel collided with a steep, submerged kerb, and she was catapulted over the handle bars, landing in a painful, wet heap by the side of the road. She felt a sharp crack above her left ankle just before her head made contact with a large, upturned cobble, and she swam into unconsciousness.

*

1872.

The Manchester Courier

14th July 1872

BODIES WASHED AWAY AS MEDLOCK BURSTS ITS BANKS

Two days of uninterrupted torrential rainfall have resulted in the worst flooding in Manchester for more than half a century. Devastation has been visited on all parts of the city but the hardest hit has been Philips Park, the adjoining cemetery and the communities bordering all sides.

It was at half past twelve yesterday when

the floods came. The banks of the River Medlock were overflowed to an alarming extent. The first intimation of the flood was the sweeping away of a footbridge near to the park. It must have been very strongly fixed, for it not only bore the rush of the flood for a considerable time, but it resisted it to such a degree that the water backed up for a considerable distance.

Once the bridge collapsed, however, there was nothing to hold the mighty forces of the water at bay. Not even a Moses could have saved the day. The flood increased in depth and power, and at length swept in a fierce torrent over a large portion of ground apportioned to the Roman Catholics at the Bradford Cemetery, carrying away not only tombstones, but actually washing out of their graves a large number of dead bodies.

Indeed from the first indication of danger, so far as workers on the banks of the Medlock were concerned, dead bodies were observed floating down the river, and those watching could easily see that these bodies had been disinterred out of the Bradford cemetery. It is impossible to calculate precisely how many had been swept out of their final resting place but the number is not short of seventy-five. In response to the flooding, work will begin at once on the construction of a culvert, fashioned from red terracotta-brick, to form a broad, continuous channel, which will from now on carry the river between the park and its adjoining cemetery.

When Esther came to, the rain had stopped, but the sound of water gurgling all around her filled her waking senses. She lifted the bicycle from on top of her and pushed it to one side. She tried to stand, but the pain in her left ankle shot through her with such force that it caused her to gasp out loud. She tried to take stock of her situation.

She was on the edge of Philips Park Cemetery, some way from the nearest street. She looked around in every direction but could see no one. She tried once more to stand and found that if she put as little weight as possible onto her left leg, she could gingerly make her way slightly further along, where there were signs of road repairs. Perhaps, she wondered, there might also be a workman's hut nearby, in which she might take some shelter until she could work out what she might do.

As she neared it, she saw that a deep pit had been dug, the sides of which were all shored up with wet and heavy sand bags. She peered down into it. Below, at a depth of about six to eight feet, she calculated, she could just make out a red brick culvert, covered with mud and slime, from which water now oozed in a slow but persistent trickle through a narrow crack. It was this crack, she assumed, that was awaiting repairs. There was something else there, too, grey and solid, which she couldn't properly make out, and yet which appeared to her to be oddly, disturbingly familiar. She knelt at the pit's edge and leant down lower in order to try and get a closer look at what it might be. At that precise moment, she heard the sudden violent retort of a rifle firing, so loudly it seemed to bounce off the brick and stone all around her, startling a clatter of rooks in the leafless trees at the edge of the park. She looked around and, as she did so, she lost both her grip and her balance, and fell backwards into the pit.

The jolt as she landed knocked all the breath from her body, and once again she found herself slipping away. Her head swam, and it was several seconds before the world, this new, dark, enclosed version of it, righted itself, and her eyes began to make out where she was. Although the base of her back was sore, she didn't think she'd incurred any further damage, and she looked about her to see if there might be some means of escape.

The walls of the pit were more or less sheer, but even though the sand bags had been packed and wedged so tightly, it was, she believed, possible to fashion finger and toe holds to enable her to climb her way back up. Or rather, it would have been, had her ankle been able to take her weight, but it was quite unable to do so. She suspected it was broken, or possibly dislocated, with the tibia and talus no longer maintaining their anatomical relationship, in which case it could be that the distal ends of the tibia and fibula were what had been broken. She was thankful for her first aid training acquired during her shifts as a VAD at Brook House, but frustrated that, although she may well have the basic knowledge to diagnose her condition, here at the bottom of this pit, which was, she realised, slowly but steadily filling up with the muddy water emanating from the crack in the culvert, she had none of the means at her disposal to treat it.

She looked more closely at her surroundings, which in fact more accurately resembled a trench than a pit. Its construction reminded her of how Arthur had described the trenches that they built out along the Western Front, whole networks of them, leading out from the rear supply lines towards the different units, branching off this way and that. As much of their time was spent in constructing these tunnels, Arthur had explained, as in actual fighting, thank goodness. They must have looked like an army of moles, shovelling the earth aside as they burrowed their way beneath what had once been grazing land, arable land, land for growing things. Now nothing grew there, except for hopes and dreams, of what had once been there. The Manchester Regiment soon established a reputation for being expert tunnel-diggers and trench-builders. Hardly surprising, wrote Arthur in one of his early letters back home, considering so many of us had been miners. They'd even given their trenches names, as reminders of landmarks back home – Deansgate, Market Street, Hanging Ditch, all radiating out from Piccadilly. What might this small cul-de-sac of a trench be called, mused Esther, so narrow and cramped she could barely stretch out her whole length? Melland Road, maybe, whose confines she had at times railed against?

She remembered why she had ridden so blindly out of the flat earlier that afternoon, upon receiving that letter from Arthur's Commanding Officer. The sentiments expressed by Lieutenant Foulkes, although sincerely meant, and to which she would reply with gratitude at some point when she felt calmer, contained everything that so outraged her, the assumption that somehow Arthur's death had not been in vain, had not been such an unforgivable waste. Now that the war was over, nobody could really say what had been achieved, what it had been for in the first place, why it had been felt necessary to sacrifice the lives of millions of young men like Arthur, who left behind them so much unfulfilled promise. Surely, she thought, if the war was to serve any useful purpose at all, it must be to change the old order of things, to make society more democratic, more egalitarian, recognising that there was so much more that unified the peoples of the world than divided them, as Arthur had pointed out in his letter about that Christmas Day truce? And where better a place to start on that road towards a new order than here in Manchester?

She tried once more to stand, but the pain in her ankle prevented her. The sun had briefly dipped below the cloud and was shining into the trench where she lay sprawled in one corner. Its beam fell upon that grey object she had dimly seen when looking down into the trench from above. She had forgotten about it, but now the sun revealed it clearly. It was a skull. Poking through the mud walls where sand bags had not been so firmly stacked, she now began to perceive other human bones, a rib, a femur, a tibia, not unlike her own that she felt certain had been broken. She was not frightened by this discovery, merely further convinced in her sense of things needing to change. She had not been a Christian for many years now, her doubt surfaced before the war even, and her faith withered and was hardened by it. She looked at these grey bones, unearthed by the day's sudden storm, caught in the last dregs of sunlight, and wondered how they came here. What cataclysm had washed them from their burial plot? Or what misfortune had left them to lie where they fell, until they were picked clean as now? When Lieutenant Foulkes talked of the special bond between Arthur and his Captain Owen, he little knew of what he wrote.

She held the skull in the palm of her hand and manoeuvred it so that the final rays of the sun fell upon it, before speaking out loud:

> "*Move him into the sun –*
> *Gently its touch awoke him once,*
> *At home, whispering of fields half-sown.*
> *Always it woke him, even in France,*
> *Until this morning, and this snow.*
> *If anything might rouse him now,*
> *The kind old sun will know…*"

The sun was sinking lower. She stretched her arms as far as she could reach above her head, trying to keep the last drop of sun upon the skull in her hands.

> "*Think how it wakes the seeds –*
> *Woke once the clays of a cold star.*
> *Are limbs so dear-achieved, are sides*

Full-nerved, still warm, too hard to stir?
Was it for this the clay grew tall?
O what made fatuous sunbeams toil
To break earth's sleep at all?"

And as she finished speaking, the sun left the trench completely. She lay at the bottom in near darkness. The skull rolled from her hands into the shadows, where a rat scurried past it, intent upon a journey of its own. Esther, for the first time since the war began, felt the tension in her body leave her, and she wept, without any attempt to prevent herself.

How long she cried for, she could not say. She may even have cried herself into exhaustion and sleep. She did not know. Suddenly, however, her senses were ratcheted into high alert by the vivid and lurid appearance at the top of the trench of a face, a face lit by a burning torch, the face of a man. His skin was dark, a deep chestnut reddish-brown, with streaks of dirt smeared across the brow and cheeks. The hair framing the face was unusually long, almost black, flecked with faint traces of grey, beneath a wide-brimmed hat, from which different bird feathers sprang up, raven, magpie, buzzard, owl. His eyes were dark, cavernous almost, and the whites of them, illuminated by the dancing flames of his torch, showed yellow and slightly bloodshot. His appearance was rendered yet more demonic by the absence of two front teeth, so that as he stretched his lips to speak, he revealed arrow-sharp fangs.

"Catch," he called, and threw a length of a rope down towards her. "Now, tie," he instructed, and he made the shape of a circle with his free arm around his waist. "And here," he indicated, gesturing beneath his shoulders.

Without a moment's hesitation, Esther did as she was shown, and when she had finished and the rope was securely tied and fastened, she looked back up.

"Loop and throw," he commanded, and Esther dutifully worked the remaining rope into something resembling a cowboy's lasso and tossed it up towards him. He then briefly disappeared, while he secured the end of the rope around the trunk of a tree further up the slope towards the park. When he returned, he proceeded, very slowly and surprisingly gently, to haul Esther up towards the surface, inch by inch, pausing regularly to check that she was fine for him to continue. Finally, as she neared the top, the man reached down towards her, placed his hands upon her hips and lifted her the few remaining feet onto the footpath beside the trench.

A relieved but exhausted Esther thanked him and he nodded. He offered his hand to help lift her to her feet, but she raised her hands, their palms open towards him, and shook her head. "I'm afraid I've injured my ankle," she said. "I can't stand."

He nodded again and stooped to examine her.

"Which?" he asked.

She pointed to her left. With exquisite tenderness he took off her shoe and carefully held her foot in his hands. As he tried to turn it outwards slightly, Esther winced, and he stopped.

"I think it's dislocated," she said. "It needs putting back. I'm a nurse. Or rather, I assist nurses. I've watched it being done. But I don't seem able to do it to myself."

He regarded her carefully and rapped his clenched fist against his chest. "Horse doctor," he said. "Back in home country."

She looked in his eyes and seemed to see him riding out of a dark forest into a vast grassy plain, with distant views of high mountains.

"Lakota," he explained.

It was not a word she'd heard before but its meaning was clear. "Go ahead," she said. "I'm ready."

With a sharp, swift twist he pulled the ankle back. The pain was severe but quick. When he had finished, her body began to shake and her teeth to chatter, as if having at last been given permission by her to do so. The man opened a hessian bag slung across his shoulder, and from it pulled a thick, yellow blanket. He spread it over her, from her feet right up to her chin. It smelled of dried leaves, human sweat and wood smoke, and immediately she started to feel warmer. He placed his hands on the sides of her shoulders. "Back soon, he said. "Wait here."

He ran a few yards up towards the brake of trees, which marked the boundary with the park, and disappeared amongst them. She heard the sound of a branch being cut and then he returned. He had selected a firm spar of alder, from which he was expertly stripping the bark, removing all the sharp notches. He came back to her side, measured a length of cord, which he snapped with his teeth, and proceeded to apply the spar to Esther's left leg, tying it firmly with the cord to make the beginnings of a splint. He then jumped back into the trench from where he had rescued Esther, emerging just a few moments later brandishing one of the bones she had disturbed when she fell, a femur, which he then attached to the spar of alder, before strapping the whole tightly and expertly to Esther's leg.

"Bone will give more strength, more support."

Esther nodded, scarcely able to speak.

"Now, I take you home," he said.

Esther bowed her head. "It's quite a way," she said, finding her voice once more. "Too far to walk, even with you supporting me, and much too far for you to carry me."

"How did you come here?" he asked.

She pointed to the bicycle and its buckled front wheel.

He went across to it, picked it and examined it. "I fix this," he said. "Enough to make it move again," and at once he began to straighten the various spokes of the wheel until it was able to spin more or less freely. "Come," he said. "Sit side saddle and I steer."

"In a moment," she said. "Let me get warmer first. This blanket is helping. I don't suppose you have any water, do you?"

He took a leather bottle from the hessian sack and poured a few drops into an old tin mug. "Not too much at first," he said. "I will make fire," he said, "heat water, add leaves, herbs. Then home."

She nodded her thanks.

While he busied himself, Esther was able to look about her and take in a little more of who her rescuer was. He wore a long black overcoat, which appeared to have more patches than original cloth. The pockets were bulging with what might have been rabbits, but on closer inspection she realised were moles. Lying on the ground beside him was a long pole with a cross-piece at the top, from which hung several more moles, all now neatly laid out in rows. Next to that was a coil of wire netting, wrapped around what she assumed might be some sort of trap, but not one with those appalling ferocious sets of iron teeth she had seen other men use, this looked more like a cage to collect them in, after they'd been tempted along the wire tunnels. Finally, there was a shotgun, its barrels broken for safety, close to where he now squatted, attending to the fire.

"Was that you who fired a gun shot some time ago?" she said, tentatively.

He looked up. "Might have been."

She smiled ruefully. "It was that which made me stumble into the trench."

He said nothing, merely blew on the flames as the fire caught and took hold. She watched him crumble what looked like bits of plant matter into the mug of now hotter water. "Drink," he said. "Slowly."

She raised the mixture to her lips. It smelled tangy, acrid, and the taste was not altogether pleasant. But she drank as she'd been instructed.

"Is this what you do," she asked, "catch moles?"

"Sometimes. I came to this country a young man. Part of a Wild West Travelling Show. I did not like. I miss my home. One day I run away. I dream of going back." He laughed, mirthlessly. "Not possible. So I stay here instead. Follow the three rivers. Fish. Hunt. Make myself useful. There were more farms back then. People look for me with the seasons. Lambing. Shearing. Milking. I stick the pigs. Flay the hides."

"Catch the moles?"

"Yes."

"Why?"

He looked at her curiously.

"I've often wondered," she began, "what harm do they do? Apart from spoiling rich folks' lawns?"

"They harm roots. Stop things growing."

"But don't they do good things too?"

He nodded and smiled.

"What?"

"You ask many questions."

"I just want to know things."

"Moles clean out soil," he said. "Eat grubs and insects. But also worms. Earth needs worms to make soil rich."

"Are there lots of them?"

"Too many. That is why I…"

"I never knew. You don't see them, do you? But they're right here, under our feet all the time, building their tunnels, burrowing away."

"And if we do not take a few from time to time, their tunnels make the land collapse. Think. Houses tumbling like playing cards. Streets crumbling to dust. Whole cities disappearing."

"Does it hurt them?" Esther asked. "When you kill them?"

The man picked up his gun, cocked the barrel. "Not with this. It is quick."

They were silent for a while. The fire crackled. Esther drank her mixture under a hunter's moon.

"Where do you live?" she asked.

He pointed back into the trees. "I make camp," he said.

"Did you...?" She faltered. She wasn't sure if she wanted to know the answer to the question that hung on her lips.

"You want to ask about the war," he said.

Esther nodded.

"Yes," he said. "I went. They needed blacksmiths, help with horses. But then they needed me for different things."

Esther looked at him hard. His eyes reflected the rising flames from the fire. She saw in them shadows of men, crouched on all fours, burrowing through the mud, trying not to be seen as they scuttled away from the battlefields. And then she saw a larger shadow, of a man with feathers in his hair, rising up out of the ground, training the sights of his rifle on these blind, scurrying moles, taking aim, then firing.

The man kicked dirt into the fire, putting it out.

"Time I took you home," he said. "Come," and he stretched out his hand towards her.

She took it, then he scooped her into his arms and carried her towards the bicycle, which was leaning against a tree. She leant into his shoulder. She felt safe. He placed her carefully onto the saddle and then began to wheel her, back the way she had come, back towards Melland Road, back towards her home.

They made their way mostly in silence. Only when they reached the last corner did they speak again.

"What's your name?" she asked.

"People call me Tommy," he said. "Tommy Thunder."

"I'm Esther."

"Where I come from," he said, "names have meaning. When I was a child, I would run and chase the storms. My father called me 'Chasing Thunder'."

Esther smiled. "I like that," she said.

"And what does Esther mean?"

"I believe it means 'star'," she said, "but I don't think my parents thought about that when they named me."

"Look," he said, and pointed to a star shooting across the sky. "That is how I will remember you. Burning brightly somewhere else, even if I never see her."

"We've reached my home, Mr Thunder," she said shyly. "Thank you."

He walked to the front door, knocked sharply, then returned to Esther and lifted her off the bicycle. When the door opened, Esther's three brothers stood there, astonished, as Tommy Thunder handed her across the threshold. She turned to bid him goodnight, but he had already gone.

Later that night, when Esther had finally succeeded in persuading Frank, Harold and Jim that she was quite well enough to be left alone, she wrote a letter to Lieutenant Foulkes to thank him for his kindness, without giving the slightest indication, she hoped, of how she truly felt, and then steeled herself to look inside Arthur's kit bag. In amongst his various things she found, buried at the bottom, two books. First was a well-thumbed copy of Houseman's *A Shropshire Lad*, which had accompanied him throughout the war, and in which he had underlined several favourite passages. It fell open upon one verse, beside which Arthur had written in pencil, "to be shared with Esther":

"There pass the careless people
That call their souls their own;
Here by the road I loiter,
How idle and alone…"

But he wasn't alone, she thought, not in the end, just as I was not earlier this evening, when I encountered my own strange meeting.

The second book was a slim volume of Voltaire's *Candide*, in a translation by Smollett, seemingly a gift to Arthur from Captain Owen, for on the fly-leaf was written the inscription, *"To a dear friend, from W."*

Esther knew of it by reputation but had never read it. She opened it, imagining herself reading it as Arthur might have, at night, by firelight, under a cold, wintry sky, not so very different from where she had been sitting just a few hours earlier. She wondered if Arthur had reacted as she was doing now, with growing rage and incredulity, following Candide's journey to various foreign fields, after he was tricked into leaving behind the Eden of his home, in his increasingly gullible pursuit of *El Dorado*, the Promised Land, where all was always for the best, in this, the best of all possible worlds, goaded and cajoled by the ridiculous posturing Professor Pangloss, whose pomposity and hyperbole continually reminded her of the opportunist Lloyd George, with his own high blown, empty rhetoric and his recent snap "coupon" election, an election she still could not take part in, filled with hollow promises of "a happier country for all" and "a land fit for heroes", before Candide finally comes to his senses, rejecting all of it, realising instead that we must all of us simply return, back to whatever place we now called home, and cultivate our garden.

Esther finished reading the final page and closed the book. She shut her eyes and rubbed the bridge of her nose. They had no garden at Melland Road, but they had the life they had made for themselves. She would look after her father in his failing years. She would support her three remaining brothers until they had each left home and were supporting themselves and their own families. She would cherish the memories of Freddie and Arthur. She would shore up their lives with the sand bags of work, so that they would not be swept away by the rising flood. And when the waters began at last to subside, she would set her face to the world, climb back up on that bicycle, and pedal where the road took her, to wherever she was needed most.

*

It was a raw, cold early morning, the sky an iron grey, Friday 27th December, 1918, three years to the day since Ruth's funeral, not that she was known to the young man who approached the western end of Philips Park Cemetery as the bells of the nearby church of St Jerome's tolled eight o'clock. John Jabez Chadwick stood by the Gothic arched entrance, looking up at its central, rising spire, collecting himself before he walked in.

It had taken him more than six weeks since the official Armistice had been signed to make his way back. First there had been nearly a fortnight of necessary tasks and duties to be completed before his unit had been given their official orders to stand down. There had been the injured to be accounted for and escorted to train depots for transfer back to Blighty, the fortifications to be dismantled, the armaments to be packed away and got ready for transportation, and then there had been the various prisoners to be processed. Finally, they had assembled for one last bugled parade at which their Commanding Officer, his voice thick with emotion, had told them what splendid chaps they had all been, before wishing them all *Bon Voyage*.

Having survived Passchendaele with the Lancashire Regiment, Jabez had been transferred, together with several of his comrades, to the newly created 14th British Corps under the command of General Babington, whom they rarely saw. They joined forces with brigades from the French, Italian and

Czechoslovak armies for a combined assault against retreating Austro-Hungarian troops, culminating in victory at the Battle of Vittorio Veneto. Jabez had crossed the River Piave, where he had witnessed at first hand members of the crack *Arditi* corps, who had fought the battle almost entirely by swimming, often for more than sixteen hours at a stretch, armed only with a knife and two hand grenades.

Since then Jabez had, in concert with others from his Unit, walked back over the Dolomites, across the flat, open plain of the Po valley. Before they had set off, they had been assigned one final harrowing task, to round up all the remaining horses and shoot them. But they had refused. They waited till their C/O had gone, before untying their tethers and setting them free to gallop into the high passes, where uncut grass still grew, and the mountains rumbled and shook. They then proceeded to follow in their wake, right across the wide yoke of Italy, until they reached Turin, where they were able to board a train to Genoa, from where a troop ship took them to Marseille, where they then took the first of a series of further trains, with long, slow miles of walking in between, first to Lyon, then to Paris and finally to Calais, where they were crammed onto an already overcrowded ship, which docked, with some difficulty, in Dover.

Once there it took a further three days before all of the various papers had been stamped, travel vouchers issued, and they were able to make their separate journeys home across all the waiting counties of England. By the time Jabez finally stepped down from the overnight Milk Train onto Manchester's London Road Station, there were just two of them still together, who had made that epic journey all the way back from North-East Italy. His pal, Clifford, was from Bolton, and so, following a firm handshake and a promise to stay in touch, which both of them knew they would probably not keep, each anxious to pick up the threads of their former lives, leaving the horrors they'd witnessed deeply buried, Jabez walked the final two and a half miles back to his home alone, as the dawn's grey light slowly crept towards him.

On an impulse, just as he passed through Holt Town, heading down Rowsley Street, towards Grey Mare Lane, he decided to make a short detour. He doubled back down Sarah Ann Street, Glass Street and Topaz Street, before crossing a patch of waste ground leading to Forge Lane, which led him onto Mill Street, which eventually took him to Philips Park Cemetery, where he now stood, looking up at the imposing Gothic arched gateway.

Six months before, a letter had reached him from Joan, the elder of his two sisters, informing him that their father had finally succumbed to the emphysema, which had been troubling him for years. His father, John, had been a miner, but when his lungs first began to trouble him, he had left the pit to assist his own father, also called John, as Assistant Park Keeper, rising to the position of Head Keeper when the son of the legendary Jeremiah Johnson, the park's original gardener, who had succeeded the great man upon his death, died himself. Jabez had from time to time worked beside his father at weekends and in the evenings, finding the fresh air and proximity to growing things a welcome balm and reparation from his long days spent underground as a miner and, now that the war was finally over, he had begun, on his long journey home from the Dolomites, to harbour dreams of taking up the position of Head Keeper and Gardener at the park himself. In the ruin and devastation of the trenches, he had seen once green fields churned into grey mud, bleached by rotting bones and corpses, where nothing grew, nor ever seemed likely to again, and in those few snatched moments of sleep he would muster during those long, dark years, he would dream of Philips Park and Tulip Sunday.

But when the war took hold, the park was given over to allotments and the growing of much needed food for those left behind, particularly when German submarines patrolled the oceans and blockaded the ports, and as he passed it in the cold morning light, it looked barely recognisable to the scenes he had conjured in his wartime dreams. Now, he hoped, there'd be an appetite for colour to return to these drab streets.

His father had been temporarily relieved of his duties at the park and had returned to the colliery. Although he had, for the most part, been assigned to surface work, nevertheless his health had deteriorated almost immediately, and so it was no real surprise to him when Joan wrote to tell him of his passing. "He was not in pain," she had written, "not at the end, and his last thoughts were of you, wishing you safe passage and return…"

And now he was back. He had not of course been able to attend the funeral, and so he thought he would visit the grave now to pay his respects, before finally walking back up into Quixall Street, where his mother and sisters would no doubt have been daily wondering when he might return. An extra hour now, he felt, would make little difference.

After less than a quarter of an hour's searching he came across a row of more recent headstones and in among these he found his father's. A bunch of fairly fresh tulips lay on the grave, probably placed there on Christmas Day, he thought. He knelt by the plot, slightly rearranging the blooms, for several minutes, trying to think back to happier times before the war, but found that he was quite unable to do so. His mind was still too full of all it had seen in more recent years.

He thought he was quite alone, but the sudden snapping of a twig caused him to look up from his reverie. He rose and turned around. About twenty yards away from him, a young woman was standing behind another of the more recently tended plots. She was supporting herself by resting her forearms on the back of the headstone, leaning her head upon them. A pair of rooks was cawing in the growing light. Mindful of her need for privacy, Jabez stayed where he was, waiting to see if she might move, before deciding what he might next do, whether to bid her good morning, wishing neither to startle nor ignore her. Had he been a regular visitor to art galleries, which he was not, she would have struck him immediately as the figure in Henry Alexander Bowler's notorious painting *The Doubt: Can*

These Dry Bones Live? But although he would not have been able to place the painting, nor note the lack of any butterfly of hope alighting on the headstone, he instinctively recognised, from the expression on her face as she lifted her head from her arms, the same crisis of faith she appeared to be experiencing, for he felt it too, acutely so. This war, which had supposedly been fought to safeguard for posterity the ideals of England as some kind of lost Eden, to rebuild Jerusalem among these dark Satanic mills, had shaken such beliefs to their very core. Jabez may well have dreamed of planting tulips once more in Philips Park, but not so much as a return to the past, more a desperate hope to see things grow again, flower, however briefly, their seeds harvested for future blooms.

The young woman, he noticed, was also carrying a bunch of tulips, which now she let fall from her fingers, as she stirred to move away. She was not, he also noted, crying, but, like him, was dry-eyed. He decided he would, after all, make his presence known to her.

"Good morning."

She looked up at him as if she had seen a ghost.

"Forgive me, Miss. I didn't mean to startle you…"

"It's quite alright, sir. I was thinking of someone else, and then suddenly, there you were."

"I remind you of someone?"

"No. Not really. It's the uniform, I suppose."

"You're thinking of someone you lost perhaps?"

She smiled thinly and shook her head. "Not in the way you think." She indicated the headstone. "My mistress was buried here three years ago this very day.

She were only twenty-one. Her fiancé died in France just a few weeks before that, and her father was interned on th' Isle of Man, where he died around t' same time. And then I moved to look after my mistress's mother, who herself died just a fortnight ago."

"I'm very sorry."

"Thank you. And you?"

"My father," he said, pointing back to where he'd been standing. "While I was away."

"And you've just got back, I take it?"

He nodded. "This morning. I'm on my way home now."

"Is it close?"

"Very. But I'm not expected."

"You sent no word?"

"I didn't know for sure when I'd arrive."

"Have you travelled a long way?"

"Yes."

They looked steadily at one another for the first time. Each of them saw sorrow, but more than that, strength.

"What will you do?" she asked.

"I don't know."

"Me neither. I were thinking as I walked here this morning of all t' different paths I might've taken. The what ifs, whether any o' t' different things that have happened might've been prevented if I'd done summat other than what I did…"

"You shouldn't blame yourself. Things happen that are outside of our control."

"They still affect us, though, don't they?" She threw this last remark at him with surprising force. "I'm sorry," she said. "It all feels such a waste," and she threw the flowers angrily to the ground.

Jabez stooped to pick them up. He pointed to a small section of one of the flowers just beneath the bloom. "Do you see this?" he said. "This is the seed pod. Once it's dried and brown, it's ready to be removed from the plant stem. Then you can harvest the seeds and plant them in the soil. It takes a long time – four to six years sometimes – but in the end, they grow."

"Into tulips?"

He nodded. "But they may not look anything like the original flowers they were taken from. They might be a different shape, or a different colour. The soil, the shade, the weather, so many things, all make a contribution, but in the end, they just become what they are, themselves."

"For want of a nail the shoe was lost."

"For want of a shoe the horse was lost."

"For want of a horse the rider was lost."

"For want of a rider the message was lost."

"For want of a message the battle was lost.

"For want of a battle the kingdom was lost."

"And all for the want of a nail," concluded Mary.

Jabez bent down and removed a nail from his own shoe. "This has been bothering me for weeks," he said, smiling.

"You'd best not lose it then."

"I'm Jabez," he said. "John Jabez Chadwick."

"Pleased to meet you, Jabez. I'm Mary. Mary

Flynn."

"But your mistress was German?"

Mary regarded him carefully before she replied. "She had a German name. But she were born here. In Manchester."

"We're all of us from somewhere else to begin with."

"Like in the Bible? All those begats?"

"I wouldn't know about that."

"What then?"

"Like seeds. Carried on the wind. Drifting on the ocean. Dropped by birds onto ships. We all get mixed up."

"Like Mrs Schneider's stews, with all their different ingredients. The longer you leave them, the better they taste."

"And these hybrids are stronger, tougher, more resilient, better able to withstand blight or disease."

"How do you know so much about tulips?"

"My father. He used to be the gardener here."

Mary lowered her head.

"Yes. I see…"

Jabez waited a moment before continuing.

"And you? Will you be going back to… the Schneiders, was it?"

"I don't think so."

He gave a slow, broad smile.

"In that case, Mary Flynn, can I walk you anywhere?"

"Well now, kind sir…"

"Are you teasing a soldier?"

She raised an eyebrow. "I'm staying at the Station Hotel in Denton. I've been charged with closing up the shop my mistress's parents used to run near there. There's no one left to inherit it, so it's to be sold. I'm to clean it all up and make it ready for the agents."

"But that's nearly five miles."

"I'm not helpless," she said, laughing.

"I didn't mean that you were."

"And you've got a home to go back to…"

"Yes. My mother and sisters."

Mary nodded, taking this in.

They stood in silence for a while before Mary turned to go. After just a few steps, she paused and turned back towards him.

"Perhaps you might like to see the shop?" she asked.

"If you can spare the time," he replied.

"Oh I think so," she said, a sparkle in her eye. "I should be finished by tomorrow afternoon. Call on me then. You can't miss it. There's a sign in the form of a giant pair of spectacles hanging above it. I'll be waiting underneath them at four o'clock."

"Keeping an eye out?"

"Two eyes."

Jabez gave Mary a smart salute. Smiling, she curtseyed, and then went on her way. She was, he noticed, carrying one of the tulips still in her left hand. Perhaps, he hoped, perhaps they might collect the seeds, propagate them, water them and feed them, and watch them grow together.

Just as he was about to turn, a flight of Avro 504s roared overhead, leaving a pair of vapour trails looping across the sky. Jabez and Mary looked up, then back to each other, and waved.

4

7th May 1922

After the first Tulip Sunday since the war had been officially declared open by the Right Honourable Mr John Edward Sutton MP, the large crowds happily dispersed around Philips Park to marvel at the floral displays nurtured to their peak by Jabez, or to sample the fairground rides brought in especially for the day from nearby Belle Vue, or to partake of the delicious array of refreshments provided by the Manchester Mothers Union, or to listen to the Victoria Brass Band, or simply to take the air and promenade along the many serpentine paths, which wound around and through the thirty-one acres of park land.

Esther had arranged with her brothers that they would take over the supervision of their father for an hour, while she went to speak with Winifred, whom she had espied during the opening ceremony. She made sure he was settled with a cup of tea by the refreshment tent, where Jim, her youngest surviving brother, was already waiting for them. Their father was a well loved, popular figure, and soon several of his old work mates from the mine, accompanied by their families, came to pay their respects and wish him a good morning.

"How do, Walter?" they said.

"Oh, mustn't grumble," he replied.

"What's yours?" they asked.

"Tea," said Walter, feeling Esther's watchful eye

upon him.

"Coming up," they answered, tapping the side of their nose with a knowing forefinger.

Esther, satisfied that he would be fine for a while, hurried back to the Bandstand, where she had arranged in pantomime with Winifred during Mr Sutton's speech that they would later meet. The band had broken into a stirring rendition of Cecil Spring-Rice's *I Vow to Thee, My Country*, with which the listening throng had spontaneously begun to sing along.

"*I vow to thee, my country*
All earthly things above
Entire and whole and perfect
The service of my love..."

It still struck Esther as strange, even after four years, that such patriotic fervour persisted, as she looked around at the shining faces singing all around her. It was partially the tune, she supposed, which was, even she would admit, quite glorious, but one that she preferred, as Holst had arranged it, without words, yet still they continued.

"*The love that never falters*
The love that pays the price
The love that makes undaunted
The final sacrifice..."

She caught sight of Winifred on the far side of the Bandstand and waved. The two women then made their way between the pressing crowds until they found each other in an awkward flurry and embrace. Was Winifred too listening to these words, wondered Esther as they disentangled themselves from one another, making sure their hats were safely secured as they sought a less crowded spot where they might speak more easily?

"The love that asks no questions
The love that stands the test
That lays upon the altar
The dearest and the best…"

It had been more than a year since they had last seen one another. The truth was that, since Arthur had died, they realised that it had chiefly been he who had created the bond between them, and that to see one another only reinforced that fact and proved painful to both of them. The hymn continued. The crowds were less sure now of the words of subsequent verses, which were taken up by the Choir of St Jerome's, who stood on the steps leading up to the Bandstand.

"And there's another country
I've heard of long ago
Most dear to them that love her
Most great to them I know…"

Esther and Winifred waited as the song continued, aware that it was useless to try and compete against it, better to let it run its course.

"We may not count her armies
We may not see her King
Her fortress is a faithful heart
Her pride is suffering…"

Winifred, she noted, seemed perfectly content to listen. Her face was turned back towards the choir. A slight breeze blew wisps of her hair across her face which, in silhouetted profile against the May sun, looked the very picture of a faithful heart and a suffering pride.

"And soul by soul and silently
Her shining bounds increase
And her ways are ways of gentleness
And all her paths are peace…"

When the hymn was over, the crowds began to drift away. Winifred composed herself and turned back towards Esther.

"Thank you," she said, "for letting me listen. I know you probably hate it."

"I think 'hate' is rather strong," Esther replied.

"You know what I mean. Shall we walk down one of these paths of peace?" she continued, smiling and linking her arm through Esther's. "Let's admire the tulips."

The band had switched to a medley of tunes from popular operettas – Offenbach, Lehar, Romberg. At that moment they were playing a selection from *A Desert Song*, and Esther smiled too, as she tried to picture the high, dry mountains of Southern Arabia, here in this frequently wet and grey East Manchester, but couldn't, not even when they were blessed with such rare warmth and sun as they were today.

Winifred was chattering brightly and Esther realised she hadn't heard a word. They were approaching a wooden bench overlooking the central pond. "Let's sit here," she said. "Now – tell me, Winifred, how are you? Truly?"

Winifred paused and looked back at her friend. "Truly? I'm lonely, that's how I am."

Esther nodded. "Yes. I see."

"My mother died – finally – a blessing really, she didn't know who she was any more, and so it's just me. I've got my job of course…"

"Yes," interrupted Esther. "How is that?"

"Well, I've been there nearly three years now. As you know, as soon as the war ended, all of us bus conductresses were given our marching orders. 'Thank you very much, but there are returning soldiers wanting work now'." Winifred paused. "I really enjoyed that job, you know? I got to know the whole of the city. The way it's spreading, it's wonderful to behold. Like a giant blanket being laid across us all, saying, 'Come on in, it's lovely'."

"It's not all lovely, though, is it?"

"No, dear, of course it isn't, but don't let's quarrel, not today. I just meant that if you have a pot big enough, and you throw in enough ingredients, eventually they'll all mix in. It might taste a bit queer at first, but given time, you get used to it, even grow to like it."

Esther took Winifred's hand that was still linked through her own arm and squeezed it. "So tell me about this new job of yours."

"I'm a telephonist. At the Royal Exchange. When it first started, nearly fifty years ago now, it all used to be boys, but they soon learned they couldn't be trusted, and so it's only women now. Even the Chief Supervisor's a woman – a Miss Brent: Edwina. Started on the switchboard, just like me." Winifred laughed briefly.

"What are the other women like? Have you made any friends?"

She shook her head. "They're mostly younger than me. And that's what I'm saying, Esther. I'm twenty-six now, and already these girls, they think of me as an old maid. And what's worse, I agree with them."

Esther said nothing.

"Look around us," Winifred continued, "here, today, in this park. It's mostly women and children. The only men are either old, or…" She gestured hopelessly in the direction of a row of disabled veterans, legless, pushing themselves on low handmade trolleys, shaking tins in front of them.

"There are some younger men," ventured Esther awkwardly.

"But they're all spoken for. Look."

It was impossible to deny. Esther scanned the park below them. Each young, whole man she saw was walking with a young girl or woman on his arm.

"The truth is," Winifred said in a low voice, "being

engaged to Arthur gave me a clearer sense of who I was. I got used to the idea of being half of a couple, and now, even though he's gone, that feeling hasn't. I want to be a wife, Esther. I'm sorry if what I say upsets you."

"No. I understand. I do, really."

"Don't you ever feel the same need?"

Esther paused. "To be honest," she said at last, "I don't think about it. I know that's not an answer, but it's true. I'm just too busy."

"Looking after all your men?"

"Don't be bitter, Winifred. It's work that will rescue us. Me with my father and brothers, you with your switchboard."

"I suppose you're right."

"Whether I am or not, it's what we've got, isn't it? And we must make the best of it."

"But doesn't it get you down?"

"Honestly? No. My father is poorly all of the time now, but he still gets great pleasure from such little things."

"Like what?"

"Like the sun coming up in the morning. Like the taste of simple food – a soft boiled egg, a sausage toasted on a fork in front of a fire. Hearing stories of the pit from the boys when they come home from work. Outings like today."

Winifred nodded.

"But it's a very quiet life, whereas you... you're at the very heart and hub of a great exchange, connecting thousands of people every day, right around the world. Isn't that a wonder?"

"And it all started here," said Winifred. "The very first telephone exchange was set up on Shudehill, in Dantzic Street, in 1878. There's a plaque in our office that reminds us every day," and she smiled.

"That's better," agreed Esther. "Let's take a look at what else there is here today. I've only got half an hour before I'll have to get back to my father." The two friends linked arms once more and walked off down a different path, along the Avenue of Black Poplars, towards the Amphitheatre, where the fairground rides and stalls awaited them.

As they approached the line of hoopla stalls, tombola tables, ice cream vendors and coconut shies, they became aware of a particularly large crowd gathered around what first appeared to be a busker, but on closer inspection turned out to be something altogether stranger.

An American Indian brave, assorted bird feathers round his head, war paint streaking his face, chest and arms, buckskin waistcoat decorated with mythical winged and beaked creatures, fringed trousers, moccasins, was dancing. Across his eyes he wore a mask with a large eagle's head painted upon it and between his teeth and inside his mouth he carried an array of tiny musical instruments, with which he emitted a dizzying mix of different bird calls. In his hands he carried a drum and shaker, while around his wrists, elbows, knees and ankles were tied bells and castanets and small cymbals. As he whirled around he appeared to carry a whole forest of wild life inside him, whose sounds transported the crowds to places they could only dream of. They stood entranced, transfixed, children and grown-ups alike, until, with a final flourish, he threw everything high into the air, catching each of them separately with a long pole as they fell, before bowing deeply to generous applause.

He then sat cross-legged on a rough mat with an abstract design of zig-zag stripes around its edges, his various wares arranged around him, and proceeded to sell his hand-made toys and instruments to anyone who'd buy them.

It was as he took off his eagle mask that Esther gasped in the sudden recognition that this was none other than Tommy Thunder.

She turned excitedly to Winifred. "I know this man. He was my knight in shining armour the night I broke my ankle. He rescued me, made a splint for my leg, then wheeled me all the way home on Arthur's buckled bicycle. I never thought to see him again."

She made her way through the excited gaggle of children towards him.

Without looking up at her he said, "And how is your foot?"

"It is quite recovered. Thank you."

"You walk with a slight limp."

"It's nothing," she said. "How are you?"

"As you can see," he said, spreading out his hands, "busy."

"Still catching moles?"

"Not so much these days."

"And chasing thunder?"

He looked up at her directly for the first time. "Do you see storm clouds?"

She smiled and shook her head.

She rejoined Winifred, who was all agog with curiosity, but before she could ask even one question, they were both interrupted by a different voice behind them.

"Miss Winifred? Miss Esther?"

They turned as one.

"Do you remember me?" It was a young woman. She was carrying a small child in her arms.

It was Esther who replied first. "Mary! Is it really you? How long has it been?"

"More than six years, nearer six and a half."

"And who's this little cherub?" asked Winifred, her eyes shining.

"This is Toby, my youngest," she said, kissing the top of his head, as he squirmed to get down.

"Youngest?"

Mary's smile broadened even further. "He has a sister – Harriet. Over there, see? Riding on her Daddy's shoulders," and she beckoned towards Jabez. "This is my husband – Mr Chadwick. Jabez. And Jabez, these two ladies were good friends to Miss Ruth. Miss Blundell and Miss Holt."

"Please call me Esther."

"And Winifred."

They all shook hands.

"I'm delighted to meet you, Jabez," said Esther.

"What do you do?" asked Winifred.

"Why Winifred, you weren't paying attention during the Right Honourable Mr Sutton's speech earlier, were you? Jabez is Head Keeper of the Park. It is him we must thank for all the magnificent flowers on display here today."

"Yes indeed. Congratulations, Jabez."

"Thank you, Miss – Winifred."

"And not just on the flowers, but on all of this." Winifred looked around, beaming at Jabez and Mary, their two small children, and the unmistakeable evidence from Mary's figure of a third along the way. "You do know," she continued, looking first at Jabez, and then back towards Mary, "that you are the luckiest man in the world?"

"Of course he does, Winifred," said Esther, as Jabez nodded, blushing.

"He'd better," said Mary, and they all laughed together.

Just then Toby began to grizzle and Mary's attention was drawn completely towards him. "He needs feeding," she said. "If you'll excuse us…"

"And I too must be getting back. My father will be starting to feel anxious. Goodbye."

They all shook hands once more and Winifred watched as Mary, her husband and children sought their privacy, while Esther headed off in the opposite direction towards the Refreshment Tent, before all were swallowed up by the crowds.

Winifred remained where she stood. Despite the throngs of people buffeting her this way and that, she felt quite alone.

Giovanni Locartelli wheeled his ice cream van along the Avenue of Black Poplars looking for the best spot to pitch it. After changing his mind several times, he finally settled on a spot overlooking the Central Lawn.

"Here, Claudia," he announced. "We shall set up here."

Claudia, his daughter-in-law, was following behind, struggling with baskets of food and two small, excited children – a girl aged six with dark hair, even darker eyes and a sulky, pouting mouth, and a boy aged three, who was wriggling and straining like a dog on a leash, trying to escape his mother's hand.

"Giulia," said Claudia, "keep an eye on your brother while I help *Nonno*."

Giulia glowered. She had wanted to wear her new white dress, but her mother had forbidden it, telling her that she must save that for the Whit Sunday Walks in three weeks time, and so she was forced to wear what she wore for church each week instead. Three weeks! That was a lifetime away. She couldn't possibly wait till then, but she was dragged out of her reverie by her mother's fierce voice.

"Giulia! Please!"

When she adopted this tone, Giulia knew she must absolutely be obeyed, or there would be serious consequences to face. She might even be forbidden to wear the new white dress at all.

She scanned the crowds for her brother, who had finally managed to extricate himself from his mother's clutches and immediately run off towards the Boating Lake at the bottom of the hill. Giulia caught sight of him and tore down the slope.

"Paulie! Wait!"

She reached him just in time to prevent him from launching himself head first into the lake and lifted him by his waist into the air, so that his feet flapped and dangled like a fly which had just been caught in a spider's web.

"Come along," she said, dragging him reluctantly up the hill. "Let's see if *Nonno* might have an ice cream for us."

Paulie instantly set off, running back up the hill towards his mother and grandfather and the promise of an ice cream, while Giulia looked around. None of the little girls she could see looked prettier than she did. Perhaps this old dress wasn't so bad after all, she thought.

The Victoria Brass Band was now playing a series of rousing military marches, as current servicemen from The Manchester Regiment paraded around the Bandstand, up the entire length of the Carriage Drive, passing cheering crowds, many of them waving white handkerchiefs, until they reached the brow of a small hill, where the Lord Mayor and Lady Mayoress of the city awaited them on a raised dais, next to the four large cannon brought back from the Crimea, which marked the entrance to the park. Having raised their colours, they stood in strict formation, in the shape of a letter

'M', as each of the cannon was fired, before receiving the order to stand down, at which all the soldiers freely mingled with the crowds, who spread themselves around the various attractions once more.

The band began to play a selection of old time music hall favourites, all of them with a floral theme – *Roses of Picardy, When She Wore A Tulip, Lily of Laguna*. The conductor turned away from his musicians to face the crowds, encouraging them to sing along to each new tune.

Elsewhere, beside the Ornamental Boating Pond, announcements were made to signal the start of the Children's Sports Day. Mary had wandered there with a happily fed and sleeping Toby, whom she pushed along the path in his pram, holding Harriet's pudgy hand as she toddled precariously alongside, while Jabez was keeping a very excitable Meg firmly on her leash, for she would have joined in all the races and tried to jump inside the sacks with the boys, or snatch the eggs from the little girls' spoons.

"Let's sit and watch from here," said Mary, as a tottering Harriet flopped obligingly down into the soft, dry grass.

The warmth of the sun was delicious and Mary surreptitiously eased the sleeves of her blouse up towards her elbows and lifted her hair away from the back of her neck. A sleepy bumble bee was drowsily basking inside a small patch of yellow tulips nearby and Mary was trying to distract Harriet's attention from getting too close to it.

"Please take your marks for the Under 10's Girls'

Egg and Spoon Race," announced the kindly Brown Owl from the Gorton Girl Guides, who seemed to be in charge of the children. "On your marks, get set, go!" And she blew a sharp blast on her whistle, which startled Harriet, so that she forgot completely about the bumble bee and watched the race instead.

Mary's attention was drawn to one particular girl, who lagged a little way behind the rest. Her tongue curled out from the side of her mouth in fierce concentration. She never once dropped her egg from her spoon and, while her other speedier competitors up ahead of her kept spilling theirs and had to be sent back to where they started, this girl doggedly kept going until she was almost at the front. Just as she was passing them, Meg decided to give her an encouraging bark, which so surprised her that she turned her face in the dog's direction and, in doing so, dropped her egg. With a slight frown she stooped to pick it up, but by that time Harriet had already seized upon it and was just about to pop it into her mouth, when her mother intervened. The girl stood patiently, one hand on her hip, the other holding out her spoon. Her face was in shadow, framed by the sun. It was only as she reached further towards them that Mary saw it. Blooming brightly on her left cheek was a strawberry mark.

Esther collected her father from the Refreshment Tent, where he was already flagging, she could see.

"Come along, Father," she said, helping him to his feet. "Let's go and catch our tram, and you can tell me what you'd like for your tea."

He was a little unsteady, whether from fatigue or perhaps one too many beers in the warm sunshine, and he gratefully took his daughter's arm.

"Yes," he said, "I'm ready. Perhaps Freddie and Arthur will be waiting to meet us when we get there…"

Esther patted his hand, and the two of them made their way beneath the Black Poplars and out towards the outdoor swimming pool, which was filled to overflowing. Alongside, a pair of Indian elephants were patiently plodding back and forth, giving rides to the children. Mr Blundell paused.

"What is it, Father?" asked Esther. "Would you like a ride on one of them?"

"I did once, you know?"

"Really?" It was not always easy these days for Esther to know what her father claimed to remember had actually happened or not, but she was intrigued. "Tell me about it." Maybe it would take his mind away from his dead sons.

Winifred had still not moved from where Esther and Mary had parted from her. She surveyed the myriad of paths criss-crossing the park but couldn't decide which one she should take. Suddenly she heard a raucous noise erupting from one of the larger tents on the Central Lawn below. Attracted by its promise of colour, excitement, gaiety and life, she decided she would investigate.

Soon she was swept along on a tide of similarly

curious onlookers, who surged down the hill towards the tent. Winifred found herself hemmed in on all sides. The press of people was so strong that, for a time, her feet were lifted from the ground, as she was carried forward by the crowd's momentum. In her struggle to maintain her balance she did not at first register that nearly all of the people were men. There were very few women she could see and none were unaccompanied. Finally she reached a narrow flap, opening into the tent, through which they were all funnelled, like being squeezed through a tube of toothpaste.

It was dark inside the tent, after the brightness of the sun outside and, as her eyes adjusted, she began to make out the source of the noise. There in the centre of the tent, raised some three feet high, was a boxing ring. Inside it stood a small ferret-faced man in an ill-fitting dinner suit, holding a megaphone loosely by his side. Behind him, in one corner, already stripped and prepared for action, was one of the contestants, bouncing on the balls of his feet and shadow boxing. The ferret-faced man raised the megaphone to his lips.

"My Lords, Ladies and Gentlemen, please welcome to the ring The Clayton Collier, The Manchester Miner, The Bradford Bull, your very own local hero, the one, the only, Vic "The Volcano" Collins!"

Mary picked up the egg from the grass and placed it gently into the small girl's spoon. She had a grave expression on her face. Her eyes remained firmly fixed on the egg to make sure it did not fall off once more.

She gave a careful, solemn curtsey and said politely, "Thank you, Ma'am," before heading back into the race.

"You're most welcome," called out Mary to the little girl's back as she made her way towards the finishing line. She hardly dared breathe or blink, in case she disappeared.

By the outdoor swimming pool, a line of boys had gathered with mounting anticipation, among them the nearly nine year old George Wright. The elephants had just given their last ride of the day and were being scrubbed down by their keepers, who led them to the poolside. The boys pressed closer together, barely able to contain their excitement.

"First to run's a cissy," called out George, as the elephants dipped their trunks into the cool, inviting water.

Winifred was transfixed. She had never before witnessed a boxing match. But the sight of Vic Collins, the sweat glistening on his chest and biceps as he casually danced around the ring, the broad confident smile as he acknowledged the roar from the crowd that greeted him, the way he rested his arms along the top of the ropes as his trainer gave him one last rub down, was utterly mesmerising. She felt transported. As the referee called the two boxers together for the start of the fight, he pushed back from the ropes and appeared to look directly at her. He brought his gloves to his lips, kissed them, then thrust them out towards her. She was overwhelmed.

A steward awkwardly approached her.

"You can't stand there, Miss," he said. "You're blocking people's view."

"Oh. Sorry." She looked about her, not quite understanding where she was, or what she should do.

"Strictly speaking, I shouldn't let you in." He pointed to a notice. "No ladies or children unaccompanied."

"I see." She supposed she should make to leave, but her feet seemed unable to follow her brain's instructions.

"But seeing as how you know Vic Collins, I suppose it'll be alright."

"But I don't."

"Well, he seems to know you," he laughed, then winked. "Just stand there, where the other ladies are." He pointed to a row of men in sharp suits, who were all urging last minute encouragements towards Vic. On their arms were several young women, their faces rouged, their hair bobbed, and their profession apparent.

Esther and her father had reached the park gates at Mill Street. They turned for one last look at Tulip Sunday.

"It's been a fine day, Esther," said Walter.

"Yes, Father. It has." She surveyed the happy crowds enjoying the sunshine and remembered the words of Tommy Thunder. She looked back up to the still cloudless sky. "Let's enjoy it while we can," she said and took off her hat. She unpinned her hair and let it fall down her back.

"You remind me of your mother when you do that," he said, smiling. "She loved a bit of sun."

"Come on," she said. "We don't want to miss our tram."

Mary's gaze followed the little girl with the strawberry mark until she'd rejoined the others, a whole gaggle of them, Mary now saw, all wearing identical white pinafores over utilitarian grey dresses, revealing well scrubbed bare legs below the knee, a few now streaked with grass stains.

In the centre of them stood a small, round, smiling nun, who clapped her hands, put a finger to her lips, before going through a series of different hand gestures – waggling the fingers, placing them on the top of her head, putting them down by her sides – which the girls all dutifully copied until they were all neatly standing in pairs ready to depart.

Mary realised it was now or never.

"Jabez," she called, "please can you mind the children? There's someone I have to see," and she hitched up her dress and ran smartly across the lawn towards the nun and the children.

Puzzled, Jabez watched his wife heading off across the grass, gathering Harriet and Toby to him, while Meg strained at her lead, her bark giving voice to her master's perplexity. Together they watched Mary introduce herself to the nun and then engage in what looked like an urgent, breathless conversation. They saw the Sister's face turn from a frown to a wide smile of delight as she gave Mary a spontaneous hug. Then they looked at each other in wonder and surprise, as the Sister appeared to beckon to one of the girls, who dutifully approached her. The Sister bent down to the little girl's eye level and spoke to her seriously for a few moments, before she indicated Mary and gestured to the girl that it was quite alright for her to go and talk to this unknown woman. The girl stood before Mary, her hands in front of her lap, with fingers interlaced, while Mary said a few words to her. The girl then curtseyed and ran back to join the line of other little girls. Mary held out her hand towards the Sister, who took it in both of her own and clasped it warmly and firmly. Mary then nodded her head several times quite quickly before taking her leave and walking back towards Jabez, Harriet, Toby and Meg.

At the swimming pool the tightly packed scrum of boys were jiggling up and down, their faces screwed tight, holding their breath, shaking their closed fists in front of them, as the elephants dipped their trunks into the water for the umpteenth time.

Before, they had contented themselves with idly spraying the water over their backs and swaying their heads from side to side. Now, at a signal from their handlers, they drank for longer and deeper. The boys held onto each other tightly. This, surely, was the moment. George closed his eyes and held his breath.

Back in the Boxing Tent, the bout was ready to start. The timekeeper rang his bell, the referee made the two boxers touch gloves, then the contest began.

In truth it was not a contest at all. Roared on by the partisan home crowd, Vic, quite literally living up to his nickname, exploded from his corner and tore into his opponent like a force of nature. His punches came so fast that his arms seemed a blur. He landed sickening blows to the other's face and head and body. Winifred was sure she heard the snapping of rib, the splitting of lip, the crushing of jaw. The force unleashed by Vic was truly volcanic. Being so close to the ring, Winifred was spared nothing of the fight's visceral nature. When Vic landed a blow full square on his opponent's nose, the blood arced across the air, caught in the shafts of sunlight that slanted in from outside, before spattering the canvas, as well as those in the crowd closest to the action, including Winifred, whose dress, gloves, and face even, were caught, stippled in pinpricks of crimson.

And still Vic relentlessly poured in the punches. The other fighter had somehow got his arms looped in the ropes of the ring so that he was unable to fall to the canvas, which would have been a mercy. Instead he had to endure wave after wave, blow after blow, from Vic's seemingly unstoppable flow. Eventually, the referee, at much risk to his own safety, waded in and managed to call a halt to the proceedings, just as the bell for the end of Round One was rung. The fight was stopped, Vic declared the winner, and the crowd stormed the ring, hoisting him onto their shoulders, parading him triumphantly to all corners.

And this time the boys were not disappointed.

The elephants aimed their trunks directly at them and sprayed the water all over them. The squeals of delight from the boys, now completely drenched and soaked to the skin, were only drowned by the delighted trumpeting of the elephants. George ran roaring in search of his parents, Hubert and Annie, shaking himself dry all over them, like a shiny wet terrier.

Meg barked and jumped up in excitement as Mary returned across the grass. Her eyes were shining.

"What is it?" asked Jabez.

"Lily," she said. "I've seen her. She's being well taken care of. She's happy, she's healthy, she's loved."

Jabez wrapped his arms around her. "This calls for a celebration," he said. "Ice creams all round."

"Oh Jabez," she said, laughing, "we can't afford such treats twice in the same day."

"Who said anything about paying for them? Come on," he said, tapping the side of his nose. "Follow me."

Giovanni Locartelli was holding his grandfather's pocket watch in his left hand, the only physical thing linking him back to the old country, scrutinising it intently. As the second hand wound its way around towards the top of the dial, he looked up. Just then the clock on St Jerome's Church began to toll the hour.

"Six o'clock," he announced to anyone who would listen. "From now on, ice creams are free!"

There was a gasp of delight from the people nearby, who formed themselves into an orderly, if excitable, queue, while news of the surprise offer spread around the park like wild fire. Soon there were dozens of children, together with their tired, harassed parents, milling around the tiny ice cream van, painted in pink and gold fairground letters: "*Locartelli's – Finest Ices in Manchester.*"

"*Paparino,*" whispered Claudia, as the crowds around the van grew and began pushing against it. "What are you doing? We'll never be able to serve all of these people. They'll get angry and never come back."

"No," he replied, switching at once to Italian, so that fewer people would understand him, "they will be disappointed, but so impressed by our generous offer that when they hear just how delicious our *gelati* are, they will come back again – earlier, and they will pay for them."

Claudia tried to deal with the mass of customers as best she could, while her father-in-law proceeded to sing loudly – and to her ears embarrassingly – choruses from his favourite Neapolitan love songs.

Esther and her father climbed aboard the tram that would take them back to Melland Road. Almost at once her father fell asleep. Esther looked back on a day full of surprises. It had been good to see Winifred again, after such a gap, but her demeanour had troubled her. She must try and find a way to see her more regularly if she could, although with Winifred's work at the telephone exchange and her father's distress every time he saw her, this would not be so easy. Perhaps she might persuade Winifred to join her at her monthly meetings at the Lit & Phil. These she had been able to resume once her services were no longer needed at Brook House, which had closed its doors to wounded soldiers once the remaining patients had died, recovered sufficiently to be able to return home, or had been transferred to longer term convalescent units, if they had families who could afford such care...

But it had been wonderful to have been able to spend most of the day out of doors. The park had looked magnificent. Mary's husband had done a fine job. She recollected that she had seen him before the war, at the pit, where he had been friendly with her brother Harold, and how, when he joined up, Harold had come home very quiet and shaken. He had wanted to go too, she could tell, but then the news came about Freddie, and he knew that two brothers away fighting was enough for any family. Mining was a scheduled occupation after all, and he had persuaded himself – as had Frank and Jim – that they were each doing their bit by staying at home to bring up the coal for the country's war effort. Looking at her father peacefully sleeping now made her realise again just how thankful she was that Harold had come to that decision without need of further pleading or persuasion from her...

But Jabez had survived, and here he was now, back at home, combining his work as a miner with his duties at Philips Park, where his skills were evident for all to see and admire. He was thriving, so touchingly proud of Mary and his children. It had been good to see Mary again...

She pondered the thought that probably the soil that lay all around here was fed and nourished somehow by the coal underground, and that the tulips benefited from this special relationship. The charcoal undoubtedly provided nutrients that would feed the earth, but what of all the other chemicals it harboured? Esther, through her reading and the various lectures she attended, had become increasingly aware of the potential longer term damage caused by some of the toxic by-products of mining. Her father's damaged lungs were clear proof of that, but she chose to keep these thoughts to herself...

She would have liked to discuss them with Tommy Thunder. He would no doubt have had something wise and enigmatic to say about them. Fancy seeing him again, and wearing that bird mask, which had somehow seemed the most natural garb in the world on him...

As the tram made its slow way back towards Gorton, stopping frequently as it did so, to let people off who had all decided to leave Tulip Sunday when she and her father did, she continued to mull over these thoughts in her head. She would work it out with Winifred somehow...

Winifred found herself caught up in the mayhem and melee following Vic's one round triumph. As he was being carried shoulder high right around the ring to the non-stop roars and cheers of the crowd, she was swept along and, before she realised quite what was happening, she ended up, along with a dozen others, inside a recess at the back of the tent, which served as a changing room for the boxers.

The boys lowered Vic to his feet and, with a painted girl on each arm, he swung around to face her. He placed his still gloved hands on each of her shoulders and pulled her towards him. His face and torso were a pin cushion of blood and sweat, glistening gold and red. Steam rose from him like a stallion after a hard race. Every pore of him seemed to issue a vital, vibrant sense of absolute invincibility. She had never, she knew, been so close to such raw, physical power, and she found it intoxicating.

"Hello, hello, hello?" said one of the painted girls.

"Who's your lady friend?" sang the other.

" Something the wind blew in," said the first.

"You're a fish out of water, darling," said the second. "The Ladies is round the corner if you want to powder your nose."

"She'll get a fright when she sees herself," added the first and dabbed a bead of blood with her finger from Winifred's face, which she offered for general inspection, before lewdly licking it.

"That's enough, girls," said Vic. "Leave the lady

alone."

The painted girls "oohed" their derision.

"You'll have to beg their pardon, Miss. They're not used to polite society. Nor am I, to tell the truth of it. But I think you're in the wrong place," and he beckoned one of the stewards across.

Winifred gathered herself together and said, as quietly but as clearly as she could manage, "Where would be the right place?"

Eventually Giovanni instructed Claudia to send the remaining people away, explaining that they had no ice cream left, and to point out the address of their shop painted on the side of the van – 4 Loom Street, Ancoats – where they could buy all manner of delights every day of the week.

He was just about to pull down the shutter when he spied Jabez and his family waiting nearby.

"Jabez!" he boomed, then in *sotto voce*, "Come round the back. Claudia," he whispered, "some ice creams for my good friend Mr Jabez Chadwick and his wife and children."

"I thought you had none left," said Jabez.

"For them, I don't," Giovanni replied, indicating the departing crowds, "but for you, I do. *Benvenuto.*"

Claudia fashioned two cones, one each for Jabez and Mary, and then broke off two tiny pieces of wafer dipped in a little ice cream for the children.

"You must let us pay you," said Mary, glaring at Jabez.

"No, no, no," beamed Giovanni. "I couldn't dream of it. This has been a great day for Locartelli," he said. "Tulip Sunday." He spread his hands and looked about him. "It brings thousands of people back to the park, so many of whom buy our ice cream, and it is all thanks to your husband."

Mary looked at the two men. "How do you know each other?"

"I..." began Jabez, "I knew Signor Locartelli's son in the war."

Giovanni pointed to a small photograph pinned on the wall inside the van, which showed a young, dark-haired man, smiling into the camera, shielding his eyes from the sun, so that much of his face lay in shadow. Claudia looked down.

"Your brother?" asked Mary.

Claudia shook her head. "My husband."

Mary put an arm around her shoulder.

"These flowers," said Giovanni, looking back towards the gradually emptying park, "thousands and thousands of them. *Bellissima.*"

Leaving the park, too, were the two elephants and their handlers. The one at the back had linked its trunk to the tail of the one in front, and together they processed down Stuart Street and Rowsley Street, Palmerston Street and Viaduct Street, before turning into Dark Lane and Temperance Street, Harkness Street and Dolphin Street, until they crossed Ardwick Green and made their final way down Hyde Road to Jennison's Zoological

Gardens, Belle Vue.

Looking out of the tram window, Esther saw them just as she and her father were turning onto Gorton Road, and she gently woke him, so that he might catch a last glimpse of them.

He nodded and smiled. "I rode on one of those once," he said.

"You must tell me about it," she said again, but he had already drifted back to sleep.

It was eight o'clock in the evening, and the park was now quite deserted, except for Jabez, Mary, Harriet, Toby and Meg, as Jabez did his final rounds, checking that people had gone and locking the two main gates. It was exactly twelve hours since he had done the self-same journey first thing in the morning with just Meg for company, having spent the whole of the previous night there, beating its bounds, not knowing for sure how this first Tulip Sunday since the end of the war would go. It had been a big responsibility, but one he had relished, and he was quietly proud of all the compliments he had received during the day, from the members of the Parks & Gardens Committee, Mr John Edward Sutton MP, even the Lady Mayoress, right down to his mates from the pit, who'd all clapped him on the back and offered to buy him a pint. If he'd accepted every offer, he would not have been able to stand, let alone be making this final round of the park.

But there was one last action to be carried out, one he'd been saving till now, when everyone had gone, and only he, Mary and the children were still here.

"Have you finished?" asked a weary Mary. "Only the children are exhausted. And so am I."

"Almost," said Jabez. "There's just this one thing."

Will it take long?"

"That depends."

"On what?"

"You'll see. This way." And he led them away from the path, down what was little more than a grass track, which was barely visible.

"Where are we going? Is it far?"

Jabez put his finger to her lips. Both children were now fast asleep, and he signed to Mary to lay them on the grass. Her eyes widened and she was about to speak, when he pressed his lips to hers. "Shh," he whispered, and then he pointed.

Further into the trees, where it was now almost completely dark, Mary could just make out a faint smudge of colour. Jabez took her hand in his and together they crept like mice towards it.

When they reached it, Jabez helped Mary down to the ground, where she might see close up the source of the colour. A carpet of multi-coloured, wild tulips covered a narrow patch of earth some ten yards square. They were low-lying, close to the soil, beneath a small stand of pine trees, which Jabez had allowed to grow in this little known corner of the park.

Mary looked at Jabez.

"These are from those seeds we took from that bunch of tulips you were carrying the first day we met in the cemetery by Ruth's grave."

"Really?"

Jabez nodded. "They're hybrids," he whispered. "Tougher and stronger than the original flowers. That's why there are so many different colours."

"And will they spread?" she asked.

"There's no reason why they shouldn't," he answered. "If they're allowed to."

"Then let's allow them to," she said, and she leant across him, placing her hands upon his face. "I love you, John Jabez Chadwick."

"And I love you, Mary Flynn."

"Then isn't it about time you made an honest woman of me?"

They wrapped their arms around one another, laughing, as they lay beneath the pines, the earth cushioned by the fallen needles, their children asleep beside them in the grass, and made love next to the wild tulips under the reddening Manchester sky.

Belle Vue Zoo & Pleasure Gardens

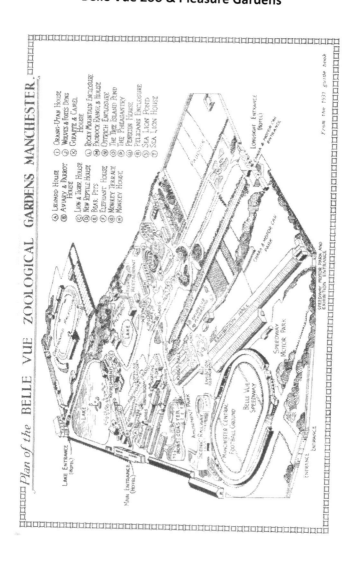

TWO

Belle Vue

5

1872

Waverley Auction Rooms, Edinburgh
10th May 1872

Grand Sale of Exotica

from

Wombwell's Travelling Menagerie
including

**Lions, Lionesses, Bactrian Camels, Kangaroos
Dog-Faced Baboons, Scarlet Macaws, Emus
Capuchin Monkeys, Tasmanian Devils, Raccoons
Bengal Tigresses, Boa Constrictors, Hyenas
Leopards, Ocelots, Brown Bears, Wombats
Porcupines, Coatimundi, Nylghau, Llamas**

AND

MAHARAJAH

The World Famous Asiatic Elephant

*

"Sold!" The auctioneer's hammer comes firmly and decisively down. "For seven hundred and ninety-seven pounds and ten shillings, to Mr James Jennison of Strawberry Gardens, Manchester, one baboon, one lioness, one nylghau – that's an antelope to you and me, Madam – and one ten year old Asiatic elephant, what goes by the name of Maharajah!" And he raps his gavel one more time to a smattering of applause.

James Jennison, sitting on the front row of the Waverley Market Hall, smiles broadly, lights up a cigar, shakes the auctioneer by the hand, and then poses for the newspaper photographer, who happens to be obligingly at hand.

"Congratulations, Mr Jennison."

Jennison turns around. The voice, with its unmistakeable, patrician Edinburgh timbre, belongs to a tall, thin, lugubrious-looking fellow in a frock coat and top hat. "I hope you will be well satisfied with your purchases. I represent the estate of Wombwell's Travelling Menagerie, and we have now successfully disposed of all of their assets, the elephant being the last – and most prized – of all of the items."

"Thank you, Mr… er?"

"Flay, sir. Cornelius Flay of McGadden, Flinders and Flay. At your service." He removes a single goat's kid glove and offers a pale, reptilian hand, which Jennison accepts with no pretence of concealing his distaste.

"It was the prospect of the elephant, of course, that drew me here in person. When a Jennison says he wants a thing done, he likes to make sure he does it. In person. So here you find me." He casts an approving eye over Maharajah as he is about to be led away by his handler, a flamboyant character bearing more than a passing resemblance to Buffalo Bill Cody, complete with a long mane of silver hair and goatee beard to match, who lingers meaningfully. "He's just the attraction our expanding enterprise needs," continues Jennison, blowing a perfectly shaped smoke ring, which exactly frames Mr Flay's elongated head.

"Which is…?" enquires Flay, flapping ineffectively at the smoke.

"The soon-to-be-renamed 'Belle Vue Zoological & Pleasure Gardens', the first such establishment anywhere in Great Britain. Manchester, as with most things, will once more be at the vanguard of progress and change."

"Quite so," says Flay, with evident displeasure. "May I introduce you to the animal's handler – Mr Lorenzo Lawrence."

"Your servant, Sir," replies Lorenzo, with a bow and a flourish.

Jennison nods in his direction. "Don't I know you?"

Lorenzo inclines his head modestly. "Perhaps, Sir."

"Yes. I've seen you before. But not with an elephant. Lions and tigers. You put your head right inside a lion's mouth. Damned impressive. Made the wife and daughters faint. How did you manage it?"

"A lion tamer's secret, sir," demurs Lorenzo. The more he speaks, the more Jennison detects the faintest trace of a different accent. Antipodean perhaps? "But elephants are my first love. From when I was a boy in Sydney."

Jennison smiles to himself, pleased to have picked up on it.

"Sir…?

By Jove, he's angling for a job, thinks Jennison. One has to admire the chap's nerve.

"Lawrence will meet you at the station in two days time, Mr Jennison, to make sure all of your animals are loaded safely onto the 10.15 train to Manchester," says Flay, clearly keen to bring proceedings to a close.

"Excellent," replies Jennison, puffing further on his cigar. He cursorily shakes Flay's now re-gloved hand, then approaches Lawrence. "Until Tuesday morning then," he says, smiling, and then takes out another of his cigars, which he proffers towards the animal trainer.

"Thank you, sir." Lorenzo waits until both Flay and Jennison have gone, before rolling the cigar like a connoisseur between his fingers, drinking in its aroma, and affording himself a quiet smile. "This game's not over yet," he adds, to no one but himself.

Two days later, at the appointed hour, Jennison stands on the platform of Edinburgh's Waverley Station. He flips open his pocket watch just as the train driver releases from his cab an ebullient hiss of steam, which rises to the glass domed roof of the station, before settling in a cloud around everyone boarding the train, saying farewell to friends and loved ones, or, in the case of Mr Jennison, making sure that it leaves on time with all of his special cargo safely secured.

As the Guard blows his whistle and waves his green flag towards the engine at the front, signalling that all is now ready to depart, there is a sudden tremendous commotion erupting from one of the goods wagons towards the rear of the train. Jennison rushes down the platform, just in time to see Maharajah kicking his way desperately out of the carriage, dragging a dishevelled and disconcerted Lorenzo Lawrence behind him.

"It's no good, sir. He just can't settle. What with all the noise of the engine, the whistles and the steam, not to mention the shunting back and forth, he's spooked."

"I assure you, sir," interrupts the Guard, "nothing like this has ever happened before, and we've been transporting animals safely, without mishap, for decades."

"But have you tried with elephants before?" asks Lawrence.

The Guard reluctantly concedes that they haven't.

"There you are, then," says Lawrence, spreading his hands, allowing his grip on Maharajah's tether to loosen momentarily. The elephant, now quieter, waits patiently on the platform, seemingly unperturbed by the shouts and cries of alarm from other passengers now crowding around him. "There's nothing for it, Sir. He'll just have to walk to Manchester. Accompanied, of course," he adds, removing his hat and bowing.

"I fear you are correct, Lawrence," replies Jennison, his lips pursed sternly. "Guard, please alert the Station Master that I need a word – urgently. Compensation will be required, mark my words. My solicitor will be writing to him directly."

"Of course, sir. If you'll just allow me to signal to the driver that he is clear to depart, I shall escort you to his office directly."

His whistle is blown, his flag is waved vigorously

once more. The engine gives three sharp blasts, followed by a further hissing of steam, before it slowly thunders into motion, as the platform gradually clears.

Amid the bustle and distraction, nobody notices Jennison slip a sovereign to Lawrence, who tips his hat, and returns to Maharajah, still waiting patiently and calmly.

"We should reach Manchester in ten days, sir."

"*Bon voyage.* Telegraph me if your schedule alters," and he raises his cane to the Guard, who directs him towards the Station Master's office. "We want to be sure to offer you the appropriate welcome."

Lorenzo pockets the sovereign and immediately sets off, walking along the actual railway track of the North British Line, which operates the route between Edinburgh and Manchester. There's only one scheduled journey per day and so Lorenzo knows he will have an untroubled walk at least for one day. Maharajah follows on behind him, cheered by enthusiastic crowds who line the track until they leave the city behind.

The Edinburgh Daily Review confidently predicts that the elephant can easily cover thirty miles each day. This would mean an arrival in Manchester in six days at the most, but Lorenzo halts in Stow, where they spend the night, or Stow-in-Wedale, to give it its full name, a Scottish Borders town some seven miles north of Galashiels. They peel away from the railway line and cross the old Pack Horse Bridge, which marks the entrance to the town. They pass the Church of St Mary, with its one hundred and forty foot high clock tower, which tolls the hour as they approach it. Maharajah answers with a trumpet of his own. They camp for the night next to Our Lady's Well, just south of the village.

The second day sees the pair cover the twenty-six miles from Stow to Hawick. Lorenzo leaves the railway line behind and follows the course of the River Tweed until they reach its confluence with the smaller Teviot. For much of the day they hardly see a soul, skirting the ruined abbeys of Kelso, Jedburgh and Melrose, their progress like the passing of one age and the ushering in of another.

The Daily Review continues to cover their journey for its readers, but now curiously refers to Maharajah as Big Ben, a name not taken up by anyone else. When they finally reach Hawick, at about six o'clock in the evening, another large crowd awaits them. The elephant appears to be completely untroubled by the pressing throng. Not even the youngsters who run alongside are able to provoke him. The paper reports that Lorenzo is "greatly pleased by their numerous escort", and that he proceeds to sign autographs. They put up for the night at *The Bridge Hotel*, which has an arch high enough for Maharajah to pass through into the coaching yard behind, where they can rest without further disturbance.

The Hawick Express now takes up the tale, describing Maharajah as "the best of specimens", and the following morning they set off on the next stage of their journey, from Hawick to Langholm, via what the *Express* reporter describes as "the wild desolation of Mosspaul", in fact a popular location with the local gentry for shooting and fishing. Happily there is no country squire tempted to take a pot shot at Maharajah, and Lorenzo picks up the railway line from Waverley once more, as they follow the Esk Valley between Scotland's Southern Uplands, skirting the four hills of Warblaw, Tinpin, Castle and Whita, before dropping down into Langholm itself, or Muckle Toun, as the locals have it, resting for the night in the shadow of Glanckie Tower, stronghold of the Armstrong Clan, who offer Lorenzo and Maharajah shelter and protection.

Day four heralds their crossing into England and their arrival in Carlisle, where for once the pair cause little interest. No local newspaper reports on their journey. The sight of elephants walking along the country's highways is not, after all, such an uncommon sight in 1872. At the very same moment that Lorenzo marches Maharajah south to Manchester, Lizzie the African Elephant, of Mrs Edmonds' Travelling Menagerie, is staying at an inn in Staffordshire where, such is the antipathy towards her from the locals, she is forced to flee under cover of darkness from their hail of stones and pellets. Happily no such misfortune befalls Maharajah, who is welcomed in every village, cheered through every town, with songs sung about him, and music played to greet him.

The fifth day takes them through the spectacular scenery of the Lakeland Fells to Penrith, and from there, on the sixth, they climb the remote, high passes over Shap, before the long, slow descent into Kendal, where brass bands salute them in the stable yard of *The*

White Hart, a coaching inn close by the swift-flowing River Kent in the heart of the town.

The next day *The Kendal Mercury* describes how they set off early in the morning, "Lorenzo in front" with "Maharajah jogging along at a good pace behind".

They stay the seventh night at *The Commercial Hotel* in Lancaster, where once again they are fêted, but their arrival the next day in the bustling mill town of Preston appears to pass unnoticed. No contemporary records can be found, but its distance from Lancaster suggests that this was their likely destination for that night.

It is on the ninth day, the penultimate leg of their epic walk from *Auld Reekie* to *Cottonopolis*, that one of its defining events takes place. They are travelling the main highway between Preston and Bolton, a recently metalled road, which throws up large clouds of earth with every pounding hoof beat of Maharajah's unvarying stride. The two of them can be seen arriving for miles around, the dust storms they create forming a haze, which renders them almost as a mirage.

Just as they are exchanging the realms of one private estate for another, they reach one of the many tolls that mark their way. Lorenzo pauses. Maharajah waits patiently behind him. The toll keeper regards the pair suspiciously and refuses to lift the bar until a large sum of money is handed over. Lorenzo tells this story many times, and it is one that grows with each telling, as does the size of the amount being demanded from the recalcitrant toll keeper. They embark upon that well-trodden path of ritual banter.

"A penny for you," says the Toll Keeper, "a guinea for the elephant."

Lorenzo hands over his penny. "This is for me, as a foot passenger, but nothing for the elephant."

"A guinea," reaffirms the Toll Keeper.

"Nothing," repeats Lorenzo.

"Ten shillings then."

"Nothing."

"Five shillings."

The same defiant shake of the head from a tight-lipped Lorenzo.

"Then what are you prepared to pay?" demands an increasingly exasperated Toll Keeper.

"Like I say. Nothing."

"But look," says the Toll Keeper, throwing down his hat to the ground in frustration, and pointing towards a sign board detailing the various duties for different types of cargo and passenger.

"For every last of wheat, rye, barley, malt, or any other grass, seed or pulse, a person is obliged to pay the rate of one shilling," he reads.

"But I have none," replies Lorenzo.

"For every barrel of salted beef, cod, herring or other provisions, fourpence."

"We carry no barrels."

"For every pipe, puncheon, or piece of wine or spirits, two shillings. For every hogshead of ale, beer, or porter, and so on in proportion for larger or smaller quantity, sixpence."

"We have none, more's the pity," says a smiling Lorenzo.

"Here we have it," shouts the Toll Keeper, jabbing a finger at the board. "For each sheep, pig or other small animal, threepence." He looks back at Maharajah, frowning. "Ah, now we come to it – for each horse, mule, cow or ox, sixpence." He folds his arms, as if his point is proven.

"I can read perfectly well, thank you," declares Lorenzo, "so please save yourself the trouble of continuing. Where, I pray, does it say 'elephant' anywhere on this list of Rates of Merchandise?"

The Toll Keeper looks back towards the Board and glares at it, as if willing the necessary wordage to materialise before his eyes.

"I can see that you refer to 'any other small animal', but nowhere do I see reference made to 'any other large animal', from which I can only conclude that, since there is no mention anywhere of the rate for an elephant, he must pass for free."

The Toll Keeper hurumphs indignantly. "It's not natural," he says, "and nor is that," he adds, waving his arm towards Maharajah.

The elephant, startled at being shouted at in this way, now takes matters into his own hands. He pounds his foot in front of him, lowers his head and, with a mighty trumpeting roar, he charges the toll, lifting the bar with his tusks and tossing it dismissively to the ground.

Lorenzo bids the terrified Toll Keeper a cheery good day and, together, he and Maharajah proceed on their way jauntily towards Bolton, Lorenzo singing and Maharajah waving his trunk joyfully in time.

This incident quickly becomes the stuff of legend, and interest in Maharajah's imminent arrival in Manchester soars. *The Bolton Evening News* welcomes "the heroic pair" into their midst. Having "smashed his railway wagon in Edinburgh", then "uprooting the door posts of an inn stable in Carlisle", (a later addition to the tale by Lorenzo), "he was put to the necessity of lifting a toll gate from off its hinges", for, as *The Evening News* is at pains to point out, "all gates are open to him free", adding by way of explanation, "inasmuch as the gate keepers cannot rate him as horse, cow, ass or sheep, for which alone they have legal authority to charge". Inspired by this and other accounts, the celebrated artist and Royal Academician, Heywood Hardy, exhibits *The Disputed Toll*, depicting Maharajah leaning patiently over the gate, which proves the hit of the season.

The following day Mr Jennison takes out an almost full page advertisement on the front page of *The Times*:

"The Fine Male Indian Elephant, named Maharajah, purchased at the sale of Wombwell's Menagerie, at Edinburgh, will ARRIVE at the BELLE VUE Gardens THIS DAY, at approximately 2 o'clock, having travelled by road from Scotland, via Carlisle, Kendal, Lancaster and Preston."

They have been walking for ten days.

By the time Lorenzo leads Maharajah down Hyde Road on the last half mile to Belle Vue, the crowds have swelled into the thousands. Mr Jennison has arranged for a series of massed bands to lead the way. Song sheets have been distributed among the assembled throng, containing the words to a specially written song to celebrate Maharajah's arrival, which local children have been practising all morning. As Lorenzo and Maharajah finally come into view, the entire crowd takes it up, singing to the tune of *Boney Was A Warrior*.

Maharajah Elephant
From Edinburgh
Packed his trunk and down he went
To Manchester

People flocked from miles around
To Belle Vue Fair
To hear the Maharajah sound
In Manchester

A travelling menagerie
Sold him to
The owner of the Strawberry
Belle Vue Zoo

They put him on a special train
The people cheered
But when he jumped right out again
They fled a-feared

Maharajah Elephant
From Edinburghr
Packed his trunk and down he went
To Manchester

The first day he walked out to Stow
Till daylight's end
Led by old Lorenzo
His faithful friend

From Stow to Hawick the second day
These pals did roam
Waving crowds did line the way
From there to Langholm

Everywhere they made folk smile
They clapped and sang
And when they entered Great Carlisle
The church bells rang

Maharajah Elephant
From Edinburgh
Packed his trunk and down he went
To Manchester

They trudged through moorland peaks towards
Great lakes, small tarns
At night they slept in stable yards
At inns and barns

To Penrith, Shap and Kendal Town
They boldly go
Maharajah hoses down
Lorenzo

One day the Keeper of a Toll
Would not permit them through
They feared they'd not achieve their goal
To reach Belle Vue

But Maharajah Elephant
With trunk swung high
Raised the gate so through they went
And waved good bye

Maharajah Elephant
From Edinburghr
Packed his trunk and down he went
To Manchester

Past Pendle Hill to Preston Guild
From Lancaster
Every vantage point's been filled
With crowds pressed there

And if you want your picture took
Beside this famous pair
Pay a shilling for good luck
And ride around the square

So let three cheers ring all around
Lorenzo
Maharajah's trumpet sounds
Away they go

Maharajah Elephant
From Edinburgh
Packed his trunk and down he went
To Manchester

6

1882

"Walter?" whispers Mrs Blundell as she raps once sharply on the boys' bedroom door. "Are you awake?"

There's no answer.

She knocks again, twice this time. "Walter? Time to get up."

There still being no reply she marches briskly in. The tousled shapes of her various sons stir reluctantly in the two large beds. She approaches the one closest to the window and peers down, prodding one of the recalcitrant shapes. Her eldest, William, opens an eye.

"Where's Walter?" she asks once more, inspecting the space between William and his still pretending-to-be-asleep brother Samuel, the space where she expects to find Walter's toes in this bed shared by three of her sons in their top-to-toe arrangement, a space now empty.

William points a finger to the floor. "Already down," he grunts, before turning over to occupy some of the space vacated by Walter.

Mrs Blundell raises an eyebrow and then looks across the room towards her two youngest in the smaller bed along the far wall. She's tempted to throw back the curtains on this glorious spring morning but relents. It is a Sunday after all, and her boys work hard at the pit all week. They deserve their lie-in.

She makes her way past the tiny box room, partitioned off from the bedroom she and her husband occupy, together with the baby, and looks in on the two girls. Ada, the youngest, is up already. She is earnestly brushing her doll's woollen hair and talking to it in hushed whispers, while Dorothy, thirteen and almost grown, is just waking up.

"Hello, Mother? Is it time already?"

Mrs Blundell nods. "Tha's got ten minutes. I'm just seeing to Walter."

Downstairs she finds him, sitting on the back step polishing his shoes. He's put on his Sunday clothes and even made an attempt to comb his hair, using a bit of water to try and coax it, unsuccessfully, to lie flat. She spits on her finger and smoothes the wayward strand into place. Walter squirms as she does so but says nothing.

"Can tha' see tha' reflection in 'em yet?" she adds, pointing towards his shoes.

Walter grins. "Almost."

"I've packed thee a crust and some dripping," she says and indicates a screw of paper on the kitchen table.

"They're giving us tea."

"I know, lad, but I daresay tha'll be clemmin' for summat afore then."

"Thanks, Mum."

"Are thee excited?"

He nods sheepishly.

"Make sure tha' behaves tha'self, and do as Miss Aspinal tells thee."

"Yes, Mum."

"Here's tha' sister. She'll keep an eye on thee, won't tha', Dor?"

"He'll be alright, Mum, tha' needn't worry."

"He'd better be," and she wags her raised forefinger warningly towards him.

Dorothy has got up, washed and dressed herself in less than five minutes. She's even had time to tie in a new ribbon she's been saving especially for today. She breezes into the kitchen just as Walter has finished polishing his shoes, which he lifts for her inspection.

"Can I see my face in them?" she asks.

"Tha' can," he says, "but who'd want to?"

He darts behind his mother as Dorothy chases him round the kitchen, finally cornering him by the back door, where she ruffles his recently combed hair.

"Give over, the pair of you," scolds Mrs Blundell, trying to flatten back Walter's hair as best she can. "Now – be off with you." She thrusts the paper bag with the bread and dripping into Walter's hands as the two children skip off up the ginnel next to their house onto the street. "Enjoy yourselves," she calls after them. "Be good."

And they're gone.

It's the first Sunday in May, and Dorothy and Walter are walking the short distance from where they live in Lower Openshaw to the Barmouth Street Methodist Chapel, where they go every week for Sunday School. But this week is different. After Sunday School is over, they're all being taken to Belle Vue for the Chapel's Annual Summer Outing for Local Children, in the charge of Mr Aspinal, the Minister, and his sister, Miss

315

Agatha, together with a number of other ladies from the Chapel. They will visit the Zoo, where they will look at the lions and tigers, the zebras and giraffes, the penguins and pelicans. There will be a Chimpanzees' Tea Party and the promise of Elephant Rides, and the day will be rounded off by a Wild West Show. Walter doesn't think he has ever been so excited.

To get the children in the mood, Miss Agatha reads them the story of Daniel in the Lion's Den and asks them to draw a picture of it. Walter, already imagining himself at the Fair, shows Daniel putting his head right inside the lion's enormous gaping, grinning mouth, complete with razor sharp teeth and a gold crown upon his head.

Eventually Sunday School is over. Miss Agatha lets them all run around outside the Chapel for five minutes, while the grown-ups gather together everything they need. Dorothy, as the senior girl, then self-importantly claps her hands and organises the children into pairs for the crocodile in which they'll walk to Belle Vue. With a mischievous grin she places Walter next to little Alice Owen, much to the silent mirth of the other boys, at whom Walter scowls threateningly.

But this is all forgotten as Miss Agatha raises her Bright Red Parasol with a cheery "Follow me", and away they all go, each pair holding hands. Little Alice Owen matter-of-factly pulls the sleeve of her cardigan over her wrist, so that her hand does not have to make actual contact with Walter's already sticky paw, having just polished off the last piece of his mother's bread and dripping. Once they have set off she proceeds to chatter brightly and constantly, and quite soon Walter, too, is enjoying himself.

"How old are you?" she asks.

"Eleven,"

"It's my birthday today," she says.

"Oh. Happy Birthday."

"Thank you."

"How old?"

"It's not polite to ask a lady her age."

"You're not a lady."

"But I will be. One day."

"You'll have to marry somebody rich to be a lady."

She throws him a sideways look. "Ten," she says. "I'm ten."

"Does Miss Agatha know? Mebbe they'll have a cake."

"Do you think so?"

"You never know."

"With ten candles?"

"You could close your eyes and make a wish."

"I will." And she closes them tightly, then opens them once more and mimes blowing out the imaginary candles.

"What did you wish for?"

"That's a secret."

"I know what I'd wish for."

"What?"

"Not to have to go down t'pit."

Alice shudders. "Is it really dark?"

"We carry candles so it's not too bad. But if they ever go out, which they do sometimes, then it's blacker than the blackest night. Like someone's pressed their hand upon your eye."

"Are there ghosts?"

"I've never seen any. But some of th' older lads reckon there is. When I first went down, they set me for a trapper."

"What's that?"

"It's for t' littl'uns. We sit in a squashed up dark hole, all on us own, and open and close a small shutter, to let air in and out, wi' just a candle for company, which blows out sometimes. Then it's easy to believe there's ghosts."

Alice shivers. Her pale face, sprinkled here and there with freckles, framed by her unruly mass of red hair, which she keeps tucking behind her ear, goes paler still.

"But I don't do that no more. Not since I grew a few inches."

"What do you do now?"

"I'm a putter. I push t' wagons up and down t' tracks. But first I carry t' canary," he says. "In a little cage."

"Oh, I should like to see that."

"It chirps away and hops about from one foot to t'other."

"Does it sing all the time?"

"Ay, mostly. It's when it stops you've got to worry."

"Why's that?"

"It acts as a sort o' warning, in case there's any poisonous gases about. Then we have to walk backwards, the way we've just come, till we get out of that tunnel and into a different one."

"And does the canary start singing again?"

"Sometimes," he says, coughing a little.

Alice squeezes his hand tightly.

After a while Walter speaks again. "What about you? What do you do?"

She lowers her head. "Tomorrow I start at t' mill with me mother and sisters. I'm to be a piecer."

"What's that?"

"Tying yarn threads together when they break. My mum says I'll be good at that, cos I've got small, quick fingers." And she digs one of them into Walter's ribs and tickles him.

After he has batted her away from him, he asks, "And what else?"

"What d'you mean?"

"Well, them threads can't be getting broken all the time, can they?"

"A bit of scavenging, I s'pose. Picking up bits o' cloth from under t' machines. We have to scamper and crawl beneath t' looms while they're still working and collect everything we can. My mum says it's all wet and slippery from the oil, so we have to go about in bare feet, so as we don't slip."

"My mum used to work in t'mill. She lost a finger when t' mule jammed."

The two of them look at one another.

"Let's not think about that," she says. "What are you looking forward to most about today?"

"All of it," he says.

"Me too. But what, if you could only do one thing, would you choose?"

"I'll tell you after," he says. "Then I'll know."

As soon as they arrive, at the Longsight Street entrance, they all climb aboard the Miniature Railway, which takes them around the perimeter of the park. Walter has a chance to sit with the other boys, but he finds he's quite happy to stay with Alice, who wants to sit near the front, so she can pretend to be the driver.

They chug through the formal Italian Gardens, noticing signs for The Maze, before the little engine, puffing steam and whistling as it passes the crowds of people, pointing out the various wonders they see at every turning, crosses an ornate bridge over a stream, arriving at the Aviary, where the children all get out.

"This way," booms Miss Agatha, holding her Bright Red Parasol up high, so that they can all follow her, past the peacocks and parrots, pelicans and birds of paradise, into the House of Tropics, where there are chameleons, which change colour right before their eyes, snakes, one of which is claimed to be fifty feet in length, which can swallow tiny children whole if they don't behave themselves, says Dorothy, and basking crocodiles, which open their huge mouths wide with a smiling yawn, to reveal row upon row of teeth as sharp as knives, before they reach the Firework Lake.

"Will there be fireworks tonight?" chorus the children.

"Maybe," replies Miss Agatha. "If you're very good."

They then board a paddle steamer, named the *Little*

Britain, which circumnavigates the lake, winding between a series of small artificial islands, where miniature landmarks from around the country are displayed as life-size models, complete with tiny people, which cause Alice to clap her hands with delight. Big Ben, which chimes every time a boat passes by, The Tower of London, which raises its drawbridge just as they approach, Buckingham Palace, complete with a tiny Union Jack and a gold coach with the Queen inside, drawn by four white horses, Edinburgh Castle, with its canon firing, and Stonehenge, with dancing druids, while frolicking in and out of the water are real, life-sized sea lions, one of whom leaps right onto the deck to the excited squeals of the children nearby, to be fed by one of the zoo keepers, before flopping back into the water, just as the steamer passes a model of St Paul's Cathedral.

"Oh," she exclaims, "how I should like to visit these places one day!"

"I reckon as how it's a model of Manchester they should put on one of these islands, for there's nowt to beat her, and in the middle there'd be a tiny Belle Vue, with a little paddle steamer chugging around, with thee and me leaning on t' rail, waving…"

"Like this?" asks Alice, and she starts to wave furiously.

"Ay," says Walter, "just like that," and he joins in, laughing.

The boat disembarks at the *One Shilling Tea Rooms*, where a brass band is playing and, in the far corner, a long table is all laid out ready with knives and forks.

"Here we are," announces Miss Agatha. "Now – is anybody hungry?"

"Me, Miss!" they all shout as one.

"Well sit yourselves down – quietly and tidily please. Let's show everybody here that the Barmouth Street Methodists' Sunday School children have the best table manners in the whole of Manchester."

Dorothy helps the youngest ones to sit up close to the table and then comes around to join Walter, only to find Alice already sitting next to him. "Oh," she says, "I thought you were meant to be saving a place for me, but I see you've found yourself a little friend?"

Walter blushes, even though he knows she's only teasing him.

"Well – aren't you going to introduce me?"

"I'm Alice Owen," says Alice, getting to her feet, "and today's my birthday, and Walter's being very kind to me."

"Is he now? I'm glad to hear it." She tousles the top of Walter's hair before waltzing off to join some of the other older girls."

"Is that your sister?" whispers Alice.

"Worse luck."

"Isn't she pretty?" She stares, wide-eyed, after her.

"I think you're pretty," stammers Walter, and then blushes even more.

He is saved from further embarrassment by the arrival of their lunch, which turns out to be a huge plate each of fish and chips with mushy peas, provoking a delighted round of applause from everyone.

Just when everyone has finished and nobody thinks

they could possibly eat another mouthful, Dorothy, led by Miss Agatha, walks towards the end of the table where Alice is sitting, carrying a large round Victoria Sponge cake, with ten lit candles fluttering in the rush of air as she approaches.

"*Happy birthday to you,*" sings Dorothy.

"*Happy birthday to you,*" join in all the other children.

"*Happy birthday, dear Alice…*" There is the briefest of pauses before…

"*Happy birthday to you!*" sings everybody in the whole restaurant.

"Make a wish," commands Miss Agatha, and Alice duly obeys, closing her eyes, her face beaming with pleasure, lit by the warm glow of the candles.

When she and Walter played this game for pretend earlier, Alice wished for her very own pony and trap, something she knew she would never have, but now, when she is asked for real, she makes a wish that she hopes really might come true.

"I wish," she says, secretly to herself, "I wish I might see Walter Blundell again."

But for now, the afternoon holds further delights.

First there's to be an Elephant Ride.

A memory of elephants waits patiently as the children are lifted, six at a time, onto the wooden howdahs, which have been fastened with ropes and covered in rugs, on their gently swaying backs. Dorothy makes sure that Walter and Alice are safely stowed aloft, before settling herself alongside.

"What's our elephant called?" asks Alice.

"Maharajah," replies his handler. "And I am Lorenzo. Now – are you ready?"

"Yes," chorus the children, and Maharajah trumpets loud and long to signal he's about to set off.

They swing from side to side as though they're sailing on the ocean. From their new great height, they can see over the hedges of the Maze, where people are trying to find their way into the centre. There's only one true way, with many false turnings leading to dead ends. The children take great delight in calling out wrong instructions to the lost and baffled crowds below.

Walter imagines himself an Indian Prince riding out to battle, while Alice pictures herself as a princess, wearing a jewelled sari.

"This isn't just any elephant, you know?" says Dorothy. "This is the famous Maharajah! Isn't it, Mr Lorenzo?"

Lorenzo, patiently walking beside them, nods importantly.

"Did you really walk all the way from Scotland together?" she asks.

"That we did."

"In only ten days?"

"We could have done it in less, if it weren't for all the crowds lining the streets the whole way, tossing us cakes."

"Do you like cake, Mr Lorenzo?" asks Alice.

"Why no, Missy, not me. But Maharajah does."

"Really?"

"You don't happen to have any cake with you now, do you?" he asks, winking at Dorothy.

"Yes, I do," shouts Alice. "I've some birthday cake!"

"Well how did you know that today is Maharajah's birthday?"

"Is it?" Alice is beside herself with excitement, while Dorothy stuffs her handkerchief into her mouth to stop herself from laughing.

"D'you think you might spare some?" asks Lorenzo.

"Here!" shrieks Alice, and she tosses a piece of her cake high into the air, then watches, thrilled, as Maharajah calmly catches it with his trunk and transfers it immediately to his mouth. Alice's heart is so filled with pleasure that she feels sure it will burst.

But there are more pleasures still that await them.

For next comes The Wild West Show.

Maharajah deposits them by a large Circus Tent, and Lorenzo helps them down. Miss Agatha is waiting for them all with her Bright Red Parasol held high above her head.

"This way," she calls. "Quickly now, we mustn't be late. Fine words butter no parsnips. Time and tide wait for no one."

They make their way inside the tent and sit on the front two rows of wooden benches just a few feet away from the sawdust-covered ring. No sooner have they sat down, when they hear a bugle ring loud and clear, heralding the arrival of the Cavalry. Six riders on horseback gallop around the ring, firing rifles in all directions, sometimes riding without hands, or standing in their stirrups, or even sliding off to one side and shooting from underneath their horses.

They rear up on the horses' hind legs, before whinnying and cantering out of the ring to be at once replaced by a group of cowgirls, with wide felt hats, buckskin waistcoats and skirts, and decorated leather boots, who perform a synchronised routine of ever more impressive rope tricks with their lassos, at one point skilfully aiming them over the heads of various children, capturing them like a buffalo, Alice included. One of them is then introduced as "Little Miss Sure Shot", who enters with a shotgun and asks for a volunteer from the audience. Dorothy puts up her hand and is led out into the centre of the ring, where a blindfold is tied around her eyes and an apple placed on top of her head. To a prolonged and tense roll of drums, Little Miss Sure Shot turns her back on Dorothy, takes aim instead through a mirror held up for her by another of the children, and the crowd holds its collective breath, while she counts – one – two – three – before shattering the apple to thunderous applause.

Little Miss Sure Shot is then followed into the ring by a tribe of American Indians. The braves wear many-coloured head dresses, with war paint on their faces, and carry ferocious-looking tomahawks, which they whirl above their heads, or spears decorated with feathers and tassels, which they throw high into the air, catching them as they fall, while the squaws, with long black braids and moccasins on their feet, stitch and weave fantastical patterns onto buffalo hides, before they all begin singing and dancing in a big circle.

Walter and Alice sit entranced throughout. At first Alice thinks she wants to be a cowgirl, with a wide felt hat and leather boots, riding the palomino mare, but then she thinks maybe an Indian, with braids and feathers in her hair, while Walter loves nothing more than the sound of the bugle, signalling the return of the Cavalry. He watches that bugle blower like a hawk. He reckons, with practice, he might just be able to do that himself. At the same time he finds himself drawn towards the quiet nobility of the Indian braves and, just before it is time for them all to leave, he notices something shining in the sawdust of the ring. He stoops to investigate and notices it is a feather from one of their head dresses, an eagle's feather, he imagines, and places it inside his jacket pocket for safe keeping.

After the show is over, the children pour out of the tent, red-faced and hot with excitement, chattering all at once nineteen to the dozen, replaying their favourite moments over and over again. The noise grows so loud that in the end Miss Agatha is forced to blow her whistle, raise her Bright Red Parasol high into the air with her left hand, while putting the forefinger of her right onto her lips, bidding the children to do the same.

"Now," she says, "let's all be Indian braves and squaws tracking through the forest, making not the slightest sound lest our presence is detected. Imagine my Bright Red Parasol is a head dress, and Dorothy here, who is going to carry it, is wearing it. She is your Chief and you will all follow on behind her in Indian file as we make our way through this thicket to Firework Lake."

Unable to contain themselves, many of the children immediately whoop and holler and ululate, till finally they settle into the game and creep silently through the park.

While they are thus preoccupied, noses to the ground, eyes darting left and right, Alice hears, or thinks she hears, a twig cracking in the undergrowth, leaves rustling in the bushes. She pauses, listens – nothing. But as she carries on once more, she swears she hears it again. She looks to her right, from where the sound seems to be emanating and, for the briefest of moments, the shortest of seconds, she is certain she sees four pairs of feet scurrying alongside her. Later she feels as though she is being watched, glimpses a row of faces staring at her from between the branches of a rhododendron bush, but when she goes to take a closer look, there is no one there. Just as they emerge from the cover of brake and gorse, back into the open grassland once more, she again feels sure they are being followed, tracked, but when she turns around, all she can see is a tight knot of four rats they must have disturbed burrowing back into the thicket.

They all sit huddled together on the grassy slope overlooking the lake, which affords them a clear, uninterrupted view of the fireworks, which begin just as the sun is setting. There are rockets and Catherine wheels, Roman candles and rainbow fountains.

The children "ooh" and "ah" in wide-eyed wonder and delight until, finally, the fireworks are finished, and it is time to go home, the showers of sparks and embers floating down to the ground beside them as they walk, reflecting in their shining eyes, the smell of smoke and ash filling their nostrils and clinging to their clothes and hair. It is a day that none of them will ever forget.

When they get back to Barmouth Street Chapel, the Reverend Aspinal is there to greet them, together with several mothers or older siblings, waiting to walk the younger children back to their homes. In the melee of goodbyes and thank yous, Walter doesn't get chance to speak to Alice one last time. He turns around and she's already gone. His shoulders slump but, just as he takes his sister Dorothy's offered hand in his, he hears a pair of tired footsteps running up behind him. It's Alice.

"I just wanted to say thank you. I've had a lovely birthday."

Walter's smile is almost too wide for his face. "Good luck at the mill tomorrow," he says, and he presses into her hand the feather he had saved from the circus tent.

She looks at it like buried treasure, places her hands upon his shoulder, rises up on tip toe and plants a delicate kiss upon his cheek, before running off to join her waiting mother, her red hair the last remaining light in the gathering dusk.

"Come on, lover boy," say Dorothy, tugging at his sleeve. "Father will be wondering where we've got to."

"And how was he, our Dor? Did he behave hisself?"

"He did, Father. Miss Aspinal said to say to thee that all the children had been a real credit to their families and the Chapel. Tha'd've been reet proud of 'im today."

"I'm allus proud o' thee, Walter, tha' knows that."

Walter tries, but fails, to stifle an enormous yawn.

"Sorry, Father," he says. "It must be all that fresh air I've had today."

"Ay, well it's work tomorrow and an early start for all of us. Best be off to bed, I reckon, Mother?"

"Come on, Walter. Up the dancers. Get undressed and say your prayers."

Walter kneels beside his bed. His younger brothers are already fast asleep in the other one, and Walter thinks luxuriously of the next few hours he'll have to enjoy his bed all to himself, before his older brothers come up and climb in on either side of him, shoving him into the middle.

After his usual nightly litany of "God bless Mother, God bless Father and all my brothers and sisters", he opens his eyes and then, on hearing his mother's footsteps just outside the door, quickly adds in a fierce whisper, "And God bless Alice Owen."

His mother comes in and looks at him with a smile.

"I'm glad tha's had such a good day, lad," she says. "Off to sleep with thee now."

"Mum…?"

"Yes, love?"

"Might you just…?"

"What?"

"You know?"

She tuts and shakes her head.

"Please?"

"Very well. Just this once," and she sits beside him, ruffles his hair, and very softly begins to sing.

"Buzzer's blowin', Walter lad
Lights are blazin' down below
Come on, best get ready, lad
It's almost time to go

Sithee, Owd Wilson's shut 'is gate
'Enry Arkwright's crossin' t' fold
Come on, lad, best not be late
Though mornin's dark an' cold

You'll find a bun on t' cellar sill
Kettle's boiled and t' fire's been lit
Daylight's breakin' over th'hill
Come on, lad, it's time for t' pit

Stand upon thy own two feet
Time to earn tha' daily bread
Clogs are rattlin' down the street
Come on, lad, now rest thy 'ead

Buzzer's blowin', Walter lad
Lights are blazin' down below
Come on, best get ready, lad
It's almost time to go…"

7

1892

The Reverend Mr Neville Aspinal stands before the altar of Barmouth Street Chapel with a warm smile upon his face. He signals his sister, Miss Agatha, seated at the organ, to begin playing, as the radiant bride, her arm linked through her proud father's, walks up the aisle towards him. The groom, nudged by his ever alert best man, steps nervously forward to meet her. Behind the bride, the matron of honour quietly organises the assorted bridesmaids, ranging in age from fifteen down to just six years old, to make their way as they have practised, each carrying a small posy of tulips before them.

"I now pronounce you man and wife," concludes a still smiling Reverend Aspinal, and the happy couple turn to face the congregation, looking as though they can scarcely believe their good fortune at having found each other.

Miss Agatha plays Mendelssohn's *Wedding March*, as the couple walk back down the aisle, followed by the matron of honour, still carefully guiding the bridesmaids, past all the smiling, weeping relatives and out onto the steps at the front of the Chapel, where a friend of the best man has already set up his camera on its tripod.

The photographs will record the groom fidgeting awkwardly at the unaccustomed collar and tie, looking nevertheless handsome in his conveniently well-fitting, borrowed suit, (apart from the trousers finishing a couple of inches above his shoes, revealing a fresh pair of charcoal grey socks), his attention quite rightly fixed only on his bride of just a few minutes, who smiles directly towards the camera, confident and composed. She wears neither veil nor bonnet. Instead she wears a garland, woven with laurel and fern, plaited with white flowers, around her red hair, for once allowed to hang loose and free, and there, prominent in the centre, is a bird's feather, which is the talking point of all the ladies there present.

As the photographer continues to organise different groupings – "Now can we have the groom's family... now the bride's... now the bridesmaids... now everybody for one last time..." – Walter and Alice have eyes only for each other. Then, as the best man is gathering people together for the short walk to where the reception is to be held, Dorothy, having carried out her matron of honour duties to perfection, approaches Alice and kisses her cheek.

"Let me be the first to congratulate you, Mrs Blundell."

Alice laughs. "I'm not sure I shall ever get used to that," she says.

"You'd better," quips Walter, and they are all laughing once more.

The best man signals to Walter that they're ready and Walter stands behind Alice, covers her eyes with his hands, and gently guides her towards the road.

"For you," he whispers, as he takes away his hands. "You once said this was something you wished for."

There before her, waiting patiently just outside the Chapel gate is a pony and trap.

Alice cannot contain herself and skips from foot to foot. "Walter, this must be costing a fortune. Are you sure we can afford it?"

"We're not going on a honeymoon, so we're saving on that, and I've been putting a bit by each week into the Co-op. The divvy from that has paid for this," he says, gesturing towards the pony and trap. "Madam, your carriage awaits."

He helps her climb up, then gets in beside her, as Dorothy leads everyone in the throwing of rice. The driver clicks his tongue, flicks the reins, and the pony immediately sets off at a trot. Alice can almost believe she has gone to Heaven and allows Walter to put his arm around her and give her a kiss, in full view of all the relatives.

The reception, which is rather a grand term for a tea, is to be held at the Hyde Road Hotel, just inside the entrance to Belle Vue. It has been made possible because the proprietor is a Methodist and a good friend of Mr Aspinal. He has arranged for the Function Room to be made available without charge, while Miss Agatha, marshalling an army of wives, has organised the sandwiches and the tea.

Walter and Alice, by benefit of the pony and trap, arrive ahead of everyone else, who are all walking on behind, but Walter has anticipated this. He is about to tip the driver but is declined.

"All taken care of, Sir. My best wishes to you and your new wife for your future happiness." He clicks his tongue once more and the pony heads back out of the park.

"This way," says Walter. "We have another short journey before we arrive at our destination," and he leads Alice towards the Animals Enclosure where, waiting for them on the path, is a silver-haired gentleman standing alongside an Asiatic elephant.

"Wanting a ride, Sir... Madam?" asks the silver-haired gentleman, with the slightest suggestion of a wink.

"Thank you, Lorenzo. Right on time."

Alice climbs the wooden steps leading up towards the howdah, followed by Walter, who makes sure she is safe and comfortable before signalling they are ready.

After a few moments, Alice finds she is once again accustomed to the graceful, swaying motion and looks around her, feeling exactly like that Indian Princess she had dreamed of being ten years before, when she last sat atop an elephant. Walter is so happy witnessing her silent pleasure, he finds he has no words he can say either, the two of them king and queen of all they survey.

Eventually it is Alice who finds her tongue.

"We first met riding on an elephant led by you, Mr Lorenzo, ten years ago. I don't suppose you remember us, we were only children then," she said.

"I give many children rides," he said. "But ten years ago, that would have been when Maharajah was still alive?"

"Yes. Maharajah was the name of the elephant we rode. What happened to him?"

"He grew old, Madam, that's all. He caught pneumonia and he died. But he had a good life, and this elephant you are riding on today – Sultan – he learned everything from Maharajah, and between us all, we keep him alive by remembering him, yes?"

"Yes indeed, Mr Lorenzo."

They pass The Maze, as they did that afternoon of the Sunday School outing, but instead of looking down on lots of lost individuals seeking an escape, they see only a courting couple, who have found the centre and have it all to themselves. Walter and Alice take their cue from them and kiss passionately.

After the tea and after all of the speeches, the party is accorded one final treat, with the arrival of an uninvited, but very welcome extra guest – Belle Vue's one and only, perennially popular Consul the Chimpanzee. He enters wearing a Norfolk jacket with matching waistcoat and plus fours, riding a tricycle, smoking a *meerschaum* pipe and playing the violin all at the same time.

When the children clap their hands, he claps his own in response, and he even sits on the lap of one of the older bridesmaids, puckering his lips as if wanting a kiss. Most people roar their pleasure, and the more they applaud and cheer, the more incorrigible become Consul's antics, but not everyone approves. While Alice declares herself "delighted that so distinguished a gentleman as Consul should honour them with his most esteemed company on this, the happiest day of her life", some of her Walter's mining pals are less enthusiastic.

"Monkey see, monkey do," says Jake, Walter's best man.

"Bread and circuses," says Cyril, Jake's uncle and something of a scholar.

"What are you on about?" asks Alan, who started down the pit the same day as Walter, and who is just beginning to be a little the worse for wear after imbibing a few too many times from the hip flask in his pocket during this determinedly Methodist teetotal reception.

Delighted to have a captive audience, Cyril explains. "The Roman emperors would keep the working people down by giving out free food during mass public spectacles. To distract them from realising how they were being exploited." He points towards the chimpanzee, now turning somersaults through a wooden hoop. "Bread and circuses."

"It's only a bit of fun," says Alan, "and we all need that from time to time."

"Ay," says Jake, "I reckon tha's not wrong, but things are changing. There's summat in the air. Mark my words. A new century's comin'."

"And if a monkey can learn to smoke a cigar, who's to say what the likes of thee and me can do, if them who's in charge nobbut let us?" adds Alan.

"Who says anything about lettin' us?" says Cyril, darkly, leaning in closer to the other men. "Why not take what's rightfully our own?"

Walter catches Alice's eye looking towards them from where her parents are sitting with a concerned expression. "No politics tonight, eh lads? Save it all for another time," and Consul cartwheels towards the top table, where he helps himself to a piece of the wedding cake.

Less than a year later Consul is dead. The Belle Vue animal doctor privately speculates whether his early death might be due to too many cigars and his fondness for chocolate, but keeps his opinions to himself, while the Jennison brothers speedily purchase a replacement from Wombwell's Travelling Menagerie, naming him immediately Consul II.

The celebrated Lancashire dialect poet, Ben Brierley, writes a eulogy to the ape, which he publishes as a Penny Broadsheet, on sale at street corners right across Manchester, from Oldham to Wigan, Bolton to Ashton.

IN MEMORY OF CONSUL

The Belle Vue Chimpanzee, who died aged 5 years

by

Ben Brierley

Hadst thou a soul? I've pondered o'er thy fate
Full many a time: yet cannot truly state

The result of my ponderings. Thou hadst ways
In many things like ours. Then who says
Thou'rt not immortal? That no mortal knows,
Not even the wisest – he can but suppose.

Tis God alone knows where "The Missing Link"
Is hidden from our sight; but on the brink
Of that eternal line where we must part
For ever, sundering heart from heart,
The truth shall be revealed: but not till then.
The curtain, raised by the Almighty when
Mankind must answer for the deeds of men.

ONE PENNY

Published by F.G. Wright & Son, Portugal Street

Sold by all Newsagents

Later that night, after they have all returned to their houses, Walter carries Alice across the threshold of their newly acquired flat on Melland Road, rented from the recently formed Sutton Dwellings Trust, founded to provide homes for working class families in England's industrial cities. He stands her on her feet and together they look around them at their clean, if sparsely finished new home.

"I love you, Mrs Blundell," says Walter.

"I love you too, Mr Blundell," replies Alice.

"My beautiful Indian Princess."

"My handsome Indian Brave."

They smile at the memory. He lifts her up into his arms once more, her red hair falling across both their faces, and carries her into the bedroom, to follow where hope and instinct lead them.

8

1902

"My Lords, Ladies and Gentlemen, a very warm welcome to you all on this, the first Sunday of September when, in keeping with our custom, we are holding our 50th Annual British Open Brass Band Championship, and once again we are delighted to be hosted here at the Belle Vue Zoological Gardens."

The Chairman of the Federation leads the audience of more than sixteen thousand people crowded into the open grounds beside Firework Lake in an enthusiastic round of applause.

"Celebrating fifty years of this most prestigious competition, as we do today, marks an important milestone, not only for our growing federation, but for the story of brass bands as a whole in England. When we began, eight bands contested for the honour of First Prize and to have their name inscribed upon this magnificent silver cup. The first ever winners were The Mossley Temperance Band with their unforgettable rendition of *The Heavens Are Telling* from Haydn's *Creation Oratorio*, still remembered fondly by those who were fortunate to have been present that afternoon, as indeed I was as a young boy and, looking up at the clear blue skies that we are blessed with today, the heavens are once again telling us that we are sure to be in for a musical treat and extravaganza this afternoon, for this year no fewer than twenty bands, including, for the first time, one from our neighbours in Wales, will be competing for the Senior Trophy, currently held by the Kingston Mills Band."

Another burst of applause interrupts him.

"A very popular, local band from just down the road in Hyde, who I see have brought with them many supporters this afternoon."

A loud roar of approval greets this acknowledgement.

"And so, without further ado, would you now please welcome our esteemed judges for this year's competition, Messrs Frederick Vetter, Carl Kieffert and George T.H. Seddon, all of whom I am sure are well known to many of you here."

The audience applauds politely as the adjudicators take their places in the front row.

"This year's Test Piece, to be played by all the bands, in addition to a programme of their own choosing, has been specially commissioned to mark our fiftieth anniversary, our Golden Jubilee. It is *L'Ebreo*, composed by Giuseppe Apolloni, and arranged for brass ensembles by Charles Godfrey Junior."

Murmurs of recognition ripple around the auditorium.

"And now, will you please welcome to the stage the first of our competing bands this afternoon? In keeping with the tradition first accorded by the late Mr John Jennison, Founder of these magnificent Pleasure Grounds, that honour goes to last year's winners and current holders of the Senior Trophy, the Kingston Mills Band and their conductor, Mr Alexander Hargreaves."

Waiting anxiously by the side of the stage is Walter.

It is ten years now since he and Alice married, and much has happened in the interim. Walter still works down the pit. No longer a putter or trapper, he works right at the coal face, a driller and a blaster. Now he is a man, just passing thirty, he has the respect of his fellow miners, but with respect comes responsibility, for he is now also a father.

Alice has six children in eight years, five boys and a girl, Esther, the apple of Walter's eye, who rides on his shoulders, who gives him his baggin before he sets off for work, who stands on the front door step when he comes back home, hands on her tiny hips, not letting him pass until he's taken off his boots, who reads everything put in front of her with a hunger that's insatiable, and who is not quite six years old. And now, after a two year gap, Alice is pregnant again, expecting in less than a month's time, but insisting that Walter still plays in the championship this year, especially after his success of the previous autumn, when Kingston Mills, his band, won for the first time.

Ever since watching the Wild West Show more than twenty years before, Walter has been in thrall to the bugle. Hearing all about it in the weeks that followed, Walter's father made enquiries and learned that Reddish Band had a boys' brigade, with a stock of instruments available to borrow. When he is twelve, Walter attends for the first time…

"See if tha' can fetch a sound from this then, young 'un," says the bluff conductor, thrusting an old B♭ trumpet into his hands.

Within seconds, Walter's face turns a bright puce with the effort, but nevertheless he manages to extract a note from it that is not anywhere near as strangulated as the conductor has been expecting.

"Not bad, young 'un. I reckon tha'll manage. But tha' might find this a bit more to tha' liking," and he tosses him a smaller instrument, which Walter quickly learns is called a cornet, and at once he is smitten.

He practises all hours of the day and night, much to his brothers' dismay, but he earns his father's approval, and so that soon quietens his brothers, who are all dragooned by Dorothy to attend his first concert, playing carols in the Barmouth Street Chapel. Reverend Aspinal singles him out for particular commendation, while Miss Agatha is seen to be dabbing her eyes with a handkerchief after Walter's solo rendition of *Once in Royal*. Even his brothers offer grudging praise afterwards.

By the time he's fourteen, he's already playing in the Reddish Senior Band, and after one particular concert in the Bandstand of Philips Park for Tulip Sunday, his old conductor calls him over.

"That were grand, lad," he says, "reet gradely. But there's summat I 'ave to tell thee."

Walter looks up, concerned by the strange change of tone in the old man's voice.

"There's nowt else I can teach thee, lad. If tha' wants to improve, tha' needs to join a better band."

Walter's eyes widen in surprise.

The old conductor leans in towards him. "Now don't be telling t' rest o' t' band I said this, will thee, lad?"

And so it is arranged for Walter to have an audition to join the celebrated Kingston Mill Band, who are based just four and a half miles away in Hyde, which he sails through with flying colours, and it comes as no surprise to anyone, except perhaps Walter himself, when he's selected to play the cornet solo part in the Test Piece for the 1901 Competition, Charles Gounod's *Mirella*, arranged again, as are so many of them, by Charles Godfrey Junior.

On the day of the competition he feels no nerves, just excitement. Alice is sitting in the audience, with all of their children, who are as good as gold throughout, even baby Freddie, and when he's finished playing his solo, he scans the first few rows until he spies them. Alice's eyes sparkle in the September sunlight, so that not even when they are announced as Winners of the Senior Trophy, and he is carried shoulder high through the cheering crowds afterwards by other members of the band, can his happiness match that moment when Alice looked directly at him, nodding her head with such quiet pride, just after he had sat down…

But this year she will not be sitting in the audience. She is too near her time, and besides, this pregnancy has not been like the others. For much of it she has been sickly and tired, the light in her eyes has lost its glow, and as he leaves the house that morning, she can barely lift her head to say goodbye or wish him luck.

Esther waits for him by the front door, holding out his cornet case for him.

"Good luck, Father," she says with a serious expression in her large, dark eyes.

"Thank you, Esther," he replies, taking the case from her. "Now," he continues, bending down so that his eyes are at the same level as hers, "I want you to be a very grown up girl today and look after your mother."

"Yes, Father, I will," she says solemnly, "but isn't Auntie Dor coming?"

"Soon. In about an hour. So I'm putting you in charge till she gets here. Alright?"

"I am only five, you know."

"But very nearly six. And the cleverest girl I know." He lifts her high above his head, swings her round twice, before setting her down again and stepping out towards Belle Vue.

Now, as he hears the Federation Chairman announce the start of this year's competition, he is surprised to feel butterflies in his stomach. Instead of excitement, he experiences doubt. There's a tricky triple-tonguing section in *L'Ebreo* and he doesn't feel confident. As he climbs onto the stage with the rest of the band, the palms of his hands are sticky and his mouth feels dry.

When it comes to his solo he navigates his way past all the various hurdles and challenges, but he knows he hasn't played it as well as he might have. The fluency wasn't there, the phrasing was awkward, and the arc of the piece not realised. The other band members congratulate him afterwards, but he merely shrugs, looking towards Alex, their conductor, who says nothing. They both know they'll not be retaining the Senior Trophy this year, which will be awarded instead to their old rivals, The Black Dyke Mills Band from across the Pennines, near the other Bradford, but at this moment neither of them knows this, for just as they are putting away their instruments in the tent by the side of the stage, Esther is running towards him.

"Auntie Dor says you've to come home straight away. Mother's started. The baby's on its way," and she takes hold of Walter's sleeve and pulls him as hard as she can.

Three quarters of an hour later, after Walter has carried Esther on his shoulders and run all the way back to Melland Road, the midwife comes through from the bedroom with a worried look on her face.

"Go and fetch Dr Warren," she says.

Walter heads straight back out.

When he returns, the doctor joins Dorothy and the midwife in attending to Alice, whose cries are frequent and loud. He finds Esther has sat the rest of the children in a circle on the floor in the parlour and is getting them to sing as many nursery rhymes as she can think of, so that they don't have to listen to their mother's distress. He sits down to join them, but Esther turns to him gravely and says, "It's alright, Father. You wait in the kitchen, in case you're needed there."

Four hours later it is all over.

Dr Warren takes Walter to one side. "Your wife has had a most difficult time," he says. "You don't need me to tell you that, you must have heard. She's quiet now, though, and the midwife is seeing to her."

"Can I go to her?"

"Later. Let her rest first."

"What about the baby?"

Dr Warren shakes his head. "I'm sorry," he says, putting his hand on Walter's shoulder. "She wasn't ready to be born…"

Walter feels himself trembling. He sees his cornet, lying on the floor where he left it by the back door when he came in, and picks it up. He steps outside into the small yard and feels the night air on his face and arms. It's already dark and a few stars are showing in the sky. A huge harvest moon rises, bruised and orange, as Walter brings the cornet to his lips and tries to play, as quietly as he possibly can, a deep, yearning lament. As the notes climb into the night, it is almost as if he can see them, like shooting stars, falling from a nearly spent firework, forming a direct line between that boy who first heard such notes more than twenty years before, sitting holding the hand of an excited girl closing her eyes, making a wish, before blowing out the candles on her birthday cake, one by one.

But the line stretches deeper and further, longer and higher. He hears it in the hammer as it rings against the coal face, feels it in the air, humming with the singing wires of the pithead, the earth shaking beneath his feet in the rumble of falling rocks far off underground. He watches it forge a river of fire in the blacksmith's yard, weave a thousand threads in the clattering loom, weld together sparks of light in the overhead tram cables, sees it crackle as rail tracks bend and buckle, the deep vibration coming through the soles of his boots, a wild elephant storming out of the forest, hooves trampling the spine of the country, a storm cloud of dust pursuing him, escaping the exigencies of a cruel past, scouring the land for a new home. He traces their slow rise and fall, the cadence of telegraph wires, looped and laced above the city, the twisted stitch of lives across the years, raining out of the sky, catching each note as he plays it, gathering them all together, thistledown on the wind, trapped infinitesimally between his fingers, through which he blows, to see them dance and fall, back into the earth, like tiny seeds, which might lie dormant for centuries, or poke through the soil tomorrow.

Almost as if he is his own Pied Piper, Walter lets the notes he plays lead him back into the house, through the kitchen, past the parlour, into the bedroom, where Alice is sleeping, and there he stops. He lets each note leave his lips to light again those candles on the cake, those wishes that still burn brightly and will not be extinguished. He sits beside her and takes her hand in his.

After a few moments he feels her fingers gently squeezing his.

She opens her eyes.

She smiles.

"I'm sorry," she says."

He kisses her forehead.

"We're complete," he says.

"Play for me again," she says.

He lifts the cornet to his lips. She sleeps.

9

1912

The Daily Dispatch

31st May 1912

IS THIS THE END FOR LORENZO THE LION TAMER?

On a busy Whit Holiday Monday at the Belle Vue Zoological Gardens a sudden surge from the hundreds of people queuing for The Scenic Railway, the park's recently opened new attraction, caused one of the two elephants working that day to panic and run towards the terrified crowds.

In the ensuing mayhem of pachyderm bodies, Lorenzo Lawrence, in trying to bring the rushing elephant to a halt, was crushed between the two mighty beasts and badly broke a leg.

Lorenzo, a world famous lion tamer, is perhaps best remembered as the man who accompanied Maharajah the Elephant on his famous walk from Edinburgh to Manchester forty years ago. Maharajah died in 1882, since when Belle Vue has housed several other elephants, all of whom have been handled by Mr Lawrence.

But could this accident bring to an end his illustrious career?

Recovering afterwards in Manchester

Infirmary, Lorenzo pointed to his suspended leg entirely cast in plaster of Paris and quipped:

"This is what happens when an irresistible force meets an immovable object!"

*

The following weekend Esther reaches the gates to Belle Vue before they are open. Outside a newsboy is selling copies of *The Clarion*. Esther debates with herself whether she can afford to buy one. It only costs a penny, but she will have to forego any refreshment once inside the Gardens, but the local library no longer subscribes to it, bowing to local complaints from the Independent Labour Party, who complain that its articles go too far, are seditious even, by which they mean they support women's suffrage, which they, in their alliance with Mr Churchill's Liberals, currently do not favour, not since the split in the WSPU, and Mrs Pankhurst's emphatic support for more direct action. "Deeds not words" has become the rallying cry, and it is that which has brought Esther to Belle Vue so early this Sunday morning. She takes a penny from her purse and hands it to the newsboy.

The gates are unlocked and she hurries inside, finds a bench to sit upon and greedily starts to devour her copy, page by page.

The lead article, by the paper's founder, Mr Robert Blatchford, is a detailed analysis of present day Germany. There has been much talk of the possibility of war, which Esther fervently hopes will not come to pass. There are many German families on the eastern side of the city, most of whom have been living there for generations. They have German names, some of the older ones even still bear traces of a German accent when they speak, but there is far more that they share than that which divides them. This mix of different peoples, different religions and cultures from right across the world is one of the things Esther admires most about Manchester, its ability to welcome all comers, shape and accommodate the times, encourage new ideas, new ways of thinking, its ever expanding boundaries like open arms, embracing the globe like a large stewing pot into which it continually stirs new and unfamiliar ingredients until, over time, their taste becomes second nature.

That is not to say the old divisions between the social classes have all been swept away. Far from it. Mr Blatchford laments with great eloquence the suffering he witnesses daily in the desperate slums that still prevail beside the city's rivers and canals, stagnant with filth, where typhoid and cholera are always rife, while, literally a stone's throw away, the rich build their high walls behind which they can plant their perfumed gardens to mask the stench of disease.

"You don't see anything like that in Germany," he writes. "Is this how we are preparing to fight for the existence of our Empire? What use will these ragged, famished spectres be when we have our backs to the wall?"

Not that he is advocating war. No, he merely fears that the country is already inexorably sleep-walking into it, unaware of the longer term consequences. "I want to convince the people of this country that war is coming and to urge them to use the power of the ballot box to persuade our politicians that this horrible war can, and must, be prevented."

He saves the worst of his ire for the evils of conscription, which he fears will be an inevitable consequence of any large scale war with Germany. "I have seen our soldiers used for strike-breaking, and conscription will only pit man against his brother, instead of working together for the common good of all."

Esther avidly reads page after page, hungry for every nuance of argument and opinion. Now she reaches what she has been hoping she will find – further information about the Women's Suffrage March planned to commemorate the fifth anniversary of the infamous Mud March, when women from all points of the compass walked across Britain to gather for a rally in London, more than three hundred thousand of them converging on Hyde Park, braving the cold and the rain, not for one moment put off by the sea of mud they were forced to wade through to listen to the speakers, Mrs Pankhust and Miss Christabel among them, their passion and purpose winning over several thousand more waiverers. How Esther wishes she could have been there – or here, in Belle Vue, the previous year, 1906, when Miss Adela Pankhurst heckled Mr Churchill so incessantly he was obliged to sit down.

Now, *The Clarion* dissects the opposing arguments of the two factions of the Movement that have emerged,

Mrs Pankhurst and Christabel on one side, Sylvia and Adela on the other – as well as a growing number of calmer, more moderate voices, whose rejection of the more extreme, violent actions of the glass smashers, the paint throwers, those who would fling themselves beneath the galloping hooves of the King's horse, has begun to win over some senior politicians, Lloyd George among them, voices such as Millicent Fawcett, Elizabeth Garrett Anderson, and the woman scheduled to speak at today's rally at Belle Vue, Hannah Mitchell, who had been one of Miss Adela's fellow hecklers back in 1906.

Esther walks purposefully towards the platform which has been erected, from where Mrs Mitchell will make her speech. Although she is not due to speak for another two hours, crowds are already beginning to gather, as well as a large contingent of constables anticipating possible trouble.

Esther is continuing to make her way forward, determined to secure a good spot for later, when she thinks she recognises Mrs Mitchell herself, speaking with the organisers. She opens *The Clarion* to check. There is a photograph inside, she is certain. Yes. There's no mistake. Esther looks up from the newspaper. As she does so, her eyes meet those of Mrs Mitchell's, who walks towards her with a warm smile.

"Are you here to help?" she asks.

"No. Well – yes," stammers Esther.

"Either you are, or you are not," remarks Mrs Mitchell.

"I mean yes – of course – I am willing to do

anything to help, but in fact I have come to listen to you speak. I've just been reading about you in here." She holds up her copy of *The Clarion*.

Mrs Mitchell smiles. "How old are you, if you don't mind me asking?"

"I'm almost sixteen."

"Younger than I was when I first began reading Bob Latchford's rantings."

"You don't agree with what he writes?"

"Not always, no. But he never fudges. And I like that. What's your name?"

"Esther Blundell."

Mrs Mitchell holds out her hand. "I'm Hannah. Tell me, Esther," she continues, picking up the newspaper, "which side of the great divide are you on?"

Esther thinks for a moment before she replies. "I'm not really sure."

"A good answer," says Hannah, smiling, "but sometimes you have to take a stand, decide just how far you…" and she gently jabs a finger towards Esther, "…are prepared to go to stand up for what you believe in."

Esther nods. "I wouldn't want to go to prison," she says.

"Nor would anyone."

"You did," replies Esther, unthinkingly.

"Yes. But I didn't want to."

"You knew you risked the possibility, though, when you interrupted Mr Churchill?"

"I'm not sure that I did, to tell the truth. I just got so incensed by the man's obstinacy – no, worse than that, his smugness." She smiles again at the memory.

"What happened? Can you tell me?"

Just at that moment, one of the organisers begins hammering nails into the platform in order to secure the lectern that is being prepared for the speakers later.

"Let's sit down away from all this noise and commotion," says Hannah, "over there by the Tea Room, and then at least we can hear one another."

"If you're sure you've got time?"

"Now there's a question, and no mistake. Time... When I was your age, I was in such a rush." She pauses briefly, as if deciding whether or not to confide in this eager young girl, who looks up at her now, hanging on her every word. "Sit here," she says, "opposite me, where I can see your face. There's something about you that reminds me..."

"Of what?"

"Of me, Esther. Of me."

Esther looks down at her hands placed on the table in front of her. "Please tell me," she says.

"What?"

"Whatever it was you were going to."

Hannah waits a moment, then nods imperceptibly. "I was born Hannah Webster in 1871, one of six children, on a remote farm in Derbyshire. I went to school for just two weeks. Two weeks! My father taught me to read. He loved his books, and I inherited my passion for them from him. But he was a farmer, so he was always busy, up before the sun, out in the fields till long after it was dark again, so I barely saw him. When I did, he'd ask me what book I'd been reading that day. Well – I hardly had time, my mother worked me so hard every day, washing and scrubbing, cooking and mending, but I didn't want to disappoint him, so I'd volunteer to do my brothers' chores for them in return for looking at their school books when they came home each day. But my mother saw what pleasure this gave him – she was jealous, I think – and she treated me even crueller. In the end I could stand it no longer and one morning I just walked out of the door and never went back."

"How old were you?"

"Younger than you are now. Just fourteen."

"I'm so lucky in comparison. I'm also one of six, and the only girl, but I've never been made to feel less important than them."

"And yet you have a sadness about you, Esther…"

Esther swallows hard. "My mother died. Two years ago."

Hannah takes her hand in her own. "I'm sorry."

"She'd not been well for years. Not since she lost a baby." She takes her hand away and wipes her face roughly with the back of it. "That's why I don't want to risk going to prison. I've my father and brothers to look after." She looks back at Hannah, almost defiantly.

"Yes. I can see that."

"What happened next? After you left home?"

"Well… I tramped over the hill, hardly conscious of the distance. I just kept walking, going where my feet took me, and they brought me here, to Manchester. I knew now I had to rely on myself. I knew also that I was ill-equipped for whatever was to come, uneducated, untrained, and quite alone. Somewhere on that moorland road I left my childhood behind."

Esther privately wonders how the woman sitting opposite from her managed to get from that lost and frightened young girl on the moor to one of the leading figures among the Manchester Suffragists. She may only be approaching her sixteenth birthday, but she has seen enough of the harshness of inner city life to know the fate that awaits so many young girls in similarly precarious situations.

As if reading her mind, Hannah resumes her story. "I was lucky," she says. "My older brother took me in. He found me stumbling off the moor, and his wife secured me employment as a maid in the local schoolmaster's house. From there I went to Bolton to work as a dressmaker's assistant. I spent every free hour I had, which wasn't much, borrowing books from the library there. It was then that I started reading *The Clarion*. I heard about a Public Meeting being held in the town. It was entitled *A Brighter Future*, and I remember thinking we could all do with that. The speaker was a woman, not much older than I was, but so much better read. Katherine Conway, her name was. Such a slight figure. Tiny. But what a voice. The kind that makes you want to lean forward in your seat and hang onto every last syllable."

Esther realises that that is exactly what she is doing at that very moment and almost laughs. "What did she talk about?" she asks. "Can you remember?"

"I've never forgotten. She was a Marxist and a feminist, but more important than either of those, she was an optimist. She desired warmth and colour in human lives. More bread, yes. But roses, too. When she spoke, she made it possible for you to imagine beauty and culture in a more justly ordered state."

"Yes," says Esther in vigorous agreement. She is thinking how bleak their lives are at home, now that her mother has died. The light has gone from her father's eyes, the cornet has been put away and not been played for years. There is only work, grinding hard work, from which he and her brothers return each evening, grey and exhausted. Esther finds solace in the books she reads from the library, but this is a lonely pursuit, carried out in the isolation of her bedroom in a precious hour at the end of each day. She yearns for like-minded others, with whom she might hold conversations that range beyond the confines of domesticity, where she might test out her still-forming ideas and opinions. It is why, she now understands, she has sought out this rally today, in the hope that the spark which has been kindled within her might find some necessary oxygen to fan it before it is extinguished.

"That was my Road-to-Damascus moment," continues Hannah. "I began attending more and more meetings, joining more and more societies. Some I realised were not for me, but some I stuck with. One of these was the Labour Church, and that's where I met Gibbon Mitchell."

"Your husband?"

"Ay, my husband. But don't you be getting any starry-eyed, romantic notions. Married life, as lived by my brothers and sisters and other friends, held no great attraction for me. But I wanted a home of my own.

Perhaps if I had understood my own nature better, I might not have married. I soon realised that marriage – at least as far as men understand it – requires a certain amount of self-abnegation from a woman, which was quite impossible for me. But I was young, full of hope that the kind of marriage being advocated by Socialism, a measure of comradeship, as opposed to the traditional notion that a woman must be subservient to a man, might be the kind of Utopian state that Gibbon and I might inhabit. I was naïve."

"Do you have children?"

"You ask a lot of questions."

"I'm sorry. It's just that – I know from observing my mother – when a woman has children, her own life tends to disappear, whereas you, you continue to live a full and public life."

"We've just one child. At my insistence. It was a difficult birth. I've come to realise that although birth control may not be a perfect solution to all of life's social problems, it is the first and the simplest way for us women to obtain at least some measure of freedom over our lives."

"And acquiring the vote…?"

"… may lead us down the path of much needed reform. *Ad meliora.* To things getting better."

"*Acta non verba*?"

"That's a question I still can't answer."

"But you left the WSPU?"

"Because it became undemocratic."

"You went to prison for them."

"And would have stayed there, had my husband not

put up my bond, which I was most displeased with him for…"

Esther is speechless. It is a window into a world she has previously glimpsed only through books and pamphlets, and now it is sitting right opposite her, here in Belle Vue.

"Yes, we shall be judged in the end by our actions more than our words, but it is through our words that we may inspire others to action, and I believe we can inspire more people to take bolder actions by not alienating them through violence or destruction. We are revolutionaries, not terrorists."

"I imagine at times you must have found yourself caught between a rock and a hard place."

"Yes. Navigating that narrow passage between Scylla and Charybdis is not without its challenges. But beyond, if we make it that far, lie calmer waters. *Dum spiro, spero.* Where there's life, there's hope."

Later, when Esther has listened to all the speakers at the rally, applauded till her hands have become sore, and when she has waved to those several hundred of them who are making the Anniversary March to London, she has walked back home, to Melland Road, acutely aware of the gulf between the reality of the life she inhabits and the life she'd prefer to pursue, but that, just possibly, the way to achieve the latter might be found through the way that she lives the former.

It is with a lighter step and a gladder heart that she has made her way home than she has known since her mother died. She will urge her father to play the cornet again, to teach it to Harold, who has always shown a keenness for it. She will try not to scold Freddie so much, but to help him find less reckless ways of testing himself against his brothers. She'll encourage Jim with his reading, help him to make sense of the hieroglyphs that dance before his eyes. She'll try to be more patient with Frank, especially when the pen he holds in his huge ham hands explodes, spattering walls and floor with spider-trails of spilt ink. She'll look to be more imaginative in devising new ways for each of them to take a bath more regularly, without it sounding like she's nagging. She'll make sure they don't rush off back out again straight afterwards, but wait at least until their hair has dried a little, for they've all begun to show signs already of developing the same chronic cough their father has, and she will promise herself to show more interest in the next young lady Arthur wants to invite for Sunday tea. She might find she has more in common with them than she is prepared to admit, if she will only give them a chance. She finds herself humming one of the anthems she heard earlier at the rally that afternoon, adjusting her step to its rhythm as she sings the words out loud.

"Shout, shout, up with your song!
Cry with the wind for the dawn is breaking.
March, march, swing you along!
Wide blows our banner and hope is waking…"

10

1922

Tulip Sunday.

Walter and Esther climb aboard the tram that will take them home. Walter is so tired he falls asleep almost as soon as he sits down. His head lolls onto Esther's shoulder. He's had a good afternoon. People he's not seen for many months, years even, have come to him and spoken to him. He's caught up with their news, been introduced to new arrivals, lamented sad departures. He's talked, drunk (more than he probably should have), smoked (when Esther's not been watching), coughed as a result, and reminisced.

"D'you remember when we…?"

"And when you…?"

"And when I…?

"When…?"

He's enjoyed the flowers, and the sunshine, and the children's races, and the ice cream. He's listened to the music – "not a bad band, not Championship material, but not bad nevertheless". Harold's doing quite well, that cornet solo was quite promising. He's remembered his own playing days, the trophies, the cups, the rivalries. He knows he's seen Jim and Harold and Frank, all courting now, but he mixes them up, their lady friends, the Ediths, the Ethels, the Elsies, and sometimes, he's certain, he's seen Freddie and Arthur. They're with him now, sitting on the seat in front, making faces out of the window. They think he's not spotted them, but they're in for a surprise. He must remember to tell Alice when he gets back how Harold got on, for she'll want to know.

"Have they all been good, Father?" she'll ask.

"She's looking better, don't you think?" he says to Esther.

"Who, Father?"

"Your mother, of course. Don't you think so?"

"You're tired, Father."

And he is, it's true. He's drifting off again. He's watching the Cavalry at the Wild West Show, galloping round and round the ring, chasing the Indians, who shuffle and dance and stand fast, the light of distant mountains in their eyes. He's picking up a feather. He'll save it for later. For Alice.

"What's this for?" she asks holding it out in front of her.

"For luck," he says, and he is lucky, the luckiest man alive, he thinks, as he watches her walk down the aisle, the feather plaited into her wild red hair.

The tram stops with a jolt and he opens his eyes. They're at the top of the rise at Ryder Brow. He sees mountains in the distance. The girl sitting next to him he can't quite recognise. She's holding a feather in her hands. "Where did you get that?" he shouts, and the whole bus looks round. "You stole it. Give it back." And he tries to wrestle it from her with his fingers, which pluck lost trumpet notes from the air. The girl beside him places her hands over his and gradually his fingers grow still, the melody slipping away from him. Yes, he thinks. I know this woman, I just can't put a name to her...

Esther waits until he seems to be calmer and then gently extricates her fingers from his grip. She smoothes the vaned feather in her hand, the feather given to her that afternoon by Tommy Thunder. She holds it up to the window to let the light pass through it, so that it becomes quite translucent. The central shaft, the rachis, to which all the vanes attach, rises from the calamus, the quill at the base. It is infinitely intricate, each vane comprising untold numbers of barbs, each barb further divided into barbules, all branching off towards the barbicels, tiny hooks, which connect each feather to its neighbour. Esther studies it carefully, so delicately wrought, so fragile, yet so strong. It reminds her curiously of a mine, the central shaft carrying the full weight of all the different tunnels branching off it, towards each of the precious, exposed seams, threaded like lacewing under their feet. Tommy Thunder told her that an eagle has seven thousand feathers, every one of which it needs to help it fly. That night he rescued her from the flooded trench, he talked of how he watched them as a boy, in his home, a far off country over the ocean, whole kettles of them riding the high thermals, and how his father had taught him never to take more than a single one down with his bow, or rob a nest of all its eggs. She recalls that night now, how she lay in the mud, tugging at a thigh bone protruding from the earth, washed away by the rising flood, that she might use for a splint. She looks at this feather now, and suddenly it seems to her that the rachis is itself like a bone, acting as a support for all the vanes and barbs, barbules and barbicels, just as her own bones serve as a vessel for muscle and tissue, ligament and nerve. Remove just one and the whole skeleton collapses, and she thinks how precarious the whole arrangement is, how they dig their way down, deep into the earth to extract the black coal, whose dust settles on their hair, their skin, lodges in their lungs, until it is all hollowed out, like an empty honeycomb, with just a trace of memory, voices echoing in long abandoned tunnels.

She looks through the tram window at the row upon row of houses stretched out before her as far as she can see, all built because of, and on top of, these underground mountains of coal. She remembers walking with her father once as a child, back home from Debdale Park, from the bandstand there, where he'd playing in a concert one Sunday afternoon, passing the Gorton Reservoir, which she can just make out now if she cranes her neck as far as she can to the left. They were crossing over Hyde Road towards Ryder Brow. They had just reached Levenshulme Road when the ground opened up right in front of them. Her father pulled her back just in time, hurried her round the corner until the noise died down and the dust cloud cleared. There before them was a vast sink hole, more than forty feet deep. She remembers holding tightly to her father's hand as they edged towards the crater's rim and peered down into the guts and entrails of the earth.

"Subsidence," he said. "It's like dominoes. You brush against one and the whole row tumbles, one after the other."

She thinks back to another time, twenty years ago,

when her mother lost her last baby, and Walter played the cornet outside in the yard, at the back of the house, his notes pulled up from deep underground, before floating up and away, high into the night sky.

He jerks awake beside her.

"Look," he says, and points towards the two elephants ambling trunk to tail along Hyde Road, with a white-haired trainer twirling a silver-topped cane, back towards Belle Vue after giving rides to the children in Philips Park all afternoon.

Walter turns excitedly to Esther. "Do you remember when we had a ride on one, on that Sunday School outing?"

Esther smiles. "That was with Mother, Father. Not me."

"Oh," he says, tapping his forehead anxiously. "Aren't you my mother?"

He hears a woman's voice singing.

"Buzzer's blowing, Walter lad
Lights are blazing down below
Come on, lad, get ready now
It's almost time to go…"

1932

For the PERFECT FAMILY DAY OUT
Belle Vue
ZOO PARK
MANCHESTER
Open Daily 10am till Dusk

Enchanted Gardens
Aviary   Reptile House   Aquarium   Penguin Pool
Deer Paddocks   Performing Sea-Lions   Gibbons Cage
Elephant Rides   Polar Bears   Lions & Tigers

Fun Fair Speedway
Boating Stock Cars
Music Dancing
Boxing Wrestling
Greyhounds Fireworks

DON'T MISS THE EVENT OF THE YEAR
GRAND WHITSUNTIDE OPENING
THE NEW CYCLONE RACER
THE TALLEST, FASTEST ROLLER COASTER IN BRITAIN

HOLD ON TO YOUR HATS, IT'S...
THE BOBS

ONE SHILLING PER RIDE

Printed by F.G. Wright & Son

*

It was Mary's idea.

"Let's celebrate," she'd said. "A family outing. We deserve it."

"Do we?" asked a surprised Jabez. "What's the occasion?"

"An anniversary."

Jabez scratched his head. "We were wed in the autumn, not in the spring."

Mary smiled. "I know that. But this weekend will be three years to the day since we came to live here."

She was referring to the move from Garibaldi Street into the Head Keeper's Lodge at the entrance to Philips Park.

The previous incumbent's spinster daughter died and, allowing for a brief period afterwards in which her family had been able to take away some mementoes, the Parks & Gardens Committee of Manchester Corporation approved the recommendation by its Chair, Mr Julian Pettigrew, to grant permission for Jabez and his family to take possession immediately after Easter. But there had been further delays. The Corporations's Inspector of Properties had deemed the property unsafe until essential structural work was carried out on its roof and walls, and Mary and Jabez were forced to endure another two frustrating years of waiting, until finally the great day came.

"It still needs some work," said Pettigrew, as he formally handed over the keys to Jabez. "Miss Harrison lived here alone for some years, as you know, after her father died, and nothing's been done to the place since well before then. But I don't expect you'll mind."

"No, Sir, and Mrs Chadwick will be delighted. She'll have plenty of ideas for brightening it up a bit."

"Quite so. The Corporation has checked the

essential structure – roof, walls, guttering etc – and will carry out the necessary repairs forthwith, but as for the inside, well – that's entirely up to you."

"Thank you, Sir."

Mr Pettigrew shook Jabez by the hand, gave him the keys, tipped his hat with his cane, and then made his way back to the car, which was waiting for him around the corner on Mill Street.

In the weeks that followed, Mary was like a woman possessed. No sooner had she closed the door behind the children, Harriet and Toby, as they left each morning for school, than she set to with a will. She'd pack her cleaning things and walk across to Philips Park. If Jabez was already there, working on the flower beds, or pruning the bushes that lined the paths, or lopping branches from the trees, she'd wave and perhaps even join him for half an hour when she knew he might be taking a break, methodically munching his way through the lunch she'd prepared for him each morning. He liked, she noticed, to save a few crumbs for the small birds, which thrived in the park, whose names he'd try and teach her, but which she could never retain, unlike Harriet, who lapped up such information, and who'd eagerly recount to her father any sightings she might make to and from school, mostly scraggy starlings, sparrows or blackbirds, though occasionally a flight of geese or ducks passing in formation above the smoke from house or factory chimneys. If she accompanied her father to the park, though, there was a much greater variety, all manner of finches, tits and warblers, woodpeckers in the black poplars and pines, egrets and herons taking off from the ponds. But generally Jabez did not like to be disturbed while he was working, preferring instead to stroll more leisurely afterwards, pointing out things the children might otherwise miss, newts and tadpoles in the spring, returning flocks of field fares in the winter, swallows and swifts in the summer, bats in the evenings. He particularly treasured those final moments of light before darkness fell completely, when the water in the brooks sounded closer and louder, when all manner of nocturnal flutterings were beginning to emerge, when the gates were locked and the public had left and the park was theirs. Now that they were to move into the Lodge, Jabez would be almost full time in the park, but he would still carry on working a couple of days each week underground at Bradford Colliery. After the rigours and deprivations of the General Strike three years before, the mine had gradually returned to full production and was taking on more men again. There would always be a couple of shifts he could do each week, and he was pleased to continue. Not only would he miss the company of the other men, most of whom he'd known all his life, but coming up for air after ten hours of hard, back breaking labour excavating a new seam, where it was so hot he had trouble even breathing, made him appreciate the open spaces and fresher air of the park even more.

And so, for the fortnight after Mr Pettigrew gave Jabez the keys to the Lodge, Mary would go each day to air it and clean it, wash its curtains, beat its rugs, sweep its floors, and then scrub and polish every square inch of all of its four rooms, each of them larger and lighter than their house in Garibaldi Street, which they'd lived in for more than ten years. She stripped the peeling wallpaper, then filled in the various cracks in the plaster, before coating them with a layer of sugar soap. Once she was satisfied the walls were dry and ready, she applied two coats of distemper throughout. On the last day, just before heading off back for the children, she called Jabez over to inspect what she'd done.

"Well…?" she said.

"Ay, lass," he said, nodding. "It'll do." He tried to keep his face straight for as long as possible, but his serious expression cracked as Mary flung a dish cloth at him. He put his arms around her and drew her close. "How about we christen the place?" he suggested.

Mary laughed. "I've the children's tea to fix first. You'll have to hold your horses till we've moved in properly."

"We'd best be quick about it then," he said, as he tried to steal an extra kiss.

The next weekend Jabez arranged with Giovanni for Claudia's elder brother Matteo, along with her thirteen year old son, Paulie, to use his cart to take all of their stuff from Garibaldi Street over to the Lodge. Matteo was a Jack-of-all-trades. Among the very many things that he did for his large extended family, he was also a rag-and-bone man, and early on the Saturday morning he turned up bright and early. Harriet and Toby could hear the clip-clop of hooves striking the cobbled street and rushed outside to greet him, walking alongside his old mare, Bombola, who was contentedly chewing oats from her nose bag. Jabez and Mary, with Matteo's help, loaded everything they possessed onto the back of the cart, while Harriet, Toby and Paulie took it in turns to sit upon Bombola, as they walked the two and a half miles from Garibaldi Street in Ancoats to the Lodge at Philips Park.

"Why do you not have an Italian name like your Uncle Matteo?" Harriet asked Paulie.

Paulie shrugged. "Because we are English, my mother says. We must stop looking back to the old country, she says. Our future is here now, so I must have an English name. Paul. But they keep calling me 'Paulie'. Which I don't like. I prefer Paul."

"And a Manchester accent too," remarked Harriet, smiling.

"Oh yes. I even support United," he said.

"Best keep that quiet," laughed Harriet. "Our dad's a City fan," and she ran on ahead, with Paul chasing after her.

They were all of them in high spirits. Not even the pitying or disapproving looks from certain passers-by who, regarding their assorted belongings – chairs, table, wardrobe, bed – suspected they might be doing some kind of moonlight flit, could dampen their enthusiasm. Nor when a few drops of rain began to fall as they skirted the edge of Bradford Colliery. Matteo simply stretched a length of tarred canvas over everything stacked on the back of the cart, and they all began to sing at the tops of their voices.

"Take me back to Manchester when it's raining
I want to wet my feet in Albert Square
I'm all agog for a good thick fog
I don't like the sun, I like it raining cats and dogs
I want to smell the odours of the Irwell
I want to feel the soot get in me hair
Oh I don't want to roam, I want to get back home
To rainy Manchester…"

By the time they reached the park, the rain had stopped.

In less than a couple of hours, everything was unpacked and in its new place. Mary brewed some tea, and she and Jabez sat on the recently donkey-stoned front step to drink it, surveying their domain like a king and queen, while Matteo led Harriet, Paul and Toby for rides on Bombola around the park.

"Come," said Jabez after they'd finished their tea.

He took Mary's hand and he led her away from the Lodge towards the clump of pines that stood nearby.

"Look," he said, and pointed.

The patch of wild tulips he'd planted there, using the seeds harvested from the bunch held by Mary on the day they first met in the cemetery adjacent to where they now stood, had proliferated and spread, with more colours than ever.

Mary turned towards him. She took his face in both her hands and kissed him.

Now, three years later Mary was waiting at the kitchen

table for Jabez when he came in from work. She was holding a leaflet in her hand.

"Let's celebrate," she'd said. "A family outing. We deserve it."

Jabez studied the leaflet. It was a poster advertising the Grand Opening of a new ride at Belle Vue Funfair. The Bobs. They'd never been, not as a family. The hours Jabez worked excluded the possibility as a rule, but on many an evening they'd sat on the brick wall at the back of Garibaldi Street, from where they could get a distant glimpse of the nightly fireworks displays.

"Well?" said Mary, "what do you think?"

"Please!" urged Toby, who'd been hopping impatiently from one foot to the other.

"As always," said Jabez, "your mother is in the right of it."

Even Harriet became caught up in the excitement as the four of them danced and sang around their new home.

Two weeks later they arrive just as the gates are opening. Already a queue has been forming ahead of them, and it takes nearly half an hour before they finally step through the turnstile into the Gardens.

Jabez looks at the long line snaking around The Bobs and turns to the others. "Let's leave them till later. Save the best till last, eh? What else is there?"

Toby has got the list off pat. "Well," he says, "there's the Scenic Railway, the Water Chute, Shoot the Rapids, the Caterpillar, Jack & Jill, the Dodgems, the

Ghost Train, the Flying Sea Planes, the Ocean Wave – and for the girls, there's the River Caves."

Harriet rolls her eyes.

"Is it too early for ice creams?"

"Never too early for them," replies Jabez with a wink.

Toby's jaw hits the floor.

"Of course," says Mary, "if you have an ice cream, you'll have to wait to finish it before you can go on a ride."

Toby screws his face, wrestling with the dilemma.

"I think I might have the perfect solution," says Jabez. "Let's have our ice creams while looking round the Zoo."

"Let's go to the Aviary first," pipes up Harriet. "I want to see the parrots."

"And the pelicans," adds Toby.

"And the penguins," says Harriet.

"Then the lions and tigers," says Jabez.

"And an elephant ride to finish off with," smiles Mary.

"Finish?" asks Toby, faintly alarmed.

"Before we begin on the rides," concludes Jabez. "Come on, let's see if Giovanni's here – we might get an extra scoop each."

And off they all go, mingling with the crowds until they are no longer distinguishable on this Manchester Whitsun Bank Holiday.

They do all that they've listed and more, and when it

comes to the final ride, The Bobs, it's the middle of the afternoon, and the press of the people has lessened. Mary watches Jabez, Harriet and Toby queuing up in front of her, Toby's voice rising higher and higher with excitement, until he almost takes off, his cheeks hot and red and all puffed out, like one of those robins that hop right up to their front step sometimes, where Harriet likes to sit, as silent and still as Toby is noisy and restless, holding out bread crumbs in her hand to feed them. From time to time Mary fancies she sees a young girl with red hair and a strawberry mark upon her cheek, and she wonders if it might be Lily, who must be sixteen now, she thinks, shaking her head in wonder at the passage of time, but each time any of these girls turns her head, Mary sees it is not her.

The Bobs rears up before them, stark and dramatic against the afternoon sky. No garish colours necessary, just white paint and the dark metallic skeleton of the track, rising like a mountain, with shadowy gulleys, sunlit peaks, unimaginable twists, scaling impossible heights, plumbing unreachable depths, beneath a simple, unadorned sign: "The Bobs", picked out in a blood-deep red. The sound of it rattling through its thunderous caverns, the sight of it bucking and rearing like a wild horse, sent a shiver and a thrill through each of them as they waited in line, inching ever forward.

"Why's it called the Bobs, Father?"

"Cos it costs just a shilling a ride."

"Really?"

"Really."

"And is it the highest roller coaster in England?"

"So they say."

"And the fastest?"

"In Europe."

"And it's right here. In Manchester."

Eventually they reach the front of the queue and squeeze themselves into the wooden carriage, Jabez and Toby in front, Mary and Harriet behind.

"Hold onto your hats," calls Jabez. "That's what the sign says."

"But I haven't got a hat," answers Toby.

"Hold onto your head then," says Harriet.

And then, slowly at first, it starts to move.

The grinding, creaking rack-and-pinion pull of the chain, winding them all inexorably towards the summit, reminds Jabez instantly of the headstocks at the pit, and he wonders if his son is already imagining a life underground, as will be the futures of so many of his classmates at school. As it crests the brow of that first climb, it pauses briefly, as if, like a living thing, it has not yet decided whether to go back or continue. It hovers teasingly. Harriet just has time to look around her – that last deep breath before the plunge – and she sees Belle Vue spread below her, the people like tiny ants scurrying to some hidden purpose, and beyond to the streets that fan outwards across the whole city, almost as if she were at the epicentre of the entire world. She even catches a glimpse of her school, the Central Grammar School on Kirkmanshulme Lane, which she started the previous autumn, having been allowed to sit the entrance exam and passing it with ease. The horizon expands.

Then, having teetered this way and that, the Bobs makes up its mind. It drops its cargo like a boulder, plummeting almost vertically towards what feels like the entrance to Hades. Now everything becomes a blur of twisted metal, splintering bones, a series of thunderous roars, as the beast twists them this way then that. They feel its deep surge of power rumbling from within, its gravitational pull a force they cannot resist, its fiery breath of grease and metal hot upon their faces.

The ride lasts barely five minutes, but when Jabez, Mary, Harriet and Toby step away from the cart at the finish, their ears still ringing, their bodies still trembling, it is as if they have seen their whole lives flash before their eyes, and they are high with exhilaration.

"Can we do it again?" asks Toby at once.

Mary and Jabez exchange a grin.

"Maybe another day, son. Time we were heading home, I think."

And in truth Toby is not disappointed. For though in later years he will ride The Bobs many times, the experience will never quite match this first time.

It is early evening. Many of the crowds are leaving Belle Vue by its various gates, but just as many are streaming in, for the night is young, and the Pleasure Gardens have further thrills on offer that night.

Jabez is relieved they are leaving now, for the crowds arriving for the big fight are rowdy and raucous, already well-oiled from the sound and look of them. They are jostled by them as they squeeze through the turnstile, and as they walk away from gates, they can hear more of the roaring boys steaming round the corner, with the painted girls shrieking on each arm, already revving up for the night ahead.

Once inside the Gardens the Roaring Boys and the Painted Girls push their way to the front of the queue, climb the steps leading into the Kings Hall and, from there, head straight for the bar. The fight's not scheduled to start for another couple of hours, and there are more drinks to be had, associates to be met, bets to be laid off before then.

Alone in a far corner sits Winifred. She's now a familiar sight, recognised by many, though known by few. She keeps herself to herself and, when one of the Painted Girls raises her glass of port and lemon towards her, she does not acknowledge it.

"Stuck up cow," she hears her say, or rather reads her lips.

She takes no notice. She's humiliated herself so many times in the past decade that such remarks wash over her now.

Ten years.

Has it really been ten years since she first saw Victor and the ground, quite literally, shifted beneath her feet? She mentally checks and yes, she's right. Ten years since she stumbled by chance into that crowded Boxing Booth on Tulip Sunday. Was it just chance, she wonders? She doesn't believe in fate, not after what happened to Arthur. A happy accident then. Well, she thinks, draining her glass and ordering a refill, Victor has made her happy at times, deliriously so, but she's also never been more miserable...

*

After she'd recovered from the shock of that first meeting with him – more of an encounter than a meeting, for few actual words were spoken, but the connection that had passed between them was undeniable, like an electrical current that shot through her whole body – she hurried back home as rapidly as she could, the crowds parting before her like the Red Sea, fearful of this blood-spattered, disarrayed madwoman suddenly in their midst.

She was still shaking when she finally reached her house on Pearl Street more than an hour and a half later.

She had no recollection of how she got there, no sense at all of the four and a half miles she must have walked. She shut the front door behind her, leant her back against it and slowly sank to the floor, grateful that her mother had not lived to witness such public shame and humiliation.

Eventually she picked herself up and began the long process of boiling up water for a bath. While the first pans were heating, she hastily undressed, tearing off some of the buttons from her blouse in her sudden urge to be rid of their bloodstains and sweat. She wrapped her dressing gown around her, but even with that on, and despite the warm May evening, she still felt cold. Her body was shivering and her teeth were chattering. Finally the water was ready and she poured it steaming into the tin bath she'd dragged in front of the now lit stove in the back kitchen, unpinned her hair, removed her robe and eased herself gratefully into the almost too hot water, where at last her body began to relax.

She stayed there a long time. When she climbed out and had dried herself thoroughly, she felt sufficiently recovered to examine her thoughts and feelings with more calmness and composure. She went upstairs to her bedroom and looked at her reflection in the full length mirror on the inside of her wardrobe door. She was not unduly distressed by what she saw. She had a firm body, a trim figure and, for the most part, unblemished skin. A small scar beneath her right collar bone and another just below her rib cage were reminders of her near miraculous escape from the explosion at the munitions factory. Her face was pale, the cheeks a little hollow with dark shadows under her eyes, but such was the face of most women these days, still emerging from the aftermath of war. But she was also, she observed coolly, with a tight pursing of her thin lips, twenty-five years old, almost twenty-six, practically an old maid and, with so many hundreds of thousands of young men lost to the fighting, her prospects for finding an eligible replacement for Arthur as a future husband were not good. Statistically the odds were stacked against her. She looked again at her reflection. Nobody else, she realised, had ever gazed upon it, not even her mother since she was a little girl. Certainly not Arthur. Their courtship had been traditional. Sunday afternoon walks in Horse Close Wood, or over to Dodgeleach Brook, or along the banks of the River Tame, her arm linked through his, polite conversation tethering minutes of nervous, anxious silence, an awkward tea, more often than not with Esther and all of the brothers smirking behind the backs of their hands, and then a chaste kiss good night. After he'd joined up, and his sweet, formal proposal, down on one knee on the edge of Denton Wood, there'd been more urgent embraces, and on his few, all too brief periods of leave, they had clung to each other more hungrily, but his hands had never strayed, and nor had she encouraged him to try. They had saved their passion for their letters, each of them waiting out the war's end for when they could marry and their love could find more unbridled expression. That he should have been killed in the final week of the war had only added further weight to her loss, to the awful sense of waste that overwhelmed her.

That was almost four years ago now, and it was as though, until this afternoon, her life had been on hold, locked in the unfulfilled promises of the past, the one photograph she had of the two of them, posing as a couple after they had announced their engagement, a cruel mockery. But this afternoon what she had experienced in the Boxing Tent at Philips Park bore no resemblance whatever to the feelings she had had for Arthur. Yes, there'd been times with Arthur when she'd felt desire – the brushing of fingertips beneath the dining table during one of those torturous Sunday teas, the closeness of their fully clothed bodies at a Midsummer's Eve dance – but at the time these had all felt like stations of the cross, until they could meet at the altar. As she looked at herself now in the mirror, all outward signs of the encounter with Victor removed, she acknowledged, with shameful clarity, that what had been aroused within her must be satisfied, or she would risk becoming what some of her younger colleagues at the Telephone Exchange already whispered about her when they thought she couldn't hear them, a dried up, withered old spinster.

She made enquiries and drew up a list of all the boxing gyms in Manchester. Given the strength of his local following at Tulip Sunday, and recalling how he'd been introduced as the North West Miners Boxing Champion, she decided she would begin her search in the east of the city, in gyms close to Bradford Colliery. Her first two visits bore no fruit but at her third she struck gold. The Ardwick Lads' Club on Palmerston Street.

She was surprised on entering the building that the first face she saw was a painting of Arthur Balfour, former Prime Minister of Great Britain, who had once been the local MP, and who was still the Honorary President of the Club, but if she thought such a whiff of gentility might protect her from further humiliation, she was quickly disavowed of any such hope. Having ascertained that yes, Vic Collins did train regularly at the gymnasium there, and that yes, he was expected to be there later that evening, she was informed in no uncertain manner that this was a Lads' Club, strictly men only, and that women were not allowed under any circumstances, with no exceptions.

"At what time do you expect him to arrive?" she asked.

The man at the front desk, cigarette stub tucked behind one ear, was studying the racing page of the local newspaper and merely shrugged. "Couple of hours maybe."

"Might it be possible to leave him a message?"

"Suppose," he said, not looking up from his paper. "Can't guarantee he'd get it, though."

"Then can I wait here to see him before he goes in?"

"Doesn't come in this way."

"Oh? Is there another entrance I should wait at then?"

"Round the back." He jerked his head indeterminately. "But I wouldn't go there if I was you."

"And why is that?" asked Winifred as defiantly as she could manage.

"D'you need me to spell it out for you?"

With as much dignity as she could muster, Winifred turned on her heel and exited the club. As soon as she was outside she took a deep breath and paused. Isn't this what she'd been trying to do, she asked herself? Track him down? Having successfully done so, was she now going to quail at the first obstacle? She was prepared for it to be difficult. She had braced herself for the likely mortification. She had steeled herself for the probable rejection and the accompanying public embarrassment, but she was equally determined not to sit and moulder away alone at home every evening, not just yet at any rate. The connection she had felt so acutely when she had first seen Victor, several weeks ago now, she was certain she had seen reflected in the boxer's eyes, if only for a moment, before that look was replaced by a less ambiguous glint. She had to put her intuition to the test, to ascertain once and for all whether these last few weeks of such bitter longing had any basis in reality, or whether they were just ridiculous fantasies.

She set her mind to action and walked briskly around the back of the building, where she discovered a fire escape, an iron staircase leading up to an open door, from the other side of which she could hear the unmistakeable sounds of gloved fists hitting bags, of skipping ropes fizzing through the air, of shouted instructions and loud curses. Under the fire escape, leaning against the wall, stood a small group of young men in vests and shorts, some of them with towels draped around their shoulders, smoking cigarettes, being spoken to strenuously by slightly older men wearing bowler hats and coloured jackets over patterned waistcoats, and hanging on their arms, the painted girls she recognised from Tulip Sunday.

As Winifred approached, they all fell silent and stared. One of the girls openly started to laugh.

"Look what the cat dragged in," she said. "Little Miss La-di-Dah."

"What's that funny smell?" said another. "At first I thought it must be the Gas Works, but it's much worse than that." She was now standing very close to Winifred and spoke directly into her face. "It's the smell of respectability."

"After a bit of rough?" called the first of them.

Winifred said nothing. What could she? For one thing they were right, and for another she knew that as soon as she opened her mouth, their suspicions would be confirmed. But in the end she knew she had to face them down, or she'd never get anywhere, and she'd only regret it once she'd got home. She'd come this far, and now she was being given an opportunity to pull back, to retreat, only her pride damaged, and not pursue this folly any further, but something in her rebelled at giving up so easily. Her resolve hardened. She stood her ground and waited, while the smoke blown into her face from the girls' cigarettes cleared.

"I'm looking for Victor Collins," she said.

"Aren't we all?" said one of them.

"But is he looking for you?" said the other.

"He might be," said a voice from behind, and immediately the men put out their cigarettes and brushed past Winifred to surround him.

"There you are, Vic. We've got great news. Jack Phoenix has agreed to come over from Ireland for a fight next month. This is a real step up in class, Vic."

"Later," said the voice. "Aren't you going to introduce me first?"

Winifred turned round to face him, and at once she knew she'd been right. The same electricity flooded her veins. She smiled, held out her gloved hand, which he took, playfully kissed, and smiled back.

"To whom do I have the pleasure?" he asked, still holding onto her hand.

Winifred said nothing at first, savouring the moment.

"Winifred," she said eventually, and then, astonishing herself with her own boldness, "Winnie. Win."

"I like to win," said Vic.

"You live up to your name then."

They held each other's gaze, until Victor leaned in towards Winifred and whispered in her ear. "And so do you," then added for everyone else to hear, "Come on up and watch me train."

"She can't do that, Vic, you know the rules," said one of the men.

"Fuck the rules," said Vic, took hold of Winifred's hand and led her up the fire escape steps into the gym, where the wall of heat and sweat hit her like a fist. She stood in the doorway, knowing that if she were to take that next step and enter, it would be unequivocal, exchanging one world for another. She looked back down at her feet, while Vic waited inside, and deliberately, consciously, took note as she placed one foot firmly across the threshold, followed by the other.

Later that night in bed Winifred is wide awake. She can almost feel the blood coursing through her veins. She lies absolutely still, in case the slightest movement she might make should wake Victor, who is sprawled asleep half on top of her, his head comfortably lodged between her breasts. Winifred loves the weight of him, the rise and fall of his breathing synchronised with her own, as she begins to learn the map of him beneath her fingertips. Occasionally he makes a gentle whimpering sound, like a dog when it is dreaming, and she holds him closer to her. She hopes he will not wake for hours yet, for she fears if he does that he might simply get up and leave, especially if she has fallen asleep herself, for isn't that what men do in situations like this?

When he first entered her, the pain was sharp but brief, and soon she discovered a way of matching her rhythm to his that she found delicious. Afterwards he was surprisingly tender. He did not simply roll over to one side and light a cigarette, but stayed close to her, kissing her gently on her lips, her eyelids, her neck, her body, before gradually slipping into sleep.

When morning finally came, he awoke and still he did not leave. They made love again, this time much more slowly, and she took even greater pleasure in it.

Finally, as he was finishing getting dressed, she went downstairs to the kitchen and found it the most natural thing in the world to make them both some breakfast, which he took his time over eating, before lighting at last that inevitable cigarette.

"You'll be late for work," he said.

She smiled. "I've time yet."

"Don't come to the gym again," he said.

She looked at him questioningly.

"You've seen the sort of girls who hang out there."

"Perhaps I'm one of those girls."

He reached swiftly across the table and took her face in both his hands. "No," he said, harshly. "You're not." They held each other's gaze a long time. "*Parker's*," he said abruptly, as he moved towards the front door. "The café on St Mary's Gate. Tomorrow. Half six." And he was gone.

Of course, he didn't turn up.

Winifred waited an hour and a half, by which time she began attracting pitying looks from the waiters, and then more pressing enquiries about when she might vacate her table.

Over the next few days she drifted about in a state of uneasy limbo. If she couldn't return to the gym, she wondered, how was she going to see him again? How would she find him? After nearly a week, she began to come to her senses. This won't do, she told herself sternly. You traced him once before, you shall do so again. The thought of giving him up did not cross her mind. When she had stepped so deliberately into the gym, she had crossed the Rubicon. She had left one life behind and entered another entirely.

Emboldened, she made her way back home one evening after a particularly trying day at the Telephone Exchange, when she had had to endure the endless gossip of some of her younger colleagues poring over patterns for a wedding dress for one of them, and resolved once more to take matters into her own hands. When she saw him, loitering outside her front door as she turned into Pearl Street, she found she wasn't the least surprised.

"Where were you?" she asked. "I waited."

"Oh," he said, looking away, "something turned up."

"You'd best come in then," she said, inserting her key into the lock.

Without a pause, he threw down his cigarette, trod on it with his foot, and followed her inside.

As soon as the door was closed behind them, they were onto each other in a flash, greedily kissing and fumbling with each other's clothes. He took her where she stood, thudding into her against the back of the door, hurriedly withdrawing from her just before he came.

They stood there, panting, laughing as they caught their breath. Winifred wiped the unfamiliar sticky substance from the inside of her thigh with her hand, and placed her fingers into her mouth, savouring the salty slipperiness.

And so a pattern evolved.

They would make no firm arrangements. She would come home from work to find a hastily scribbled note posted through the letter box suggesting a time and a place, or he would be waiting for her as she came out of the Telephone Exchange, leaning nonchalantly against a lamp post, chewing a match stick. Sometimes they'd see each other several times in a week, and then not at all for a fortnight. She kept her promise not to go to the gym, but this did not prevent her from watching his fights. He dispatched Jack Phoenix in three rounds, quickly followed by two other opponents, both of whom Vic stopped in Round One. Other women would attend these contests, apart from the Painted Girls, and Winifred learned how to navigate her way between the trainers, handlers and various hangers-on to be admitted to Vic's changing room before and afterwards. She remained something of an outsider, viewed with a mixture of suspicion, amusement and incomprehension by the rest of his rag-tag entourage, but recognised and accepted, if not exactly welcomed.

She still shocked herself at just how thrilled she was by the actual fights themselves, the whirlwind of flailing fists which characterised Vic's aggressive boxing style as he stormed out of his corner at the start of each round, the frisson of fear and arousal which accompanied the vivid splatter of blood sprayed upon the canvas, the steam of sweat rising from the boxers' faces and bodies, the baying ring side spectators, and the visceral, deep-throated roar which greeted every jarring blow and knockout. After each contest, Victor would crow like a cockerel to the delight of the crowds, who'd crow back to him as one. To Winifred these made Victor less the conquering hero, more the boy who never grew up. Peter Pan. Peter Pan, who needed her, she came to understand, like Wendy, for affirmation, bedtime stories, and to help him stitch back his shadow. For a time this was enough for her too, but gradually, despite willing it to be otherwise, she found she needed something more than this perpetual Neverland, something with a future.

She first tried to raise this early one cold winter's morning, when Victor was pulling on his clothes. Ice patterns had formed on the inside of the bedroom window, and their breath was making frosty statues as they spoke.

"Must you go yet?" she asked. "It's still dark."

He nodded. "I'm on earlies."

"I don't understand."

Victor paused, aware he'd been caught off guard, a child in the act of spilling a previously sworn secret.

"Earlies?"

He sat down beside her on the edge of the bed. "Why do you think they announce me as 'North West Miners Champion'?" he said. "I still work down the pit."

Winifred sat up. She realised just how little she knew about his life apart from those times they were together.

"I need the money," he said. "It's as simple as that. The fights pay well but they're not every week, and I have bills to pay the same as everyone else."

"D'you mean, like rent?"

"Ay," he said, "among other things."

"What other things?" she asked, her senses suddenly

on high alert, the hairs on the back of her neck rising.

"Not now, love," he said, patting her arm gently. "I'll be late. Another time, eh?"

She lay back down, frowning, and it was only when she heard the front door close downstairs, and heard his footsteps echoing along the cobbled street outside in the still dark not-quite-morning, that she realised he had not kissed her goodbye.

They met again a few days later at *Parker's*. Despite his no show on that first occasion, it proved a convenient trysting place, clean, respectable, reasonably priced and, most importantly of all, anonymous. It was not that Winifred was ashamed of being seen with him, more that she liked the fact that it was clandestine, theirs and theirs alone. They had a loose arrangement that they would each try to be there every Monday evening, whether they had arranged anything or not, and Winifred religiously turned up. Occasionally Victor didn't, but mostly he did. Sometimes Winifred considered not turning up herself, just to test Victor's resolve, but when it came to it, she couldn't resist. Seeing him, being with him, whether just talking or making love, which was where it usually led, had become like a drug she couldn't do without, and she suspected – hoped – it was the same for Victor also.

And so, while she waited for him to show on this particular Monday evening, the waiter having shown her to their usual table and brought her customary glass of sherry, she rehearsed what she hoped she would have the opportunity to say to him when he arrived. She wanted to support him in whatever way she could, she would say, so that he could put all of his energies into being a boxer full time, so that he might train more and so progress to better class opponents, maybe even contest titles. To enable that, she would propose, why don't you live with me, so that you can save on rent? I earn a decent wage, she would say, and if you were fighting better class opponents, you could command higher fees and earn more yourself. Then, if it works out, she would suggest, we might think about getting married... The boldness of what she was considering even surprised herself. The thought of a woman proposing marriage to a man, and offering to support him financially, if only initially, might not go down well with most men, they might feel threatened, emasculated, but Victor wasn't most men, she countered, he didn't abide by the standard rules, he'd see that what she was proposing made sense, was an expedient, which both of them could benefit from. It was this independent, maverick streak in him that was a large part of his appeal for her. She was just going over her arguments one more time, when in he walked, sat down opposite her and, before she could say anything at all, began to speak.

"There's something I've got to say," he began. "No – don't interrupt. Let me finish first." He took a deep breath. "The thing is – I should've told you before things went so far with us..." He paused, took a deep drag on his cigarette, which he then stubbed out in the ash tray on the table, and looked at her directly, taking hold of her hands in his as he spoke. "I'm married," he said.

Winifred slowly withdrew her hands from his. Everything suddenly seemed very far away. She looked around her. She saw men and women arriving and departing, sitting down and standing up, eating, drinking, speaking to one another, discussing, arguing. She saw waiters weaving among the tables balancing trays up each arm, laden with cups and saucers, glasses and plates of food. Outside the café she saw more people passing by in both directions, with the busy flow of traffic beyond, trams and buses, horses and motors. She heard a train rumbling across the bridge over Knott Mill on Deansgate, she felt the earth trembling beneath her feet. Someone close by laughed loudly and tipped back her head, while her companion, a large, bald red-faced man mopped his brow with a handkerchief. A waiter, trying to avoid another customer's sudden outstretched arm flung back with expressive violence, dropped his tray, which fell with a clatter, spinning like a coin, catching the light as it eventually came to a halt, while what was on it flew high into the air, before falling in slow motion, each separate glass smashing into hundreds of tiny shards as they hit the floor, reflecting the café and its customers in a series of dancing, broken fragments. The sounds too decelerated in Winifred's ears, dropping in pitch, so that it felt like she was watching animals in a zoo. She looked back towards Victor, who was still speaking. She knew that he was, because she could see his lips moving, his tongue occasionally striking his teeth, but she could no

396

longer hear the words he was saying. She tried to stand up, but the world just tipped away from her, like a sink hole collapsing in on itself right before her feet. She felt a sudden rush of bile from her stomach, which she couldn't prevent from rising into her mouth. The ceiling flipped like a spinning top, and as she tried to stand, she knocked against the table and chair, both of which crashed over, and the patterned marble floor rushed to meet her as she fell.

The next thing she knew she was lying on a couch in a private room at the back of the café, a waitress was gently sponging her stained overcoat, while Victor stood, looking down on her with anxious concern.

"I'm so sorry," she said. "I haven't eaten all day." She became aware of the waitress. "Thank you. I'm sure I can manage for myself now."

The waitress scurried away, leaving Winifred and Victor alone.

"I should go," she said, after a long and awkward pause.

"Wait," said Victor, sitting down beside her. "Hear what I have to say first."

Something in the urgency of his tone told her she should stay.

He lit a cigarette, took a deep breath, and then began to speak.

"Her name's Martha," he says. "I met her on my first home leave. February, 1915. *The Station Café* on London Road. I'd just stepped off the train. Fancied a cup of tea before hitting the town. I was meant to be visiting Mabel – my sister. She's ten years older. Looked after us when we were kids. After my mum died. And now that my dad had died too, she was all I'd got left. But I didn't fancy it. 'Tha's a soldier now, our Vic,' she'd said on my last leave. 'I reckon tha' can fetch for tha'self from now on. But tha' can keep tha' things 'ere, till after t' war's over an' tha' gets tha'self fixed up wi' some place of thy own.' That's what she's like, our Mabel. Calls a spade a bloody shovel and no time for sentiment. Well – that were fine wi' me, so I was in no hurry to get myself there. Next morning'd do. So – I'm about to order a cup of tea, when I notice this girl, serving behind t' counter. Pretty thing, she were. Nice smile. She asked if I wanted sugar. I shook my head. 'That's a shame,' she said. 'Aren't I sweet enough for you?' We laughed. 'That's better,' she said. 'You look almost human when you smile.' I asked her what time she got off. 'You don't mess about, do you?' she replied. 'Why put off till tomorrow what you might do today, that's my motto.' She laughed again. 'I do like a man in uniform,' she said. 'So masterful.' That's how it started. Just joking around."

He doesn't tell Winifred about the previous few weeks at Langemarck, how terrible they'd been. The long slog of Ypres. He'd lost so many mates during that particular show, and here he was back on leave, with no place he could call home, and a pretty girl making it clear she was up for it. Whatever it might be.

Instead he says, "I wish I could say it were love. Or at least a bit of romance. But I shan't lie to you, Win.

Just a quick fuck under th' arches on t' London Road. I never thought to see her again, and she wasn't laying any claims on me neither. Couple o' days later I'm back on t' Troop Train to Dover, crossing t' Channel, then back to join my unit. So why not, I thought?"

Vic was with the Engineers. "Sapper, that's me," he'd say, to anyone who cared to ask. His job was to build the trenches. Dig out the earth, shore up all the walls with pit props and sand bags. "Not that much different to being down t' mines," he'd say. "Blastin' tunnels, makin' t' roof safe. We're like an army of bloody moles," he'd explain, especially when the ale was flowing, "burrowing our way through t' mud. But it's important to get 'em right, make 'em strong, secure."

It was like a whole city out there, a real rabbit warren of lanes and ditches, some all geared up for the duration, with oil cloths for roofs, "to keep t' radio transmitters dry," he'd say, "but more so officers'd got somewhere roomy, like, to shave and give their orders from, wi' all t' comforts of home." He must've built mile upon mile of trenches, each one getting narrower and narrower, "till you get to those just below t' front line, from where all t' pals wait to be given t' word to charge, over t' top, for King and Country…"

Winifred put her finger to Victor's lips. "I don't want to hear about the fighting," she'd say if ever he spoke about such times.

Victor had nodded then. She'd told him about Arthur, and he respected that.

Now he lights another cigarette, then carries on.

"Shells'd come over and make one hell of a mess, so we sappers, we'd be spending all of our time rebuilding 'em, where t' sides'd caved in, or water'd rushed through. It were just like when a mine flooded if you were opening up a new seam. We 'ad to work like devils, pluggin' all t' gaps an' proppin' up t' walls. We 'ad quite a reputation. 'Send for Private Collins and his Moles,' the officers'd shout..."

Victor has retreated into his memories again, and Winifred is content to let him stay there a while. She knows he'll get back to the matter in hand, and if he doesn't, she'll make sure that he does.

"One of 'em," he continues, "a Captain Willis, looked on us as some kind of lucky charm, me especially, an' 'e sort o' took me under 'is wing. I told 'im I used to box a bit, back at 'ome. Well, you should've seen the look on 'is face. Like Christmas and Birthdays all rolled into one. 'Splendid,' 'e exclaimed. 'We'll have to hold a Championship.' An' 'e did. Whenever things were quiet for a bit, he'd set up a kind of ring on a bit of open ground far away from t' front line, and I'd be pitched against all-comers. As long as I kept winnin', he'd arrange things so I didn't get to go out over t' top more than I 'ad to. I wa'n't complainin' about that. I were no shirker, an' I worked damned 'ard fixin' those trenches every single night, cleanin' up all t' mess..."

He pulls on his cigarette, thinking back.

"I did my fair share o' soldierin' too, but if sometimes me an' my pals got pulled out of a night time sortie into No Man's Land, well – that were fine wi' me."

He looks away again, conjuring it all up before him.

"The boxin' weren't exactly what you might call Queensberry Rules. Bare-knuckle, near enough, just a few strips o' calico saved from our puttees'd be wrapped around our fists, an' away we'd go 'ammer an' tong, tryin' to knock seven bells out of each other. I never lost. A few bloody noses an' black eyes, sore ribs an' split lips, an' I were winded a fair few times, but no one got the better of me. That's how I come by my nickname, Vic 'The Volcano' Collins, an' it sort o' stuck. The thing is, I reckoned that if I flailed my arms fast enough, an' threw as many punches as I could in t' shortest possible time, mebbe I could just keep one step ahead of whatever might be comin' down… "

He pauses. He knows he is avoiding the real issue, and he can see the patient expression on Winifred's face becoming taut and strained. He doesn't tell her the real story about how he acquired his nickname, about the ambush, a couple of days before the Second Battle of Ypres began, when one of those night time sorties into No Man's Land to lay signalling wire, was rumbled and went terribly wrong. An advanced party of the enemy took them all by surprise. Taking advantage of a moonless night, Victor was alerted by a sudden hail of sniper fire, and the next thing he knew their trench had been overrun by up to fifty German soldiers, who were laying into them with their bayonets and rifle butts. This was hand to hand combat, visceral and real, right there in his face, so unlike the featureless anonymity of tank and shell, howitzer and mortar, canon and pounder.

Up close and personal, feeling the heat of body and breath, an eye-gouging, tongue-ripping, neck-snapping kind of war, when instinct kicked in, senses on high alert, every hair follicle and skin cell bristling, like the twitching of barbed wire snagged by the slightest gust, the knife to the heart, the fist to the face, Victor wading in up to the elbows in gore, the windmill arms, the pressed boot to the head, full weight exerted, forcing it down, deeper and deeper, into the mud till nose and mouth were blocked, and all life drained away, all that is except his own, so that when he thrust himself harder and harder into Martha under the railway arches on the London Road, her cries of pleasure drowned by the goods trains rattling overhead, or into the inexhaustible stream of girls and women in the French and Belgian villages, he felt immortal, newly alive with each coupling, and he crowed like a cockerel to usher in the day.

Winifred waits for him to return to her, takes his face gently in her hand and guides it towards her. "Martha?" she says.

"Ay."

She knows what's coming, can guess the letter, the stark words on the page which, even when the ink begins to smudge in a sharp squall of rain as he reads them, refuse to disappear.

"It were Mabel who wrote first. 'You bloody idiot,' she said. 'You're in a right mess, now, aren't you? Well, lad, I hope you'll do the decent thing…?' The decent thing," adds Victor with a shake of the head. "To be fair to 'er, Martha didn't ask for 'owt. Just wrote a few months later to say she'd 'ad a boy, and did I mind if she called 'im Joe?"

Winifred says nothing. She knows there's more and waits for him to finish.

"I married her on my next leave. Mabel grudgingly minded the baby, so as we'd look like dozens of other rushed weddings in the Registry Office at Ashton Town Hall that weekend – a soldier home on leave marrying his sweetheart." He stubs out his cigarette bitterly. "Martha stayed with her mother after, said she'd look for somewhere we might rent together once the war was over, but seeing as how there was no way of knowing when that would be, she'd wait till it actually finished, if it was all the same to me…"

"And did she?" Winifred can't bear to ask the questions but neither can she help herself.

"She went to the Manager at the Colliery and got herself put on a list."

"And that's the real reason you still work down the pit as well as box?"

"I can't just leave 'em to fend for theirselves. The boy needs a roof over 'is head."

"And a father."

"Yes."

"How old is Joe now? Seven?"

Victor nods. "The truth is, Martha and I quickly realised we 'ad absolutely nowt else in common. She can hardly bear t' sight o' me now. Nor me her," he adds, looking away again.

"Your sister was right. You did do the decent thing. But you don't have to stay there. Not any more.

Divorce her. You can still provide for Joe. He can come and stay with us sometimes. After we're married."

Victor grabs Winifred's wrist. "Are you not listening to me? That's not going to happen."

"Victor, please. You're hurting me. What do you mean, it's not going to happen?"

"Because she won't divorce me, that's why. Don't you think I 'aven't asked her? God knows I've given 'er cause enough. It's not like you're the first woman I've been unfaithful with."

He releases her wrist. Winifred rubs it painfully. "I know that," she says quietly, "but…"

"But what?" He juts his chin towards her belligerently.

"I also know that it's different for you with me, isn't it? Than with any of the others?"

She holds his gaze a long time. Eventually he looks away, takes another cigarette from the packet and tries to light it, but his hands are shaking.

He nods.

"Say it," says Winifred, then repeats it louder. "Say it."

"Yes," he says finally. "It's different."

He tries again to light his cigarette. She takes his hand in her own, they strike the match together. It sparks and she guides it towards the cigarette, gently clamped between his lips, and watches the end glow.

Ten years later Winifred is sitting in a corner of the bar at The Kings Hall, Belle Vue, less than two hours

404

before Victor's fight is scheduled to start.

It's been five years now since Victor tried to persuade Martha to grant him a divorce for the last time.

"What did she say?" asked Winifred, hardly daring to hope.

"Nowt," he said. "She just laughed. Like she always does. 'You've made your bed,' she said, 'you'll have to lie in it'. Fuck it. I've left her."

Winifred lifted a hand to her mouth. "But what about Joe?"

"He's not a baby any more. He's twelve now, just a few weeks shy of thirteen. He'll be leaving school next year an' joining me down t' pit after that. He knows how things stand between 'is mother an' me. I reckon he'll be a lot better off wi'out his mum an' dad shoutin' at one another all t' time."

Winifred held her breath. "And where will you go?"

Victor looked at her. An amused smile passed his lips. "Where d'you think, you daft beggar?"

She felt all the tension leave her body, a tension she realised she must have been holding on to for years, and began to cry.

"And here's me, thinking you'd be happy."

She looked across to him. His smile broadened.

"It won't be all plain sailing," he said. "I know that. But marriage is only a bit of paper, eh love? And it's not all that it's cracked up to be neither."

Winifred was now laughing too, wiping her eyes, agreeing.

"I'm not much to write home about," he said finally,

"but I'm all yours. What do you say? Shall we give it a go?"

She nodded. "We'll work it out," she said.

Victor was right. It wasn't all plain sailing. While Winifred's neighbours had turned a blind eye to the occasional visits of what they referred to behind her back as "her gentleman caller", they strongly disapproved of him being next door on a permanent basis, "living in sin", as they termed it, and things proved equally tricky for her at work, at the Telephone Exchange. The irony was that had she and Victor been free to marry, in all likelihood her bosses would have asked her to leave, for theirs was a policy which did not employ married women, and so she was grudgingly permitted to stay, while at the same time being repeatedly and pointedly passed over for any promotion prospects that might otherwise have come her way. When, once, she questioned this, though nothing was mentioned in so many words, she was left in no doubt that the company regarded itself as being what they referred to as "custodians of Christian morals", and throats were awkwardly cleared and her interview was concluded with a perfunctory "Will that be all, Miss Holt?"

But she had a job, as did Victor. He still worked down the pit, he continued to train at the gym at Ardwick Lads' Club several nights a week, and he fought regularly, every two or three months. He remained undefeated, but still only against undistinguished opponents, and then came his big chance. This night. The Kings Hall. Against Leonard "Len" Benker Johnson.

Born, like Victor was, in Clayton, less than two miles from Belle Vue, Len now lived in Moss Side, though for most of the time he was on the road. Unlike Victor, Len boxed full time. He began when the Crossley Engine Works, where he was a foundryman, went on strike, and he fought a couple of amateur bouts in a booth at Gorton Fair run by the legendary Bert Hughes, both of which he won by a knockout, persuading him to try his luck as a professional. His career took him all over the country, then all over the world. In England he fought in London, Leeds, Sheffield and Birmingham, as well as frequently in Manchester, while he also fought many times in Australia, where he defeated Tiger Jack Payne to become the British Empire Middleweight Champion, a title he defended successfully three times, and in Europe, where he defeated Maurice Prunier and Pierre Gandon in France, Leone Jacovacci and Giuseppe Malerba in Italy, Jack Etienne and Louis Westrenraedt in Belgium, Ignacio Ara in Spain and Piet Brand in Holland, before returning to England to defeat Michele Bonaglia of Italy at Belle Vue to become the Champion of Europe also.

But because Len was of mixed race, neither of these titles was recognised by the British Board of Boxing Control. In the eyes of the public, though, he was hailed a true champion and became something of a folk hero.

Disillusioned by the boxing establishment, Johnson toured his own booth, challenging all comers, competing as frequently as twice each month, and the top fighters in the country were all keen to pit their skills against him. Among these was Len Harvey, the official champion of Britain, Europe and the Empire, who recognised in Johnson a fighter of rare ability and courage, and who had agreed to a title fight with him at the Royal Albert Hall in London the next month. The whole of boxing was talking about this bout, a rematch from when Johnson had defeated Harvey some three years before, even though the Board of Control still refused to sanction it, and Leonard "Len" Benker Johnson was using this fight tonight against Victor as a warm-up just a fortnight before.

As soon as the contest was announced, the excitement in the city grew to a fever pitch. Two home grown heroes. One a true champion, no matter what the authorities might say. The other an undefeated local legend, albeit against far less distinguished opponents. Most pundits favoured Johnson to win, but Victor had his followers, passionate and plentiful, who saw this as his long-awaited big chance.

Now, with only an hour to go, Winifred sits nervously in the bar. She orders a second drink, something she never does, and takes it to the window. Outside the crowds are arriving in huge numbers. She looks beyond them to The Bobs, its hulking silhouette starkly etched against the night sky. She watches the winding gear cranking ever tighter as it hauls each wagon up towards the summit, hears the clanking of its chains groan and squeal, before plummeting earthwards with a sickening jolt. Her own stomach is performing similar somersaults when she hears a voice behind her.

She turns. It's Joe. He'd promised to come and here he is, scrubbed and spruced up, for a night out on the town, with shining cheeks and brylcreemed hair. He leans and kisses Winifred on the cheek. Since Victor left his mother, he's been a regular visitor to her house – *our* house, thinks Winifred now, a family house, if not quite in the conventional sense, an unexpected, unlooked for bonus, and so highly cherished.

"Look at you," she says, holding his shoulders and leaning back to take him all in. "You look so handsome."

Joe's shining cheeks redden. "It's a big night," he says. "Thought I'd make an effort."

He is seventeen now and works down the pit with his father. The labour has made him fill out, grow a couple of inches.

"How's he holding up?"

"Alright, I think. I've not been to see him."

Joe knows that she would like to, just to let Victor know she's there, with him all the way, but that before a fight his father prefers to be undisturbed, on his own, just his trainer from the gym, going through their usual pre-fight rituals, the bandaging of the fingers before tying on the gloves, the rubbing of embrocation into every muscle, a last final work-out with the rope. The trick with Victor is to keep all that pent up energy sealed in as tightly as he can, before the volcano erupts once that first bell is rung. If he were to let it blow before then, he'd have nothing left to expend once the fight begins.

The bar is filling up, the crowds clamouring for that last drink before entering the hall. Joe sees Winifred glance towards the clock on the wall. Less than half an hour to go.

"Come on," he says," let's go in."

They make their way past the gauntlet of the Painted Girls. The presence of Joe does not escape their notice, but he seems not to hear their crude remarks or, if he does, he pays them no heed.

Once inside the Hall itself, Winifred is struck at once by the wall of heat, the rising tide of expectation crashing like waves in the peculiarly echoing acoustic of the venue, together with the unmistakeable smell of ale, sweat, excitement and fear, all of which threaten to drown her. She feels her skin and clothes becoming moist. She tries to remember to breathe but is immediately assailed by the overwhelming fug of tobacco smoke, through which she must peer as she and Joe make their way towards their ringside seats. Each step down the raked auditorium takes her closer to the ring which, the nearer she gets to it, rises up higher before her, so that by the time she reaches it, the canvas floor is barely above the level of her eyes.

The sound of the technician throwing the switch to bring up the full, fierce glare of the arc lights directly overhead resonates around the Hall, and the crowds begin a ritualised drumming of feet upon the wooden floor, which grows louder and louder, drowned only by the loud fanfares that greet the arrival of the two boxers. Follow spots pick out each one as they enter down different aisles, making their royal progress towards the ring, applauded and cheered by the jumping crowds. Victor passes right by Winifred and Joe, acknowledging them with the briefest of nods, before climbing at last into the ring, where immediately he begins to shuffle and bounce from foot to foot, the hood of his dressing gown over his head, shadow boxing furiously. Even though she cannot see his face, Winifred senses just how wired he is. Johnson meanwhile is much calmer. He's used to such occasions, takes in the cheers and adulation, raises his right arm in an acknowledging wave, effortlessly vaults the ropes, landing lightly and silently onto the canvas like a cat, and then proceeds to patrol the perimeter as if marking his territory, re-staking his claim.

The Master of Ceremonies pulls down the microphone lowered to him from above and begins to introduce the two contestants.

"My Lords, Ladies and Gentlemen, the Kings Hall Belle Vue warmly welcomes you all tonight to the fight that everyone's been talking about, a true Clash of the Titans, between Two Sons of the City, Manchester's Finest, in a ten round middleweight contest, here at the Home of Boxing. In the red corner, please show your appreciation for the Local Hero, the Undefeated North West Miners Champion, Vic "The Volcano" Collins!"

His words rises to a climax and are greeted by a deep, guttural, warrior-like roar from the many hundreds of Victor's supporters, an army of voices thundering their way up from a deep mine miles underground.

"Vic, Vic, Vic, Vic," they chant, on and on, like a mighty machine pounding at a rock.

Victor continues to shadow box, not once breaking his focus or concentration, not allowing himself to be distracted by what he hears or feels surging through him.

"And in the blue corner, making a welcome return to The Kings Hall, scene of so many of his spectacular triumphs – who will ever forget his demolition of Gipsy Daniels, the British Light Heavyweight Champion, or the way he dispatched Roland Todd, the former Cruiserweight Champion of Europe, in such spectacular fashion, before packed houses here at Belle Vue? Will you please welcome The Crossley Cannonball, The Moss Side Machine Gun, The Peerless Prince of Darkness, A True Champion, The One, The Only, Leonard "Len" Benker Johnson!"

The roar which greets this surpasses even that of Victor's, but each set of fans, as passionate as they are in support of their own favourite, bear no rancour towards their opponent, applauding the other with genuine warmth and admiration.

The referee calls the two fighters together in the centre of the ring as he gives them their final instructions. Victor is still shifting his weight constantly from foot to foot, while Johnson stands calm and still. There seems no animosity between them, no nose-to-nose stares, just quiet respect and, with a final touch to each other's gloves, they retreat to their corners, discard their robes, listen to the last second advice from their trainers, as they wait for the bell for the first round to signal the start of the contest. The crowd can barely contain its excitement. The stamping and cheering give way to the full-throated bay of a hunting animal as the bell at last sounds and the two fighters launch themselves into the centre of the ring.

Victor storms out a hurricane as he always does, his arms flailing like pistons in a blur of speed and power. If anything, he's faster than he's ever been before, but Johnson is wise to him. He dances lightly, backwards round the ring, keeping Victor at bay with a series of long, raking jabs. The contrast in styles could not be more marked. The sheer volume of punches thrown by Victor means that inevitably some of them land, but only glancingly, none of them tellingly, most being blocked by Johnson's gloves and forearms. The round appears to end in the merest blink of an eye, and both fighters practically jog back to their corners.

Winifred and Joe look at one another, catching their own breath.

"A good start," shouts Joe above the din and racket all around them.

"Do you think so?" asks Winifred.

"Definitely," says Joe. "This was never going to be a pushover. Johnson's a different class from those who Dad normally fights."

"Yes," agrees Winifred, "you're right," and she tries to manage a smile.

Two of the Painted Girls are parading round the

edges of the ring, holding up cards announcing the imminent arrival of Round 2 – a new innovation being tried by the promoters at Belle Vue – swaying their hips from side to side, clearly enjoying the wolf whistles and cat calls.

The bell for the second round sounds and it's a repeat of what happened in the first: Victor chasing Johnson round the ring, throwing punch after punch but landing few, with Johnson keeping him at bay with the same insistent disciplined jab.

Round 3 produces the same pattern. The intensity of the contest is unrelenting and the crowd is completely caught up with the tactical battle, appreciating the contrasting styles and skills of each.

Then, towards the middle of Round 4, Victor's pace begins to falter and slow, barely perceptibly, but sufficiently to be picked up on by the *cognoscenti* close to ringside, who whisper to one another worriedly, and even more so by Johnson himself, who seizes upon this slightest hint of hesitation by Victor immediately. He steps forward for the first time, advancing decisively, landing three probing jabs into Victor's face, which momentarily stop him in his racks, before he gathers himself and launches his most furious assault yet to finish the round strongly, but when the bells goes at the end, it does not escape Winifred's notice that whereas Johnson turns on his heels and positively bounces back to his corner, Victor is breathing heavily.

The *cognoscenti* nod knowingly to one another, and at once the odds against a win for Victor lengthen in the Hall.

Joe tries to be encouraging. "Did you see the way Dad came back after taking those three blows to the head?" he says excitedly.

Winifred shakes her head. She can't bring herself to answer. She had flinched with each one of those blows and still feels too winded to speak. The truth is Victor has barely had to fight beyond three rounds, and never at this intensity. Normally his fights finish before then, with Victor having overwhelmed his opponents with his power and speed, the "volcano" effect, the sheer force of his will. Once or twice, she recalls, he has fought beyond that, and although she knows he has trained for this fight by concentrating almost exclusively on developing and increasing his stamina, suspecting it would last much longer than he is used to, she is more concerned than she can bring herself to admit to Joe by how hard Victor is breathing still in his corner, when the bell rings for Round 5.

Victor once more charges out of his corner, but he is less controlled than he has been, his desperation to try and finish the bout quickly writ large on every punch he throws, and Johnson begins to pick him off easily. After less than a minute Johnson is advancing towards Victor once again, landing that long left jab with alarming ease and penetration. Winifred turns her eyes away as Victor's head rocks back with each blow he receives. Unlike the first two rounds, this round seems to last a lifetime, the ring feels suddenly smaller and Victor is now the one retreating, being picked off by Johnson like apples from a tree.

Round 6 sees Johnson attacking from the start.

Victor's defence simply cannot cope with Johnson's jab, and Johnson is now emboldened to throw in some right hand blows as well, hooks and upper cuts to the body and head, and Victor's eyes are starting to puff up and close. A free-flowing combination of lefts and rights from Johnson towards the end of the round has Victor back against the ropes completely defenceless and unable to halt the unstoppable surge of blows he is taking. The crowd is on its feet and is shouting so loudly that the boxers do not hear the bell, and the referee has to intervene to prevent Johnson from finishing the contest there and then. Once more he dances back to his corner, while Victor can barely see his way back to his own.

Winifred looks down at her feet, covering her ears with her hands. The Hall appears to be swimming around her, like one of those rides in the fairground just outside, or that time when she fainted in *Parker's* after Victor had first told her he was married. She becomes aware of Joe's arm around her shoulder, lifting her back to sit up straight.

"It looks bad, I know, but you can't let Dad see you looking so worried. If he looks this way, we've got to smile, clench our fists, give him a thumbs up, let him know we still believe in him, that he can still win."

"But he can't, Joe. Not this time."

"It only takes one punch. Dad won't give up, you'll see."

When Round 7 starts, it looks as though Joe might be right after all. Victor comes out swinging and succeeds in landing a strong right to Johnson's head, which clearly shocks him. He quickly resumes his defensive pose, patiently waiting to pick off Victor with more jabs, and it doesn't take long before Victor once more runs out of steam. It's as if he can barely lift his arms, as though his gloves are weighted with iron hammers that lower his guard and leave him open to Johnson's attacks, which now come in wave after wave. Blow after blow lands home. One particularly powerful punch to the stomach makes the crowd audibly gasp, as if they themselves have been hit, and doubles him up, which Johnson follows up immediately with a left upper cut and a right to the head, and Victor is on the canvas, the first knock down he has ever experienced.

He looks about him, trying to get his bearings, blinded by the overhead lights and the flashing, popping cameras exploding all around him. In between each flash and pop he sees faces shouting, screaming, urging him to get back up. He catches sight of Winifred, her hands drawn up to the sides of her face, her clothes spattered in blood, *his* blood (for Johnson doesn't appear to have a mark on him anywhere), her eyes pleading with him – but to do what? Throw in the towel or somehow keep going? Instinct drags him back to his feet just as the sound of the referee's voice counting "seven – eight – nine" reaches his consciousness. The referee looks into his eyes, appears to be satisfied that the fight can continue, and then stands back, as Johnson once more comes roaring back for the kill, scenting the fight to be nearly over. Another combination of rights and lefts to the head and body send Victor crashing to the canvas once more.

This time, he knows, there's no getting up. The referee counts relentlessly on. "Five – six – seven…" The crowd are on their feet, stamping and cheering. Johnson stands respectfully in a neutral corner waiting for the inevitable. But just at that moment, Victor is quite literally saved by the bell, which sounds for the end of the round. The referee had only reached "eight" and so the contest is technically not over. Victor's trainer leaps into the ring and helps him to his feet and back to his corner. In the now less than one minute before the start of the next round he frantically tries to revive him, all the while shouting instructions, not knowing whether they are being heard or not.

All too soon they are on their feet for Round 8. No volcano charge from Victor this time. In a cruel reverse of the opening exchanges it is now Johnson who comes relentlessly forward, while Victor tries to defend as best he can, using the ropes to dodge beneath Johnson's long arms, holding his own arms high to form a shield for his face and body. But inevitably Johnson's superior ring craft shows through. He begins to find his target with increasing accuracy as the round wears on and Victor's stamina again begins to drain away from him. His arms drop for the briefest of moments, and immediately Johnson pounces and unleashes another shuddering series of punches, all of which land and leave their mark. Victor's body is showing purple bruises around the ribs. Both eyes are almost completely closed. There is a cut above his right eyebrow, which is flowing freely, the blood running into his eye, even though it can barely open. His nose is spread across his face, and his lips are split.

As the round nears its end, there is nothing it seems that Victor can now do to prevent blow after blow from raining down upon him. Johnson has him pinned against the ropes, which Victor, an image rising from the dim recesses of his memory, loops around his arms, just as he remembers an opponent did against him in a tent on Philips Park ten years ago one Tulip Sunday, the day he first saw Winifred, and clings on to them tightly, so that whatever punches Johnson throws at him, he will not be knocked out.

When the bell mercifully brings the round to a close, Victor can barely move. The crowd rise to their feet in a salute to his courage. Johnson acknowledges this and sportingly helps Victor back to his corner before returning to his own, a gesture that brings even more cheers and applause from the crowd.

Winifred is in shock. Even Joe can think of nothing to say now. In her heart she wants the referee to intervene, to stop the fight, to tell Victor that he can't continue, but she knows that that is not the way of things, nor what the rest of the crowd, or Victor, would want. She can only hang on and wait. Two more rounds to go. Just six minutes. But she knows they will seem more like six hours.

The applause has not ceased throughout the break between rounds, and Victor's supporters begin again their deep-throated rallying cry of support for their champion.

"Vic, Vic, Vic, Vic!" On and on, so that even Johnson's supporters are moved to take it up too.

Johnson looks around, recognising the mood in the Hall. He nods his head and smiles, raising his gloves as if to urge the crowd to keep on chanting.

"Vic, Vic, Vic, Vic!"

For the final two rounds Johnson delivers a master class. He dances round the ring, flicking out remorselessly that long left jab, every one of which lands somewhere on Victor, following them up occasionally, though not relentlessly, with a few rights to both body and head. Each one stops Victor in his tracks, but Johnson takes great care now not to unleash anything so powerful that would knock him out, nor does his apparent leniency appear patronising or demeaning. On the contrary, for two rounds he continues to show his beaten opponent the utmost respect, ruthlessly exposing Victor's defensive shortcomings, while honouring his courage with dignity.

As the fight nears its end, the crowd count down as one the final ten seconds and, when the final bell is rung, the applause and cheers for both boxers is prolonged and loud. The referee immediately holds up Johnson's arm as the clear winner, who at once walks across the ring to where Victor is out on his feet and raises his arm in genuine admiration. Victor acknowledges the ovation he is receiving as best he can, but as his trainer intervenes to help him back to his stool in his corner, he collapses in complete exhaustion.

The trumpeters play a victory fanfare to accompany Johnson's noble progress around the ring, from where he bows to all four sides of the auditorium, receiving the acclamation of the still cheering crowd, before being carried aloft in triumph. This has been a useful warm up for his important rematch with Len Harvey in London in a fortnight's time, one that has not taken too much out of him, his face unmarked, his breathing easy, his body having barely broken a sweat, but perhaps more than he realises at this moment of victory, for he will lose the bout with Harvey narrowly on points.

Victor meanwhile finds he is unable to rise from his stool. His legs have buckled beneath him, his breath is shallow and laboured, and his face is cut and swollen almost beyond recognition. Joe rushes to his father's side and, together with his trainer, helps Victor painfully slowly to make the seemingly interminable walk back to the changing rooms at the back of the Hall. Mostly this goes unnoticed, except for those members of the crowd he passes directly, who fall silent, gasp inwardly at the sight of his injuries witnessed in such close proximity, or murmur their heartfelt words of tribute to him, none of which he registers or hears. By the time he reaches the changing room, Winifred is already there, waiting for him with towels and sponges and bowls of hot water.

A doctor has been summoned, who examines him carefully. He talks of facial contusions, abrasions, lacerations, a broken nose, several fractured ribs, possible subdural *haematoma* and urges immediate admission to hospital. At the mention of this Victor becomes increasingly agitated, so that Winifred is required to calm him with gentle hands and soothing words that no one hears but him.

Afterwards she speaks privately with the Doctor, who finally acquiesces that Victor can perhaps be treated at home, so long as Winifred does exactly what he prescribes, insisting that Victor will require a long period of absolute rest if he is to recover, which he may never fully do, and that he must – no room whatsoever here for argument or negotiation – never box again.

"You have my word," says Winifred.

A taxi is arranged, and they quietly slip away through a side door.

They don't hear the sudden commotion that has erupted above them, as the taxi arrives to take them home.

A mob of more than five hundred masked blackshirts storm into the main body of the Hall, accompanied by a large number of police officers, who appear to be acting as their protectors, forming a cordon to separate them from the confused audience still inside. Marching down the central aisle is none other than Oswald Mosley. A loud chorus of boos greets him as more and more of the crowd recognise who he is. Aping Mussolini he goose-steps his way into the boxing ring, now surrounded by his bodyguards all of them brandishing baseball bats and other wooden clubs, pulls down the microphone and begins to address the stunned and angry throng.

In the preceding weeks Mosley and his blackshirts have been increasingly active across the city – in Hyndman Hall in Salford, at Queen's Park in Harpurhey, even at the Free Trade Hall in the centre of the city, in a mockery of that establishment's noble, radical tradition. He'd opened new branches of the British Union of Fascists in Stretford, Altrincham, Rusholme and Hulme, Blackley, Oldham, Bury and Rochdale, even in nearby Ashton, although there he'd been given short shrift by angry miners, many of whom fill The Kings Hall tonight. Fascist slogans had been chalked up in Boggart Hole Clough, Platt Fields, as well as Philips Park. Jabez had reported the defacements to Mr Pettigrew, and the Manchester Parks Committee had complained to the Police about the escalating costs of having to continually whitewash the offending remarks, but still the enforcers of the law seemed inclined to turn a blind eye (and ear) to his anti-Jewish speeches, his racial slurs and comments, and his constant stirring up of hatred and vitriol. Now he stands before the baying mob at Belle Vue, comparing those who try to speak against him to the animals in the zoo outside.

"Christians, awake!" he cries, but before he can say anything more, several members of the audience have begun to orchestrate a wall of noise of their own in an attempt to drown him out.

"Down with Fascism," they chant. "Down with blackshirt thugs," while a group of them has the presence of mind to spirit Len Johnson back to the changing rooms safe and unseen.

Mosley continues to try and make his speech, but despite the microphone, his words go unheard. He begins to resemble a demented marionette with his stiff arms gesturing wildly, while all around him the crowd begins to sing with fervour and pride *The Red Flag* and *The Internationale*.

> *"The people's flag is deepest red*
> *It shrouded oft our martyred dead*
> *And 'ere their limbs grew stiff and cold*
> *Their hearts' blood dyed to every fold…"*

The blackshirts, rapping their clubs into the palms of their hands, begin to advance towards the crowds who remain unmoved and who continue to sing undaunted.

> *"Then raise the scarlet standard high*
> *Beneath its folds we'll live and die*
> *Though cowards flinch and traitors sneer*
> *We'll keep the red flag flying here…"*

The blackshirts are now standing inches away from the crowd on all four sides of the ring, while Mosley continues to rant and rave unheard. The crowd stands firm, still singing right into the masked faces of the blackshirts. Mosley releases the microphone and totters nervously, a doll about to topple over, his hands flapping like a seal's by his side, his mouth opening and shutting, as if gasping for air. The crowd stops singing. There is a moment's silence, taut and stretched as a humming electric wire, like The Bobs outside just before it plunges to its very first stomach churning drop, and then both sides launch themselves at one another. Chairs are thrown through the air, or cracked against ribs and skulls. The police, sensing a potential bloodbath, rush towards the blackshirts, creating a narrow corridor through which they might usher their leader away to safety, quickly following on behind in close and desperate pursuit, running the gauntlet of the mocking taunts and jibes from the crowds held back behind the wavering thin blue line of the constables, who beat their own hasty retreat as quickly as they dare, while the crowd delights in singing after them, supporters of Victor and Johnson united as one, celebrating courage and dignity in the face of injustice and prejudice, as the cowards flee, vanquished and humiliated, their tails between their legs, nursing their sore heads and bruised pride.

"Pack up all your cares and woe
There they go, running low
Bye-bye, Blackshirts

Let somebody shine the light
We'll be singing home tonight
Bye-bye, Blackshirts…"

Back in Denton Joe and Winifred help Victor to navigate the slow, painful ascent to the bedroom. Winifred undresses him as carefully as she can. The slightest touch is an agony to him. Eventually he slips into a deep and troubled sleep, with disorienting dreams of falling down a deep long abandoned mine shaft, its walls collapsing in around him, losing himself in the maze of trenches he had once dug on the Western Front, each of them leading to a dead end where, waiting for him, was Leonard "Len" Benker Johnson with another howitzer fired straight at him, and a woman's voice mocking him mercilessly, "Tha's made tha' bed, tha'll have to lie in't," over and over, gradually becoming another, urging him to "do the decent thing, do the decent thing", and then a gentler, stronger voice saying, "It's different with me, different with me", before opening curtains at a window, a silhouette against the sun streaming through, gradually slipping into focus, her pale face leaning over him, looking into his eyes, as her hand gently sponges his face and forehead with tiny drops of cool, welcome water. "We'll work it out," she says. "We'll work it out."

He opens his dry, cracked lips and tries to speak, but his throat doesn't seem able to work properly. The woman squeezes a few more precious drops of water onto his lips, places one hand at the back of his neck and helps him to lift his head a few painful inches from the pillow.

"I'm all yours," he says, his voice barely a whisper. "I'm all yours."

In a different bedroom five and a half miles away upstairs in The Lodge at Philips Park, Jabez and Mary are wrapped in each other's warm embrace, unaware of the violent events which have unfolded at Belle Vue since they left at the end of their big day out with the children, who sleep peacefully in the next room, having watched the distant fireworks from the window at the top of their house, dreaming of Shooting the Rapids, the Scenic Railway, Elephant Rides and the Ghost Train, and the unforgettable thrill of that first plummeting fall on The Bobs, and the dizzying climb back up afterwards.

"I love you, Mary," whispers Jabez.

"I love you too," smiles back Mary, pulling Jabez towards her.

12

1942

Inside Studio 1 of Broadcasting House in Portland Place, London the red light flashes and the six pips of the Greenwich Time Signal commence, followed by the reassuring, sonorous chimes of Big Ben. Outside the glass booth of the recording studio the producer counts down with his fingers then points back to the news reader inside to begin.

LIDELL:

Good evening. This is the BBC Home Service. It is now time for the nightly 9 o'clock news with me, Alvar Lidell, reading it.

As has been our custom since 1940 we shall begin this broadcast with a minute's silence in which we invite listeners across the world to dedicate their prayer or contemplation to those serving overseas.

The minute's silence passes.

LIDELL:

British Forces of the Eighth Army under the command of Field Marshall Montgomery have launched a major counter offensive against Rommel's 21st Panzer Division at Gazala in the Cauldron.

Heavy bombing raids have been carried out by the Royal Air Force over several major industrial sites in Germany, mainly concentrating on Essen.

In the Pacific US Naval forces have engaged the Japanese fleet under the command of Admiral Nugamo around the island of Midway. Both sides have suffered heavy losses but the island's airbase remains operational.

Here at home the British Coal Industry has been nationalised the better to coordinate the transport of supplies to where they are needed most.

And on a lighter note, tomorrow sees the opening of a new exhibition at the Victoria Museum of Manchester, where the skeleton of the much-loved elephant Maharajah will be on public display to commemorate the sixtieth anniversary of his death. Maharajah famously walked all the way from Edinburgh to Manchester seventy years ago in 1872 to become a major attraction at the Belle Vue Zoological Gardens. Now Mancunians will be able to see their beloved friend once again for free and pay their respects…

*

Harriet switches off the radio in the sitting room of The Lodge in Phillips Park and continues her knitting. She is eager to finish it this evening, so that she can enclose the new socks in the letter she's been writing to Paul, her fiancé, currently in an undisclosed location because of the war.

... tomorrow I am taking the children on a visit to the museum to see the skeleton of that old elephant who used to give rides at Belle Vue. They're so excited. All day they've been asking me questions. "Miss, will it be scary? I don't like ghosts." I reassure them of course that it's not a ghost, but once one of them starts, it's like the opening of the flood gates, and it's all they can think of. "Miss, will it chase us?" "Miss will it come back to life?" They're always asking me questions about dying these days. Hardly surprising, I suppose. But a trip outside the school will be good for them, a break from the usual routine, and it is a genuinely interesting artefact of local history. We were even on the 9 o'clock news tonight. Little Gracie was just going to bed when she heard it, and it made her even more excited than she already is.

I think I'll sign off now, my love. My parents ask me to send you their love and best wishes for a safe return, which we all hope will be soon. It's been too long since we last saw one another, but receiving your letters more than makes up for it. I am always amazed – and grateful – when I read that you got my latest letter. It's impossible to imagine, when I pop the envelope into the post box at the entrance to the park, that it somehow wends its way to you. I wish I knew exactly where you were, so I could look at the spot on the map in an atlas, but I understand the reasons why you are not allowed to say.

All my love, as always, darling. Wish me luck for tomorrow!

Harriet x

*

Mary watches Gracie getting herself ready for school the next morning in a state of surprise and astonishment, a state she's been in ever since she was born just over nine years ago.

The first surprise was that she was conceived at all, the night the family came home from their trip to ride The Bobs at Belle Vue in such high spirits, which Mary and Jabez had carried with them right through till morning. After she'd lost her third child, almost at full term, not long after that first Tulip Sunday twenty years before, she was told that it was unlikely she'd have any more children. There'd been more miscarriages since, but usually early on, before she'd had time to start hoping, and so when she became pregnant again, she steeled herself for what she was sure would follow. But the weeks passed, and then the months, and Mary continued to bloom. The pregnancy proceeded almost like Harriet's and Toby's had, and she and Jabez crossed their fingers and dared to dream. "If it's a boy, we'll call him Robert," joked Jabez, "and if it's a girl,

Roberta." "No we won't," laughed Mary, playfully punching her husband on the arm.

When Grace was born, a month early – "you've always been in a hurry," they'd tease her later – she was small but strong. Her first cries were lusty and loud. "This one's going to make sure she gets heard," joked the midwife, but Mary could see right away that something wasn't right with her left leg. It didn't kick like the other one. It was smaller and thinner.

The Doctor diagnosed polio. "But not too severe," he added, "and we've caught it early. Only her leg seems to be affected, and there've been some exciting new approaches to treatment lately, especially in America, so there's plenty of cause for hope."

Dr Edlin took a special interest in Grace from then on and was always on hand to give advice on massage, exercise, diet. "Make sure she gets plenty of fresh air," he'd say. "You're lucky living so close to the park. Let her sleep outdoors during the day if the weather permits, and make sure you keep her active."

The midwife had been right about Grace the moment she was born. She never failed to let her parents know exactly what she needed. She knew where she wanted to be and she was in a constant rush to get there. She was quickly hauling herself up and trying to stand, or climbing over her brother or sister, demanding to be carried if she couldn't get where she wanted under her own steam. By the time she was talking, she was leading them all a merry dance, and it was if she had always been a part of their happy family.

As soon as he could Dr Edlin encouraged her to

wear a calliper and, with the extra balance and support this provided, Gracie, as she had come to be called, was soon charging about at a rate of knots. Nor was she daunted by school and the prospect of being different or shunned, and very quickly she made friends. The children there, like the family at home, simply stopped taking notice of her disability.

And so that morning Mary watches from the doorway as Gracie gets dressed, puts on the calliper by herself, comes down the stairs three at a time, polishes off her breakfast in seconds, and announces that she's ready.

"But I'm not," calls Harriet, coming into the kitchen.

"Well hurry up!" orders Gracie.

"Is that the way you speak to your teacher?" asks Harriet, pinning up her hair and pretending to be stern.

"You're not my teacher till we get to school," Gracie answers back. "Till then you're only my sister."

"Your older sister," Harriet reminds her. "Have you forgotten what they say about respecting your elders and betters?"

"You may be older, but that doesn't make you better."

"That's enough of that, young lady," says Mary, lifting her finger in warning. "It's not too late for me to decide you can't go to school today."

Gracie knows it's never a good idea to cross her mother, especially when that finger is raised, and she sits down mutinously on the front step. But she's too excited about the prospect of their trip to the Museum today to be downcast for long. "How are we getting there?" she asks.

"Bus," replies Harriet. "The Council's put on a series of specials for all the schools. Come on, Gracie, put your coat on. We don't want to be late, do we?"

Gracie glares back indignantly. "That's what I've been saying all morning."

Mary waves them off from the front door of the Lodge, then goes back indoors, and suddenly all is calm after the hullaballoo of first Toby setting off for the pit, then Jabez going out to the park, and finally Harriet and Gracie leaving for school. She relishes this quiet oasis, but only for a moment. She likes to be busy and there's always plenty to do. She knows that Harriet won't be living with them much longer. She was so proud of her when she went to the Grammar School, and from there to the Elizabeth Gaskell Teachers' Training College. There'd never been any question as far as Jabez was concerned.

"We mustn't stand in her way," he'd said. "Schools always need teachers, and I reckon as how our Harriet'll be as good as any."

Toby too was proud of her and never resented for a second that his own future inevitably meant leaving school as soon as he could to go down the pit and start earning money. He'd never been much of a scholar himself, but he saw the value in it for those who took to it. He already saw the road ahead for him following much the same course as his father's had – the pit and the park – and being a miner meant that he was spared conscription, although he could go if he chose to, again just like the decision his father had faced in the last war.

But for now he was content to think he was doing his bit just as much down the mine as he would be if he were stuck out in the middle of nowhere, or wherever it was Harriet's Paul had been sent. Toby thinks Paul is a decent bloke, though he'd never say that to Harriet of course. Mary too thinks that Paul's a fine young man and, if he's spared, he and Harriet will make a fine couple. But all this waiting, this putting a part of your life on hold, is not a good thing, she thinks, and her mind goes back to those times she spent with Ruth in Denton, when they were both just girls, the same age as Harriet is now, when all those hopes were wrecked, and not for the first time she wonders what might have happened to Lily, who will be twenty-five now, thinks Mary. Whenever she passes a young woman in the street with a strawberry mark on her cheek, she finds herself wondering. "Could she be...? Might that be her...?" No, it doesn't do good to invest too much hope in the future, she thinks. Better to take what pleasures are to be found in the moment...

She stands up, scolding herself. "None of this dreaming about the past is going to get the washing done today, is it?" she says out loud, and she rolls up her sleeves and begins to carry the water that's been boiling out towards the scullery at the back.

It's a double decker bus that takes Gracie and her classmates from Church Street School, Clayton to the Manchester Museum, and Gracie sits by a window on the top, from where she can look down on the city streets, still recovering from the Blitz of a year and a half ago.

From Tartan Street, they proceed down Stuart Street towards Grey Mare Lane, which leads on to Pottery Lane, crossing Hyde Road, where they take a short detour past Belle Vue.

"How many of you have been to the Zoo?" asks Harriet, standing at the front of the top deck of the bus.

Several hands are raised.

"And how many of you have been since the War started?"

No hands go up this time.

"I'm not surprised," she says.

"Can anyone tell me why? Yes, Thomas?"

"It's not open as much."

"That's right, Thomas. And why is that, do you think?" Harriet looks around, waiting to see if anyone might have an answer. She knows that Gracie knows, but she also knows that Gracie will not put up her hand, for fear of being labelled the teacher's pet. Instead she alights upon the boy who comes in early each morning to help the caretaker light the stoves in all the classrooms. "Bromley?"

"Well, Miss, when t' war started, they was worried a bomb might fall on t' Zoo, and all th' animals'd escape, so there'd be lions and tigers and polar bears roaming wild in t' streets, Miss."

The other children laugh at this, which Harriet quickly suppresses with a stern look.

"Actually, children, Bromley is quite right. That's exactly what the authorities did fear, and so they posted soldiers in the grounds, with orders to shoot to kill if any animal escaped. Thankfully, that is something they've not had to do yet. If you look over the wall to your left, you might just catch sight of them marching up and down."

The children all rush to the left hand side of the bus, craning their necks to see if they might catch sight of the soldiers.

"There's one," cries Amy, always an excitable child.

"Don't be daft," says big John Blay, who was something of a gentle giant in the class, a good head higher than all the rest, with a warm smile and a slow way of talking. "That's just one o't' keepers wi' a rake to pull out all t' shit from t' cages."

The children are beside themselves with giggles at the use of the rude word.

"I shall pretend I haven't heard that, John Blay," says Harriet, "but I shan't if I hear it again – from any of you." The class is immediately silent.

"Sorry, Miss."

"Now – who can tell me what rations are?"

A forest of hands goes up, including Gracie's, noted with quiet pleasure by Harriet, but overlooked all the same in favour of Anita, who rarely says a word.

"Anita?"

"It's what we can't have, Miss. They give us coupons we can swap for food, but it's never enough to go round."

"That's one way of putting it, Anita. Well done."

"Last week," calls out Hartley, Bromley's older brother and one of the livelier boys, "our Gertie came home wi' a pair of nylons."

"Black market," shouts Jessie knowingly.

"No," says Hartley, "one of them G.I.s."

There is immediate uproar, which it takes Harriet some moment to quell. "Thank you, Hartley That will do. We none of us like the idea of having our food and clothing, our coal and petrol rationed, but Mr Churchill thinks it's the only fair way of making it possible for all of us at least to have a little, even if it doesn't always feel quite enough. What's our motto, children?"

"Make do and mend," they all chime back obediently.

"Very good. And the animals in the Zoo have had to make do with rations as well as us. No bananas for the monkeys. No millet for the parakeets. No fish for the seals. The keepers tried smearing strips of meat with cod liver oil…"

"Ergh! Yuk!"

"The seals didn't like it either. But they learned to adapt. Like we've had to."

They leave Belle Vue behind, head down Kirkmanshulme Lane, where Harriet sneaks a sly peep at her old school, cross Stockport Road to Dickenson Road, and finally turn right onto Wilmslow Road towards the University and the Museum.

As the children troop off the bus, Harriet asks the other teacher if she wouldn't mind keeping an eye on Grace, in case she needs help climbing the marble steps into the upper gallery of the Museum, where Maharajah's skeleton is on display, but she needn't have worried. Gracie bounds ahead at the front, her characteristic, lolloping gait singling her out immediately.

The Museum Guide is waiting for them at the top of the staircase and quickly organises the children to sit cross-legged on the floor in a circle around the skeleton. After retelling the story of how Maharajah walked from Edinburgh to Manchester with his keeper Lorenzo, and then furnishing them with various facts and figures about the number of bones, the length of the tusks, the elephant's height, she hands out sheets of paper and pencils and asks them to draw him from where they are sitting. Immediately the children become quietly absorbed, and several tongues protrude from mouths, faces screwed in concentration.

Gracie has deliberately placed herself right in front of Maharajah, looking up through the tusks towards his mighty head, with its enormous eye sockets, which seem to be staring directly into her. Those large caves where the eyes should be, and the black hole from where the trunk would once have swung, remind Gracie of the heavy rubber gas mask she has to carry around with her at all times, like they all do.

She gazes back for a long time, trying if she can to unlock some hidden secret from those dark recessed pits, as deep as mine shafts.

After a while, the Museum Guide approaches her, sees that she has yet to draw anything at all, and asks if she is alright. She has that well-meaning but annoying habit, Harriet notices, of seeing Gracie's calliper on her leg and then immediately talking to her in an artificially cloying and pitying way. She bites her tongue, knowing that Gracie is well used to dealing with this.

"Yes, Miss," she replies, smiling sweetly. "I'm just studying him before I begin."

The Museum Guide withdraws, satisfied, and Harriet grins.

Meanwhile Gracie does indeed pick up her pencil, which she chews absent-mindedly, turning her attention away from Maharajah's skull to the rest of him. The bones, she notices, are not white, like the pictures of human skeletons she's seen in books, not bleached, but coated with a sheen of many different colours – yellows, browns, oranges – which blend to form a patina not unlike beaten metal. Like everyone else, what overwhelms her at first is the sheer size of some of the individual bones. The bone joining the knee with the foot alone is taller than she is, while the rib cage looks like the hulk of a great ocean-going ship. But she is also struck by the delicacy of some of the smaller bones, like those in the feet. How could such tiny bones, she wonders, hold up such a mighty beast, and she looks down at her own withered leg, which cannot bear the weight of even someone as small as she is without the support of her calliper, which she rubs now instinctively, affectionately.

This starts her thinking about how the skeleton itself is keeping upright in front of her. Just as she knows how floppy a body would be if it didn't have bones inside it, she also guesses that without the skin to stitch them all together, the bones might just collapse. She looks hard at the elephant, and she notices a series of thin metal poles attached at various points, which have been carefully positioned to keep the skeleton in an upright position without you really noticing them.

Just then the sun shines through the tall stained glass window at the back of the Display Hall, immediately behind Maharajah's head from where Gracie is sitting on the chair that has been provided for her, which she is using even though she doesn't really need it. The sun bounces off the skeleton's spine right into Gracie's eyes, and she pushes the chair back to avoid being dazzled. The noise of it scraping across the marble floor of the Museum echoes loud and long. To Gracie it sounds exactly like an elephant trumpeting. The chair tips back and Gracie falls clumsily, shielding her eyes from the blinding sun, which encircles Maharajah like a golden crown. The skeleton appears black in its penumbra and seems to Gracie very much alive once more, bucking and roaring, as it charges out to greet her, its thundering hooves shaking the earth beneath her, throwing up huge dust clouds, opening great craters of upturned rock and ruin.

Harriet is there in an instant, not so much to help Gracie, who she knows will be fine, but to intercept the Museum Guide, who will undoubtedly make a fuss. The other children barely notice, so intent are they on trying to pin down the elephant in pencil on paper.

On the bus ride back to school afterwards, the children are full of excitement about their day in the Museum, their voices chittering like birdsong, all except for Gracie, who is unusually quiet, preferring instead to stare out of the window at the bombed streets below.

Manchester has not received much in the way of air raids for nearly eighteen months now, not after that initial wave of terror during the Christmas of 1940, when the *Luftwaffe* blitzed her night after night for several weeks. But the city still bears the scars.

Gracie looks out at row upon row of windowless, roofless houses, some little more than skeletons themselves, but not reconstructed, like Maharajah, simply left to stand – or fall – where they are. Piles of rubble, mountains of bricks, lie everywhere, some of them roped off, with "Warning – Danger" signs, but most of them unguarded, from scavengers scrabbling for shrapnel, or looters on the look-out for scrap metal. Children climb unsupervised like the monkeys in Belle Vue, leaping sure-footed from crumbling ceiling joists to second storey door jambs. They lasso lengths of rope to bent and leaning lamp posts, swinging their way across this broken landscape as if it was their natural habitat, skirting the craters with their unexploded bombs or land mines, avoiding the sink holes where roads have collapsed in on themselves, revealing the lost layers of lives and years, from where smoke still rises. Tired and desperate women push old prams through the still tumbling bricks, picking up whatever they can find, to sell or exchange for food, or to remind them of what they once had. Old men stand on what before had been street corners, lost and loitering, while members of the emergency services, together with local volunteers, the ARP Wardens, St John's Ambulance, Red Cross, WRVS, try to bring what relief they can.

Gracie watches men and women with tin hats upon their heads carefully sifting through the ruins, painstakingly brushing away the fine film of dust from the surfaces to try and understand just what happened here, placing each of their findings, however tiny, into small canvas bags slung across their shoulders. One of them sits on a pyramid of bricks, drinking tea from a tin mug, sorting through her pickings. A man with glasses and a tweed jacket sits beside her with a clipboard, checking each item she shows him against a list.

"What are they doing?" she asks Harriet just as she's passing.

"I'm not sure," she replies. "I think they might be archaeologists, from the museum or university."

"What's archaeologists?" asks Gracie.

"They're people who try to find out about those who used to live here hundreds of years ago and what kind of lives they led by looking at the things they left behind, things that tend to get buried by who comes afterwards."

Gracie takes this in. "Like the bits and pieces of pottery we sometimes find in the park at home?"

Harriet nods. "That's right, yes."

Gracie likes to make up stories about them, who might have used them, what their names were, where they went to after they'd left. "I wish museums did that," she says, "tell us stories, rather than just putting things in a glass case, so that you can't touch them."

Harriet smiles sadly. "Sometimes I wish they'd just leave things alone." She looks down to the half demolished street below, with the archaeologists rummaging through its grief and desolation. "There's a time and a place."

"There's no time like the present," says Gracie. "That's what Mum says."

"Yes she does," says Harriet, "and I expect she's right. When the war's over, they'll clear all this away and build new streets with new houses, and then it won't be possible to go digging underneath."

Harriet's attention is drawn by Bromley and Anita squabbling over something towards the back of the bus. Gracie returns to her scrutiny of the scene of smoke and ruin below, and notices, clambering determinedly over the rubble, a small but growing number of rats, their noses twitching with curiosity at this new country rising out of the upturned earth.

Mary watches Gracie and Harriet walking across the park towards her. It is one of her secret pleasures to be able to observe them unseen, marvelling at Gracie's complete matter-of-factness about her polio. Her rolling, galumphing gait is a joy and a wonder to behold. Mary loves how, when Gracie sets her mind to something, nothing will deter her from pursuing it until she has mastered it. She's like a dog with a bone – which reminds her, she must save some scraps for Tag – and she calls out to them both from behind the last load of washing she's just finished pegging out. She's been washing all day, but she wants to take advantage of these long, light June evenings, so she's done more than she would usually do.

She waves and Gracie waves back, breaking into her equivalent of a run, which has the same rhythm as when children pretend they are riding horses, leading each step with the same foot and slapping their hip.

"Had a good day, love?"

"Yes, Mum," both girls answer simultaneously, then laugh.

"Has she been good?" Mary asks Harriet.

"I'm always good," protests Gracie indignantly.

"Except when you're bad," retorts Harriet, trying to keep her face straight, but Gracie knows she's being teased and lets the remark go.

"It was fantastic at the Museum, Mum. Can we all go again? Maybe on a Saturday?"

"We'll see," says Mary.

"It's free," adds Gracie, knowing that this might be what is most persuasive.

"You'll have to ask your father."

"I'll ask him now," says Gracie, whooping her way into the park, where she knows she'll find him sooner or later.

Harriet shakes her head. "That girl," she says, "I don't know where she gets her energy from. Want some help with tea, Mum?"

"If you could peel a few potatoes, love, that'd be a start."

Mary and Harriet disappear indoors as Gracie heads down the Avenue of Black Poplars, calling for her father, who's working on the allotments in the bottom field. All the flower beds have been turned over to vegetables for the duration of the war, a task Jabez takes as much pleasure in as he did preparing the bulbs for Tulip Sunday, which has not been held for the last three years now.

Within seconds their dog, Tag, comes bounding towards her, and wherever Tag is, Dad is sure to be not far away. Tag, like all of their dogs, is a black and white Welsh collie. First there was Jabez's brother Jack's Meg, and after Meg came Peg. Gracie dimly remembers Peg, she thinks, and she's already decided that the one after Tag will be Tig.

"Good boy," she says, as he jumps up and licks her hand.

She hears her father's sharp, high whistle, which Tag responds to directly, returning towards Jabez, while Gracie hurries on behind.

"Father?" she calls.

"Eh up," he replies, "summat's up."

"What do you mean?" she asks.

"If tha's callin' me "Father", it can only mean one o' two things – either tha's in trouble, or tha' wants summat. So which is it, young 'un?"

"I want to ask you something please."

"Best get on wi' it, then," he says, resting on his spade, while Tag explores some interesting new smells.

"Will you take me to the Museum?"

"Tha's only just been. What dost tha' want to go back again so soon for?"

"Why are you talking funny? You sound like Uncle Jack."

Jabez smiles and ruffles his daughter's hair. "I'm only joshing," he says. "That's how he used to talk to

me when I were a nipper, if ever I asked 'im for 'owt."
He takes an apple from his pocket and starts to peel it
with his pen knife. Gracie watches him in silence as he
manages to take it off in a single sweep. When he's
finished, he hands it to her, and she holds it up to the
sun, which appears to shine right through it as it dangles
from her fingers like a snake skin.

"Will you teach me to do that?" she says.

"Ay," says Jabez, "when you're ten."

"Why ten?"

"That's the age Toby was when I first taught him,
that's why. Nine's too young for handling pen knives."

Gracie nods. It's an answer that satisfies her. Her
father hands her the apple and she quietly starts to eat it.

"What's all this about the Museum then?" he asks
her after a while.

Gracie waits a moment before she replies, trying to
think how best to put into words these thoughts which
have been rolling round her brain.

"I want to know where I come from," she says in the
end.

Jabez smiles. "If you're talking about the birds and
the bees, you'd be better asking your mother, or your
sister."

"I don't mean babies, Dad. I'm talking about me,
you, all of us. Where did we begin?"

"I don't rightly follow you, girl. Best sit down and
tell me what you mean."

Gracie flops down in the grass. She looks across to
Tag and sees him scrabbling furiously at a patch of
earth under one of the bushes. Jabez emits another

sharp whistle and the dog immediately bounds towards them both, looking exceedingly pleased with himself. In his mouth he is carrying a bone, which he sets down between his paws when he reaches them and contentedly starts to chew it, making small pleasurable noises in the back of his throat.

"That," says Gracie suddenly. "That's what I'm talking about. Bones."

Jabez scratches his head. "You're a puzzle, and no mistake."

Gracie takes a deep breath.

"When we were at the Museum today," she says, "we had to sit in a circle round Maharajah's skeleton. I sat right at the front, staring up at its huge skull, and I thought – how do they know? How do they know that this is Maharajah's skeleton, as opposed to any other elephant's? What makes it special? Different from all the rest? Then, when we were going home, we walked through a room which had lots of other skeletons in it – pigs, horses, cats, dogs – and I got to thinking. I reckon I could tell our Tag apart from any other dog. I'd know him anywhere, with his floppy ear, and his white face, and the black circle round his eye. But if he was dead, and we buried him, like we did with Meg and Peg, and then someone came along and dug him up, like Tag has with this bone he's got now, would I still recognise him? Or would his skeleton be just like any other collie dog? How would we know it was him? And then I thought – what if someone dug up my skeleton? They'd see I had one leg shorter than the other, but apart from that, what else would they see? There's more to me than just my leg, Father, isn't there? Isn't there?"

Gracie has worked herself up into quite a state and is threatening to cry. Jabez knows from experience that it's best not to intervene, but to let her talk herself to a finish when she gets like this, for she'd only shrug him off, get crosser and more upset, and then not be able to complete her train of thought.

"And then on the way back, we passed a bomb site, and there were these people going through the ruins picking out things they were finding there."

"Looters?"

Gracie shakes her head. "Harriet said they were…" and she screws up her face trying to bring the word back to her mind. "… ar-chae-ol-o-gists." She lets her breath exhale. "Harriet says they dig up the past and tell stories about it from the things that they find, and that they work in the Museum, and that's why I want you to take me there." She looks at him directly, a fierce expression on her tear-streaked face. "That's what I want to be when I grow up."

Jabez waits a long time, until she's sure she's finished, then nods his head.

"Seventy years ago," he says, "in 1872, the same year that your Maharajah made his long walk all the way from Scotland, there was a great flood here. The Medlock burst its banks and washed everything in its path clear away, including many of the graves from the cemetery next door. Hundreds of bodies were swept away by the mud and the water. It must have been a shocking sight to behold, all those bodies floating past. The Corporation did what they could, but they couldn't recover them all, and in any case I imagine they all got mixed up somehow. So you see, Gracie, we're sitting on bones right now, right here, under our feet, and nobody knows who's who or what's what, not exactly. That's partly why things grow so well here. I sometimes come across them when I'm digging a new bed, or Tag does – like he has now…"

The dog looks up at the mention of his name and barks, once, happily, before resuming on his gnawing.

"But that's not a…. human bone, is it?" asks Gracie.

"No, love, probably just a badger's, or a fox's. But the thing is, Grace, you can't tell every single person's story, not by yourself, there's just too many. You need to tell your own story first – where you've come from and where you've got to – and then pass it on. That's all any of us can do, leave our marks in the land for others to follow…"

"Walking in the footsteps of ghosts…"

"Standing on the shoulders of giants…"

"Like Maharajah," smiles Gracie. "I like the sound of that."

Jabez smiles back. "Just over twenty years ago," he says, "after the last war had finished, I did a long walk myself."

"Did you?" asks Gracie, her eyes on stalks. "Longer than Maharajah's?"

"Much longer," he replies. He picks up a blade of grass, rolls it between his fingers, then blows on it to make a high-pitched whine, which hums in the air. Tag looks up at the sound, ears pricked, and trots over towards them. "All the way from Italy. From a high mountain pass, where I set free a herd of frightened horses and watched them gallop away in every different direction. I walked west, following the course of a big river, then north past an even higher range of mountains and into France. Everywhere I went I passed people on the road, who'd loaded up what little belongings they had left onto carts and were looking to make a fresh start, find a new home. I passed burnt out villages, ransacked towns, abandoned farms. I walked through fields of mud as deep as my waist, where nothing grew and all the trees were dead stumps, and I trampled over bones as plentiful as pebbles on a beach. And in the end I came back here, to the cemetery over there, to pay my respects to my father, and that's where I met your mother, who was laying a bunch of tulips by the grave of a friend of hers. And that's how come you and me are sitting here now having us this conversation."

Gracie runs her fingers through Tag's ears. "Everyone's got a story to tell, haven't they? When I grow up, perhaps I can help people to tell theirs."

They sit in silence a while, listening to the bees murmuring in the flowers close by, watching the swifts swooping down upon invisible insects, until they hear the loud, metallic clanging, of somebody hitting a pan with a ladle.

"Come on," says Jabez, helping Gracie to her feet. "That'll be your mother calling us in for our tea. She won't want us to be late."

The following Saturday Jabez takes Gracie not to the

Museum as she'd asked, but further into the city, to St Peter's Square and the Central Reference Library.

"This all used to be fields once," he says as they step off the bus. "St Peter's Fields. A great battle took place here. Plenty of stories waiting to be told about that, Gracie."

He leads her up the steps into the library and he takes her straight to the enormous circular domed Reading Room on the first floor. Her eyes try to drink it all in.

"You wait here," he says, "while I ask the librarian to fetch us a particular book I want you to look at, and see if you can read what's written round the ceiling."

He goes off to the Information Desk, positioned in the centre of the Reading Room like the central hub of a wheel, and leaves Gracie standing there, craning her neck to try and read the curly Gothic script snaking round the dome above her, the letters laced and looped together like the apple peel when her father's removed it in a single cut and hung it on the kitchen dresser to catch the light.

He returns carrying a book that is almost as big as Gracie. He lays it down on one of the desks, which lie along the various spokes of the wheel, leading out from the hub in the centre. Inside it is full of old maps of Manchester, including one of Philips Park. The librarian accompanying her father hands her a pair of gloves to put on before she is allowed to touch the book. The librarian then brings across a folder of other maps, all seemingly pencil-drawn on what look like sheets of stiff tracing paper, which he proceeds to place, one on top of the other, so that right before her eyes, Gracie is transported back in time, to the flood of 1872, to when Philips Park was first laid out in 1844, and then back and back, before there was a park, before work on the Ashton Canal was begun, to when there were farms and orchards and open countryside. Gracie is entranced.

"Everything lies under our feet," explains the librarian. "The more we dig, the more we find, and the more we find, the more we learn about who we are, and where we come from."

Jabez thanks the librarian and then turns towards Gracie. "Do you still want to be an archaeologist?" he asks.

She nods her head vigorously.

"Then tell me what it says on the ceiling," he says.

Gracie looks back up, shields her eyes against the light streaming through the glass window in the centre of the domed ceiling and reads, haltingly at first, then growing in confidence.

" *'Wisdom is the principal thing. Therefore get wisdom and within all thy getting get understanding. Exalt her and she shall promote thee. She shall bring thee to honour when thou dost embrace her. She shall give to thine head an ornament of grace. A crown of glory shall she deliver to thee...'* 'Grace'?" she adds smiling, and Jabez winks back at her.

"Come on," he says, "let's have another look at these maps."

An hour later they are making their way down Peter

Street towards Deansgate, from where they can catch their bus back home. As they pick their way through the bones of skeletal buildings still standing after last year's bombing, poking their way bravely through the rubble, they gradually become lost among the crowds of people gathering around the Saturday morning markets, eyes fixed firmly on the ground to avoid the pot holes and cracks, diggers and miners both.

13

1982

When Bradford Colliery closes in 1968, despite having more than a hundred years worth or more of coal still waiting to be mined, over two thousand workers lose their jobs. Most seek alternative employment in other local industries, some take early retirement, but a few, like Derek, have mining in their blood and want nothing else. Having survived the explosion in 1953, when he was trapped underground for two days in total darkness, Derek – Walter's great grandson through Harold – can sympathise with those that seize this chance to get out for good, but for him the experience created a bond, something unspoken, but deeply felt, that he still sees in the expressions of others, recognised and shared, and it is not something he can do without.

Derek uproots his wife, son and daughter, therefore, none of whom are very happy about it, and moves them fifteen miles east, to Glossop, to work in the Ludworth Moor Mine just outside the town. He quickly settles in to the new routines – one mine is much like another. He makes friends, drinks at the local Miners' Welfare, supports Stockport County, provides for his family.

He stops playing the cornet, though, for although the Glossop Old Band has a fine tradition, he's recently developed what he can only describe as "wobbly eye". His hands have started to shake too. Not all the time, but when he's tired, or stressed. He goes to see his doctor, who sends him to an optician, who diagnoses something called Acquired Nystagmus. It's very rare, he says, it affects less than one in two thousand. Why me, asks Derek? Why indeed, wonders the optician. You're a miner, you say? Derek nods. The optician explains that nobody is really certain what causes it in adults – some children are born with it – but you do hear of it among miners, something to do with working in near pitch darkness all day, then having to adjust to bright daylight afterwards. Then why don't all miners get it, asks Derek? That's what we don't understand, says the optician. Do you drive? Derek shakes his head. Good, says the optician, because if you did, I'd have to advise you to stop. There's no cure, I'm afraid, but with glasses and drops we can slow its progress. Will I go blind? Not necessarily. Let's just take things one step at a time. What about this wobbly eye, asks Derek? Can you stop it? We can minimise it. And what about work, says Derek, for the first time a note of anguish in his voice? I've got to work. The optician nods. Yes, he says, I understand that. Let's keep it under review, shall we?

And so Derek does keep on working, and he learns to control the dizziness, the blurring vision, by a very slight nodding of his head and turning his eyes upwards just a little when he feels a wobble coming on. He doesn't tell his family. He just says that he has to wear glasses from now on, and that he can fit goggles over these when he's at the coal face.

But he stops playing the cornet.

He hands it down, as it has been to him – from Walter to Harold, from Harold to Alan (his father), and from his father to him – now to his daughter, Florence, for her sixth birthday. "You're never too young to start," he tells her. It's New Year's Day, 1972.

Ten years later Florence, now sixteen, attends Glossop High School. She's bright, clever, has lots of friends and is pretty. The sixth form boys have begun to notice her and she enjoys flirting with them, but already she's begun to look beyond the confines of this small Derbyshire town. The city lights of Manchester beckon. In two years time, if she continues to work hard, university seems like a real possibility. If she goes, she'd be the first person in her family ever to go. She smiles. She likes the sound of that and she settles to her cornet practice.

She plays for her School Band, and they've just been invited to play at the North West Youth Brass Band Competition to be held on 14th February 1982 at the Kings Hall, Belle Vue. Valentine's Day. If she plays her cards right, she might get a Valentine's Card from the principal trombonist, and if *he* plays *his* cards right, he might just get a kiss for his trouble.

The day dawns, and Derek walks with Florence to the school, where a coach is waiting to take the band to Belle Vue. He intends to get the bus later in the day to be there in time for the performance. He works for Lancashire Chemicals now, as a sheet metal worker, in the centre of the town, the Ludworth Moor mine having closed the previous year. His eyesight has deteriorated further, but the tremor in his eyes and hands is, for the most part, under control, though not so much this morning, as they reach the school gates.

"Wish me luck," she says, noticing, but saying nothing.

"You don't need it," says Derek. "You'll be champion."

"Thanks, Dad," she says, letting go of his hand.

"Hold the line," he says, just as she's turning to join the rest of the band on the coach. "Don't think about all them complicated triples, just hold the line."

She nods. "I'll try."

When they reach the Kings Hall, their teacher tells them that they've been drawn last to play.

"You know what that means," he says, "don't you?"

They look at him blankly, as if to say, isn't it obvious?

"No," he says. "Remember me telling you? They're pulling the Kings Hall down right after this concert. This is the very last event the old place is ever going to stage, and you'll go down in history as the last band ever to play here."

They laugh. "The Who, The Stones, The Clash and us," quips the Principal Trombonist, winking at Florence.

Consequently, they have time to kill before it's their turn. Florence and the Principal Trombonist (whose name is Pete, which will be forgotten when Florence will look back on this day, years later, though the events will remain sharp and clear) walk around what's left of Belle Vue. The Zoo shut down five years before. The last animal to leave was Ella May, a fifteen year old elephant who, the newspapers said, was seen to shed a tear as she boarded the train to depart. The Fun Fair closed a year ago, when the much loved, famous old Scenic Railway was finally torn down, the Bobs having been sold to an Amusement Park in Colorado. Only the Greyhound and Speedway tracks remain, and they lie half a mile outside the grounds. And after today, the Kings Hall too is to go. Florence and the Principal Trombonist watch a crew of men already erecting scaffolding around its walls, with hoardings advertising the name of the demolition company. On the fairground PA, Madness are singing *Welcome to the House of Fun*.

"This must have been quite a place in its day," says the Principal Trombonist.

Florence shoots him a sidelong glance. "Didn't you ever come here?"

"No," he says. "This is my first visit – and my last, from the look of it."

She shakes her head, amazed. "We used to come here every year. I practically grew up here. I remember this one time – I must have been only six, I'd just started playing the cornet – we went to the Flea Circus. It was in a tiny tent, which only let in a few people at a time."

"How come?"

"Because they're fleas, duh! You can hardly see them."

"So how did you know they were there?"

"Because of what they did. *'Professor' Tomlinson's Mighty Fleas'*, the sign read."

"Gross. It makes me itch just hearing about them."

"I know. They had chariot races, they were harnessed somehow – you couldn't see anything – but the chariots'd move about an inch a minute. They rode bikes, pulled mini garden rollers, they even had sword fights."

"What?"

"Yeah – fencing fleas! They scrabbled about with pins stuck in pieces of cork."

"It sounds to me like a huge con."

"Maybe. I was only six, remember. When it shut down, they blamed it on "improvements in domestic living conditions". We were all living in cleaner houses, see?"

"That's what the Welfare State does for you. Puts fleas out of a job. Or maybe we all just wised up a bit."

"Come here," she says, and pulls him towards her. "Don't shatter my childhood illusions..."

They return to the Hall in good time and Florence goes through her usual ritual of scales and exercises to warm up her fingers and lips in the room set aside for them, where the Band prepares to go on stage. There is the usual last minute banter of jokes and then, as one, they all fall silent. The Chairman of the Federation steps forward to the microphone.

"And now it is with both pleasure and sadness that I introduce on stage the last band ever to play in this famous old hall. Will you please put your hands together to give a good old fashioned Belle Vue welcome to The Glossop High School Band!"

As they take up their positions on stage, the applause thundering over them, Florence looks out into the auditorium, where she spots her Dad, nodding his head towards her from the front row and smiling. She smiles back. She feels no nerves, just excitement, as she always does before a performance.

Their teacher gently raps his lectern with his baton. Then, when he's certain every single pair of eyes is focused on him, he raises his hands and brings them in to start.

They are note-perfect. Derek watches Florence from his front row seat, sees her stand to take her solo, hears her hold that line, reaching right back in time, to an afternoon a hundred years ago, right here in Belle Vue, when Walter first heard that bugle blown from the back of a stallion thundering around the ring, and gave a lucky feather to his childhood sweetheart, whose likeness seems resurrected in the same red hair, a loose strand of which now falls across Florence's lightly freckled face.

They take their bows as the audience rises to its feet, shouting for more. They are applauding the Glossop High School Band, yes, but also all the other bands who have played here, since the Kings Hall, named for both Edward VII and George V, was first opened in 1910, and before that, when the Championships were held in the open air, and when Walter had led the Kingston Mills Band to triumph in 1892.

"More," the audience continues to roar, and the conductor seizes the moment. He turns back to the band, says something inaudible to them, they smile and he raises his arms once more, signalling they are about to begin again. The audience sits back down in hushed anticipation.

And so The Glossop High School Band begins the last ever tune to be played in the old Kings Hall. As soon as the first notes descend from the stage, the audience sighs and spontaneously applauds. The conductor turns to face them and with his baton invites them to sing along.

"Should auld acquaintance be forgot
And never brought to mind
We'll take a cup of kindness yet
For Auld Lang Syne..."

As the crowds stream away afterwards, the demolition crew begin to make the necessary preparations to tear the Kings Hall down.

Derek is full of praise for Florence, and Florence thinks she'll risk taking advantage of his glowing good mood and ask if she might go into the city that night with some of the members of the band. She doesn't mention the Principal Trombonist specifically, but after she gave him his Valentine Day's kiss, he hinted that he might have access to tickets for *The Hacienda*, where New Order are rumoured to be playing.

"Don't be too late," says Derek, smiling, and

watches her troop off with her friends.

He looks back towards Belle Vue. A heavy February snow moon is just visible above the high outer walls. A wind is picking up. He can still hear the fairground's PA system. Bucks Fizz are singing *The Land of Make Believe*, whose last notes are quietly trailing away. The demolition crew send the giant wrecking ball swinging into the black and white timbered façade of the Kings Hall, smashing through its concrete awnings, louder than the loudest rock bands, the deep rumble of its destruction, as walls and roof, having withstood the hammer blows and upper cuts of boxers and wrestlers down the decades, all the Len Johnsons, Henry Coopers, Brian Londons, the Jackie Pallos, Big Daddies, Giant Haystacks, splinter and collapse, sounding like distant thunder, rolling across the city, along its rivers and canals, roads and railways, past its statues and landmarks, down through all the layers of years, kicked up and disturbed by the never ending passage of feet, human, horse and elephant, the ceaseless flow of traffic, the unstoppable march towards the future, out of a past being excavated that very moment by one Dr Grace Chadwick, archaeologist in charge of the recently uncovered Roman fort at Castlefield on the edge of Deansgate, which she formally declares the country's first Urban Heritage Park.

Back at Belle Vue, the giant wrecking ball swings and smashes once more into the skeletal hulk of the Kings Hall.

The Navigable Levels, Worsley

circa 1885

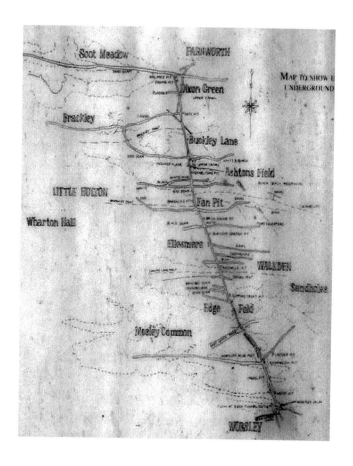

THREE

The Delph

14

Tommy Thunder peeps through a crack in the flap at the back of the tent. They have just completed their last ride of the day. By now he calculates they must have done more than a thousand such rides. They have been at Belle Vue for more than twenty lunar months, and it must be at least another twenty since they last glimpsed their homeland, or walked upon familiar earth, watched the sun rise and set over the plains of their forefathers, from where they were scooped up in a net suspended from an American Elm, carted off to Rapid City, where they were dumped in a cattle truck and transported by railroad to St Louis to become part of the Wild West Show. Here, in Manchester, there have been weeks where they have scarcely seen the sun at all.

He watches through the flap until the ring is empty. This afternoon there has been an especially lively audience. Mostly children, whose wide-eyed wonder he can still find pleasure in, even in this enforced and cramped existence. He sees hope and wisdom in their open-hearted innocence. Today he noticed a small girl with hair as red as flame, her face dappled with freckles, reminding him of his first horse, a gift from his father, a skewbald filly, who rode out to meet each new day head on. The red-haired girl was sitting in the front row, next to a young boy who, although he was held in thrall by their dances and songs, kept stealing glances at her. When they stood up to leave, he gave her something, which made her face light up with joy, and Tommy Thunder is curious to know what that might have been.

At the end of every show he places a feather down in the centre of the sawdust. Sometimes this is trampled on by horses, or snatched up by monkeys, or swept away by the ring boys, or sometimes it is simply left there, abandoned, unnoticed. Tommy Thunder will then stoop to collect it, placing it in his leather bag, along with everything else he keeps there – pebbles, leaves, string, matches. But today he thinks might be different. He walks out into the ring. There is nothing there. Yes, he thinks, I was right. The boy presented it to the girl, and she accepted it for what it was, treasure, a gift, the possibility of flight.

Tommy returns quickly to the stable block where they are all locked in each night with the horses and tells the others what he has found. Or rather, not found.

"It's a sign," he says to them. "We leave tonight. Now. At once."

The others nod. They have been waiting for this moment. They are ready.

The others.

Leaping Fish, Fire Catcher, Reads The Moon.

And Chasing Thunder.

Water, Fire, Air and Earth.

Like Chasing Thunder, who is known to all now just as Tommy, they each have their English names. Leaping Fish is Sammy, after the salmon. Fire Catcher, Freddy Catch, or Catch for short, and Reads The Moon is simply Moon, misnomers all from early half-heard

468

introductions, clumsy attempts at strange-sounding words, as ill-fitting as the clothes they now each wear, patched cotton shirts, heavy duty work trousers, moleskin coats, hobnailed boots instead of moccasins.

Tommy, Sammy, Catch and Moon look at each other without a word. They will wait not a second longer. It is time. They slip the bolt and run, silently into the park, just as the fireworks are sparking over the lake.

They hug the perimeter wall of the park, breaking into open ground only where they have to, as now, while they skirt the crowds, whose upturned faces have eyes only for rockets and Roman candles. They reach a brake of rhododendron bushes just as the fireworks are finishing. Tommy notices the boy and the red-headed girl again. She has placed the feather in the tangle of her hair. She looks like a young squaw. Tommy smiles. Behind him the others grow impatient. Catch steps on a twig, which snaps audibly just as the last few sparks of light are falling in the sky. The girl turns in their direction. Tommy is sure that just for a moment she sees them. He throws a pebble a few feet away, disturbing four small rats from the undergrowth, and the girl's attention is drawn away. When she looks back, Tommy, Sammy, Catch and Moon are gone.

They head for the river, the Medlock, follow its course. They pass factory after factory piled cheek by jowl along its short length towards the centre of Manchester, coal mines, cotton mills, tanneries, gas works, brick works, wire works, dye, soap and rubber manufacturers, foundries, paper mills and tar companies, each of them pumping waste and sewage directly into the river, which is sluggish, clogged and dead. Noxious fumes and toxic vapours fill their nostrils. Dead fish float on the surface, a crusted, poisonous sludge of disease and decay.

They creep past the yards and cellars of Little Ireland, where the river oozes beneath the city streets and railway arches, holding their breath as they delve into tunnels under Piccadilly, before heading along Shooter's Brook, briefly following the River Tib, where they leave the water's edge, making their way via Hanging Ditch, over Shude Hill, to the back of the Cathedral. Manchester is peppered now with people from across the globe. It's not unusual to see Chinamen with their pigtails, Hassidic Jews with their long beards and braids, Punjabis with their turbans, Arab, African or South Sea Islander, their dark skins etched blue with tattoos, yet still they feel uncomfortable, conspicuous on the streets. There are just too many, the crowds are too thick. There is too much light, too many opportunities for discovery, for awkward questions, the risk of apprehension. They duck behind Victoria Station to join the Irk, which they follow as far as Ducie Bridge, where it slimes its way into the Irwell.

There is little traffic along the river now that night has fallen. The occasional coal barge, or coracle, disturbs the surface of the water. Sometimes they pass a lone walker, a courting couple, a waterman tying up till morning. They retreat to the shadows of wharf walls, or cling to the sides of bridges. They can lie motionless for minutes at a time if they have to, render themselves invisible to people passing within just a few feet of where they hide. Sammy wishes they had a canoe for he is in his element in water, even water as foul as this, while Catch would like to be carrying a torch, following its flames as they dance along walls and tow paths, but Tommy urges caution, favouring darkness and silence. Moon, older than the rest, proceeds more slowly, placing one foot doggedly in front of the other, seeing an altogether different journey in his mind, conjuring spirits from the air, thick once more with fumes and vapours.

"Two dawns," he says and begins to sing, an incantation from the ancient days in the old tongue.

"Run like coyote
Fly like the eagle
Swim like the beaver
Wait like the wolf…"

Two dawns.

The second dawn sees them leave the river. The air is less pungent, the ground less built upon. They see trees for the first time since they made their escape. Their feet walk on grass. Fields open up before them. They are on the edge of Chat Moss. To the east lies Worsley Old Hall, to the south the Bridgewater Canal. To the west the overgrown tangle of Mosley Common, and to the north the coal fields of Ellenbrook. In the lee of Lady Hill, close to Rands Clough and Alder Wood, they make camp by Worsley Brook.

"Here," says Tommy, and he places a feather upright in the earth.

*

Three years pass.

For the first year they answer a long buried ancestral call and move with the seasons, but they soon come to realise that here, on the flat string of mosses which tie the land between the river and the canal, the Irwell and the Duke's Cut, there is little difference to be found wherever they make camp, and that distances are short enough to render the nomadic life redundant, and so they settle on a spot a few miles further downstream, close to the confluence of the Irwell and the Mersey, in a clearing on the edge of a copse of sycamores.

They cut down branches, trim and fasten them with stripped bark into staves, form them into a circle of tepees, interwoven with more pliable saplings for extra strength and stability, then covered with deer hides for warmth and shelter. They hunt, they fish. Sammy makes a coracle of willow and birch. They cook over open fires kept burning throughout the winter by Catch on the banks of the river, where brown trout are plentiful. They become familiar landmarks to their neighbours, the farmers on the mosses, the bargemen on the water, the miners trudging homewards from Ellenbrook.

Tommy makes the rounds of farms from Warburton

to Worsley, ploughing, planting, harvesting. He digs potatoes, hand crafts hay ricks, catches moles. At the Earl of Ellesmere's farm he heals an injured horse. News spreads like wild fire, and soon he's in demand from Barton to Rixton for his ointments, potions and whispering.

Catch finds work at the forge, where he demonstrates a fabled gift for conjuring fire, moulding the hot coals and liquid fire to fashion weather vanes, ploughshares, hammer heads, horse shoes. He embarks upon a secret task, telling no one, not even Tommy, who is like a brother to him, in the midnight glow of the forge. It is a task for a lifetime, but in this, Catch, whose temper in all else is hot and quick, is quietly patient.

Sammy ventures further and further downstream, knows every creek and current, can recognise and name every heron, egret, swan, watches the wind riffle the water with each change in the weather or season. Like a beaver he builds floating dams of fallen trunks and branches, tied with rope and net to intercept the trout before the pike can, which he brings back each evening for Old Moon to gut and grill over one of Catch's fires.

They plant cereals – barley, rye and winter wheat. They count the birds that arrive with each season – the swallows in spring, the swifts in summer, the redwing and field fare in autumn, the long-tailed tits in winter – and observe how they mix beside those, like them, who stay year round, and those rarer, more exotic visitors, who wonder whether these new found shores might welcome them home. Rooks squabble in the sycamores, sparrows scritter in the hedges. Partridges squawk in the wheat field, waxwings gorge on the rowan berries, and the last corncrake in Lancashire creaks like a rusty gate, a watch too tightly wound. All fall still and silent as a wake of red kites swoops and dances on the high thermals.

Old Moon sings in the starlight. His cracked voice rises with the sparks from Catch's fire up towards the night sky, where it hangs like a new constellation. Reads The Moon sings the moon.

"Stars on the water
Necklace of light
Fires in the darkness
Face of the moon…"

The first year they set up permanent camp Tommy Thunder hears a bird booming in the reed beds across the water, a fabled bird he hears the locals speak of, though they rarely see it, and names the copse of trees in whose shade they now dwell after it, Bittern Wood. He plants a seed from the American Elm there, which he has carried with him since their capture beneath it on the Dakota Plains.

Winter clenches the land in its fist. Frosty wind makes moan. Earth stands hard as iron, water like a stone. The river ices over. Sammy sees fish trapped and swimming beneath. They have had no time to gather winter fuel. Moon sits wrapped in a blanket by the glowing embers of a fire even Catch struggles to keep alive. Ice crystals form on their eyebrows and beards. Their frozen breath is caught in coils of smoke, struggling to loosen their shackles from the earth like hungry ghosts. One morning they emerge from their tepee to find half a dozen pigeons hanging from a low branch, which immediately they pluck and cook. The next day a pair of coneys and a small sack of root vegetables are left in the fire's ashes. Sammy, curious to know who their secret benefactor is, sits up all through a third night, is just upon the point of being overtaken by sleep as a thin dawn prises a crack in the eastern sky, when he hears a twig snap close by. He can just make out a child creeping from the Bittern Wood. She is picking her way gingerly over the frozen ground, careful not to slip or fall, holding out before her a makeshift nest of bantam eggs, which she carries like treasure. Sammy wonders if perhaps she is a spirit, a phantom, an angel. She pushes the eggs gently through a flap in their tepee before heading back towards the copse. Sammy puts his hands to his mouth and makes the cry of an owl, but she makes no response, shows not the slightest sign that she's heard him at all, before she is gone, swallowed by the shadows of trees in the Bittern Wood.

On Candlemas Eve Tommy is summoned by the Earl.

His prize black mare has slipped on the ice and cannot get up. Jenks, his Bailiff, is advising a swift and merciful dispatch, a bullet straight between the eyes, but word of Tommy's skills has reached the Earl, who is anxious to try this last throw of the dice. The mare was his wife's, who died last spring, and is a daily reminder to him of her grace and beauty. Jenks is reluctant to call on the services of someone he believes to be little more than a savage but knows when it is wise to quarrel with the Earl. This is not such a time, but he makes his feelings plain to Tommy nevertheless when he delivers the Earl's message.

Tommy listens. He hears the disapproval in the Bailiff's tone, but cares only for the mare. "Tell your master I come at nightfall. Keep the mare warm. Cover her with blankets. Make sure she is tied fast. She must not try to stand. Light fire beside her. Crush sage and rosemary leaves. Feed them to the flames. Let her breathe in the smoke."

He spends the next few hours brewing a tincture from yarrow and goldenrod. He makes a poultice from pulped potatoes, mixed with ground burdock root.

When he reaches Worsley Hall, he finds the mare in a pitiful state. Her coat is dull and matted with sweat. Her breathing jolts in short, painful rasps. The cuts on her legs and body are deep and raw. Tommy can see deep welts where barbed wire and snags of blackthorn are still attached. She thrashes wildly when anyone approaches. Her legs have been hobbled and tied so that every time she tries to stand, she only damages herself further. Jenks is standing by with his shotgun, trigger finger primed and itching.

Tommy asks everyone to stand back. He takes a knife from the bag slung across his shoulder, a knife with a blade sharpened and polished by Catch at the forge, and walks carefully towards her. He speaks in a low voice, words from his own tongue, words that sound like distant thunder rumbling in the sky overhead. He cuts the ropes that bind her and at once she is up, rearing and bucking, before her legs give way once more and she teeters, toppling like a great elm as she falls. Jenks rushes to the Earl.

"Your Lordship, please. She's suffered too much." He raises his shotgun.

"Wait. Allow our horse doctor more time to do his work. There are always new things to be learned. Entertain the stranger at our gates, Jenks…"

Tommy edges closer to the mare. Her rolling eyes are a maze, where she is becoming lost. Tommy looks deeply into them, trying to find her. Steam rises from her flanks. Her hooves scrabble for traction on the ice. Tommy crouches at her side. He places his right hand on her neck and holds it there until she calms herself. With his left hand he begins to stroke her muzzle very gently, whispering to her all the while. Finally her eyes grow still. She comes back to herself and focuses just on Tommy before her. He continues to speak to her, tenderly, as if to a lover. No one but the mare can hear him. He leans in closer to her, whispers directly in her ear, and then rests his own head next to hers. He waits until the pulse in both their temples matches, joins, converges as one, slow and steady. When he is sure of her, he takes the tincture and the poultice from his bag, gently applies them, one then the other, directly to the wounds upon her legs and sides, until the bleeding stops. He looks over his shoulder, back towards the others, a finger to his lips, and then beckons the Earl and Jenks towards him, signalling to Jenks to lay his shotgun on the ground first.

"Help me to lift her to her feet," he says. He turns to face Jenks. "You – take the weight of this leg in your hand. Then, together, we walk her to her stable." He now addresses the Earl, handing him the tincture and the poultice. "Rub these on the wound three times each day. Feed her oats. Feed her apples. Keep her warm."

"How long...?" asks the Earl, his voice barely a croak.

"Ten days till scars fade. But scars in here..." and he taps the side of his head... "who can say? Maybe never. Her hunting days are over. Let her rest. Let her eat grass all day long in sun and in shadow."

Once the mare is settled, lying on a bed of fresh straw in her stable, the Earl takes Tommy to one side. "Thank you. Where did you learn such skills? That was one of the most remarkable sights I have ever witnessed."

"My grandfather. Chief."

The Earl nods. "I never really knew mine. He died when I was still just a boy. I have a photograph of him in the house welcoming the Queen when she came to stay here thirty years ago. Now I am honoured to greet a Prince. Will you join us for supper?"

"I should get back."

The Earl nods once more, then takes a sovereign from his waistcoat pocket, which he holds out towards Tommy.

Tommy shakes his head.

"If not money, is there something else I might offer you for services rendered?"

Tommy pauses a moment. "May we plough the field beside our camp?"

"Certainly. By all means. Consider it yours."

The two men shake hands, each satisfied with the deal that has been struck. Tommy makes his slow way back across the frozen fields towards the Bittern Wood beneath a haloed moon.

The following day Tommy inspects the field. It is small, about four acres, and roughly square, a furlong in length from north to south, east to west, and on slightly higher ground from their camp with little risk of flooding. He learns from an old tenant farmer called Nathaniel, for whom Tommy has picked seasonal fruit the previous two summers, that the field has lain dormant for several years, the grass scythed for silage and that is all. Tommy wonders what other seeds he will awaken when he ploughs it, in addition to the wheat and barley he will sow.

Winter still grips the ground in its icy claw. He decides to spend the whole day there, familiarising himself with its curves and contours, watching for the birds and animals who visit it, who will be his neighbours, with whom he'll share its bounty. The first things he notices are the lines of mole hills, which criss-cross the land like railway tracks. He smiles. These he will let live. Moles in a field are as sure a sign that worms lie buried there as a canary in a coal mine will indicate the presence of a poisonous gas. Worms. The ploughman's friend. A worm is a piston, aerating the soil with each muscular contraction, creating drainage, pulling down leaf mould, making it more fertile.

The field is bordered on three sides by hedges, on the fourth side by the wood. Nathaniel tells him the hedges were planted a hundred and fifty years ago, when the land around was first enclosed, by one of the Earl's ancestors. They are made up of hawthorn and blackthorn, intertwined with ivy. Nathaniel can't remember when they were last properly pruned and re-laid. Tommy will ask Catch to help him with this task in the coming days, while they wait for the land to warm up, before he begins the ploughing. He sees a number of small birds huddling for warmth inside the hedges. The ground's too hard for pecking and Tommy fears for these birds' survival if this cold snap continues. Birds whose English names he's beginning to learn – chaffinch, sparrow, blackbird and robin, whose red breast reminds Tommy of a drop of blood against the white land. He asks Nathaniel if he might bring some seeds and lumps of fat to hang in balls from the low branches to help them through the winter, and Nathaniel smiles and says that he will. The drilling of a woodpecker in the wood close by draws Tommy's gaze from the field so that he almost misses the tiniest movement in the grass a few yards ahead of him, as a hare eases herself out of her form on the fringe of the field beneath a corner of the hedge. For a split second Tommy is looking directly into her huge eyes. She stops the vigorous washing of her face with her front paws and remains completely still, the only movement being the quivering of her fur in the sharp east wind. The rooks in the wood fall silent. The hare then bolts for cover just as a sparrowhawk, its bladed wings torqued back behind its head, knifes the air above him, before spiralling back up into the sky, its beak empty on this occasion. The air settles once more and the rooks start up their customary skrike and squabble.

Over the coming weeks, winter reluctantly yields the field to Tommy, inch by frozen inch, as its vice-like grip slowly uncurls. He gets to meet more visitors. A pair of red-legged partridges saunters between the molehills like a country squire and his corpulent wife. Long-tailed tits gorge themselves at the feeding table Tommy has set up, sprinkled daily with Nathaniel's seeds. A yellowhammer hops up onto a gate post, from whom Tommy learns his familiar call. "A little bit of bread but no cheese." Half a dozen wagtails patrol the patches of groundsel and chickweed, shepherd's purse and speedwell, whitlow grass and dog's mercury, which have begun to carpet the outer edges of the field, beneath the snowdrops under the hedges. Two jack hares have joined the jill Tommy saw that first day, who vie for her attention. Tommy squats on the edge of the wood to watch her fend off their advances. They rear up on their hind legs and box like children, paddling their front paws fiercely towards each other, though Tommy sees scrits of fur fly then rise, like thistledown, before floating away on the wind, as the jill chases away each jack. A kestrel arrives every afternoon, an hour or so before the sun slips down beyond the distant black hills, which are in fact the towering spoil tips of Ellenbrook. It hovers motionless above him before swooping down on some unlucky mouse or vole, and always, always, the rooks call above him. At first light Tommy waits for them to emerge, black wraiths from the white mists of morning, rising from the river, their voices rusty nails rattling in a tin.

Easter is early this year, and by March the earth is ready. Tommy makes several holes with a piece of iron railing, wide enough and deep enough for his bare arm only, which he plunges down into each one of them, holding it there for as long as he can bear it. He is satisfied. The temperature has risen below the surface sufficiently to accept the seeds he will plant and the worms have done their job. The soil is dry and does not cling to his skin as he pulls out his arm.

Nathaniel has fetched up an old plough frame. Catch has wrought two new blades of gleaming, polished iron for the coulter and the share, which he fixes to the beam, and the Earl has arranged for Tommy to have the use of a pair of his Clydesdales for four days, the length of time it should take him to plough the whole field, one acre for one man in one day. Nathaniel has run him through the basics and has even offered to do the job for him, but it feels important to Tommy for him to do this task himself, to mark the planting of their first crop in this strange new land, staking their claim to just one small piece of it, as he and Catch, Sammy and Moon are welcomed more and more into this community of farmers, bargemen and miners, where their long flight has landed them, in this new home in the Bittern Wood by the confluence of the three rivers.

Collar, traces, breeching and girth. Surcingle, martingale, crupper and tugs. Terrets, lines, bridle and curb. Pedestal, overcheck, shadow roll, bit.

Tommy hears Nathaniel intoning these names like a litany, but mostly he listens to the horses, whinny and snort, nicker and neigh, studies the statues formed by their breath, tunes to the rhythm of head and hoof, mane and tail. Nod, stamp, shake, swish.

A grey mist rises from the river, settles like a blanket over the field. A pale sun leaches through a thin bandage of cloud. He hitches the horses quietly to the plough, picks up the reins, waits. A heron lifts lazily from the wood. Tommy watches its slow orbit of the field, sees it land beside the sighting post he set up yesterday, framed between the head-piece and the whippletree, connecting the harness to the plough.

Tommy waits.

The horses wait.

The bells on their collar jingle.

The brasses glint on the martingales. They hang from their straps and wink in the sun.

The light dances, startling the heron, which croaks, alarmed, before taking off in a heavy, slow motion.

Tommy takes this as his signal to strike out. He clicks his tongue, jiggles the reins and guides his team towards the first sighting post.

He walks slowly, steadily, not looking down, but keeping his eye firmly fixed on the stake. Nathaniel has impressed upon him never to fight the plough. To get the blade to suck in, he must raise the handles. To go deeper, raise them more. If he pushes down too far, the plough will come out of the earth. To control the plough requires the gentlest of touches, Nathaniel warns him. Never jerk, or wrestle with it, he tells him. To steer to the right, simply raise the left handle. To go left, raise the right handle. The horses know, he says. Tommy nods.

Upon reaching the stake at the far end of the field, Tommy stops. He tips the plough over to the right and lets it ride on the ploughshare and the right handle. At the same time he turns the horses around to the right. He makes a big circle to pull the plough back out of the way as he turns. He stops the horses right alongside the upturned sod from the first furrow. He guides the near horse next to the soil, just three inches away from it. Then he steadies and sets off for the other end of the field. The strip he now turns over lies slightly on top of the first one. He has successfully opened up the field.

He ploughs all day.

Every time he reaches the end of the field he turns his horses to the right. He puts the near horse in the furrow just ploughed. He looks along the length of it, lying between the horses, raises both handles, then starts again. He walks in the furrow he is making, while the near horse walks in the one he is covering.

Old Moon walks behind, sowing the wheat seed in each upturned furrow.

All day.

Up and down. Back and forth.

The sun makes its slow arc across the sky, tracking their progress.

Tommy ploughs till it dips behind the Bittern Wood and the field is in shadow.

He has completed one land.

He detaches the harness from the horses, stowing it under oilskins at the field's edge. He leaves the ploughshare buried in the earth overnight. To keep out the damp air, Nathaniel advises, and inhibit rust. He leads the horses back to the Camp, where he lets them graze and drink and rest till morning.

The next day he starts again.

And the next.

And the next.

Tommy ploughs. Moon sows.

At the end of the fourth day, he has turned the whole field.

Old Moon sings in the twilight.

"Horse and furrow
Earth and sky
Rain and ploughshare
Yoke the year…"

*

Early on the fifth day, Tommy, Catch, Sammy and Moon make their way to Lady Hill, where folk from all the outlying farms and villages have gathered to greet

485

the sun this Easter Sunday morning, the dawn of the vernal equinox.

As the sun climbs above the ridge of the hill, everyone looks back. All the mills, smokestacks, chimneys and cooling towers of Manchester, black silhouettes against a blood red sky, rise up like broken teeth. The people turn towards the Earl. Before he gives the signal for the ritual to begin, he gazes back towards the city and wonders how much longer before its incessant creep, a mere seven miles away now, will finally overwhelm them, here in their lost Eden. With a sigh he lowers his white linen handkerchief. The gathering turns as one, each taking from their pockets a highly decorated egg, a specially painted Pace Egg for Easter, which they roll down the steepest slope of Lady Hill. Every possible diversity of design is represented there, like banners at a tournament, the flags of all nations. Some bounce off rocks beneath the surface of the grass and dance in the sharp morning air, while others glitter brightly against the frost covered hillside, their colours and patterns whirling kaleidoscopically as they make their individual descents to the valley bottom, where some crack, some shatter into dozens of fragments, while some remain whole, to survive a second rolling. The people follow their eggs down to the foot of the hill, pick up the remains of their shells and exchange tips and tactics for making them tougher and stronger this time next year.

They then process to the lawn at the front of Worsley Hall, where refreshment and retiring tents have been erected in a circle around a flat central area. A brass band is playing. Dogs and children run pell mell, helter skelter. For a split second Sammy thinks he glimpses the Spirit Child, the Phantom Girl, the Angel, skittering among them, and then she is gone, as everyone gathers for the play, the jag, the mumming.

Rattling stones in pans and kettles, the Mummers enter the field. A lone violin hails their arrival. They wear costumes of many coloured rags and feathers. Horned masks conceal their faces. Each emits a low keening drone as they form a circle and clear the way. Once they have arrived they start to sing, in strange, discordant harmonies.

MUMMERS:
Good people pray heed our petition
Your attention we beg and we crave
And if you are inclined for to listen
An abundance of pastimes we'll have
We are come to relate many stories
Concerning our forefathers' time
And we trust they will drive out your worries
Of this we are all in one mind

The whole assembly now takes up the song, for they have heard it sung every year for longer than they can remember.

Many tales of the poor and the gentry
Of labour and love will arise

There are no finer songs in this country
In Manchester, Salford likewise
There's one thing more needing mention
Our dances we dance all in fun
So now that you've heard our intention
We'll play on to the beat of the drum

The Mummers begin to whirl around in a frenzy of noise and colour, cracking their sticks against one another, before forming them into the shape of a star, through the centre of which leaps Jack-in-the-Green.

This first figure, Jack, whose ribbons are green and brown, whose mask and beard are plaited with twigs and leaves, bark and branches, steps forward, emitting ghostly bird-like cries.

JACK:
In come I, Jack-in-the-Green
To welcome you all to this pleasant scene
Into the future, out of the past
What once was first shall later be last
So let us all join hands in a ring
To dance in the dawn, this first day of spring

The Mummers engage in a wild, ungainly dance, full of shrieks and shouts. They carry long staves with trails of coloured strips of cloth crowned with birds' nests, which they shake menacingly towards the crowds, who gleefully recoil.

JACK:
> And if you don't believe what I say
> Step in St George and clear the way

To great cheers and further rattling of the kettles and pans, a figure clad in red and white steps forward, carrying a sword and shield.

ST GEORGE:
> In come I, St George
> A man of courage bold
> With my broad axe and sword
> I won a crown of gold
> I'll fight the fiery dragon
> And drive him to the slaughter
> And by these means I'll win
> The King of Egypt's daughter

The rest of the Mummers form themselves into a great train, carrying a lurid snake's head mask before them, with wild eyes and a long protruding tongue. They conspire to make a series of roaring, hissing sounds, their movements and gestures conjoined in a rhythm of wheels and pistons. Old Moon, watching with Sammy from the side, remembers the coming of the Iron Horse across the plains of South Dakota.

St George stands alone, defiant, facing down the great leviathan. He waits till the very last second before plunging his sword towards the snake's head mask. With a piercing scream of brakes, the hot scrape of metal grinding on metal, a great fountain of sparks arcing the sky, the snake cracks apart, opens, splits and separates, to reveal a towering ANGEL, trembling with white wings, waiting to greet St George. High upon her stilts concealed by a long white dress is the silent girl who left her gifts at the water's edge. Sammy sees and recognises her at once. She is not, he now realises, a child, but a young woman. She looks out, past him and over the heads of everyone, towards the distant horizon where the city's smoke stacks bellow and rise.

One of the Mummers holds up a large metal sheet, almost as wide as his outstretched span. He takes its weight in his arms and slowly starts to shake it. The metal ripples, catching the light of the still climbing sun, and from it emanates the low groan of distant thunder. Out of the crowd steps a Mummer in black and burnished gold.

TURKISH KNIGHT:
    In come I, the Turkish Knight
    Come from Turkish lands to fight
    I come to fight St George
    That man of courage bold
    And if his blood be hot
    I soon will make it cold

The two figures of St George and the Turkish Knight circle slowly around one another. The rattling sound of stones in pans and kettles grows louder and louder.

St GEORGE:
>Battle to battle with thee I call
>To see who on this ground shall fall

TURKISH KNIGHT:
>Battle to battle with thee I pray
>To see who on this ground shall lay

They launch themselves towards one another in a clash of wood and metal, sword and shield. With a single blow the Turkish Knight strikes St George a blow across the top of his skull. St George sinks to the earth in an agonised slow motion. The crowd sighs.

JACK:
>Is there a doctor to be found
>To staunch this deep and deadly wound?
>Doctor, Doctor, where's the Doctor?

To the surprise of Sammy, Moon and Catch, Tommy Thunder enters the arena. Though heavily masked and disguised by his rags and feathers of charcoal grey, they recognise his gait, his way of stalking the ground in long, measured strides. He carries a pair of bones in his right hand, which clack repeatedly as he makes his way around the circle's edge towards the centre, a figure of ghosts and mists, frosts and spider webs. Over his shoulder he carries his own bag, from which he now produces the bottle which once contained the tincture to cure the wounds on the Earl's prize black mare. When he speaks – words whose meaning remains unclear to him, words the Earl has taught him when first he asked him to join the ranks of Mummers – it is the tone he remembers, from Moon when experiencing a vision.

DOCTOR:
>Yes – there is a doctor to be found
>To cure this deep and deadly wound
>I am a Doctor pure and good
>And with my head I'll staunch his blood

JACK:
>Thou sayest thou art pure
>But Doctor, Doctor, what canst thou cure?

Tommy performs a jerky dance as he speaks, a marionette crow seeking out carrion.

DOCTOR:
>I can cure…
>The itch, the stitch, the spots, the pox
>All manner bellyache, rashes and gout
>There be nine devils in
>I kick ten devils out

He holds the tincture bottle high and creeps towards the slain St George, still lying prostrate on the grass.

DOCTOR:
>I have a little bottle here by my side
>The fame of which spreads far and wide
>The stuff therein is elecampane

'Twill bring the dead to life again

He kneels beside St George, cradles his neck with the back of his hand, tips the tincture bottle towards his lips.

DOCTOR:
A drop on his head
A drop on his heart
Arise, bold fellow
And take thy part

The violinist begins a slow lament, which shifts into a rhythmic, quickening jig. The Mummers advance towards the body of St George. They each lay their birds' nest sticks above the body in the shape of a star once more. When the music reaches its climax, St George leaps through the centre, resurrected and transformed, to loud, approving cheers.

Two more Mummers emerge from the crowd. The music continues to gain in speed.

BEELZEBUB:
In come I, Beelzebub
Bashing and banging with my club

DEVIL DOUBT:
And in come I, Little Devil Doubt
With my shirt-tail flap hanging all about
I dither, I dather

I blither, I blather
Oh what a racket I make

BEELZEBUB:
We run up and down
The streets of the town
Till every last soul is awake

The music is now demented and manic as Beelzebub and Devil Doubt dart in and among everyone in the crowd.

ALL: (*singing*):
Turkey Rhubarb
Turkey Rhubarb
Turkey Rhubarb I sell
We come from Old Turkey to make you all well
And if you don't know us we'll sing this again
We are the celebrated Turkey Rhubarb Men

They sing the song a second time, with all the crowd joining in. At the end Jack-in-the-Green steps forward.

JACK:
We've come to the end of our Pace-Egging play
We wish you much joy this Easter Day
We pray you be happy and wish you Good Cheer
And hope we will see you again next year

All the Mummers bow solemnly, before leading a procession towards the Great Barn, where trestle tables are laid out with plates of Easter biscuits and simnel cake.

The Earl catches up with Tommy just as he is taking off his cloak and mask.

"You'll always find a welcome here," he says.

Tommy thanks him, then asks after the mare.

"Good," says the Earl. "Her wounds are barely visible. She is managing daily walks around the yard now. She's itching to gallop."

Tommy shakes his head. "Wait till the May blossom is out," he says. "Then put her in a paddock. She will tell you when she's ready."

The day draws to a close. Tommy finds Old Moon sitting under the shade of an ancient yew tree in the churchyard. Together they make their way back to the camp. They see Catch drinking ale from a jug. He tells them Sammy has already left, but that he will stay a while longer.

The sky is almost dark by the time Tommy and Moon reach the Bittern Wood.

Tommy settles Moon, then heads back to the field for his ritual walking of its perimeter, followed by an hour or two's watch of its nightly visitors.

From the wood he hears the eerie ecstasy of foxes mating. A tawny owl is hunting. He feels the rush of silent wings disturb the air. The moon is full, its dark marks the unmistakeable outline of a hare. He looks for the jill in the field, where shoots of early wheat show sharp and clear in the frosty light, but he cannot see her. Perhaps she really is dancing in the moon, he thinks, and smiles. He senses a movement just a few feet in front of him. It is the recently born leveret, now fully weaned and nibbling at the night time grass. He watches her excrete a slim, dark faeces, which she then proceeds delicately to eat. As far as Tommy knows, the hare is the only creature to do this, extracting double the nutrients for every morsel of food. He is so absorbed in watching her that he fails to spot the approaching danger until it is too late. Out of the woods, black apocalyptic wings against the moon, the sparrowhawk swoops, as swift as if fired from a bow, its beak deadlier than any arrow's tip, and plucks the leveret from the field in less than a heartbeat. Before Tommy's eyes can even blink, it is gone. A wisp of cloud now covers the moon, as if the hidden hare can't bear to look.

> *"Fur and feather*
> *Beak and claw*
> *Blood from moonlight*
> *Feeds the earth…"*

*

Hinge and latch, lock and key. Poker, fender, ash pan, grate. Nut and bolt, nail and screw. Files, rasps, axe heads, horse shoes. Horse shoes, horse shoes, always horse shoes.

Catch is apprenticed to Ezekiel Flint of the

Worshipful Company of Blacksmiths, Zack to his friends, Mr Flint to Catch. Catch first sees Flint when he enters the dark of the forge, drawn by the deep red glow of iron and fire, a man mountain, head and neck like a buffalo. Flint asks him to lift the anvil in the far corner of the smithy and carry it to him. "A smith must be able to carry his own anvil," he says.

A horse comes in to be re-shod. Flint barks instructions over the hammering, roaring, hissing and cooling for Catch to fetch this, for Catch to lift that, for Catch to keep out of his way. Later, when the horse is led back out into the yard, Flint orders Catch to spit on the now red hot anvil, then studies the sizzle.

"Ay, lad. I reckon tha'll do."

In the weeks that follow, they work alongside each other for ten hours a day, bare-chested, glistening with sweat, casting huge red shadows on the far wall of the forge. Catch only speaks if spoken to first, and Flint rarely speaks at all, unless it is to complain about shoddy work, and as the weeks turn into months he has less and less cause to do so. Catch takes the white hot metal from the heart of the forge and beats it, hammers and bends it, into every shape imaginable. From it Flint fashions all manner of objects – gates, grilles, railings, farm implements, tools, religious items – but for Catch, always, every day is horse shoes.

On his first day Catch watches Flint beat out a set of horse shoes in the blink of an eye, punch six nail holes into each with unerring accuracy. While these cool, hissing in the huge water trough, Flint examines each hoof, prises off the old shoes, chips off the compacted dirt and stones with a hoof pick, wire brushes the foot clean, scrapes the dark, outer layer of the sole to reveal the softer white underneath, trims any excess hoof wall with a pair of nippers, rasps and flattens the level of the sole, sizes the shoe to the hoof, bending, cutting and shaping to fit, then drives the nails through the holes in the cooled shoe to fix it to the foot. He can completely shoe a horse in two hours.

"The secret," he says, "is never to hurry."

Catch smiles. He knows when he's being conned. By the end of a month he can re-shoe a horse in an hour and a half.

But it's a repetitive, back-breaking business, and no mistake. For the first year, horse shoes are all that Flint will let him make. Anything fancier, anything requiring a bit of artistry, he keeps for himself. When Catch challenges him one day and asks to make the new weather vane for the Church of St Mary the Virgin in Ellenbrook, after the old one has blown off in a storm, Flint smiles and shakes his head.

"Tha's a cheeky beggar, I'll say that for thee. What did I tell thee? Never to hurry. Mebbe next year, youth."

And so Catch devises himself a plan. At the end of each day, when Flint finishes early, for Catch to lock up and rake out the ashes from the grate, and set up the coals for the next day's fire, Catch stays on to work the dying embers, using iron cut-offs and scrap, to cast a black feather for each horse shod that day. He keeps these feathers in a large ammunition chest, at the far end of the forge, where Flint rarely goes. In twelve months he has crafted more than three hundred of them, from every bird imaginable, picked up where he finds them, pigeon, crow, blackbird, gull, jackdaw, lapwing, magpie, rook. As the nights stay lighter longer, he likes to take them out at random, hold them up, study their separate shapes and forms. Sometimes he will close his eyes, run his fingers slowly along each vane and wing tip, testing the way the metal curves and joins, and see if he can detect its identity from touch and feel alone.

One night he stays longer than he intends, falls asleep and wakes with a start as Flint kicks open the heavy wooden doors to let in the morning and begin to light the fire. He says nothing. He goes about his customary rituals as if he hasn't noticed Catch in the corner. Only when he has set the giant pair of bellows in motion does he call him over.

"Here," he says, "cop a hold of these."

While Catch pumps the bellows up and down, up and down, Flint wanders over to the ammunition chest and rummages through Catch's collection of iron feathers. He looks at the jackdaw's for a full thirty seconds.

"Not bad, youth," he remarks, tossing the feather back into the pile. "I reckon tha' might make that weather vane over at Ellenbrook after all."

From that day forward Flint shares all the work which comes into the forge equally between them.

Catch is now making not just weather vanes, but gates, railings, pole hooks, chains, mountings for lamps, couplings for trains, shafts for wagons, rail splitters, fork tines, coal scuttles, bread ovens. He still makes horse shoes, a hundred a fortnight, and he still makes a feather for each of them, which now he places, embedded within, or set alongside, every object he finishes. They become his signature, his mark, and soon these feathers can be found right across the parish, if you know where to look, in church porches, beneath boot scrapers, on barge plates, and always, always, on weather vanes, turning in the wind.

But in one place they do not appear. For all his appreciation of Catch's skill, Ezekiel Flint does not offer him a partnership. There is no crow's feather, or magpie's, or rook's, yet to be seen in the sign which hangs above the forge door, and Flint is not getting any younger.

"I reckon I'll have to sell up when I'm done," he says one day. Catch knows that Flint has no son, that he regrets this, but he also knows the forge is a going concern, would fetch a tidy sum if put up for sale, enough to keep Flint from the ever present threat of the workhouse's embrace, and that there's no way he, Catch, will ever be in a position to buy it himself.

More and more he's begun to look upon the flat marshes stretching between their camp in the crook of the Irwell and the mines at Ellenbrook as home. He no longer dreams of the South Dakota plains, nor does he feel the old ancestral pull of the seasons, or the need to be always on the move. He sees Sammy staking out the rivers, brooks and canals, marking out some kind of territory he can call his own. He sees Tommy watching the nightly progress of the wheat in his field, and he sees his own shadow lengthening across the land as he picks his way across the moss towards the forge, taking pleasure in familiar landmarks, saying good day to people he passes along the roads. And then he hears Old Moon singing the old songs, in the old tongue, rocking back and forth, his voice floating up towards the stars, and begins to understand the old ways are slipping away from him, but that they will never leave him entirely. He thinks of his name, the name that now he's known by, and wonders how he came by it. What is left for him still to catch, that he must chase and fight to keep? He looks up at the sign above the forge door – Ezekiel Flint: Blacksmith – and knows that this is not where his future lies. But it will do for now.

He continues on his way along the raised bank above the moss. His eyes track possible pathways across the treacherous marshes, where the mud is so thick and deep he once saw a horse stuck fast in it, unable to pull itself free, slowly sink beneath the surface and disappear, leaving not a trace of itself. No. He's not ready to risk losing himself in the mire, not until he can see a new fire to catch, a new piece of ground on which to pitch camp, leave his mark, where someone he's not yet met might place a candle in a window to guide him home, past these will o' the wisps, these swamp lights, lit by the methane gases from the moss, these Jack o' Lanterns, who carry their flickering ghost lamps along the corpse road.

He pauses, sees a pheasant feather lying on the path in front of him, picks it up and tucks it in his hat, before stepping out back towards the camp, the creeping lure of Manchester glowing ever brighter.

*

Chat Moss was once even more treacherous than it is when Catch walks across it to and from Flint's forge.

The Delph. The delved place. A sandstone ridge between Worsley and Salford which had been quarried for centuries. It provided the stone for the Bridgewater Canal more than a century before. Cut by hand using pick and shovel, hammer and drill, and, later, gunpowder. Spoil from the construction was used to reclaim Chat Moss, transform it from an impassable swamp to a land that could be crossed on foot, if you were careful and knew the secret ways.

The Delph. Also the entrance to a series of underground canals, known as the Navigable Levels, dug at the same time to connect the many small mines all within reach of the Bridgewater – Edge Fold Pit and Chaddock's Pit; Wharton Pit and Sandhole Pit; Fan Pit, Wood Pit, Tongues Field Pit; Buckley Lane and Brackley Pit; Crippen Croft and Turnpike Lime; Cinder Field and Linnyshaw; Tub's Engine, Magnalls, Ellesemere Air and Ellenbrook, and, further back along the Irwell, Clifton Hall and Agecroft.

The Navigable Levels serve three main purposes – they transport coal from the face of each pit directly to the Bridgewater, they drain the mines, and their run-off feeds back to the main canal. Sammy finds work there, plying the more than fifty miles of underground channels. Less than six feet in height, seven in width, and barely a foot in depth in places, he navigates the narrow subterranean darkness of this latter day River Styx in a specially designed boat, with both ends shaped as a prow, to enable him to row in both directions, its constricted shape with visible ribs showing through earning it the nickname of "starvationer".

Sammy paddles his starvationer the entire length of all three of the Navigable Levels from Worsley to Farnworth, Walkden to Boothstown, transferring between levels via a complex series of locks on water-driven inclined planes. He spends all his daylight hours underground and much of his night-time ones by the river's edge, back at the camp, repairing nets, trawling the Irwell for trout and grayling, chub and dace, perch and pike, and the seething beds of eels. He rarely leaves his twin-prowed canoe, his starvationer, what little sleep he snatches, he takes within the confines of its beam, its deck upturned above him.

His eyes have grown accustomed to searching in the darkness. He sees the water flickering on the arched tunnel roofs inches above his head. He can grade in an instant the different shades of black – coal, canal, clay and stone – recognise at once the looming shapes of lock and chute, kerb and capstan, and see the whites of another pair of eyes at fifty paces. His fingers trace initials carved in the stone, in the farthest reaches of the Levels, as far from The Delph as it's possible to get. He encounters strange figures crudely daubed upon the tunnel's walls, men and women, birds and fish, horses and ploughs, and all the other creatures from the upper air, and finds the bones of long-trapped birds, gnawed on by nocturnal rats. All his senses heighten and fine tune. He can smell the soil above his head as it freezes and thaws, the differences in coal dust from one pithead to another, the welcome breath of air when he's nearing The Delph. He hears the water dripping from above, rain that fell a century before, seeping its way through the rock, before landing in separate, echoing drops in each bend of the hewn caves of the Levels, whose every nook and cranny he recognises in the particular quality of each unique drip. He knows where all of the colonies of pipistrelle bats reside and feels the rush of air as they swoop past him towards their feeding grounds beyond The Delph. In Queen Anne Pit, by Stirrup Brook, he unearths a hoard of Roman coins, which he gives to Tommy to take to the Earl, who proclaims it treasure trove, donates it all to the Manchester Museum, save one, with the head of Diocletian still preserved in its well-worn, much-exchanged bronze, which Sammy gives to Old Moon.

On one particular cold and starless night when, but for the change in air, Sammy hardly marks the transition from rowing the Navigable Levels to emerging out of The Delph into the Worsley Brook, and from there to the sluggish waters of the ink black Irwell, he hears, smells and feels, rather than sees his journey back to the camp, while his large lemur-like eyes dilate and adjust. As he approaches the final crook in the river's bend, beyond which the camp lies waiting, he sees the orange sparks from their always lit fire dancing in the sky, and he hears the hoarse rasp of Old Moon singing one of the ancient songs in the lost tongue.

"*Flow like the river*
Turn like the earth
Rumble like thunder
Fall like the rain…"

Sammy checks the nets – like he does every night. He hauls the traps he placed that morning until they flop on the bank, coiled and wriggling – like he does every night, and then he sits on the upturned keel of his starvationer to inspect the catch – like he does every night. But tonight something is different. The nets are heavier than usual. At the centre of the seething silver is something dark and still. He clears away the tangle of trout and grayling, striking each head skilfully, once, before tossing them into an open barrel, until he reaches the black heart at the centre of his catch. The moment his fingers first touch it, brush against its slick sheen of fur, he knows it. An otter. Curled in a tight whorl. Head buried beneath its tail.

His first thought is that it must be dead, but as he lets his hand hover lightly above its silky pelt he can sense a pulse, a quiver, shuddering through it. He quickly grabs it in both his hands, holds it firmly round its body, while it jerks and thrashes. It is weak. Normally, he knows, a healthy otter would be impossible to quell, would sink its sharp teeth into his flesh, but not this one. It calms, quietens, allows him to relax his grip and stroke the top of its head and along its throat, until soft bubbles of formless sound oscillate the night air. A waxing half moon begins to emerge from behind a cloud, and Sammy brings the otter, a female he can now see, closer to him. He looks directly into her dark, unblinking eyes. There is an expression there he seems to recognise, slow and patient, like time. The last remaining wisps of cloud leave the moon completely. It shines down pitilessly on the two of them, locked together as the minutes pass. An owl hoots close by. The sound releases them from their strange embrace. The otter wriggles free from Sammy's grip and leaps back into the river. Without a conscious thought he dives in after her. Now he is in *her* element and the tables are turned. She is flying as much as she is swimming. She slaloms in and out of the reed beds, she butterflies above and below the surface. The water cascades along her body, individual droplets holding a thousand images of her simultaneously, like the shards of a broken mirror, in which Sammy sees himself also, reflected back but tiny, floundering in her wake. But he is called Leaping Fish for a reason. He breasts the dark river like a skimming stone, before gulping a lungful of air to plunge beneath the water, where all is dark, tracking her by vibration more than sight, then back up into the air, straining to catch a glimpse of her. She is toying with him, he realises, doubling back at each bend in the river to check he's still behind her, still in hot pursuit.

They approach the weir where the Irwell meets the

Mersey. The water tumbles over sharp rocks, the current is forcing him back, caught in the vortex of its broiling, roaring maelstrom. Using every ounce of strength that's left him, Sammy leaps, a running salmon returning to spawn. He surges high above the rapids, reaches at last the calmer upstream current, but she is gone, nowhere to be seen. No tell tale bubbles break the surface. Sammy swims in ever decreasing circles, slower and slower, his arms and legs so heavy they can no longer support him. Somehow he drags himself to the bank, heaves himself on shore, and lies face down in the wet earth.

It takes several minutes for his breathing to begin to return to normal. Slowly his other senses recover. He hears a twig snap a few feet away, then another. The soil beside him sighs with the imprint of a small foot being placed upon it. He feels a hand softly caressing the back of his neck, and then some strands of hair brushing across his face as he is gently turned over onto his back.

He slowly opens his eyes.

A face is looking down on him, anxiously searching his every flicker.

He wonders if he's drowned, or dreaming.

She reminds him, in her expression, of the otter, whose body he held as the moon crept out from behind a cloud.

The same waxing half moon, which shines above him now, which frames the face of the girl.

The phantom girl.

The spirit child who left them food that first winter

they arrived, when they had nothing, when they almost starved.

The angel.

The child who is not a child, but a young woman.

Here. Now.

Bending over him.

Looking into his face.

Smiling.

He wonders if she might be a selkie.

Half girl, half otter.

The smile broadens. As if she is reading his thoughts.

She stands. He tries to lift himself from the earth. She places a finger to his lips. He lies back down again. She walks away, towards a wooden hut further up from the river's edge. He calls after her. She doesn't respond. He calls again. Still she doesn't answer, doesn't turn.

She comes back in a few moments, carrying a bucket of water and a ladle. She places one hand behind his neck, and with the other brings the ladle towards his mouth. He drinks.

"Thank you," he says, as she turns away, back towards the bucket.

She says nothing. She hears nothing.

He understands.

The girl is silent. She cannot speak. She is mute. Mute and deaf.

When she brings the ladle back towards him, he sits up, faces her, makes sure she can see his lips.

"What – is – your – name?"

She smiles. She picks up a stick and writes in the

sand.

E – V – E.

Sammy laughs. "I can't read," he says.

*

On a warm midsummer's evening in June Tommy is packing up after a day's work at the Hall. The ornamental lawns have been overrun with moles and Tommy has been brought in to deal with them. Moles, he thinks, not for the first time. Useful in one place, unwanted in another. The irony is not lost on him. He takes great care to dispatch them as quickly, as painlessly, as possible, making sure to find as many uses for them once they're dead as he can, to give a better reason for their dying. As he lays the bodies out upon the grass he silently asks forgiveness from each one.

He remembers the words of his father, when he took him on his first buffalo hunt. "Everything as it moves, here and there, now and then, pauses. The bird as it flies pauses in one place to make a nest, and in another to rest in its flight. A man when he goes out into the world pauses as he wills, until that final pause, which is not of his choosing, but is decided for him. So it is with the sun, who journeys across the sky, falls into darkness with the night, but returns the next day."

The Earl is standing on the terrace looking out across the lawn towards the city in the distance. A barge is chugging below on the junction of the river with the canal. Beyond, the sun's last rays are picking out sheep and cattle in the fields, the orchards heavy with fruit. He comes down to join Tommy.

"I have a painting in the Hall which shows exactly this scene," he says. "More or less. William Wylde. Ours is just a copy. The original's in the Royal Collection. It was commissioned by the Queen after she stayed here. She stood exactly where we're standing now, looking at this very view. She was enchanted by it, I seem to recall, Prince Albert even more so. He'd just opened The Great Exhibition that summer. He lit a cigar and pointed towards the mills and factories of Manchester in the distance, turned to my father and said, 'That's the future, George. And where we're standing is the past. What happens when they meet, eh?' Well, the city's closer now..." He pauses, puffing on his own cigar, and looks down at the neat row of mole corpses laid out on the lawn. "But this is not the past, Tommy, is it? It's the here and now."

"My father says time is a circle."

"Sounds like an interesting fellow, your father."

"Yes, sir."

"Change is coming, Tommy. Mark my words. Great change."

"Change is always coming. What is it your priests tells us? In life, we are in death."

"Quite so. But what to do about it, that's the real matter, is it not? Do I embrace it, or do I resist it? Do I cling to our old ways, or do I ring in the new?"

"A man cannot halt the tide."

"But he can harness its power, can he not? Build dams, dig tunnels, change the course of rivers?"

"He can. He does."

The Earl walks a few steps away, thinking. Absent-mindedly he blows a smoke ring from his cigar, which gradually forms a frame around his head. "Have you walked across Chat Moss, Tommy?"

"Not as often as Catch, but yes, I have."

"So have I. Though not for some time. What do you make of the place?"

"Lonely."

"Yes. Some say haunted. Do you believe in ghosts, Tommy?"

"The dead are always with us."

"I'm inclined to agree. I didn't used to. Dismissed such talk as mumbo jumbo. But out on the Moss, one hears things, sees things."

"Yes."

The Earl wafts away the smoke and turns urgently back towards Tommy. "Tell me."

"Cries."

"What sort of cries?"

"Like a soul that is lost."

"My elder brother Henry, the second Earl, would have said you were merely hearing the call of the curlew, which was quite a common sight on the moss when I was a boy."

"It's the same thing. Birds carry souls in flight."

"Hmm." The Earl considers this for a moment. "And what did you see?"

"Bodies."

"Yes?"

"Floating to the surface. Long dead."

"Bodies?"

"Yes."

"Not skeletons?"

"No. There is skin covering the bones."

"You could make out their faces?"

"Yes."

"It's the peat. It preserves things."

"Memories."

"Yes."

"Ghosts."

"Yes. I suppose."

"People who lived here."

"Worked here."

"Under the earth."

"Digging the tunnels."

"Yes. Sammy has described these tunnels to me."

"He's been there?"

"He follows the rivers, the canals."

The Earl stands right up close to Tommy. "What did *he* see? What did he find?"

"He's still looking."

The Earl is urgently searching Tommy's face, as if for answers, then turns aside, tossing his now finished cigar into a flower bed, which Tommy picks up while the Earl is facing away, and places in his bag. He likes things to be tidy, and he doesn't like waste.

The Earl comes back to himself. "I can't decide what to do."

Tommy says nothing. He will let the Earl talk himself to a standstill or a decision. "Whichever course of action I take," the Earl continues, "I will be harming

the interests of some, improving the lot of others."
Another pause. "I fear I have inherited my father's habit
of vacillation. I succeeded him in becoming the
Member of Parliament here, and the well being of my
constituents, just like my tenants, I take most seriously,
but the choice I am now faced with means that if I act in
one way, the happiness of my constituents will be at the
expense of my tenants, while if I pursue the alternative,
the opposite will apply. I am caught between a veritable
rock and a hard place."

"What would your father have done?"

"That's just it, you see. He was for ever changing
his mind. Take the Corn Laws. A wicked, insidious act.
At first he opposed their repeal. He thought he was
guided by the interests of manufacture rather than
agriculture. 'I presume that a man who is in the centre
of a largely rural population,' he said, 'will look to its
wishes and apparent interest. I shall do likewise. If he
looks to his ricks, I shall look to my chimneys and those
of my neighbours.' Change, you see?" He knows
Tommy cannot possibly be following what he is saying,
but he feels compelled to continue. "My father looked
on industry as the future and farming as the past. But
his decision caused great suffering. People could not
afford the price of bread, and they starved. Everywhere.
But especially in the city, whose interests he thought he
was championing." The Earl looks in the direction of
Manchester, regards its columns of smoke inking in the
horizon. "And so he changed his mind."

"It takes a wise man to admit when he is wrong."

"Or a weak one."

Tommy spreads his hands.

The Earl waits, as if contemplating something, then speaks quickly. "Come. I want to show you something."

He leads Tommy inside the Hall, the first time Tommy has ever stepped across its threshold. The Earl stops in front of a framed facsimile of what looks like a letter, written in a confident, elegant hand. "Can you read?"

Tommy shakes his head.

"This is my father's final speech to Parliament. The Prime Minister had asked him to move the Loyal Address in which that cruel law would at last be repealed. Peel chose my father because he thought it would sound stronger coming from someone who had changed his mind."

Tommy nods in agreement.

"Permit me to read you an extract:

'I myself have been compelled to be a somewhat close observer of the connexion between the prices of provisions, and the employment and happiness of the people. Accident has cast my lot in the midst of a dense population, with respect to a large portion of which, this accident has made me a distributor of work and wages; and I have seen the operation of what I believe to be the connection between the prices of provisions, and the happiness and employment of the people in various conditions. Five years ago high food prices, artificially regulated by government controls, led to great social unrest. I saw this for myself in the manufacturing districts of South Lancashire, and I

can tell you, no one who witnessed this could wish to see its return. As a consequence, I stand before this House today a fervent advocate of free trade. My observation has led me to believe that if you, as a Government, undertake to control and regulate the supply of the means of subsistence to the community, you will find that it is difficult, nay, impossible for you, to spread the public table with what profusion you may, to satisfy those who would still retire from the feast with appetites not altogether satiated, and with minds not fully convinced that they have had sufficient for their health, and that all that remains for them is to pray that they may be truly thankful. The abundance, which you call sufficient, but which no man can call excessive, is, after all, but a matter of comparison. There are dark spots and weak places in various parts of our social system: let us not be blind to them, or neglect the duty of exposing them, with the view of mending and improving them. Let us not fling in one another's teeth difficulties, remedial or irremedial, for the sole purpose of party or of faction. Let us not fling in the face of one class a Cheshire agricultural worker; or a manufacturing labourer from Lancashire in the face of another. To meet the cases of both - to give them, in the first instance, food - to give them other luxuries which many of them still need - air, water, drainage - to give them all the physical and moral advantages possible; let that be our employment and our duty, and let us endeavour to perform that office by ridding the country of those subjects of angry discussion to which I have *referred'.*"

The Earl has tears in his eyes as he finishes. Tommy moves to one side out of respect. He wonders if the Earl's emotions are caused by pride or fear.

"It is difficult to live up to the expectations of our fathers," he says.

The Earl looks Tommy directly in the eye. "What should I do?"

"What does your heart tell you?"

The Earl takes a step back, struck by the simple force of that simple question. But unlike his father, he knows that the choice facing him now is an irrevocable one. Once the decision has been made, there will be no second chance this time, no possibility to change his mind.

"How is your field?" he asks instead. "The wheat must be almost ready to cut."

Tommy nods. "Soon, I think. Eight weeks."

"Come to the Harvest Home," says the Earl, gripping Tommy's elbow. "I shall have made my decision by then."

Tommy picks up the dead moles, which he has strung together on baler twine, attached to a cruciform pole, and makes his way back to the camp beneath the Midsummer moon.

*

It is as hot a summer as anyone can recall.

Nathaniel scratches his head and tells Tommy he's not known such a long dry spell for half a century. Flint curses in the smithy as the sweat pours from him, for they have to keep the forge burning however hot it is outside. There are always horses to be shod. Even Sammy feels the heat stretching out its long fingers deep into the heart of the Navigable Levels. The walls and roofs drip with slime and condensation, as if the tunnels themselves are perspiring. It's a dog-panting, tongue-lolling, snake-basking kind of summer, a clay-oven, earth-baking, brook-emptying, tar-melting kind of summer. Even the bees seem fat and slow, heavy and drowsing in corn flowers, poppies, cockle and marigolds starring the wheat field. The wheat itself has been sun-roasted to a burnished gold from its tender green of a fortnight before. It bows its collective head, ears tipped with flame, and seems on the point of collapse, but its stalks stand straight still. Its roots, microscopic tendrils, burrow deep. The field holds deep artesian wells from decades past of winter rain, reservoirs of memory.

The nights are barely any cooler. Windows are flung wide open at the Hall. The horses fret and stamp in their stables. Old Moon lets the fire go out at the camp. The land lies suspended. Not a breath of wind ripples the surface of the water. Not a sound disturbs the soporific hush in the Bittern Wood. As the sun begins to bleed across the sky striking the air with its tinder box, the dawn chorus sounds parched and dry, almost as if the effort of waking has drained the birds of any energy to call or sing. Only a rogue magpie desultorily hopping by the edge of the wheat field emits its dry death rattle. One for sorrow.

"Suck a pebble
Stave your thirst
Bones and ashes
Slake the soil..."

It is Eve who notices it first.

Sleeping in the crook of Sammy's arm, her head resting on his chest, which rises and falls, rises and falls, with the gentle rhythm of his breathing, she feels something stir deep in the earth below her. The vibration ripples outwards until the surface of the ground beneath them trembles, like a trapped bird held in her fingers.

Tommy jerks awake.

The hairs on the back of his neck stand up. The skin along his arms prickles. He lays his ear close to the earth and listens. His long buried ancestral instincts are re-awakened and he starts to run, living up to his name, chasing thunder.

The dogs in Nathaniel's yard begin barking without warning. In the top pasture the cows are spooked. They try to leap each other's shadow.

Flint, at his forge since before dawn to try and make the best of the early morning, before the heat of the day reaches its zenith, when he will feel like he could simply thrust his poker up into the sky and it will be hot enough to turn the iron red then white, feels the ground rock beneath him, so that for the first time since he himself was a young apprentice, scarce beginning at his trade, misses his stroke, his hammer striking the anvil only, instead of the horse shoes for the Earl's prize mare.

Chat Moss is drier than at any time in living memory. Catch has taken to exploring newly revealed banks and pathways as the swamp shrivels and the marsh retreats. He rises while it is still dark, while it is still cool enough to move through the heavy, drugged air. He walks deep into the Moss's heart, uncovers adders, lizards, and rare butterflies, the heath fritillary, speckled wood and painted lady, almost steps on a bed of eels writhing their way across dry land in search of a safe passageway back to the river, and from there to the sea. He passes hand built shacks of wooden planks and rusted corrugated, raised on stilts, connected by flimsy pontoons to the normally hidden web of levees. Rolling-eyed dogs, tethered on chains, bay and snarl as they pick up his scent on the thistledown air, but the sun is too intense for them to keep it up for long, and soon it is all they can do to raise their fly-blown, mangy heads for the most cursory of glances, a token, deep-throated growl, before collapsing back in the dust of their broken-stepped stoops, seeking what little shade they can muster.

Occasionally Catch sees people, distant figures, dots in the land, scratching their heads over empty traps, brittle bone-dry nets. Sometimes they see him and wave an arm as if to say, who are you? What are you doing here? Whatever it is, know that you're not welcome. But their gestures are limp, short-lived, half-hearted, and all too soon they turn their backs and let him drift on by.

He sees hand painted signs nailed up on wooden poles warning him to "Keep out, you!" A dead crow, weighted beneath a cloud of fly, hangs from a fence post.

On this particular morning, when he is so far deep in the fat, bloated belly of the Moss, so far from Flint's Forge or his own Camp that he is completely lost, not a landmark in sight anywhere, he hears the unmistakeable sound of a shotgun being cocked, its hammers being pulled back, and a voice, slow and mean, asking, "Where the hell do you think you're going?" followed by, "Turn around real slow," and then, "Do I know you?"

Catch does exactly as he's bid. Facing him from just a few feet away, the shotgun aimed right between his eyes, is a figure he can't make out. Face in shadow, with the sun directly above and behind. The land is lower here, the lowest point on the Moss, and still wet, even in this Sahara of a summer. Now that he is not moving, standing stock still, face to featureless face, trying to work out what his next move might be against this dark shadow, mirage in the sun, shimmering just a few feet away from him, his feet begin to sink slowly into the soft, peaty earth. Black ooze rises thickly about his ankles. He tries to lift his left foot free, but this slightest of movements elicits an immediate response from his captor, who fires an immediate warning shot which strikes an abandoned, rusting horse shoe, floating on the surface barely inches away from Catch's foot. He freezes, but then is forced to lift his right foot from the mud, to adjust his balance and save himself from sinking further. A second gun shot pings against a second horse shoe, poking through the slime. Its echoes ricochet and bounce across the Moss.

It's then that Catch hears something else. His attacker hears it too and lowers the shotgun. A low, deep rumbling from far below, directly under where they are standing. They feel it as strongly as they hear it. A juddering within the rock face of the earth. The land appears to tilt. They hear a low, creaking moan. The rickety wooden steps leading up to the bleached weatherboard stoop splinter and crack, and then the whole ship of the shack begins to list to starboard, as slowly, but unstoppably, it starts to sink into the unforgiving, sucking swamp of Chat Moss. The silhouette with the gun clings desperately to the door of the dwelling, which has swung open, but the wood, rotten from the perpetual damp that in most years permeates the Moss and now brittle from the recent weeks of rainless sun, snaps and separates, so that the figure is flung into the black, peaty ooze of the marsh. Catch instinctively hurls himself towards the falling figure, which he grabs around the waist, so that the two of them land temporarily dazed, when there is a second jolt and the land attempts to right itself.

The two bodies try to disentangle themselves from one another, slipping and scrabbling in the mud as their feet and hands flail to gain what traction they can, but only manage to effect an even tighter embrace. Catch now has for a brief moment a slight advantage of height. It is he whose face is blocked out by the sun, and for the first time he can see his assailant clearly.

Two things strike him immediately and he is not sure which of them shocks him more. His attacker is a woman, and the woman is black.

Eve wakes Sammy as soon as she feels the second vibration, shaking the earth even more strongly.

He feels it too. It drags him from the pit of sleep, an electrical impulse charging his senses to high alert. Then he hears its low rumble and is instantly awake. He senses, from the pattern of the sound and the flow of the tremor, its source and is on his feet at once. He races down to the water's edge and launches the starvationer in the direction of The Delph. He rows as silent and stealthy as a wolf following a new scent. As soon as he reaches the entrance he is aware at once of a backwash. The normally static Stygian treacle of the canal's surface this morning resembles a tidal bore. Water is splashing against the walls of the tunnels, and as Sammy reaches the junction, less than five hundred yards in, where the channel makes the first of its numerous forks and divisions, he can tell at once the source of the disturbance, and he paddles as hard as he can against the flow in the direction of Lumn's Lane.

Tommy runs.

He runs through the dry, crackling forest of the wheat field. Red legged partridges, making their customary morning patrol between the towering avenue of stalks, hop out of his way in a flurry of noisy, indignant effrontery, before dusting themselves down and continuing their stately *passegiata*. A harvest mouse, delicately balanced on a ripening ear at the tip of a wheat spike, has to perform a perfectly executed somersault from its high wire trapeze to avoid being trampled underfoot. A surprised corn bunting flutters awkwardly from the heart of the field. Its startled song rasps like the jangling of keys on a rusty ring. It alights precariously on a nearby fence post, its yellow bill appearing to rearrange the necklace of dark spots across its speckled breast.

Tommy runs along the edge of the Moss, sure-footedly skipping from rock to stone, watched by a family of natterjack toads basking in the sun, lazily darting their tongues to catch clouds of insects disturbed by Tommy's progress. He runs towards an embankment shimmering in the heat haze, whose position shifts and tilts as another vibration rocks the earth, but this does nothing to impede Tommy's measured, even pace. He runs up the embankment without breaking stride, and now he has reached the railway which links Manchester with Liverpool, the first ever railway, built more than fifty years before, strung across Chat Moss on a series of floating rafts.

Tommy turns east, runs along the track, from sleeper to sleeper, lengthening his stride, quickening his pace, towards the plume of smoke he can see rising on the horizon.

Tommy runs.

Tommy runs, chasing thunder.

Tommy runs.

Back in the heart of the Moss, where the swamp has not fully dried.out even under this season of blazing sun, where the quagmire still grips and torques, where the ground gives way to invisible quicksand in less than a footstep, Catch and his assailant still wrestle and cling in a lover's embrace.

She regards Catch with the same astonishment as he imagines must be written across his own features, but there is no time for further speculation. Every time one of them tries to scrabble for a foothold, gain some traction in the shifting, cloying mud, they are sucked in deeper, until at last, in panic and anger, she yells to him.

"Let go of me, you fool! All your thrashing about is only making it worse. Try to stay still."

Something in the woman's tone, the certainty behind her exasperation, makes Catch instinctively do what she says. He releases the hold he has of her around her waist and immediately she pulls herself out of the bog and onto a tufted patch of more stable marsh grass close by.

"Spread yourself over as wide a space as you can."

Once more Catch obeys. Spreadeagled in this way he can sense at once the rate of his sinking beginning to slow, but at the same time it leaves him feeling particularly vulnerable, completely at the mercy of this strange amphibious creature crouched above him. Out of the sun he sees her raise her shotgun and point it back towards him. Perhaps she really is about to shoot him, he thinks, and he instinctively starts to brace his body. Instantly he begins to sink once more.

"*Enfin,*" she says, "grab the barrel," and she extends the gun towards him. With a desperate lunge he closes the fingers of his right hand around it. "Now the other," she commands. He tries to extricate his left arm which, with a great sucking sound from the mud, he manages, only for the fingers of his right hand to start to slip. Somehow he wraps both hands around the gun, as the woman pulls him towards her, inch by inch, towards drier land and safety. Catch is a big man, made even bigger by his time at the forge and heavier by the mud clinging to his clothes, but the woman is strong and, after several slow, agonised minutes, she finally succeeds in dragging him clear.

"*Merde,*" she exclaims, followed by a further torrent of French and Creole expletives.

The two now face each other on the bank, eyes locked, her hands on the butt of the shotgun, his on its barrel, still pressed against his stomach. Beside them her shack continues to list. With a final shuddering sigh it loses its battle to remain upright and keels over creaking into the bog, disappearing plank by rotten plank, until all that is left to denote it was once there is the hand painted warning sign.

"*Keep out, you!*"

The harder Sammy paddles, the more backwash he creates. He must pause from time to time to allow the water to settle and to listen again to the sonic echoes reverberating round the tunnels. He wishes he'd been named for the bat, rather than the fish, to have made the task easier.

After more than an hour he reaches the side-arm which serves Lumn's Lane. He tries to operate the lock that will transport him to the next level down, but it isn't working. He is forced to make a detour via Agecroft which, when he reaches it, is already thronging with people.

By the time Sammy is stepping out of his starvationer at Agecroft, Tommy has already been at Lumn's Lane for more than half an hour, during which each minute has felt like a lifetime. The scene resembles a battlefield.

Clifton Hall Colliery is owned by Messrs Andrew Knowles & Sons Limited. Its entrance is on Lumn's Lane, by which name it is universally known, in Weaste on the edge of Salford, just three miles from Worsley. It has been open for fifty years, operating successfully and growing in size and production. The depth of the shaft is five hundred and forty yards and there are now three main seams – Doe Mine, Quarters Mine and Trencherbone Mine. It lies close to Clifton Junction

Station on the Lancashire & Yorkshire Railway, as well as being linked to the Bridgewater Canal by the Navigable Levels. But now, as Tommy surveys the wreckage, all sense of order and direction is gone.

It was just after seven o'clock in the morning the first of the underground explosions occurred.

Mr Hindley, the manager on duty, is explaining to anyone who asks that all the miners at Lumn's Lane use the patent safety lamps, but admits that yes, sometimes, naked flames are still carried down, especially if conditions are, as he terms them, "remarkably good", when there is "no danger of gas accumulation". Today, it seems, was deemed just such a day, despite what has happened since indicating the contrary. He has removed his jacket and is mopping his face and brow with a linen handkerchief, which earlier that morning was white, but is now smudged and black.

A second explosion occurred just after the morning shift had started. Guard rails on the sides of the pit mouth up at the surface were blown clean away and the cages used to descend to the three seams were rendered useless. More than two hundred men and boys are now trapped underground. The sound of the explosion was heard more than two miles away, but the shaking of the earth, the shock waves caused by the blast, were felt much further afield than that. These are what have brought so many people to the pit, eager to offer what help they can, Tommy among them.

Ezekiel Flint arrives just as Mr Hindley is arranging for a kibble, a large bucket used for bringing coal to the surface, to be lowered down the mine and calling for volunteers. Zack and Tommy, together with Aaron Manley, a local pitman not working this shift, step forward.

"Right," says Hindley grimly. "We'll need a blacksmith," he adds, looking at Zack, and someone who knows the seams – like you, Manley." He turns now towards Tommy, whose reputation is known. "And yes, we'll probably need assistance with any ponies that are trapped."

They proceed towards the bottom in a series of jerks and jolts, as the chain to which the kibble is attached is laboriously winched by hand. Before they have descended two hundred yards, the smell of the gas rising up towards them becomes increasingly noxious. By the time they have reached the bottom, it is completely overpowering.

"Firedamp," groans Manley.

"Cover your faces," gasps Hindley, "and don't, whatever you do, strike a match."

The deeper they go, the darker and fouler it gets.

When eventually the kibble hits hard rock at the foot of the pit, they are tumbled out like dice from a shaker.

The scene that greets them is a nightmare.

They stumble over dead bodies, piled one on top of another. Worse than that, as they grope their way through the dark, trying not to breathe any more than they have to, their hands grasp severed limbs, fingers, a foot, an arm, a stump of leg.

Flint turns away and works at once to free one of the cages, so that it might be used to carry those still living back up to the surface as quickly as possible. The groans of the maimed and dying echo all along the three seams. They ricochet around the tunnels like canon fire. Manley and Hindley move among them, trying to bring what comfort they can. They are badly burned, some of them beyond recognition, and all are suffering with the effects of afterdamp, carbon monoxide poisoning.

Tommy's ears pick up the faint pawing of a hoof scraping against the seam wall, the pitiful, rasping breath of a pit pony in pain. Tommy finds it partially submerged in a rising rush of water unleashed by the explosion from one of the Navigable Levels. He grabs its tether and pulls it from its murky, debris-strewn roar. It clambers to its feet, then charges the cage which Flint is trying to free from fallen rocks. Tommy leaps across and wrestles it to the ground once more before it can damage Flint or itself further. He calms it, whispering gently in its ear, and slowly helps it back to its feet. It stands unsteadily, its balance precarious. Tommy creeps round to the front of it, his hand never for a moment leaving its wounded side, and puts his head close to the pony's muzzle. He breathes out slowly, sending the flow of unpolluted air from deep within his lungs directly into the pony's nostrils. It rears backwards a step, whinnies, then returns to Tommy, who breathes into it once more. The pony lifts its head as if seeking a source of air not so thickly contaminated with the coal gas. Finally, it turns itself around and, still hobbling, makes its slow and painful way towards the partly blocked entrance to the Doe seam.

By this time Flint has freed the cage, and he and Manley begin helping the worst of the injured into it.

The painstaking process of hauling the dead back to the surface takes the rest of the day.

Meanwhile Hindley has ascertained from those men able to speak that no one was in the Quarters seam, which is in any case completely blocked, but that the Trencherbone seam has collapsed, and that there is no hope of reaching anyone still there. Tons of rock have fallen and another explosion threatens to bring some of that down upon where they are now gathered.

"Follow the pony," says Tommy.

They all turn towards him, and he points towards the Doe seam.

"He's right," says Manley. "It's our best hope."

While Tommy keeps hold of the pony, Manley pulls away as much of the rock from the entrance as he can, and then he and Hindley help the injured through.

And so begins the long walk of all the remaining survivors along the Doe seam. It is a torturous route. Parts of it are flooded and they have to submerge themselves completely, holding their breath for several yards, only to re-emerge gasping, gulping lungfuls of poisonous air, which only weakens them further. Some are overcome, fall back into the water and drown. On and on the others trudge. The path narrows even more, so that they must edge sideways, each holding on to the fellow in front, a ghostly file of prisoners of war chained to the rock face. After more than a mile of this painful, inch-by-inch progress, they reach a turning, which the pit pony immediately takes. The path is wider, drier and there is a chink of light winking at them from above.

"Yes," gasps Hindley. "This leads to Agecroft. It's an old connecting road between the two mines."

From somewhere near the back of the line one of the men begins to sing, faltering and hesitant at first, but gradually growing in strength, an old chapel hymn.

"Lord in the morning thou shalt hear
My voice ascending high
To thee will I direct my prayer
To thee lift up mine eye..."

Another voice begins to join, then another, and another, as the miners, weary but not unbowed, continue their slow march up the seam towards the distant, growing light.

"Up to the hills where Christ is gone
To plead for all his saints
Presenting at his Father's throne
Our songs and our complaints..."

The pony stumbles on the scree of loose stones skittering down the path, and Tommy pauses to allow the pony to settle and gather itself once more. He lets the men go by, hearing them sing as they pass, their mouths barely moving, mumbling these words learned at the hearth as much as from the pulpit, sung in the fields as well as down the mines. He waits until the last one has gone by, and then follows them up the path.

Back at the Camp, Eve is watching Old Moon. His hands are trembling. He beckons her towards him. She can tell at once he has a fever. His skin is cold and clammy despite the heat. With his fingers he talks to her, urges her to relight the fire. He describes wild flowers he needs her to bring to him, which she crushes with a sharp stone against a low flat rock. She grinds the petals, stems, seed heads and roots into a sticky ball, which Old Moon chews and then spits out into the fire. An acrid smoke rises from it, which he breathes in deeply, while signalling for Eve to step away from the fumes. His eyes roll back in his head. Eve watches him climb awkwardly to his feet. Her instinct is to be at his side, support him, prevent him from falling, but he waves her away. Slowly he starts to dance, clumsily but rhythmically, stamping the earth, his feet taking him unerringly towards the wheat field. Eve follows him there.

Old Moon dances to the centre of the field, where the wheat is as high as his waist. He stops. He runs his fingers through the waving stalks and starts to revolve in a series of slow turning circles. Although she cannot hear him, Eve can see that his lips are moving. He is singing. Telling the field what he sees.

He sees a great wave. A wall of water covers the land. He sees tall ships sail upon it, men and women from across the world. He hears them speaking in many languages…

He sees the distant city, its mills and smoke stacks, its mines and factories, its towers of steel and glass, creeping ever closer, lining the banks of the shining water…

He sees great flying machines and armies marching to war. Where once the wheat grew in the field, he sees mud and bones. He hears boots and orders, shouts, explosions. He sees craters and rockfall, bodies floating in water. He smells poison on the wind…

The vision fades. He looks around him. The wheat perspires. Soon it will ripen and then it will be cut down. There is blood in the margins. The scarlet cups of poppies all aflame, burning coals fallen from the sky, pulled out of the earth.

He sees a woman running through the grasses towards him. Eve. She takes his arm, steers him back towards the safety of the Camp.

The rescued miners continue their slow march back to the surface, where the air is sweeter, their voices growing in strength and hope.

"Lord, crush the serpent in the dust
And all his plots destroy
While those that in thy mercy trust
For ever shout for joy…"

Up above, those who are waiting for news hear the distant singing and fall to their knees. One by one they add their voices to the choir.

"O may thy Spirit guide my feet
In ways of righteousness

Make every path of duty straight
And plain before my face…"

And then they are there. The men and boys stumble into the yard at Agecroft Pit, stagger into the arms of those who have been waiting for them, coughing and collapsing. Tommy, bringing up the rear with the exhausted pit pony, climbs out into the upper air in time to hear the final verse, sung with gratitude and exhaustion.

"The men that love and fear thy name
Shall see their hopes fulfilled
The mighty god will compass them
With favour as a shield…"

Up at the surface Sammy has been able to mobilise the other starvationers and bargemen to bring in medicines and alert the authorities. By late afternoon a hundred and twenty two men and boys have made the long, slow, painful march up the Agecroft shaft to the shield and compass of the various offices of state, the mine owners and politicians, constables and fire fighters, reporters and photographers.

A further sixty-two men are winched back to the surface at Lumn's Lane, but many of these do not survive their injuries. Flint is the last to step down from the final cage.

Back at Agecroft there are no extravagant demonstrations of grief, nor wild outpourings of joy when husbands are at last reunited with wives, mothers with sons, only the subdued sobbing of children, the blank dismay on the faces of the women whose men have not returned, and the settled melancholy visible in the men who have. Tommy rubs soothing salves and ointments into the pony's open wounds. Its recovery offers a small crumb of comfort to the silent children, who take turns to stroke its matted mane. Tommy ties a piece of muslin loosely around its eyes to protect them from the unaccustomed light.

The Inquest, held at *The Mechanics Institute*, Pendleton, lasts nine days.

The Coroner, Sir Philip Voss, concludes that "an explosion of a large amount of inflammable gas emitted from a goaf in the Trencherbone Mine, to the eastern side of Number Two Level, ignited at a lighted candle in the working place of an unnamed pitman."

No blame or responsibility is apportioned.

The final death toll is a hundred and seventy-eight. A hundred and fifty nine die from burns, gas or from the injuries they incurred, nine die on the road to Agecroft from further suffocation or drowning, eight die later at home from the shock caused by burns, and two die in Salford Hospital from carbon monoxide poisoning.

The Earl opens up a part of Worsley Hall to house the long term sick or wounded, and Jenks arranges for baskets of food to be sent to all the families.

*

When Catch arrives for work the next morning at the forge, Flint is waiting in the open doorway. A patch of pink chamomile, faded and dusty, lies beneath his feet, which he scuffs at with his still mud-splattered boots. He picks up a clump and rubs it between his fingers, then lets the crushed seed pods float back down to the earth.

"Tha's work to do, youth," he says, without looking up. "Tha's much to make up for after missing yesterday. I daresay tha'd cause."

Catch looks down.

"How's tha' reading coming on?"

Catch shrugs.

"It's time tha' learned then." Flint points to a wooden sign hanging just inside the door, which Catch has seen but never paid much heed to. "My grandfather put that up," continues Flint. "He were quite a scholar in his day. You can read the grain in a piece of wood, he'd say. Or the sediments of stone in a rock. Or the colour of iron in t' forge."

Catch nods. He understands this way of reading.

"But sometimes, my grandfather'd say, tha' needs words in a book to see a truth that otherwise stays hid. Is tha' following me, youth?"

"I think so."

"Good." Flint points back to the sign. "So he hung this up when I were a young 'un and made me get it by rote. It says:

'For though the chamomile, the more it is trodden on, the faster it grows, yet youth, the more it is wasted, the sooner it wears.' Shakespeare."

Catch looks up at the meaningless caterpillar trail of letters, squinting his eyes against the sun. He knows – if he's to be his own man, this is something he must master.

"Think on, lad. Look at this each day till tha' can recognise the different letters."

"Yes, Mr Flint."

"Now – get cracking. Tha's new guard rails to make for Lumn's Lane Pit."

*

Her name is Clémence Audubon Lafitte.

"But you can call me Clem," she says in rich, honeyed tones. "Everybody does."

They learn her story over several days as she stays with Catch at the Camp. She shoots rooks in the Bittern Wood, which she plucks and roasts over the re-lit fire. She mends nets with Eve while Sammy plies the still-again waters of the Navigable Levels. She guts trout and skins eels. She can swear and curse in several languages. Her black eyes are like tunnels, her rare smiles the light at their end. At night she and Catch make long, slow love. Her kisses taste of woodsmoke and molasses, from which Catch comes gasping for air.

Her lineage is a labyrinth. Her grandfather is the Creole pirate Jean Lafitte, who ransacks the Florida coast, briefly raises the flag on his own independent republic in Galveston, before the Texas Rangers force him to flee to the Louisiana bayous, where he holes up just south of the Cane River for the next twenty years with Marceline Fontenot, his mulatto mistress, one quarter African, one quarter Spanish, and two quarters Biloxi.

Moon interrupts to ask her something in a language none of them understand. Except Clem, who answers with a broad grin spreading across her face.

Sammy, who has been conveying everything she's been saying to Eve, using the private language of hand and finger gestures they have developed between them, asks Clem what Moon has said.

"He spoke to me in Biloxi, a Sioux language akin to Lakota."

"What did he ask?"

"If the buffalo roam through Louisiana."

"And do they?"

She shakes her head, laughing. "Only snakes and alligators."

Sammy translates for Eve, who nods.

Lafitte continues to capture Spanish ships in the Gulf of Mexico, operating openly out of New Orleans, where he attracts the attention of Simon Bolivar, who invites him to provide security for the burgeoning state of Great Columbia, protecting and escorting her merchant ships around the coastal waters of Cuba and Honduras. Before he disappears from the Bayous for good, he fathers thirteen children, the eldest of whom, Aristide Baptiste, is snatched as a boy by plantation slave catchers, who transport him to Audubon, east of Baton Rouge. There Aristide meets and marries Obosa, the daughter of slaves from the Bight of Benin.

"That's where I was born," says Clem, "and that's how I got the name of Audubon, after the plantation."

Escaping after the Union victory at Appomattox, Aristide and Obosa make their way north, through the Carolinas, to Jamestown, following the Patapsco River, where they both get jobs below decks on the Old Bay Line, ferrying passengers along the Chesapeake towards Baltimore on paddle steamers.

"When I first came here and saw the same boats all along the Duke's Cut, I thought I was dreaming."

"This is where they first were built," says Sammy. "So the bargemen tell me. They say Manchester is first in all things."

"I took it as an omen," says Clem, "a good one. My folks loved working on the river, and I got to see all the rich ladies in their fine gowns…"

It is in Baltimore that Aristide is introduced to George Washington Murray, kingpin of the new black élite beginning to emerge after the Civil War, owner of numerous businesses, with the ear of several influential politicians. Murray takes a particular interest in Clem, who by this time is a pretty, precocious seven years old. He persuades Aristide that the best opportunity for his daughter's advancement lies not in Baltimore, not, even, in the Union, but in Europe, in England, where he, Murray, has links through his contacts with a number of mill owners in Manchester, philanthropists who are keen to support the education of girls. Clem is placed in the charge of Mrs Anne Needham Philips, sister-in-law of Mark, Manchester's first Member of Parliament and champion of public parks, part of the wider Philips-Hibbert clan, who between them control much of the Lancashire textile industries. After a tearful farewell to her parents at the docks of Harpers Ferry, Clem is escorted by Mrs Philips, first by ship to the West Indies, where she meets and befriends one of the granddaughters of Charity Henry, the black woman with whom the Hibbert patriarch, Sir Thomas, has a thirty year relationship. Clem then sails with Mrs Philips to Liverpool, from where she takes her first railway journey to Manchester.

"That's when I saw Chat Moss," she says. "The train travels really slowly over the Moss, and I looked out of the window, and it reminded me of the Bayous where I was born."

"But no alligators," signs Eve.

"No," laughs Clem.

In Manchester Clem is taken to the Philips house at 10 St James Square and begins her formal education.

"For ten years," she says, "everything went fine."

But then Caroline Philips, the daughter of Robert and Anne, with whom Clem has forged an almost sisterly affection, becomes engaged to Arnold Otto Costigan. At a ball to celebrate the announcement, Clem is asked to dance by Caroline's fiancé.

"Mr Costigan," she says, dropping a curtsey and lowering her eyes.

"Please," he replies, smiling in a manner Clem finds most disagreeable, "call me Otto. I believe we may dispense with unnecessary formalities, don't you?"

He pursues her relentlessly throughout the evening, eventually capturing and cornering her in a back stairs corridor. When, with the aid of a well placed knee to the groin, she prevents him from having his way with her, he returns to the party, but she knows that he'll come back. His balls may ache but his injured pride hurts more. As soon as he has gone, Clem packs a few belongings and leaves that same night without a word. Otto, she knows, will be persistent. Like a charging boar he may not be so easy to thwart a second time. She has no thought as to where she might go.

"Just somewhere that no one would find me," she adds.

She remembers her first sighting of Chat Moss, the low, wet landscape that reminded her of where she was born, and purchases a railway ticket to Liverpool. As the train slows almost to a halt traversing the floating embankment across the Moss, she opens the carriage door and jumps. She finds an abandoned wooden shack in the centre of the marsh, and that is where she stays.

"And that is where you found me," she says, looking at Catch. "*La vie douce.*"

"*Tanyan yahi,*" smiles Old Moon.

"Welcome," agrees Tommy.

"*Philamayaye,*" she replies. "*Merci.*"

And it hasn't been so bad, she thinks. Better than she could have imagined when she first ran away from St James Square. People leave you alone on the Moss, she reflects. They don't ask questions, just accept you for who you are. No, it hasn't been so bad. She's

541

managed. She's survived. And now she's found herself a soul mate, when she wasn't even looking for one. *La vie douce*. She takes Catch by the hand, leads him past the flickering embers of the fire deep into the heart of the Bittern Wood, where a fox and vixen cry out to one another under the stars, singing their pleasure.

*

For two weeks Tommy checks the wheat daily with Nathaniel. He shows Tommy how to roll an ear between the palms, split it between thumb and forefinger. If a pale, milky substance oozes stickily out, however tiny the amount, the wheat is not ready. At the end of a fortnight it is hard and dry like a nut. Nathaniel nods his head.

"Tomorrow," he says. "Tha' must cut it tomorrow. A day or two early and it's no use for t' miller. He just cannot grind it. A day or two late and it sprouts and starts to rot. Tomorrow it is, lad. I'll get folk ready at dawn."

Tommy decides to stay in the field all night. It will be his last chance to observe the birds and animals who've made it their home. After tomorrow, they'll be seeking pastures new. He wanders into the centre of the field, lies down and waits.

He hears the chaffinches before he sees them, their metallic chink chink, like the rattling of a ladle against a pan announcing supper time, and before long he sees a small flock of them pulling at the seeds from the grain. Tommy is content to share his bounty. The acrobatic harvest mouse is back, scaling a single stem then riding with it as it bends low enough to allow him to scuttle off between the towering stalks, evading the beady-eyed blackbirds scooting close to the ground, two males squabbling over territory. The rooks begin their noisy carouse, out of tune drunks reluctantly staggering homewards, not caring if they keep all the neighbours awake. A buzzard circles lazily above the field, its bright eyes piercing the wheat in search of late night vole or shrew. Two of the rooks swagger up towards it, their mob a braggadocio of bluster and bombast, but it is sufficient to deter the buzzard, who ascends the high thermals beyond their reach. There'll be other nights.

All is quiet at last in the Bittern Wood, and Tommy settles to watch the nocturnal wanderings of the wheat field. A badger, nose to the ground rooting out grubs, blindly passes within a few feet of him, not seeing, intent as he is on his own predestined trail. The red-legged partridges, sitting on their nests, blink in the moon's huge glare. An owl brushes past his ear, silent and swift. It barely disturbs a molecule of air in its nightly hunting.

Tommy waits. The hours pass. He can hear the water trickling loudly on the edge of the Camp. He thinks of how its character has changed in recent weeks. He pictures Old Moon, sitting on a rock, wrapped in a blanket, watching the last embers of the fire floating up to mingle with the stars. He imagines Eve and Sammy, Clem and Catch, curled up in each other, the rise and fall of their bodies matched in the slow, rhythmic tides of dreamless sleep. And he thinks of himself, alone in the wheat field. It's not as if he hasn't had a woman. He's had a number. But not since they made their permanent Camp here by the Bittern Wood. Before, in the time when he lived a more nomadic life, moving from farm to farm with the seasons, there was usually a woman. They seemed to understand he would not stay, his need to keep on the move, and they would stand in a doorway, or from a thicket of trees, and wave. Sometimes there would be tears, but not often, and sometimes, even less so, a harsh word or angry gesture, but mostly there would be a slow smile and a turning back to where they had come from, wondering if perhaps he might return the following spring with the swallows, or in autumn with the redwings, and once or twice he has done, and been welcomed back, without rancour. But now that he no longer migrates himself, he's sought out no one. He recognises that he has become known here, something of a fixture, with a role, a possessor of skills that are needed, and that if he were to pick a mate here, she would come with ties and responsibilities. He wonders when, if ever, he might feel ready to embrace such affiliations.

These night time musings are interrupted now by the sight he has been hoping and waiting for, and his patience is rewarded. There are hares dancing in the moonlight. Since the sparrowhawk took her young a few weeks back, the jill, Tommy sees, has had two further pairs of leverets, who stop their dancing just a yard or two in front of him, whiskers bristling, fur trembling. Their cratered, three-sixty eyes stare unblinking into his. He wonders where they will make their home after tomorrow's reaping.

He has watched them closely all summer. The leverets are precocial, capable of feeding themselves independently from the moment they are born. The jacks mate with multiple jills, who are superfoetate, able to conceive while already being pregnant. They give themselves as many chances as they can to secure their futures.

Is that what he is doing? If so, what kind of future is he trying to build? Or is he simply unready or unable to commit? The leverets bound away from the returning owl's curiosity. The wheat trembles beneath silent wing beats. Tommy thinks about tomorrow.

*

"Whet!"

On Nathaniel's command two dozen men and a handful of women armed with scythes stand to attention, running their whetstones along each blade so that the sparks fly. They place the stone in a small pouch slung across their backs, then raise their scythes as if shouldering arms.

Nathaniel crouches low, spreading his arms out wide. "Wait for it," he warns, drawing out each word, "and...." He signals to Clem, who fires her shotgun up into the sky. "Begin!"

An army of rooks explodes out of the trees. With military precision, the scythers advance as one along the first long edge of the field, swinging their blades in a remorseless, regular rhythm, left right, left right, four lines of pendula marching in columns, cutting in clockwork. When they reach the end of that first length, Nathaniel's Sergeant-Major voice rings out across the field.

"Halt! Whet! Wheel turn! Advance!"

They make their way along the second edge, Tommy among them. He is in the second rank, can feel the swish and sway, swoop and cut, of blades carving the air around him, the tall stalks of wheat falling before them.

"Halt! Whet! Wheel turn! Advance!"

They proceed as one along the third edge.

"Halt! Whet! Wheel turn! Advance!"

Tommy can feel the line that holds them, senses they are all linked in a chain of walking, raising, cutting, felling, a golden swathe of destruction in their wake, stained with the red of poppy and campion, corn cockle and pimpernel.

"Rest!"

They have now completed one full circuit of the field. Its outer edge is flattened. Mice and rats, rabbits and voles retreat from the tidal wave of reaping, deeper into the field's heart, though some are left behind, to be caught by dogs, or shot at by children with air guns. The scythers pause, take a flask of ale from the sacks on their backs and drink long and deep. The sun rises higher in the cloudless sky and beats down fiercely. The scythers tie wet cloths upon their heads and along the backs of their necks.

"Whet!"

After a brief pause, Nathaniel calls them back to

order. They line up in formation once again, ready to begin their second circuit.

"And – begin!"

It seems to Tommy that the column moves faster now. Refreshed by the beer, with the knowledge that from here on in each side length will become progressively shorter as they edge their way inexorably towards the centre of the field, they march in step. Their raised scythes glint and dazzle, the blades sharpened and polished by the wheat with each killing cut.

"Halt! Whet! Wheel turn! Advance!"

Flocks of birds follow their every step – rooks and jackdaws, crows and seagulls – growing larger with each step they take, screaming and clamouring, swooping and diving, seizing the swarms of insects, spiders, rodents and smaller birds, exposed by the reaping. Inevitably some of them edge too close and a scyther's blade will slice off a head or wing, speckling the cloths on their heads with crimson, but nothing can stop the ceaseless pendulum swing of the blade, the pitiless ticking of the clock, nothing except Nathaniel's command.

"Halt – and rest!"

More ale is drunk, more animals dive for the cover of the still uncut wheat, more stragglers are shot at. The birds retreat to the wood, waiting for the ritual to start up again. Which it does within minutes. They have now done two complete circuits. As they close in on the centre, the lengths of each of the four sides grow correspondingly shorter. Two more circuits should see them reach the heart.

"Right, reapers," calls Nathaniel. "We're close enough now. Two more courses and that should do us. No need for any more whetting. I reckon we're sharp enough now. To your stations!"

They resume their positions, scythes lifted aloft.

"By the left – and march!"

The pace is quicker now, the turning sharper, and the slicing of the blades a ballet.

The rooks and jackdaws, seagulls and crows return in an instant, wheeling in a dizzying, daring aerobatic display. The scythers sweep through them, a choreography of beak and claw, talon and wing, danced to a symphony of scream and screech.

"Halt!"

And suddenly all is still, all is silent. A small stand of wheat no wider than a man's span is all that is left. The birds hover above, waiting. The children surround it with their air guns. Nathaniel has one arm raised. All the reapers train their eyes upon him, waiting for his signal. Slowly he lowers his arm, and with him the reapers lower their scythes as one. Nathaniel walks directly towards Tommy.

"Your field, lad, so you must make the last cut."

Tommy nods. He approaches the remaining stand of wheat. As he draws up closer to it, he becomes aware it is seething. Rats, voles, rabbits, shrews. And there in the centre, trembling, is the leveret he saw the previous night.

He wheels around. In a single, slow circular motion, he cuts the top of the wheat only. He plunges his hands into the stems that remain and plucks the leveret from within. As he does so, the other animals make a mad dash for the safety of the hedges which border the field. The dogs are released to chase them, and for several minutes all is mayhem and confusion, a cacophony of squealing, barking, shouting and shooting. Tommy is able to slip away unnoticed to carry the leveret to the comparative safety of the wood. When he returns, peace and calm have descended once more upon the field. The captured rabbits are piled high in baskets to be taken home to various kitchens where they will be hung, later to be plucked and skinned and cooked. Crows and magpies swoop upon the remaining corpses of rats and mice. Children chase each other around the flattened field, until the heat of the day exhausts them, and they flop upon the piles of stalks, listlessly throwing blades of wheat up above their heads and watching them fall slowly in the drugged, motionless air. Women are sharing out the baggin of bread and cheese and a raw onion for lunch, washed down with further jugs of ale.

Nathaniel instructs the men to bring in the threshing and winnowing machines. Some of the women gather up the cut wheat into sheaves, while others bind them with twine, and stook them into piles. Most years they would leave them like this for a couple of days to dry out thoroughly, but such has been the force of the heat and drought this summer that there's simply no need to wait. Jenks drives the traction engine that will power the machines, hissing and snorting into the field, the Earl's pride and joy, recently purchased from Richmond & Chandler of the Victoria Works, Salford, its newly polished wheels, boiler and funnel gleaming in the fierce noonday sun, slowly becoming enveloped in billowing clouds of steam.

Flint has sent Catch along to keep an eye on things, in case the machines break down and there might be emergency repairs to carry out. But everything works in synchronised perfection, with everyone knowing their allotted role, men, women and children alike, feeding the cut wheat first into the mechanised thresher, which removes the grain from the stalk, loosening the seeds from the husks, and then into the winnower, which separates the wheat from the rest of the chaff. Catch marvels at the beauty of the engineering, the poetic arrangement of yoke and wheel, belt and pulley, sieve and fan, auger and elevator. The foundry man is cousin to the smith, he thinks, and the seed of an idea is planted.

They work till sunset. Loaded carts transport the winnowed grain to the manorial mill at the Hall. The field is stripped bare, as slippery and sharp as polished glass, with just the stumps of stubble poking through the baked earth like tiny daggers. Tommy, Catch and Clem are the last to leave. Sammy, Eve and Moon will be waiting for them back at the Camp. As they are closing the gate by the Bittern Wood, Clem sees a straggle of rats nosing through the stubble. She raises her shot gun.

"Wait," says Tommy. "How many do you see?"

"Six, by my count," she replies.

"Six?"

"*Oui.*"

He looks around, spreading his arms about him as if

trying to hold the whole Camp in his embrace.

"Room enough for all," he says.

She lowers the gun, and they all walk home together, beneath the huge red harvest moon.

*

People gather on the Ornamental Lawn in front of Worsley Hall for the annual Harvest Home. The Farnworth & Walkden Brass Band, affectionately known as The Old Barnes, after its original benefactor, Sir Thomas Barnes, who thirty years before gifted land for the development of Farnworth Public Park at the other end of the Navigable Levels, is playing hymns on the terrace. The combined choirs of St Mary's in Ellenbrook, St Andrew's in Boothstown, as well as St Mark's in Worsley, are singing at the request of the Earl.

> *"Come, ye thankful people, come,*
> *Raise the song of harvest home;*
> *All is safely gathered in,*
> *Ere the winter storms begin;*
> *God our Maker doth provide*
> *For our wants to be supplied;*
> *Come to God's own temple, come,*
> *Raise the song of harvest home…"*

All the local tenant farmers and their families, together with the estate workers, line up on the Lawn to be presented to the Earl. It is on days such as these, feast days, high days and holidays, on which he misses his late wife acutely. She was so much better at this than he has ever been. She always knew what to say to people, remembered who had had a baby recently, or whether a grandparent had been ill. Whereas he has difficulty even recalling names. Faces, yes. He recognises those and can bid them a 'Good morning', but names, no. Luckily he has Jenks at his side, who can prompt him as he proceeds along the line.

"It has been a good crop this year," he remarks to Nathaniel, who touches his cap as the Earl pauses to speak.

"Yes, sir. As good as I can remember, sir. Potatoes, swedes, carrots, cabbages, all at record levels, sir."

"Excellent – Nathaniel, isn't it?"

"Yes, sir."

"And how is your good lady?"

"Mustn't grumble, sir. She's helping with the refreshments, sir. I'll be sure to pass on your kind wishes."

"Jolly good."

"Oh, and sir – if I may…?"

"Yes, Nathaniel?"

"The wheat field by the Bittern Wood has had a particularly good yield this year, sir. We shan't be going hungry this winter, sir, none of us."

"Excellent."

The Earl moves further along the line. The choirs continue to sing.

"All the world is God's own field,
Fruit unto His praise to yield;
Wheat and tares together sown,
Unto joy or sorrow grown;
First the blade, and then the ear,
Then the full corn shall appear:
Lord of harvest, grant that we
Wholesome grain and pure may be…"

The Earl pauses to listen. He turns to his Bailiff. "That's the land we set aside for Tommy Thunder, is it not, Jenks?"

"Yes, sir."

"Is he here this afternoon? I don't see him."

"He's with the horses, sir."

"Yes, of course."

The Earl takes the watch from his waistcoat pocket to check the time. It is attached to an Albert chain, presented to his father by the Prince Consort himself on the occasion of his visit to unveil the statue of the Queen in nearby Peel Park, which the Earl has inherited from him.

He turns once more to Jenks. "What time am I meant to be addressing the assembled throng?"

"Half past three, my Lord."

The Earl looks at the line of people still stretching before him.

"Best get a move on then, for I'd like a word with Mr Thunder before then."

Jenks inclines his head. "Whatever you say, sir."

"For the Lord our God shall come,
And shall take His harvest home;
From His field shall in that day
All offenses purge away;
Give His angels charge at last
In the fire the tares to cast;
But the fruitful ears to store
In His garner evermore…"

The Earl finds Tommy in the paddock at the back of the house. He is walking the prize black mare around its perimeter, whispering to her all the while.

"Ah – Tommy. I thought I might find you here. What do you think of her, eh? She's doing well, is she not?"

"Yes, sir. She is."

"All thanks to you."

"You're not thinking of riding her to hounds again, are you, sir?"

"No, no. It's the life of leisure for her now. As you requested. But…"

"Yes, sir?"

"I was wondering… She comes from excellent blood stock, you know…? Might it still be possible for her to… well…?

"To breed, sir?"

"Yes. Well?"

Tommy takes time to think before he answers. He rubs his hand along each of the mare's legs.

"How old is she?"

"Seven."

"A good age for a mare to have her first foal."

"Exactly so. Well?"

"Her wounds are healing well."

"Yes they are. And she's no longer lame, is she?"

"No, she's not."

"My cousin over at Tatton has just acquired the most magnificent Arab stallion and has offered his services. For a not insignificant fee, I might add." He chuckles.

Tommy smiles back.

"Do I take that as a 'yes'?"

Tommy nods. "So long as she's not ridden."

The Earl claps Tommy on the back and does a little dance of delight. "In the memory of my late wife," he says.

Tommy turns away, heading towards the front of the house.

The Earl calls him back.

"I've made up my mind," he says. "What we spoke about at Midsummer. I've made my decision."

As if reading the Earl's thoughts, Tommy looks directly in his eye. "Don't worry about it," he says. "We'll be fine."

"Even so, Lord, quickly come,
Bring Thy final harvest home;
Gather Thou Thy people in,
Free from sorrow, free from sin,
There, forever purified,
In Thy garner to abide;
Come, with all Thine angels come,
Raise the glorious harvest home…"

555

An hour later everyone has assembled on the Ornamental Lawn. The Earl is standing on the terrace steps. He is poised to deliver his annual address. There are rumours this year of a major announcement, of big changes. As tenant farm labourers most of the people gathered there waiting to hear what he has to say feel especially vulnerable. Might they be about to lose their livelihoods, their homes?

Some children's entertainments are coming to a close. A boy and girl from the village are singing an old nursery rhyme. The girl is dressed as a fine lady and stands on top of a pair of ladders, as if looking out from a window, while the boy wears an ill fitting soldier's uniform, all tatters and patches. Beside them Zack Flint plays a tin whistle, to which Catch beats in time with a wooden spoon against a leather bucket.

Boy:

> *Haley Paley snow on the ground*
> *The wind blows bitter and raw*
> *A poor young soldier boy dressed up in rags*
> *Came to a lady's door*

Girl:

> *The lady sat up in her window so high*
> *And fixed both her eyes upon him,*
> *Go away, go away, you poor soldier boy*
> *So ragged and dirty and thin*

Boy:

> *But, madam, I'm hungry and, madam, I'm cold*
> *The soldier boy cried from the door*

If you've got a penny please give it to me
And I never shall want any more

Girl:

The lady she sat in her window so high
Still fixing her eyes upon him,
Go away, go away, you poor soldier boy
So ragged and dirty and thin

Boy:

My father, my father was drowned in the mine
My mother she cried and she cried
Did you ever see a smile on her face
Of a broken heart she died

Girl:

She threw down a penny all into the snow
She threw down a penny or two

Boy:

Oh, I am your William that's come home from war
Your William that you never knew

Girl:

Come in, come in, you good hearted lad
You never shall want any more
For as long as I live I'll charity give
To a soldier lad so poor

Both:

Haley Paley snow on the ground
The wind blows bitter and raw

A poor young soldier boy dressed up in rags
Came to a lady's door...

The crowd applauds. The boy and girl bow and curtsey respectively before the Earl, who drops a half crown into the boy's cap and the girl's bonnet. They run back to their families and everyone's eyes turn back towards the Earl. The day falls silent. The Earl clears his throat nervously. There is a long pause. Eventually he begins.

"Welcome, one and all, to this year's Harvest Home. My thanks as ever to The Old Barnes, the Farnworth & Walkden Brass Band, and the choirs of St Mark's, St Mary's and St Andrew's Churches for entertaining us with such uplifting musical accompaniment, and to all the good ladies of the Parish and the Estate for their magnificent refreshments. You have surpassed yourselves this year and the Harvest Supper this evening promises to be most memorable.

"Mr Jenks informs me that we have enjoyed a bumper crop this summer, with exceptional yields in root vegetables, wheat, oats and barley, while in our orchards the apples, plum and pear trees are bowed down with the weight of more fruit than any of us can remember for a very long time. This is in no small measure due to the exceptionally fine, dry weather we have enjoyed these many weeks, but more than that it is a tribute to your collective hard work, your tireless devotion to the land, and your loyalty to the Estate, for which I thank you from the bottom of my heart.

"But this year has also witnessed great tragedy, great

sorrow and great loss. I speak of course of the Clifton Hall Colliery Disaster and the untimely deaths of so many men and boys, cut down like the wheat in our fields, when all of life lay before them. As the poet says, *'Death leaves a heartache no one can heal'*. But does he not also say that *'Love leaves a memory that no one can steal'*?

"Many people that day lost not only husbands and fathers, brothers and sons, but also their futures. And so it is that I have decided on a course of action that I believe will help secure all of our futures here for many decades to come."

He pauses briefly, allowing the weight of what he has just said time to sink in. He takes a sip of water provided for him by Jenks and turns back to face the sea of faces staring up at him with a mixture of anxiety and anticipation.

"Three years ago, almost to the day, I attended a private meeting at the home of that most esteemed Manchester manufacturer, Mr Daniel Adamson, in Didsbury. There, in the company of several eminent Lancashire businessmen and politicians, I listened with keen interest to two proposals put forward by two of our most prominent civil engineers, Messrs Hamilton Fulton and Edward Leader Williams. Both proposals, though differing in their preferred method, sought to achieve the same goal – the creation of a new canal, longer and deeper than any that has been constructed hitherto. It would be known as the Ship Canal and it would be able to transport ocean-going vessels from Liverpool directly to a newly built Port of Manchester.

Much of this new Ship Canal would be exactly that, a new canal, but it would also utilise existing tracts of waterway from the Mersey and Irwell rivers, as well as providing direct access to other canals, the Shropshire Union, the Weaver Navigation, the Mersey & Irwell Navigation, and of course our own Bridgewater Canal. I mention all of these details because I recognise so many bargemen in our company here on this lawn this fine autumn day, and I want all of you to know just how much thought has been put into these proposals.

"Naturally, an enterprise as large and ambitious as this gives rise to certain opposition, most notably from the railway companies and from the city of Liverpool, both of whom fear the possible loss of trade for themselves as a consequence. In the three years since that initial private meeting in Didsbury, there have been further proposals, tenders and consultations, public meetings, campaigns launched both for and against. It has been debated in Parliament. Twice a bill to allow the construction of such a canal has been defeated in the House of Commons. But as of last month, I am delighted to announce, that a third attempt has been successful. The Manchester Ship Canal Act of 1885 has now received Royal Assent."

There are loud murmurs that greet this statement amid a spattering of applause, but the faces of the people listening on the lawn remain clouded with doubt as they speculate on what this might mean for them, while they wait for the Earl to continue.

"I say that I am 'delighted' to announce this to you today by design, for I have thought long and hard in the intervening three years about the merits or otherwise of this scheme, what the benefits might be for our community here in this quiet corner of South East Lancashire on the northern ridge of the Irwell valley, less than six miles away from the greatest metropolis in the British Empire, which creeps ever closer to us. A backwater, some people call us, but they do not know the truth of our secret Eden like we do. I am proud that my ancestor, the 3rd Duke of Bridgewater, had the vision to build the Bridgewater Canal, the Duke's Cut as it is still affectionately known, arguably the world's first industrial canal, which opened up Worsley to the world. This new proposal, the Manchester Ship Canal, will link directly to our own canal, just a couple of miles away at Barton, providing us, you, with the chance to transport the coal, cotton, iron and steel products, and all of the other goods you produce not only more quickly to the markets of Manchester, but to Liverpool, and from there to the rest of the Empire and the world.

"In any new venture there are winners and there are potential losers. An engineering undertaking as vast as this requires land, land for the enormous excavations necessary to dig new channels, blast new tunnels, construct new embankments, build new locks and basins, as well as that required to widen existing waterways and house the armies of workers that will be needed to carry out this great work. And it is this aspect more than any other, which has occupied me so utterly during the past three years. So – let me say at once that not a single tenant will lose his farm, not a single labourer will lose his employment on the Estate, not a single miner, foundry worker or bargeman will lose his livelihood."

A collective sigh rises up from the sea of faces upturned towards the Earl, followed by a thunderclap of applause. The Earl lifts a hand and at once a less anxious silence falls.

"The only loss of land to this great enterprise," he continues, "will be that abutting the Bittern Wood, some forty acres or so, where we have grown most of our wheat this year but where there are no permanent dwellings. This will, however, mean the compulsory removal of the Camp by the river currently occupied by our American Indian friends, who have become such a valued and welcome addition to our family here on the Estate. I, for one, have had particular cause to be grateful for their services on more than one occasion. I am confident that I can count on each and every one of you here, if called upon, to offer them temporary shelter until they can build themselves a new encampment among us, which I sincerely hope they will. Let us all entertain the strangers at our gate."

A great cry of "Hear, hear!" rings out followed by a thunderous round of much relieved applause.

"Now – nothing will change for many months to come, possibly years. A substantial sum of money has yet to be raised before any work on the Ship Canal can commence, something in excess of five million pounds! But Manchester has found investors before, and doubtless she shall do so again, of that I am certain, so that before the end of the century we shall witness the creation of this Eighth Wonder of the World."

A further burst of applause greets this statement, which the Earl quickly raises an arm to quell.

"That is all I have to say on the matter for the present. Thank you for listening with such patience and with such attentiveness. Please now repair to the Great Barn and let us enjoy our Harvest Supper like never before, remembering those we have lost and looking forward towards the promise and hope of better times to come."

There is a brief silence as the Earl steps back from the terrace, before Nathaniel jumps up on a low wall and calls out.

"Three cheers for His Lordhip, the Earl. Hip-hip..."

"Hooray!"

"Hip-hip..."

"Hooray!"

"Hip-hip..."

"Hooray!"

The crowds disperse animatedly away towards the barn. Catch taps Tommy lightly on the shoulder.

"Where does this leave us?" he asks, a worried look on his face.

"Where it has always done," Tommy replies. "Free."

In the field adjoining the Ornamental Lawn, where the Great Barn stands, the stubble is set alight. There is scarcely a breath of wind, so the smoke climbs high and straight, up towards an already darkening sky. The fires burn in a ring. Farmers drive their cattle through the smoke, hanks of green cotton tied to their tails, for purification and good luck.

Inside the barn is decorated with row upon row of corn dollies. Each farmer has taken a few of the straws from the last sheaf of wheat to be harvested in each field, for it is here where the spirit of the corn takes refuge, and woven them into a shape, sometimes a cage, sometimes a bell, sometimes a horn, but more often than not in the likeness of a woman, the effigy of a maiden or angel. The farmer then carries this back to where he lives, hangs it upon a wall all winter long. In the spring he takes it out into the field and ploughs it into the first furrow when planting begins. In this way he ensures another good crop for the following year. But for the Harvest Supper each one is brought out and displayed in the Great Barn, where they can all be seen and revered, wakeful ghosts, guardians of the wheat fields, spirits of the corn, watching over the valley.

Tommy has not known of this custom, but Clem has.

"I'm not superstitious," she scoffs, "but why take the risk? Besides, they are beautiful, *non*?"

And so it is she who gathers the last straws of the wheat to be cut in their field and fashions them in the shape of a young hare. Tommy stands before it in silence.

When everyone is assembled inside, a band of musicians begins to play. Violin, accordion, trombone and drum. They herald the arrival of the Reapers, who enter dressed from head to toe in ragged strips of yellow and gold. Their hats are decorated with plaited corn. They carry sickles, which they flail above their heads. One of them brings a tall scarecrow in the form of a Straw Man and places it in the centre of the barn, around which the others perform an ungainly kind of Morris dance. A group of girls and young women, dressed as Corn Maidens, advance towards the scarecrow, carrying sheaves of last year's corn, which they place in a stacked pyramid of stooks around the Straw Man. They too begin to dance, weaving in and out of the Reapers. A singer steps forward.

"There were three men came from the west
Their fortunes for to try
And these three men made a solemn vow
John Barleycorn must die…"

Catch listens closely. He, Tommy and Sammy are three men come from the west, whose own fortunes seem far from being won. Since meeting Clem his hunger to become his own man has intensified. After what the Earl has just announced, he knows for sure now. He must move on. And soon.

"They ploughed, they sowed, they harrowed him in
Threw clods upon his head
And these three men made a solemn vow
John Barleycorn was dead…"

As the song progresses, the story is acted out by the Reapers and the Corn Maidens. The Harvest Dance unfolds. Catch, standing apart from the crowds, watches and listens.

"They let him lie for a very long time
Till the rains from heaven did fall
And little Sir John sprang up his head
And did amaze them all

They let him stand till Midsummer Day
Till he looked both pale and wan
And little Sir John, he grew a long beard
And so became a man

They hired men with the scythes so sharp
To cut him off at the knee
They rolled him and tied him about the waist
And served him barbarously

They hired men with the crab tree sticks
To cut him skin from bone
But the miller has served him worse than that
He's ground him between two stones

They've worked their will on John Barleycorn
But he lived to tell the tale
For they pour him out of an old brown jug
And they call him home brewed ale
Yes they call him home brewed ale..."

To cheers all round a cart is pulled into the centre of the barn by the same pair of Clydesdales used by Tommy to plough his field back in the spring. The cart is laden with three barrels of local ale, which the men make an immediate beeline for. The Reapers and

Maidens depart, merging in with the rest of the crowd, who disperse to all corners of the barn, where the various tables are waiting to tempt them with more of their wares.

As Tommy, Catch and Clem are leaving, a happily inebriated Nathaniel pulls them to one side.

"Don't you worry none," he says. "I'll see thee right."

"Goodnight, Nathaniel."

They make their way back towards the Camp. Clem carries the corn hare tucked close inside the man's shirt she wears habitually. Eve and Sammy are sitting tending to the fire when they get there, signing in their private language. Old Moon rocks by the riverbank. Tommy heads towards the Bittern Wood. It is dark now. The birds are silent. There are the usual rustlings in the undergrowth. The moon is big and bright. Three great white egrets fly across its face, black silhouettes. Catch watches them and wonders.

On the edge of the wood, by the entrance to the shorn field, the moon picks out a small sapling, clearly visible now that the wheat has all been cut down. Tommy approaches it. It is the American Elm he planted the previous spring. It has survived. He decides he will sleep out here tonight. He lays his head close to the sapling. Sleep, when it comes, is filled with complicated dreams of home.

By the water's edge Reads the Moon dreams the moon, the Roman coin with the face of Diocletian clamped in his fist.

*

Ten years have passed since Dru and Bron rode away at dawn from the camp at Mamucium towards the settlement in the confluence of the three rivers.

At first Dru fears he might be recaptured, marched back in chains and yoked once more to the testudo. He builds wooden palisades around the camp, drives sharpened stakes into the river beds to ward off any attack, places look-outs at the gates, leads night time raids against their granaries. The settlement grows, as the Roman Fort shrinks.

Three children have been born in that time. Two sons and a daughter. Cuinn, Med and Cora. They lose Med to a fever in the boy's second winter. Cuinn has seen nine summers now, Cora three. They hunt deer, raise pigs, catch fish. They grow fruit, weave wool, keep bees. Last spring they planted wheat.

More of the soldiers desert. They cross the river to join Dru and Bron and the rest of the Brigantes, telling tales of invaders from the north, Picts with painted faces, who breach the Wall and burn villages along the tidal flats at Solway.

Dru looks at Bron. She shakes her head. She's not heard of this place. Dru turns back to the soldiers. How many days march away? They shrug. Two, maybe three. But why would they come? What is there here for them that they don't have there? Once the legions pull out, they'll slip back over the Wall and vanish into their brochs. Their quarrel is with Rome, not with us, they say.

Dru scans their faces. Parthians, Scythians, Dacians. Berbers and Ethiopes. Galicians like himself. Conscript and voluntary, freedmen and runaways. All Brigantes now. He looks at Bron. He remembers asking her where she came from first. Was she born here, in the confluence of the three rivers? She shakes her head. It was empty when her father brought her. They came from over there, she says, and points to a distant line of hills, 'pennines' in her own tongue.

Everyone comes from somewhere else, he thinks, until they find a home.

This is good land, he says. Fresh water. Enough for all.

Cuinn steps forward and stands alongside his father. He squeezes juices from the stems of plants and berries onto a curved wooden shield, painting the likeness of a bee upon it, which he holds aloft, their standard.

Dru and Bron, Cuinn and Cora huddle together beside the fire. Bron is with child again and cannot sleep. She listens to the sounds of the night, the crackling of wood in the flames, the cry of a vixen coupling her mate, the screech of an owl hunting close by. Familiar sounds she associates with home.

Suddenly she senses an intruder. She picks up his scent on the breeze. She hears a twig snap by the water's edge. The other night time rustlings cease. And there in the perpetual dark, beyond the fire's penumbra, she sees them, a pair of eyes glowing in the blackness. A blink, and they're gone. No – there they are again.

Closer this time. They transfix her, rooting her to the spot. The eyes approach the fire. Now she can see a head, a body, a bobbed tail. It is four feet in length and stands more than two feet high at the shoulder, with large black-tipped ears, a long white ruff, thick silky fur, silver in the moonlight.

A lynx. The last lynx in Britain.

Bron stares at him motionless, holding her breath, the stars arching bright and clear overhead, the crab, the fish, the lion, the bull. And the lynx holding Bron's gaze, and the water chattering over stones in the confluence of the three rivers. She reaches her hand towards him. Nearer and nearer until she thinks she might touch him.

And then he bolts back to the shadows, as if he had never been, leaving nothing behind, not a strand of fur, or a print of his webbed paw. Just a fleeting, fragile memory, and a hope that she and Dru and all of them may yet make their mark upon the earth, in this far flung outpost at the edge of the known world.

She rubs her belly. She is carrying a boy, she is sure of it, and he starts to kick.

15

1887 – 1894

Manchester Guardian

22nd May 1894

QUEEN OPENS SHIP CANAL
HISTORIC DAY FOR CITY OF
MANCHESTER

Yesterday, precisely at noon, when the sun was at its zenith, Her Majesty Queen Victoria, Empress of India, officially opened the Manchester Ship Canal at the newly expanded City Docks in the magnificently refurbished Port of Manchester.

In a short address to the waiting crowds of dignitaries, well wishers and local people, Her Majesty recalled that it was more than forty years since she had last visited the city. "We now see," she went on to say, "a city that simply did not exist then. We see a city built on the best and most pioneering of industrial principles, demonstrating all those qualities of engineering and manufacture that my late husband, Prince Albert, held most dear, which he sought ever to champion, and which he found in such great abundance on his own subsequent visits to this city, when opening the Great Art Treasures Exhibition here in 1857. He told me then that Manchester was a city of the future, representing the true spirit of the age. Today that prophecy is fulfilled and Manchester, with the opportunities now afforded it by this great waterway, can truly lay claim to be the Gateway to the World. It gives me great pleasure, therefore, to declare the Manchester Ship Canal officially open."

To thunderous applause, the Queen cut the ceremonial ribbon, upon which Lord Wilbraham Egerton, 1st Earl of Tatton, cousin to the 3rd Duke of Bridgewater, called for three rousing cheers for Her Majesty. The sight of several thousand hats being lifted on high was indeed stirring, and one never to be forgotten by all who had the good fortune to witness it.

The Queen thanked the Earl and then graciously bestowed knighthoods in a short but dignified ceremony upon Anthony Marshall, Lord Mayor of Manchester, and William Henry Bailey, Mayor of Salford in recognition of their work in bringing the Ship Canal project to such a successful conclusion.

Her Majesty was then taken on a conducted tour of the city, where thousands of her most loyal subjects lined the streets to catch a glimpse of this most powerful monarch in history, proving to any doubters that, for all its Radical past, its espousal of the Chartists' cause, Manchester is more than capable of mounting a proud spectacle for every man and woman rejoicing in the name and character of what it means to be English.

After passing beneath a Grand Ceremonial Arch on Deansgate, constructed from five large ladders from the city's Fire Brigade, each of them festooned with freshly cut flowers, the Queen was heard to praise the magnificence of the stately warehouses of Messrs Watt & Sons on Portland Street, the commercial glories of Lewis's Department Store at the junction of Market Street with Piccadilly Gardens, the Gothic splendour of the recently built Town Hall designed by Alfred Waterhouse, facing which is the much loved Albert Memorial, whose pinnacled colonettes and crocketed gables house a marble statue of the Prince Consort sculpted by Matthew Noble to designs approved personally by the Queen. This sight was the highlight of Her Majesty's tour of the city. Upon arrival in the Square she alighted from the state carriage to comment favourably upon the depiction of the symbolic figures surrounding her late husband, of Art, Commerce, Science and Agriculture, innovations in each of which the Prince took a particular interest.

"The strain of purely joyous sentiment we have witnessed here today," Her Majesty declared in a short address, "in the many gracious buildings, not least this memorial to my husband, which means so much to us personally, and in the faces of our subjects who have so gallantly welcomed us here this day, is most suggestive of youth, high hope and anticipation, scarcely perhaps to be looked for in more recent years."

Let these virtues continue to be our guide on such an important and historic day not only for Manchester, but for the whole of Great Britain. The Ship Canal, the ever changing face of the city, the cheering crowds all signify a Manchester built on courage and innovation, both symbolic of the values of Her Majesty Queen Victoria and her late husband.

*

Afterwards, reflecting in her diary on the day's tumultuous events alone in her private bedchamber at Tatton Hall, where she was the most honoured guest of Lord Egerton, Victoria wrote:

"The city has altered much since my previous visit. The North seems like an altogether foreign country with its factory chimneys belching smoke night and day, a world away from the sequestered calm of Osborne House, where there is always a breeze and the comforting sounds of the sea, and yet the people seem to love me, for which I offer nightly thanks...

"When we came before, we journeyed to the city by barge on the Duke of Bridgewater's canal. We passed farms and orchards. The fields were dotted with sheep and cows, the scene could almost be described as pastoral. In the distance we could barely discern the march of industry across the land, but its effects were a constant presence: the waterside mills, the colliery *headstocks, the basins and wharves, thronging with people. I asked my good friend, Mr Wyld, to paint a watercolour of the scene, to remind us of our visit. I first encountered William's work at my Aunt Louise's in Belgium and was very much taken with it. His view of the city, entitled 'A View of Manchester from Kersal Moor', is overtly Romantic. The smoking chimneys in the distance serve only to accentuate the golden light of the sun as it sets. The goats and rustics in the foreground are most picturesque, and the painting is entirely to our taste. Albert and I mounted it into the fifth of our Souvenir Albums, which we always took such pleasure in collating during our all too brief marriage...*

"Today, only forty years later, the changes which have overtaken this same landscape are too many to report, save this: Kersal Moor has now completely disappeared beneath the continuous and unstoppable encroachment of manufacture and the houses required for those who must work in its great enterprise. Albert foretold this when we first visited, and he saw it as a good and necessary thing, but I well remember the faces of the people who pressed to see us as we were driven through the leafy expanse of Peel Park, which we had been invited to open. My husband was a great advocate of the benefits to public health of parks, and I am once again grateful to be blessed with the near constant proximity of the fresh air afforded by my beloved Isle of Wight. Albert made a

speech about the excellent work being carried out by the Sunday Schools in Manchester. I do not believe there is a city anywhere in the country with a finer record of Utilitarian success than Manchester. The overcrowding in the slums, the conditions of the houses of these hard working people, is a constant source of concern to us. The mechanics and their families who came to see us that day were all dressed in their Sunday best, ranged along the streets with flowers in their button-holes, both in Salford and Manchester, a very intelligent, but painfully unhealthy-looking population they all were, men as well as women, pale and under-nourished. We pray that this new canal will bring with it sufficient prosperity that may filter down to benefit the common man...

"We had luncheon in the splendid Town Hall in the centre of the city. The menu was a witty one, incorporating the names of some of the different docks and landmarks in the newly opened Port of Manchester into the various courses. For soup there was 'Clair à la Irwell'; for the entrees, 'Rissoles à la Latchford';for the joint, 'Baron of Beef à la Bailey'; for the vegetables 'Pommes de Terre à la Dunlop', and for the dessert, 'Souffle de Pommes à la Pomona'! Afterwards I was much taken with the architecture and the impressive murals by Mr Madox Brown depicting scenes from Manchester's history. Whilst being shown round by Sir Anthony Marshall, the *newly knighted Lord Mayor, I found myself suppressing a smile. 'Does something amuse you, Ma'am?' he enquired of me. 'No, Sir Anthony,' I replied. 'We are not amused. We are merely expressing our delight at the mosaics of bees and cotton flowers we find ourselves walking upon.' He politely demurred and withdrew. In actual fact I was smiling at the decision by Mr Disraeli to discourage us from formally opening this Town Hall some twenty years before..."*

Victoria looked out of her window in Tatton Hall. Peacocks were strutting across the lawn. One of them spread its tail feathers in a wide fan and emitted the ghostly cry of a soul that is lost. In the distance, a herd of fallow deer gathered under the trees, flicking their tails in the dappled light. Suddenly startled, as if catching a new scent on the breeze, they looked up, senses quivering, long buried instincts awakening. They had survived change before. They would do so again.

*

Seven years earlier.

Where once had stood the wheat field was now an enormous pit stretching almost to the horizon. From the brow of Lady Hill, looking across what remained of Bittern Wood, Sammy surveyed a scene of waste and devastation. The bird which had given the wood its name had long since abandoned it, its distant boom now replaced by the ceaseless pounding of steam hammers.

From his height on the hill, Sammy could make out thousands of workers, featureless columns of ants, trudging up and down the sides and all along the bottom of the great, gaping chasm before him, as the work to excavate the earth to create the miles and miles of new cuttings and channels to carry the enormous weight and depth of the Manchester Ship Canal continued day and night. It seemed, as he peered down from the giant crater's rim, that these endless subterranean exhumations reached almost to the earth's core. Far below him fires were burning. Pools of hot mud were erupting in volcanic vents, rumbling while the land shook, and everywhere was coated with a thick black slime, which the thousands of ant-like figures struggled to gain traction in, as they wheeled and carted great piles of the Moss along temporary, sinking tram roads, or up and down perilously tilted planks. Not a blade of grass remained beneath the point where the great digging machines had carved out a side of the Bittern Wood like an open wound, the tree line teetering precariously on the edge.

Sammy looked in vain for someone he could ask about where he should go, but so completely engrossed was everybody in their work, each of them certain of their own individual place in the great leviathan spread out before him, engineered cogs in the machine, which could not stop, day or night, for anyone. If a worker slipped in the mud, or buckled beneath the weight of hewn rock, he risked being trampled upon by the never-ending parade of grim-faced humanity toiling towards a single purpose.

Eventually, as his eyes adjusted to the infernal, cavernous glow all around him, Sammy began to make out certain individuals, who started to stand out, the gang masters and engineers directing operations, and there, in the heart of the maelstrom, he perceived two figures in particular. One was an authoritative-looking man, in a top hat with bushy side-whiskers, standing atop the great steam hammer. He had the appearance of an outdoor preacher, with a deep fire of conviction burning in his eyes. Next to him, bellowing instructions in a strange accent with a lion's roar, was a mountain of a man who, despite his ferocious demeanour, was clearly regarded with deep affection, as well as with the utmost respect, by all he commanded.

Sammy made his way cautiously towards them. First he had to slither down the ever moving, sheer sides of this weeping scar in the surface of the earth. Then he was forced to clamber over the chaos of rotting timbers, the carcasses of once mighty trees feeding the never satisfied hunger of fires in braziers, the wildernesses of bricks, weaving between the leaning towers of cranes and tripods straddling over emptiness, and a thousand incomplete or broken things, burrowing in the earth, scrabbling for the air, mouldering in the water, in order to reach them. The preacher in the top hat turned out to be none other than James Naysmith himself, inventor of England's first ever steam hammer, whose powerful voice urged and cajoled in time to his invention's rhythmic pounding, while the mountain man with the lion's roar introduced himself to Sammy simply as Yasser.

"Are you wanting a job?" he bellowed.

Sammy nodded.

"Been a navvy before?"

Sammy shook his head.

"What then?"

"Starvationer."

Naysmith pricked up his ears at the word. "At the Delph?" he demanded.

Sammy nodded again.

Naysmith explained to Yasser about the Navigable Levels, their history, their importance and how, following the Lumn's Lane Pit disaster, they'd been all but shut down, except for draining the maze of mines they served.

He turned back to Sammy. "Last in, first out?"

"Something like that," replied Sammy.

"Tell me about water flow and backwash," he asked.

Sammy tried to explain as best he could the way he had come to know every single yard of the Levels by its uniquely viscous current.

"You'll be needing this kind of specialist knowledge," murmured Naysmith to Yasser, "when we begin linking back up with the Irwell."

"Good," said Yasser. "But till then he can start as a setter."

"Thank you," said Sammy. "What's a setter?"

Yasser explained. "A full day's work for one man is fourteen sets," he said. "A set is a number of wagons, a train. Look." He pointed to a series of tracks roughly laid across the base of the Moss, a further twenty feet below where they now stood, where the quicksand finally gave way to solid rock. Overlapping hurdles made of branches of heather and brushwood that grew there had been covered with a mixture of sand, earth and gravel, coated with cinders to provide a surface firm enough to carry the weight of these crudely laid tracks on which Sammy could see dozens of wagons, like those he had seen at the surfaces of the various mines beyond The Delph. These wagons were drawn by horses to and from the place where the navvies were excavating at the rock face, as they pushed back the cutting inch by inch, yard by yard, mile by mile, day after day, to carry the waters of the Ship Canal once the channel had been carved, lined and secured, on rails which were extended as the earthworks grew. Each wagon in the train was filled by two men working together in harness. If the train was filled and carted away fourteen times in a day, then each pair would have filled fourteen wagons, and each individual navvy seven.

"A wagon holds up to two and a quarter cubic yards of muck – all the earth and rock and rubble we have to move every hour the good Lord allows us," interjected Naysmith, still shouting to make himself heard, "so that each man lifts nearly twenty tons of earth a day on a shovel over his own head and into a wagon."

"And that's a fourteen set day," said Yasser.

Sammy looked at Yasser and believed this giant of a man was probably capable of lifting twice that amount.

"Some men do sixteen," added Naysmith, as if

reading Sammy's thoughts.

Yasser grinned back.

"And then all that muck is brought back here, which my hammer pulverises into a kind of aggregate, which we then use to line the canal's walls and floor."

Sammy nodded. "When can I start?"

Yasser clapped him hard across the back and gripped his shoulder. "Join Zhang over there," and he pointed to a man currently working a wagon alone. "He needs a new partner."

"What happened to his old one?" asked Sammy.

"You don't want to know," roared Yasser.

Naysmith waved Yasser away. "Don't listen to him."

"His hand got trapped between two of the wagons," explained Yasser. "Squashed it, that's all. Nothing serious. He'll be back in a day or two."

And so began Sammy's time as a navvy on the construction of the Manchester Ship Canal as it cut its relentless way through the Lancashire fields on the edge of the Earl's land near Worsley.

When they had to give up the Camp, they each went their separate ways. But not before Eve had given birth to a daughter. It was Clémence who'd suggested they called her Delphine, after Sammy had told her of how he and Eve had met, when he had chased the otter out of The Delph, swum in hot pursuit of her along the Irwell to the weir which plunged down into the Mersey, where he had leapt like a salmon out of the water, beached himself on the riverbank, and there first looked into Eve's eyes.

Clem had helped with the birth, Old Moon had cut the cord, and Eve had eaten some of the raw placenta, before the rest was cooked and shared between them. The smoke rose high into the night sky, and the air was filled with Delphine's loud and healthy cry.

Sammy signed to Eve. "She has a strong voice."

In the weeks that followed it soon became clear that she responded to sounds made behind her. "She can hear too," he signed.

A grateful Eve smiled and pulled Delphine close, looking deeply into her daughter's milky, swimming eyes.

It was not long afterwards that Tommy left, returning once more to his nomadic, itinerant ways, moving from farm to farm, changing with the seasons, sometimes with Nathaniel, sometimes with the Earl, sometimes further afield, back towards Salford, making a ring around the edge of Manchester – Swinton, Pendlebury, Irlam o' the Heights and Kersal Moor, Miles Platting, Gorton, Denton and Reddish, Gatley, Handforth, Wilmslow and Warburton, and then the string of Mosses – Rixton, Glazebrook, Cadishead, Chat – and back again to Worsley. This became his migratory route, as predictable as the swallows in spring and the redwings in autumn, for the next twenty years.

Catch and Clem stayed behind to help Sammy build a cabin in Coroners Wood, just above Red Brook, a hidden, winding stream that trickled between Cadishead and Chat Moss, on the southern side of where the Ship Canal was to flow, near a place called Bobs Lane. It provided a home for Eve and Delphine, a roof over their heads, warmth in the winters, close to trees and water, where they could grow roots and catch fish, and where Old Moon could feel safe and protected.

But as soon as it was ready Catch and Clem decided to follow their own course. Catch left Zack Flint to try and secure a place of his own, switching from smithies to foundries to steel works as the opportunities arose. Sammy never saw them again.

He, Eve, Delphine and Old Moon settled to their new life in Bob's Lane, but then The Delph was closed, Sammy lost his job, and this new life needed more than just the old ways to sustain it. It needed money, and so Sammy had made his way back to what remained of the Bittern Wood to seek work as a setter on the Ship Canal, working from dawn till dusk for fourpence ha'penny a day.

Eve kept hens, fished, shot rooks and rabbits, while Old Moon dandled Delphine tenderly on his lap and softly crooned in her ear, her bubbling voice exploring all her newly discovered sounds.

"*Water flows under earth*
Fire burns leaves on trees
After the snow has melted
Green shoots will appear
And three white birds
Will fly across the moon…"

*

Six months passed.

Sammy became a regular in Yasser's gang, alongside Happy Jack, Dusty Mick, Long Bob and Frying Pan, the navvies preferring to go by nicknames rather than their real ones, and also with Zhang, Huan, Shi and Yu, as well as Asif, Nabil, Hakim and Rashid. The setters and navvies, Sammy noticed, fell into four main groups – Irish, Chinese, Arab and, overwhelmingly, Lancastrian – plus a few outsiders like himself. Each group tended to keep to their own kind, but Yasser's gang was different. Yasser hand picked his men, leading by example, urging them all to keep surpassing themselves, which they invariably did. When commencing a cutting, each of them knew their individual roles. Yasser and Sammy would stake out the intended course of the canal with rails and posts driven into the top of the hill. Jack and Mick, Zhang and Yu would dig out the upper surface until the hill was laid open, when Bob, Nabil, Rashid and Huan would excavate a gulley just wide enough for Yasser and Sammy to lay a temporary set of tram rails on which they pulled the wagon behind them. Asif and Hakim would cart away the excess muck as quickly as Yasser and Sammy could remove it, while Shi and Frying Pan followed behind shoring up the sides of the channel with a series of props driven hard into the earth. Yasser and Sammy would then force a rail back through to the upper surface, as a signal for Jack, Mick, Zhang and Yu to dig out the next stretch from above. It was hard, slow, back breaking labour, the work done almost entirely by hand. Only if the heart of a hill contained solid rock too thick even for Yasser's pick axe would they resort to using gun powder to blast their way through a particularly stubborn section. Yasser would then clear everyone from underground and bring in Zhang, who was the best explosives man on the entire site, and whose services were frequently in demand up and down the length of the canal, as it made its gargantuan progress inexorably towards Manchester.

Much of the time they worked in silence. Each picked up something of another's language, but there was little need for words. Yasser had the men well drilled with a set of rote-learned numbers of strikes upon a rail with his iron-headed hammer sufficient for clarity of instruction. Occasionally Frying Pan would sing to add a steady rhythm to which they might all work as one.

"The sea is far away where it promises to stay
And we cannot move our city to the shore
But if we can't move the town
Then we must bring the ocean down
To take the coal and cotton
Lest we should be forgotten
Bang up to the world's front door

Cos —we've got the money, we've got the men
We'll soon have the ships and we'll tell 'em then
Where there's a will there's a way, don't you know
To bring the sea to Manchester and Yo-Heave- Ho."

Sometimes, if there wasn't a use for all the tons and tons of excavated soil unearthed during the digging of a cutting, it had to be lifted up the sloping walls and dumped at the sides where, with time and weather, it might be absorbed back into the earth. This was done using the notorious barrow runs. Sammy found this aspect of the work the most thrilling, partly because, he recognised, it was potentially the most dangerous. The runs were made by laying planks up the sides of the cutting, up which barrows filled with mountains of soil were wheeled. The running was performed by the strongest of men, and Yasser felt that every member of his gang was capable of performing this arduous task and urged all of them to try their hand at it. Led by himself at the helm, they would race the other gangs. It was a matter of great personal pride that they should never be defeated. A rope, attached to the barrow and also to each man's belt, ran up the side of the cutting, and then round a pulley at the top, where it was tethered to a horse. When the barrow was loaded, a signal would be given to the horse driver at the top – this became Sammy's role – and the man was drawn up the side of the cutting, balancing the barrow in front of him. If the horse pulled steadily and the man kept his balance, everything would go well. The man tipped his barrow-load onto the side of the cutting again, this time drawing his barrow after him and with his back towards it, while Sammy ensured that the horse kept the rope taut, taking most of the weight of the empty barrow. But if, on the upward climb, the horse slipped or faltered, or if the man lost his balance on the muddy plank, then he had to do his best to save himself by throwing the loaded barrow to one side of the plank and himself to the other. If both toppled over on the same side, the barrow and its contents might fall on the man. When this happened to Dusty one time, he was the butt of the others' jokes for weeks, his pseudonym shifting from Dusty Mick to Dusty Muck. In the deep cutting they had to dig at Barton Dock, which ran through the Moss at a depth of over forty feet for more than a mile, there were more than thirty horse runs, and nearly all of the navvies were thrown down the slope several times – but none of Yasser's gang. They became so sure-footed that they earned the nickname 'Yasser's Goats'.

Mr Naysmith invented a moving platform, which ran along caterpillar treads, to take the soil up the side of the cutting without a single navvy having to go with it, but the men – and there were more than ten thousand working on the canal at this point – thought it was a machine designed to cut their wages, and broke it one night. Some pointed their finger at the long reach of Long Bob, but he only grinned when asked, and nothing could be proved. Besides, Yasser confided later to Naysmith, these barrow runs were good for morale, making a welcome break from the usual daily grind of digging and shovelling, blasting and shoring up.

It soon became necessary for Sammy to stay away from Bobs Lane for several weeks at a time, for they were frequently required to work double, sometimes triple shifts, starting each day as soon as it grew light and working late into the night. There simply wasn't time for Sammy to return home the closer they took the canal to the impatiently waiting Port of Manchester, and so he took up lodgings at Ma Grady's. But this was after he had been forced to sample the dubious delights of Peggy's Shant.

Once again it was Yasser's idea.

For most of the time the men lived where they worked. Large shanties of makeshift dwellings would sprawl across the land along the banks of the canal, hastily thrown up huts of wood and stone covered with sheets of tarpaulin. Inside they would consist of one large oblong space, where the men ate, drank and slept, sometimes more than sixty to a single dwelling. These were foul-smelling, vermin-ridden dens which, when the railway was laid across the Moss some fifty years previously, were simply abandoned and allowed to slip back into the quagmire and quicksand. It was in just such a shack that Clem had found refuge after her escape from St James Square, and which had served as her home until the Lumn's Lane Pit Disaster, and her chance meeting with Catch.

For the building of the Ship Canal the local people were more ready, and whole boardwalks of lodging houses were thrown up to accommodate the thousands of workers expected to arrive. These, too, were crude affairs, but they offered at least a crumb of comfort, a hard, almost certainly shared bed, a hot meal with plenty of ale on tap.

Sammy poked his head one night through the door of one of these. It was situated midway in one of the mud walls, on which had been painted in rough lime wash 'Peggy's Shant', not that Sammy could have read that. Opposite the door, on the inside, was a small open window with a piece of torn sacking stretched across it, and near to this were several rough benches, where four or five navvies were already sprawled, asleep or drunk or both. Two others were lying on the floor playing cards, and another was sitting on a stool mending his boots. He nodded to Sammy as he bent his head and stepped over the threshold and offered him a drink, which Sammy declined. Beneath the window stood three barrels of beer, all in tap, the keys to which were chained to a strong leather girdle around an old, toothless crone's waist, who was snoring loudly. This was Peg, and this was her shant.

The opposite end was fitted up with bunks from floor to roof like the between-decks of an emigrant ship, and in each bunk lay two or three men, their heads pillowed on their kit bag of tools. On closer inspection, as his eyes grew more accustomed to the murk, Sammy realised that some of the bodies in the bunks were women, and some were children. Many of the navvies brought their wives and babies with them, while others took advantage of the various services on offer from the scores of the Mersey Molls who had followed the course of the canal from Liverpool, as it made its way to Manchester, and from the sounds coming from some of the bunks, it was clear they were doing brisk business. In a corner a pair of rats coiled and writhed in the ashes beneath a lit stove.

Trade followed the navvies wherever they went.

Hucksters, packmen, cheapjacks, hawkers, tailors and likeness-takers all descended on the works. But the brewers and the molls were the most plentiful. Since most navvies were paid sporadically, at the conclusion of work at a given stretch, they would be forced to chalk up what they owed on a tally. This was then paid directly to the Pegs and the traders, being deducted from the navvies' wages at source, a cause of much friction and bitterness among the men, resulting in a constantly shifting turnover of the work force, for there were always new recruits eager to fill the boots of those who had left disgruntled.

Sammy quickly decided that Peg's Shant was not for him and confided in Yasser, who nodded. "Such places," he said, "are for the single man."

"Are you married?" Sammy heard himself asking.

"Not yet," winked Yasser, tapping the side of his nose. "But soon, I hope. Soon," and he roared with that infectious laugh of his. "Come," he said. "Let's see if Ma Grady has room."

Although principally a commercial enterprise, designed to bring greater profit to the merchants of Manchester, the Ship Canal was equally driven by the zeal of Non-Conformists and Unitarians, Methodists and Moravians, keen to clean up the city. Men like Sir Thomas Walker, its first Chief Engineer, and his successor, James Naysmith, saw it as their mission to offer religious guidance and spiritual uplift. They formed The Christian Excavators Union and held open air sermons by the banks of the canal, preaching hell fire damnation, while extolling the virtues of abstemiousness and temperance. The navvies never lost their rough tongue but they knew on what side their bread was buttered and, if attendance at these sermons and adherence to some simple rules concerning excess drunkenness and fornication meant that they were likely to see more of their wages come pay day, they were happy to conform, while smirking behind the backs of their hands.

Yasser's gang – Irish Catholics, Chinese Taoists and Arab Muslims – all regularly attended, regarding the services as just another part of their working week, and so the largely animist Sammy did also.

Mr Naysmith would stand on his steam hammer at the base of the latest pit which had been dug, a perfect amphitheatre around which the men would gather on the slopes leading out to the neighbouring factories and fields. His voice would boom out.

"This is a great and noble enterprise we are all embarked upon here in this place, my friends. We are forging a mighty channel to the sea. Where once a series of hills and valleys, forests and fields, lay like a barrier between our mighty metropolis and the world, now, with our combined efforts, blessed by the grace of God, we are bringing the world to us. The works of Man are indeed but trifles in the eyes of the Lord, yet here we labour to bring into being such things that did not exist before and, through these, do His bidding. As by a magician's wand, hills have been cut down, valleys have been filled up. Works have been scattered over the face of the earth, bearing testimony to the indomitable spirit of this great nation and our great city as a leader within it."

"Amen," responded those who were genuine believers.

"I believe," Naysmith continued, "there is no finer spectacle any man could witness, who like me is accustomed to surveying work, than to see a cutting in full operation, with scores of wagons being filled, every man at his post, and every man with his shirt open, working in the heat of the day, the gangers looking about, and everything operating like clockwork."

Here he paused and fixed his eyes upon Yasser, surrounded by his team, before continuing.

"I recall one particularly memorable sight. It was night. The shafts were some sixty feet in depth. Men were descending to its bottom in buckets lowered on ropes. The darkness of the cavern was made visible to those, like me, watching from above, by the numerous candles being burned by the men, and the sounds – of ringing hammer, pickaxe and chisel, the deep rumblings of the loaded wagons running along the rails, the frequent blasting of the rock, and the hoarse voices of the men calling out to one another – intermingled like a symphony. The whole scene created a *tout ensemble* of human daring, industry and ingenuity. The candles twinkled in the deep like stars on a dark night, casting great shadows of heroic figures across the cavern's walls, who flung their strong arms in a ballet of power and grace. What to some may have resembled a scene from Dante's *Inferno*, to me was more reminiscent of a great voyage to the farthest reaches of the universe, to the edges of what is known. The triumph, therefore, my friends, when after so long and perilous a delving deep within the bowels of the earth, we are enabled by the removal of stone barriers from the base to the summit of a cutting, having worked blindly and unseen from one another, to meet at last and shake hands in regions never before visited by the light of day before this great enterprise began, is a thing of wonder, more easily imagined than described, yet together we have done this."

"Amen," chorused even more men.

"Let us raise our voices then and sing together of this great pilgrimage in the stirring words of John Bunyan, who exhorts all of us 'to be a pilgrim'."

A brass band from The Christian Excavators Union played the opening bars and the exposed pit was filled with the sound of several thousand voices, from near and far, home and abroad, singing as one, united by their journeys to this city.

"Who would true valour see
Let him come hither
One here will constant be
Come wind, come weather
There's no discouragement
Shall make him once relent
His first avowed intent
To be a pilgrim…"

Over the weeks Sammy's ear tuned into its unfamiliar rhythm and words, words which reminded him of Old Moon's songs and visions, and he smiled at the prospect of sharing this with him when next he returned home.

"Who so beset him round
With dismal stories
Do but themselves confound
His strength the more is
No foes shall stay his might
Though he with giants fight
He will make good his right
To be a pilgrim…"

Sammy thought back over the years since his capture and kidnap on the plains of South Dakota, his years in the Wild West Show – dismal stories indeed – but since then they had fought with giants and had beaten them. He was making a life for himself, for Eve and for Delphine, in this strange land, which was now his home.

"Hobgoblin nor foul fiend
Can daunt his spirit
He knows he at the end
Shall life inherit
Then fancies flee away
He'll fear not what men say
He'll labour night and day
To be a pilgrim…"

But what kind of life would it be that Delphine would inherit? He watched the factories springing up weekly along the banks of this new canal they were building together and an idea began to form...

When the service had ended, Yasser put his huge arm around his shoulder and said, "It's time for you to meet Ma Grady."

*

Rose Grady knew the ways of navvies. Her father had been one himself. Michael O'Grady had crossed the Irish Sea to Liverpool and then tramped his way across the Wirral, working on the railways criss-crossing Cheshire and Lancashire, before fetching up in Ancoats, where he married Eilidh, a local girl from Angel Meadow.

On his last tramp he lost a leg beneath a fall of rock and together he and Eilidh decided to try their hand at running a pub. But this was the time of the Scuttlers, notorious criminal gangs, who fought their turf wars on the streets and alleyways right outside their front door, sometimes spilling over into fights and robberies inside. It was no place to bring up children, so they upped sticks and went back to the life they were more familiar with, a boarding house for other navvies working on the railways and canals. They dropped the 'O' and called their premises 'Ma Grady's', offering respectability and a welcome home from home for all those who found themselves in a strange land far away from their loved ones. Eilidh cooked and cleaned, while Michael set up the deals with the engineers and contractors. It was here, in a back room one noisy Saturday night, where

Rose was born twenty-one years before, the only daughter among four older brothers, all of whom worked as navvies.

Michael died when Rose was just eleven, since when she became Eilidh's pot scrubber, bottle washer and general all round help. When work began on the Ship Canal, business boomed. They acquired the next door *Braziers Arms* on Gravel Lane, and soon they could accommodate up to two dozen men at any given time. Mr Naysmith made a long-term, open-ended arrangement for Yasser and his gang to be billeted there for however long it took the Canal to progress from Barton Docks to Pomona. Now they inhabited a kind of island, with the waters of the Bridgewater Canal behind them, as they made their way the final mile towards the bottom of Deansgate in Manchester's city centre, the growing sprawl of Trafford Park to the right and left, with its chaotic tangle of factories and foundries, the sluggish River Irwell snaking in and around and between them, and the gaping hole in front of them, which was to be the Ship Canal once the last stone sluices were opened and the water allowed to fill it.

The hundred foot high clock tower of *The Royal Pomona Palace* was just visible between the rows of mill chimneys, with its unlikely Botanical Gardens just a stone's throw away, where Roman chariot races were staged, gymkhanas and dog shows, where visitors could take archery lessons, ride on the flying swings, get lost in the Hedge Maze, spy on their neighbours through the *camera obscura*, laugh at the antics of Wallet the Queen's Jester, or gaze in wonder at the exhibits in the

Human Zoo.

Rose had visited the Gardens once, as a girl, taken there one Whit Sunday by Eilidh for a rare treat. Eilidh was struggling with arthritic joints now, and so it was left to Rose to deal with the men, a task she relished, for she regarded them all as members of an extended family, exchanging banter just as she had had to do with her father and brothers.

It was here, to Ma Grady's, where Yasser brought Sammy, and where he first met Rose, who had a word and a joke for everyone, but eyes only for Yasser. Another six months had passed since that first evening, but Sammy still felt like the new boy.

"When are you going to put me out of my misery and marry me?" lamented a not so Happy Jack to Rose that first evening as she served up a plate of hot pot.

"And what would we tell that wife of yours back in Ireland if we did?" she replied, much to the general merriment of the rest of the Gang.

"Would you be so kind as to lengthen the sleeves on this please, Rose?" stammered an awkward Long Bob, holding out a much-patched jacket in front of him.

"Why Long Bob, I swear you've grown another six inches just since last week. Isn't it about time you stopped?"

"The long arm of Long Bob," joked Asif.

"Well see if you can reach into the back room with that long arm of yours," said Rose, "and give this to our Chinese friends." She handed Bob a pan of steamed vegetables, which he took to Zhang, Huan, Shi and Yu, where they were serving out bowls of rice to each other.

They preferred to cook separately according to their own preferences, and Rose was happy to oblige, so long as their bills were all paid on time by Mr Naysmith, and that went for any extra laundry or mending she undertook, like Long Bob's jacket. Yasser's men were paid slightly less than most navvies, but their food and lodgings were provided for them by the Ship Canal Company, and so they did not become enslaved to the tally men. Better fed and better housed, they were able to maintain their position as the élite gang, forging ahead with the more difficult, groundbreaking sections of the route.

Back at Barton Yasser had worked alongside Sir Edward Leader Williams himself, whose plans for the whole canal had been the preferred option, and who had designed the great turning mechanism for the Swing Aqueduct, which now carried the Bridgewater Canal over the top of the Manchester Ship Canal. Sixty-four iron rollers sat on top of the race plate held in position by a giant spider ring. Yasser had been the man to set the spider ring in place. Now the canal was approaching Pomona, there were plans to construct an even larger swing bridge on part of the Trafford Park Road, and Yasser had been requested to lead a team of men there to repeat the operation. He was going out the following day to reconnoître the site.

After supper, as was her custom, Ma Grady did the rounds of the boarding house, saying good night to the men, who all made a great fuss of her, especially Yasser, complimenting her on her excellent cooking.

"Oh," she replied, the dimples in her cheeks still

showing as she smiled back toothlessly to him, "it's mostly Rose does everything nowadays."

"That may be," said Yasser with mock solemnity, "but where did she learn all these skills, if not from her mother?" He winked at Rose.

"Don't listen to a word he says, Ma," cajoled Rose, brushing past Yasser while collecting the dishes, though smiling fondly at him as she did so. "He's a born flatterer. He's just angling for an extra helping. Which we don't have by the way," she added, poking him in the belly.

"And why wouldn't he be wanting an extra helping? He works hard all day and he's a big man. He needs his strength."

"He'll get fat."

"And what's wrong with that? I like a bit of fat on a man."

"And why's that?"

"For one thing it improves his temper."

"Well he could certainly do with that. Perhaps I'll see what's left at the bottom of the pan to scrape off for him."

"Cast not pearls before swine, Rose," said Yasser, grinning hugely as he reached for the pan.

"Quite right, Mr Wahid," rejoined Rose. "That would indeed be a waste. How about your new friend? Sammy, isn't it? Would you care for a little more?"

Sammy looked uncertainly from Rose to Yasser and back again. "I'm not sure I…"

"Don't trouble yourself, Sammy. You heard Miss Rose," said Yasser. 'Waste not, want not'," and he leant across to take back the pan.

But before he could take hold of it, Rose rapped his knuckles with the stirring spoon. "In that case I'm sure the chickens in the yard will make much better use of it."

The banter continued on into the night. Yasser helped Ma Grady up from her seat, who patted him on the arm. "The manners of children today," she said, shaking her head, "I don't know what's become of them…"

"I am not a child," called out Rose from the kitchen.

"I can't think what you see in her," said Ma Grady as she took herself off to bed.

"Who can fathom the mysteries of the human heart?" sighed Yasser in mock seriousness. "We men are but prisoners of our fancies."

"*But… a… little of what you fancy does you good,*" sang Dusty Mick, picking up his squeeze box, which signalled the end of supper. The men drifted into smaller groups of twos and threes, to smoke, play cards, write letters.

Sammy sat apart, watching the evening unfold. He was missing Eve and the baby. He wished more than ever he could read and write, and resolved to make use of the evening classes being offered by Mr Naysmith and The Christian Excavators Union in addition to their outdoor Sunday services.

Suddenly Rose was at his side with a mug of tea. "Penny for them," she said.

Sammy looked up.

"Your thoughts," she added. "Yasser tells me you

have a young baby, a little girl. You must miss them?"

"Yes," he said. "Very much."

"Drink this," she said. "Things always seem better after a mug of tea."

"Thank you."

"And you'll soon be finished, I hear?"

"Will we?"

She nodded. "That's what Yasser says."

"What does Yasser say?" said Yasser, coming across to join them.

"Nothing of any consequence," said Rose, tapping the side of her nose. "I was speaking to our new friend."

Sammy looked down.

Yasser held out his arms and Rose, smiling, allowed herself to enter their wide embrace. Sammy watched them walk outside. Outside there was a full moon, and the whole of the Milky Way arched bright and clear overhead. But Yasser and Rose had eyes only for each other.

Inside Dusty Mick had struck up another tune. One by one the men joined in to sing, each lost in his own private thoughts, their voices rising up to the night sky together with the smoke from the still lit brazier out in the yard, all the stars in the constellations mere specks twinkling in the dark waters of the canal, yet each playing their part in this great enterprise, home and the world.

"I'm a Navvy, I work on the Ship Canal
I'm a setter and live in a hut with my Sal
Or nestle in a hayrick, or shelter in a barn

And tales like these us navvies please
When not o'erdone the yarn

We have lodgers, a splendid lot of young men
In the evening around the tables are ten
Some of t' lads are strangers, ne'er been out before
But some can tell of a long, long spell
Tramping the country o'er

Our work is hard and dangers are always near
And lucky are we if safely through life we steer
But the life of a navvy with its many change of scene
With a dear old wife is just the life
That suits old Nobby Green…"

Mick finished playing and all was briefly silent, save for the lapping of the canal waters on the bank just below and the last of the wood cracking in the grate.

After a pause Yasser called out from the yard. "Who is this Nobby Green?" The others jeered and the mood was broken.

"He's here," said Rose, looking down onto the canal. Both their reflections rippled on the water.

"Then why haven't I met him?" asked Yasser.

"He's everywhere, he's all of you," she said, stirring the surface of the water with a stick, so that their reflections disappeared.

"Come to bed," he said.

Rose smiled. When the water settled again, Yasser had gone. Only her own reflection stared back at her. She shivered, turned and headed back inside and up the narrow stairs to where Yasser was waiting hopefully for her. He reached out to embrace her with his great bear-like arms, under which she deftly ducked and sidestepped her way past him.

"Good night, boys," she called out. "Sweet dreams."

Yasser clambered back down the stairs with a sigh to the amused derision of his tucked up goats.

*

Dear Eve,

When we first met, you cud read but cud not speak, and I cud speak but cud not read. I now try to learn. Mr Naysmith, he teaches me, and Rose, she helps me too. The work is hard but the men are my good friends. We dig more and more each day. I hope soon we finish, then I come home to you and Delphine.

Sammy

*

Luigi was a bellhop at *The Royal Pomona Palace Hotel*. He had just turned thirteen years old, and today was his first day on the job. In the years to come he would tell this story many times.

He stood to attention in the hotel foyer, close to the grand central staircase, trying to take a sideways peep at his reflection in the floor to ceiling mirrors that ran the length of the hallway from the revolving doors at the hotel's entrance to the ornately polished front desk, behind which stood Signor Locartelli, the Head Clerk. Signor Locartelli, or Uncle Iacopo, as Luigi had made the mistake of calling him when he first arrived, was Luigi's father's brother, and it was he who had arranged for Luigi to have this job.

"*Solo per un periodo di prova*. For a trial period only. Let's see how he gets on," he had told Carlo, his brother.

"*Si*," Carlo had replied. "*Certo. È un bravo rigazzo*. He's a good boy," and then he had added, as an afterthought, "*in fondo*. At heart."

Now, Iacopo was beginning to doubt the wisdom of bestowing this favour on his nephew. He seemed incapable of standing still, was for ever fidgeting, and kept trying to see if he could see his face in the polished brass buttons of his blue and gold uniform, the livery of all *The Royal Pomona Palace* bellhops. Bellhops, wondered Iacopo idly. Such a curious term. American, he supposed, a fad of the owner, Mr James Reilly, upon his return from New York, where he had stayed at *The Waldorf Astoria*, of which he was an ardent admirer, and about which he never tired of singing the praises, particularly the standards of service provided by the bellhops there. *Fattorini d'albergo*. Iacopo tried to instil these standards into all of his young recruits, but Luigi, he could tell already, might prove his stiffest challenge yet. He would have to have started today. Of all days. When Mr Reilly was entertaining several distinguished local businessmen, members of The Manchester Ship Canal Company, who were already beginning to plan their Grand Opening, an estimated twelve months hence, to which Queen Victoria herself had been invited, in the magnificent Tea Rooms, under the watchful eyes of Mars, Venus, Neptune and Vulcan, whose ornately painted figures looked down from the vaulted, decorated ceiling, surrounding Pomona herself, Goddess of the Orchards and Strawberry Gardens, who formed the gilt centrepiece. It was Iacopo's responsibility to ensure that all were maintained in pristine condition at all times, a duty he undertook with the utmost seriousness. Why, only last year no less a personage than the Prime Minister, Mr Benjamin Disraeli himself, had commented favourably upon the ambience, an observation which had not gone unnoticed by Mr Reilly, who had afterwards singled out Iacopo for special praise. Now, his nephew was threatening to sabotage his reputation with his constant questions, his incessant chatter, and his over-eagerness to please. He has already tripped over the suitcase of one of his guests and spilled the contents of another. Fortunately, the case had belonged to Mrs Wooding, one of the hotel's long-term residents, an extremely wealthy widow, who found the boy "charming", and who had pinched his cheek with her gloved hand, describing him as "a darling", and who had simpered at Iacopo with a "where do you find such delightful creatures?" Iacopo had merely inclined his head politely.

"Madam is most kind," he had said. "*Molto gentile*," to which she had trilled in reply how she "adored" his accent.

"*Grazie, Signora*," he had responded obligingly, but when she had gone, he glared at his nephew. "You must be careful," he hissed. "*Devi fare ancora piu attenzione del solito.*"

"*Si, Zio,*" said Luigi glumly.

"Stop calling me 'Uncle'."

"*Si, Zio.*"

"You are a bellhop, remember? I ring this bell, here on my desk, and you hop. Understand? You hop." And he banged the flat of his hand upon the bell for added emphasis.

Immediately, Luigi hopped into the air.

In frustration Iacopo rang the bell once again. In delight Luigi hopped up and down again. He liked this game. If this was the world of work, why did people make out it was so hard all the time? He hopped a third time.

Exasperated, Iacopo was tempted to box his nephew's ears and was advancing towards him from behind his desk when he heard a noise like a clap of thunder. He stopped. As one he and Luigi turned their heads in the direction of the sound. There was so much building going on in the area that Iacopo was accustomed to the constant hammering and sawing, which formed a near permanent backdrop to the day's business, so that he was tempted simply to dismiss it, but this was something different, more like an explosion. His mind went at once to the Cornbrook Chemical Works owned by Roberts, Dale & Co, frequent visitors to the hotel, less than a hundred yards away by the River Irwell. Iacopo and Luigi then looked back at one another, just as a second, much bigger explosion shook the ground beneath them. All the windows in the hotel were blown in at once, and Iacopo instinctively pulled his nephew to the floor, shielding him from the hailstorm of splintered glass, which fell like tiny needles all around them, and that was the last thing he remembered.

When he regained his consciousness, Luigi was still buried beneath him under a layer of white plaster dust as well as the shards of glass. Iacopo lifted him up and – *grazie al cielo* – his eyes fluttered open.

"*Zio...?*" Luigi absent-mindedly brushed the plaster dust from one of the buttons on his jacket. The two of them looked about them. The hotel was in ruins which, Luigi observed, were reflected in the surface of his jacket's brass buttons.

*

THE ✿ TIMES

22nd June 1889

FATAL EXPLOSION AT MANCHESTER CHEMICAL FACTORY

An alarming and destructive explosion took place at noon yesterday at the Cornbrook Chemical Works, Ordsall, Manchester, belonging to Messrs. Roberts, Dale, and Co.

Up to a late hour yesterday the exact

cause of the disaster had not been placed beyond doubt, but it appears that a fire had broken out a few minutes before in one of the laboratories, and it is supposed that sparks fell among some explosive mixtures.

A fireman in the service of the firm, named James Martin, was found dead with a brass jet in his hand, as though he had been hastening to his work when an explosion followed. He was killed by a wall being blown down on top of him.

There were two explosions in succession, one a few seconds after the other, the second being the more violent, but both were of such force as to shake down walls and do other serious damage in all parts of the works, while the effect for a considerable distance around was to break windows, furniture, and fittings of houses and cause persons to rush into the streets, including along the Trafford Park Road, where workers for the Manchester Ship Canal Company were doing reconnaissance work for the construction of a new Swing Bridge to cross the great canal once it is completed.

A dense volume of smoke was seen issuing from the works, and the city's Fire Brigade were soon there in great force. The buildings were partly of brick, and were found already in ruins from the shock, but flames were issuing from several places and, the smoke being charged with chemical gases, the firemen had not a little danger and difficulty to contend with. The apprehension of further explosions did not deter them, and they worked with admirable steadiness for some hours till the fire was overcome, not only in the chemical works, but also in the neighboring premises of Pomona Gardens, which had been ignited in a dozen places by the lodgement of burning material. Both the *Agricultural Hall* and *The Royal Pomona Palace Hotel*, the scenes of many local festivities and of political gatherings of importance, were seriously damaged by the fire.

The wreck of the chemical works blocked the roadway, and the firemen had great difficulty in getting near those buildings with the engines. Some of the workpeople, of whom there were about fifty at the works at the time, had to jump from storey to storey as the staircases were destroyed. It is possible that some passers by may have been overwhelmed by the falling walls or struck by the stones, bricks, iron piping, and other fragments which were shot to great distances by the explosion.

Great damage has been done in Ordsall Lane to the mills of Messrs. Haworth, the dyeworks of Messrs. Worrall, and the chemical works of Messrs. Harvey. About a score of workmen and girls were treated at the Salford Hospital for cuts and contusions received either while in the mills or walking near them. An as yet unnamed man, a navigator on the Canal, was reported to have suffered serious burns as a result of the debris from this second explosion.

Fortunately the scene of the blast was in a

comparatively open space, but the vibration was severely felt over a large area, the outer walls being blown across the road for more than twenty yards. Some of those fragments fell on the roofs of buildings on the other side of the Irwell, including *The Braziers Arms*, which is an utter wreck in its interior, the contents being broken and flung together in all the rooms, although nobody was reported injured.

Thousands of persons flocked to the spot and detachments of the 13th Hussars and the 1st Lancashire Fusiliers were engaged in keeping back those who pressed too near either for their own safety or for the work of the firemen and police to proceed unimpeded.

*

Nabil had taken on the role of Gang Master for the day while Yasser was away with Mr Naysmith inspecting the site of the proposed Trafford Park Road Swing Bridge. Nabil was down at the base of a new cutting they were opening up in one of the basins that were to form part of Salford Quays, a major docking area for the berthing of ocean going ships once the Canal was completed and open for business. He had just signalled for a pause in the incessant hammering so that he might detect whether Sammy and Shi, who were measuring out the route at the surface, had broken through yet.

It was in that rare moment of silence that he felt the vibration beneath his feet. They all did. They looked to Nabil for further instruction. Then they felt the second vibration, much stronger and more prolonged than the first had been. They gazed in the direction of where the sound had originated and saw a column of black smoke rising. Without a second glance they all ran as one, towards the column of smoke, which lay close to Ma Grady's, the isle of Pomona, and the Trafford Park Road.

They reached Ma Grady's first. The windows were blown in, the door was swinging on its hinges, and much of the furniture inside – the tables, chairs, benches and bunks – were lying in pieces. Petals of ash and charred paper were floating all around them in a grey haze. Covering their mouths, they ventured further inside, up the narrow stairs, where they saw Rose kneeling on the landing beside a prostrate Eilidh.

"She's not hurt," gasped Rose, her face and arms smeared with soot and grime, "just shaken. But Yasser," she said, then stopped. "I don't know…"

Sammy and Shi did not need to hear a further word. At once they were off and running, clambering through the debris strewn across Ordsall Lane and Commercial Road, as they picked their way towards the Trafford Park Road.

Back at Ma Grady's Nabil calmly took charge. Frying Pan helped Rose carry Eilidh to the bedroom, clear away the brick dust and fragments of broken glass, so they could lay her down on the bed, and then fetched Rose water and whatever else she asked for. Dusty Mick and Long Bob swept and cleaned every surface inside *The Braziers Arms*, while Asif, Zhang, Rashid and Wu set about removing all the broken glass from the windows and covering the open gaps with slats of wood, which let in bars of light as well as filtering out at least some of the noxious smoke that was swirling in poisonous plumes all around. Hakim and Happy Jack repaired and re-hung the front door, while Nabil climbed up onto the roof, securing any slates that had slipped or loosened.

By the time Sammy and Shi reached the Trafford Park Road, it was difficult to tell where the road had once been. Great slabs of stone lay strewn in haphazard piles. Wagons and carts had overturned, spilling their goods and wares. Horses were skittering everywhere in a blind panic, those that were not trapped and whinnying beneath their smashed and scattered shafts and felloes, splinter bars and tail boards. Men were moaning, crushed under the weight of broken cart wheels, while passers-by attempted to attend to injured children, lying shocked and frightened by the roadside. A detachment of soldiers was trying to clear a safe passage to allow members of the Fire and Ambulance services through, while an old man, dazed and wandering amidst the tumult of noise and smoke and chaos all around him, stooped to pick a fallen apple that was rolling slowly towards a gutter and quietly bit into it.

Sammy wove his way through all of this, his feet swift and sure, not pausing an instant, eyes darting this way and that, as he desperately tried to seek out Yasser. Shi kept finding himself distracted by the different people he came across, each of them needing his help, so that the two of them quickly became separated.

Sammy ducked under a police cordon of constables linking arms, dodged between the mounted soldiers, until eventually he found himself near a small wooden footbridge linking the road with the isle of Pomona across a narrow stretch of the Irwell. He called out Yasser's name, again and again. Just as he stepped upon the bridge he thought he heard a voice faintly answering him from close by.

"S-a-m-m-y…"

He looked about him, and there, on the opposite bank of the river, he thought he detected the lifting of an arm from among the rubble. He ran further towards the middle of the bridge, but it at once began to collapse beneath him. But Sammy – *Leaping Fish* – rode the bridge as it fell towards the river, leapt lightly from one broken rock and rusted grille to another, which poked through the sludge of the river's thick, polluted surface, with pockets of marsh gas ignited by the explosion shooting up their flames around him as he danced his way rapidly between them, flitting across them like stepping stones, until he reached the other side, where Yasser's arm was still protruding from beneath a recent rock fall.

Sammy pulled the rocks away one at a time, as fast as he could, taking care not to bring about further falls, until more of Yasser's body was exposed and uncovered, first the arm, then his chest, then his legs, and finally his head, which was cut and badly burned. He was alive, but barely.

Scanning the earth close by for something that might help, Sammy's eyes alighted upon two things – an old railway sleeper and a rusting wheelbarrow. He flung the sleeper across the stepping stones he had just danced across, calculated that it might stay for just a few minutes before it either slipped off or was sucked beneath the surface. Using all the strength he could muster, wishing he was Catch, or even Yasser himself, he somehow heaved Yasser into the wheelbarrow, lined himself up with the edge of the railway sleeper, took a deep breath and then, emitting a deep-throated battle roar learned from his father back in South Dakota, he launched himself across the water.

"*Hoka hey!*"

Just as he reached the other side, the sleeper slipped from under his feet and sank, gurgling, into the stinking depths of the river.

Shi, who had heard Sammy's Sioux war cry, was instantly there by his side. He cleared the way before them so that Sammy could run the barrow the half a mile back to *The Braziers Arms*, where Nabil saw them first from his position on the rooftop and called out to the others. Long Bob and Zhang rushed out to meet them. Quickly but carefully the four of them carried Yasser upstairs to where Rose was waiting for him.

*

Reproduction of in-house Manchester Police Newspaper Article:

"THE INQUEST"

24th June 1889

The Manchester Deputy Coroner opened an Inquiry into the cause of the death of James Martin, fifty-four, who was killed by the explosion at Messrs. Roberts, Dale and Company's Cornbrook Chemical Works, Ordsall, two days previously.

Mr. J.M. Bates, barrister, who represented Roberts, Dale & Co., expressed their deep regret at the explosion, which had deprived them of one of their most valued servants. His clients were present to render to the court and to Colonel Majendie, the Government Inspector, every assistance in their power.

The cause of the explosion was wholly unintelligible to them, the more so as they had manufactured picric acid in this shed for the last thirty years without danger or injury to anybody. The jury then went to view the scene of the explosion and where the dead body was found, and on their return evidence was called as to the cause of the fire, which, it is supposed, originated the explosion.

Peter Heald, a mechanic in the service of Messrs. Roberts, Dale & Co., said he was working there on Wednesday morning when he heard that a fire had broken out a minute or two before twelve o'clock. He attached a hose to the water plug, while the deceased man Martin went and held the jet in the road, just under the window where the picric stove was housed. The fire appeared to be near the centre of the sheds in the yard. Heald turned to go away as he heard the explosion, and thought the deceased was following him. When he got about twenty yards away he turned round and the whole of the works appeared to have blown up. In the shed where the fire took place picric acid, nitrate of lead, tin, crystals, and, he believed, *aqua fortis*, were kept.

Joseph Dean, storekeeper at the works, said he did not see the fire when it first broke out. He saw the fire before the first explosion. Dean went inside the shed, and stood about four yards from the fire and close to the picric stove. The fire seemed to be floating about. He had seen similar fires before, but not so large as on the present occasion.

One of the previous fires was attributed to the men smoking, an action that was strictly prohibited. When Dean first went across to that part where the accident happened, a man named Hyde had his pipe lit. Dean spoke to him, and Hyde, who was ready to go home, pulled the pipe out of his mouth and directly afterwards left the works. To light his pipe he would have had to use a match, and Dean confirmed that he had heard a stove door close just before Hyde emerged from the building smoking his pipe. Hyde was not drunk, but apparently had had "a glass or two". The men sometimes went to the Pomona Gardens for a drink, but they were fined if they brought drink on the premises.

Stephan Logan, who said he was a labourer, said he never saw Hyde smoking, nor did he think Hyde had had any drink. Hyde, a labourer, said he was working with Logan on the Wednesday, taking picric acid out of the stove and placing it in barrels. He noticed nothing unusual about the place and he was quite sober. After the stove was emptied, Hyde explained that he turned the steam half-off. He was not smoking then, nor did he light his pipe before he left the works. He admitted that he had smoked many a time in the works, and once he was caught and fined.

The inquiry was then adjourned to July 14th, by which time Colonel Majendie will have prepared his report.

*

One of the effects of the explosion was to halt further work on the Ship Canal for a number of weeks – not entirely, because Mr Naysmith could still use thousands of men to continue to strengthen and shore up those sections already dug, and there was still much work to be done in the places where it joined other waterways, but sufficiently to allow Sammy to go back to Bob's Lane and see Eve and Delphine again after an absence of several months.

While he was there he spoke to Old Moon about what had happened to Yasser. The next day the two of them went in search of the different plants and herbs which might be helpful in the treatment of burns. When he returned to Ma Grady's, Sammy took with him a sack full of the flowers, roots and stems of marigold and lavender, comfrey and plantain, as well as burdock leaves and thin strips of slippery elm bark collected from the sapling planted by Tommy three years before, which had survived the felling of much of the Bittern Wood and was now thriving.

As soon as he got back he began to prepare a range of ointments, powders, teas and infusions from the different plants for Rose to use with Yasser – the plantain and burdock to soothe the pain, the lavender oil to calm the nerves and aid with sleep, a poultice from comfrey to heal the scar tissue, cold compresses made from the marigolds to reduce inflammation and encourage the growth of new skin, and the slippery elm to help that new skin grow stronger.

Huan, Zhang, Shi and Wu took on all responsibilities for cooking and looking after Eilidh, while Happy Jack, Dusty Mick, Long Bob and Frying Pan continued to carry out the repairs to *The Braziers Arms*. Nabil, Hakim, Asif and Rashid painted stars on the ceiling of the room where Yasser lay and a frieze of the Hejaz Mountains in Southern Arabia to remind him of his homeland. They took turns to read verses from the *Qur'an* and sing ancient Sufi songs.

But mostly they stayed below, leaving Yasser with Rose, who never left his side. Night and day she nursed him, applying the ointments, refreshing the compresses, lifting sponges soaked in infusions to his dry, cracked lips, whispering to him softly – tender, secret things that nobody else could hear. Sammy was reminded of the way Tommy would whisper to the horses whenever they were sick. Yasser continued to burn up. He would shout out, strange, unintelligible cries from dark, troubled dreams, and Rose would bring her cool fingers to his brow, blow softly upon his face, croon and sing to him, as the low evening sun would creep into the room in bars of red and gold through the slatted, wooden blinds that mostly kept it shaded and cool. Rose would look up at the stars painted on the ceiling, together with an Islamic crescent moon, and look at the frieze of southern mountains on the far wall, and dream the two of them were travelling in some *caravanserai* across the desert, towards a distant ocean, where lights twinkled on the water, carrying them both towards a new home.

After nearly a week's delirium, Yasser's fever at last began to subside. When he opened his eyes, his first words were:

"Rose, Rose, where is my Rose?"

"I'm here," she whispered, "right beside you, where I've always been, and where I'll always stay."

*

```
Facsimile of:
Report on the Circumstances Attending a
Fire and Explosion at Messrs. Roberts,
Dale & Co.'s Cornbrook Chemical Works,
Ordsall, Manchester.
Gov. Report No. 1xxxi
Colonel V.D. Majendie, C.B.

    Journal of the Society of Chemical
Industry, 31st December, 1889, p. 835:
```

This exhaustive report shows that the articles manufactured on the side of the works where the explosion occurred were picric acid, nitrate of lead, nitric acid, hydrochloric acid (nitre cake and salt cake), tin crystals, tin solutions, nitrate of iron, nitrate of copper, aurin, Manchester brown, Manchester yellow, lakes for paper stainers and emerald green. Such raw materials as carbolic acid, sulphuric acid and litharge, the litharge being used for making nitrate of lead, were all present, the latter salt in very considerable quantity. Some nitrate of strontium was also present.

"A fire commenced the catastrophe, this breaking out at or near the stove used for drying the picric acid. The fire spread quickly, and in five or six minutes an explosion followed, but not one of an alarming character. This explosion came from the site of the picric acid stove as nearly as it can be located. It was followed in something under a minute by a second explosion of an appalling character, and attended with disastrous results in the shape of damage. One life was lost and more than fifty people were hurt, either as a result of serious burns received, or of injuries sustained by falling masonry or flying glass.

"There is little doubt that the fire was caused by the carelessness of a workman, who was smoking. Several theories are advanced to explain the first and lesser explosion, but the second, which was so disastrous, was in all probability due to the blazing and molten picric acid coming into contact with the litharge placed in close proximity with the nitrate of lead and nitrate of strontium.

"In view of the present disaster, it will be a matter for careful consideration whether it is not necessary in the interests of public safety to take advantage of the powers conferred by the 104th section of the Explosives Act, 1875, and to extend the definition of explosives to picric acid and all picrates, for whatever purposes manufactured, and to apply the same provisions of the Act, subject to such exceptions, limitations and restrictions as may appear reasonable. This point, however, is one which, in the interests of the trade, as of the public, demands the fullest and most careful consideration.

"As to the storage together and in close proximity of the several substances which resulted in the formation of such fearful explosives, it can only be concluded that this was an act of gross negligence."

Colonel Majendie, V.D., Govt Inspector

*

Mr Naysmith smiled warmly, regarding the happy couple standing before him.

622

"With the authority invested in me as Registrar and Reader at this Chapel, I ask you please to repeat after me."

Rose and Yasser looked at each other shyly.

"I do solemnly declare…"

"I do solemnly declare…"

"… that I know not of any lawful impediment…"

"… that I know not of any lawful impediment…"

"… why I, Rose…"

"… why I, Rose…"

"… may not be joined in matrimony…"

"… may not be joined in matrimony…"

"… to Yasser Mohammed Wahid."

"… to Yasser Mohammed Wahid."

Rose was wearing a delicately worked white cotton shawl overlaid with patterns of lace depicting a moth alighting on a laurel leaf, which Yasser had proudly presented to her that morning. She took her new husband's hand in hers, and together they walked down the steps of the Cross Street Unitarian Chapel exactly a year to the day since the Pomona chemical explosion. Outside Nabil and Hakim, Asif and Rashid, Happy Jack and Dusty Mick, Long Bob and Frying Pan, Zhang and Huan, Shi and Wu stood in pairs to form a guard of honour with raised hammers for them to walk through.

Waiting for them at the end of the line were Sammy and Eve, with an excited Delphine, now three years old, hopping from foot to foot. In her hands she clutched a posy of wild flowers picked from Pomona Gardens, which she held out towards Rose.

Everyone walked together back up to the Town Hall and gathered around the steps of the Albert Memorial Statue, where Mr Naysmith took photographs, after which Rose made a special point of introducing herself to Eve. She was fascinated by the silent world Sammy and Eve inhabited. She tried to explain to Eve just how grateful she was for her husband saving Yasser's life and saw her smile after Sammy had completed the signed translation of her words. Delphine, she noticed, happily chattered enough for the three of them.

The sun dipped below the clock tower on the Town Hall roof and everyone began to drift away, slowly meandering back to *The Braziers Arms*. When they were finally alone, Yasser and Rose stood in the yard at the back, looking down once more at their reflections on the water. This time, when they smiled, both reflections smiled back.

Yasser turned to Rose and took her tiny hands in one of his own mighty paws.

"I, Yasser Mohammed Wahid, offer you myself in marriage in accordance with the instructions of the Holy *Qur'an* and the Holy Prophet, blessings be upon him. I pledge, in honesty and with sincerity, to be for you a faithful and helpful husband."

Rose gently extracted one of her hands from his and placed it tenderly against his cheek, where a strong beard now covered that part of his face which had been so badly burned, and said:

"And I, Rose, pledge to be for you a faithful and loving wife."

"In the name of *Allah* the Beneficent, *Allah* the Merciful, let us seek refuge with the Lord of the Dawn."

The two reflections kissed in the waters of the Irwell, from where Yasser had been rescued, and retreated upstairs to the room with the stars painted on the ceiling, glittering above the Hejaz Mountains of Southern Arabia, where Rose, now loosening the white lace and cotton cloth from her head and letting it fall from her shoulders, had nursed him back to life.

*

"And so today, on this, the twenty-first day of May, in the year of our Lord 1894, it gives us great pleasure to declare the Manchester Ship Canal open."

To resounding cheers and the throwing of hats into the air, Queen Victoria cut the ribbon and the *SS Pioneer*, flagship of the merchant fleet of the Manchester Liners Company, sailed down the slipway of the Pomona Dock Number One in the newly fitted out Port of Manchester, and out into the Canal, at the start of the thirty-six miles of its maiden voyage to Liverpool, and from there to the rest of the Empire and the world.

The completion date was two years later than planned – construction had been further delayed after the Cornbrook Chemical Works by one of the harshest winters on record, so cold that ice more than a foot thick formed along the surfaces of both the River Irwell and the Bridgewater Canal, followed by severe flooding across Lancashire when the thaw finally came – and more than twelve years since the Earl had attended that preliminary meeting in the Didsbury home of Sir Daniel Adamson to first float the idea.

Now, on this bright midsummer's morning, the Earl was standing on the deck of the *SS Pioneer* as she sailed west along the Canal, passing the Trafford Road Swing Bridge, which had opened to let them pass. Alongside him was Lord Egerton of Tatton and, a little further along, together with Mr James Naysmith, a contingent representing some of the more than seventeen thousand men who had at one time or another worked on this great enterprise, who stood crowded together, cordoned off by a silk rope from the VIPs. Chief among these was Yasser. Rose stood next to him, carrying their baby daughter, Pomona, on one arm, leaving the other free to wave to the cheering crowds, who lined the route.

A great rush of pride swelled through them all. We did this, they felt, together, and, as one, they began to sing, the last of the great canal songs.

"All hail this grand day when with gay colours flying
The barges are seen on the current to glide
When with fond emulation all parties are vying
To make our canal of Old England the pride

And may it long flourish while commerce caressing
Adorns its fair banks with her wealth-bringing stores
To Lancashire, and all round the country a blessing
May industry's sons ever thrive on its shore

And now my good fellows sure nothing is wanting
To heighten our joy and our blessings to crown,
And all those lives sacrificed no longer haunting
When spring smiles again on this high-favoured town

The crowds on the quayside now loudly are cheering
Waving farewell as we sail on the tide
Beyond the horizon our end may be nearing
But till then our canal of Old England's the pride…"

Yasser pointed out to Rose all of the factories that had risen up along its banks during the long months and years of its construction, bringing wealth and jobs and people to what had been such thinly populated marshlands, where folk had had to scratch and scrabble a living, and Rose agreed, though secretly she lamented the loss of so much green. She thought of the stories her dead father would tell of his long abandoned home on an emerald isle.

As if reading her thoughts, Yasser began to speak of the mountains of the desert. "I know I shall never look upon them again," he said, "but they are all locked away in here." He tapped the side of his temple. "I can conjure them whenever I need them. But this is our home now. This is our future. A better life for our children." He lifted Pomona high into the air and swung her round above his head.

Just then they approached the Barton Dock Bridge, which had swung open to let the *SS Pioneer* pass through.

"In part thanks to you," remarked Mr Naysmith,

who had joined them briefly. "Mrs Wahid," he added, touching the brim of his hat.

"It's Ward now, sir," said Yasser.

"I see."

"Easier for folk to pronounce," put in Rose.

"And this is now our home," Yasser completed.

"Indeed. And I believe congratulations are in order?"

"Yes, sir," said Yasser, raising himself to his full height. "I'm to be a Maintenance Engineer for Manchester Liners. I start next week."

"This is most excellent news."

"I believe, sir," ventured Rose, "you may have put in a good word for Yasser?"

"I spoke nothing but the truth, Mrs Ward."

"For which we thank you, sir."

"And has Yasser told you the other piece of good fortune?"

Rose looked enquiringly towards Yasser.

"I was just about to, Mr Naysmith. Rose – look." He pointed to the shore beyond the Swing Bridge, where rows of new redbrick terraced houses were being built. "One of those is ours."

Rose found, for the first time in her life, that she was at a loss for words. She leant into Yasser's shoulder and hugged him to her.

"There's plenty of room for all of us, your mother too, and…" He glanced down towards her belly with a mischievous smile. "…any others who might seek shelter in our nest."

She playfully punched his arm, and what she might

have said next was drowned by the ship's siren as it completed its passing of the Barton Swing Bridge.

Time passed. The crowds along the shore thinned as the *SS Pioneer*'s maiden voyage proceeded along the quieter middle section of the Canal. But even here new factories were springing up – dye works, tanneries, foundries, brick kilns, tar, soap and margarine works – and clustered around them were more new houses.

They were at a point where the Canal joined the route of the Mersey. As they rounded a bend in the river, between the Cadishead Railway Viaduct and the Warburton Toll Bridge, Rose suddenly spotted someone she recognised, waving to them from the bank.

"Look," she cried. "It's Sammy."

Yasser rushed to the rail and bellowed to his friend and rescuer, standing with Eve, who was holding tightly to Delphine lest she wandered too close to the water's edge.

"*Hoka hey!*" Sammy called back and pointed towards a small hill rising up away from the Canal. There on its crest, in a clearing in a small copse of alder trees, stood a low, sturdily-built, wooden cottage, with a fire burning outside and chickens scratching around in the dust.

"Ours," shouted Sammy, pointing to himself, Eve and Delphine.

Rose and Yasser stood and waved back to them until they were just specks, dots in the distance.

When the ship had finally disappeared completely from view, Sammy climbed back up the hill to where Old

Moon was tending the fire which, winter or summer, he would never let go out. Eve and Delphine followed on behind, Delphine stopping every few yards or so to pore over each different blade of grass growing on the slope – bearded couch, creeping bent, hare's tail cotton grass, and timothy. Old Moon taught her how to split each reed and blow through it to make a high-pitched trumpet noise, which she delighted in, and then he would show her how the sound of it would make the different birds turn their heads towards it as they flew among the branches of the alder trees behind the cottage.

Sammy rubbed the crushed seed heads between the palms of his hands and blew them into the air, watching them dance on the breeze before alighting who knew where.

"I know what I'm going to do," he announced, signing to Eve as he spoke the words out loud, "now that I'm back. The Canal has split the land in two," he said, "cutting off neighbours one from another. New factories are being built all along the banks. More and more people will come to live here and to work. They will need a way to cross the Canal. I will build a boat, big enough to carry ten people, but light enough to be rowed by one. It will be called Bob's Lane Ferry, and it will be ours." He looked at Old Moon, rocking by the fire. "It will be like the old days," he continued, "living off the water and the land," and he smiled.

Eve, seeing that her Leaping Fish was happy, smiled back, while Delphine chattered on brightly beside them both.

Six months later an open boat ferried people from Bob's Lane on one side of the Canal to Locke Lane on the other, starting at half past five each morning and carrying on until eleven at night, with trips every quarter of an hour. In twelve months Sammy was ferrying more than thirty thousand people a year, each paying a penny, so that he earned a good living. Over the years he and Eve added a range of outbuildings and extensions to their shanty cottage until it became quite a settlement. Delphine took the ferry each morning on her way to the Our Lady of Lourdes school not far from Locke Lane and came back again on it each afternoon. Sometimes, Sammy would let her take an oar to help him row across.

But all of this lay in the future. That summer's evening, after the *SS Pioneer* had sailed by and Sammy had given words to the idea whose seeds had first begun forming back at the outdoor service held by The Christian Navigators Union, when Mr Naysmith had spoken to them from his steam hammer pulpit and they had sung about what it meant to be a pilgrim, they all stared into the fire, the wood splitting and cracking, the embers rising high to join the first few stars as they peeped out.

Flying across the moon, a wedge of white egrets skewered the sky.

*

Reads the Moon dreams the moon.

"River of mist hovers over dark canal
Oil slick sheen puddles with rainbows
Sludge encrusted surface chokes new life beneath...

The day grows hotter
Dead rats lie stiff among dry weeds
Flies buzz around each swelling carcass...

Row boat looms from cobwebbed mist
Ferries frightened passengers, hands covering faces
Siren voices calling from the deep...

Oil on water, sudden spark of light
Splintered wood in silent fire storm
Wall of flame rising to the sky...

Bob's Lane Ferry self-ignites..."

As Old Moon dreams, he sees horseless carriages roaring through the lanes. He sees people dressed in strange clothes, speaking words he does not understand. In the sky above his head he sees vapour trails issuing out of silver flying machines. The cottage behind him has long been torn down, overgrown with high weeds, under which lies buried a bleached and faded plank of charred wood, with the faint marks of a painting daubed upon it, streaks of light falling from a midsummer night sky.

He recognises he is dreaming of the future, of

something that has not yet come to pass, and so may never happen, long after he, Sammy, Eve and Delphine will have passed beyond sight, motes of dust in the air, feeding the soil, at one with the earth, cleansed by water, purified by fire, and so he lets the vision fade, and sleeps.

16

1910 – 1918

Sixteen years almost to the day after Queen Victoria had officially declared The Manchester Ship Canal to be open for business, her grandson King George V returned to the city to perform an opening ceremony of his own. Less than two months after ascending the throne, which saw Halley's Comet blaze a trail across the night sky, the King was invited to open the Irlam Steel Works, which sprawled along the banks of the Canal less than half a mile from where Sammy and Eve still ferried folk across from the landing jetty at Bob's Lane.

All across the city people tracked the comet, ascribing to it their own individual hopes and fears. Frederick Kaufman excitedly beckoned his fifteen year old daughter, Ruth, to view its passage through his telescope in his study at the top of their house above the Opticians' Shop in Denton.

Hubert Wright, a printer where Ancoats shook hands with Miles Platting, watched it arc its way above the city as he was walking out with a young woman called Annie Warburton, whom he had only recently met, and was so taken with it as it cast a halo of light around her dark brown hair that he went down on one knee and proposed to her there and then right outside her front door.

To her lasting surprise Annie found herself accepting on the spot, and they were married before another year had passed.

John Jabez Chadwick, still only a boy, was helping his father harvest all of the tulip bulbs late into the night in Philips Park now that the annual display was coming to a close. Each bulb seemed irradiated with light from the comet's tail.

Catch and Clem, who were caught in two minds over whether to take up an offer on a partly derelict forge near Buile Hill in Salford, having drifted from place to place and job to job for more than twenty years, ran down the cobbled streets of Weaste in hot pursuit of it. When finally it disappeared over the brow of the hill, landing, or so it seemed to them then in their fancy, directly behind the forge in question, they went the very next day to sign the papers on the lease.

"It's time," said Clem, "don't you think?"

"I always think each place we go to is the one, but then, come the spring, and I feel the need to be on the move again," said Catch.

"Not this time," said Clem. "Cam's nearly seven now. This wandering's no life for her. She needs to go to school."

Catch looked down at their daughter, who was sleepily rubbing her eyes, trailing after them on tired legs. Chamomile, named from the board hung over the door of Ezekiel Flint's forge, the lines from Shakespeare with which Catch had laboriously taught himself to read, and which soon he would write out himself and hang above the door of their own forge.

There was much work needed to be done. Standing inside it that evening, with Clem now lying the fast asleep Cam down in the straw of the adjoining barn, he looked through the gaps in the roof, where slates must have fallen off and not been replaced, and watched the last gasps of light from the comet's trail.

"Yes," he said. "You're right. We must take this as a sign." He took out a knife and began to carve notches into an old piece of wood he found.

'For though the chamomile, the more it is trodden on, the faster it grows, yet youth, the more it is wasted, the sooner it wears.'

He hung it by the broken door, which tomorrow he promised he would mend, and then bent to kiss his sleeping daughter's forehead – Chamomile – before lying next to Clémence in the soft straw, which moulded itself to their embrace.

Tommy Thunder saw it just as he was about to pull the trigger to relieve the world of one more unwanted mole and paused to trace the comet's course through both the rear and front sights of his rifle. It was time, he thought, to return to Worsley Hall, where he had not been for almost a year. The Earl would be asking for him.

Eve made a painting of the comet in the sky, with mud and flower dyes on a piece of found wood, which Sammy nailed to a post on their front porch.

And across the other side of the city, in Gorton, an excited fourteen year old Arthur Blundell came rushing indoors, his finger earnestly marking a place in his library book.

"Esther – quick! Come and look. It's a comet. See? Exactly like in this picture." He held up the illustration for Esther to study. Even though she was a year and a half younger than he was, it was important to him, she could see, for her opinion to match his own.

"Yes," she said, "you're right. Halley's Comet." She left the dishes in the sink, wiped her hands on a tea towel and followed her brother out into the yard at the back.

"It's an omen," he said. "It must be. Something momentous always happens whenever it appears."

"When was the last time?" she asked.

"Its orbit brings it to Earth approximately every seventy-five years," said Arthur, reading importantly from his book.

"So the last time would have been... around 1835?"

"Yes."

"What happened then?"

"It doesn't say," said a disappointed Arthur, "but – it appeared in 1066 during The Battle of Hastings, and some people believe that it might have been the Star of Bethlehem."

"Do they?" said Esther.

"And now a new King is on the throne."

Esther continued to watch it radiate the sky.

"It has to mean something, don't you think?" mused Arthur.

"I don't know," said Esther. "But whether it does or it doesn't, it's impressive just for what it is."

"And we're incredibly lucky to be alive to see it, aren't we?"

Esther smiled. Her older brother's sense of idealism, his need for eternal truths, for something good and honourable to believe in, was something she wished she could share, but since their mother had died, their lives seemed to be one long, unremitting grind of work, with little to bring the kind of light her brother craved, and which he now saw in this comet's trail across the sky, so that it never seemed to grow fully dark for weeks.

Arthur began to read once more from his library book.

" 'Comets are vast chunks of ice, hundreds of miles across, with particles of dust and rocks embedded within them. Most of the time their orbits take them far away from the sun, but when they get closer, the solar wind releases some of these dust particles, sweeping them into a long, curving tail'. That's what we can see now. Then, when they move further away, they freeze over into ice again. Until the next time."

And there won't be a next time, thought Esther, not for them, unless they lived into their nineties, and she didn't think she knew anybody that old. Best to grab it, then, while they could.

"Come," she said, suddenly decisive.

"What is it?" asked Arthur.

"This," she said, holding out their father's newspaper. "Read."

Arthur took the newspaper over to the kitchen lamp.

" 'On 23rd July, His Majesty King George V is coming to Manchester to open the new Steel Works at Irlam'. That's the day after tomorrow," said Arthur, looking up from the paper.

"Let's go," said Esther, taking hold of Arthur's hand, "all of us – you, me, Father and the boys."

"But what about work? What about school?"

"How often did you say that this comet is close enough to be seen?"

"Every seventy-five years."

"And how often does a King come to Manchester?"

"More often than that."

"Still…"

"All right," said Arthur, catching some of Esther's impulsivity. "Let's ask Father."

In the end it was just the two of them who went. The four younger boys – Harold, Jim, Frank and Freddie – had Sports Day at school, something they none of them wanted to miss, while their father could not be persuaded to step outside of the wall he had built around himself since their mother had died. Arthur managed to change his shift at the pit, which meant that they would not be able to linger after the King had passed through, for he would have to be back in time for work later.

Esther made them a picnic and the two of them excitedly set off early the next morning in the highest of spirits. It was an adventure, a day out, a welcome break from the usual routine. They walked the two and a half miles from home to Manchester's Central Station, from where they caught the Liverpool train, alighting at Irlam just half an hour later. Neither of them had been so far from home before, and they delighted in the views unfolding in front of them from the train. Much of the journey traced the route of the Ship Canal, finishing with a series of iron bridges which crossed and re-crossed the Canal as it joined and then left the course of the Mersey.

When they walked down the Station Approach at Irlam, there were already large crowds lining the Liverpool Road, along which the King was expected to arrive within the next hour. Rather than heading further towards Cadishead, where the main entrance to the Steel Works lay, they opted instead to turn left and walk back towards Higher Irlam, just outside *The Ship Inn*, where the crowds were thinner and where they both felt they would get a better view of him as he passed by.

The road was much quieter there, less built up, and the two of them sat on a patch of grass outside the Church of St John the Baptist opposite the inn. Esther took out the picnic, and the two of them smiled broadly.

"Isn't this grand?" said Arthur, polishing an apple vigorously on the front of his shirt.

"Ay," said Esther. "Isn't it?"

There was no other traffic, and two small children were playing whip and top in the centre of the road, their concentration so fully on their game that they did not hear the entourage of the King as it approached, and Esther had to run towards them to move them out of the way just in time, so that now she stood on one side of the road, while Arthur remained on the other.

Just then a black Daimler pulled up and, to Arthur's amazement, out stepped the King to stretch his legs. No one but Arthur appeared to spot him. The King took a silver cigarette case from his overcoat and then tapped in turn each of his pockets in vain for a lighter. Arthur had not yet started to smoke, but he had a box of matches. He stepped forward, struck one and offered it to the King, who nodded and drew deeply on his now lit cigarette. Nobody tried to intervene, or even seemed to notice.

"Thank you, my boy," said the King. "And what would you like to do when you grow up?"

Arthur smiled. He did not think it polite to inform him that he had already begun work as a collier. He thought for a moment and then he said, "I'd like to drive a car like yours, sir."

The King laughed and shook Arthur's hand. "Here's a shilling for you." Then he climbed back into his car, which drove on down the Liverpool Road to the site of the Steel Works.

The exchange between them had lasted less than a minute. Esther, in making sure the two children playing whip and top did not run back into the road, almost missed it. As the King's Daimler drove away she and Arthur looked at one another from across the Liverpool Road in near disbelief.

"Was that really...?" she asked.

"Yes," said Arthur. "It was."

Esther crossed the road to join her brother, who was staring after the black car as it slowly drove away.

"Let's not tell the others," he said. "Let it be something private. Just between us."

"If you say so," said Esther, taking in the importance of the moment for her brother.

"Look," he said. "He gave me this." He lifted the shilling up to the light.

Five years later, larger crowds lined either side of Deansgate as Arthur, having taken another King's shilling, marched with all the rest of the Manchester Regiment to overcrowded trains and trenches, to Europe and to war.

*

At the same moment that Arthur was shaking the hand of the King, Tommy Thunder was back at Worsley Hall, shaking the hand of the Earl, a hand, Tommy noted, which was not as strong as once it had been, and which had a slight tremor.

"We're none of us getting any younger, Tommy," he said.

"No, sir."

"But you look no different. Age cannot wither thee, it seems, nor custom stale."

"Sir?"

"The wandering life appears to suit you."

"It's in my blood, and the blood of my fathers."

"Quite so." The Earl paused a moment. "In fact it's blood I wish to speak to you about."

The Earl led Tommy to the paddock at the back of the house. A fine black mare was being schooled. She was meant to be trotting but she was impatient and inclined to be frisky, rearing up on her hind legs, resisting the tether.

"Recognise her?" asked the Earl.

Tommy nodded. "She has the same white star in her forehead."

The Earl smiled. "This is her granddaughter, and Star is her name."

Tommy watched her going through her paces. She seemed to sense his presence and grew calmer.

"And over there," said the Earl, pointing with his cane towards the far side of the paddock, "is my grandson."

Tommy saw a boy, aged about thirteen, leaning on the rail with a mutinous expression on his face. One leg, Tommy noticed immediately, was slightly shorter than the other.

"He thinks the whole world's against him?" added the Earl before heading back indoors. "But then what young boy doesn't? Would you mind having a word with him?"

Tommy waited until the Earl had gone and then

walked slowly around the perimeter of the paddock, his eyes firmly on Star. When he got within a few yards of the boy, he stopped and waited. After a few moments, the mare, who had now been taken off her halter and was quite alone once more in the centre of the ring, sauntered over towards Tommy, as he knew she would. He gently stroked her muzzle, scratched between her ears on the top of her poll, and then ran his other hand along the latch of her throat. Star crooned with pleasure and bumped her head against Tommy's arm whenever he paused. Eventually curiosity got the better of the boy and he came up alongside them.

"She likes that," he said.

"She does," said Tommy. "Want to take over?"

"May I?"

"Here," said Tommy, and took one of the boy's hands and guided it slowly towards that favoured spot just beyond the chin groove. Star responded to the change in touch at once and backed away, but only slightly.

"Gently now. Not so rough. Nice and slow. That's it."

The boy smiled. Star eased her way back towards him. The boy's confidence grew and his touch became more assured.

"I'm Edward," the boy said.

Tommy nodded.

Emboldened, the boy continued. "She's a beauty, isn't she?"

"I knew her grand dam," said Tommy.

"Yes, I know. My grandfather told me the story.

How she was badly injured, and how everyone wanted to have her put down but you persuaded them to let you have one more try."

Tommy said nothing, waiting for Edward to go on.

"My grandfather... he said... you – whispered to her."

"Yes."

"What does that mean?"

Tommy put a finger to his lips and shook his head.

Edward looked back towards Star, who Tommy was looking at directly in the eye. Then he leant his forehead against the mare's. The two of them remained like that, heads touching, motionless, for several seconds.

"She was meant to be mine," said Edward at last, "but I'm not allowed to ride her now. I'm not allowed to ride any horse, not even my sister Daisy's Welsh pony. Not since..."

Tommy eased back from Star. "What?"

"Everyone treats me as if I was ill."

"You don't look ill to me."

"I'm not!"

Edward turned hastily away and ran the back of a hand roughly across his eyes. Tommy let a few moments pass. Finally, without looking at Edward, he said, "What happened?"

Edward's words came out in a sudden rush. "It was last summer. I was home from school for the holidays. We were playing soldiers, me and some of the boys from the Estate. I was the Commanding Officer. The barn was the Enemy Fort. Our mission was to take it and raise our flag there. I gave the order. 'Over the top!' We all charged. One of the boys found a ladder lying against the outside wall. He and another boy lifted it up and propped it against the wall leading to the hay loft at the top. On my command we stormed the barn. One by one we climbed the ladder and leapt inside. Victory was ours. I was the last person to attempt it. I'd been holding it steady at the bottom for all the other chaps to clamber up. Then, just as I got near to the top, it overbalanced. I managed to make it inside, but the ladder fell to the ground as I did so. There was a way down from inside the loft, but for some reason we decided that we shouldn't use it. Except for Daisy. Because she was only a girl. So Daisy climbed down and – again, I can't remember whose idea this was, but I suppose it must have been mine, because I was the Captain – she stacked about half a dozen hay bales below us on the ground outside, where the ladder had been. It was decided we would take it in turns to jump down. We drew lots to see who should go first. I drew the longest, which meant that I had to go last, which was only right. As Commanding Officer I had to make sure all my men got down safely before I could join them. One by one they all jumped. Each one landed safely on the hay bales before rolling over onto the ground. Then it was my turn. I stood at the top, looking down. Suddenly..." Edward's voice began to quiver as he relived what happened next. "Suddenly... I... I froze. My feet were rooted to the spot. I wanted to jump, but I couldn't. All the boys started jeering, calling me names, a coward, and... harsher things.

Then, to make matters worse, Daisy came back up into the loft using the inside steps and said, 'It's easy, Edward. Even I can do it. Watch.' And she jumped, my baby sister, and made it look as easy as anything, but still I couldn't do it. The shouting grew louder and louder, until, in the end, I covered my ears so I wouldn't have to hear the names they were calling me, and shut my eyes, and then... then... I'm not sure whether I jumped or I just lost my balance, but the next thing I knew I had landed on the ground. I had missed the hay bales and my foot was caught in one of Jenks's traps he puts out for the foxes, and..." He stopped. His breath was coming in short, sharp rasps, and his cheeks were hot and red.

Tommy waited until the boy's breathing grew calmer. Then he looked him directly in the eye, just like he had done earlier with Star, and nodded.

Edward spoke again in the quietest of voices.

"I've never told anyone before. Not the whole story."

Tommy now leant his forehead against the boy's.

"That was a brave thing to do," he said.

"But I'm not brave," wailed Edward. "I'm a coward. I'm a disgrace to the regiment."

"Who has told you this?"

Edward turned away sheepishly. "Nobody. But they would do. If they knew the truth."

Tommy said nothing for a while. He turned back to Star, who was impatiently pawing the ground, seeking attention. When he had checked her front hoof and removed a small stone from it, he said, "So what are

647

you going to do?"

"I can't do anything. They won't let me."

"Who won't?"

"Everyone. I can't play rugger or cricket at school. I'm not allowed to march with the Cadets, and now that I'm home, I'm supposed to stay indoors and study."

"Why?"

"They say I mustn't do anything in case I make it worse."

"Make what worse?"

"My foot. My leg."

Tommy shook his head. "I don't think the problem is with your leg."

"Look at it!" shouted Edward. "It's shorter than the other. It's useless. I can't do anything."

"That's not a reason. That's an excuse."

Edward stood, open-mouthed.

Tommy continued slowly. "I don't think you want to."

"Of course I do. I'd give anything to…"

"I don't believe you."

"What?"

"Then why are you giving up?"

"I'm not giving up. I've told you. They won't let me."

"Who?" Tommy spread his arms out wide. "Who won't let you? There's no one here, Edward. Just you and me."

Edward said nothing. Tommy waited. "You say that Star was meant to be yours?" he said.

Edward nodded.

"Then what's stopping you? Come into the paddock and ride her now. With me."

"I can't."

"Why not?"

"I might fall off."

"Yes. You might. But if you do, you can get back up and try again till you do."

"I can't."

Tommy led the mare closer to the boy.

"When I was your age," he said, "I was always angry. I had no patience and I wouldn't listen to anyone. I always thought I knew best. My father called me 'Chasing Thunder' because of it. One day, when there was a storm, he sent me out into the plains and said, 'Since you are always chasing thunder, now try and see if you can catch it'."

"And did you?"

"Of course not. You can never catch the thunder. But it didn't stop me trying. I'm still chasing it today. Now – climb upon Star's back. See how patiently she waits for you."

"But there's no saddle…"

"What do you need a saddle for? Or reins? Coil your fingers through her mane and gently squeeze her sides with your legs. She'll do the rest."

Edward looked at Tommy a long time, waiting for some sign that he might let him get away without trying, but Tommy said nothing. Gingerly he approached Star.

"Look her in the eye," said Tommy. "Let her know you're here."

Edward did as he was bid. Then, very slowly, he walked around to the mare's left, took hold of her mane with his own left hand, before placing his left foot into Tommy's cupped hands, which carefully eased him over Star's back.

"Now – just sit for a while. Get used to seeing the world from up there."

Edward nodded. His body was still tense, but gradually his breathing slowed. When Tommy felt he was ready, he walked a few paces away from them, turned and clucked his tongue. At once, Star began to walk. Edward's face lit up.

"That's it," said Tommy. "Try to find her rhythm and move yourself to it. Good."

"Can we stop now?" said Edward after they had gone once round the paddock.

"How about a little trot first?"

Before Edward could protest, Tommy made a different clucking sound and Star at once broke into a slow, steady trot. Edward clung even harder to her mane as he bounced up and down upon her back.

"Grip more strongly with your knees. Rise, then fall. Rise, then fall. That's it. Good. Now you're getting it."

Round and round the paddock they went. Trotting, walking, trotting again, finally risking a canter.

The Earl appeared at the corner of the house. Tommy signalled for him not to make his presence known. He withdrew into the shadow cast by one of the high gables and watched with growing pride as his grandson rode the fine black mare round and round in the late afternoon. Edward's face was set in fierce concentration. Even when, as the sun began to set, he slipped from Star's back, landing in a heap on the hard trampled grass, nothing could take away from him that expression of determined happiness.

Elsewhere in the grounds of the park, the last frantlings of the peacocks filled the evening air, as the comet, with a futile, final flourish, blazed brilliantly in the night sky before it fizzled and died.

*

Just as the peacocks were keening their last lonely farewells to the departing comet in the grounds of Worsley Hall, Delphine was looking out at the same night sky from the window of her new lodgings in Stretford, near Seymour Park.

It was a small, plain, unadorned room at the top of a recently built tall Edwardian terrace in Lime Grove. It reminded her of a nun's cell in a convent, and the comparison was not unappealing to her. Her time at Our Lady of Lourdes School had prepared her for a life of service and devotion. There was no paper on the walls, which were washed in a clean white paint. There was a small chest of drawers for her few clothes, on the top of which stood a simple wash basin and jug. On the back of the door were a couple of hooks on which to hang a coat and dressing gown, and on the wall above the narrow single bed hung a framed print of Holman Hunt's *The Light of the World*. Mrs Snook, the landlady, was a widow who still dressed predominantly in black. Although her appearance was somewhat formidable, Delphine had discovered that she was soft spoken and kind. She had shown her where the bathroom was on the floor below and had taken great pains to go through the strict rota concerning ablutions. Hot water was limited, she had explained, and Delphine, or Miss Fish, as she was insisting on calling her, was one of six guests. Each guest was given an allotted evening for when they might take a bath. Her own was always and unchangingly Sunday. Delphine was accorded a Thursday. The other guests, all of them female, all professional women, had elected to see to their own breakfasts, but that she, Mrs Snook, would provide a cooked supper at 6.30pm every weekday evening, as well as lunch on Sundays. The total cost would be five shillings and sixpence a week, payable on Mondays.

"I trust this arrangement will prove acceptable to you, Miss Fish?"

Delphine had replied that it did.

Now, as she opened the window to let in the still warm night air, she looked around her new domain with much satisfaction and excitement. The sweet scent of Mrs Snook's rose bushes, which grew in a neat row directly in front of the house, drifted up into the room. Delphine was twenty-two years old. She was not only beginning a new job the next day, or settling into her new home that evening, she felt she was at the start of a new life altogether, on the cusp of irrevocable change, and it was exciting.

When she reached twelve, she could have left school, as did most of her contemporaries, to work on the land or in any of the growing number of mills and factories, which had spread along the Ship Canal, which provided her father with a good living, in spite of the ramshackled state of the home they lived in, but she chose instead to stay on. Sister Rona was delighted to have her as her assistant, looking after the little ones, listening to them as they struggled with their alphabet, helping with their sums or their handwriting. By the time she was sixteen, a special corner of the school room had been set up by Sister Rona just for Delphine, who became more or less solely responsible for the younger children. Perhaps because of her own somewhat unusual and isolated upbringing, she was particularly adept at bringing the shyer ones out of their shells. Nor was she ever intimidated by any of the bigger boys. She could run faster than most of them, climb trees more easily and swim like her namesake. And so Sister Rona encouraged her to set her sights higher. The year Delphine turned sixteen saw the purchase of Sedgeley Park, a gracious house near Prestwich, just five and a half miles to the north of Manchester, by the Faithful Companions of Jesus, a teaching order of nuns, with whom Sister Rona was in contact. Two years later the Order opened an extension in the grounds, which could house eighty-six trainee teachers in residence. In 1906, a week after her eighteenth birthday, Delphine became part of their first intake of students.

Sammy, Eve and Old Moon walked with her the short way from Bob's Lane to Cadishead Station. When the train pulled out, Delphine leaned out of the window waving to them until they were just distant dots on the horizon, and then disappeared altogether. It was the first time she had ever been on a train. Once, when she was twelve, she had walked with Sammy as far as Patricroft to visit his friend Yasser. It had taken them nearly three hours. When they got there she had enjoyed playing with Yasser's daughter, Pomona, and afterwards they had promised to write, but where she lived, with Sammy and Eve and Old Moon on the banks of the Canal, didn't have a proper address, and so that had not after all been possible. That journey – they walked back later the same day just as it was growing dark, her father not keeping to roads, but following his own internal compass, using trees and hills as landmarks, checking the position of the stars – had been the only time she had ever been more than a couple of miles from home.

In spite of that she did not feel frightened or nervous about the prospect of making her way unaccompanied to Sedgley Park. On the contrary, she was excited. It was an adventure. She got off the train at Manchester Central and, following instructions given to her by Sister Rona, she made her way across the city to Piccadilly, marvelling at the crowds, the thronging traffic of horses and wagons, trams and buses, and the occasional automobile, stopping to take in some of the buildings, *The Midland Hotel* on Peter Street, the Watts Warehouse on Mosley Street, Lewis's Department Store at the corner of Market Street. From Piccadilly she took her first tram, which shook and rattled its way down Oldham Street, turned left at Stevenson Square onto Hilton and Thomas Streets, between the entrances to Exchange and Victoria Stations, passing the Cathedral and the black granite statue of Oliver Cromwell, before climbing up Shude Hill, where the streets were crowded with tightly packed market stalls. For the first time she saw Jewish people. A friendly older gentleman with a long grey beard and plaited side locks which, she learned, were called *payots*, sat beside her, reading a book printed in Hebrew. He sensed her curiosity and took pains to explain things to her and point out various landmarks, including the Sephardi Synagogue on Cheetham Hill Road. She greatly enjoyed their conversation, which removed any traces of apprehension she might have been feeling, and he was able to point out the stop where she was to get off for Sedgley Park. There were just so many new things to experience, absorb and learn from and, as she walked the final half mile through the leafy park towards what was to be her new home, she felt determined not to let a single opportunity pass her by, or waste a single second of her time there.

As well as the training she received, she made many new friends. The girls came from a wide variety of places and backgrounds, though none had had quite the kind of childhood Delphine had experienced. None could climb a rope in the gymnasium with as much ease or agility as she could, none could handle a row boat on the lake in the park as expertly as she could, and none knew extracts of Lakota chants like she did. But many brought with them levels of sophistication she simply could not match, the books they had read, the music they had listened to, the museums they had attended. At weekends and in the holidays she went on cycle rides into the hills of Derbyshire, or the Trough of Bowland, and hiking excursions to the Yorkshire Dales and the Westmorland Fells with the Audreys, Margarets and Marjories, who became her confidantes.

But it was the teaching that drew her, pushed her and inspired her. She understood that she had found her vocation and, while many of the other girls dreamed of the marriages they would one day make, she allowed herself no such romantic distractions. She had a calling. Like God for the Sisters who taught her, she had the care and nurture of young minds, to which she was wedded, in sickness or in health, till death did her part.

Her first position upon completing her training was at the nearby St Philip's School on Cavendish Road, Broughton. It was something of a baptism of fire. The children were rough, well used to being on the receiving end of what their parents referred to as "a good hiding", an approach they expected and, at times, encouraged the teachers to mete out with daily regularity. But Delphine refused to walk down that route, and although at first the children could not believe their luck, thinking she was someone they might easily "play up", they quickly learned to recognise that she was firm and unyielding in lots of other ways. She quite simply assumed the highest standards of behaviour from them all. "Do unto others" was a favourite maxim, and the children soon learned that to receive an expression of disappointment from Miss Fish, if they failed to live up to her always high expectations of them, was far worse than any administering of the ruler or the cane.

After she had been at St Philip's for two happy years, she was called one afternoon into the study of Sister Basil, the school's headmistress.

"Ah, Miss Fish. Do sit down. Tea?"

"Thank you, Sister."

"Milk? Sugar?"

"No sugar, thank you."

"I see you are as abstemious as you are conscientious. I find I may permit myself one lump at the end of a particularly trying day."

Delphine inclined her head.

"Tell me, Miss Fish. Are you happy with us?"

"Oh yes, Sister. Very."

"I thought as much." Sister Basil paused and took a sip of her now sweetened tea.

"Is there something amiss, Sister?"

Sister Basil put down her tea cup and looked directly at Delphine.

"I have observed, Miss Fish, that you have a particular talent for drawing out those pupils who are what we might describe as 'reluctant learners'."

"Thank you, Sister. I believe that all our children have special qualities."

"Even Billy Pick?"

The two women smiled. Billy was the latest in a long line of Picks, who frequently came to school unwashed, unfed and unshod. In addition, Billy, despite being seven years old, had not yet mastered the art of language and proceeded to try and communicate using only animal-sounding grunts, whose meaning was stubbornly elusive. Except to Delphine, with whom Billy appeared to have struck quite a rapport, and who he trailed after devotedly.

"I noticed you adopting some form of sign language with him yesterday, Miss Fish."

"Yes, Sister."

"Surely you did not learn that from the Faithful Companions?"

Delphine smiled. "No, Sister. I learned it at home."

"Elaborate for me, if you will."

"My mother is deaf and dumb, Sister. I believe since birth. She is not able to make a sound of any description, and so we have learned, my father and I, to develop our own private form of communication, involving signs, gestures and much facial expression." She smiled again.

"Remarkable. I did wonder if there was something of that nature in your background, for you seemed so assured, so unself-conscious in your dealings with young Master Pick."

Sister Basil sat back in her chair, looking thoughtfully to one side, while she finished her tea. Delphine waited for what she might say next. After almost a minute, Sister Basil turned back towards Delphine.

"In addition to my duties as Headmistress here, I have been for some years a Trustee on the Board of *The Manchester Institution for the Deaf and the Dumb*. Or *The Royal Manchester Institution*, as we are now called, since the late Queen so graciously conferred that title upon us just over a decade ago. We have two schools presently – a High School, for older children, in Bolton, and the one in which I take a keen, personal interest, Clyne House, a residential establishment for Infants, in Stretford. It is most pleasantly situated in what remains of the former Botanical Gardens, close to where *The Royal Pomona Palace Hotel* once stood."

Delphine let out a short involuntary gasp.

"Miss Fish, are you quite well?"

"I beg your pardon, Sister. I know of where you speak."

"Indeed."

"Not the school. I did not know there was a school there. But Pomona – my father worked there for a time."

"I see. Well, Miss Fish, I happen to know that there is a situation coming up at Clyne House. One of our teachers there is leaving this summer to be married. I wonder, therefore, if you might be interested in applying for the position? We should of course be most sorry to lose you here, but I have observed your very special gifts, Miss Fish, and I would hate to stand in the way of any possibility of advancement for you – and advancement it would most assuredly be, for as a specialist school we need to attract the very best of teachers and reward them accordingly. I believe that you have the makings of such a teacher."

"Thank you, Sister."

"You would have to be interviewed of course, but my recommendation will count for something, I have no doubt. Might you be interested, Miss Fish?"

Delphine did not have to think twice. This was more than she could have hoped for when she left Sedgley Park just two years before. "Yes, Sister, I would be delighted to apply."

Now, as summer was tipping into autumn, Delphine was sitting in her small upstairs room at Miss Snook's contemplating her first day at Clyne House the next day. Once again, as she counted down the hours before she was to start, she felt no nervousness, just more excitement to be taking this next fork in the road, to be beginning this next chapter of her still young life.

Before travelling to Seymour Park she had made a brief return to Bob's Lane to let her parents know about this new opportunity. As she explained to her mother that she would be teaching deaf and dumb children to speak, she saw a myriad of expressions flit across her face, like so many clouds racing across a summer sky, revealing at last the clear, unbroken light of the sun.

*

Four more years passed.

War had been declared. The Harvest Home in the Great Barn of Worsley Hall was a more muted affair as a consequence. Early optimism that hostilities would be over by Christmas had given way to a grimmer reality. Tommy watched from the sides. There was no boisterous singing of *John Barleycorn* this year, nor did any Corn Maidens dance. He was on the point of leaving when one of the grooms informed him that the Earl was requesting to see him.

He was indoors, sitting in a chair with a rug pulled over his knees. As Tommy was ushered into the drawing room, he was coughing. Tommy could see at once that his days were numbered. He would not see another Harvest Home.

"Tommy? Is that you? Come near to the window, so that I can get a better look at you."

Tommy stood by his side.

"I want you to promise me something."

Tommy nodded, waiting as another painful bout of coughing wracked the Earl's shrunken body.

"Pass me that water, will you?" The Earl flapped his hand in the direction of a glass on a small table nearby. The same hand then shook as he raised the glass to his lips.

"It's about Edward," he said at last. "He's desperate to go across to France, do his bit and all that. He applied for a commission the day after war was declared, but was turned down on account of his leg. Can't say I was sorry myself. But now that it's clear it's no flash in the pan, but that we're in it for the long haul, no matter what those damned fools Haig and Kitchener might say to the contrary, I reckon they won't be quite so choosy in the future, and that if Edward applies again – which I am certain he has every intention of so doing – they'll let him in this time."

"Yes, sir."

"That'll make his day of course, but it will break his poor mother's heart. Mine too..." He broke off, seized by yet further coughing. Tommy waited, saying nothing, until the Earl had regained his composure.

"He wants to prove himself, sir."

"Yes, I know," replied the Earl bleakly.

The two of them looked out of the window, each recalling an afternoon more than four years before when Tommy had coaxed Edward to ride the black mare bareback.

"That was a marvellous thing you did, Tommy. I've never forgotten."

"It was down to the boy, sir. In the end. He could have given up. But he didn't."

"He's stubborn, I'll grant you that," and he smiled thinly. "And there's another thing," he said, rousing himself from his reveries.

"Sir?"

"The horses. They're requisitioning the lot. It upsets me, Tommy. From what I've heard, it's a nightmare over there, a real hell on earth. Worse for the horses, for they don't have any choice, do they?"

Tommy looked away. He could see horses working the fields in the distance. A pair of drays were hauling a wagon laden with barrels. Ponies were pulling barges behind them along the Bridgewater Canal. The Earl's Arab thoroughbreds were all stabled in the yard.

"Will they take all of them, sir?"

"They'll let us keep some, for the work on the farm, they'll have to, but they'll take as many as they can…"

Tommy knew what was coming.

"If Edward gets his commission, will you go across too? To keep an eye on him? You could go on the pretext of seeing to the horses – they'll need skilled hands like yours – but be on hand for Edward, in case he needs you. He's my only grandson, Tommy, and there's no one I can trust his care to more."

Tommy turned back to face him. He knelt down in front of him, so that his head was on a level with the Earl's.

"I promise."

The Earl nodded. He placed his hand on one of Tommy's and grasped it as firmly as his weakening strength would permit him, blinking back a tear.

The two of them remained in the drawing room, not speaking, until the sun set behind the avenue of elms, which lined the drive up to the house.

Four weeks later The Earl had died, Edward had received his commission, the majority of the Estate's horses had been requisitioned and Tommy Thunder volunteered as a "rough rider", to break in the young horses and look after the general welfare of the others required for active duty by The Manchester Regiment.

He marched behind Edward, now a Subaltern, leading those horses not being ridden by the officers, to thousands of cheering crowds along Deansgate in Central Manchester. Edward's horse skittered occasionally, not used to being in such close proximity to so many people, but Edward kept her calm and steady for the most part, grateful that he had followed Tommy's advice of placing leather blinkers on either side of her eyes, to keep her attention focused mainly on what was happening in front of her.

An officer whose name Tommy did not know, but

whose picture he had seen on the many posters affixed to walls and lamp posts, staring out and pointing an accusing finger at all who happened to look upon his face, was standing on a raised dais directly opposite Kendal, Milne & Faulkner's Department Store, taking the salute from the men as they paraded past. This caused a delay in their progress along the route and for quite some time Tommy was forced to wait until the Regiment could move on once more. Tommy looked about him. Opposite the Field Marshall there was a momentary break in the crowd. Tommy saw two women standing in a shop doorway. They reminded him of the way Lakota women would wave their braves off to war back on the Plains when he was a boy. One of them was in great distress and was being comforted by her friend. She sank to her knees, and an old dog, not unlike the late Earl's golden retriever, which had been hidden from view by the woman who had just fallen to the ground, padded across to her to offer comfort. For the briefest of moments Tommy's eyes met those of the still standing woman, and then their company was moving on again, and they became lost from view.

Having taken the salute the Regiment proceeded to the Cathedral, the Collegiate Church of St Mary, St Denys and St George, where a special service was to be held in their honour, conducted by His Grace the Most Reverend Edmund Arbuthnott Knox, 4th Bishop of Manchester, with choristers from The Bluecoat School built by Humphrey Chetham and bequeathed to the city some two hundred and sixty years before. The Bishop spoke much of duty and sacrifice, history and tradition.

Tommy heard very little of it. He remained outside the Cathedral, with the horses and a large company of men, who grew restless, eager to be back on the move, once the interminable service had ended. The horses stamped and whinnied, shaking their manes. They sensed, as Tommy did, that a great army had passed this way before, shaping the fate of the city just as they were doing this day…

On the far corner of the Cathedral Green, close to the Hanging Ditch, unseen by Tommy, stands Old Moon.

Old Moon closes his eyes, hearing the march of armies, the Jacobite pipes and drums, as a hundred years after the founding of the Bluecoat School, whose choristers are singing this very morning, the forces of Bonnie Prince Charlie, having crossed the Irwell by the old Salford Bridge, to capture the town without a fight, muster on the Green.

He sees men in Highland dress and a woman before them with a drum at her knee, and he hears her singing, the notes dancing on the air, drowning out the Bluecoat Boys.

"From Long Preston Peggy to Manchester went
To join the bold rebels it was her intent
For in brave deeds of arms did she take much delight
And therefore she went with the soldiers to fight

The Prince called his servants who on him did wait
Go down to yon maiden who stands in the gate

Who sings with a voice which is soft and so sweet
And in my high name do her lovingly greet
So down from his master this servant did hie
For to do his bidding and bear her reply
But ere to this handsome young virgin he came
He took off his bonnet and called out her name

Oh Long Preston Peggy your beauty's adored
By no other person than by a Scotch Lord
And if to his wishes you will now comply
All night in his Chamber with him shall you lie…"

Old Moon leans on a rail, listening to the voices rising up through the years from beneath the Hanging Ditch. Around the corner, on The Shambles, stand two inns, *The Bull's Head* and *The Angel*. In *The Angel* the Whigs and Hanoverians mutter darkly, while in *The Bull* the High Tories and Jacobites openly begin recruiting.

"All gentlemen that have a mind to serve His Royal Highness Prince Charles, here's five guineas in advance…"

From inside *The Bull* on this day a hundred and seventy years later, Old Moon hears a woman's voice saucily singing through the open doorway.

"On Monday I walk out with a soldier
On Tuesday I walk out with a Tar
On Wednesday I'm out
With a baby Boy Scout

On Thursday a Hussar
On Friday I walk out wi' a Scottie
On Sunday the Captain of the Crew
But on Saturday I'm willing
If you'll only take the shilling
To make a man of any one of you…"

A torn poster, peeling from the lamp post Old Moon is leaning against, flaps in the wind.

"Take the King's Shilling
Your Country Needs You…"

In less than twenty-four hours more than three hundred men enlist to form the first ever Manchester Regiment. They will march on London to stake the claims of Charles Edward Stuart to the British throne.

There is dark talk in the taverns, much shouting and the thumping of fists on tables. Old Moon hears a young girl's voice, anxious and frightened, searching for her father. He sees her standing before the Court Leet in the upstairs room of *The Bull's Head*.

State your name.
Lizzie Byrom.
What is your age?
Fifteen, sir.
Do you swear to tell the truth, the whole truth and nothing but the truth, so help you God?
I do, sir.

The Manchester Leet for the 25th of November 1745 is now in session. You may proceed, Lizzie Byrom.

I was affrighted by the noise, sir, and I called out to my father.

"Papa, who are all these men? What do they mean by their beating on our door?"

"Pay them no heed, Lizzie. Tis but a party of horse come in."

It was my Lord Pitsligo's Horse. I tell 'ee, sir, I saw Mr Walley there, and Mr Foden, and Hugh Sterling – him as was 'prentic'd to Mr Hibbert – and the Deputy too, sir, who did billet them. My Papa could see I was afear'd, sir, so he took care of me to the Cross at Market Street Lane. 'Twas a very fine moonlit night, sir. The streets were exceeding quiet, with not one person to be seen or heard.

"Lizzie, you must stay with your uncle this night. Take care not to venture out of doors, but if you do, steer well clear of Acresfield. They bury the Reverend Hoole on the morrow, who was even unto his death our most fierce opponent, ever blackening the good name of our Young Pretender, denying him his true and rightful claim."

"Where will you go, Papa?"

"To consult with Mr Croxton, Mr Fielden and others, about how we may keep ourselves out of any scrape."

The next morning, at eleven o'clock, we all of us, my uncle, mamma and sister, went once more up to the Cross, for there was such commotion, sir. They were all beating up for the Prince, sir, a great clamouring of

668

pipes and drums. At first there did come small parties, led by a young girl no older than me, sir, whom folk did call Long Preston Peggy, and so it did go, sir, till about three o'clock, when the Prince himself did come, at the head of the main body, so many I couldn't count 'em, sir, breakin' over the town like a great wave. The Prince went straight to Mr Dickenson's, where he now lodges, the Duke of Athol to Mr Marsden's, the Duke of Perth to Gardside's. There came an officer to us in Highland dress at the Cross and read us the manifests. The bells they rung, and a great bonfire was lit, so that all the town was illuminated. Papa joined us then, my mamma, sister, uncle and I, and together we walked up and down amid a great throng. At four o'clock the Prince was proclaimed King, and after, we went to my aunt's, where we stayed till eleven o'clock, sir, making St Andrew's crosses. We sat up making till two o'clock, sir, enough to give out to all the folk the next day, sir, when the men would all set off for London…

Old Moon is accidentally jostled by an angry mob surging out of *The Bull's Head* and knocked to the ground. A small but vocal group of protestors are holding a rally outside *The Angel*, holding up banners, calling on people to sign a petition against the war – Christian Pacifists, Irish Nationalists, and other various anti-militarists. Scuffles break out between some of the protestors and the jingoistic crowds lining the streets to cheer the new recruits.

Old Moon feels his head spin. His eyes glaze over.

The hands on the clock tower of the Town Hall in Albert Square begin to turn backwards. At first quite slowly, then quicker and quicker, until they become a blur, a Catherine wheel spitting out sparks, its spiked flails trundling down the streets, scattering the people.

He sees two men quarrelling.

"The King should be subject to the will of the people."

"The King is subject to no earthly authority. He derives his right to rule directly from the will of God."

"One man, one vote."

"An absolute monarch rules absolutely."

"By the Grace of God."

"Please note. I, Sir Thomas Tyldesley of Morley's Hall, Astley, Lieutenant-Colonel to His Majesty King Charles, do not bandy words with a common weaver."

"Richard Perceval is my name, sir, from Levenshulme. We are all of us equal before God."

Curses are uttered. Blows are exchanged. A knife is brought out. Richard Perceval lies dead in a pool of his own blood, the first fatality in the English Civil War. Within hours the whole city is under siege. A state of conflagration and disorder prevail.

Lord Strange leads the Royalist forces over the Salford Bridge. He commandeers a fine house by the Dean's Gate, and there does set up quarters.

Fall back, fall edge is the cry. Tis fiddlers and revels day and night.

Church bells are rung to summon the Manchester militia under the command of General Rosworm, a

German, veteran of the Thirty Years War, Lutheran and loyal Ironside. Two hundred Parliamentarians gather on the higher ground in the churchyard of St Mary, St Denys and St George, from where they can view any Royalist attack.

"We have small comfort, for it rains hard. Our food, when we can get it, is berries; our drink, water; our beds, the earth; our canopy, the clouds. We pull up the hedges, pales and gates, and make good fires."

Psalms can be heard being sung across the city.

"Praise the Lord, all ye nations
Praise the Lord, all ye people
For His merciful kindness is great towards us
And the truth of the Lord endureth for ever..."

For three days and three nights they repel the Royalist attacks. For a further three days and three nights there is waiting. Fires burn across the city where Strange and his men have ransacked and rampaged. Rats scurry down alleys, or over the rooftops, in search of safety and shelter.

Then on the morning of the seventh day the attack comes at last.

The sky rings out to cannon and culverin, to volleys of musket and flintlock, snaphance and arquebus. Arrows from long bow and crossbow rain down. As the smoke clears, the streets echo to the charge of boots on cobblestones. Sparks fly as halberd clashes with pike, lintstock strikes spontoon.

"Let the high praises of God be in our mouths

And a two-edged sword in our hands
To bind our king with chains
And his nobles with links of iron…"

Old Moon sees the tattered remnants of the Royalist army slink away back across the Salford Bridge, the torn banners streaming in the wind, the russet-reds of the soldiers retreating…

…and then returning, the bedraggled tartans of the Jacobites, who never reached London, turning back dejected in Derby, heads low, bodies bent into the teeth of a gale…

…the rag-tag dribs and drabs of khaki-clad soldiers, despondently dragging weary bodies home from France, no crowds to cheer them home as when they went, down half-remembered lanes to quiet, empty villages, where fields lie fallow and unploughed, and no church bells ring…

…as they do this morning.

Old Moon picks himself up from the ground, dusts himself down, waiting for his eyes to focus. He feels the earth shake beneath his feet. He sees the great mills and warehouses in the city tumbling all around him, showering him with brick and plaster dust. Gaping holes open up before him. Flames billow out of top storey windows. He hears the clamour of horns and klaxons, sirens wailing. Women are running through the streets between the burning buildings. Babies are crying. Dogs whimper as they scrabble to rescue a child from beneath fallen masonry. Until finally his eyes clear.

He walks back along the Hanging Ditch just in time to see the last of The Manchester Regiment marching in a column into the nave of the Cathedral, whose doors swing open wide, like an ever-hungry mouth.

Bishop Edmund Arbuthnott Knox sounded the clarion call from his pulpit inside.

"Our texts this day are from St Paul's Epistle to the Corinthians and from Numbers. First, Corinthians: *'For if the trumpet give an uncertain sound, who shall prepare himself to the battle?'* "

A woman carrying a banner of the Christian Pacifists Union, who had been part of the fracas during the vigil outside on Hanging Ditch, stood up and shouted from the rear of the nave.

"But does not St Paul then go on to say, *'There are, it may be, so many kinds of voices in the world, and none of them is without signification'?*"

"Indeed he does, Madam, but he also warns, *'So likewise ye, except ye utter by the tongue words easy to be understood, how shall it be known what is spoken, for ye shall speak into the air'?*"

The woman was forcibly removed by the cathedral's sidesmen, having to run a gauntlet of insult and disapproval from the crowds pressed close to the church doors.

Seemingly unmoved, Bishop Knox continued his

address.

"And now from Numbers, chapter 32, verse 6: *'But Moses said unto the Sons of Gad and to the sons of Reuben, Shall your brethren go to war, and shall ye sit here?'*"

After receiving the final blessing from the Bishop, The Manchester Regiment marched the final mile to the railway station, singing proudly as they went.

> *"Onward, Christian soldiers*
> *Marching as to war*
> *With the cross of Jesus*
> *Going on before*
> *Christ, the royal master*
> *Leads against the foe*
> *Forward into battle*
> *See his banners go…"*

Tommy was busy assisting with the loading of the horses onto the wagons at the back of the Troop Train. Edward's horse became increasingly agitated by the bustle and confusion, the constant shouting and sudden hisses of steam. Tommy had to place a hood upon her head to calm her. He worried how she would fare when faced with the much louder noise and greater smoke of battle.

Eventually all were loaded aboard and Tommy took his own place in one of the carriages reserved for the farriers, sadlers and other rough riders such as himself.

There were no spare seats, so he was forced to stand in the corridor along with a dozen others. The train at last began to pull slowly out of London Road Station. Tommy leant out of the window, reflecting on the promise he had made to the Earl, and wondered if he would ever return to this city, whose surrounding towns and villages had been his home for the last thirty-five years. Or would he, if he survived, seek pastures new?

Just as the steam was clearing he saw a young woman standing apart from the waving crowds. She was urgently searching for someone. When her eyes fell upon him, they remained there, and her stare bore right through him. He knew he should recognise her, but he could not place her. She was, he realised, one of the women with whom he had formed a temporary attachment during his nomadic wanderings from village to village, but he could not now remember her name. Once she was sure she had Tommy's full attention, she lifted up a small child, a boy, less than two years old, and held him high above her head, her eyes unblinkingly fixed upon him. Tommy watched them till they disappeared from view. He sank back into the corridor of the moving train. The industrial landscape sped by in a blur, the whole of Manchester cloaked in a thick, impenetrable pall. Somehow, he knew, he must try and make it back.

*

Reads the Moon dances the moon.

He walks by the moon's light, navigating by the

stars. Those long-buried, hard-wired instincts guide his footsteps back to the confluence of the three rivers.

His eyes do not see the ugliness of soot-stained brick or stone. His nostrils do not register the stench of tanneries or dyes, of effluent or rotting corpses. His ears do not hear the clamour of anvil forges, steam hammers, clattering looms, the roar of coal rushing along steel chutes from pithead to canal basin, the rumble of trains thundering over iron bridges. He does not feel the press of people on every side. His feet seek out the soft imprint of bare earth, and so he starts to dance.

His last dance.

All the ghosts dance with him, stamping to the rhythm of fire and water, earth and air, the old ancestral voices crowding in on him, carrying him with them, as the smoke of industry coils around him, its unstoppable progress a spiderweb of song and story, mud and memory, a mighty leviathan, whose appetite is never sated.

On and on he dances.

Deer bolt in the clearings. Starlings flock in their thousands to begin their nightly murmuration, and the men of Manchester march to war.

And still he dances.

Dances till his last breath, his final gasp, and he sinks slowly to the earth, which covers him, is fed and nourished by him, tissue, blood and bone, till all that remains is a much thumbed, shiny worn Roman coin.

"I wish I were a little swallow
And I had wings, and I could fly
I'd fly back home to one who loves me
And try to pass my troubles by

But I am not a little swallow
I have no wings, neither can I fly
I'll lie down here and sleep till morning
None shall wake me ere I die…"

*

THE TIMES

POPPIES BLOOM RED OVER THE GRAVES OF HEROES

30th July 1917

It is an old legend that roses never blow so red as over a hero's grave. The same must now be true of poppies.

Nowhere does the ground flame quite so brilliantly as it does around Warlencourt, on the dreadful expanse above the Bazentin Ridge towards High Wood in the valley of the Somme, where men of The Manchester Regiment passed by on the first of this month.

Elsewhere the scarlet is half veiled in the mist of flowering grasses, and mixed with them are a profusion of other blossoms, yellow ragwort, hawkweed, sow thistles, and ladies' bed straw, mauve scabious, purple vetch and knapweed, tall campanulas, blue chicory, vipers' bugloss and cornflower, and nearer to the ground pale field convolvulus and pimpernel, with everywhere white yarrow and chamomile.

No yard of all this ground but last year was ploughed up by shells, and beaten and ploughed again, so that much of the soil which now lies on the surface must have been thrown up from many feet below, and then churned and churned and churned again. Yet the grasses and the flowers are as in any rich meadow at home. But there are no villages, no landmarks beyond the occasional tree stumps which once were woods, only the wide, forlorn expanse, where there are no human beings, as if this valley were the heart of some new continent, which man had but just discovered. All larger things were destroyed and swept away by war, and only the little things, like plant seeds and insects' eggs, were able to survive.

There are places where crops flourish, patches of an acre or more being covered with oats or barley, or wheat, all three growing strongly and hardly less close than if they had been truly sown, which seems impossible. More likely they survive from many summers ago and, self seeded, have held their own well against the wild things which riot around and among them. In one place a solitary potato was growing strong, sprung presumably from some stray from a German field kitchen.

Next to poppies the most abundant flower is the chamomile. It grows on the roads and beaten paths by which the armies used to travel on, to and from their lines, so that, looking across the country, amid the deep green and other waving colours, the course of an old track may still be traced where it runs like a pure white ribbon, fringed with its flowers. Their fragrance, when trod upon, almost overwhelms that other all-pervasive odour of decay.

But strangest of all in nature's haste to hide the ravages of war are the shell holes. Many still remain half filled with water, in which a luxuriant pond life has developed. Tiny whirligig beetles perform mazy dances on the surface, and water boatmen skate across, just as in any village pond at home. Around the water's edges, white butterflies crowd to drink. When disturbed, they rise up in clouds till the air is full of them, like a child's snow globe.

*

Tommy's war was horses. Horses and moles. Moles and mud and meadows. Ploughing and harvesting. Feeding the living. Speeding the dying.

Back in Buile Hill Catch's war was horse shoes. Clem's too.

More than three quarters of a million horses were

requisitioned for transport overseas to the various fronts across the globe, and the need for horse shoes was insatiable, shipped by the wagon-load week after week, month after month, year after year. To cope with this never ending demand, Catch commandeered Clem, and together the two of them worked side by side at the forge, day and night, night and day, while Cam, approaching thirteen, became their Jill-of-all-Trades.

Catch complained that the work was robbing him of his touch, his finesse, his hands no longer capable of the subtlety they once possessed. He was only fit for horse shoes now, he would say, as he crashed bone weary each night into bed beside Clem, who would hold them in her own now coarsened fingers, rub them a while, then smile.

"Oh I don't know," she'd say, "they still have their uses," and she'd wrap his great arms around her, and they'd rock together till dawn, while she sang to him the French Creole songs of her childhood.

"J'ai passé devant ta porte
J'ai crié.bye-bye à mon beau
Y'a personne qui m'a répondu
Oh yé yaille, mon cœur il fait mal…"

Tommy never saw action. Not first hand. But he heard it plenty. And he saw the effects of it. The dead and the dying. The bodies stretchered back from the Front. He also saw the mending. The healing and the hoping. These he assisted with. And when there was no more hoping to be had, he assisted there too.

But for the most part he helped with the horses. By 1918 he ran teams of them, ploughing the fields behind the lines, the ones still left unshelled, to grow the food they needed, the oats and wheat and barley, just like back at Bittern Wood. And root crops for the men. Potatoes and carrots, swede and rhubarb. The horses ploughed with gas masks for blinkers. And still the seasons turned.

Sometimes a horse might get sick or be wounded beyond further care. Then they'd send for Tommy. To provide quick and painless dispatch. Sometimes, they'd be overrun with moles, burrowing between the rows of young wheat. They'd send for Tommy then too, for the same speedy solution. And sometimes there'd be others, tunnelling beneath the barbed wire, looking for escape, and a short cut back to home. Tommy would provide that too. Quietly, compassionately, without fuss.

It was what turned out to be the final month of the war. The Austro-Hungarian army, having been routed at Vittorio Veneto, signed the Armistice with Italy and the Battle for the Sambre Canal in Northern France was entering its final decisive phase. It was a Tuesday. November 5th. Bonfire Night. With still many Guys in the line to be burnt.

Tommy's horses were busy transporting field ambulances for the wounded as they were being carried back from the fighting. Among them was Edward, now Captain Egerton. He lay on a wagon, covered in blankets, his head bandaged. He was smoking a cigarette. He saw Tommy first and called him over.

"Bloody awful show," he said. "Ambushed. Crossing the canal. Blame myself. Should have seen it. Warned often enough. More than a thousand bought it. Me too, eh Tommy?" He started coughing and Tommy was forced to take his cigarette, while he tried to lift him to a sitting position. Edward winced as Tommy pulled him upwards, then smiled weakly.

"That's better. Do you think I might have my cigarette back, old chap? Thank you."

He closed his eyes and inhaled deeply. Tommy took advantage to look quickly beneath the blankets. It was worse than he feared. A harassed-looking nurse from the VAD hurried past. Tommy tried to find out from her what was being planned for Edward.

"They'll operate," she said. "He'll lose both his legs."

"What are his chances?" asked Tommy.

"He'll live. Probably," she said. "Though what for precisely I'm sure I couldn't say," she added. Then she paused and collected herself. "I'm sorry. I shouldn't have said that. But today has just been... well... You haven't got a cigarette, have you?"

Tommy lit her one.

"Thanks. I needed that. Right." She took out a handkerchief and briskly wiped her eyes. "Best get back inside," she said indicating the hospital tent. "Mustn't let the men see me like this. Brave face and all that. Here," and she handed him back the unfinished cigarette. "I expect your friend could do with that more than I."

Tommy returned to Edward and placed the cigarette

between his lips for him, removing the finished one that was dangling from his fingers. Edward opened his eyes.

"Do you remember that afternoon you got me to ride bare back in the paddock at the House?"

Tommy nodded.

"I probably wouldn't have been here today if it hadn't been for you."

Tommy turned away.

"No, no," said Edward, "you misunderstand me. Bloody grateful. Wouldn't have missed it for the world."

"Your grandfather would be proud of you."

"Would he? Really? Do you think so?"

"Yes. He would."

The two men looked at one another a long time. Tommy placed a hand on Edward's shoulder. It was Edward who spoke again next.

"I say – I was wondering…"

"Yes?"

"Do you still… catch moles?"

Tommy nodded. "If I'm asked."

Edward looked at him pleadingly.

"But you are not a mole."

Edward turned away again, drawing on his cigarette. "No, I suppose not."

Tommy leant over him and whispered softly in his ear. "You are a horse. And when there's nothing left that can be done to save a horse, to leave him with a life worth living, then they come to me. I am going to wheel this cart to the corner of the field, far away from all this noise and confusion, where it's quiet, and we can be…

just the two of us. You and me. Like before. When you found your courage. I can do this for you now. If that is what you want."

Edward closed his eyes once more, then nodded.

Catch no longer cast an iron feather on the anvil for every single horse shoe that he made. There were simply too many. But whenever he had a spare moment he would fashion another and toss it into the heavy munitions box, which had accompanied him and Clem throughout their years of wandering, and which now lay in a corner of the forge. There must have been more than a thousand of them.

It was while he was trying to sort through them one September evening in 1918, in an effort to try to close the lid on the box, so that he could stand on the top of it to reach down a new tin of nails from a shelf high up, that Cam called to him from the doorway. He was so lost in his thoughts that he didn't hear her, and so she was forced to come closer. She tapped him on the shoulder. Startled, he dropped the box, and dozens of the wrought iron feathers clattered onto the hard earth floor.

"What are these?" she asked, picking them up and holding them to the light.

Her father explained.

"They're like the three in the kitchen."

He nodded.

"One for each of us."

"Yes."

"Why do you keep so many of them?"

"I thought I'd make something with them one day."

"Like what?"

He shook his head.

"A weather vane for the top of the church?"

"No."

"Why not? It'd turn in the wind. I'd like that."

"I don't want to make something useful."

"What then?"

"Something just for its own sake. Something beautiful."

"Like *Maman*?"

"And you."

"You'd better get started then."

She scrunched up her face and wrinkled her nose. He laughed.

"What did you want? Just now, when you came in?"

"Oh, nothing really. Supper's nearly ready, that's all."

He nodded and she wandered off, still holding one of the iron feathers. He managed to close the lid on the box, stood on it and reached down the tin of nails. When he stepped back down, he paused. Cam had been right. It was about time he made a beginning.

Outside he could hear her singing one of her mother's Creole songs.

"*Moi j'm'ai mis à l'observer
Moi j'ai vue des lumières allumées
Y'a quelque chose qui m'disait j'devrais pleurer
Oh yé yaille mon cœur il fait mal…*"

At nights Catch would sometimes dream he passed by an open door. He would call out, "Hey there, Beautiful?" But no one would answer. He'd pass by again. He'd see candles lit in the window, but still no one was there. When he woke, his heart would be aching and he'd pull Clem closer to him.

When he walked out of the forge into the yard, Cam was still singing. When she saw him, she stopped and pointed up to the sky.

"Look," she called.

Three great white egrets were flying across the moon.

"Make them," she said, laughing, and skipped indoors.

Yes, he thought. Why not?

"There were three men came from the west
Their fortunes for to try…"

For the next eight weeks Catch worked every night to fashion the three birds, using as many of the more than a thousand iron feathers as he could to build up the complex structures of the wings, layer upon layer.

"They look like angels' wings," whispered Cam to him late one evening.

Catch nodded and kissed the top of her brow.

"When will they be finished?"

"Soon, I think. Tomorrow maybe."

He had used a couple of hundred to create each of the three long necks and outstretched bills, and a couple of hundred more to mould a large, round full moon, pitted with craters and mountains, whose shadows formed the faint outline of a hare.

On the last night he painted the rest of the moon a whitish yellow, so that the black iron feathers of the birds would fly across it as silhouettes.

Tuesday 5th November. Dusk.

Catch applied the final finishing touches, attaching the three birds to the backdrop of the moon. His hammer rang upon the anvil loud and clear, echoing across the evening sky.

Tommy wheeled Edward to a far corner of the field unnoticed amid the chaos all around.

Edward gripped Tommy's arm. "Will they know?" he asked.

Tommy shook his head. "They will think it was a sniper's bullet. That you endured pain without complaint. That you died with honour."

"Will it hurt?"

"You'll feel nothing. I promise you."

Edward closed his eyes once more. He tried to conjure up memories from his life, his early golden childhood at the Old Hall, cut short all too soon by his being sent away to school, the accident in the barn, riding Star around the paddock bareback, but he found that he couldn't. They all bled into one. School, the Army – which was which? It was all of it finished. What, he wondered, would have been waiting for him, if he had managed to make it back in one piece? Would he have recognised it? Would he have wanted it, to carry on just the same as it had always done, to the last syllable of recorded time? The men under his command, who he had tried to get to know during these last four years, they understood far better than he ever could the true nature of sacrifice. He hoped he hadn't let them down.

"I'm ready now," he said at last.

Tommy placed his hand upon Edward's brow and closed his eyes, turning his head gently to one side. He lifted his Bell Gun, the humane device he carried with him for the horses, unscrewed the firing mechanism, inserted a single lead shot into the vented barrel, placed the chamfered, bell-shaped muzzle against Edward's temple, then fired. It pierced the skull with no significant exsanguination, passing through the cerebral cortex and *cerebrum* into the *medulla oblongata*, the brain stem. It took less than a second. Death was instantaneous.

Tommy bowed his head briefly, then walked swiftly away.

The sound of the single gunshot barely registered amid all the other noise of shouts and shells exploding, but for Tommy it cracked across the sky, resounding as clear as the ringing strike of a hammer on an anvil.

Far across Europe, beyond the Alps, across the valley of the Po River, in the lee of the Dolomites, it ricocheted like a peal of bells, of promises kept, as Private John Jabez Chadwick released a troop of working horses to run free across the wet grasslands towards unknown destinations and an unseen future.

Back in Buile Hill, Catch hung his great work, his three great egrets flying across the moon, from a beam at the back of the forge, where they hung and slowly turned, glinting in the sun's last rays, while Clem and Cam lit candles, placed them in a circle directly underneath the iron birds, and sang.

"Quand j'ai été cogné à la porte
Quand ils ont rouvert la porte
Moi j'ai vue des chandelles allumés
Tout l'tour de ton cercueil…"

Leaving and returning, leaving and returning. The three of them for ever in flight. Suspended.

17

1919

It was a perfect, almost midsummer's day. Warm with a gentle breeze. High clouds scudded lightly across otherwise clear blue skies. Delphine opened the window wide in her top floor lodgings on Lime Grove and breathed in the warm, scented air from the roses below, which were now in full bloom, and whose fragrance was sufficient to mask the less pleasant smells that more generally wafted in from the Manchester Ship Canal in the middle of June.

She had lived there happily for nine years. Other lodgers had come and gone, so that she was now the longest-serving resident – the Mother of the Marshalsea, as she had quipped to Miss Poulter, the most recent arrival, who was due to take on Delphine's room from the following week, for Delphine was leaving.

Mrs Snook had been most perturbed when Delphine broke the news.

"But Miss Fish, are you no longer happy here?"

Even after nine years of seeing one another almost daily, they had never progressed beyond these formalities. Delphine did not in fact know what Mrs Snook's first name might be. She had on a few occasions picked up letters from the mat addressed to Mrs T. Snook, but the 'T' almost certainly stood for 'Thomas', the name of Mrs Snook's late husband.

"On the contrary, Mrs Snook, I have been most

happy here. But I have had the good fortune to secure a new and improved position at the University, which will require me to live closer to where I shall now be working."

This response produced nothing more than a tight-lipped, "I see", followed by: "I shall nevertheless require a week's rent by way of compensation."

"Of course, Mrs Snook."

And so now here she was on her last weekend in Seymour Park, packing up her few modest possessions into two medium-sized suitcases. She looked around the simple, white-washed room which had been her home these past nine years and smiled – her nun's cell, as she had thought it – and which had suited her very well. Over time she had added one or two ornaments of her own, a row of books on the top of the chest of drawers, plus the only two photographs she possessed, one showing herself as a small child, sitting beside Old Moon at the water's edge near Bob's Lane with her parents busy working in the background, Sammy repairing nets, Eve gutting a fish, and the second of Yasser and Rose's wedding, a group of people standing in front of the statue to Prince Albert by the Town Hall. In this photograph Delphine was little more than a baby, having been picked up by Rose, who was smiling and cooing towards her. She had not seen either of them for many years now. She knew that their daughter, Pomona, had caught tuberculosis and died when she was young, and that their son had been away in the war. She hoped he had returned safely. She must write to them, she thought, and let them know her new address.

Now that everything had been packed the room seemed very bare again. Only the framed print of *The Light of the World* remained, looking down on her as it had these nine years from above the narrow bed. There had been several times during the past few years, especially when news from the Front had been bad, when she had wondered if Holman Hunt, in depicting Christ's face in such dark shadow, and in showing him preparing to knock at a long unopened door, overgrown with weeds, had not somehow been prophesying the severe crisis of faith which had befallen so many of her generation as a consequence of so much seemingly futile loss and destruction.

She tried to shut away such depressing thoughts. Today was not a time for them, not on such a perfect a day as this. This was the first summer since the Armistice and it felt to Delphine, as she passed people in the streets, that there was a new buoyancy in their mood, a spring in their step, and a feeling of cautious optimism about the future.

This was matched by her own good fortune in having so recently secured her new position, which she would be commencing in a week's time, leaving her plenty of time to settle in to her new lodgings.

The University had decided to open a new Department of Audiology, the first in the country, and Delphine was joining their inaugural team. She had taught at *The Manchester Institution for the Deaf & Dumb* in Stretford for nine years, and in that time she had become widely recognised as a teacher with rare gifts of patience, understanding and the ability to communicate with often unreachable children. There were sharp divisions of opinion among teachers, academics and doctors regarding the best and most appropriate methods for teaching deaf children to "speak". Some advocated signing, but the majority view was strongly and vehemently opposed to it, arguing that it reduced people to the level of animals, that speech and spoken language was what distinguished humans and rendered them unique as a species. Delphine argued the contrary position, maintaining that it was a teacher's duty to enable her charges to communicate in the best way that they could. For some this meant speech, certainly, but for others, like her own mother, who was mute, speech was not a possibility. For her, and for others like her, signing was the only way to allow them access to the rest of the world, while for others a mixture of the two proved the best approach. She was eagerly looking forward to animated debate and discussion with her soon-to-be-met new colleagues, and to pursuing her own independent research into the area.

She had found herself quite commodious rooms in Upper Brook Street, less than five minutes walk away from the University, a sitting room, bedroom, kitchen and bathroom, and she smiled at the prospect, looking around her nun's cell at Mrs Snook's for what would be her penultimate night there. Yet this modest room had seemed like luxury when compared to the ramshackle nature of her parents' cabin at Bob's Lane which, when she had been a child, had been her whole world, with each day bringing new adventures and fresh discoveries. Tomorrow she would go and visit them, give them her good news, spend the day with them, then return to Lime Grove for her final night there, before carrying her two suitcases the following day to Upper Brook Street.

The next day, a Saturday, she rose early, for the journey to Bob's Lane was not a straightforward one. It was going to be another warm day, and by the time she had walked the half mile from Lime Grove to the station at Throstle's Nest Junction, skirting the edge of Seymour Park, where the leaves on the trees were already starting to acquire their blowsy, late summer demeanour, she was beginning to perspire. This was not helped by the train being so crowded, despite the early hour, that there was no seat to be had. She was forced to stand pressed too close for comfort to an overweight, red-faced gentleman, who repeatedly mopped his forehead with a less than clean handkerchief with unnecessary exuberance. The train took on more and more passengers at each of the next six stations, so that, by the time they reached Timperley Junction, she thought she might expire. It was with considerable relief that she stepped out onto a much emptier platform, where she had to wait twenty minutes for her connection on the Skelton to Glazebrook East line which, when it arrived, was mercifully quiet. Forty-five minutes later she alighted at Cadishead Station. Having climbed down the steps from the Cadishead Viaduct it was then a short walk along the Liverpool Road, past the bandstand in the park, where a gaggle of ragged children could be heard screeching as they rode the lethal Witch's Hat, until she turned into Bob's Lane and dropped down towards the Canal. It was a walk she could have made blindfolded.

As soon as she reached the ferry, she sensed that something was different. It was more than six months since her last visit home, but as a rule very little ever changed. It was this constancy that she clung to almost like a faith. The first thing she noticed was the boat itself. It was tied up against the bank, where it bobbed forlornly. Usually her father would have been there too, waiting to carry passengers across, or fetch them from the opposite bank. On the rare occasion he might be called away somewhere else, her mother would have been there in his stead. They operated the ferry seven days a week from seven in the morning till eleven at night. Week in, week out. Autumn, winter, spring and summer. Today neither of them was there, yet standing on the opposite shore, clearly needing to come across, stood a young man, looking up and down the canal, as if he might summon assistance from thin air.

"Hello?" he called out. "I'm looking for the boatman. Do you know where he might be found?"

"Yes," shouted back Delphine. "I'll just…" The rest of what she said was abruptly drowned out by a piercing blast from the siren of one of the Manchester Liners' ocean going ships, which hove into view on its way to the city from Liverpool. She had to wait several minutes until the vessel, a tanker from Aden, had passed between them.

"Yes," she began again. "I know where they live,"

she explained. "I'll just go and see what's keeping them. I shan't be long."

And with that, she hitched up the hem of her skirt and ran diagonally up from the water's edge towards a small copse of trees on the brow of a low hill, through which the young man thought he detected the outlines of a small settlement of wooden cottages. He took off his jacket and sat on the iron capstan to which the ferry's rope would be tethered while its customers stepped aboard, had it been operating as normal.

She had not gone more than fifty yards, however, when she suddenly stopped, turned around, and ran as adroitly down the slope as a mountain goat – almost as if she had been born on such terrain, the young man mused.

"I'll fetch you first," she called, untying the rope as she spoke, "and then go and investigate why they're not here afterwards. You've been waiting long enough."

"Thank you. That is most kind of you, Miss – er…?

"Fish," she called back.

The young man smiled. For a moment he was sure she had said "Fish".

"But please call me Delphine." She felt oddly exhilarated. It must be the sun, she thought, and smiled too.

"Delphine?"

"Yes."

"Are you French?"

"No."

By now she was already rowing across the canal and was answering his questions in between strokes.

What an extraordinary young woman, he thought. Why, she handles that boat like a sailor. Or perhaps *matelot* would be more appropriate, and he chuckled to himself at his own joke.

"And what," she began, still rowing, "might I..." (another pull on the oars) "...call you?"

"Oh," he said, somewhat taken by surprise. "That's rather a difficult question to answer." Heavens, he thought. What kind of fellow will she think I am? Only rogues and vagabonds are evasive about their names.

"Are you," she asked, "an actor?"

He burst out laughing. "No," he said. "Not the sort you mean anyway."

"I see," she rowed. "What sort... of actor... are you...?"

"I haven't quite decided," he said, a little less loudly, for now she had almost reached him.

"Names are complicated," she agreed, leaping lightly out of the boat. She gestured with the rope towards the capstan, on top of which the young man had placed one foot. "Excuse me."

He stepped out of her way as she deftly looped the rope around it with a single throw. She was evidently much at home here, and he felt oddly wrong-footed.

"Take mine," she said.

"Miss?"

"My name. My father is a Sioux Indian." The young man's eyebrows shot up. "It's not every day you hear that, is it now? And they don't have names, not in the sense we understand them. His father called him 'Leaps Like A Fish', because he loved to swim in the stream near their camp, and when he tried to explain that here, someone thought he was describing a salmon. So – Sammy he became. Sammy Fish. And my mother, well – she doesn't have a last name. She can't speak. She's a mute. So she couldn't tell us anyway, even if she had one."

She paused for breath. She'd never told this to anyone. Yet here she was, confiding in a perfect stranger.

"And Delphine?" he asked, his eyebrows returning to their more usual position.

"Ah," she said, and stopped. No, she thought. I shan't explain that. "It's personal," she said. "Private."

He nodded. "I can respect that."

"Thank you." She looked at him squarely. "Have you decided what your own name is yet?"

"Well…"

"Hop aboard," she said, "then you can tell me while I ferry us back across. It's hard to row and speak at the same time."

He stepped into the flat-bottomed boat and perched along the stern, while Delphine, facing him from the prow, began to pull on the oars. Her hair had become unpinned and, from time to time as she rowed, she tried to blow stray wisps away from her face.

"I'm thinking of changing it," the young man said eventually. "My name, that is."

"Why? Are you on the run?"

"No," he said, more forcibly than he intended, "but it feels as though I may as well be."

He was silent for a while and then, as if having

taken a decision, he began once more to speak.

"My name is Franz Halsinger," he said. "As you can no doubt discern, that is a German name. After the sinking of *The Lusitania*, I was interned. On the Isle of Man."

"Oh, I'm sorry," interrupted Delphine. "I thought that was such a wicked and unjust thing to do. It made me feel ashamed to be English."

"That's just it. I was just seventeen at the time. I was born here, so I'm just as English as you, and yet, at the time, although I was angry, I could sort of understand why it was being done."

"I don't agree. I hate the idea of labelling people like that. We're each of us individuals, regardless of geography. Unique. Special. That's what I tell my children."

"Your children?"

"I'm a teacher."

"I see."

"Or I was."

"Was?"

"Never mind. You were telling me your story."

"My father was quite an old man. At least that's how he seemed when I was a boy. My mother died when I was very young. I don't remember her. Just my father. We always had to be quiet around him. So he was not taken away, like I was. I was put on a ship with hundreds of others, all of us frightened, confused, not understanding what was happening, and then we were taken across the island to a camp, where we were to be held for the duration of the war."

"It must have been terrible."

"Actually it wasn't that bad. Once we got there. It was fairly relaxed. The Camp was large so it didn't feel hemmed in. We worked on a farm close by. We could play sports, make music, read books. It was…"

"What?"

"Not so much the loss of liberty as the loss of years. More than four years of my life taken from me. It's the waste as much as the injustice that still rankles with me."

"Yes. I can see that."

They had almost reached the other side of the Canal now. He had fallen silent. He sat there, hunched up, facing but not looking at her. He reminded her of a snail who had just pulled in his horns, who was carrying a heavy burden upon his back, like a shell he had constructed around himself, and which had now formed a second skin. He had extraordinarily pale skin, like something that has been deprived of sunlight for too long, that you might come across if you turned over a dead branch in the wood, with translucent, blinking eyes.

"What have you been doing since the war ended?"

He looked up, startled, when she said that. "That's just it. Didn't you know? No, I suppose not. They won't have reported this in the newspapers. I'm only just on my way home. They wouldn't let us leave till a week ago. They wanted to deport me back to Germany. 'But I'm not from Germany,' I kept telling them. 'I'm English. I was born here.' Eventually they agreed. The ship docked in Liverpool yesterday. We had to make our own arrangements once we got there. There was a telegram. It was sent to the ship's captain, who handed it to one of the stewards, who gave it to me just as we reached shore…"

"What did it say?"

"It was from my father's solicitor, informing me that my father had died a week ago…"

"Oh, I'm so sorry."

"…and that he'd left everything to me when I turn twenty-one."

"And when's that?"

He looked directly at her for the first time in a while. "Today."

She said nothing.

They had now crossed the Canal. Delphine automatically threw the rope around the windlass and jumped ashore, steadying the boat while Franz got to his feet. She stretched out a hand which, after a brief pause, he took and stepped onto the waiting jetty.

"What will you do now?" she asked.

"I'm sorry. I hadn't known I was going to say any of this. You've been most kind, allowing me to. So – to answer your question, I think the first thing I'm going to do is to change my name."

Now it was Delphine's turn to raise her eyebrows in surprise.

"Why?"

"I feel like a fresh start. I have no family. But I'm lucky. For I have money. My father was a wealthy man. I want to put these last four wasted years behind me and never speak of them again."

Delphine nodded. "What to?"

He smiled. "Franz Halsinger will become Francis Hall. Very English, don't you think?" he added wryly.

"What happened to 'singer'?"

"I haven't quite decided yet. But I will not lose him altogether."

"Well – good luck," she said, and held out her hand towards him. He considered it a moment, then shook it, quite formally.

"Thank you."

"Do you know where you will go first?"

"To Manchester, that is all. I have been following the line of telegraph poles all the way from Liverpool." He pointed towards a long line of them stretching beside the Canal, before departing from it again as the Canal, following the course of the Mersey at this point, took a bend in the river. They looked like sentries standing in a row, to attention, on guard.

"Whatever for?" she said, laughing.

"That is another story, and too long in the telling. I have detained you enough."

"In that case, I'll go and see if I can find out what's been 'detaining' my parents. Goodbye."

He watched her hitch up her skirts once more and run off up the slope towards the copse of alder trees on the top of the hill. When he could no longer see her, he turned back towards the line of telegraph poles marching across the land and lit up a cigarette. He would smoke it and then be on his way.

Delphine was nearing the crest of the hill. The copse was strangely quiet as she entered it. Even the rooks seemed to be taking a siesta in the heat of the afternoon and were snoozing dustily in the sun, which made dappled patterns on the ground as she approached her parents' settlement. Flecks of light fell onto her hands and arms where she had rolled up the sleeves of her blouse. Motes of dust danced in the air, which hummed with the low drone of insects.

The fire which, even after Old Moon vanished, was always kept alight, whatever the season, for it was still their only source of heat for cooking, had been left to go out – quite recently, from the faint glow Delphine could still see in the ashes – and the wooden porch was littered with her parents' usual detritus – ends of rope, a box of tools, empty eel traps stacked in a heap. It was as if they had suddenly decided, on a whim, to take themselves off on a trip. They did this sometimes. But Sammy's narrow, wooden starvationer canoe lay upturned a little way off from the huts.

Puzzled, Delphine called out their names.

A pair of rooks cawed back desultorily. Otherwise nothing.

Perhaps they'd gone for a walk. It was a beautiful day after all, and Eve liked to pick wild herbs and flowers from the tangled carpet of undergrowth beneath the alders for use as medicines if needed.

Delphine called again.

Frowning, she decided to look indoors. The door was not locked, was never locked, and she swung it open and stepped inside to its shaded cool.

The smell hit her at once. That overpoweringly sweet, sickly smell which, even if you've never encountered it before, instinct tells you at once signifies death. She covered her mouth and nose with her arm and made her way towards the room at the back where they slept.

They were lying facing one another, arms wrapped around their bodies in a tender embrace, lips touching, eyes closed.

They had not been dead long – perhaps a day – for there was no decay, no indignity. A few flies buzzed around, but not too many yet. *Rigor mortis* had begun to wear off and there were no signs of bloating or extending. But for the lack of any rise or fall of breathing, they could almost have been asleep.

Delphine backed slowly out of the room. She could not bear to see them like this. It felt like an intrusion into that most private and intimate of moments. Which one of them, she wondered, had died first, had watched the other slip away, before patiently waiting for their own turn? She supposed it must have been the Spanish flu, which was on everyone's lips these days.

Once she had finally left the room, she suddenly turned and ran, out of the hut, through the copse, and down the hill towards the jetty, where she could see the young man was still standing, smoking a cigarette.

"Franz," she shouted. "Francis."

He was just finishing his cigarette and gathering himself to set off once more, when he heard her shouting his name, his names. He turned and saw her hurtling down the slope towards him like a hare attempting to outrun a pack of hounds.

Four hours later the two of them were sitting on the rickety steps leading up to the front porch of the wooden hut that had once been Delphine's home. Francis, as Delphine was now quite used to calling him, had lit two more cigarettes, one for himself and one, now, for Delphine. They sat side by side, smoking in silence, each in their own private thoughts. Their hands, arms, faces and clothes were smeared with dust and earth, but so dry had been the summer this would quickly brush away.

"Thank you," she said at last.

He smiled thinly.

"I don't know what I should have done if you'd not been still here."

"Someone would have come."

"Perhaps."

They became quiet once more. Delphine drew deeply on her cigarette. She was not a routine smoker, but appreciated the sense of calm the tobacco spread through her, though her hands, she noticed, were still shaking.

"I could have managed to dig the graves," she said, "but not to carry the bodies."

Francis said nothing. The nightmarish unreality of what she had told him, and then asked him to do to help her, was already starting to evaporate in the wreaths of smoke drifting above their heads.

She had torn two strips of cloth she had found lying about. "Tie this around your face," she'd said, and he'd obeyed without a second thought. These were not the first dead bodies, he'd seen. An old man had died while he had been interned at Knockaloe. Someone had found him sitting on a rock overlooking the Irish Sea, holding a carved toy wooden boat in his hands. They'd thought at first he was sleeping and had tried to wake him. Then they'd realised. Francis had been commandeered by one of the guards to help carry the old man back to the Camp on a stretcher. But he'd been covered with a blanket, and so Francis had seen very little of him. This had been very different. There was no mistaking the irrefutable deadness of Delphine's parents, their bodies so delicately but irredeemably locked together. His first thought, he was ashamed to confess, had been whether they were still infectious. Delphine assured him that she did not think so. She was extraordinarily calm, he noted, given what had happened. She was, and had always been, a practical person. She knew what had to be done, but physically she could not manage to carry this out without the helping hand of a second person.

She had stood at the foot of the bed, looking down on where her parents lay, turned back to Francis and said, "Don't worry. I'm not asking you to lift the bodies. Or touch them even. I don't want to separate them."

"Do you want me to fetch an undertaker? Or a priest? Or stay here while you do so?" He was looking distinctly nonplussed and not a little green. Suddenly, he clutched the piece of cloth even closer to his mouth. "Forgive me," he had said, and then rushed from the room.

Delphine heard him retching outside and waited while he composed himself before joining him on the porch.

"I'm sorry to ask this of you. I'm not thinking straight."

"Please. I understand. This must have been an enormous shock."

"Thank you. Let's sit here for a while, and let me try to explain what needs to be done."

They sat on the step and he waited for her to begin.

"I told you on the ferry that my father is – or, rather, was – a Sioux Indian."

"Yes. I remember."

"Lakota tradition instructs that when a person dies, he must be left untouched for a day…"

"But…?

"…to give his spirit time to leave the body."

Francis nodded.

"Then he must be buried, as close to where his body was found as possible, unless that was within a further day's journey from his home. I don't believe they've been dead for more than two days, judging from the…" Her voice was beginning to tremble. "…lack of decomposition."

Francis looked away.

"He would want them to be buried according to tradition, and so what I'm proposing is… that we bury them just there," she said, and pointed towards a tree about ten yards away from the hut.

Francis again said nothing. He found that his mouth was terribly dry.

"What I'd like you to do please," Delphine continued, "is help me to drag the bed they're lying on over to that spot." She spoke slowly, deliberately, as if by naming each separate task dispassionately, she might lessen the enormity of what she was suggesting. "Then we shall need to dig a hole deep enough and wide enough for them to be lowered into. And then cover them over with the freshly dug earth." She looked at him directly, her face devoid of all ornamentation. "Please."

Francis stood up. "Yes," he said. "But I suggest we dig the grave first. I assume they had spades?"

Delphine fetched them one each, and for the next two hours they dug wordlessly. The alder tree beneath which the bodies were to be laid offered a welcome shade, and they worked as quickly as the dry, baked earth allowed them to.

Eventually, when they decided they had dug deeply enough, Delphine handed her spade to Francis. "Wait here," she said and walked off in the direction of one of the many small outbuildings clustered around the main hut. A few moments later she came back with two thick coils of rope.

Francis nodded and followed her back towards the house, re-tying the cloth around his face. They found three old railway sleepers, which they lay across the steps leading from the porch down to the ground below. They tied a length of rope to each of the legs of the bed and then, with agonising slowness, they proceeded to drag it, inch by painful inch. They slid it precariously down the three sleepers, then hauled it across the hard earth towards the open grave. Once there, they transferred the three sleepers to form a shallow ramp for the bed to slide down into it.

They then stood side by side looking down. Francis delicately retreated back towards the hut, leaving Delphine some time to be alone. She looked for the last time upon them. Their locked embrace had survived this last journey, and this is how she would remember them for ever afterwards, the two of them as one in death, as they had been in life.

At last she turned away, walked briskly back towards the hut, stepping past Francis and going inside, from where she returned with a thick blanket Old Moon had habitually wrapped himself in during his long night time vigils by the fire, which she delicately placed over the bodies of her parents.

"I can manage by myself now," she said, beginning to shovel the earth back into the grave. "Thank you."

Francis walked back towards her, picked up the second spade and, without saying a word, loaded it with more earth.

Now they had finished. They sat back on the rickety steps and smoked their cigarettes.

"Will you be all right?" he said after several minutes.

She nodded.

"What will you do?"

"I'll stay the night," she said, "sort out the house."

"Do you want me to stay and help?"

She shook her head. "No. I'd rather do it by myself. Thank you. You've done so much. But I'd like some time alone now, I think."

"Yes," he said. "I can understand that." He stood up and began dusting himself down.

"Where will you go?"

"I'll just keep following those telegraph poles," he said, then tapped the side of his nose. "I have a plan."

She stood up and faced him. "I've shaken your hand and wished you luck once already today. May I do so again?"

"Of course," he said, as he took her offered hand.

They held each other's gaze a moment longer, and then he put his jacket back on, turned and walked quickly away. When he reached the bottom of the slope, he stopped, looked back towards her, gave a short wave, before setting off once more in the direction of Manchester, whose distant factories and smoking chimneys added an even redder glow to the evening sunset.

Delphine sat for a long time on the steps after Francis had gone, looking down the short hill towards the Ship Canal, watching the light dancing on the water. It reminded her so keenly of so many similar nights she'd spent there as a child. In the past ten years she'd not been back more than once or twice a year, and after this night she would not, she realised, be returning again.

She felt suddenly exhausted. Her arms and legs were stiff and heavy with all the exertions of the day, and the realisation that both her parents were dead, at a single stroke, was just finally beginning to dawn. She was shivering. Delayed shock, she supposed, and she began to cry. She had been so happy when she set off to see them at the start of the day, excited to be sharing her news with them of her new position at the University. They may not have fully understood the nature of what she did, but they were always so pleased and proud of her achievements, especially her mother, who knew that what her daughter now did for her work had been influenced by her own condition. Inspired is how Delphine would have described it. Her mother's isolation had been so acute but, as far as she had been able to tell, had not appeared to distress her at all. It was a fact she simply accepted, along with being orphaned from when she was still only a child. Communication was never easy for her, especially when it came to relating things that may have happened in the past, even with the unique system of signing which she and her father had developed between them, and which Delphine had picked up before she had learned to talk herself, and so she knew next to nothing about that time before she met Sammy, only what her father had told her, and he was not a man for talking. He told her about how she visited him and Moon and the others when they were near to starving one winter, how she would come in the nights and leave tiny gifts – a pair of rabbits, an eel and some fish, a pigeon – but that they never saw her. They thought she must be a spirit, some kind of angel sent to watch over them, and then, just at dawn one morning, Sammy had seen her carefully carrying a nest of eggs, creeping barefoot in the snow, before she seemed to disappear right in front of him, and so he had been convinced that, yes indeed, she truly must be a spirit. Her mother would smile secretly at her when Sammy told this story, widening her eyes, but when Sammy told her how they met a second time, her expression would grow serious, and her gaze would be fixed entirely upon him. He was paddling out of The Delph, he would say, it was still dark, and the moon was shining on the water, lighting his way back to the Camp. He went to check the nets, as he did every night when he got back, and on this particular night, caught in the mouth of one of them, was an otter. Her eyes were your mother's, he'd say to Delphine, and Eve would shake her head. She leapt into the river pulling Sammy in after her. He almost drowned trying to keep hold of her, as she dived deep beneath the surface of the river, until finally, gasping for air, he leapt against the current over the weir – "like a salmon," Eve signed, laughing – and landed on the shore, his arms flapping like a beached trout. "Your mother's a selkie," he would say, "she brought me back to life…"

And now they were both dead. Delphine had never really believed that tale, not even when she was a child, but she never tired of hearing it. Hers had been a childhood like no other when she compared it to those of the other children in her school at Our Lady of Lourdes. She and Sammy and Eve and Old Moon had lived out of time, like lost babes in the woods. She had thought little of it at the time, having known nothing else. Now, she understood it had been special, unique, priceless beyond measure, and now, it was over, and she missed it. The pain she felt was so strong she thought it might never leave her. She did not think she wanted it to.

She knew what she would do. She wiped her face with the back of her hand, not at all caring how she must look, stood up and tried to shake the stiffness from her limbs. She would light a fire, and she began collecting twigs to get it started. She knew there would be a stack of cut logs piled in one of the outbuildings, and sure enough there was. Soon the fire had taken hold and flames rose up to the darkening sky overhead. She listened to all those remembered childhood sounds of rooks settling in the alders, of foxes barking in the wood, of wood cracking in the heat, and closed her eyes. Mixed in with these familiar, comforting noises drifted the lonely wailing of a ship's siren, passing along the Canal below. It reminded her of another sound, one she thought she had forgotten, the haunting, eerie boom from Bittern Wood. They were all of them, she felt, singing farewell to her parents. She tried to conjure up Old Moon as she sat there, searching for those old ancestral words.

"*E – ah – kah – di – wah – da – ho*
E – lo – hi – wakan – ho
E – ah – kah – di – wah – da – ho
E – lo – hi – wakan – ho…"

She woke with a jolt while it was still dark. The eastern sky was just beginning to show the faintest traces of white against the black. The moon was waning and the stars arched clear and bright.

She was gripped with a sudden certainty of what she must now do. She found an unlit branch, plucked a handful of dry grass, which she attached to the branch with a mixture of sap from dandelion leaves and her own spit. Then she walked through every room of the hut, followed by all of the different outbuildings that made up the settlement, searching for any keepsakes. As she suspected, there was very little to be salvaged – the net which had captured the otter, the nest which had carried the eggs – and nothing else. She missed the board on which Eve had painted Halley's Comet, but she spotted the jars stored at the back of the woodshed. They were large demijohns, almost fifty of them, but instead of wine or beer, they held coins, pennies, saved from the fares of passengers who they'd ferried across the Canal for more than twenty years. Her parents had little need for money, preferring instead to barter and trade, living off the earth, but Delphine had no idea that they had accumulated so much. At a conservative estimate she calculated there must be more than two hundred pounds in these jars, more than twice her own annual salary as a teacher. She thought of all the little luxuries some of these pennies might have bought to make their lives easier, but knew that that was simply not their way.

Well – she knew where it now might do some good. She did not need it for herself. Her salary at the

University would be ample for her own needs, but *The Manchester Institution for the Deaf* – just imagine the equipment and materials this amount of money could furnish it with. She resolved she would return and collect it somehow, but for now she needed to keep it safe. And so, for the second time in less than twenty-four hours, she found herself digging a pit, on this occasion by moonlight, where before it had been in the fierce heat of the sun. She covered the mound with some of the logs from the woodpile. Nobody would find them, of that she was certain.

Now there was one final thing remaining to be done. She placed the net and the nest inside the starvationer canoe, which she dragged away from the rest of the buildings. Another Lakota funeral rite, one which she had not described to Francis, was that, after the bodies had been buried, it was often the custom to burn the place where the person had last lived, together with all their belongings, to help them on their journey to the spirit world. It was not that Delphine believed any of this. She definitely didn't. The war had banished any faith she might once have had. But she knew it was what Old Moon would have done quite naturally, and she felt instinctively it was what her parents would have wished.

She lit another branch and carried it across to the main hut. It did not take long for a fire to catch. Her parents' home had been a tinder box, and within a matter of minutes the conflagration was huge, with flames rising high into the sky, consuming the buildings like greedy snakes. And just as quickly it died away again. By the time dawn crept across the sky, all that remained of the settlement was a smouldering skeleton of charred and bleached bones, which would soon be sucked back into the earth and reclaimed.

Francis followed the line of telegraph poles which tramped across the land for the next two hours after he had said goodbye to Delphine.

It had been a shattering experience, and the walk was helping to settle his nerves once more. There was no doubt that an unexpected encounter with death threw things into perspective. He was more determined than ever to make up for the lost years of his internment. Time had passed so slowly in the Camp, even more so once the war ended, followed by all the endless prevarications over the decision to allow him to return to England and to Manchester. Now, as he walked across the fields between the various towns and villages strung together by the telegraph wires and the remorseless spread of the city, he speculated over the relativity of distance, speed and time. When his father had been the age Francis was now, the fastest one could travel was contingent upon the speed of a horse on land, or a ship across water. But the last few years had brought automobiles, aeroplanes and now these telegraph wires. The world was getting smaller. Louis Bleriot flew across the Channel in just fifty minutes, and Francis could send a message by telegraph from Manchester, which could be received in Glasgow less than fifteen minutes later.

The ship's captain, when he handed Francis the telegram with the news that his father had died, talked to him enthusiastically about Guglielmo Marconi, the electrical engineer who had sent the first long distance telegram when he alerted the world about the sinking of the *Titanic*.

"Radio," said the ship's captain, "that's the coming thing. You mark my words…"

This made an immediate impression upon Franz Halsinger, and he decided then and there to change his own name, reinvent himself, look to the future, not to the past. Franz Halsinger would become Francis Hall, and he would open premises which specialised in the latest technical innovations – photography, telegraphy, radio – which he would call Hall & Singer. When people asked him who or where Mr Singer was, he'd narrow his eyes cryptically and drop a casual remark about "a sleeping partner". The thought of this made Francis smile as he continued his journey. A sleeping partner indeed, a nod to his relinquished ancestry, which had unjustly led to the loss of these last four years, the bitterness of which would now spur him forwards into the future, singing in the humming wires overhead.

"He who owns the air waves, owns the message," he repeated to himself as he placed one foot in front of the other, a phrase that would become his mantra, guiding him as surely as the evening star, towards an as yet unknown destination.

When he reached a junction at the small town of Flixton, where the telegraph poles divided, following two directions, he reached inside his jacket pocket, pulled out a coin and tossed it. Heads or tails. If heads, he'd go left; if tails, right. Tails. He turned at once to the right, whistling as he marched along.

He walked all night.

By dawn, just as Delphine was discovering the demijohns of pennies at the back of the woodstore, Francis arrived in Denton. He strode down Hyde Road past a row of shops, which were all still closed. Above them, grocers and bakers, ironmongers and pawnbrokers lay fast asleep. Only he, Francis Hall, was wide awake. Opposite him stood a jeweller's – or, to be more precise, a jeweller's, optician's and engravers. It was, he noticed, with timely satisfaction, for sale. He smiled. He recognised a kindred spirit, someone who had seen the need for diversification, for moving with the times, for responding to the changing tastes of customers' needs. He, Francis – how he liked the sound of this new name as he continued to roll it around his tongue – he also would diversify, but he would not merely move with the times, he would shape them. He would not simply respond to changes in taste and need, he would define them.

He looked up. Above the shop's Gothic-scripted sign was a large pair of round, rimless spectacles. He was delighted by them. All-seeing eyes staring out across the city into the future. He would keep them. First thing Monday morning, he would be knocking on the door of the property agents handling the sale.

It was still early. The first rays of the sun were already beginning to warm the day. Delphine placed the net and the carefully wrapped nest into the prow of the starvationer. She sat inside it and pushed off from the shore with the oar and began to paddle.

She caught a glimpse of herself reflected in the surface of the water and hardly recognised who she saw. What a difference a single day had made. The extreme physical and emotional exertions of the previous day, coupled with the fires, had turned her into something resembling a pirate, an outlaw, a highwaywoman, or, perhaps, a Sioux warrior, for that is how she felt, rather than someone who was about to join a new academic team at the University of Manchester. Her clothes, which had been one of her best outfits, were now dishevelled and torn. She had ripped the hem of her skirt to stop it from trailing further in the dirt and, to risk the chance of it tripping her up, she had looped it between her legs and tucked it into her waist band. She had discarded her jacket, now rolled up and stowed at the back of the canoe, and she had undone the top two buttons of her blouse, as well as rolling up the sleeves, so that it was now more like a man's work shirt. Her hair, which had become completely unpinned and fallen loosely onto her shoulders, she had tied back in a kind of turban with the strip of cloth she had used to cover her face the previous day when in close proximity to the bodies of her parents. She had cast off her shoes and stockings, so that she could enjoy the feeling of the warm air over her bare legs and feet which, like her arms, bore the marks of the events of the last day. But these were but superficial compared to the deeply etched lines of sorrow smeared across her cheeks and brow, like war paint.

She had grown up by water, and although it had been several years since she had last paddled a canoe, her muscles retained the memory of what she must do. She passed a heron at the Canal's edge, which took off in that slow, uncertain, cumbersome way they had, before gaining height with sure, slow, strong wing beats, while she too found her rhythm and began to plough the water with increased confidence, each long pull through of the oar recalling a remembrance of times past, propelling her towards where she knew she must go next.

She reckoned it was approximately five miles to her first port of call, the Barton Swing Aqueduct, where the wide sluggish waters of the Manchester Ship Canal passed beneath the older, narrower passage of the Bridgewater. At her current rate of progress, she thought she should reach that in a little over two hours.

She rowed through the centre of the channel when she could, enjoying the freedom of the open water. It being a Sunday, there was less traffic than would have been the case on a week day, but she still had to be watchful to steer clear of the coal barges plying up and down, and the occasional large liner making its unstoppable way towards the Port of Manchester. She would hug the shoreline whenever one of these leviathans approached, careful not to be tipped by the surge of their wake, for the starvationer was a narrow vessel, not designed for such open water and easily capsized. The effort and concentration required to reach the Barton Bridges took her mind momentarily away from her grief.

She passed beneath the Cadishead Railway Viaduct, where just yesterday she had skipped down in such high spirits, before navigating her way through the cross currents where the Canal stopped sharing its course with the Mersey, which flowed off towards the meadows of Flixton, until she reached the Irlam Locks. These were manually operated by a series of stone sluices, which powered mechanically driven vertical sets of steel roller gates, supported by masonry piers, designed to maintain a continuous water flow along the Canal's length. Delphine was anxious that the increased turbulence caused by the sluices might sink her, and so she was forced to lift the canoe onto the bank and drag it along the tow path until she had passed the locks completely. One of the gate keepers saw her struggling with it and offered his assistance, which she gratefully accepted, relieved that, while he may have looked at her curiously, he asked her no questions. He must have seen far stranger sights than me, she thought, as she resumed paddling, once she was clear of the locks.

But in less than half a mile, she had to repeat the entire process again in order to negotiate the Barton Locks system. It was more crowded here, and she was attracting more attention. She could sense the eyes of the men upon her bare legs, but there was nothing for it. She had reached her first port of call. If she was to achieve the mission she had set herself, she would have to withstand their stares. She untucked her skirt from its waist band and let its folds unfurl and fall back towards her feet, covering her calves at least. She put on her shoes and walked towards them.

It was Yasser she had come to see. It was his help she was seeking. But she did not know where he lived, only that it was near the Barton Bridge. She gambled he would be sufficiently well known for her to receive directions, and her gamble proved correct. At the mere mention of his name, all their dark looks and mutterings dissolved into broad smiles and immediate offers of help.

"Yasser? Of course..."

"Why didn't you say so...?

"Any friend of Yasser's..."

"Follow this road here...

"Take the first right..."

"Number sixty-four..."

"We'll look after your boat till you come back..."

"Look, boys. It's a starvationer..."

"I've not seen one of these in years..."

"How did you come by it...?"

"Don't worry – it'll be safe here..."

She thanked them profusely and followed their directions. It was just after ten o'clock and the streets were quite busy with families on their way to Chapel or to Church, dressed in their Sunday clothes. As she approached them, one or two of the older gentlemen bid her "good morning" and touched their hats, but most averted their gaze, steering a wide berth.

She reached Yasser's house in a little under ten

minutes, but now that she stood before its front door, a doubt crept over her. She had not seen him since before she left for Sedgeley Park, more than a dozen years ago. Would he still remember her? And even if he did, would he be able to help her? Would he think her idea was foolish?

She raised her hand to the brass knocker and knocked twice upon it. It was quieter here, and the sound of it echoed startlingly. She waited nervously. She heard footsteps approaching the door, but it was Rose, not Yasser, who opened it.

"Can I help you?"

"Rose?"

"Yes?"

"You... don't recognise me, do you?"

"I'm sorry, but no, I don't." Rose looked at this dishevelled young woman, stammering on her doorstep with some concern.

"I'm Delphine... Sammy's daughter."

"Delphine! Yes! Now I can see it's you. Come in, come in. Yasser? Delphine's here. Sammy's girl. Come on through. What on earth's the matter? You look like you've been dragged through a hedge backwards. I'm sorry, but it's true. You look a real fright. What's brought you here?"

And then everything happened at once. Rose took hold of her and led her down the hallway into the kitchen, where Yasser, still wearing only a vest and trousers, was bringing in a sack of potatoes from the yard at the back which, when he saw Delphine, he dropped on the table and gave her an enormous hug, lifting her into the air.

"Put her down," said Rose, "and go and put a shirt on."

"Delphine doesn't mind, do you, Delphine?"

"Ignore him. Now you sit down while I put the kettle on."

Then a young man walked in. "Hey, Ma – what's all the noise? Oh hello?" he said, spotting Delphine.

"This is Sammy's girl," said Yasser. "You remember me telling you about Sammy, don't you, Jaz?"

"Yes, yes. I remember. Pleased to meet you."

"Our son," said Rose over her shoulder. "Hejaz."

"But I prefer Jaz."

"And today we are celebrating," boomed Yasser, fastening up the last buttons on his shirt with his big, clumsy fingers, so that one of them flew off and landed on the floor by Rose's feet.

"What am I going to do with you?" she tutted, picking it up and placing it in a drawer.

Yasser continued unperturbed. "Our son has a new job. Draughtsman at Metro-Vickers." He beamed widely.

"Congratulations," said Delphine to Jaz.

"Thank you."

"He starts tomorrow. So today we celebrate. Proper Sunday dinner." Yasser stepped back out into the yard and promptly returned with a freshly killed chicken, which he placed onto the table next to the potatoes. "And you must join us," he commanded, at which point Delphine began to cry and, to her eternal embarrassment, once she had started, she could not stop.

An hour later everything was resolved.

Rose had ordered Yasser and Jaz out of the kitchen, Delphine had managed to explain all that had happened in the past twenty-four hours, and she nervously outlined her plan of what she wanted to do next.

Yasser's response had been immediate and unequivocal. "Anything," he said to her. "Anything at all. You only need to ask and Yasser will see that it's done. Your father saved my life. Everything I have," he said, looking around him at Rose and Hejaz, "I owe it to him."

Delphine bowed her head.

"You need to get started then," said Rose, "if you're to be back before it gets dark."

"Yes," said Yasser. "We go at once."

"And you must stay the night," added Rose. "We shall have our dinner when you get back." Delphine opened her mouth to protest. "Not another word," said Rose. "Now go."

Delphine walked back to the Barton Locks with Yasser, where the men, good as their word, were waiting for them.

"The boat is here," said one of them as they approached. "No one has touched her."

"Good," said Yasser, and he had a brief word in the ear of another of them, which Delphine could not hear.

"I'll see to it, Yasser," said this second man and

immediately went on his way.

Yasser picked up the starvationer as if it were a toy, then turned to Delphine. "Follow me."

He led her through the labyrinth of the lock gates back towards the Ship Canal, whose tow path they followed for about a hundred yards, before taking a steep flight of stone steps up towards the aqueduct, which carried the Bridgewater Canal. When they reached the top, Yasser turned to Delphine and said, "I build this. Your father – he help me."

Delphine nodded. They paused a few moments. Yasser was clearly remembering those times.

"Now," he said, pointing away from the aqueduct, "your path is this way, away from the Ship Canal. You will come to a lighthouse. On your right. Then you go under an iron footbridge. Soon you reach Worsley. Very pretty. At Worsley there is a junction. Go right. Take the short loop. This leads to The Delph. Two miles in all. At most two and a half. Should take you an hour. Perhaps a little more. Then you will need time. For yourself. For your parents. Another hour. Someone will be waiting for you. He'll say, 'Yasser send me'. Bring you home."

Delphine took Yasser's hand. "Thank you."

He steadied the canoe and she stepped in.

"God speed," he called, as he gave her a strong, firm push, and she was away.

The Bridgewater Canal was much narrower, much quieter than the Ship Canal had been. Before long she passed the Lighthouse, as Yasser had said, and then the iron footbridge. The canal bent slowly to the right as it neared Worsley, which was indeed pretty. The banks were much greener. Willow trees hung gracefully down towards the banks. Swifts dived and swooped all around her, feeding on insects. Dragon flies hovered near the surface of the water, beating their wings so quickly they were almost invisible, barely a blur, before darting away.

She reached the junction and took the right fork as Yasser had directed, and in a few hundred yards, she saw it, a low brick arch emerging from the undergrowth on her left. She slowed the starvationer almost to a stop and manoeuvred it delicately into position, so that she was facing the arch directly.

This was The Delph.

The entrance to the Navigable Levels. The more than fifty miles of underground waterways dug out by hand over the centuries, one above the other, which her father had rowed every single yard of thirty-five years ago. From where, one moonlit night, he had emerged to follow an otter, a selkie, with eyes the colour and shape of her mother's, out along this stretch of water where now she, Delphine, hovered. The Delph. After which she'd been named.

She peered now into that impenetrable darkness and knew what she had to do. The water stretched ahead of her and out of sight. Like the entrance to the Underworld. She placed her left hand against the low inside wall of the arch – it was cool and damp – while with her right hand she lowered the oar to see how deep the water was beneath her. It struck earth less than three feet below the canoe. It felt firm. There was nothing else for it. There was no bank nearby from where she might stretch across. She reached inside the prow of the starvationer and took out the delicate bird's nest, which she carefully balanced on the top of her head. She placed the oar alongside her inside the craft, drew her knees up towards her, swung herself slowly to one side, breathed in deeply, then lowered herself into the water, steadying herself with her right hand against the side of the boat, while her left hand held onto the nest on her head. It was icily cold beneath the arch, as if the sun never quite reached here, making her legs feel instantly numb. The earth on the bottom of the canal remained firm and held her weight. She worked her way round towards the starvationer's stern and placed the nest on the narrow flat section at the rear. She checked that the net and oar were safely stowed inside, and then she paused. She shut her eyes, focusing all of her thoughts on these last few moments where she felt in close physical contact still with her parents. Then she opened them. With a single determined push, she propelled the starvationer deep into the tunnels of the Navigable Levels, retrieving the bird's nest just before it passed out of reach, watching till the Stygian darkness swallowed up the narrow canoe for ever, reclaiming it for its own. She listened to the slosh and slap of the water lapping against the brick walls inside made by the starvationer on this, its final voyage. She waited and listened, till she heard it no more.

She waited several minutes more until the cold had

spread through her entire body, forcing her to bring her vigil to its end. She waded slowly towards the shore, still carrying the nest in front of her. Then she heaved herself out of the water. She sat on the bank, shivering. It was done.

Bees droned unseen in the grass beside her. A rat passed just a few feet away, taking no note of her, as it scurried purposefully in search of its next meal. She heard a blackbird singing. It was perched on the top of the low arch marking the entrance to The Delph, where, a few moments before, she had been standing. She watched it scoot low across the ground and land a few feet away from her. It bobbed its head up and down, then hopped a little closer to her. Deciding it was safe to stay, it began to study the grass around its feet. With a sudden, darting lunge, it swooped down and tugged a worm from the earth, which wriggled and squirmed in the bird's yellow beak.

Delphine watched all this with a detachment that surprised her. The sun was beginning to sink in the sky. But it would rise again tomorrow.

"Excuse me, Miss. Are you Delphine? I am Asif. Yasser sends me."

Delphine roused herself from her reverie and turned in the direction of the voice. A man was walking towards her, looking at her somewhat nervously. As well he might, thought Delphine, for she was still wet and shaking from her minutes spent in the water.

"I come to take you back," he said.

"Yes. Thank you."

He stretched out a hand to help her to her feet, which she gratefully accepted. She followed him up the slope of the embankment to where a cart was waiting. It was a kind of rulley, the sort of multi-purpose wagon that might have been used for transporting sacks of coal or flour, and probably was. Delphine could see a patina of coal dust and flour grains on the surface of the cart. Another man, with his back towards her, was arranging a few of the sacks to act as a seat and back rest for her, while the horse, an old brown mare, was contentedly chewing grass as she waited. The man turned round and Delphine was surprised – and pleased – to see that it was Hejaz.

"Here," he said. "Let me help you aboard."

"I'm fine," she said. "I can manage. I used to climb trees all the time when I was a child." She placed her hands on the top of the cart, put one foot on the central hub of the back wheel, and pulled herself up, showering Hejaz with water as she did so.

"I'm sorry," she said. "I feel like a wet dog, shaking myself dry."

"You're soaked," remarked Hejaz with some concern. "What happened? Did you fall in?"

"Not fall – jumped."

Hejaz was silent. "Did you… do what you came here for?" he asked quietly after a few moments.

"Yes," she nodded. "It's all done now."

"Then we'd best be on our way. Asif?"

Asif climbed up onto the front of the cart, picked up the reins and, with a click of his tongue, the old brown mare set off down the path by the side of the canal.

"I brought this," said Hejaz, holding up a blanket. "It's not the cleanest, but it's dry. I think you should wrap it around you – keep yourself warm. It'll take about three quarters of an hour for us to get back home by road."

"Thank you." She reached out towards the blanket, just as he was handing it over, so that her own hands accidentally clasped his. His cheeks reddened and he began to cough, forcing him to move further away down the cart.

"It's very good of you to come and meet me like this," she said, after his coughing had subsided.

"I was concerned. We all of us were. It's a terrible thing that's happened. My father's very upset."

"I didn't know that Sammy had…"

"Saved his life?"

"No. He never said."

"My father never speaks of it either."

"And you, Hejaz…"

"Jaz – please."

"Jaz… you have not long returned from the war?"

"Yes."

And I imagine that you never speak of that either, thought Delphine. All these things which are not spoken of, simply locked away inside of us, it cannot be good, she reflected. She thought of the children she taught, imprisoned within their walls of silence. And then she thought of her mother. She had seemed happy enough, but who could really tell what was truly going on inside her head? Now she would never know. She remembered only how alive her eyes were, darting constantly, making sure they never missed a thing, a myriad of emotions flickering across them in an instant, like a butterfly dancing on wild flowers in sunlight. By contrast Jaz's face was a cloud of shadows.

"Where did you serve?" she asked him tentatively.

"Aden," he said dully.

"Oh... that must have been... awkward, I imagine?

"Yes," he said, "it was," but he didn't elaborate.

"Congratulations on your job," she ventured, after a further pause. "I'm sorry I've delayed your celebratory dinner."

"It's only a clerk," he said. "Nothing to celebrate."

"Look upon it as a start perhaps."

"Yes." He did not seem too convinced, and they continued once more in silence.

Sammy and Eve had had no expectations of Delphine at all, and so she could never be a disappointment to them. She sensed just how keenly Jaz needed his father's approval.

"Your father's immensely proud of you," she said.

Jaz said nothing. No matter what he did, or what his father said to him by way of praise, he felt he would never fully deserve it, a pale shadow next to Yasser's blaze of light.

When they finally got back, it was dark and Delphine was cold, in spite of the blanket. Her teeth were chattering as she thanked Asif, who nodded and drove off without a word. Rose was waiting at the door.

"Come in at once," she said, putting her arms around her. I've heated some water. Take off those wet things and have a long hot soak. Yasser's lit a fire and brought the bath into the back room in front of it. I've put a towel and a change of clothes in there ready for you. And before you say anything, it's no trouble. Don't argue." She steered Delphine directly in front of the fire, while she brought in kettles and pans of hot water from the kitchen.

Half an hour later Delphine was wrapped in a towel in front of the fire, feeling warm and sleepy. There was a gentle knock on the door. Rose popped her head round.

"Can I come in?"

"Please do."

"Is that better?"

"Immeasurably. I can't thank you enough, all of you, for all you have done for me today. I turned up out of the blue, standing on your doorstep like some wild scarecrow, and you rescued me."

"We're happy to have helped, but just so sad to hear what happened. You were incredibly brave, doing all that you did."

"It didn't feel brave at the time. It was what had to be done. I couldn't have managed without the help of Francis."

"He sounds an interesting man," said Rose, with a hint of mischief in her eyes.

"He's ten years younger than me."

"Even more interesting," laughed Rose.

"Stop it," said Delphine. "Anyway, he struck me as the kind of man who's not interested in women."

"Oh…"

They each sat on the sofa, staring into the fire.

"Did you," said Rose at last, "manage to do what you had to do out at The Delph?"

Delphine nodded. "It seemed... I don't know... fitting..."

Rose's eye was caught by the bird's nest, which Delphine had placed on the sideboard. "What's that?" she asked.

Delphine explained.

"That's a beautiful keepsake. Is it the only thing you've kept?" asked Rose.

"It's enough. They had so little."

"They had you," said Rose, and she gently held her to her. "And now, I think it's time you went to bed. You must be exhausted."

"I'm sorry about your celebration dinner."

"Don't worry about it. There'll be other times."

"It was very good of Jaz to come and meet me like that. Did Yasser ask him to?"

"No. It was his own idea."

"It was very kind."

"He *is* kind," said Rose, "always thinking of others."

Delphine stood up, stretched and yawned. "Does he have a young lady?"

Rose smiled. "Not yet."

"I can't think why not."

"And what about you? Do you have a young man?"

Delphine shook her head. "I have my work," she said.

The next morning Delphine prepared to leave, to make her way back to Seymour Park. Mrs Snook would have been concerned that she had not returned the previous evening.

"Thank you again," she said. "For everything."

"Is nothing," said Yasser. "Anything. Any time. Just ask."

"Well," said Delphine, "if you're sure. There is one other thing…"

She told him about the buried jars filled with pennies and her wish to donate them to *The Manchester Institution for the Deaf.*

"Leave this with me," said Yasser. "There are bargemen I know, who owe me favours. I meet you at Bob's Lane. Next Saturday at noon."

Yasser was as good as his word. A week later Delphine stood on the jetty at Bob's Lane, having retraced her steps by train to Cadishead that morning, watching a coal barge steam its way towards her, with Yasser waving from the foredeck.

She had wondered how she might react to being back at the scene so soon after she had buried her parents, but she felt surprisingly calm. It was as if the rituals of burning their settlement and returning the starvationer to The Delph in accordance with their traditions had been a kind of cleansing for her. She felt empty, numb, but pleased to be carrying out this final act.

The barge moored up to the jetty. They passed the

raised mound of earth, which marked the grave of her parents. Yasser stood by it in silence, head bowed, for several seconds, before rejoining Delphine. She showed him where the demijohns had been buried, and he and the bargemen set to at once with unearthing them and carrying them aboard. With a minimum of fuss, as soon as this was completed, they turned around and began to chug their way back towards the Pomona Docks, which was the closest landing point to the school. Delphine stood at the stern, looking back, till the jetty at Bob's Lane could no longer be seen, and then joined Yasser further along the deck.

"Asif will be waiting for us with his cart. He will drive you across the bridge to the school."

"Thank you again."

Yasser nodded. He was quieter than usual, and this quietness grew stronger the closer they got to Pomona. When they arrived, he helped Delphine down onto the dock.

"Come," he said, "I show you something."

He led her quickly to Dock Number 3, where the Pomona Lock connected the Manchester Ship Canal to the Bridgewater, close to the Trafford Park Road Swing Bridge. He pointed.

"This was where your father rescued me," he said. "Before all this was built. The explosion...." He paused, then turned back towards her. "I thought you should see it."

Delphine nodded. She stood quietly, looking out over the scene. Cranes were unloading goods from one of the great ships the Canal had brought here in huge nets, which passed over their heads before being emptied directly into the wagons of goods trains, hissing with steam, ready to be transported across the city. Stevedores from Africa, Arabia and Asia, from Russia, Poland and Italy, as well as England, Wales and Ireland were climbing ladders, wheeling carts, lifting sacks, running up ramps, down in the holds and up on the gantries, shouting in several languages simultaneously. This was Yasser's world. He was at home here, just as surely as she was not, and it was the actions of her father, rescuing him from the rubble all those years ago, which had made that possible. She looked again at the tumult of movement all around her and began to see pattern and order. She listened more closely to the cacophonous babble and began to hear music and concord.

"I take you to Asif now," he said.

They embraced warmly before Yasser departed abruptly. Within seconds she lost sight of him, swallowed up by the seething swirl of Pomona's Docks.

Two days later Delphine woke early and excited. She flung back the curtains in her new flat on Upper Brook Street and an impatient sun streamed through the windows. She had still not finished unpacking. Her clothes had not been hung up, her cups and plates not yet put in cupboards, her cutlery not in drawers, but she did not mind. There would be plenty of time for all of that. Only the bird's nest had found its place, on the mantel above the hearth. The rest could wait.

She settled a bunch of bright tulips in a vase on the table, the single indulgence she'd permitted herself, and smiled. She collected her briefcase, checked her hat in the hall mirror, opened the front door and stepped purposefully across the threshold, out into the morning. The University Audiology Department was just a five minute walk away. The sounds of the city were waiting to accompany her. As if an unseen conductor had raised his baton, she began to walk, her footsteps finding a rhythm to match the pulse of the times, rising up to greet her from the earth.

18

1932

Tommy Thunder stands outside the gates to Belle Vue. The sun has set and a green moon hangs low in the sky. People are beginning to leave. A sudden surge of angry, shouting men in black shirts thrust him to one side, baying like wounded dogs, closely pursued by another pack, many coloured, their faces shining, taunting the blackshirts, who skulk away along the Hyde Road.

It is fifty years since Tommy has last stood here, when he and Catch, Sammy and Moon made their dash for freedom.

Now he had returned.

From time to time his nomadic wanderings would bring him in the vicinity, as he followed his yearly rounds, but he had never thought to visit again the scene of their escape, until tonight.

The lights are being switched off inside Belle Vue, one by one. The gates are locked and the park is plunged into darkness. He peers through the bars, remembering. He fancies he hears the cries of elephants, the howls of monkeys, the hooting of eagle owls.

It's time enough, he thinks.

Lately he's been waking up each morning with a damp chill in his bones, which even the warmest of suns seems unable to shake off. There's a permanent film across his eyes, so that it seems he views the world each day through a mist, a cloud, which never quite disperses. His coughs are deeper now, with a pain that wracks his chest.

It's time.

Yesterday he found himself below a brake of trees not far from here, which stirred a memory. It was not somewhere he visited regularly. More than a dozen winters had passed since he was last there, just after he'd returned from France and started up his wanderings again. Some men had dug up a section of road to mend a broken water main. It was as he passed the pit they'd dug that he was reminded of it, how he'd found a young woman who had crashed her bicycle and fallen into a similar hole. She'd broken her leg and he'd had to improvise a splint for her using a thigh bone she had found from an old skeleton unearthed by the trench diggings. He remembered how furious she'd been, not with her accident, but with the world. He'd admired that sense of fury and outrage, her tears of rage against the waste, as he'd carried her back to her home. He wondered what had become of her.

There were others like her too, who he'd encountered over the years, men and women and especially children, whose faces now were beginning to blur. His had been a solitary life for the most part, but one of his own choosing, a freedom bought dear at first, those early winter months beside the Irwell, before the gradual dawning that this was now his home, this sprawling city whose net spread wider than any Sammy might cast into the river, where he might slip between the cracks, disappear among its fringes, in the reeds among the shallows, carve himself a niche, find himself a sort of home, a looked-for visitor, returning with the seasons, like the great white egrets flying from the west across the moon.

And so, yesterday, when he passed the men mending the broken water pipe, he had looked down into the hole, and it had seemed to him as he watched them dig, that their bodies dissolved away, and he saw only bones, bones that were ready to go back to the earth and feed the soil, his bones.

Yes, it is time, he thinks.

He turns his back upon Belle Vue's locked gates and starts to walk, his last walk. He will walk, he tells himself, all through the night, through the next day, until he can walk no further, until he reaches his final resting place, where he might wait out the days. The thought of no longer wandering, staying in one place, suddenly appeals.

Over the years he has come to know all the highways and by-ways of the city, the hidden tracks between the factories, the foot bridges over the lock gates, the tunnels beneath the rivers and canals. He knows each stream and brook and tributary, each copse, each park, each private estate, where to trap eels, where to catch moles, where the waters are clean enough for trout still to be caught, where the wild hares run over the fields.

He decides to take a circuitous route. He will avoid the main thoroughfares and their press of people. Instead he will follow the margins where earth and water merge. He makes his way to the Medlock, following the route he took with Sammy, Catch and

Moon fifty years before. Much has changed since then, but Tommy has witnessed all those changes, watched them unfurl like lichen on stone, like rust on railings, like a caterpillar crawling from its egg. He feels the deep thrum of the mine workings from Bradford Colliery, which spread like steel-meshed spider webs beneath his feet. He follows the Medlock till he reaches London Road Station, where the river flows beneath the city's streets. Where Piccadilly meets Portland Street, he pauses beneath a street lamp outside *The Queen's Hotel*, "favoured of kings and princes", an advertisement reads, where, from inside, he hears a woman's voice singing songs that remind him of Clem. He listens, remembering, until an Italian commissionaire in red and gold livery requests him in no uncertain terms to move on.

He turns hurriedly into Little Lever Street. From there he follows the scum of the Rochdale Canal for half a mile, crossing and re-crossing it via its many footbridges, his boots clattering on the iron walkways from where he looks down through the rusting grilles to the jostle of coal barges below. At Ducie Bridge he delves into the warren of yards and cellars trapped within the stench of putrefaction from the tanneries down to where the River Irk flows, or rather, stagnates, its surface a thick crust of sludge from the effluents dumped there night and day. He sees eels grown sluggish and fat from the grease and oils emptied into it from the maze of mills and chemical works along its banks. He stoops low through the bricked up culverts alongside Victoria Station where the river finally slurps its way into the Irwell, which Tommy has made the object of this first part of his journey.

From here he means to retrace his footsteps all the way back to the Bittern Wood on the edge of the Worsley Old Hall estate. He does not know the current Earl of Ellesmere, the 4th, Lieutenant-Colonel John Francis Granville Scrope Egerton, the Viscount Brackley, Edward's older brother, who Tommy has never met. After the war, after what he did for Edward, Tommy no longer included the estate as part of his seasonal perambulations. The 3rd Earl had died, shortly after the war began, a few days after he had asked Tommy to go out to France to keep an eye on both his grandson and his horses. Once the war had ended, after he had helped Edward to die bravely, Tommy felt that he had kept his promise. It would have proved too painful to return.

Instead he moved from farm to farm, town to town, estate to estate, as the seasons turned and his various services were needed. He felt comfortable in his wandering, liked the pattern imposed by changing weather, enjoyed returning to remembered woods and streams, familiar fields and orchards, and seeing the same faces. Sometimes he'd simply set up camp on the edge of a settlement, light a fire, catch fish, shoot rabbits, and then sell what he didn't need for himself to local people, setting up on the steps of a market hall, or simply going from door to door. Such times reminded him of the early days, with Sammy, Catch and Moon, and he'd find himself wondering what became of them. He'd not seen Moon or Sammy for more than thirty summers – maybe they were already dead, Old Moon must be, he thinks – but he still saw Catch from time to time, when his tramp took him to the edge of Buile Hill. They'd nod if they saw one another, but rarely speak, for they'd each taken their own road, though Clem would always find a word, or a song, and invite him into the forge for supper. He's not seen them in a while. He can't remember the last time. They had a daughter, whose name Tommy cannot now recall, a strong-willed girl with her mother's independent spirit. He wonders what became of her.

Now, as he passes Victoria Station, he is reminded of a different woman, the one holding the child above her head, staring at him from the station platform, as he boarded the Troop Train bound for Dover, then for France. His son, he'd assumed. On his return he'd looked for him, as he imagined him grown, in the faces of the young boys and, later, young men, he might see at his regular stopping-off points. Sometimes he thought he caught an expression in the eyes, or a certain set of the mouth, or a familial hook in the nose, but he could never be sure. Once he was especially drawn to a young man he saw performing acrobatics, riding bareback on a string of horses in a travelling fair on Hollins Green, but he couldn't get close enough to be certain. And even if he had, what would he have said? 'You don't know me, but I might be your father'? No. And so he said nothing, while the sorrowful and reproachful looks he received from different women as he moved from place to place only served to make him seek further solitude and separateness. There'd been no other women since he returned from France…

He reaches the Irwell at last at Hunt's Bank. He ducks under several bridges – Cathedral, Blackfriars, Chapel Wharf – before he takes the path beneath Woden, alongside the Upper Reaches of the Ship Canal, where it shares its course for a time with the river. He navigates his way through the labyrinthine passageways of the docks at Ordsall and Pomona. Armies of men rise up from the ground to carry out night time repairs on the many ships moored up there. Welders, with iron helmets on their heads, wield their cutting torches through the rusted metal, issuing sparks of fire, which blaze in rainbow arcs across the sky like shooting stars. A night watchman on his rounds patrols the docks' perimeter. His lantern swings from side to side as he walks, casting lurid shadows on the basin walls. For a split second Tommy's dark face is illuminated in its dancing beam, startling the night watchman, who thinks he might have conjured a devil from the deep, and scurries away. Tommy presses back against a walled up recess beneath a narrow archway and watches cold, black drips of slime slowly swell, hang pendulously, before they burst, dropping one by one from the low, brick roof into the stagnant pools beside his feet, where a rat gnaws companionably on the laces of his boots. He gently prods it aside, smiling as he observes the delicate, fastidious interplay of whisker and paw.

He emerges from the docks to follow, briefly, a stretch of the Bridgewater Canal, bending south like a downturned mouth. It has started to rain. He hears it first, a gentle pitter patter on the surface of the water, before he feels it fall upon his face, quickly becoming heavier. He turns up his collar and leans into the wind.

He leaves the canal at Taylor's Bridge, winding his way between paper mills and printing works, feeling the rhythm of their ceaseless twenty-four hour presses pounding through his body as he proceeds towards Gorse Hill. It was here, in Gorse Hill, where once he was ambushed and set upon by a gang of drunks staggering out of the pub, for no other reason than he happened to step in their way. He rolled himself tightly into a ball, trying to offer the smallest target that he could to them, and lost two front teeth for his trouble. Each time he finds himself on these streets now, he's careful not to loiter. He cuts through narrow ginnels and unlit entries between the streets and houses, disturbing a cat on its nightly ransack of the dustbins. These lead him to the back of Longford Hall, a regular seasonal stopping off point for him, where he has picked fruit in autumn and raked ponds in winter.

On and on he walks until the dawn begins to break. It has rained all night. A pale sun tries to poke through the cloud, a leaked bandage across the bruised sky. He slips through a gap in a hedge, which takes him, via the Southern Cemetery, to Turn Moss, from where, after crossing through its bogs and marshes, he is able to follow the course of the River Mersey, past its muddy junctions with the Ousel and Stromford Brooks, along the backs of Urmston Meadows. In the distance he can see the smoke stacks and towers of the oil refinery at

Partington, belching plumes of red flame up into the wounded sky. On the flooded field beside the river an old horse is just beginning to wake, its front hoof delicately poised like a ballet dancer, but one whose dancing days are long over, its body retaining the last vestige of ancestral muscle memory, its head wreathed in smoky coils of dew-soaked breath.

He leaves the river at Shaw Town, crosses the Penny Bridge, just as the early morning milk train thunders underneath, enveloping him in a cloud of steam which, when it clears, reveals a large, rolling-eyed dog blocking his path, barking furiously. Tommy lowers his head to the same height as the dog's, making sure his eyes are looking away, until the dog does not feel challenged or threatened, becomes quiet and calm, even allowing Tommy to stroke him playfully behind his ears, before letting him pass. He walks through Acre Gate, past the candle factory, where a line of thirty women, all in single file, with scarves tied on their heads, walk in the grey half light of morning towards the still locked gates, then on to Calder Bank, where new houses are being built for the steel workers in nearby Irlam. He is skirting the flat wetlands, looping around Bent Lanes, until he can at last rejoin the old, somewhat abandoned course of the Irwell, a section not subsumed within the Ship Canal, dredged and overgrown, little more than a rank, muddy, slow-moving ditch, before it peters out into Salteye Rill. His destination is very close now. He can almost smell it. Salteye Rill cuts a wide arc around the graveyard at Peel Green. Across two more fields and he glimpses

Worsley Brook, threading its way towards The Delph between the old, semi-derelict Barton Hall and the new Aerodrome, where an Avro Baby bi-plane, manufactured just a few miles away at Woodhead, has just taken off. Tommy looks up and the aircraft is still low enough for him to see the pilot, a young woman with bobbed, red hair, who blows him a kiss before pulling down her goggles and circling around the hundred foot tall octagonal tower of St Catherine's Priory, and then soaring off through the low morning cloud into which she disappears. Beyond the tower lies Winton Park, Alder Forest and the final open ground of Cleaveley Marsh, across the other side of which Bittern Wood awaits him.

Bittern Wood.

The bells in the spire of St Mark's, close by Worsley Green, strike midday just as Tommy reaches it. It is much reduced since the time he, Catch, Sammy and Old Moon first set up their camp there, with the field where he planted and harvested the wheat having been swallowed up by the spread of the Ship Canal and the further creep of mills and factories along its banks. But although the field is gone, the wood remains.

Bittern Wood.

Tommy enters the deep hush of it.

He enters from its western edge. It is smaller than he remembers it. Parts of it have been felled. But it is still large enough to lose himself in, and find himself too perhaps, he thinks.

Rooks call from the trees, which creak and groan as he walks between them. The wood is carpeted with the last of the bluebells, shot through with wild garlic and campion. The trees are a mixture of sycamore, ash, but mostly beech, whose leaves are still new, with that freshly-washed green, which will last just a few days more, before they acquire their customary summer dustiness. The ground is wet from the overnight rain, with droplets of water catching the light. Buckler ferns gracefully uncurl from the earth, where they resemble giant green seahorses swaying gently in the breeze. Everywhere there are butterflies, their paper thin wings opening and closing delicately as they feed on the young shoots of buckthorn and ground sorrel – wood whites, speckled yellows, orange tips, pearl-bordered fritillaries and the camouflaged grizzled skippers, wings the colour of mottled barks – rising in clouds, then settling, as Tommy passes through them. He disturbs an adder sliding noiselessly from the undergrowth. He bends low to look at it. The two of them regard each other warily, before the adder coils its way back beneath a fallen branch, covered with clustered feather moss, into which it disappears. He sees the tell-tale signs of moles, whose upturned mounds of earth signify their recent presence. A good sign. He smiles. This is fertile soil. Things will grow here. He lays his ear against the surface of the earth and listens. He fancies her hears the sounds of worms dragging down leaves and beech nuts to munch, excrete and fertilise.

Tommy reaches the eastern edge of the wood. He has taken this route deliberately, hoping to save this next sight till last. He wonders if it has survived the years. He steps out into a clearing, and there it is – the American Elm he planted from a seed brought over with him from South Dakota, now thirty feet high, its roots shallow but extensive. He runs his hand along its rough, coarse bark, striated in alternate ridges of grey and white. Its leaves are notched ellipses, forming a broad umbrella canopy, through which the sun is throwing dappled light, as it flits in and out of a large black cumulus cloud massing on the horizon.

A wide-antlered fallow buck is grazing beneath it. He looks up as Tommy walks out from the wood, his white tail twitching. Unconcerned, he continues to crop the grass. A peacock's haunted cry rises up from the grounds of the Old Hall half a mile to the north and hangs suspended. The deer lifts his head. The earth holds its breath.

A sudden crack of thunder splits the air. The deer bolts, as if chasing after it. Tommy tilts back his head, offering his face to the rain, which once again begins to fall.

It is time.

He takes a fletch of feathers from his rucksack. He sticks each one fast in the ground, spacing them an inch apart, until he has no more left. They form a perfect circle. Like the moon. He stands back, examining the effect as the rain falls heavier.

It is time.

He lies down in the centre of the circle, his head and feet fringed with feathers. He folds his arms across his chest and closes his eyes. He hears the voice of Old

Moon singing by the camp fire, the words rising with wood smoke.

"The blossoms fall in the orchard
The flax threads fall from the fingers
The soldiers fall in the battle
All things fall

I see a man ride a horse
I see a horse plough a field
I see a field grow with corn
I see the corn clutch a hare

I see a hare hide in the moon
I see the moon shine on a dog
I see a dog hunt for a man
I see a man scythe down the corn

The moonlight falls on the mountain
The poppies fall in the meadow
The heroes fall in the forest
All things fall

I see a worm on a hook
I see a fish eat a worm
I see a man catch a fish
I see a worm eat a man..."

Tommy sees eggs rolling down a hill. A lame boy riding a black mare. A hawk plucking a leveret from a wheat field. He sees young girls dressed in white with angels' wings hauling the harvest home. Men in columns sharpening with stones the blades of scythes glinting in the sun. Poppies staining the golden corn with red. He sees a woman holding her child high above her head. The light go out in Edward's eyes. Egrets flying across the moon. He sees horses riding round and round a circus ring. A small boy picking up a feather. A red haired girl with freckles placing it in her hair.

A few hours later the rain has stopped. The sun sinks beneath the blanket of cloud. It shines through the crown of leaves in the Bittern Wood. It lights up the base of the American Elm, where Tommy lies irradiated in a ring of feathers.

A skewbald filly, with no saddle or bridle, approaches him circumspectly. She stretches her neck across the feathers down towards his body. She gently nudges him with her large head. She nudges him again. And again. She places her muzzle close up to his face and breathes soft, warm air directly into his nostrils.

Nothing.

The skewbald filly steps back out of the circle, throws back her head and whinnies to the sky. From the other side of the Bittern Wood a loud booming call answers her. She tosses her mane, rears up on her back legs, then gallops away down the hill and out of sight.

Tulip continues in:
Volume 2: Nymphs & Shepherds
(Ornaments of Grace, Book 3)

Dramatis Personae

(in order of appearance)

CAPITALS = Major Character; **Bold** = Significant Character;
Plain = appears once or twice

JOHN JABEZ CHADWICK, known as Jabez, Head Gardener
Philips Park, married to Mary
Harriet, Jabez & Mary's daughter
Toby, Jabez & Mary's son
Julian Pettigrew, Chair Manchester Corporation Sub-
Committee Public Walks, Gardens & Playgrounds
Right Honourable Mr John Edward Sutton MP for
Manchester Clayton
Hubert Wright, a printer, married to Annie
Annie Wright
George Wright, their son
MARY FLYNN, married to Jabez
ESTHER BLUNDELL, daughter of Walter, a miner
WALTER BLUNDELL, Esther's father
Freddie Blundell, Esther's younger brother
ARTHUR BLUNDELL, Esther's older brother, fiancé of
Winifred
Frank, Harold, Jim Blundell, Esther's middle brothers
WINIFRED HOLT, Esther's friend, a munitionette, later tram
conductor, then telephonist, Arthur's fiancée
Miss Annie Briggs, a suffragette
Mrs Evelyn Manesta, a suffragette
Mrs Lillian Forrester, a suffragette
Judge at Trial of Suffragettes
Mr Friedrich Kaufman, Ruth's father
Mrs Helga Kaufman, Ruth's mother
Iris McMaster, Nurse at Manchester Royal Informary
CHARLES TREVELYAN, Doctor at Manchester Royal Infirmary
RUTH KAUFMAN, mother of Lily

Cecil Young, Ruth's fiancé
Mr Young, Cecil's father, owner of Victoria Mill
Mrs Young, Cecil's mother
Nurse Jenkins, who looks after Friedrich
Young red-haired girl on Isle of Man
Mrs Woakes, midwife's handywoman
PC Ernie Wray
Mr Hart, Hospital Registrar
Lily Shilling, Ruth's daughter
Sister Clodagh, of St Bridget's Orphanage
Mr Henry Schneider, husband of Ruth's mother's cousin
Mrs Klara Schneider, Ruth's mother's cousin
King George V
Queen Mary of Tek
TOMMY THUNDER, a Native American horse doctor
Giovanni Locartelli, known as Nonno, Claudia's father-in-law
Claudia Locartelli, née Campanella
Giulia Locartelli, later Lockhart, Claudia's daughter
Paul(ie) Locartelli, later Lockhart, Claudia's son
VICTOR COLLINS, boxer, miner, soldier
Marco Locartelli, Claudia's husband
Maharajah, an elephant
James Jennison, owner of Belle Vue, 1872
Lorenzo Lawrence, Maharajah's handler
Mrs Blundell, Walter's mother
Dorothy Blundell, Walter's sister
Mr Aspinal, Minister of Barmouth Street Chapel
Miss Agatha, Mr Aspinall's unmarried sister
ALICE OWEN, later Walter's wife
Mr Blundell, Walter's father
Hannah Mitchell, pioneer suffragist
Matteo Campanella, Claudia's brother
Martha, Victor's estranged wife
Joe Collins, Victor's son
Leonard 'Len' Benker Johnson, boxing champion
Alvar Lidell, BBC Newsreader
GRACE CHADWICK, Jabez and Mary's youngest daughter

Derek Blundell, Esther's Great Nephew
Maureen, Derek's wife
Florence Blundell, Derek and Maureen's daughter
Principal Trombonist, Pete
SAMMY, aka Leaping Fish
Freddy CATCH, aka Firecatcher
OLD MOON, aka Reads The Moon
Eve, later Sammy's wife
3rd Earl of Ellesmere
Jenks, the Earl's Bailiff
Nathaniel, a farmer
Ezekiel Flint, a blacksmith
CLEM, Clémence Audubon Lafitte, daughter of a slave
Mr Hindley, manager of Lumn's Lane Mine
Sir Philip Voss, Coroner
Dru
Bron
Cuinn, eldest son of Dru & Bron
Med, younger son of Dru & Bron
Cora, daughter of Dru & Bron
Queen Victoria
James Naysmith, inventor of the steam hammer
DELPHINE, Sammy and Eve's daughter
YASSER WAHID, Yemeni foreman on Ship Canal
Happy Jack, Dusty Mick, Long Bob, Frying Pan, Irish labourers on Ship Canal
Zhang, Huan, Shi, Yu, Chinese labourers on Ship Canal
Asif, Hakim, Nabil, Rashid, Yemeni labourers on Ship Canal
Eilidh 'Ma' Grady, landlady of The Brazier's Arms
ROSE GRADY, Ma's daughter, later Yasser's wife
Luigi Locartelli, bellhop at Royal Pomona Palace Hotel, later Head Porter at The Queen's Hotel, brother of Marco
Iacopo Locartelli, Luigi's Uncle
CHAMOMILE 'CAM' CATCH, Clem and Catch's daughter
Edward, 3rd Earl's grandson
Sister Basil, Headmistress at St Philip's School, Broughton
His Grace the Most Reverend Edmund Arbuthnott Knox, 4th

Bishop of Manchester
Lizzie Byrom, supporter of Bonnie Prince Charlie
Sir Thomas Tyldesley, Royalist
Richard Perceval, Puritan
Woman Peace Protester in Cathedral
Harassed VAD Nurse
FRANCIS HALL, formerly Franz Halsinger
Jaz, Yasser's son

The following are mentioned by name:

[Jeremiah Harrison, former Keeper of Philips Park]
[William Gay, Designer of Philips Park]
[Crowds attending Tulip Sunday 1922]
[Mrs Pettigrew]
[Edward Hopkinson MP]
[Tiny Girl splashing in pool]
[Legless War Veteran]
[Bugler from Victoria Brass Band]
[Mark Philips MP, after whom Philips Park is named]
[Disabled Soldier]
[Art Gallery Attendants]
[Frederick, Lord Leighton, artist]
[George Frederick Watts, artist]
[Dante Gabriel Rossetti, artist]
[John Everett Millais, artist]
[Edward Burne-Jones, artist]
[Briton Rivière, artist]
[John Melhuish Strudwick, artist]
[Arthur Hacker, artist]
William Holman Hunt, artist]
[Clerk of Manchester Assizes]
[Dr Peregrine Gray, witness at trial]
[Protesting Suffragettes in Courtroom]
[Foreman of Jury]
[Emmeline Pankhurst, founder of WSPU]
[Ethel Smyth, leading suffragist]
[Mr H.H. Asquith, Prime Minister]

[Soldiers of The Manchester Regiment]
[Cheering Crowds on Deansgate]
[Chief Constable Sir Robert Peacock]
[Strangeways Prison Officer]
[Female Workers at Charles Mackintosh}
[Female Munitionettes, Hooley Bridge]
[Mrs Holt, Winifred's mother]
[Janet, Winifred's cousin, waitress at The Midland Hotel]
[Mr Randall, Manager at Hooley Bridge]
[Doctor & Nurse, examining munitionettes]
[Director of Propaganda Film about Munitionettes]
[Lillian Gish]
[Cinema audience, The Palace Denton]
[Billy, small boy in rioting crowd]
[Rioting Crowd after Sinking of The Lusitania]
[Two older women in rioting crowd]
[Women picking through damage after the riots]
[Traumatised Woman with Doll]
[Angry Mob outside Kaufmans' Opticians]
[Middle-aged gentleman with umbrella]
[Mr Gould, a glazier]
[VAD Nurse, Field Hospital Salonika]
[Arthur's C/O]
[City Art Gallery Visitors]
[Flower seller, Hyde Road Denton]
[Millicent Fawcett, signatory of Christmas Letter]
[Emily Hobhouse, co-signatory]
[Dorothy Smith, co-signatory]
[Isabella Jones, co-signatory]
[Percy, a soldier in Arthur's unit]
[British & German soldiers in Christmas Truce]
[Arthur's C/O]
[Walter Deverell, artist]
[German Internees en route for Isle of Man]
[Guards on board ship and at camp at Knockaloe]
[Manx Police Officers]
[Gustav, Friedrich's Uncle]
[Friedrich's father]
[Manchester Estate Agent with black moustache]
[Vicar at St Lawrence's Church, Denton]
[Biddy, Ruth's nanny]

[Internment Camp Doctor]
[Charles' relatives]
[Scipione Riva-Rocci, Italian physician]
[Dr Eberhard Frank, German physician]
[Mary's parents]
[Postman delivering The Tulip]
[Two boys playing in street who deliver note to Winifred]
[Midwife's mother]
[Two women drinking in The Grey Horse]
[Cab Driver]
[Gentleman with cane, Charles' neighbour]
[Miss Franks, receptionist at Manchester Royal Infirmary]
[Tram Conductor]
[Man with a match]
[Rouged women on Pink Bank Lane]
[Reverend Theobald Crowe, Minister at St Lawrence's Church, Denton]
[Reverend Archer, Minister at St Paul's Church, Clayton]
[Gravediggers]
[William Dyce, artist]
[Stallholders, Denton]
[Postman]
[People queuing for tram]
[Ford Madox Brown, artist]
[Pilots & Flight engineers in Woodford]
[Sir Anthony Ashley Cooper, Royal Commission]
[Mr Thomas Livesey, former owner of Bradford Colliery]
[Three young women who die in pit accident, 1846]
[WW1 Pit-Brow women]
[Wounded Soldiers in Brook House]
[Nathan Daniels, chemist at Hooley Hill]
[Frank Slater, fellow chemist]
[John Morton, lab assistant]
[Dead and injured workers at Hooley Hill]
[Sylvain Dreyfus, co-founder of Hooley Hill]
[Policeman at scene of explosion]
[Young man injured in explosion looked after by Winifred]
[Alderman Heap, Mayor of Ashton]
[Lord Beaverbrook MP for Ashton]
[Brass bands of The Manchester Regiment & Salvation Army]
[250,000 mourners]

[George Formby Snr]
[Capt. Wilfred Owen, poet]
[Passengers on trams]
[Kaiser Wilhelm II]
[Lieutenant James Foulkes, Manchester Regiment]
[Tommy Thunder's father]
[David Lloyd George, Prime Minister]
[General Babbington, 14th British Corps]
[Jabez's C/O]
[German & Turkish prisoners-of-war]
[Soldiers of French, Czech and Italian armies]
[Members of crack Arditi Corps]
[Clifford, Jabez's pal]
[Joan, Jabez's elder sister]
[Jabez's father, John]
[Henry Alexander Bowler, artist]
[Choir of St Jerome's Church, Clayton]
[Miss Edwina Brent, Chief Supervisor at Manchester Telephone
Exchange]
[Younger telephonists]
[Lord Mayor & Lady Mayoress of Manchester, Tulip Sunday 1922]
[Brown Owl, Gorton Girl Guides]
[Children in egg-and-spoon race]
[Ferret-faced MC in Boxing Tent]
[Crowds in Boxing Tent]
[Elephant keepers, Philips Park]
[Boys squirted on by elephants]
[Steward in Boxing Tent]
[Men in sharp suits in Boxing Tent]
[Painted Ladies in Boxing Tent]
[Vic's opponent in Boxing Ring]
[Auctioneer, Waverley Auction Rooms, Edinburgh]
[Cornelius Flay, of McGaddan, Flinders & Flay]
[Guard at Waverley Station]
[Passengers, Waverley Station]
[Station Master]
[Crowds cheering Maharajah at Hawick]
[The Armstrongs of Glankie Tower]
[Mrs Edmonds, owner of Lizzie the African Elephant]
[Crowds cheering Maharajah in Kendal]
[Toll Keeper]

[Crowds cheering Maharajah in Bolton]
[Heywood Hardy, Royal Academician]
[Crowds cheering Maharajah in Manchester]
[William Blundell, Walter's older brother]
[Samuel Blundell, Walter's second older brother]
[Children on Sunday School Outing]
[Mrs Owen, Alice's mother]
[Zoo Keepers]
[Circus performers in Wild West Show]
[Little Miss Sure Shot]
[Bugler]
[Bridesmaids at Walter & Alice's wedding]
[Best Man]
[Driver of pony and trap]
[Wedding Guests]
[Courting Couple in Belle Vue Maze
[Consul the Chimpanzee]
[Jake, Walter's Best Man]
[Cyril, Walter's Uncle]
[Alan, Walter's friend, a miner]
[Ben Brierley, Lancashire Poet]
[Chairman British Brass Bands Federation]
[Audience for Belle Vue Brass Band Open, 1902]
[Messrs Frederick Vetter, Carl Kieffert, T.H. Seddon, Judges of Brass
Band Open]
[Charles Godfrey Junior, musical arranger]
[John Jennison, Founder of Belle Vue]
[Kingston Mills Brass Band]
[Mr Alexander Hargreaves, conductor Kingston Mills]
[Bluff conductor of Reddish Band]
[Black Dyke Mills Band]
[Dr Warren]
[Crowds queuing for Scenic Railway, 1912]
[Newsboy]
[Robert Blatchford, founder of The Clarion]
[Christabel Pankhurst]
[Adela Pankhurst]
[Elizabeth Garrett Anderson]
[Hannah Mitchell's parents]
[Hannah Mitchell's older brother and wife]
[Derbyshire schoolmaster]

[Bolton dressmaker]
[Katherine Conway]
[Gibbon Mitchell, Hannah's husband]
[Hannah Mitchell's child]
[Speakers and Audience at WSPU Rally, 1912]
[Queues for The Bobs, 1932
[Arthur Balfour, former PM, President of Ardwick Lads Club]
[Desk Clerk of Ardwick Lads Club]
[Boxers and Trainers in gym]
[Waiters at Parker's]
[Jack Phoenix, a boxer]
[Two further defeated boxers]
[Customers at Parker's]
[Mabel, Victor's older sister]
[Captain Willis, Victor's C/O]
[Soldiers in Vic's unit]
[Girls in French and Belgian villages]
[Martha's mother]
[Victor's sister, Mabel]
[Manager at Bradford Colliery, 1920s]
[Winifred's neighbours]
[Bert Hughes, Gorton Fair]
[Tiger Jack Payne, boxer]
[Maurice Prunier, boxer]
[Pierre Gandon, boxer]
[Giuseppe Malerba, boxer]
[Jack Etienne, boxer]
[Louis Westendraedt, boxer]
[Ignacio Ara, boxer]
[Piet Brand, boxer]
[Michele Bonaglia, boxer]
[Len Harvey, boxer]
[Crowds for Boxing Match at Kings Hall]
[Technician, Kings Hall]
[Master of Ceremonies, Kings Hall]
[Gipsy Daniels, boxer]
[Roland Todd, boxer]
[Referee, Kings Hall]
[Trumpeters, Kings Hall]
[Doctor, Kings Hall]
[Oswald Mosley]

[Blackshirts, followers of Oswald Mosley]
[Police officers, Kings Hall]
[Field Marshall Montgomery]
[Admiral Nugamo]
[Midwife at Gracie's birth]
[Dr Edlin, the Chadwick family doctor]
[Thomas, child in Harriet's class at Church Street School, Clayton]
[Bromley – ditto]
[Amy – ditto]
[John Blay – ditto]
[Anita – ditto]
[Hartley – ditto]
[Jessie – ditto]
[Gertie – Bromley and Hartley's elder sister]
[Manchester Museum Guide]
[Scavengers and looters among rubble of Blitz]
[ARP Wardens, Red Cross, WRVS, St John's Ambulance workers in bomb sites]
[Woman drinking tea from tin mug]
[Man in tweed jacket with glasses and clipboard]
[Gracie's Uncle Jack, Jabez's brother]
[Librarian at Central Reference Library]
[Crowds on Deansgate]
[Derek's doctor]
[Derek's optician]
[Derek's son]
[Glossop Old Band]
[Alan Blundell, Derek's father]
[Glossop High School Brass Band]
[Florence's music teacher]
[Madness]
[Professor Tomlinson's Flea Circus]
[Audience at Brass Band Concert in Kings Hall]
[Bucks Fizz]
[Demolition Crew]
[City centre crowds, inc. Chinese, African, Punjabi, Jewish, South Sea Islander]
[Tommy Thunder's Grandfather]
[Tenants on the Earl's estate]
[Mummers]
[William Wylde, Royal Academician]

[Tommy Thunder's father]
[2nd Earl of Ellesmere, the 3rd Earl's elder brother]
[Sir Robert Peel, Prime Minister]
[People who dwell on Chat Moss]
[Men and boys trapped underground at Lumn's Lane]
[Manley, an old miner]
[Police constables, fire officers]
[Jean Lafitte, Clem's grandfather, a pirate]
[Marceline Fontenot, Lafitte's mulatto mistress]
[Texas Rangers]
[Simon Bolivar]
[Aristide Baptiste]
[Obosa, a slave, Baptiste's wife]
[George Washington Murray, black businessman in the Carolinas]
[Mrs Anne Needham-Philips, Mark Philips' sister-in-law]
[Sir Thomas Hibbert, slave-owner]
[Charity Henry, Hibbert's mistress]
[Robert Philips, Anne's husband, Clem's guardian]
[Caroline Philips, Robert & Anne's daughter]
[Arnold Otto Costigan, Caroline's fiancé]
[Harvesters at Bittern Wood]
[Farnworth & Walkden Brass Band, aka The Old Barnes Band]
[Choirs of St Mary's Ellenbrook, St Andrew's Boothstown, St Mark's Worsley]
[1st Earl of Ellesmere, 3rd Earl's father]
[Prince Albert]
[Lord Wilbraham Egerton, 3rd Earl's cousin at Tatton]
[Boy and Girl who sing Haley Paley]
[Mr Daniel Adamson, proposer of Manchester Ship Canal]
[Hamilton Fulton, architect]
[Edward Leader Williams, architect]
[Reapers & Corn Maidens at Harvest Supper]
[Parthians, Scythians, Berbers, Dacians, Ethiopes, Galicians at Mamucium]
[Anthony Marshall, Lord Mayor of Manchester]
[William Henry Bailey, Civic Mayor of Salford]
[Messrs Watt & Sons, Portland Street]
[Alfred Waterhouse, designer of Manchester Town Hall]
[Matthew Noble, sculptor]
[Queen Victoria's Aunt Louise of Belgium]
[Ford Madox Brown, painter of the Manchester Murals]

[Navigationers and their families in Peggy's Shant]
[Hucksters, packmen, cheapjacks, hawkers, tailors, likeness-takers, brewers and molls following the construction of the Ship Canal]
[Sir Thomas Walker, Chief Engineer of Ship Canal]
[Michael Grady, Ma's late husband, Rose's father]
[Wallet, the Queen's Jester in Royal Pomona Botanical Gradens]
[Mr James Reilly, owner of Royal Pomona Palace Hotel]
[Benjamin Disraeli, Prime Minister and Guest at Hotel]
[Mrs Wooding, long term guest at Hotel]
[Messrs Roberts & Dale, owners of Cornbrook Chemicals]
[James Martin, fireman at Cornbrook Chemicals]
[Workers at Cornbrook Chemicals]
[Sightseers of explosion at Cornbrook Chemicals]
[Fire & Police officers dealing with explosion]
[13th Hussars and 1st Lancashire Fusiliers holding back the crowds at explosion]
[Deputy Coroner, Manchester]
[Mr J.M. Bates, Barrister at Enquiry]
[Colonel Majendie, Government Inspector]
[Peter Heald, mechanic at Cornbrook Chemicals]
[Joseph Dean, storekeeper at Cornbrook Chemicals]
[Stephen Logan, labourer]
[Crowds at the opening of Manchester Ship Canal]
[Pomona, Rose and Yasser's daughter]
[Two children playing whip and top on Liverpool Road, Irlam]
[Daisy, Edward's sister]
[Farm boys playing with Edward]
[Mrs Snook, Landlady of Delphine's flat in Lime Grove, Stretford]
[Female guests at Lime Grove]
[Sister Rona, Delphine's teacher at primary school]
[Jewish stall holders on Shudehill]
[Old gentleman who sits on tram next to Delphine]
[Audrey, Marjorie, Margaret, trainee teachers at Sedgley Park]
[Billy Pick, pupil at St Philip's]
[3rd Earl's daughter, Edward's mother]
[Lord Kitchener]
[Choristers at Manchester Cathedral]
[Army of Bonnie Prince Charlie]
[Long Preston Peggy]
[Woman singing Recruiting Song in The Bull's Head]
[Magistrate at Court Leet]

[Lizzie Byrom's father]
[Lord Pitsligo]
[Mr Walley]
[Mr Foden]
[Hugh Sterling]
[Mr Hibbert]
[Lizzie's uncle]
[Mr Croxton]
[Mr Fielden]
[Bonnie Prince Charlie]
[Mr Dickenson]
[Duke of Athol]
[Mr Marsden]
[Lizzie's mother]
[Lizzie's sister]
[Christian Pacifists, Irish Nationalists, Anti-Militarists]
[Lord Strange]
[Royalist forces]
[Two hundred Parliamentarians]
[Retreating Jacobite army]
[Farriers, sadlers, rough riders, London Road Station]
[Young Woman at station holding up Tommy's baby]
[Soldiers at the Front]
[Miss Poulter, guest at Mrs Snook's]
[Thomas, Mrs Snook's late husband]
[Deaf children taught by Delphine]
[Delphine's colleagues at The Manchester Institution for the Deaf
and Dumb]
[Overweight, red-faced gentleman on train]
[Children playing in Cadishead Park]
[Mr & Mrs Halsinger, Francis's parents]
[Ship's Captain on Isle of Man ferry]
[Louis Belriot]
[Giuglielmo Marconi]
[Gatekeepr, Irlam Locks]
[Workmen at Barton Locks]
[Older gentlemen in Barton en route for Church]
[Bargemen on Ship Canal]
[Stevedores from across the world at Pomona Docks]
[Men mending broken water pipe]
[4th earl of Ellesmere]

[Young man performing acrobatics on horseback at Hollins Green]
[Night Watchman, Ordsall]
[Gang of drunks at Gorse Hill]
[Headscarved women at Candle Factory, Acre Gate]
[Aviatrix with bobbed hair, Barton Aerodrome]

Acknowledgements
(for *Ornaments of Grace* as a whole)

Writing is usually considered to be a solitary practice, but I have always found the act of creativity to be a collaborative one, and that has again been true for me in putting together the sequence of novels which comprise *Ornaments of Grace*. I have been fortunate to have been supported by so many people along the way, and I would like to take this opportunity of thanking them all, with apologies for any I may have unwittingly omitted.

First of all I would like to thank Ian Hopkinson, Larysa Bolton, Tony Lees and other staff members of Manchester's Central Reference Library, who could not have been more helpful and encouraging. That is where the original spark for the novels was lit and it has been such a treasure trove of fascinating information ever since. I would like to thank Jane Parry, the Neighbourhood Engagement & Delivery Officer for the Archives & Local History Dept of Manchester Library Services for her support in enabling me to use individual reproductions of the remarkable Manchester Murals by Ford Madox Brown, which can be viewed in the Great Hall of Manchester Town Hall. They are exceptional images and I recommend you going to see them if you are ever in the vicinity. I would also like to thank the staff of other libraries and museums in Manchester, namely the John Rylands Library, Manchester University Library, the Manchester Museum, the People's History Museum and also Salford's Working Class Movement Library, where Lynette Cawthra was especially helpful, as was Aude Nguyen Duc at The Manchester Literary & Philosophical Society, the much-loved Lit& Phil, the first and oldest such society anywhere in the world, 238 years young and still going strong.

In addition to these wonderful institutions, I have many individuals to thank also. Barbara Derbyshire from the Moravian Settlement in Fairfield has been particularly patient and generous with her time in telling me so much of the community's inspiring history. No less inspiring has been Lauren Murphy, founder of the Bradford Pit Project, which is a most moving collection of anecdotes, memories, reminiscences, artefacts and original art works dedicated to the lives of people connected with Bradford Colliery. You can find out more about their work at: www.bradfordpit.com. Martin Gittins freely shared some of his encyclopaedic knowledge of the part the River Irwell has played in Manchester's story, for which I have been especially grateful.

I should also like to thank John and Anne Horne for insights into historical medical practice; their daughter, Ella, for inducting me into the mysteries of chemical titration, which, if I have subsequently got it wrong, is my fault not hers; Tony Smith for his deep first hand understanding of spinning and weaving; Sarah Lawrie for inducting me so enthusiastically into the Manchester music scene of the 1980s, which happened just after I left the city so I missed it; Sylvia Tiffin for her previous research into Manchester's lost theatres, and Brian Hesketh for his specialist knowledge in a range of such diverse topics as hot air balloons, how to make a crystal radio set, old maps, the intricacies of a police constable's notebook and preparing reports for a coroner's inquest.

Throughout this intensive period of writing and research, I have been greatly buoyed up by the keen support and interest of many friends, most notably Theresa Beattie, Laïla Diallo, Viv Gordon, Phil King, Rowena Price, Gavin Stride, Chris Waters, and Irene Willis. Thank you to you all. In addition, Sue & Rob Yockney have been extraordinarily helpful in more ways than I can mention. Their advice on so many matters, both artistic and practical, has been beyond measure.

A number of individuals have very kindly – and bravely – offered to read early drafts of the novels: Bill Bailey, Rachel Burn, Lucy Cash, Chris & Julie Phillips. Their responses have been positive, constructive, illuminating and encouraging, particularly when highlighting those passages which needed closer attention from me, which I have tried my best to address. Thank you.

I would also like to pay a special tribute to my friend Andrew Pastor, who has endured months and months of fortnightly coffee sessions during which he has listened so keenly and with such forbearance to the various difficulties I may have been experiencing at the time. He invariably came up with the perfect comment or idea, which then enabled me to see more clearly a way out of whatever tangle I happened to have found myself in. He also suggested several avenues of further research I might undertake to navigate towards the next bend in one of the three rivers, all of which have been just what were needed. These books could not have finally seen the light of day without his irreplaceable input.

Finally I would like to thank my wife, Amanda, for her endless patience, encouragement and love. These books are dedicated to her and to our son, Tim.

Biography

Chris grew up in Manchester and currently lives in West Dorset, after brief periods in Nottinghamshire, Devon and Brighton. Over the years he has managed to reinvent himself several times – from florist's delivery van driver to Punch & Judy man, drama teacher, theatre director, community arts co-ordinator, creative producer, to his recent role as writer and dramaturg for choreographers and dance companies.

Between 2003 and 2009 Chris was Director of Dance and Theatre for *Take Art*, the arts development agency for Somerset, and between 2009 and 2013 he enjoyed two stints as Creative Producer with South East Dance leading on their Associate Artists programme, followed by a year similarly supporting South Asian dance artists for *Akademi* in London. From 2011 to 2017 he was Creative Producer for the Bonnie Bird Choreography Fund.

Chris has worked for many years as a writer and theatre director, most notably with New Perspectives in Nottinghamshire and Farnham Maltings in Surrey under the artistic direction of Gavin Stride, with whom Chris has been a frequent collaborator.

Directing credits include: three Community Plays for the Colway Theatre Trust – *The Western Women* (co-director with Ann Jellicoe), *Crackling Angels* (co-director with Jon Oram), and *The King's Shilling*; for New Perspectives – *It's A Wonderful Life* (co-director with Gavin Stride), *The Railway*

Children (both adapted by Mary Elliott Nelson); for Farnham Maltings – *The Titfield Thunderbolt, Miracle on 34th Street* and *How To Build A Rocket* (all co-directed with Gavin Stride); for Oxfordshire Touring Theatre Company – *Bowled A Googly* by Kevin Dyer; for Flax 303 – *The Rain Has Voices* by Shiona Morton, and for Strike A Light *I Am Joan* and *Prescribed*, both written by Viv Gordon and co-directed with Tom Roden, and *The Book of Jo* as dramaturg.

Theatre writing credits include: *Firestarter, Trying To Get Back Home, Heroes* – a trilogy of plays for young people in partnership with Nottinghamshire & Northamptonshire Fire Services; *You Are Harry Kipper & I Claim My Five Pounds, It's Not Just The Jewels, Bogus* and *One of Us* (the last co-written with Gavin Stride) all for New Perspectives; *The Birdman* for Blunderbus; for Farnham Maltings *How To Build A Rocket* (as assistant to Gavin Stride), and *Time to Remember* (an outdoor commemoration of the centenary of the first ever Two Minutes Silence); *When King Gogo Met The Chameleon* and *Africarmen* for Tavaziva Dance, and most recently *All the Ghosts Walk with Us* (conceived and performed with Laïla Diallo and Phil King) for ICIA, Bath University and Bristol Old Vic Ferment Festival, (2016-17); *Posting to Iraq* (performed by Sarah Lawrie with music by Tom Johnson for the inaugural Women & War Festival in London 2016), and *Tree House* (with music by Sarah Moody, which toured southern England in autumn 2016). In 2018 Chris was commissioned to write the text for *In Our Time*, a film to celebrate the 40th Anniversary of the opening of The Brewhouse Theatre in Taunton, Somerset.

Between 2016 and 2019 Chris collaborated with fellow poet Chris Waters and Jazz saxophonist Rob Yockney to develop two touring programmes of poetry, music, photography and film: *Home Movies* and *Que Pasa?*

Chris regularly works with choreographers and dance artists, offering dramaturgical support and business advice. These have included among others: Alex Whitley, All Play, Ankur Bahl, Antonia Grove, Anusha Subramanyam, Archana

Ballal, Ballet Boyz, Ben Duke, Ben Wright, Charlie Morrissey, Crystal Zillwood, Darkin Ensemble, Divya Kasturi, Dog Kennel Hill, f.a.b. the detonators, Fionn Barr Factory, Heather Walrond, Hetain Patel, Influx, Jane Mason, Joan Clevillé, Kali Chandrasegaram, Kamala Devam, Karla Shacklock, Khavita Kaur, Laïla Diallo, Lîla Dance, Lisa May Thomas, Liz Lea, Lost Dog, Lucy Cash, Luke Brown, Marisa Zanotti, Mark Bruce, Mean Feet Dance, Nicola Conibère, Niki McCretton, Nilima Devi, Pretty Good Girl, Probe, Rachael Mossom, Richard Chappell, Rosemary Lee, Sadhana Dance, Seeta Patel, Shane Shambhu, Shobana Jeyasingh, Showmi Das, State of Emergency, Stop Gap, Subathra Subramaniam, Tavaziva Dance, Tom Sapsford, Theo Clinkard, Urja Desai Thakore, Vidya Thirunarayan, Viv Gordon, Yael Flexer, Yorke Dance Project (including the Cohan Collective) and Zoielogic.

Chris is married to Amanda Fogg, a former dance practitioner working principally with people with Parkinson's.

Printed in Poland
by Amazon Fulfillment
Poland Sp. z o.o., Wrocław

50823746R00456